SHORT NOVELS
OF THE
MASTERS

BOOKS BY CHARLES NEIDER

FICTION
The Grotto Berg: Two Novellas
Mozart and the Archbooby
A Visit to Yazoo
Overflight
Naked Eye
The Authentic Death of Hendry Jones
The White Citadel

NONFICTION
Beyond Cape Horn: Travels in the Antarctic
Edge of the World: Ross Island, Antarctica
Suzy: A Childhood
Mark Twain
The Frozen Sea: A Study of Franz Kafka

BOOKS EDITED BY CHARLES NEIDER
Essays of the Masters
The Travels of Mark Twain
Tolstoy: Tales of Courage and Conflict
Life as I Find It: A Treasury of Mark Twain Rarities
The Selected Letters of Mark Twain
Mark Twain: Plymouth Rock and the Pilgrims and Other Speeches
Antarctica: Firsthand Accounts of Exploration and Endurance
Man Against Nature: Firsthand Accounts of Adventure and Exploration
Great Shipwrecks and Castaways: Firsthand Accounts of Disasters at Sea
The Fabulous Insects: Essays by the Foremost Nature Writers
Papa, by Susy Clemens
The Autobiography of Mark Twain
Great Short Stories

SHORT NOVELS
OF THE
MASTERS

EDITED WITH AN INTRODUCTION BY
CHARLES NEIDER

Cooper Square Press

Notes from Underground, by F. M. Dostoyevsky, translated by Bernard Guilbert Guerney, is reprinted by permission of Vanguard Press, Inc., from *A Treasury of Russian Literature*, edited by Bernard Guilbert Guerney. Copyright, 1943, by Vanguard Press, Inc.

A Simple Heart, by Gustav Flaubert, is reprinted from *Three Tales* by Gustav Flaubert, by permission of Alfred A. Knopf, Inc. Copyright 1924, by Alfred A. Knopf, Inc.

The Death of Iván Ilých, by L. N. Tolstoy, translated by Aylmer Maude, is reprinted by permission of the Oxford University Press.

Ward No. 6, by Anton Chekov, translated by Bernard Guilbert Guerney, is reprinted from *The Portable Russian Reader*. Copyright, 1947, by the Viking Press, Inc.

Death in Venice, by Thomas Mann, is reprinted from *Stories of Three Decades*, by Thomas Mann, by permission of Alfred A. Knopf, Inc. Copyright, 1936 by Alfred A. Knopf, Inc.

The Dead, by James Joyce, from *Dubliners*, included in *The Portable James Joyce*, is reprinted by permission of The Viking Press, Inc.

The Fox, by D. H. Lawrence, is reprinted from *The Portable D. H. Lawrence*. Copyright, 1923, by Thomas Seltzer, Inc.; 1947, by The Viking Press, Inc.

Published by Cooper Square Press
An Imprint of the Rowman & Littlefield Publishing Group
150 Fifth Avenue, Suite 817
New York, New York 10011

Distributed by National Book Network

Library of Congress Cataloging-in-Publication Data
Short novels of the masters / edited with an introduction by Charles Neider—1st Cooper Square Press ed.
    p. cm.
    Originally published: New York : Carroll & Graf, 1989.
    ISBN 0-8154-1178-2 (pbk. : alk. paper)
    1.   Fiction—Collections. I. Neider, Charles, 1915–

PN6120.2 .S465 2001
808.83—dc21   2001028421

Manufactured in the United States of America.

TO MARK NEIDER

CONTENTS

Introduction

THE TALES in this volume are limited to from fifteen to fifty thousand words. There is no agreement among editors or critics on the length limitations of the various fictional genres, and I have therefore set up my own criteria. The characteristics of the short story are its brevity and its full and immediate impact. It seems to me that narratives longer than fifteen thousand words generally fail to achieve such characteristics. I see no useful distinction between the long story and the short novel. The value of our definition of short novel is that it permits the collection in one volume of the longer but unnovelistic works of the modern masters. The usual anthology of short novels would probably exclude *The Dead* and *A Simple Heart*, which readily find admission to volumes of short stories. It seems to me of some value to study the works of the masters in the intermediate genre, when they were on vacation, as it were, from the strenuous exertions of the novel and yet too eager, full, and ambitious for the limitations of the short story. It is not difficult to understand why James called the intermediate genre the "blest *nouvelle*," and why the masters are partial to it. The short story is capable of poetic moments, but it is essentially a miniature form, like miniature painting, and cannot achieve heroic effects or such delightful orchestral attenuations as are achieved by the tone poem. The novella permits the master to improvise fully. It is just the balance of concentration and dilution which imparts to it its special and ingratiating flavor.

There is at present no generally preferred term for the intermediate form. My own preference is for *novella*, which, it seems to me, possesses certain advantages over *short novel*, and I shall therefore use it in its Anglicized form frequently in this introduction, although, for the convenience of readers, *short novel* is used in the title of our volume. *Novella* originally designated, in Italy, short tales such as those by Boccaccio, and first made its way into English when the Italian tale found favor with masters like Chaucer. The term *novelette* partly supplanted it. *Short novel* I consider inadequate because of its dependence on what is etymologically a newer and itself dependent form — *novel;* but mainly because, by robbing the intermediate genre of the dignity of its independent verbal identity, it tends to obscure the real aesthetic distinctions between the novella and the novel. I dislike *novelette*, which strikes me as pejorative; it looks and sounds trivial and is too long:

3

besides, its obviously diminutive form of *novel* also tends to blur distinctions and suggest dependence. *Novella* has a number of striking advantages over these terms. It is euphonious, dignified in sight and sound, of good length and fine color. To use it again is to revitalize it with its own rich tradition.

In Herman Melville's *Benito Cereno* the protagonist, an American, is a spectator of a foreign drama. The same situation exists for the protagonist of James's *The Aspern Papers*. This is not as accidental as it may seem. The American artist born before the middle of the last century was not inclined to look inward or at his own culture. It was a culture which estranged Melville and finally sterilized him, and frightened James sufficiently to make him settle abroad for most of his creative life. As an outsider, the artist became accustomed to being a spectator. Since much of his native spectacle was unpalatable to him he observed other, more pleasant cultures. Melville wrote of charming Pacific islands and primitive peoples. James wrote mainly of a super-civilized Europe. When either tried to deal with the "home situation" he found himself emphatically rebuffed. The artist's prying eye was resented by the Philistines. The artist, unhappily, lacked a great tradition to sustain him against this resentment. Dostoyevsky, Tolstoy, and Chekhov were more fortunate. In Russia a great literary beginning had been made early in the century. The nation was looking inward and was curtailing the importation of foreign languages and ideas; it was spiritually settling down to a long period of isolation. A Turgenev was savagely attacked by both Dostoyevsky and Tolstoy for his sympathy with the West. Soon it would be Russia who would be ogled as France and Germany had been, and ogled by the astonished West. Before long the pan-Slavs would have their Western artistic and philosophic disciples, and Nietzsche would cry out that Dostoyevsky was his teacher; Mann, gazing at his photograph of Tolstoy, would murmur about his sympathy with the East; and André Gide would be ecstatically steeped in the study of his master Dostoyevsky. It is not accidental that the protagonists of *Notes from Underground* and *The Death of Ivan Ilych* are indigenous, the authors underlining the fact that they are Russian types. In these tales the conflict is internal and it occurs on native soil. The American tales are adventure stories; the Russian ones are stories of inner crisis.

One other author in our collection was born before the middle of the nineteenth century — Flaubert. Although he was perennially in arms against the bourgeoisie, he had merry company. The bourgeois could harass the French artist but could not easily vanquish him. In his legal battle with Flaubert over *Madame Bovary* the bourgeois emerged badly mauled. The artistic tradition in France was long and great, and the artist found protection in high places. Baiting the bourgeois was a sport, like baiting the bear. The fact that one could go on baiting him was proof of the French artist's superior position. French culture was old and stabilized, worthy of studying itself. Flaubert painted it in a series of tableaux. He was a spectator by choice, in a sense. *A Simple Heart* evidences the cool touch of the distant master, secure in his profession and his art. There is neither an outer nor an inner conflict. The interest lies in a maidservant's predictability.

With the exception of Chekhov, the remaining authors of our collection all belong to the third quarter of the century. Chekhov's *Ward No. 6* echoes the novellas of Tolstoy and Dostoyevsky, but it is milder than both; it can afford to speak quietly after their denunciations. In Mann's *Death in Venice* the spectator of a foreign drama becomes also the leading actor in it, experiencing an inner crisis: a balance of forces is achieved between the spectacle and the experience. In the nation of Goethe and Schiller the artist is poet and teacher in one. Art has attained respectability, but in its devotees the criminal impulse, although suppressed, is still the motive force, and at a moment of climax may spring out and destroy its possessor. Joyce's *The Dead* also portrays a spectator who experiences an inner crisis; but Gabriel's crisis is more cultural than personal. The Ireland which suppressed Joyce and sent him into voluntary exile has emasculated Gabriel, an artistic type, who lacks the strength of revolt and exile as well as the weakness of complete surrender. Kafka's *The Metamorphosis* follows the tradition of Dostoyevsky's underground, although with an expressionistic rather than a realistic vehicle. Lawrence's novella follows several traditions, largely English; but in his depiction of the mental underground he is indebted to Dostoyevsky.

It is noteworthy that of our ten novellas, nine strike the note of defeat — all save Lawrence's; and that nine are concerned with physical death — all except Dostoyevsky's, which describes spiritual death. Three contain the word *dead* or *death* in their titles. Death need not, of course, be considered a defeat; but in almost all these tales it is related to defeat, the authors utilizing it symbolically to carry the weight of their pessimism. All decry the modern world, which they describe as petty, materialistic, soulless. In Melville's novella, death overtakes the representative of a decayed but cultured aristocracy, a man doomed by rebellious barbarians. In James's, it removes from the scene one of the last survivors of a heroic era, leaving the narrator to face the uninspired, shriveled present one. In Tolstoy's, it is the punishment for a typical modern hero: the materialistic, bureaucratic, self-centered civil servant. In Dostoyevsky's, the protagonist is crushed by the modern world of oppression, the city, alienation. In Chekhov's, death symbolizes the extinction of sanity, reason and idealism, destroyed by the Philistines. In Flaubert's, it is the reward of a good and faithful member of the peasant class who has exhausted her life in devoted but largely unrecognized service to a member of the bourgeoisie. In Mann's, an untimely death is the price of an artificially heroic life in an unheroic age. In Joyce's, death symbolizes the loss in Gabriel of youthful idealism, imagination, poetry; he is a product of Irish Babbittry. In Kafka's, death takes the idealistic son, a commercial traveler unfit for the modern hustling world. And in Lawrence's, it removes from the stage the one hindrance to Henry's progress; Banford is an Edwardian, and Lawrence destroys her. Lawrence's optimism sounds brassy compared with the pessimism of the other masters.

The creative practices of our masters range from Flaubert's aesthetic idealism to Lawrence's aesthetic realism. For Flaubert, the flesh stands in the way of the ideal, and it must therefore be renounced with unyielding asceticism. For Lawrence, art approximates biology. It is a product of the body's rhythms. There is no ideal to be achieved except the natural bodily expression in improvisation. If the artist is not satisfied with a draft, he must ask his body to assume another attitude and improvise all over again. Mann is the referee between these extremes. He sees art as a mediation between nature and spirit, body and idea. The Platonic ideal of Flaubert exists but can never be wholly reached by man. On the other hand, art is also partly a product of bodily functions. The artist suspends himself in the void of nonbelief and permits himself to be acted upon simultaneously from above and below. In doing so he performs a moral service, that of humanization of the idea and spiritualization of the body; the artist is the supreme humanist. For Joyce, there is a Flaubertian ideal to be striven for ascetically; but this ideal is closely linked with humanity; it is a repository of human dreams. The artist is the keeper of the myth. In him the race finds its articulation and self-realization. Chekhov sees the artistic gesture as a high human act, mental and physical, and as such capable of constant improvement like any other. He disbelieves in the existence of a Platonic realm. Melville and the early Tolstoy agree with him. The converted Tolstoy believes that the artist should be a functionary subordinated to moral needs. For him there is a moral ideal which it is the artist's duty to work toward. James is an aesthetic idealist: the artist's duty is to seek the ideal by observation and by a play of mind. For Dostoyevsky and Kafka the artist performs a purgative function. When humanity becomes dammed up with supercharged feelings and notions, the artist, as the most sensitive and the consecrated valve in the structure, explodes to save it. His is a suicidal mission of a religious sort.

I

HERMAN MELVILLE

(1819 — 1891)

Herman Melville is the greatest modern practitioner of the novel of realistic romance in the tradition of Defoe, and of the novel of the sea in the tradition of Smollett. He managed partly to fuse the two differing traditions of Defoe and Sterne, from the latter gaining technical and personal freedom as well as a symbolistic tendency. Among his novels, *Moby Dick* owes most to Sterne. Melville perversely yearned to imitate his friend Hawthorne, who worked in the Sterne tradition and was followed in this by James; but when he permitted himself actually to attempt imitation the result was unfortunate. It was Joyce who carried forward the task of fusion begun by Melville. Although Melville's influence on Conrad, Stevenson, Hudson, and Masefield has been carefully noted by critics, his influence on Joyce has been underrated. One ought to recall the stylistic affinities — the love of sounded and specialized language, of language for itself, the broad vocabulary, the genius for dialogue, the onomatological obsession — and such striking similarities as the use of the interior monologue and the play form in *Moby Dick* and in *Ulysses*.

Melville's experiments in symbolism and literary metaphysics upset his public, which was not ready for them. The age was addicted to stories of romance and travel. A great writer was presumed also to be a great journalist. *Two Years before the Mast* was a vast success, and as long as Melville followed its pattern he was acclaimed throughout the nation. But from the beginning he was a troublemaker: he offended the clergy and the French with *Typee* and the Navy with *White-Jacket*. He made his weight felt: he introduced new words, such as "taboo," into the language, and reforms into the naval code, becoming responsible for the abolition of flogging. The deluge of abuse began with *Moby Dick*. With *Pierre* it began to overwhelm him. The public muttered that the brilliant writer of romances had soured: worse than that, he had turned wicked. And Melville entered the desert of neglect.

One of the stories of his last period is startling in its modernity. Kafka would have been proud to have written *Bartleby the Scrivener*, with its mixture of laughter and tears. This "story of Wall Street" is an indictment of the soulless activities symbolized by the thoroughfare. Bartleby, the disillusioned tabellion, dies — with his excess of the spiritual he has long been on the side of death — with a Jamesian gesture of renunciation. He just "prefers not to," to the destined end. And Melville sighs "Ah Bartleby! Ah humanity!" From such a pre-expressionistic effort in the short fictional form, Melville turned to the superbly descriptive and romantic *Encantadas*, as if to exhaust his versatility. And during this same unhappy period of his life he composed *Benito Cereno*.

Benito Cereno, a psychological masterpiece of the ambiguity of appearances, appeared anonymously in *Putnam's Monthly Magazine* in 1855 and remained unacknowledged until the following year, when it was included in *The Piazza Tales*, a volume of Melville's short stories. Together with *Billy Budd*, it stands at the artistic apex of Melville's shorter fiction. With the posthumous and unfortunately unfinished work it has many affinities besides the fact that both take place at sea, at the very close of the eighteenth century, and are concerned with mutinies. The theme of the noble figure overwhelmed by the world's unreason was a familiar and dear one to Melville, who perhaps saw Benito and Billy as personifications of his dark literary fate, which began with expurgation and charges of immorality, one journal proclaiming him "a wretched profligate," and ended with almost total neglect. Benito succumbs in a monastery as a result of his torture by the powers of evil, who rose to engulf him in so dramatic a manner as to fire the imagination of a Melville brooding upon the oceans of calumny then engulfing him. Billy is the victim of sudden passions and an iron naval code, Claggart being the instrument of evil who inflames and dooms him. Billy is a sacrificial lamb slaughtered to appease the monsters of necessity and hard destiny. His fate is less sentimentalized and more classically tragic than Benito's. But then he is the handiwork of a man of seventy-two, who in a mild hour at the end of his life closes the circle by returning to artistic beginnings, while Benito is the creation of a man still violent, powerful — and very angry.

Aside from one flaw, *Benito Cereno* is the architectural delight of Melville's fiction. The often burdensome documentation of novels like *Typee*, the sometimes embarrassing effusions of *Mardi*, the flawed point of view of *Moby Dick* are handicaps not evident in *Benito Cereno*, in which the construction is excellent and in which the slowly increasing psychological weight of the tale, due to its careful architecture, is beautiful and orchestral. The flaw is the bulky mass of depositions, which are anticlimactic after the running narrative. The depositions were taken almost word for word from a document which was the inspiration for the novella.

It was common for Melville to base his narratives on personal experience together with a good deal of research. In *Benito Cereno* he depended heavily on a published account, Captain Amasa Delano's *Voyages and Travels*, which appeared almost forty years earlier. Chapter 18 of the account forms the groundwork of Melville's story. Melville, of course, symbolizes, dramatizes, and psychologizes the raw material with great skill and purpose. He changes the names of the two ships from *Tryal* and *Perseverance* to *San Dominick* and *Bachelor's Delight*: brightens Benito's character, blackens that of the Senegalese; invents the oakum pickers, the Ashantee hatchet polishers, and the shaving scene; and studs his narrative with symbolic devices and pieces of psychological business. By calling the Spanish ship *San Dominick* he suggests monasticism, feudalism, and fanaticism. He describes the ship as resembling "a white-washed monastery after a thunderstorm, seen perched upon some dun cliff among the Pyrenees," and the figures peering over the bulwarks as seeming like "Black Friars pacing the cloisters."

His method of symbolizing the theme of the ambiguity of appearances and the reversal of good and evil may be exemplified briefly in an early description of the Spanish ship: "But the principal relic of faded grandeur was the ample oval of the shield-like stern-piece, intricately carved with the arms of Castile and Leon, medallioned about by groups of mythological or symbolical devices; uppermost and central of which was a dark satyr in a mask, holding his foot on the prostrate neck of a writhing figure, likewise masked." Melville also symbolizes the contrast between American democracy and Spanish monarchy. The American captain is portrayed as naïve and blunt, a healthy practical man bent on helping his neighbors while making an honest dollar. The Spanish captain is pictured as overrefined, given to ritualistic gallantry and circumlocution. The Spanish ship, symbolizing the empire, is rotten, and the Spaniards are the victims of colonial revolt. Ironically, the democratic Americans restore the feudalistic Spaniards to power.

At the risk of committing *lèse-majesté*, I suggest that Melville was so absorbed in the symbolistic aspects of his theme that he allowed himself to be guilty of meretriciousness in deviating too far from the truth. In the real Delano's account of his adventures with the Spanish ship there are several expressions of profound sympathy for the slaves. Not that Delano by any means condoned the mutiny; however, he understood the beastliness of their condition and the fact that the Spaniards were their oppressors. He made it clear what butchers the Spaniards were, how they tried to slaughter the remaining blacks after the Spanish ship was recaptured and how Cereno himself was guilty of treachery, cruelty, and violence. Melville glosses over extenuating circumstances in an effort to blacken the blacks and whiten the whites, to create poetic images of pure evil and pure virtue. The result is sometimes unfortunate in the feelings it arouses against the Negroes.

I do not mean to suggest that Melville is lacking in compassion or social insight; only that, with his fixed ideas of ambiguity, ambivalence, and masquerade, he is swept away by artistic and thematic considerations to a point where he *seems* to lack compassion and an acute awareness of the truth. There is contrivance, too, in *Ivan Ilych* and *Ward No. 6*, but always to heighten the truth and the sense of compassion, never to diminish them. However, this is a minor sin in a virtuous artist. If anyone doubts the existence of Melville's compassion, then he cannot have read the heart-rending chapter of *Redburn* called "What Redburn Saw in Launcelott's-Hey," a description of the dead and dying poor in Liverpool, concluding with the eloquent, "Ah, what are our creeds, and how do we hope to be saved? Tell me, oh Bible, that story of Lazarus again, that I may find comfort in my heart for the poor and forlorn. Surrounded as we are by the wants and woes of our fellow-men, and yet given to follow our own pleasures, regardless of their pains, are we not like people sitting up with a corpse, and making merry in the house of the dead?"

The language of *Benito Cereno* is restrained and formal, possessing a dry beauty, yet perilously close to Melville's last unhappy style.

With Melville as with Joyce, language was always the real hero and he reveled in it, producing at his best a rubied surface, with a powerful, masculine, auditory rhetoric, alliterative and onomatopoetic. Melville's real tragedy is not that he withdrew from his early subjects into the metaphysical mists of *Pierre* and *The Confidence Man*, but that he permitted himself to stiffen inwardly in recoiling from the public's misunderstanding of him, and let his language grow formal and stale. He learned to grow ashamed of his riotous gifts; he yearned to write like Hawthorne; he constricted his vigor and violence in the strait jacket of puritanical English, abandoning idiom, slang, the earthy tone color of his genius. *Benito Cereno* is bathed by the twilight of that genius, but it is a genius still sufficiently great to make this product one of the masterpieces of our literature.

II

HENRY JAMES

(1 8 4 3 — 1 9 1 6)

If Melville is characteristically a "masculine" writer, with great drive, color, and earthiness, in the line of Defoe, then Henry James, following the tradition of Sterne through Thackeray and Hawthorne, is a "feminine" artist whose chief characteristics are subtlety of insight and nuance, a high intellectual quality, and remoteness from the cruder if more basic concerns of life. Melville is the type of artist whose artistry seems to find expression despite the man; whereas James is above all the artist, his daily and yearly existence running a poor second to his art. In Melville's life, "events" were of importance; in James's, they were singularly absent, despite his travels and his considerable social side; and these factors are importantly reflected in their work. Their dissimilarity is further suggested by the difference in their language. Melville's is Elizabethan; James's is of a less virile century, with its lambent style, intellectual sinew, and its wit rather than humor.

James is a master of the novella form, of which he was extremely fond. Of *The Aspern Papers*, that limpidly beautiful and exciting example of the "developmental" novella as against the "anecdotal" short story, he wrote in one of his prefaces to the New York edition of his collected works: "I saw it somehow at the very first blush as romantic . . . that Jane Clairmont, the half-sister of Mary Godwin, Shelley's second wife, and for a while the intimate friend of Byron and the mother of his daughter Allegra, should have been living on in Florence, where she had long lived, up to our own day, and that in fact, had I happened to hear of her but a little sooner, I might have seen her in the flesh." The fact which "kindled a flame" was that a gentleman, an ardent Shelleyite, had designed to become Miss Clairmont's *pensionnaire* with the hope of enjoying priority, in the event of her death (which seemed imminent), in bargaining for Shelley manuscripts which he supposed her to possess.

In one of his notebooks, in an entry dated January 12, 1887, James wrote: "Hamilton (V. L.'s brother) told me a curious thing of Capt. Silsbee — the Boston art-critic and Shelley-worshipper; that is of a curious adventure of his." He speaks of the American's adventure with Miss Clairmont and her niece and says he believes there is a little subject there, "the picture of the two faded, queer, poor and discredited old English women — living on into a strange generation, in their musty corner of a foreign town — with these illustrious letters their most precious possession." Further on he continues: "The interest would be in some price that the man has to pay — that the old woman — or the survivor — sets upon the papers. . . . The Countess Gamba came while I was there: her husband is a nephew of the Guiccioli — and it was à *propos* of their having a lot of Byron's letters of which they are rather illiberal and dangerous guardians, that H. told me the above . . . ."

James always required — one might almost say demanded — a minimum of suggestion for the inspiration of his art. The discoveries of the fabulist, he would assert, "are scarce more than alert recognitions." The fabulist comes upon the interesting thing "because he had moved in the right direction for it . . . ." Of *The Aspern Papers* he wrote many years after its publication: "So it was, at all events, that my imagination preserved power to react under the mere essential charm — that, I mean, of a final scene of the rich dim Shelley drama played out in the very theatre of our own 'modernity.' This was the beauty that appealed to me; there had been, so to speak, a forward continuity, from the actual man, the divine poet, on; and the curious, the ingenious, the admirable thing would be to throw it backward again, to compress — squeezing it hard! — the connexion that had drawn itself out, and convert so the stretched relation into a value of nearness on our own part." For reasons of delicacy, James shifted the scene of the tale to Venice and made the leading characters Americans.

James's behavior in the presence of the particle of fact which stimulates the imagination may be strikingly contrasted with Thomas Mann's. James immediately withdraws from actuality, whereas Mann ardently embraces it. According to Mann himself, almost all the symbols, scenes, characters, and events in *Death in Venice* actually presented themselves to him in the life, and his main task was that of vision, organization, and style. Similarly in *Tonio Kröger*. This dissimilitude in behavior toward the inciting experience suggests an important distinction in their attitudes toward art and life.

James's art is in large measure Platonic; that is, idealistic, although its fabric is skeptical realism. Mann's, in contrast, is realistic and often naturalistic, while his thought is idealistic in the German metaphysical tradition. James's artistic development was in the direction away from facts and events. His great interest was improvisation; he wished to test to their utmost the many permutations and combinations, all purely imaginative, of any given situation, without the clutter of "facts." It was a kind of geometric fascination. James loved to feel the unbounded imagination at play; he delighted to see how far the bubble could be stretched without bursting. This "pure" type of flight Stephen Spender likens to music. The suggestion is apt, although it rankles a little because of the fact that James, according to reliable reports, was altogether unmusical. It was really the great engineering feat that James adored: to see how long and how light he could make his span across the river of prosaic reality. But there is a grave danger in extremely extended invention: the stress may be too great and the bridge may fall. It seems to me that just this occurs in *The Turn of the Screw*.

To speak of music again: in music each moment must please in itself at the same time that it carries the larger flow of delight. In the verbal arts the necessity to please en route, as it were, is satisfied largely by the extent that language approaches poetry. In prose fiction many instruments play their roles — suspense, characterization, et cetera — and these inevitably limit as well as encourage invention. The more they are challenged by improvisation the more the language must be poetic to sustain the immediate delight. Now the characteristic beauty of James's language lies in its exquisite prosiness — as against, say, Melville's poetic prose. Therefore James can afford less than poetic-prose fabulists to exceed the limits of the prose-fictive conventions. Music, after all, *is* time, while prose imitates and represents time. Prose must above all represent or communicate. When what it com-

municates is simply sheer invention, this is a signal that the improvisation has become too attenuated, that the bridge is down.

"Nothing is so easy," writes James, "as improvisation, the running
on and on of invention; it is sadly compromised, however, from the
moment its stream breaks bounds and gets into flood." He modestly
neglects to say that it is peculiarly easy for *him*. He believes that the
merit of *The Turn of the Screw* is that "it has struggled successfully with
its dangers." Perhaps he would very much like to believe this because
it is uncompromised invention "without the possibility of ravage, without the hint of a flood," which was here his goal. For me the tale is
swamped by excessive manipulation. My recommendation of an example of a successful Jamesian span is *The Aspern Papers*.

It is difficult to regard James's flight from the inspirational fact without a certain probing curiosity. One wonders what his gesture symbolizes, what it unconsciously represents. Is it a distaste for reality,
based on the equation of reality with vulgarity, crudeness, imperfec-
tion? Does James withdraw with such passion because he hopes to
attain in his private world of form and plastic beauty a larger measure
of happiness than he can hope to obtain in the public one? That is, is
his creative method a function of his view, of his awareness and judgment, of life? If so, then perhaps a greater understanding of it will
enlighten us a little regarding the private James.

At what point does James take flight from fact? And just what kind
of facts inspire him, acting as triggers which release the flow of his fan-
tasies, as well as the simultaneous flow of the artistic disguises which
veil their true nature? Here is an interesting field of study for the student of James. I would hazard that for James reality, as a complex of
symbols and as a whole symbol itself, was closely married to the notion
of sex and particularly with heterosexual relations and that his flight is
always from this "nasty" world into the "purer" realm of celibacy,
chastity, renunciation — or, that is, narcissism and latent homosexuality. The seed of fact, I suspect, must for James always be capable of
secret homosexual symbolic expansion. One *senses* the latent homosexuality in almost all of James's work. A large number of his male
characters are like the obstetrical toad, which takes over some of the
female's duties by wearing a string of eggs round its middle. Perhaps
much of the beauty of the work is due to this latent homosexuality, to
the beautiful gestures and forms with which it disguises itself. But this
is not to suggest that James was altogether unaware of his masks. It is
part of the challenging complexity and greatness of the man that he

was capable of turning his microscope and his irony upon himself as well as upon the world he observed.

In *The Turn of the Screw* the homosexual symbolism is starkly evident, once one rejects the supernatural conventions and accepts the evil servants as still alive. In *The Pupil*, another novella, the boy Morgan has caustic insight into his parents. In a sense he is against them and for Pemberton, his tutor. The two are subtly in league against the parents, who are portrayed as disorderly in person and morals, and vulgarly heterosexual. Morgan and Pemberton are pictured as finer, of nobler stuff, of higher conscience and aesthetic perception. Morgan is intent on exposing his parents' wickedness to Pemberton, or at least on forcing Pemberton to admit his knowledge of it. He wishes to form an alliance based on this knowledge and on their difference from the parents — a situation with homosexual overtones. Morgan says, "We must be frank, at the last; we *must* come to an understanding. I know all about everything." Morgan, who has a weak heart, dies because of his sudden joy on learning that he is at last free to go away with Pemberton — presumably to a lovers' relationship. As so often in James, money plays an important role. His concern with money in his work has been but one of the causes for the charges of snobbery leveled against him. His defenders have argued with effect that in his life James was not unduly concerned with money; that money *is* important in the moneyed society which he best knew; and that by supplying his people with it James enabled them to enjoy the higher life of aesthetic and moral discrimination which only leisure affords. What has been overlooked by commentators, to my knowledge, is the symbolic value (ordure) of money in James, symbolic in a mythical and psychological sense.

James and Dostoyevsky: one is not likely to find with ease another literary pair so emphasizing dissimilarity. And yet unlikeness sometimes conceals analogy. Dostoyevsky, too, is a great improviser whose works have their germ — but only their germ — in reality. He is full of the hot "idea," however, while James is definitely not. T. S. Eliot said of James that he had a mind so fine that no idea could violate it; and Charles Peirce, the American scientist, wrote of him to William James: "He is a splendid fellow. I admire him greatly and have only discovered two faults in him. One is that his digestion isn't quite that of an ostrich and the other is that he isn't as fond of turning over questions as I am, but likes to settle them and have done with them. A manly trait too, but not a philosophical one." James himself once wrote in a letter: "Thank God, however, I've no *opinions* — not even on the Dreyfus case. I'm more and more only aware of things as a more or less mad panorama, phantasmagoria and divine museum." But the "idea" and the "non-idea" are not so far apart as they may seem, the Dostoyevskian "idea" being an explosive manifestation of psychic energy, and the "non-idea" of James being a shunning disguise for the release of similar energy in a quiet and aloof nature. In Dostoyevsky, too, there is the constant tone of latent homosexuality, as in *Crime and Punishment.* Such a tone is not lacking in *The Aspern Papers,* which seems on the surface no more than a story of intellectual and aesthetic curiosity, but which is permeated with the sense of the narrator's desire to "reach" Jeffrey Aspern's person more than his literary effects. The small oval portrait of Aspern, which the narrator finally possesses, is of suggestive symbolic interest, as well as the narrator's references to it during the climactic scene with Miss Tina.

The Aspern Papers stems from James's beautifully mellow middle period, the popular one of *Daisy Miller* and *The Portrait of a Lady,* in which he is more genial than in his late and difficult manner. Here he has still a certain interest in façades and events; and his warmest self enters his work, that fine, tender, relatively uninhibited self of the letters. In his last period he was more daemonic, less sparing of himself and his reader. It, too, produced its masterpieces, such as *The Beast in the Jungle* and the great novels. There he finally achieved his goal, merciless objectivity in the study of the aesthetic sensibility. An ascetic artist like Flaubert, his concern with facts and data was now very different from Flaubert's. Flaubert collected facts as if they were precious stones and put them together into scintillating mosaics. His philosophy of impersonality was embodied in the objectivity of the fact. James came to consider the fact to be an indissoluble hindrance to the smooth flow of sensibility. His philosophy of objectivity was embodied in the impersonality of the aesthetic sensibility. He came to regard action as the hardest of facts, as composed of facts and creator of them. Action is therefore sedulously avoided in the presentation; only as reported by a sensibility does it dissolve into the necessary fluidity which permits James's standard of style. The world as intellectually perceived, but not in terms of mere "ideas" and "platitudes of statement" — this came to be his aesthetic and dramatic problem. Sensibility as discrimination, intellect as sensibility, the ultimate union of emotion and idea: these are James's province and victory. Facing direct and immediate experience, James was rewarded with ignorance and blankness. But when he averted his eye, pretending indifference, the rays struck it at the corner and enriched him with his finest illuminations.

III

FEODOR MIKHAILOVICH DOSTOYEVSKY

(1 8 2 1 — 1 8 8 1)

In 1864 there appeared in three numbers of *The Epoch*, a Russian magazine edited by Dostoyevsky's brother Mikhail, one of the great novellas of all literature, Feodor Dostoyevsky's *Notes from Underground*, of which André Gide has written: "I believe that with these *Notes* we reach the height of Dostoyevsky's career. I consider this book (and I am not alone in my belief) as the keystone of his entire works." Thomas Mann calls the work an "awe- and terror-inspiring" example of Dostoyevsky's "sympathy" and "frightful insight." "In its contents," he continues, "it comes closest to Dostoyevsky's great and completely characteristic products."

As usual with Dostoyevsky, his work was produced in trying external conditions. In this instance his first wife was dying slowly and painfully of consumption, and often her screams filled the apartment. Nevertheless he went on with the work and was even able to write to Mikhail in April, 1864: "The story lengthens. Sometimes I dream it will be trash. However, I am writing with fervor. I do not know how it will turn out. Yet in this matter what is needed is much time. . . . I am afraid that the death of my wife will take place soon, and this will cause a necessary interruption in the work." A little later he writes, "What am I to do? Surely it's not possible to print it unfinished. It is impossible. It cannot be divided. However, I do not know what will become of it — perhaps it will be trash. But personally, I place strong hopes in it. However bad it may be, yet it will produce a powerful effect. I know it. Perhaps it will be very fine."

Although all his life Dostoyevsky cried out for more leisure for the production of his art, it is likely that unconsciously he required desperate circumstances for its conception and completion. He envied Turgenev and Tolstoy their ability to create in peace, taking as much time as they needed to correct, implement and polish, and casually waiting for publishers to make an offer; while he, because of poverty, invariably had to offer his work to editors of magazines even before it was fully conceived, and then had to meet deadlines as the sequences appeared in monthly installments. Dostoyevsky was convinced that events were against him, that his destiny had played him false. But it is quite possible that at bottom he understood that this destiny was at least partly his own creation, and that he thrived on external turmoil, which supported the inner turmoil that gave birth to the products of his genius.

Freud, in his *Dostoyevsky and Parricide*, one of the most brilliant essays in the Dostoyevsky literature, has suggested convincingly that Dostoyevsky's sense of guilt was a result of an Oedipus fixation, and that because of this guilt he felt the urge to punish himself. Freud explains his gambling mania as an onanistic compulsion and a titanic self-punishment, stressing that Dostoyevsky invariably played until he lost all, and that afterward he worked at his best, having relieved himself temporarily of his guilt feelings. Freud suggests that Dostoyevsky compulsively assumed external burdens (such as his brother Mikhail's debts and the support of his family) because of his need for punishment, and that consequently he was able to flourish in situations intolerable to normal men. Dostoyevsky's unquenchable optimism, even in the most monstrous occurrences, can be seen as due to a feeling of relief caused by his punishment. It is probable that the editorial conditions — especially the constant and nerve-destroying deadlines — under which his work was produced were also secretly his own creation, part of his vast unseen system of self-punishment. Dostoyevsky's work had to be born in fear and trembling. Its greatness resides in its tension, and this tension seems to stem from his sense of guilt and his efforts to expiate for the unknown crime. Dostoyevsky's life-pattern required the element of last-minute miraculous escape, the prototype of which was possibly his experience before the firing squad, with the last-minute commutation of sentence. The function of his epilepsy, which Freud calls his hystero-epilepsy or serious hysteria, rather than true organic epilepsy, was among other things to intensify his sense of guilt after suddenly releasing him from it.

In *Notes from Underground* Dostoyevsky presents most bluntly, forcefully, and in consummate fashion his conceptions of the underground man and the double, conceptions that single him out from novelists of the nineteenth century. Nietzsche's two masters, Dostoyevsky and Schopenhauer, are rebels against nineteenth-century mechanical optimism, which relied on the dictates of reason and the postulates of a mechanistic universe. They emphasized the irrational in man. Dostoyevsky's objections to the revolutionary programs of his time were that they were mechanically amelioristic, and that they regarded men as ciphers in a neat equation, to which the revolutionists alone possessed the key. Dostoyevsky's "hero" in the *Notes*, pendulating between sadism and masochism, outdragoning the world one moment and outflunkying it another, in his malediction denounces rationalism and asserts the force of the mysterious and powerful underground impulses in man, which are often "unreasonable" to the extent of being suicidal.

Dostoyevsky is the precursor of two other students of the underground, Lawrence and Kafka. He is greater than they because of his polarity: he is also exquisitely aware of the saintly aboveground. In his dualism he owes much to Hegel, whom he admired tremendously. Dostoyevsky conceived of his underground man as a social phenomenon — and primarily a Russian one, the result of hundreds of years of Russian oppression and repression. He believed that freedom could be attained by faith and humility rather than by science and reason; but despite his desperate search for faith he died wavering between belief and despair. His hero's philosophy is a philosophy of malice, a malice that is the sadistic side of the unconscious. He believed — and the researches of Freud have proved him correct — that only by an acceptance of the unconscious, the underground, can man win freedom and health. As an artist he knew that the underground, the abyss, the Abaddon, is the source of all creativity as it is of criminality.

Dostoyevsky's double is a portrait of a split personality. The double is *the* inhabitant of the underground. He is the wild neurotic, hopelessly trapped by his ambivalence, torn by conflicting criminal and ethical impulses. At times Dostoyevsky actually projects a double, as in *Crime and Punishment*, and as in his first novella, entitled *The Double*, an amazing *tour de force* of paranoia which he composed in 1846, shortly after *Poor Folk*, the first novel which brought him sudden fame. *The Double* was not well received by the critics and the public. It seemed a disappointment coming from one who was expected to wear Gogol's mantle. And this estimation has continued consistently, despite Dostoyevsky's enthusiasm for the work. Perhaps the tale was too modern, too daemonic, too irrational; perhaps it is still these things. Its psychological penetration, its invention and richness, its portrait of the world as nightmare, are astonishing, aside from the fact that it was created by a youth of twenty-five, more than a century ago. But the best thing about it — the stroke of genius — is that its point of

view is undeviatingly that of the irrational. There is a moral difference between portraying a madman from the outside, clinically, and
from the inside, poetically. The first insists he is an aberration from
rational society; the second, that he is a victim of irrational society.
Golyadkin is seen as society's victim; and here is the author's defense
of the underground man: that he is the result of an attempt at rationalism in the midst of an irrational society which pretends to be reasonable.
This, incidentally, is one of Kafka's basic themes.

Dostoyevsky believed that the underground man was the hope of
Russia's spiritual redemption, and that by casting him out, by shunning him, she was destroying herself. Chaos as the mother of redemption, the pit as prelude to rebirth, the abyss as creative, sin as the basis
of saintliness: these were among his leading themes. Dostoyevsky is
without doubt the profoundest student of the abyss in modern literature.
His works constitute a great portrait of the artist as criminal and saint.
Golyadkin of *The Double* is as modern and as lost as Gregor of *The
Metamorphosis*. His loneliness is terrible. He is tormented by guilt and
by fear of the world. He is a spiritual brother of the hero of the *Notes*,
between whom and the world the wall of incommunicability is as great
as if he had been transformed into a monstrous bug. As Golyadkin
slowly succumbs to his modern and symbolic disease, he is accused of
lying, treachery, maliciousness. The charges are correct, but they disregard his mitigating qualities and the fact of his illness. Society glibly
accuses him because it has decayed; in its decadence it finds it natural
and easy to suspect the accused of the worst and to find him guilty
without trial — the pattern in Kafka.

Dostoyevsky, the orgiast whose emotional life constantly reached
extremes — the mechanism of the epileptiform attacks is significantly
similar to that of the orgasm — was not attracted to "reasonable"
people and events, a fact which partially explains his hatred of the
even-tenored, self-possessed Turgenev. Many of his characters live
a life of undignified otiosity. He is frankly a sensationalist. His work
has the kind of fascination one finds in the tabloids. The difference,
of course, lies in his understanding, imagination, compassion, richness
of detail — and his art. Amazingly enough, everything he touched
seems a *tour de force;* and yet his people and events possess an undoubted
reality. His world is not beautiful; it is even deliberately unpoetic.
But, like the creations of all great geniuses, it impresses one with its
self-sufficiency. It is obsessive and fantastically vertical; also enormously aural. The emphasis is always on dialogue rather than on

narration and visual imagery.   His works are not epical, like Tolstoy's.
They are colossal, loutish dramas portraying a hemmed-in, distorted
universe full of the "idea," in contrast with the pagan corporeality of
Tolstoy's world.

IV

LEO NIKOLAEVICH TOLSTOY

(1 8 2 8 — 1 9 1 0)

Leo Tolstoy possessed to an awe-inspiring degree the genius of insinuating himself into the very center of life. James, on the other hand,
avoided the middle — it startled and perhaps terrified him; at any
rate it stultified him. His treatment of death is typical. One rarely
feels that his people actually die. Like the exploited Indians, they
"bite the dust." In Tolstoy there are no euphemisms for death.
Tolstoy understood and portrayed death more vividly and profoundly
than any other novelist — perhaps because he was more alive than
his literary competitors. To be half alive is to be half dead, and
consequently only half afraid of death. Tolstoy was wholly alive,
an incredible Antaeus, prodigious in his appetites; and his mortality
was a terrible burden to him. His vitality is felt everywhere in his
work, even in his portraits of corpses, and in his ascetic musings on the
mortifications of the flesh. In fact, one of Tolstoy's corpses is more
alive than the average novelist's athlete.

James was an aesthete, like Turgenev and Flaubert. For Tolstoy
the philosophy of the aesthete was repugnant. Turgenev's deathbed
appeal that Tolstoy return to art, which he had renounced, was for
Tolstoy merely the final and most effective proof that Turgenev was the
unreconstructed littérateur. With all his genius for understanding
humanity, Tolstoy seemed unable to grasp the fact that Turgenev, with
his modicum of vitality, was accomplishing a hero's labor in being the
artist on so fine a scale; that he himself, Tolstoy, was the product of his
energy, even its slave, down to his philosophy; and that he was contemptuous of the aesthetes because he possessed sufficient energy to
outdo them in art and was still dissatisfied with art because of the
energy that remained. Melville, born nine years before him and half
a world away, shared with him a fabulous lust for life, creative genius,
and a terrifying sense of death, as well as a distaste for aesthetes.

Melville and Tolstoy — epic artists, abounding in life. Both began their careers mightily, and both ended them in clouds of mysticism in their efforts to appease the dragon of death.

In 1879 Tolstoy completed an astonishing testament which he called *A Confession* and in which he depicted, step by step, his journey on the spiritual road to Damascus. Like Saul of Tarsus, he found himself converted to Christianity, although of so unorthodox a variety that he was later excommunicated by the Russian Church. While possessing everything he had supposed he could wish for — money, fame, health, love — he suddenly found his life impossible and his past a vanity of vanities. Among these vanities he included his great artistic works, which he now regarded as sensual abominations. What brought him to this cataclysmic change, which was to dominate the second half of his life, was fear of death — not death in the abstract, nor through accident or disease, nor as the final scene in his personal drama, but death as an aggressive, invisible, monstrous pursuer: death in the form of elemental urges to self-destruction, in a form so cunning and insidious that he had to shun rope and rifle and similar instruments for fear he would suddenly annihilate himself.

Tolstoy sought means of escaping this impulse to death. From science he derived no comfort because, in his opinion, it was incapable of revealing to him the meaning of life. Nor did metaphysics help. He found refuge finally in religious faith. In the testament, after reviewing his life of ambition, vanity, and lust, he quotes Socrates, Schopenhauer, and Ecclesiastes to support him in his conversion. From Socrates he sets down, "We approach truth only inasmuch as we depart from life. . . . The wise man seeks death all his life and therefore death is not terrible to him." Schopenhauer he quotes on the advantages of renouncing the universal will and its specific manifestation, the *Wille zum Leben.* Then he presents the Vanity of Vanities peroration at length. It is all extremely touching, honest, and human. But what interests us in the confession at the moment is its illuminating relation to the extraordinary novella of Tolstoy's in our volume.

According to the Tolstoy authority Ernest J. Simmons, *Ivan Ilych* was probably begun as early as 1882, although it was not completed until March of 1886. It is considered the first important work of art that Tolstoy produced since finishing *Anna Karenina* in 1876, and by many is judged to be his most successful artistic work of the period of his conversion. Its effect on publication was great, in Europe at large as well as in Russia. Romain Rolland wrote that it impressed the French public as few Russian works had, and that he had witnessed the sensation it caused among the middle-class readers in the French provinces, "a class apparently indifferent to literature and art." He called Ivan Ilych "the representative type of the European bourgeoisie of 1880, which reads Zola, goes to hear Bernhardt, and, without holding any faith, is not even irreligious, for it does not take the trouble either to believe or to disbelieve, it simply never thinks of such matters."

While it is true that Ivan Ilych is the "representative type of the European bourgeoisie," what is just as true is that he is in many respects Tolstoy himself. For in *The Death of Ivan Ilych* Tolstoy portrayed symbolically a drama whose title might be, a little facetiously but no less descriptive for that, "The Near-Death of Leo Tolstoy." In this novella he set down the artistic equivalent of his didactic confession of three years before — a fact which has apparently gone largely unremarked. Aylmer Maude, Tolstoy's friend, English translator, biographer, and editor, underlines the relation between the novella and Tolstoy's essay *On Life*, which appeared in 1887. But while this essay does indeed have a close connection with the tale, particularly in its emphatic discussions of death and fear of death, it is mostly a tract and not autobiographically intimate in the sense that *A Confession* is. And its tone and structure are utterly dissimilar to the structure and tone of *Ivan Ilych*, while those of *A Confession* — and this is the striking thing — are amazingly like them, even to the style. This intimacy is by no means surprising in Tolstoy, in view of the fact that his fictional works are so highly autobiographical that a Russian critic said that all of Tolstoy's work constitutes one enormous, unceasing confession. The spiritual kinship between this aristocratic confessionalist and Goethe, another confessionalist and pagan genius of the body, has been beautifully memorialized by Thomas Mann.

What happened to Tolstoy in the process of his conversion was that he became appalled by his vanity and beyond that by his sense of individuality. From his great favorite, Schopenhauer, he inherited a shame of his Western singularity and he desired to tear away that "web of Maya" of which Schopenhauer so eloquently writes and which he borrowed from Oriental philosophy, the solipsistic web which makes each individual secretly believe in his immortality and which prevents him from merging with his fellow humans in a mental flow of utter communion.

The theme of *Ivan Ilych* is essentially a simple one: that of the web of Maya in a certain stratum of Russian society and the spiritual regeneration of one of the soulless bureaucrats as a result of losing the web in the primal experience of pain and death. In *Ivan Ilych* Tolstoy hoped to abandon his previous Olympian objectivity and to write a propaganda piece. Appalled by his former vanity, he wished to regenerate his readers by exposing the web of Maya for them under the terrifying spotlight of death. The chief desire of Ivan Ilych and of his class is to live a pleasant and regular life. Such a life involves deadening oneself, forgetting one's childhood, envying one's neighbors, and living a life of lies. In a crisis, however, nature has its revenge; for it is then that an Ivan Ilych wants sympathy, understanding — and above all the en-ennobling effect of the truth. He wants the acknowledgment that what is happening to him may happen to anyone else, and that at any rate death is everyone's destiny. He has been forced by the rigors of events to lose his web. But from others he gets only lies and loneliness and spiritual vacuity. Up to the last hours he clings to his solipsism; but when, during the final torment, he loses his web through paternal and filial love, fear of death disappears and he finds peace; he is able to yield his broken self to the universe of which he becomes an indis-indistinguishable part.

Such a moral, at any rate, was Tolstoy's intention, although I doubt if the propagandist overcame the artist in this case. It is true that we quake with fear and trembling during the contemplation of this novella and are purged as if by a Greek tragedy. But certain reservations re-remain. Tolstoy roars out with vengeance like a jealous Jehovah or like the angry Hebrew prophets modeled after Jehovah. He bludgeons Ivan Ilych with death in punishment for his simpering life and by im-implication says to the reader, "This is what he got and what you'll get too if you don't look out!" Then, as if death is not enough, he scourges Ivan Ilych with physical torment. "Never mind the afterlife," he grimly suggests. "Since you refuse to try for heaven on earth, I'll show you fire and brimstone." By his excess he tends to awaken in the reader, as in Ivan Ilych's family and friends, that very sense of the web of Maya which he is intent on destroying. In sheer self-defense one breathes, "Thank God this is not happening to *me*."

A shrewder propagandist might emphasize rewards rather than threats. A superior moralist might have regenerated Ivan Ilych by a beautiful and appealing mystical experience; but Tolstoy must utilize death — for it is death which obsessed *him*. Curiously, Tolstoy himself did not die as a result of his anxiety attacks and his suicidal depression. Why, then, does he have Ivan Ilych die? Granted that Ivan Ilych is no

genius and is incapable of sudden spiritual regeneration through less
than cosmic impulses, yet why does Tolstoy punish him with that which
he himself escaped? The answer may be that the portrait of death is
extremely affective. A deeper reason is that Tolstoy was always the
pagan, the seer of the body, and that ultimately the inner artist, with
epic casualness, obscured the moralist and portrayed with consummate
skill and penetration a chapter in the physical history of man. Tolstoy
remained faithful to himself, at bottom, as the genius of the rational,
just as Dostoyevsky continued to be the genius of the irrational.

It has often been said of Tolstoy that in him life and art are one, and
this has become a truism which has discouraged analysis of his work.
Where life and art are seemingly *not* one, as in James, the close commentators are legion, perhaps because it is ever so much easier to
analyze art, which is subject to intellectual manipulation, than life, at
which one can only gawk in impotence. But of course life and art are
not really identical, not even in Tolstoy. In the great Russian master
it happens that the *illusion* of life is tremendous, suggesting that the art
is tremendous too. Perhaps a few comments on the art of *The Death of
Ivan Ilych* are relevant here.

It is first of all a marvelous stroke to make the epilogue the prologue
— that is, to present the post-mortem section first, although this necessi-
tates marring the unity of point of view (the rest of the story is strictly
Ivan Ilych's). In this opening section very few of the trivial details are accidental; they subtly heighten the sense of the fragility of
life. The newspaper announcing Ivan Ilych's demise is "still damp
from the press," as if the paper, just born, has a life of its own. The
particularities of existence are emphasized to contrast with the abstraction of death. Sensualism, vanity, triviality — these are given
special attention, and they strike the tinny note of mortality before
Ivan Ilych's life is placed on the scene. The section swarms with life
and yet is remarkable for its economy. In the work of an aesthete,
economy seems a strategy, while in Tolstoy it impresses one as a proof
of his enormous vitality, as if he has so much to say that he must forever
hurry on.

As for the credibility of Tolstoy's tale, it is extraordinary. Note how
Tolstoy increases credibility by startling insights into the seemingly irrelevant. Of Ivan Ilych's daughter he writes, "She had a gloomy,
determined, almost angry expression, and bowed to Peter Ivanovich
as though he were in some way to blame." Of Ivan Ilych's son he
writes, "His tear-stained eyes had in them the look that is seen in the

eyes of boys of thirteen or fourteen who are not pure-minded." And
he lavishes brilliant touches on Schwartz, a minor character, and on a
shawl and a squeaking sofa. The strategy behind these details is to
make the reader feel that if Tolstoy can handle such minor items so
accurately, he must surely be able to handle the more obvious and important ones even more truthfully. Besides, by concentrating on the
irrelevant, Tolstoy obtains the tone of nonchalance he desires. He is
like the conjuror who makes his audience concentrate on his right hand
while all the while he is secretly producing his effects with the left. We
see at play in this first part the discriminating, manipulative skill of
genius. Note that the details are always materialistic ones, to emphasize the dull materiality of the corpse. In the very first pages Tolstoy
sketches all the important motifs of this essentially musical composition.
All lead up to an overwhelming climax: it is a weaving of orchestral
tissues into one great crescendo, as Ravel said of his *Bolero*.

As for such an apparently innocent matter as proper names, note the
subtle development of the Ivan theme: there are Peter Ivanovich and
Ivan Egorovich, the repetition of the name suggesting that all these
fellows are of the same cut as Ivan Ilych, and that although they may
refuse to recognize the fact, they are exposed to the same fate that overtook their colleague. It is Peter Ivanovich who is the spectator at the
widow's house; it could have been Ivan Egorovich, except that it is
subtler to make Peter Ivanovich the spectator since it is his patronymic
which is Ivan, rather than the more obvious first name. Note also that
Schwartz is referred to only by his surname. This helps to suggest his
extreme irregularity. Schwartz is completely hedonistic, while Peter
Ivanovich, like Ivan Ilych, is a middle man, and has momentary
doubts, even feelings of terror.

Of Tolstoy the man and artist (as distinguished from the moralist)
what was said of James may be repeated: he had a mind so fine that
no idea could violate it. In Tolstoy's case this statement means that
he would permit no notion to obscure his animalistic, intuitive, thoroughly autobiographical view of life. For example, Tolstoy realized
the importance of childhood memories for himself and consequently
derived the conclusion that they were important for everyone in pro-
portion to his worth. When he says of Ivan Ilych, "All the enthusiasms of childhood and youth passed without leaving much trace on
him . . ." he knows what a terrible indictment this is, for to have lost
one's childhood, with its eagerness, poetry, idealism, is to be spiritually
dead. For Tolstoy, childhood and youth were forever the restorative

springs to which he returned for inspiration and health. He never lost his loyalty to his brother Nicholas' fable of the green stick. As a very old man, more than three quarters of a century after first hearing the fable, Tolstoy requested that he be buried at the spot of the green stick, and there his body was placed, on the grounds of the ancestral estate.

That Tolstoy's extensive knowledge of life was great is clear in the novella we are discussing. He is easily capable of examining a man's full life — in the second part of *Ivan Ilych* the summation narrative is Flaubertian — and at the same time thoroughly instrumenting it with specific apparatus and the rhythms of a particular class. Tolstoy is expert at portraying types. His people are always characters in society, acting in accordance with the rules of their set, in contrast with Dostoyevsky's alienated, individual figures.

Tolstoy said somewhere of Chekhov that the latter began with contempt for his heroine in *The Darling* and ended by falling in love with her. This was a tribute to Chekhov's sympathy. Tolstoy's sympathy is equally great. The angry Jehovah has compassion for the suffering Philistine. The illumination, the understanding, is so profound in Tolstoy that we hate no one; we can only understand and pity. We no more despise Ivan Ilych's wife than we condemn Anna Karenina's husband. Nor do we hate the doctors, showing their virtuosity in the face of Ivan Ilych's calamity; we understand that they are the slaves of their class. (Tolstoy's implied attack on the doctors here, by the way, does not constitute an attack on science, regardless of his attitude to science as expressed elsewhere, or his intentions here. It is the medical bureaucracy he is condemning, not the ideal which it debases. Tolstoy, however, was antiscientific during his religious period. Both he and Lawrence tended to confuse science with scientolism.) Whereas it is hard to feel hatred toward Tolstoy's people, it is easy to love them. Tolstoy himself is obviously fond of the peasant Gerasim, with his simple and profound acceptance of death. For Gerasim, living close to the soil, death has none of the terrors it has for the parasitic middle class. Gerasim is the earth itself. When he holds Ivan Ilych's legs, the latter feels better: the strength flows back to him from the earth. Gerasim recalls Eroshka in *The Cossacks*, and both recall the influence of Rousseau on Tolstoy.

V

GUSTAVE FLAUBERT

(1821 — 1880)

Flaubert wrote of *War and Peace* that in parts it is marvelous, even Shakespearean, but he deplored its formlessness as well as certain of the author's ideas. Flaubert, the devotee of form and style, the aesthete whose inspiration was intense but relatively narrow — Flaubert, the friend of Turgenev, Tolstoy's "enemy," is at the artistic antipode from the gigantic Russian. Although he was first published relatively late in life — *Madame Bovary* appeared when he was more than thirty-five — Flaubert wrote from early childhood. His youthful compositions were effusively romantic. In his maturity, after establishing his characteristic style, his efforts were severely restrained, with a maximum of understatement. His mature manner wearied its creator, requiring massive erudition, infinite patience, and constant application, and granting none of the joys of fervor in the task. By 1874 Flaubert was exhausted physically and spiritually. The fall of France in 1870 seemed to have wounded this "nonpolitical" man more than he could have imagined. Besides, he was very lonely; he had lost his great friend Louis Bouilhet in 1871 and his mother and Gautier the following year. He began work on *Bouvard and Pécuchet*, the subject of which had interested him for thirty years, intending it to be a short novel. But the new opus constantly made unexpected demands of him. In 1875 he magnanimously gave his fortune to his niece, whose husband was in financial difficulties. Overcoming the new difficulties this step involved, he plodded along on the enormous documentation of the novel-in-progress. Finally he decided to rest. He wrote to Zola that he would go to Concarneau to interrupt the labors which were tormenting him. The rural atmosphere calmed him, and he began writing *The Legend of Saint Julian the Hospitaller*. In 1876, after a sojourn in Paris, he returned home to Croisset, where he wrote *A Simple Heart*. He completed in eighteen months *Trois Contes*, which includes, in addition to the titles just mentioned, *Herodias*.

What he sought during this interruption on the tedious and exacting *Bouvard and Pécuchet* was an invigorating rural scene, the luxury of remembering things past and an escape from the mortifying present. Like the enervated Aschenbach of *Death in Venice*, he was fleeing from the task which oppressed him. His years of discipline, of suppressed emotion, threatened to have their revenge. Like Aschenbach, he decided not to span the bow too far. He found his rural scene in the countryside of his childhood; lingered over souvenirs of a faded life which now seemed incredibly rich; and made his escape from the present by writing two tales of the distant and heroic past. But in *A Simple Heart* he commemorated the personal days that were gone. His niece, Caroline Commanville, has written: "During his final years my uncle experienced an urgent desire to recall his youth; and after his mother's death he wrote *A Simple Heart* in an effort to do so. He painted the town where she was born, the hearth at which she had played, his cousins, the companions of his childhood; and all this gave him great pleasure and produced some of his most touching passages, revealing, perhaps for the first time, the man behind the writer. In the tale there is a scene in which Madame Aubain and Félicité arrange the trifling possessions that had belonged to Virginie, and are deeply moved. A large black straw hat of my grandmother's stirred in my uncle a similar emotion. He would take down the hat from its nail, look at it silently, his eyes filling, then carefully replace it."

As usual, the composition of the tale was not easy. Flaubert wrote to Madame des Genettes: "My *Simple Heart* moves along very slowly. I've written only ten pages. In order to get hold of some documents I made a little trip to Pont-l'Évêque and to Honfleur! The trip filled me with sadness, I found myself in a bath of memories. How old I am, my God! How old I am!" The tale was inspired by his friend George Sand, who suggested that all writing need not be critical and ironic; but she died in 1876 without seeing this most moving of Flaubert's work. He was at pains to show that he had a heart. In one of his letters he wrote: "*A Simple Heart* is just the story of an obscure life — the life of a poor country girl, devout but mystical, devoted but without enthusiasm, and soft-hearted as a crumb of bread. . . . All this is by no means ironical, as you are probably thinking, but, on the contrary, very serious and very sad. I wish to excite pity, to move feeling hearts to tears — being a person of feeling myself. Ah yes! The other Saturday, at George Sand's funeral, I burst into a fit of sobbing when I kissed little Aurore, and again afterwards when I saw my old friend's coffin."

In Flaubert's case the restraint of the novella form imposed on him an added discipline which saved him from the excesses of his novels. For this reason his novellas are the finest specimens of his art. Flaubert, by the ascetic practices of his craft, surpassed his natural literary self; but his asceticism portrayed him as a humorless fanatic, when in actuality he was really a man of sensibility. His three novellas have the kindly function of ushering before us a balanced portrait of man and artist.

For all their acknowledged greatness, Flaubert's novels have for me certain characteristics which detract from my appreciation of his genius. At times his literary *pointillisme* stultifies; it does not permit the mind to take flight; it lacks the northern mystical magic. Mann's marvelous feat is his fusion of Flaubertian detail with Germanic suggestiveness. Flaubert went too far in his reaction against the romantics; he confused abstraction with suggestion and, unfortunately, too often exorcised the latter from his work. His constant emphasis on the concrete causes the depressing effect of sheer materialism, unalleviated by thought or fancy.

A few years before his death, Flaubert said, "I am the last of the Fathers of the Church." He was speaking of his artistic monasticism; and it is just this characteristic which often deprives his work of a humanistic tone. Henry James once wrote of Flaubert: "He is sustained only by the rage and the habit of effort; for the mere *love* of letters — let alone the love of life — appears at an early age to have deserted him. Certain passages in his correspondence make us even wonder if it be not hate that sustains him most." But hate is perhaps too strong a word. "Flaubert has tenacity without energy, just as he has self-love without vanity," wrote Turgenev to George Sand. Croce is harsher: "This freedom from all interests, which was impotence towards all interests . . . ."

What is found so objectionable in Flaubert is his seeming disrespect for the human personality, or perhaps his real failure to appreciate it. He uses people as beads for his grand necklace, just as he uses exotic details to flavor his historical romances. In his novels he too often seems to lack what the great Russians possess in such plenitude and which thrusts itself up through their lust, their criminality, and their pagan vigor — a deep respect, a profound mortification before the miracle of the universe. The Russians seem more moral in their excess than Flaubert in all his moderation. On the other hand, there are Russians like Turgenev. But even Turgenev, the Europeanized Russian, is gentle, humble, "soulful." James called him "the beautiful Russian genius"; whereas he disliked Flaubert, who was uncouth in manners, violent in criticism, and capable of opening the door to James in a dressing gown not even properly girdled, through which the undergarments peeped out in unseemly fashion.

A Simple Heart is richer in humanity than any other work of Flaubert's, as though the gentle fluid of sympathy cast a soft glaze over the details, dimming their outlines and letting them enter our consciousness unobtrusively. In *Salammbô* the details are chilly; one is struck by their strange brilliance, but the effect is too often merely intellectual. In *A Simple Heart* Flaubert comes close to the nostalgic warmth of Proust without sacrificing discipline, apparent impersonality, or meticulous form. A strong feeling of sadness permeates this prose, a feeling not altogether related to Félicité's sad fate. It is a sadness larger than that connected with an individual life; a philosophic sadness whose source is the contemplation of the rhythm of life and death, and whose especial twinge stems from the remembrance of life upon the threshold of death. Félicité's existence might be Flaubert's; his was nearly as devoid of external events as her own, and as full, in its umbratile course, of the delights of sacred devotion. He himself, at the writing of the tale, was only four years from death, and very lonely. He was speaking with a personal accent when he wrote: "Then years slipped away, one like another, and their only episodes were the great festivals as they occurred — Easter, the Assumption, All Saints' Day . . . and one by one the old acquaintances passed away: Guyot, Liébard, Mme. Lechaptois, Robelin, and Uncle Gremanville, who had been paralyzed for a long time."

A Simple Heart is, in symbolic terms, Flaubert's personal summing up. It is also his religious statement. Flaubert was actually religious, although he shunned doctrine and belief; religious as Kafka was, as anyone is whose life is consecrated to selfless ends of truth and beauty. Félicité's life is a devoted one, despite the coldness of her employer, that sourhearted mistress of the simple heart. She is capable of infinite sympathy. She merges her destiny wholly with those she loves and serves. Her name characterizes her: she made of her miserable existence something worth while after all, by sheer faith and selflessness. Compared with the vanitarianism of his bourgeois contemporaries and with what he called in disgust their *muflisme*, their muckery, Félicité's selfless devotion, her adjustment to nature's ways, her ready acceptance of death, must have seemed to Flaubert to comprise a life comparable to his own, with its monastic elements — suffering without self-pity, surrender to an ideal. It is no accident that Flaubert portrays a noble figure here in the form of a maidservant; almost all of the *good* people in his contemporary novels are of the peasant class, the poor rural folk who are still uncorrupted by the materialistic Second Empire mania

for self-advancement. His peasant people are no Emma Bovary, waiting for her amorous odd-come-shortly. It is in the nature of Flaubert's
duality that he can never create without irony. For all his sympathy
with Félicité and his concern that the reader be sympathetic too, she
remains a figure to be pitied, seen from the author's liberated height.
There is never a possibility of identification with her, as there is with
Dostoyevsky's poor and benighted.

The working methods of the man who drained the quaggy romantic
novel of its subjective slush are legendary. His tireless search for the
exact word is a part of every serious modern writer's conscience. The
manuscript and notes for *A Simple Heart* comprise several drafts,
worked over so thoroughly that they are almost illegible; detailed
notes on pneumonia; on the habits and care of parrots; on religious
rituals; and an extensive scenario, sketching the action, tone, and general details. An interesting flaw in the tale is Félicité's thought that
"the Father could not have chosen to express Himself through a dove,
for such creatures cannot speak; it must have been one of Loulou's
ancestors, surely." Friends of the author, on hearing him read the
manuscript, protested that such subtle thinking was out of character.
He agreed, and labored for hours to construct a new sentence. But he
could not fashion one whose rhythm and sonority satisfied him; and
rather than mar the beauty of the style, he permitted the solecism to
stand.

Flaubert was not of the fortunate race of creators, like Melville or
Mozart, who sing without seeming effort. He was rather akin to a
Beethoven, who often began with banal phrases. Melville poured
forth his winy, ululant, or silently glistening language like an Elizabethan; but he was not careful about form, in which Flaubert conspicuously excelled. *A Simple Heart* shows clearly those qualities which
attracted and influenced Maupassant: the matter-of-fact style, the
wealth of suggestive detail, the case history with a carefully designed
point stripped of the accidentals of actuality. But Maupassant lacked
the fire and spiritual exaltation of his master. He was too corrupted
himself to infuse his portraits of corruption with Flaubert's noble irony,
the Swiftian irony which is a desperate cry of idealism threatened with
extinction.

Much has been made, as a source of wonder, of Flaubert's strange
yearning for the opposing poles of romanticism and classicism, exoti-
cism and realism. It is, of course, just this polar tension which is characteristic of all genuine artists and it is to be accepted as a familiar

pattern. Flaubert was nauseated by the banality of bourgeois existence, yet was so fascinated by it that he portrayed it extensively in *Madame Bovary, Sentimental Education,* and *Bouvard and Pécuchet,* although with great torment, with signs of profound masochism. He yearned for romantic release, yet condemned himself to the most exhausting, most classical, most disciplined of styles, reserving only his letters for gushing, sometimes ungrammatically expressed sentiments. When, in disgust with his own age, he retreated, in *Salammbô, Saint Anthony,* and *Saint Julian,* to more expansive ages, he catalogued them as laboriously as he did his own age of inventories and cold facts.

VI

ANTON PAVLOVICH CHEKHOV

(1 8 6 0 — 1 9 0 4)

Flaubert's acerbity toward ignorance and prejudice is matched by Chekhov's mellowness and sympathy. Flaubert, divorced from the bourgeoisie, had the distance to despise it. Chekhov, born into the peasantry, had the compassion to love and aid it. The disciple of Gogol, Dostoyevsky, and Tolstoy, and the synthesizer of the familiar elements of their work, Chekhov, whose philosophy of life and art was so different from Lawrence's, was beginning to come into his own in the year that D. H. Lawrence was born. He was on the way to being no longer the composer of funny trifles for the humorous sheets; he was feeling his way toward a more serious and more painstaking and extended art. All his life Chekhov abhorred the kind of subjectivism which was so dear to Lawrence. He once wrote: "Bias has its foundation in man's incapacity to rise above particularities. . . . The artist must be only an impartial witness . . . . I am not a Liberal, nor a Conservative, nor a meliorist . . . . I should like to be a free artist . . . ." This is a statement which James would have heartily underwritten. At twenty-three Chekhov was already writing to his brother Alexander, "Subjectivity is an awful thing — even for the reason that it betrays the poor writer hand over fist." Four years later he wrote: "To chemists there is nothing unclean on earth. And a writer has to be just as objective as a chemist; he must renounce subjectivity and remember that muck-heaps in a landscape play a very respectable part, and that evil passions are as peculiar to life as good ones." The criticism that he made in a letter to Gorky in 1898 could be aptly applied to Lawrence. "I shall begin by saying that, in my opinion, you do not use sufficient restraint. You are like a spectator in the theatre who expresses his rapture so unreservedly that he prevents both himself and others from listening." As for science, of which Lawrence was violently contemptuous, Chekhov wrote, at the age of thirty-nine, "My acquaintance with the natural sciences and with the scientific method has always kept me on my guard, and I have tried, wherever possible, to take the scientific data into consideration; and where this was impossible I have preferred not to write at all. . . . I do not belong to those fiction writers who take a negative attitude toward science; nor would I belong to the order of those who arrive at everything by their wits."

As Chekhov well understood, his art was intimately related to his study and practice of medicine. "Medicine," he wrote, "is my lawful wife and literature my mistress." It is no accident that doctors figure prominently in his work and in the great novella included in the present volume. Chekhov possessed what Lawrence so obviously lacked: a gentle sense of humor. Although he was as idealistic as Lawrence, he was unable to sustain Lawrence's youthful optimism into middle age. His idealism became strangely mixed with pessimism, but not of a vitriolic sort. He was never the satirist, always the gentle ironist. A somber autumnal tone settled over his mind and was movingly and beautifully reflected in his work. Not that he ever acquired the stolidity of fatalism; on the contrary, he was always vastly although quietly responsive to suffering and he impressed sensitive observers with a quality of saintliness. Chekhov knew the lower depths of his society, just as Lawrence did. He was born the son of a former serf, and almost all his life was burdened by poverty. Lawrence, the son of a collier, turned away from his native class in most of his writings, preferring to deal with the middle and upper classes. This was a measure of escape from an unpleasant reality, as was his voluntary exile from England. Chekhov chose to remain and observe. His studies of the Russian peasantry are among the soundest of their kind. He painted the peasants as a peasant might see them, not from above in the manner of Turgenev and Tolstoy. His compassion for them was impressive, yet he never sentimentalized. He described them honestly: as wretched, cruel, amusing, ignorant, tender, sturdy, fatalistic, diseased, holy. He never failed to include the humanistic touch of his humor, which he inherited from Gogol. No other Russian writer except Gogol possesses so fully the genius for arousing laughter mixed with tears.

It is obvious that objectivity was not a fixed idea with Chekhov, as it was with Flaubert. Nor was it part of a technical revolution. Essentially his emphasis on objectivity is an expression of his insistence on plain truth. He believed, like a scientist, that only with the aid of the raw truth could disease be correctly diagnosed. Yet his interest was far from being Zolaesque. He is not merely a scientist or a poet, but an original fusion of both. His work is an effective antidote to the loose belief that science and poetry or science and humor do not mix. He did not need to labor as Flaubert did to achieve objectivity: it seemed to be his birthright. For the most part he composed swiftly — hundreds of stories, novellas, and a few great plays — and left behind him a large heritage for so short a life. In his last decade he took better care of his genius and rewrote often. Whereas before then writing had been like singing, now it was tormenting drudgery. But the work benefited. While growing richer and more somber, it also became more thoughtful, secure, moving, beautiful, true. Yet even in the early days writing was not altogether a lark. In a letter to his brother Alexander he said, "Don't envy me, dear brother! Writing gives me nothing but twitches!"

Everyone knows that Chekhov is famous for his plotless, uncontrived stories; that he is a master of the story form and literary father of many modern writers. His method, however, had its pitfalls. Sometimes his striving to be natural caused him to write in a formularized manner, and occasionally his stories ended so abruptly that they were not stories but unfinished sketches. Still, at his best he could infuse his tales with the quality of psychological completion so pleasing to his audience. In these stories the reader is not shocked by incompletion, but is invited to accept incompletion as a poetic commentary on life, a heightening of a vision of life. Chekhov suggests endings by means of his musical overtones, and the chords are resolved not in the text but in the reader's consciousness.

Like Kafka and Lawrence, Chekhov gave his life away to tuberculosis. When he experienced his first hemorrhages he refused to be examined by a doctor or to treat himself. Later, when he was seriously ill, he constantly failed to obey his doctors' orders. Once he talked with Tolstoy for an hour and brought on a severe hemorrhage shortly after a very serious one earlier that day. His end was tinged with Chekhovian irony. He died in the Black Forest, where he had gone for his health. He awoke in the middle of the night and asked for a doctor. His wife fetched one. Chekhov said to him, smiling.

"*Ich sterbe.*" The doctor called for champagne. Chekhov sipped it, gave up the glass, and with a tender smile turned on his side, facing the wall, and died. His body was shipped to Russia in a railway refrigerator car conveying oysters.

In 1892 Chekhov wrote the following remarkable comment in one of his letters: "I am finishing a story, a very dull one, as woman and the element of love are completely lacking. I cannot bear such stories. I wrote it somehow without intending to, from light-mindedness." The story referred to is *Ward No. 6*, a fascinating psychological, symbolic, and social study, one of his greatest creations. The somber realism with which it opens sets its tone. The details are authoritative. But it is not only the technical power which is attractive; as always in Chekhov, it is the personality which lures the reader. We somehow feel assured that as long as Chekhovs exist, the world cannot be altogether black. Chekhov creates a sense of darkness with a portrait of the real, and dispels it with his hidden spirituality. This dualism of the event and its poetic interpretation is in large part the cause of his subtle tension. His reporting is always of the best; we feel compelled to nod approval of it, we drink it in, feeling intellectually curious, feeling we ought to be acquainted with disease for our souls' sake. Chekhov is never content to remain with disease, he moves a step forward into the poetry of disease. In Chekhov we come again and again upon the beauty of ugliness. The details may be painful; but the whole effect is aesthetically satisfying. This is the result of style; and here style is profoundly the man.

There is much akin to Dostoyevsky in the present novella. Where else but in Dostoyevsky would one expect to find a doctor arguing desperately about life with a madman? Or a madman's speeches powerfully, movingly indicting a whole society? This Ivan Dmitrich, this paranoiac of marvelous reasoning ability, whose insanity resides in his overpowering fixed ideas, this symbol of reason and idealism who castigates Andrew Ephimich, his doctor, the symbol of bureaucratic sloth, sentimentalism, self-pity, vanity, passive cruelty (all parts of the Russian disease early analyzed and satirized by Gogol) — this character seems to be a fugitive from Dostoyevsky's underground. How surprising that the tale should have been written by the gentle Chekhov. One can believe him when he says, "I cannot bear such stories." But he did not write it out of "light-mindedness." Against his will, "without intending to," yes. For he seems to have been possessed. Which is only another proof of the great complexity of his personality and the versatility of his art.

VII

JAMES JOYCE

(1 8 8 2 — 1 9 4 1)

Chekhov is an artist not marked by an unusual degree of daemonism, yet there are important points in common between his work and that of the Flaubert disciple, Joyce, the most daemonic artificer, with the possible exception of Proust, of our century.   Joyce's use of the "epiphany," a striking psychological illumination, is similar to Chekhov's method of floodlighting his characters.   And his work as a young man is as plotless and as uncontrived as the mature Chekhov's.   Joyce also has something in common with James.   A *Painful Case*, among the finest of Joyce's stories, displays his psychological depth and strikingly recalls James's *The Beast in the Jungle*.   Both tales portray the sterile life of a man who, having renounced the proffered love of a woman, destroys her and condemns himself to spiritual death.   James's story concludes with an action unusually violent for him: his protagonist throws himself face downward upon the gravestone of his friend.   Joyce's story ends with violence of tone: "He gnawed the rectitude of his life; he felt that he had been outcast from life's feast."   Working apparently in realms so distant from each other, these two expatriates met forcefully on the theme of renunciation.

The Dead is Joyce's only tale which may be called a novella by our definition.   It is unique for other reasons as well.   Although he included it in *Dubliners*, a volume of short stories, it was written a few years later than most of the stories, and it does not altogether fit the intention of the volume.   The intention, Joyce announced to his publisher, "was to write a chapter of the moral history of my country and I chose Dublin for the scene because that city seemed to me the centre of paralysis.   I have tried to present it to the indifferent public under four of its aspects: childhood, adolescence, maternity and public life."   Joyce's "moral history" inevitably stresses three sides of Irish life: politics, religion, and drink.   *The Dead* is not lacking in them: during the course of the party Gabriel Conroy and Miss Ivors have a brief but emotional political exchange, Aunt Kate bursts out about the Pope's turning women out of the choirs, and Mr. Browne and Freddy Malins nicely symbolize the Irish inclination to spirituous liquors.   But the party is in many ways merely a preparation for the epiphany which

begins near its conclusion and reaches its climax in the stillness of the
hotel room where Gabriel and Gretta spend the night.

The Dead is the sole piece in the volume in which a domestic issue is
the central concern. This brings it closer thematically to *Exiles, Ulysses,*
and *Finnegans Wake* — all of which center on problems arising between
a man and his wife — than to the rest of *Dubliners* or to its neighbor in
time, *A Portrait of the Artist as a Young Man.* Gabriel's evening, which
began so casually and ended when his "soul swooned slowly," serves as
the mirror to reveal him to himself as an old young man, debilitated
by his surroundings, closer to the dead inhabiting the snowbound Irish
cemeteries than to youths such as Michael Furey, a young version of
Stephen Dedalus in his idealism, passion, and steadfastness of purpose.
Bartell D'Arcy's innocent song sets into motion a psychological drama
between Gabriel and his wife in which Gabriel plays an ignoble role.
The lyricism, the poetry of his wife's emotion, is contrasted with his
own self-conscious heaviness and lust. Only when he merges in mind
with the falling snow and all the dead does he find a measure of his
better self.

The novella, which begins as though it were being related to children
in a nursery and ends in sheer music, is the warmest writing in all
Joyce; and I suggest that Gabriel and his wife, but Gabriel in particular, are the most sympathetic of Joyce's creations, despite the delicate
irony which hovers over them. *The Dead*, with its deft juggling of
Paddyisms, shows Joyce at his early best. Here his realism, sobriety,
and lyricism combine in the creation of a precocious masterpiece.

Joyce composed the novella in difficult circumstances. According to
Herbert Gorman, his biographer, "Towards the end of his sojourn in
Rome the idea for a long short story (the longest he had ever written)
to be called *The Dead,* and to form the fifteenth and last section of
Dubliners, possessed him but his precarious situation was so impossible,
his days so crowded with drudgery and his mind so agitated that he
was quite put off the theme and compelled to postpone it to a future
time." Joyce was trying in Europe to win time to devote himself to a
Flaubertian consecration to art, and to use as his weapon, as Stephen
says in the *Portrait,* silence, exile, and cunning. He drew upon memories of Dublin and upon notes he had brought with him. His material,
as always, depended on actuality. Joyce's exploitation of the actual
is unprecedented in modern fiction. Although he is firmly a part of
the tradition of autobiographical fiction, he is unique in his refusal to
disguise the naturalistic sources of his material. This flaunting of

reality finds its most emphatic expression in his retention of names from one book to the next. The "Adam and Eve's" mentioned in *The Dead* also appears in the first sentence of *Finnegans Wake;* and Bartell D'Arcy of the novella figures significantly in *Ulysses*, that Dubliner's haggada of the *Odyssey*. Joyce's pattern suggests that he wrote only one book — the book of himself.

His desire to be loved by the world, despite his mask of indifference, must have been great. He was probably in earnest when he told Max Eastman that he expected the reader to devote nothing less than his entire life to the study of his works. Such self-love is not merely vanity; it is a veneration of life, a religious adoration of the self in non-personal terms. All geniuses are possessed by it. Joyce has been criticized for his indifference to the fate of his fellow men, whereas in fact he spent a lifetime wooing them. In a sense, the excesses of his work are a lover's excesses. Joyce exiled himself not only from Ireland but also from the world; but his silence and cunning were directed *at* the world. What a triumph to make the world acknowledge his anger! Joyce turned parochialism into a cult, but his hatred of Irish *muflisme* was as much a trap as Flaubert's hatred of French cant. The enemy wins if you absorb yourself too much in him; soon he absorbs you. It is love turned inside out. In the *Portrait*, Cranly says to Stephen, "It is a curious thing, do you know, how your mind is supersaturated with the religion in which you say you disbelieve." But if Joyce turned parochialism into a cult he also made that cult a monument to himself.

Stephen, in conversation with the English dean of studies, thinks: "The language in which we are speaking is his before it is mine. How different the words *home*, *Christ*, *ale*, *master*, on his lips and on mine! I cannot speak or write these words without unrest of spirit. His language, so familiar and so foreign, will always be for me an acquired speech. I have not made or accepted its words. My voice holds them at bay. My soul frets in the shadow of his language." The outsider, the alien, became the great master of that "acquired speech." Perhaps it is always an outsider who fully appreciates. What is the connection between Joyce's phenomenal mania for language and his near blindness? T. S. Eliot has written that Joyce is the greatest master of the English language since Milton — an apt statement, since Milton too was blind, as also another master of sonorities, Homer. Does the aural sense flourish as the visual one declines, or does eyesight decline because of the dominance of the ear? It has been suggested by commentators that Joyce's vision gave way as a consequence of his indifference to the world around him, and that he no longer cared to see what was happening to his contemporaries. But no one can deny that he liked to *hear* about them, a fact which weakens the theory of his indifference. Joyce's language is basically a sounded one, like Melville's. One can best appreciate this after listening to his recorded reading of "Anna Livia Plurabelle" from *Finnegans Wake*.

The sweet sonorities are already there in *The Dead;* indeed, in all of *Dubliners*. What Edmund Wilson calls the lack of the dramatic and narrative elements in Joyce's work may be the result of his linguistic mania and not, as Wilson suggests, the cause of it. Wilson believes that Joyce, unable to make his narrative move, compensated, in an effort to suggest epic greatness, by tremendous elaboration. But it is probable that Joyce's moving genius was his language obsession and that he was uninterested in drama and narrative. Each of our specialized geniuses achieves stature by permitting his mania to possess him, hoping that his extremism will insure originality and depth. Joyce had the courage to specialize, to make the one great gamble. Naturalism, symbolism, myth, psychology, erudition — these were his aids, but his driving force was language. "You made me confess the fears that I have," says Stephen to Cranly in the *Portrait*. "But I will tell you also what I do not fear. I do not fear to be alone or to be spurned for another or to leave whatever I have to leave. And I am not afraid to make a mistake, even a great mistake, a lifelong mistake and perhaps as long as eternity too." Ibsen, Joyce's early master, said that to write is to go to law with oneself. Joyce, the shaman and the pantoglot, might have countered, with some feeling, that to write is to descend into the fiery bottomless pit.

VIII

D. H. LAWRENCE

(1 8 8 5 — 1 9 3 0)

In one of the first stories D. H. Lawrence published, *A Modern Lover*, composed around 1910, when he was twenty-five, one character says to another: "Life is beautiful, so long as it is consuming you. When it is rushing through you, destroying you, life is glorious. It is best to roar away, like a fire with a great draught, white-hot to the last bit. It's when you burn a slow fire and save fuel that life's not worth having." As always afterward, his characters were speaking for him, representing various parts and phases of him; but this particular statement held true of him throughout his rather brief life. It suggests his central consciousness as well as his philosophy of life and art. Lawrence's philosophy of art was at the opposite pole from Joyce's. Joyce desired the work of art to be "static," self-contained, not designed to move people to action; whereas Lawrence wished art to influence people's modes of existence. His art does not mirror the real world as Joyce's so triumphantly does; it reflects his conception of what the world ought to be. For this reason it is more easily dated than Joyce's, more dependent on changes of intellectual climate. Even stylistically and thematically the mature Lawrence was in his early stories: in the brief hot sentences, the masterful nature descriptions, the sexual conflicts, the perception of evanescent states of mind, the obsessive interest in the present with all its minutest particulars, the weak dialogue, evidencing so convincingly that he lacked Joyce's genius for individualizing idiom, phrasing, and rhythm. Lawrence was thoroughly anti-Flaubertian in his conception of art.

Lawrence was nothing if not consistent. He wrote his things all in one gush. If dissatisfied, he attacked them afresh, beginning all over; he was incapable of minute and laborious correction. And as he worked, so he lived. He despised the "permanent" in life as he despised it in art. He was intemperate, mystical, intensely anti-intellectual, a more or less unconscious disciple of Nietzsche. In 1912 he wrote: "My great religion is belief in the blood, the flesh, as being wiser than the intellect. We can go wrong in our minds. But what the blood feels, and believes, and says, is always true." One may well have asked: Do the psychopath's, the rapist's, and the parricide's blood speak the truth? Lawrence was asserting, of course, that you cannot deny the existence of impulse, of the primitive, in man. But what did he mean by "wiser"? Better than? But for whom? Such absolutist assertions are largely the cause of his unpopularity in those circles which consider him a false prophet whose philosophy in action would lead to blood baths. His passionate followers fall into the mystical slips of their master. Richard Aldington, for example, calls him "a free spirit who loved life," in contrast to the intellectuals, whose "quasi-professorial solemnity" annoyed Lawrence. "Free" is used rhetorically; it does not really describe Lawrence, who was the slave of certain concepts, compulsive in parts of his behavior, the victim of a deadly disease. Certainly Lawrence was not intellectually free, having condemned logic and evidence. "What do I care for evidence?" he would say scornfully. "I don't feel it *here!*" And he would clap his solar plexus.

Lawrence's work is very uneven and often repetitive. Sometimes it is almost flatulent, as in his autobiographical fragment; at others it is winged, as in his prose poem on New Mexico. It is always markedly beautiful and original when dealing with nature. His vision of nature is romantic, yet in his nature motifs he comes closest to attaining Joyce's static effect. At its best his style is hypnotic, fleeting, an enchanting shimmering web. But his lapses are varied and abundant. A minor one is his sentimental addiction to the adjective "little," as if he were a giant and benevolent master. A more serious fault is the tendency to obscure his scenes by standing between them and the reader. He is too much in them, too much the sensitive flaming chap with the Biblical conscience and feminine intuition. And he is always "souped up": he uses only the highest-grade petrol. He confuses life with a nervous, electric passion. But life is also thought, lethargy, disease, meditation, work, dullness, death. Lawrence possesses little talent for character-ization. And he is notably deficient in form, architecture, and music. For these and other reasons some of his work seems as dated and un-real, in its break with the safe Edwardian past, as Fitzgerald's studies of jazz mania.

Lawrence has always been an easy target for phrase slinging. One can say of his work that it is cloak and dagger in the living room, or the hysteria of the menopause. His is the classically weak position of the artist who commits himself without a trace of irony. But therein lies also his distinction: in his willingness to be crucified on the cross of commitment at a time when ironic disdain of commitment was in vogue. Needless to say, even in this Lawrence was excessive. He shared with Joyce the latter's exile, but not his silence and his daedal cunning. Yet his example remains a challenge to all artists who would live outside the world. Whatever one's reaction to his work, respect for the man endures. The man is fascinating in all his ways, but never more so than in his egoism, which was so intense as to approach the humility of sainthood. Lawrence insisted on being loved for himself, not for his creations. In a sense he was really contemptuous of his talents. He was a passionate hero worshiper, and his hero was him-self, down to the most whimsical parts. He tried to turn whimsicality into a universal principle. He feasted at the altar of his idiosyncrasies. In him the saintly element was indistinguishably mixed with the criminal, as perhaps in every genius who is diseased.

Lawrence's output was enormous, a consequence of his belief in spontaneous creation. The act of writing was for him an almost sexually intimate affair and a kind of mystical union with the Beyond. In twenty years of productivity he brought forth close to fifty varied volumes. His theory was that spontaneous work is truer, more profound and real, that it more nearly approximates the full personality of the artist, than the Flaubertian variety. He was unwilling to concede that complete spontaneity, without the benefit of correction, forces the work to be the slave of the accidental. Yet one must admit that his occasional victories are great. By the spontaneous method he sometimes achieved an amazing freshness and grasp of the present, sometimes *saw* in so transported a manner that nothing need be forgiven him. During one such instance he created *The Fox.*

This translucent novella was written shortly after World War I. I recall how it captivated me when I first read it. It seemed to me more moving, more alert to my being, than any prose I had ever read. And I fell in love with Nellie March, so much so that I felt what seemed suspiciously like jealousy for Henry Grenfel. If the tale now seems a little time-worn, and if Nellie seems to me now something of a shatterwit, perhaps it is only because all old affairs seem a bit shabby after years of absence and cooling off. Lawrence is at his best in this tale, and there is all the typical Lawrence in it: his pansexualism, his fascination for neurotic, masculine women, his interest in the dark, "other" world close to instincts, dreams, and what Jung called the collective unconscious, his love of the triangle situation, and his mysticism. It is likely that no artist has explored male-female relations in all their adolescent subtlety more deeply and beautifully than has Lawrence. I refer not only to his handling of intimate sexual relations. Adolescent need not be a word of denigration; certainly in Lawrence's context it is not. His portrait of sex is extremely autobiographical. Lawrence wished to avoid stasis at all costs. For him the mellow relations between the sexes which follow the period of wooing and winning were as sterile as death. Only in the dynamics of wooing did he find in sex a gratification of his yearning for impermanence, explosion. Curiously enough, this fixation on adolescence — or at any rate on the primary sexual phase — is itself a form of stasis. Lawrence's breathless sentences, so different from James's, seem to be bursting from his mouth. Although at times monotonous in construction, they are not to be taken for granted: all at once they strike out like serpents and wound the reader deeply with their sinuousness and insight.

Nellie March, like all of Lawrence's favorite women, wants unconsciously to be dominated by a man. Her complexity stems from the mixture of masculine and feminine elements in her. It is precisely because she is driven to dominate that she yearns for peace and for rebirth in the rutty male. She wishes to give up her masculine traits to the man and to enter the so-called delicious realm of the subservient female. Marriage serves her as a resolution of her neurotic torment, for which she requires a powerful primitive male who, on the other hand, possesses a large feminine component, without which he would be unable to respond to her with the delicacy and intuition she demands. Lawrence's basic sexual hypothesis is the submergence of woman in man, and their simultaneous rebirth through sexual intercourse. The fox is a symbol of the male, and March's odd, unconscious pursuit of him indicates her sexual orientation. "She took her gun again and went to look for the fox. For he had lifted his eyes upon her, and his knowing look seemed to have entered her brain. She did not so much think of him: she was possessed by him. She saw his dark, shrewd, unabashed eye looking into her, knowing her. She felt him invisibly master her spirit." Then the symbol and the reality, Henry, merge. "But to March he was the fox." March averts her face from Henry and shrinks from the lamplight because she wants to be possessed by him, and she is reacting from this shamefully strong desire. Lawrence's special interest in psychoanalysis is evidenced in her two dreams, which are classic wish fulfillments.

IX

FRANZ KAFKA

(1 8 8 3 — 1 9 2 4)

There are certain interesting similarities in the lives and work of Lawrence and Franz Kafka. Both were victims of tuberculosis, both having resisted medical treatment. They were born two years apart and died within six years of each other. Both treated sex themes, both suffered from Oedipus situations, both had devoted followings, both were described as saintly and possessed by their genius. Even in contrast they illuminate each other. Kafka was modest, shy, secretive; Lawrence outgoing, explosive; Kafka rational, Lawrence irrational to an extreme.

It is difficult to understand the personal significance of *The Metamorphosis* without comprehending Kafka's relation with his father. All his life Kafka was oppressed by the belief that he was insufficient compared with his father. He was the eldest of six children. His two brothers died in their infancy, leaving the young Kafka the sole male child among three unfriendly females. At an early age he met death not as something vague in the upstairs world of adults, but as an awful gap evidencing the quicksandish nature of life. The trauma may have been in large part responsible for his early pessimism and later psychic onanism. He already suffered from being the eldest child, with all the difficulties of adjustment that this fact classically implies. Besides, he was a male in a highly patriarchal society, the son of a striving burgher casting hungry eyes about for a capable heir. He came up early against his father's disappointment. To be deprived of two sons and given a weakling: this must have been a blow for the father. Franz, flung down and trampled upon by massive unknown forces, began to revolve like a satellite around his sun-god father, transfixed by the glow that both warmed and consumed him. Seeking an attacker, he found one ready-made.

On August 13, 1912, Kafka met a young woman, F. B., at Max Brod's house in Prague, with whom he fell deeply in love. Woman for Kafka was the symbol and means of salvation, an escape from his father and therapy for himself. As a result, his meeting with F. B. had important consequences for his work. He experienced an artistic break-through a little more than a month after meeting her, discovering the theme and style characteristic of him. On the night of September 22–23 he composed the story *The Verdict* in one sitting lasting all night. It was his first genuine story, with all the accouterments of the genre, yet strikingly original. The style was the tortured and torturing expressionism; the theme, with rich variations, the quest for salvation through marriage and domesticity, the villain being the ubiquitous father image. The break-through was only a beginning. Kafka began the novel *Amerika*. By the end of November he was already reading to Brod the completed *Metamorphosis*. In this novella, the most masochistic product of his mature period, Kafka portrays himself as a gigantic bug which plagues a decent family. The autobiographical inferences are inescapable. The affair with F. B. released Kafka's pent-up masochism in the form of literary savagery and horror. An important motivation for the length of the novella must have been his creative momentum. This is clear from the essentially weak thematic development and powerful stylistic treatment, as if he were carried off by his literary strength to effects beyond his thematic interest or sincerity.

Gregor Samsa (note the parallelism between *Samsa* and *Kafka*) is an eminently good son; he is, in fact, fanatically good. And he is the economic mainstay of a parasitic family. This is a wish projection of a Kafka depressed by his economic dependence on his father. The tale is full of attacks upon the father. Its strength resides in its fertile invention and its power of empathy. It is not an "amazing story"; it differs from most horror tales because of its core of immediate and personal truth, consisting of the universality of disaster and the fear of the unknown. One feels that the actual transformation is merely symbolic of more real and deadly ones which are ever possible and which haunt even the healthiest and best adjusted of beings. There is implicit everywhere the neurotic's horror of losing control, and there are hints of fear of the lower depths of sleep, night, and dream, and also of existence in death without the release of death — a mythical echo of Tantalus. The illusion of transformation is achieved not only by a sort of bug documentation but also by the behavior of the parents and sister, who never forget that the bug is their Gregor. There are the usual perspicacious psychosomatic implications in Kafka, e.g., the gradual physical degeneration of the family under the impact of disaster, and their regeneration after Gregor's death. A slip on Kafka's part, surprising because of his meticulous care to preserve unity of point of view, is the break near the end of the tale. Kafka might have concluded with Gregor's expiration. He seems, however, to have been unwilling to forgo the opportunity of a few more digs at the family's expense. He lovingly presents them as glorying in their sudden freedom.

A critic, Paul Goodman, has recently written in a preface to *The Metamorphosis* that Kafka's animals are totems, and that the bug in the novella is a totem too. He neglects, however, to consider Freud's contribution to the understanding of totem: the conception of totem as a father symbol. The bug in the novella symbolizes the son, not the father, and therefore cannot be intelligently called a totem. Kafka's symbolism is mythical; in such symbolism, as well as in the symbolism of dreams, children are represented by vermin. It is clear that Kafka used the symbol of the bug to represent the son according to Freudian postulates; also because the notion of bug aptly characterized his sense of worthlessness and parasitism before his father. Goodman fails to use the term *totem* in its original and meaningful context: with the double taboo against killing the totem and against marrying a person of the same totem clan (parricide and incest). Kafka, in an Oedipus relation, probably experienced suppressed and often unconscious parricidal desires; yet in the novella at hand the situation is reversed, and the father is more than once on the verge of infanticide. Reversal, the use of opposites, is a favorite device of Kafka's, one found widely in folklore, in dreams, and in the unconscious mind. Its function is that of censorship.

Gregor's early dilemma is whether or not to recognize the catastrophe. Unable to comprehend it, he withdraws into the known area of his past, complaining, instead of at the transformation, against the details of his former existence. Thus Kafka stresses the mind's inability to adjust before an enormity, while ironically commenting on the importance of the "job" in his world (Gregor is unendingly concerned with his job). Kafka's fixation on the job theme arises from his own necessity to work, at cost to his creative activity. The pervading physical influence of the employer, dramatized in the novella, is a European characteristic more than an American one. It is a feature of a paternalistic, often despotic society, of closed economic frontiers and of slight fluidity between social classes. Gregor's complete transformation, both mental and physical, saves him from realizing the true nature of his tragedy. It is as though the coma of some great illness has overcome him. This mental inadequacy or ignorance is desirable for artistic reasons, for it permits Kafka to tell his story simply and unself-consciously, yet from Gregor's point of view; and it allows him to register the reactions of the family and the manager without unduly delaying the tale's movement with descriptions of Gregor's complicated thoughts and feelings. Gregor's responses are purely behavioristic: he acts as he must in his bug state; every effort is toward self-preservation, this being all that has been left him of the complicated maneuvers of human life. It is part of the strength of Kafka's *tour de force* that it never deviates from its intention, which is a thorough poker-faced documentation of the accomplished fact; while at the same time proceeding at several subterranean levels, such as the Oedipus symbolism and the complex of family relations. Whatever Gregor is, he is totally that: totally the insect, the commercial traveler, the faithful son. He is dedicated to the few roles he may play in life, no matter how minor. It must have afforded Kafka no little pleasure, ambivalent as he was, to write of a character so steadfast in his duty and his conception of his duty.

X

THOMAS MANN

(1 8 7 5 – 1 9 5 5)

It is fitting that these remarks should end with a discussion of Thomas Mann, who was the disciple of Tolstoy as well as Flaubert, whose mixture of science and poetry is akin to Chekhov's, who has often been compared with Joyce and James, who wrote homages to Dostoyevsky and to Kafka, and who was one of the latter's favorite contemporary authors. Mann's *Death in Venice* is widely considered to be one of the most perfect novellas ever written, in its immaculate style and form, and in the astonishing union of form, idea, and passion. Its perfect fusion of northern discipline with Mediterranean sensuousness, its masterly effect of growing orchestral power, its beauty of scene and linguistic envelope, make it clear that the author is a poet working in the prose medium. The novella is modern in its appreciation of music, myth, symbol, and the unconscious. On the surface it relates the death of an artist of importance, but beneath this lurks a study of the artist as a type, his devotion to discipline and form, and his yearning for bohemia and the dissolute; it is also a story of the interplay of different kinds of awareness in a complex and sensitive personality: the desperate struggle, transmuting itself at times into gleaming symbols, between the unconscious and the conscious minds.

Few modern tales cast so magical a spell, beguiling the reader by every means into a desperate and sick, even criminal although very beautiful Italian journey. Thomas Mann was thirty-six and already famous when he composed this masterpiece. As usual, he drew largely upon actuality for his creative inspiration. In May of 1911 he and his wife paid a visit to the Lido and there he experienced a number of scenes and incidents which slowly led to the evolution of the novella. He wrote later, ". . . nothing is invented. The 'wanderer' at the Northern Cemetery, the dreary Pola boat, the gray-haired rake, the sinister gondolier, Tadzio and his family, the journey interrupted by a mistake about the luggage, the cholera, the upright clerk in the travel bureau, the rascally ballad-singer, all that, and anything else you like, they were all there; I had only to arrange them, when they showed at once and in the oddest way their capacity as elements of composition. Perhaps it had to do with this, that as I worked on the story — as always, it was a long-drawn-out job — I had at moments the clearest feeling of transcendence, a sovereign sense of being borne up, such as I have never before known."

Mann was at this time the author of the universally acclaimed *Buddenbrooks*, the precocious genealogical novel in which naturalism and realism were already being winged with symbolism and music; also of *Royal Highness* and a number of remarkable stories, and of a brilliant closet drama, *Fiorenza*. Now he was about to establish himself, with *Death in Venice*, as the first writer of Germany, the carrier of all that was noblest in the German artistic tradition. In speaking of Aschenbach's art he was projecting a vision of his own development. But he was to outdo Aschenbach in every way, humanistically, in number of years, and in creative daemonism.

The novella is among other things a tissue of symbols, the primary one being death — in the form of a cemetery, cholera, the black gondolas, the sea and, foremost, five men with odd features in common. These five are the stranger in the portico near the cemetery, the sailor with the goatee, the ancient dandy, the obstinate gondolier, and the singing buffoon. The second and third are secondary symbols; their symbolic weight is carried by their physical decrepitude. The others are primary symbols; it is they who chiefly share common characteristics, one of which is a life-death dualism suggested by their aggressiveness and strength as well as by their physical appearance. All three are below medium height and of slight build, belong to the blond or red-haired type, and are strikingly snub-nosed (suggesting a death's head). All are outlanders: the first is "obviously not Bavarian," the second is "of non-Italian stock," the third is "scarcely a Venetian type." This alien status is a musical leitmotif hinting at the symbolic, mythical, unconscious meaning of journey, the journey as death. The life-death dualism is heightened by an emphasis on the naked Adam's apple and fangs and gums. A minor motif, indicative of Mann's detailed interest in such matters, is the "two pronounced perpendicular furrows" on the forehead. Mann's repetitions are carefully nuanced to avoid crudeness and to increase variation and suggestiveness. The life-death motif is epitomized by the jungle symbol. At the beginning of the story Aschenbach, yearning to travel, experiences almost a seizure of the imagination, and visualizes a jungle containing crouching tigers. Near the end he learns that Asiatic cholera springs from the jungle of the Ganges delta, "among whose bamboo thickets the tiger crouches." In this novella, as in most of Mann's work, the musical motif and the thematic symbol are indistinguishable.

The musical form is remarkably evocative. The first scene at the cemetery is like a first movement. The second section is like an adagio, the third section is accelerated. The Tadzio motif is brought in almost at once and is subtly developed while time is made to pass unobtrusively. Aschenbach's crisis, his panic, and revolution, is a fine complication to distract attention from Tadzio so that the boy's image will not grow too familiar, and to indicate how strong is the writer's passion for him. The crisis has still another and more subtle function: to indicate the futility of Aschenbach's attempts to escape his fate. He himself is the cause of the misadventure: if he had left the hotel when the porter requested, and had accompanied his trunk to the station, as was usual, the trunk would not have gone astray. The fourth section, the ecstatically lyrical one, is a renewed evidence of Mann's lyrical genius, seen throughout his career. The fifth and final section is an orchestration of all the familiar themes. The invention seems inexhaustible, the grasp of detail always rich and striking. The result in its riotous romantic color reminds one of a Strauss tone poem, as well as of Wagner, master of Mann as well as Strauss. In Mann's invention the sordid is made to seem surpassingly beautiful. Perhaps not since Plato has the homosexual motif been handled in so classical and exquisite a manner. Mann's sonorousness, texture, and weight remind one also of Brahms. It is odd that Mann has almost nothing to say of Brahms in his essays, whereas he has written so lavishly of Wagner. Both in temperament as well as in art he seems to have a greater affinity with the comparatively sober Brahms than with the ecstatic, vainglorious, exceedingly daemonic Wagner. In this musical connection, it is worth noting that Mahler was the physical and in some ways psychological model for Aschenbach.

Aschenbach is a Jamesian figure. Like the Jamesian heroes, he possesses a fine conscience and lives a life of renunciation. But whereas the Jamesian heroes generally continue to renounce, this being their tragedy, Aschenbach's tragedy is his late and sudden acceptance of disorder, the passions, and the depths. He is a symbol of the age, which is exhausted, stunted. His moral and physical decline symbolizes the decline of the European world, which is too formalistic and cerebral, a world soon to be rent by the upsurge of passion, of desperate inner need. Mann's symbol of the depths is characteristically Eastern: Tadzio is a Pole, a fact which recalls Chauchat, the Russian bohemian of *The Magic Mountain*.

Death in Venice is a study of the flight toward death, of the will to death, on the part of a man who believes that he is in complete control of himself. The flight is sketched with mythical symbols. Aschenbach is the victim of energies which he has been repressing for years. These overthrow him on two counts, moral and physical. They seduce him to the illicit level of homosexuality and, having witnessed his progressive degeneration, slay him with the plague. Fatigued by his sapping work and worn out by a lifetime of repression, Aschenbach unconsciously seeks a new life, a rebirth. That is why he heads instinctively toward the sea, symbol of woman, womb, and parturition. He travels south because the south symbolizes for him the sensuous, the feminine, and disorder, traits he has inherited from his mother, the daughter of a Bohemian musical conductor. (The coupling of music and the illicit, as well as music and the sea, is prominent in Mann's work.) Aschenbach's yearning for rebirth is suggested even by his repugnant attempts to beautify himself at the Venetian barber's. Rebirth entails death, and that is why Aschenbach must die. Aschenbach's "yearning for new and distant scenes," his "craving for freedom, release, forgetfulness" are cravings for death so that he may be reborn. Aschenbach, in brief, is the artist as Oedipus.

CHARLES NEIDER

Herman Melville

BENITO CERENO

1855

IN THE year 1799, Captain Amasa Delano, of Duxbury, in Massachusetts, commanding a large sealer and general trader, lay at anchor, with a valuable cargo, in the harbour of St. Maria — a small, desert, uninhabited island towards the southern extremity of the long coast of Chili. There he had touched for water.

On the second day, not long after dawn, while lying in his berth, his mate came below, informing him that a strange sail was coming into the bay. Ships were then not so plenty in those waters as now. He rose, dressed, and went on deck.

The morning was one peculiar to that coast. Everything was mute and calm; everything grey. The sea, though undulated into long roods of swells, seemed fixed, and was sleeked at the surface like waved lead that has cooled and set in the smelters' mould. The sky seemed a grey mantle. Flights of troubled grey fowl, kith and kin with flights of troubled grey vapours among which they were mixed, skimmed low and fitfully over the waters, as swallows over meadows before storms. Shadows present, foreshadowing deeper shadows to come.

To Captain Delano's surprise, the stranger, viewed through the glass, showed no colours; though to do so upon entering a haven, however uninhabited in its shores, where but a single other ship might be lying, was the custom among peaceful seamen of all nations. Considering the lawlessness and loneliness of the spot, and the sort of stories, at that day, associated with those seas, Captain Delano's surprise might have deepened into some uneasiness had he not been a person of a singularly undistrustful good nature, not liable, except on extraordinary and repeated excitement, and hardly then, to indulge in personal alarms, any way involving the imputation of malign evil in man. Whether, in view of what humanity is capable, such a trait implies, along with a benevolent heart, more than ordinary quickness and accuracy of intellectual perception, may be left to the wise to determine.

52

But whatever misgivings might have obtruded on first seeing the stranger, would almost, in any seaman's mind, have been dissipated by observing that, the ship, in navigating into the harbour, was drawing too near the land, for her own safety's sake, owing to a sunken reef making out off her bow. This seemed to prove her a stranger, indeed, not only to the sealer, but the island; consequently, she could be no wonted freebooter on that ocean. With no small interest, Captain Delano continued to watch her — a proceeding not much facilitated by the vapours partly mantling the hull, through which the far matin light from her cabin streamed equivocally enough; much like the sun — by this time crescented on the rim of the horizon, and apparently, in company with the strange ship, entering the harbour — which, wimpled by the same low, creeping clouds, showed not unlike a Lima intriguante's one sinister eye peering across the Plaza from the Indian loop-hole of her dusk *saya-y-manta.*

It might have been but a deception of the vapours, but, the longer the stranger was watched, the more singular appeared her manœuvres. Ere long it seemed hard to decide whether she meant to come in or no — what she wanted, or what she was about. The wind, which had breezed up a little during the night, was now extremely light and baffling, which the more increased the apparent uncertainty of her movements.

Surmising, at last, that it might be a ship in distress, Captain Delano ordered his whale-boat to be dropped, and, much to the wary opposition of his mate, prepared to board her, and, at the least, pilot her in. On the night previous, a fishing-party of the seamen had gone a long distance to some detached rocks out of sight from the sealer, and, an hour or two before day-break, had returned, having met with no small success. Presuming that the stranger might have been long off soundings, the good captain put several baskets of the fish, for presents, into his boat, and so pulled away. From her continuing too near the sunken reef, deeming her in danger, calling to his men, he made all haste to apprise those on board of their situation. But, some time ere the boat came up, the wind, light though it was, having shifted, had headed the vessel off, as well as partly broken the vapours from about her.

Upon gaining a less remote view, the ship, when made signally visible on the verge of the leaden-hued swells, with the shreds of fog here and there raggedly furring her, appeared like a white-washed monastery after a thunder-storm, seen perched upon some dun cliff among the Pyrenees. But it was no purely fanciful resemblance which now, for a moment, almost led Captain Delano to think that nothing less than a ship-load of monks was before him. Peering over the bulwarks were what really seemed, in the hazy distance, throngs of dark cowls; while fitfully revealed through the open port-holes, other dark moving figures were dimly descried, as of Black Friars pacing the cloisters.

Upon a still nigher approach, this appearance was modified, and the true character of the vessel was plain — a Spanish merchantman of the first class; carrying negro slaves, amongst other valuable freight, from one colonial port to another. A very large, and, in its time, a very fine vessel, such as in those days were at intervals encountered along that main; sometimes superseded Acapulco treasure-ships, or retired frigates of the Spanish king's navy, which, like superannuated Italian palaces, still, under a decline of masters, preserved signs of former state.

As the whale-boat drew more and more nigh, the cause of the peculiar pipe-clayed aspect of the stranger was seen in the slovenly neglect pervading her. The spars, ropes, and great part of the bulwarks, looked woolly, from long unacquaintance with the scraper, tar, and the brush. Her keel seemed laid, her ribs put together, and she launched, from Ezekiel's Valley of Dry Bones.

In the present business in which she was engaged, the ship's general model and rig appeared to have undergone no material change from their original warlike and Froissart pattern. However, no guns were seen.

The tops were large, and were railed about with what had once been octagonal net-work, all now in sad disrepair. These tops hung overhead like three ruinous aviaries, in one of which was seen perched, on a ratlin, a white noddy, a strange fowl, so called from its lethargic somnambulistic character, being frequently caught by hand at sea. Battered and mouldy, the castellated forecastle seemed some ancient turret, long ago taken by assault, and then left to decay. Towards the stern, two high-raised quarter galleries — the balustrades here and there covered with dry, tindery sea-moss — opening out from the unoccupied state-cabin, whose dead lights, for all the mild weather, were hermetically closed and caulked — these tenantless balconies hung over the sea as if it were the grand Venetian canal. But the principal relic of faded grandeur was the ample oval of the shield-like stern-piece, intricately carved with the arms of Castile and Leon, medallioned about by groups of mythological or symbolical devices; uppermost and central of which was a dark satyr in a mask, holding his foot on the prostrate neck of a writhing figure, likewise masked.

Whether the ship had a figure-head, or only a plain beak, was not quite certain, owing to canvas wrapped about that part, either to protect it while undergoing a refurbishing, or else decently to hide its decay. Rudely painted or chalked, as in a sailor freak, along the forward side of a sort of pedestal below the canvas, was the sentence, "*Seguid vuestro jefe,*" (follow your leader); while upon the tarnished headboards, near by, appeared, in stately capitals, once gilt, the ship's name, "SAN DOMINICK," each letter streakingly corroded with tricklings of copper-spike rust; while, like mourning weeds, dark festoons of seagrass slimily swept to and fro over the name, with every hearse-like roll of the hull.

As at last the boat was hooked from the bow along toward the gangway amidship, its keel, while yet some inches separated from the hull, harshly grated as on a sunken coral reef. It proved a huge bunch of conglobated barnacles adhering below the water to the side like a wen; a token of baffling airs and long calms passed somewhere in those seas.

Climbing the side, the visitor was at once surrounded by a clamorous throng of whites and blacks, but the latter outnumbering the former more than could have been expected, negro transportation-ship as the stranger in port was. But, in one language, and as with one voice, all poured out a common tale of suffering; in which the negresses, of whom there were not a few, exceeded the others in their dolorous vehemence. The scurvy, together with a fever, had swept off a great part of their number, more especially the Spaniards. Off Cape Horn, they had narrowly escaped shipwreck; then, for days together, they had lain tranced without wind; their provisions were low; their water next to none; their lips that moment were baked.

While Captain Delano was thus made the mark of all eager tongues, his one eager glance took in all the faces, with every other object about him.

Always upon first boarding a large and populous ship at sea, especially a foreign one, with a nondescript crew such as Lascars or Manilla men, the impression varies in a peculiar way from that produced by first entering a strange house with strange inmates in a strange land. Both house and ship, the one by its walls and blinds, the other by its high bulwarks like ramparts, hoard from view their interiors till the last moment; but in the case of the ship there is this addition: that the living spectacle it contains, upon its sudden and complete disclosure, has, in contrast with the blank ocean which zones it, something of the effect of enchantment. The ship seems unreal; these strange costumes, gestures, and faces, but a shadowy tableau just emerged from the deep, which directly must receive back what it gave.

Perhaps it was some such influence as above is attempted to be described which, in Captain Delano's mind, heightened whatever, upon a staid scrutiny, might have seemed unusual; especially the conspicuous figures of four elderly grizzled negroes, their heads like black, doddered willow tops, who, in venerable contrast to the tumult below them, were couched sphynx-like, one on the starboard cathead, another on the larboard, and the remaining pair face to face on the opposite bulwarks above the main-chains. They each had bits of unstranded old junk in their hands, and, with a sort of stoical self-content, were picking the junk into oakum, a small heap of which lay by their sides. They accompanied the task with a continuous, low, monotonous chant; droning and drooling away like so many grey-headed bag-pipers playing a funeral march.

The quarter-deck rose into an ample elevated poop, upon the forward verge of which, lifted, like the oakum-pickers, some eight feet above the general throng, sat along in a row, separated by regular spaces, the cross-legged figures of six other blacks; each with a rusty hatchet in his hand, which, with a bit of brick and a rag, he was engaged like a scullion in scouring; while between each two was a small stack of hatchets, their rusted edges turned forward awaiting a like operation. Though occasionally the four oakum-pickers would briefly address some person or persons in the crowd below, yet the six hatchet-polishers neither spoke to others, nor breathed a whisper among themselves, but sat intent upon their task, except at intervals, when, with the peculiar love in negroes of uniting industry with pastime, two-and-two they sideways clashed their hatchets together, like cymbals, with a barbarous din. All six, unlike the generality, had the raw aspect of unsophisticated Africans.

But that first comprehensive glance which took in those ten figures, with scores less conspicuous, rested but an instant upon them, as, impatient of the hubbub of voices, the visitor turned in quest of whomsoever it might be that commanded the ship.

But as if not unwilling to let nature make known her own case among his suffering charge, or else in despair of restraining it for the time, the Spanish captain, a gentlemanly, reserved-looking, and rather young man to a stranger's eye, dressed with singular richness, but bearing plain traces of recent sleepless cares and disquietudes, stood passively by, leaning against the main-mast, at one moment casting a dreary, spiritless look upon his excited people, at the next an unhappy glance toward his visitor. By his side stood a black of small stature, in whose rude face, as occasionally, like a shepherd's dog, he mutely turned it up into the Spaniard's, sorrow and affection were equally blended.

Struggling through the throng, the American advanced to the Spaniard, assuring him of his sympathies, and offering to render whatever assistance might be in his power. To which the Spaniard returned, for the present, but grave and ceremonious acknowledgments, his national formality dusked by the saturnine mood of ill health.

But losing no time in mere compliments, Captain Delano returning to the gangway, had his baskets of fish brought up; and as the wind still continued light, so that some hours at least must elapse ere the ship could be brought to the anchorage, he bade his men return to the sealer, and fetch back as much water as the whaleboat could carry, with whatever soft bread the steward might have, all the remaining pumpkins on board, with a box of sugar, and a dozen of his private bottles of cider.

Not many minutes after the boat's pushing off, to the vexation of all, the wind entirely died away, and the tide turning, began drifting back the ship helplessly seaward. But trusting this would not long last, Captain Delano sought with good hopes to cheer up the strangers, feeling no small satisfaction that, with persons in their condition he could — thanks to his frequent voyages along the Spanish main — converse with some freedom in their native tongue.

While left alone with them, he was not long in observing some things tending to heighten his first impressions; but surprise was lost in pity, both for the Spaniards and blacks, alike evidently reduced from scarcity of water and provisions; while long-continued suffering seemed to have brought out the less good-natured qualities of the negroes, besides, at the same time, impairing the Spaniard's authority over them. But, under the circumstances, precisely this condition of things was to have been anticipated. In armies, navies, cities, or families — in nature herself — nothing more relaxes good order than misery. Still, Captain Delano was not without the idea, that had Benito Cereno been a man of greater energy, misrule would hardly have come to the present pass. But the debility, constitutional or induced by the hardships, bodily and mental, of the Spanish captain, was too obvious to be overlooked. A prey to settled dejection, as if long mocked with hope he would not now indulge it, even when it had ceased to be a mock, the prospect of that day or evening at furthest, lying at anchor, with plenty of water for his people, and a brother captain to counsel and befriend, seemed in no perceptible degree to encourage him. His mind appeared unstrung, if not still more seriously affected. Shut up in these oaken walls, chained to one dull round of command, whose unconditionality cloyed him, like some hypochondriac abbot he moved slowly about, at times suddenly pausing, starting, or staring, biting his lip, biting his fingernails, flushing, paling, twitching his beard, with other symptoms of an absent or moody mind. This distempered spirit was lodged, as before hinted, in as distempered a frame. He was rather tall, but seemed never to have been robust, and now with nervous suffering was almost worn to a skeleton. A tendency to some pulmonary complaint appeared to have been lately confirmed. His voice was like that of one with lungs half gone, hoarsely suppressed, a husky whisper. No wonder that, as in this state he tottered about, his private servant apprehensively followed him. Sometimes the negro gave his master his arm, or took his handkerchief out of his pocket for him; performing these and similar offices with that affectionate zeal which transmutes into something filial or fraternal acts in themselves but menial; and which has gained for the negro the repute of making the most pleasing body servant in the world; one, too, whom a master need be on no stiffly superior terms with, but may treat with familiar trust; less a servant than a devoted companion.

Marking the noisy indocility of the blacks in general, as well as what seemed the sullen inefficiency of the whites, it was not without humane satisfaction that Captain Delano witnessed the steady good conduct of Babo.

But the good conduct of Babo, hardly more than the ill-behaviour of others, seemed to withdraw the half-lunatic Don Benito from his cloudy languor. Not that such precisely was the impression made by the Spaniard on the mind of his visitor. The Spaniard's individual unrest was, for the present, but noted as a conspicuous feature in the ship's general affliction. Still, Captain Delano was not a little concerned at what he could not help taking for the time to be Don Benito's unfriendly indifference toward himself. The Spaniard's manner, too, conveyed a sort of sour and gloomy disdain, which he seemed at no pains to disguise. But this the American in charity ascribed to the harassing effects of sickness, since, in former instances, he had noted that there are peculiar natures on whom prolonged physical suffering seems to cancel every social instinct of kindness; as if forced to black bread themselves, they deemed it but equity that each person coming nigh them should, indirectly, by some slight or affront, be made to partake of their fare.

But ere long Captain Delano bethought him that, indulgent as he was at the first, in judging the Spaniard, he might not, after all, have exercised charity enough. At bottom it was Don Benito's reserve which displeased him; but the same reserve was shown toward all but his personal attendant. Even the formal reports which, according to sea-usage, were at stated times made to him by some petty underling (either a white, mulatto or black), he hardly had patience enough to listen to, without betraying contemptuous aversion. His manner upon such occasions was, in its degree, not unlike that which might be supposed to have been his imperial countryman's, Charles V., just previous to the anchoritish retirement of that monarch from the throne.

This splenetic disrelish of his place was evinced in almost every function pertaining to it. Proud as he was moody, he condescended to no personal mandate. Whatever special orders were necessary, their delivery was delegated to his body-servant, who in turn transferred them to their ultimate destination, through runners, alert Spanish boys or slave boys, like pages or pilot-fish within easy call continually hovering round Don Benito. So that to have beheld this undemonstrative invalid gliding about, apathetic and mute, no landsman could have dreamed that in him was lodged a dictatorship beyond which, while at sea, there was no earthly appeal.

Thus, the Spaniard, regarded in his reserve, seemed as the involuntary victim of mental disorder. But, in fact, his reserve might, in some degree, have proceeded from design. If so, then in Don Benito was evinced the unhealthy climax of that icy though conscientious policy, more or less adopted by all commanders of large ships, which, except in signal emergencies, obliterates alike the manifestation of sway with every trace of sociality; transforming the man into a block, or rather into a loaded cannon, which, until there is call for thunder, has nothing to say.

Viewing him in this light, it seemed but a natural token of the perverse habit induced by a long course of such hard self-restraint, that, notwithstanding the present condition of his ship, the Spaniard should still persist in a demeanour, which, however harmless — or it may be, appropriate — in a well-appointed vessel, such as the *San Dominick* might have been at the outset of the voyage, was anything but judicious now. But the Spaniard perhaps thought that it was with captains as with gods: reserve, under all events, must still be their cue. But more probably this appearance of slumbering dominion might have been but an attempted disguise to conscious imbecility — not deep policy, but shallow device. But be all this as it might, whether Don

Benito's manner was designed or not, the more Captain Delano noted its pervading reserve, the less he felt uneasiness at any particular manifestation of that reserve toward himself.

Neither were his thoughts taken up by the captain alone. Wonted to the quiet orderliness of the sealer's comfortable family of a crew, the noisy confusion of the *San Dominick's* suffering host repeatedly challenged his eye. Some prominent breaches not only of discipline but of decency were observed. These Captain Delano could not but ascribe, in the main, to the absence of those subordinate deck-officers to whom, along with higher duties, is entrusted what may be styled the police department of a populous ship. True, the old oakum-pickers appeared at times to act the part of monitorial constables to their countrymen, the blacks; but though occasionally succeeding in allaying trifling outbreaks now and then between man and man, they could do little or nothing toward establishing general quiet. The *San Dominick* was in the condition of a transatlantic emigrant ship, among whose multitude of living freight are some individuals, doubtless, as little troublesome as crates and bales; but the friendly remonstrances of such with their ruder companions are of not so much avail as the unfriendly arm of the mate. What the *San Dominick* wanted was, what the emigrant ship has, stern superior officers. But on these decks not so much as a fourth mate was to be seen.

The visitor's curiosity was roused to learn the particulars of those mishaps which had brought about such absenteeism, with its consequences; because, though deriving some inkling of the voyage from the wails which at the first moment had greeted him, yet of the details no clear understanding had been had. The best account would, doubtless, be given by the captain. Yet at first the visitor was loth to ask it, unwilling to provoke some distant rebuff. But plucking up courage, he at last accosted Don Benito, renewing the expression of his benevolent interest, adding, that did he (Captain Delano) but know the particulars of the ship's misfortunes, he would, perhaps, be better able in the end to relieve them. Would Don Benito favour him with the whole story?

Don Benito faltered; then, like some somnambulist suddenly interfered with, vacantly stared at his visitor, and ended by looking down on the deck. He maintained this posture so long, that Captain Delano, almost equally disconcerted, and involuntarily almost as rude, turned suddenly from him, walking forward to accost one of the Spanish seamen for the desired information. But he had hardly gone five paces, when with a sort of eagerness Don Benito invited him back, regretting his momentary absence of mind, and professing readiness to gratify him.

While most part of the story was being given, the two captains stood on the after part of the main-deck, a privileged spot, no one being near but the servant.

"It is now a hundred and ninety days," began the Spaniard, in his husky whisper, "that this ship, well officered and well manned, with several cabin passengers — some fifty Spaniards in all — sailed from Buenos Ayres bound to Lima, with a general cargo, Paraguay tea and the like — and," pointing forward, "that parcel of negroes, now not more than a hundred and fifty, as you see, but then numbering over three hundred souls. Off Cape Horn we had heavy gales. In one moment, by night, three of my best officers, with fifteen sailors, were lost, with the main-yard; the spar snapping under them in the slings, as they sought, with heavers, to beat down the icy sail. To lighten the hull, the heavier sacks of mata were thrown into the sea, with most of the water-pipes lashed on deck at the time. And this last necessity it was, combined with the prolonged detentions afterwards experienced, which eventually brought about our chief causes of suffering. When —"

Here there was a sudden fainting attack of his cough, brought on, no doubt, by his mental distress. His servant sustained him, and drawing a cordial from his pocket placed it to his lips. He a little revived. But unwilling to leave him unsupported while yet imperfectly restored, the black with one arm still encircled his master, at the same time keeping his eye fixed on his face, as if to watch for the first sign of complete restoration, or relapse, as the event might prove.

The Spaniard proceeded, but brokenly and obscurely, as one in a dream.

— "Oh, my God! rather than pass through what I have, with joy I would have hailed the most terrible gales; but —"

His cough returned and with increased violence; this subsiding, with reddened lips and closed eyes he fell heavily against his supporter.

"His mind wanders. He was thinking of the plague that followed the gales," plaintively sighed the servant; "my poor, poor master!" wringing one hand, and with the other wiping the mouth. "But be patient, Señor," again turning to Captain Delano, "these fits do not last long; master will soon be himself."

Don Benito reviving, went on; but as this portion of the story was very brokenly delivered, the substance only will here be set down.

It appeared that after the ship had been many days tossed in storms off the Cape, the scurvy broke out, carrying off numbers of the whites and blacks. When at last they had worked round into the Pacific, their spars and sails were so damaged, and so inadequately handled by the surviving mariners, most of whom were become invalids, that, unable to lay her northerly course by the wind, which was powerful, the unmanageable ship for successive days and nights was blown northwestward, where the breeze suddenly deserted her, in unknown waters, to sultry calms. The absence of the water-pipes now proved as fatal to life as before their presence had menaced it. Induced, or at least aggravated, by the more than scanty allowance of water, a malignant fever followed the scurvy; with the excessive heat of the lengthened calm, making such short work of it as to sweep away, as by billows, whole families of the Africans, and a yet larger number, proportionably, of the Spaniards, including, by a luckless fatality, every officer on board. Consequently, in the smart west winds eventually following the calm, the already rent sails having to be simply dropped, not furled, at need, had been gradually reduced to the beggar's rags they were now. To procure substitutes for his lost sailors, as well as supplies of water and sails, the captain at the earliest opportunity had made for Baldivia, the southermost civilized port of Chili and South America; but upon nearing the coast the thick weather had prevented him from so much as sighting that harbour. Since which period, almost without a crew, and almost without canvas and almost without water, and at intervals giving its added dead to the sea, the *San Dominick* had been battle-dored about by contrary winds, inveigled by currents, or grown weedy in calms. Like a man lost in woods, more than once she had doubled upon her own track.

"But throughout these calamities," huskily continued Don Benito, painfully turning in the half embrace of his servant, "I have to thank those negroes you see, who, though to your inexperienced eyes appearing unruly, have, indeed, conducted themselves with less of restlessness than even their owner could have thought possible under such circumstances."

Here he again fell faintly back. Again his mind wandered: but he rallied, and less obscurely proceeded.

"Yes, their owner was quite right in assuring me that no fetters would be needed with his blacks; so that while, as is wont in this transportation, those negroes have always remained upon deck — not thrust below, as in the Guineamen — they have, also from the beginning, been freely permitted to range within given bounds at their pleasure."

Once more the faintness returned — his mind roved — but, recovering, he resumed:

"But it is Babo here to whom, under God, I owe not only my own preservation, but likewise to him, chiefly, the merit is due, of pacifying his more ignorant brethren, when at intervals tempted to murmurings."

"Ah, master," sighed the black, bowing his face, "don't speak of me; Babo is nothing; what Babo has done was but duty."

"Faithful fellow!" cried Captain Delano. "Don Benito, I envy you such a friend; slave I cannot call him."

As master and man stood before him, the black upholding the white, Captain Delano could not but bethink him of the beauty of that relationship which could present such a spectacle of fidelity on the one hand and confidence on the other. The scene was heightened by the contrast in dress, denoting their relative positions. The Spaniard wore a loose Chili jacket of dark velvet; white small clothes and stockings, with silver buckles at the knee and instep; a high-crowned sombrero, of fine grass; a slender sword, silver mounted, hung from a knot in his sash; the last being an almost invariable adjunct, more for utility than ornament, of a South American gentleman's dress to this hour. Excepting when his occasional nervous contortions brought about disarray, there was a certain precision in his attire, curiously at variance with the unsightly disorder around; especially in the belittered Ghetto, forward of the main-mast, wholly occupied by the blacks.

The servant wore nothing but wide trousers, apparently, from their coarseness and patches, made out of some old topsail; they were clean, and confined at the waist by a bit of unstranded rope, which, with his composed, deprecatory air at times, made him look something like a begging friar of St. Francis.

However unsuitable for the time and place, at least in the blunt-thinking American's eyes, and however strangely surviving in the midst of all his afflictions, the toilette of Don Benito might not, in fashion at least, have gone beyond the style of the day among South Americans of his class. Though on the present voyage sailing from Buenos Ayres, he had avowed himself a native and resident of Chili, whose inhabitants had not so generally adopted the plain coat and once plebeian pantaloons; but, with a becoming modification, adhered to their provincial costume, picturesque as any in the world. Still, relatively to the pale history of the voyage, and his own pale face, there seemed something so incongruous in the Spaniard's apparel, as almost to suggest the image of an invalid courtier tottering about London streets in the time of the plague.

The portion of the narrative which, perhaps, most excited interest, as well as some surprise, considering the latitudes in question, was the long calms spoken of, and more particularly the ship's so long drifting about. Without communicating the opinion, of course, the American could not but impute at least part of the detentions both to clumsy seamanship and faulty navigation. Eyeing Don Benito's small, yellow hands, he easily inferred that the young captain had not got into command at the hawse-hole but the cabin-window, and if so, why wonder at incompetence, in youth, sickness, and aristocracy united? Such was his democratic conclusion.

But drowning criticism in compassion, after a fresh repetition of his sympathies, Captain Delano having heard out his story, not only engaged, as in the first place, to see Don Benito and his people supplied in their immediate bodily needs, but, also, now further promised to assist him in procuring a large permanent supply of water, as well as some sails and rigging; and, though it would involve no small embarrassment to himself, yet he would spare three of his best seamen for temporary deck officers; so that without delay the ship might proceed to Concepcion, there fully to refit for Lima, her destined port.

Such generosity was not without its effect, even upon the invalid. His face lighted up; eager and hectic, he met the honest glance of his visitor. With gratitude he seemed overcome.

"This excitement is bad for master," whispered the servant, taking his arm, and with soothing words gently drawing him aside.

When Don Benito returned, the American was pained to observe that his hopefulness, like the sudden kindling in his cheek, was but febrile and transient.

Ere long, with a joyless mien, looking up toward the poop, the host invited his guest to accompany him there, for the benefit of what little breath of wind might be stirring.

As during the telling of the story, Captain Delano had once or twice started at the occasional cymballing of the hatchet-polishers, wondering why such an interruption should be allowed, especially in that part of the ship, and in the ears of an invalid; and, moreover, as the hatchets had anything but an attractive look, and the handlers of them still less so, it was, therefore, to tell the truth, not without some lurking reluctance, or even shrinking, it may be, that Captain Delano, with apparent complaisance, acquiesced in his host's invitation. The more so, since with an untimely caprice of punctilio, rendered distressing by his cadaverous aspect, Don Benito, with Castilian bows, solemnly insisted upon his guest's preceding him up the ladder leading to the elevation; where, one on each side of the last step, sat four armorial supporters and sentries, two of the ominous file. Gingerly enough stepped good Captain Delano between them, and in the instant of leaving them behind, like one running the gantlet, he felt an apprehensive twitch in the calves of his legs.

But when, facing about, he saw the whole file, like so many organ-grinders, still stupidly intent on their work, unmindful of everything beside, he could not but smile at his late fidgeting panic.

Presently, while standing with Don Benito, looking forward upon the decks below, he was struck by one of those instances of insubordination previously alluded to. Three black boys, with two Spanish boys, were sitting together on the hatches, scraping a rude wooden platter, in which some scanty mess had recently been cooked. Suddenly, one of the black boys, enraged at a word dropped by one of his white companions, seized a knife, and though called to forbear by one of the oakum-pickers, struck the lad over the head, inflicting a gash from which blood flowed.

In amazement, Captain Delano inquired what this meant. To which the pale Benito dully muttered, that it was merely the sport of the lad.

"Pretty serious sport, truly," rejoined Captain Delano. "Had such a thing happened on board the *Bachelor's Delight*, instant punishment would have followed."

At these words the Spaniard turned upon the American one of his sudden, staring, half-lunatic looks; then, relapsing into his torpor, answered, "Doubtless, doubtless, Señor."

Is it, thought Captain Delano, that this helpless man is one of those paper captains I've known, who by policy wink at what by power they cannot put down? I know no sadder sight than a commander who has little of command but the name.

"I should think, Don Benito," he now said, glancing toward the oakum-picker who had sought to interfere with the boys, "that you would find it advantageous to keep all your blacks employed, especially the younger ones, no matter at what useless task, and no matter what happens to the ship. Why, even with my little band, I find such a course indispensable. I once kept a crew on my quarter-deck thrumming mats for my cabin, when, for three days, I had given up my ship

— mats, men, and all — for a speedy loss, owing to the violence of a gale in which we could do nothing but helplessly drive before it."

"Doubtless, doubtless," muttered Don Benito.

"But," continued Captain Delano, again glancing upon the oakum-pickers and then at the hatchet-polishers, near by, "I see you keep some at least of your host employed."

"Yes," was again the vacant response.

"Those old men there, shaking their pows from their pulpits," continued Captain Delano, pointing to the oakum-pickers, "seem to act the part of old dominies to the rest, little heeded as their admonitions are at times. Is this voluntary on their part, Don Benito, or have you appointed them shepherds to your flock of black sheep?"

"What posts they fill, I appointed them," rejoined the Spaniard in an acrid tone, as if resenting some supposed satiric reflection.

"And these others, these Ashantee conjurors here," continued Captain Delano, rather uneasily eyeing the brandished steel of the hatchet-polishers, where in spots it had been brought to a shine, "this seems a curious business they are at, Don Benito?"

"In the gales we met," answered the Spaniard, "what of our general cargo was not thrown overboard was much damaged by the brine. Since coming into calm weather, I have had several cases of knives and hatchets daily brought up for overhauling and cleaning."

"A prudent idea, Don Benito. You are part owner of ship and cargo, I presume; but not of the slaves, perhaps?"

"I am owner of all you see," impatiently returned Don Benito, "except the main company of blacks, who belonged to my late friend, Alexandro Aranda."

As he mentioned this name, his air was heart-broken, his knees shook; his servant supported him.

Thinking he divined the cause of such unusual emotion, to confirm his surmise, Captain Delano, after a pause, said, "And may I ask, Don Benito, whether — since awhile ago you spoke of some cabin passengers — the friend, whose loss so afflicts you, at the outset of the voyage accompanied his blacks?"

"Yes."

"But died of the fever?"

"Died of the fever. — Oh, could I but —"

Again quivering, the Spaniard paused.

"Pardon me," said Captain Delano slowly, "but I think that, by a sympathetic experience, I conjecture, Don Benito, what it is that gives the keener edge to your grief. It was once my hard fortune to lose at sea a dear friend, my own brother, then supercargo. Assured of the welfare of his spirit, its departure I could have borne like a man; but that honest eye, that honest hand — both of which had so often met mine — and that warm heart; all, all — like scraps to the dogs — to throw all to the sharks! It was then I vowed never to have for fellow-voyager a man I loved, unless, unbeknown to him, I had provided every requisite, in case of a fatality, for embalming his mortal part for interment on shore. Were your friend's remains now on board this ship, Don Benito, not thus strangely would the mention of his name affect you."

"On board this ship?" echoed the Spaniard. Then, with horrified gestures, as directed against some spectre, he unconsciously fell into the ready arms of his attendant, who, with a silent appeal toward Captain Delano, seemed beseeching him not again to broach a theme so unspeakably distressing to his master.

This poor fellow now, thought the pained American, is the victim of that sad superstition which associates goblins with the deserted body of man, as ghosts with an abandoned house. How unlike are we made! What to me, in like case, would have been a solemn satisfaction, the bare suggestion, even, terrifies the Spaniard into this trance. Poor Alexandro Aranda! what would you say could you here see your friend — who, on former voyages, when you for months were left behind, has, I dare say, often longed, and longed, for one peep at you — now transported with terror at the least thought of having you anyway nigh him.

At this moment, with a dreary graveyard toll, betokening a flaw, the ship's forecastle bell, smote by one of the grizzled oakum-pickers, proclaimed ten o'clock through the leaden calm; when Captain Delano's attention was caught by the moving figure of a gigantic black, emerging from the general crowd below, and slowly advancing toward the elevated poop. An iron collar was about his neck, from which depended a chain, thrice wound round his body; the terminating links padlocked together at a broad band of iron, his girdle.

"How like a mute Atufal moves," murmured the servant.

The black mounted the steps of the poop, and, like a brave prisoner, brought up to receive sentence, stood in unquailing muteness before Don Benito, now recovered from his attack.

At the first glimpse of his approach, Don Benito had started, a resentful shadow swept over his face; and, as with the sudden memory of bootless rage, his white lips glued together.

This is some mulish mutineer, thought Captain Delano, surveying, not without a mixture of admiration, the colossal form of the negro.

"See, he waits your question, master," said the servant.

Thus reminded, Don Benito, nervously averting his glance, as if shunning, by anticipation, some rebellious response, in a disconcerted voice, thus spoke:

"Atufal, will you ask my pardon now?"

The black was silent.

"Again, master," murmured the servant, with bitter upbraiding eyeing his countryman; "Again, master; he will bend to master yet."

"Answer," said Don Benito, still averting his glance, "say but the one word *pardon*, and your chains shall be off."

Upon this, the black, slowly raising both arms, let them lifelessly fall, his links clanking, his head bowed; as much as to say, "No, I am content."

"Go," said Don Benito, with inkept and unknown emotion.

Deliberately as he had come, the black obeyed.

"Excuse me, Don Benito," said Captain Delano, "but this scene surprises me; what means it, pray?"

"It means that that negro alone, of all the band, has given me peculiar cause of offence. I have put him in chains; I —"

Here he paused; his hand to his head, as if there were a swimming there, or a sudden bewilderment of memory had come over him; but meeting his servant's kindly glance seemed reassured, and proceeded:

"I could not scourge such a form. But I told him he must ask my pardon. As yet he has not. At my command, every two hours he stands before me."

"And how long has this been?"

"Some sixty days."

"And obedient in all else? And respectful?"

"Yes."

"Upon my conscience, then," exclaimed Captain Delano, impulsively, "he has a royal spirit in him, this fellow."

"He may have some right to it," bitterly returned Don Benito; "he says he was king in his own land."

"Yes," said the servant, entering a word, "those slits in Atufal's ears once held wedges of gold; but poor Babo here, in his own land, was only a poor slave; a black man's slave was Babo, who now is the white's."

Somewhat annoyed by these conversational familiarities, Captain

Delano turned curiously upon the attendant, then glanced inquiringly at his master; but, as if long wonted to these little informalities, neither master nor man seemed to understand him.

"What, pray, was Atufal's offence, Don Benito?" asked Captain Delano; "if it was not something very serious, take a fool's advice, and, in view of his general docility, as well as in some natural respect for his spirit, remit his penalty."

"No, no, master never will do that," here murmured the servant to himself, "proud Atufal must first ask master's pardon. The slave there carries the padlock, but master here carries the key."

His attention thus directed, Captain Delano now noticed for the first time that, suspended by a slender silken cord, from Don Benito's neck hung a key. At once, from the servant's muttered syllables divining the key's purpose, he smiled and said: "So, Don Benito — padlock and key — significant symbols, truly."

Biting his lip, Don Benito faltered.

Though the remark of Captain Delano, a man of such native simplicity as to be incapable of satire or irony, had been dropped in playful allusion to the Spaniard's singularly evidenced lordship over the black; yet the hypochondriac seemed in some way to have taken it as a malicious reflection upon his confessed inability thus far to break down, at least, on a verbal summons, the entrenched will of the slave. Deploring this supposed misconception, yet despairing of correcting it, Captain Delano shifted the subject; but finding his companion more than ever withdrawn, as if still slowly digesting the lees of the presumed affront above-mentioned, by-and-by Captain Delano likewise became less talkative, oppressed, against his own will, by what seemed the secret vindictiveness of the morbidly sensitive Spaniard. But the good sailor himself, of a quite contrary disposition, refrained, on his part, alike from the appearance as from the feeling of resentment, and if silent, was only so from contagion.

Presently the Spaniard, assisted by his servant, somewhat discourteously crossed over from Captain Delano; a procedure which, sensibly enough, might have been allowed to pass for idle caprice of ill-humour, had not master and man, lingering round the corner of the elevated skylight, begun whispering together in low voices. This was unpleasing. And more: the moody air of the Spaniard, which at times had not been without a sort of valetudinarian stateliness, now seemed anything but dignified; while the menial familiarity of the servant lost its original charm of simple-hearted attachment.

In his embarrassment, the visitor turned his face to the other side of the ship. By so doing, his glance accidentally fell on a young Spanish sailor, a coil of rope in his hand, just stepped from the deck to the first round of the mizzen-rigging. Perhaps the man would not have been particularly noticed, were it not that, during his ascent to one of the yards, he, with a sort of covert intentness, kept his eye fixed on Captain Delano, from whom, presently, it passed, as if by a natural sequence, to the two whisperers.

His own attention thus redirected to that quarter, Captain Delano gave a slight start. From something in Don Benito's manner just then, it seemed as if the visitor had, at least partly, been the subject of the withdrawn consultation going on — a conjecture as little agreeable to the guest as it was little flattering to the host.

The singular alternations of courtesy and ill-breeding in the Spanish captain were unaccountable, except on one of two suppositions — innocent lunacy, or wicked imposture.

But the first idea, though it might naturally have occurred to an indifferent observer, and, in some respects, had not hitherto been wholly a stranger to Captain Delano's mind, yet, now that, in an incipient way, he began to regard the stranger's conduct something in the light of an intentional affront, of course the idea of lunacy was virtually vacated. But if not a lunatic, what then? Under the circumstances, would a gentleman, nay, any honest boor, act the part now acted by his host? The man was an impostor. Some low-born adventurer, masquerading as an oceanic grandee; yet so ignorant of the first requisites of mere gentlemanhood as to be betrayed into the present remarkable indecorum. That strange ceremoniousness, too, at other times evinced, seemed not uncharacteristic of one playing a part above his real level. Benito Cereno — Don Benito Cereno — a sounding name. One, too, at that period, not unknown, in the surname, to supercargoes and sea captains trading along the Spanish Main, as belonging to one of the most enterprising and extensive mercantile families in all those provinces; several members of it having titles; a sort of Castilian Rothschild, with a noble brother, or cousin, in every great trading town of South America. The alleged Don Benito was in early manhood, about twenty-nine or thirty. To assume a sort of roving cadetship in the maritime affairs of such a house, what more likely scheme for a young knave of talent and spirit? But the Spaniard was a pale invalid. Never mind. For even to the degree of simulating mortal disease, the craft of some tricksters had been known to attain. To think that, under the aspect of infantile weakness, the most savage energies might be couched ·— those velvets of the Spaniard but the velvet paw to his fangs.

From no train of thought did these fancies come; not from within, but from without; suddenly, too, and in one throng, like hoar frost; yet as soon to vanish as the mild sun of Captain Delano's good-nature regained its meridian.

Glancing over once again toward Don Benito — whose side-face, revealed above the skylight, was now turned toward him — Captain Delano was struck by the profile, whose clearness of cut was refined by the thinness incident to ill-health, as well as ennobled about the chin by the beard. Away with suspicion. He was a true off-shoot of a true hidalgo Cereno.

Relieved by these and other better thoughts, the visitor, lightly humming a tune, now began indifferently pacing the poop, so as not to betray to Don Benito that he had at all mistrusted incivility, much less duplicity; for such mistrust would yet be proved illusory, and by the event; though, for the present, the circumstance which had provoked that distrust remained unexplained. But when that little mystery should have been cleared up, Captain Delano thought he might extremely regret it, did he allow Don Benito to become aware that he had indulged in ungenerous surmises. In short, to the Spaniard's black-letter text, it was best, for a while, to leave open margin.

Presently, his pale face twitching and overcast, the Spaniard, still supported by his attendant, moved over toward his guest, when, with even more than his usual embarrassment, and a strange sort of intriguing intonation in his husky whisper, the following conversation began:

"Señor, may I ask how long you have lain at this isle ?"

"Oh, but a day or two, Don Benito."

"And from what port are you last?"

"Canton."

"And there, Señor, you exchanged your seal-skins for teas and silks, I think you said?"

"Yes. Silks, mostly."

"And the balance you took in specie, perhaps?"

Captain Delano, fidgeting a little, answered —

"Yes; some silver; not a very great deal, though."

"Ah — well. May I ask how many men have you on board, Señor?"

Captain Delano slightly started, but answered:

"About five-and-twenty, all told."

"And at present, Señor, all on board, I suppose?"

"All on board, Don Benito," replied the captain now with satis-faction.

"And will be to-night, Señor?"

At this last question, following so many pertinacious ones, for the soul of him Captain Delano could not but look very earnestly at the questioner, who, instead of meeting the glance, with every token of craven discomposure dropped his eyes to the deck; presenting an un-worthy contrast to his servant, who, just then, was kneeling at his feet adjusting a loose shoe-buckle; his disengaged face meantime, with humble curiosity, turned openly up into his master's downcast one.

The Spaniard, still with a guilty shuffle, repeated his question:

"And — and will be to-night, Señor?"

"Yes, for aught I know," returned Captain Delano, — "but nay," rallying himself into fearless truth, "some of them talked of going off on another fishing party about midnight."

"Your ships generally go — go more or less armed, I believe, Señor?"

"Oh, a six-pounder or two, in case of emergency," was the intrepidly indifferent reply, "with a small stock of muskets, sealing-spears, and cutlasses, you know."

As he thus responded, Captain Delano again glanced at Don Benito, but the latter's eyes were averted; while abruptly and awkwardly shifting the subject, he made some peevish allusion to the calm, and then, without apology, once more, with his attendant, withdrew to the opposite bulwarks, where the whispering was resumed.

At this moment, and ere Captain Delano could cast a cool thought upon what had just passed, the young Spanish sailor before mentioned was seen descending from the rigging. In act of stooping over to spring inboard to the deck, his voluminous, unconfined frock, or shirt, of coarse woollen, much spotted with tar, opened out far down the chest, revealing a soiled under-garment of what seemed the finest linen, edged, about the neck, with a narrow blue ribbon, sadly faded and worn. At this moment the young sailor's eye was again fixed on the whisperers, and Captain Delano thought he observed a lurking signifi-cance in it, as if silent signs of some freemason sort had that instant been interchanged.

This once more impelled his own glance in the direction of Don Benito, and, as before, he could not but infer that himself formed the subject of the conference. He paused. The sound of the hatchet-polishing fell on his ears. He cast another swift side-look at the two. They had the air of conspirators. In connection with the late questionings, and the incident of the young sailor, these things now begat such return of involuntary suspicion, that the singular guilelessness of the American could not endure it. Plucking up a gay and humorous expression, he crossed over to the two rapidly, saying: "Ha, Don Benito, your black here seems high in your trust; a sort of privy-counsellor, in fact."

Upon this, the servant looked up with a good-natured grin, but the master started as from a venomous bite. It was a moment or two before the Spaniard sufficiently recovered himself to reply; which he did, at last, with cold constraint: "Yes, Señor, I have trust in Babo."

Here Babo, changing his previous grin of mere animal humour into an intelligent smile, not ungratefully eyed his master.

Finding that the Spaniard now stood silent and reserved, as if involuntarily, or purposely giving hint that his guest's proximity was inconvenient just then, Captain Delano, unwilling to appear uncivil even to incivility itself, made some trivial remark and moved off; again and again turning over in his mind the mysterious demeanour of Don Benito Cereno.

He had descended from the poop, and, wrapped in thought, was passing near a dark hatchway, leading down into the steerage, when, perceiving motion there, he looked to see what moved. The same instant there was a sparkle in the shadowy hatchway, and he saw one of the Spanish sailors, prowling there, hurriedly placing his hand in the bosom of his frock, as if hiding something. Before the man could have been certain who it was that was passing, he slunk below out of sight. But enough was seen of him to make it sure that he was the same young sailor before noticed in the rigging.

What was that which so sparkled? thought Captain Delano. It was no lamp — no match — no live coal. Could it have been a jewel? But how come sailors with jewels? — or with silk-trimmed undershirts either? Has he been robbing the trunks of the dead cabin passengers? But if so, he would hardly wear one of the stolen articles on board ship here. Ah, ah — if now that was, indeed, a secret sign I saw passing between this suspicious fellow and his captain awhile since; if I could only be certain that in my uneasiness my senses did not deceive me, then —

Here, passing from one suspicious thing to another, his mind revolved the point of the strange questions put to him concerning his ship.

By a curious coincidence, as each point was recalled, the black wizards of Ashantee would strike up with their hatchets, as in ominous comment on the white stranger's thoughts. Pressed by such enigmas and portents, it would have been almost against nature, had not, even into the least distrustful heart, some ugly misgivings obtruded.

Observing the ship now helplessly fallen into a current, with enchanted sails, drifting with increased rapidity seaward; and noting that, from a lately intercepted projection of the land, the sealer was hidden, the stout mariner began to quake at thoughts which he barely durst confess to himself. Above all, he began to feel a ghostly dread of Don Benito. And yet when he roused himself, dilated his chest, felt himself strong on his legs, and coolly considered it — what did all these phantoms amount to?

Had the Spaniard any sinister scheme, it must have reference not so much to him (Captain Delano) as to his ship (the *Bachelor's Delight*). Hence the present drifting away of the one ship from the other, instead of favouring any such possible scheme, was, for the time at least, opposed to it. Clearly any suspicion, combining such contradictions, must need be delusive. Beside, was it not absurd to think of a vessel in distress — a vessel by sickness almost dismanned of her crew — a vessel whose inmates were parched for water — was it not a thousand times absurd that such a craft should, at present, be of a piratical character; or her commander, either for himself or those under him, cherish any desire but for speedy relief and refreshment? But then, might not general distress, and thirst in particular, be affected? And might not that same undiminished Spanish crew, alleged to have perished off to a remnant, be at that very moment lurking in the hold? On heartbroken pretence of entreating a cup of cold water, fiends in human form had got into lonely dwellings, nor retired until a dark deed had been done. And among the Malay pirates, it was no unusual thing to lure ships after them into their treacherous harbours, or entice boarders from a declared enemy at sea, by the spectacle of thinly manned or vacant decks, beneath which prowled a hundred spears with yellow arms ready to upthrust them through the mats. Not that Captain Delano had entirely credited such things. He had heard of them — and now, as stories, they recurred. The present destination of the ship was the anchorage. There she would be near his own vessel. Upon gaining that vicinity, might not the *San Dominick*, like a slumbering volcano, suddenly let loose energies now hid?

He recalled the Spaniard's manner while telling his story. There was a gloomy hesitancy and subterfuge about it. It was just the manner of one making up his tale for evil purposes, as he goes. But if that story was true, what was the truth? That the ship had unlawfully come into the Spaniard's possession? But in many of its details, especially in reference to the more calamitous parts, such as the fatalities among the seamen, the consequent prolonged beating about, the past sufferings from obstinate calms, and still continued suffering from thirst; in all these points, as well as others, Don Benito's story had corroborated not only the wailing ejaculations of the indiscriminate multitude, white and black, but likewise — what seemed impossible to be counterfeit — by the very expression and play of every human feature, which Captain Delano saw. If Don Benito's story was throughout an invention, then every soul on board, down to the youngest negress, was his carefully drilled recruit in the plot: an incredible inference. And yet, if there was ground for mistrusting the Spanish captain's veracity, that inference was a legitimate one.

In short, scarce an uneasiness entered the honest sailor's mind but, by a subsequent spontaneous act of good sense, it was ejected. At last he began to laugh at these forebodings; and laugh at the strange ship for, in its aspect someway siding with them, as it were; and laugh, too, at the odd-looking blacks, particularly those old scissors-grinders, the Ashantees; and those bed-ridden old knitting-women, the oakum-pickers; and in a human way, he almost began to laugh at the dark Spaniard himself, the central hobgoblin of all.

For the rest, whatever in a serious way seemed enigmatical, was now good-naturedly explained away by the thought that, for the most part, the poor invalid scarcely knew what he was about; either sulking in black vapours, or putting random questions without sense or object. Evidently, for the present, the man was not fit to be entrusted with the ship. On some benevolent plea withdrawing the command from him, Captain Delano would yet have to send her to Concepcion in charge of his second mate, a worthy person and good navigator — a plan which would prove no wiser for the *San Dominick* than for Don Benito; for — relieved from all anxiety, keeping wholly to his cabin — the sick man, under the good nursing of his servant, would probably, by the end of the passage, be in a measure restored to health and with that he should also be restored to authority.

Such were the American's thoughts. They were tranquillizing. There was a difference between the idea of Don Benito's darkly pre-ordaining Captain Delano's fate, and Captain Delano's lightly arrang-ing Don Benito's. Nevertheless, it was not without something of relief that the good seaman presently perceived his whale-boat in the distance. Its absence had been prolonged by unexpected detention at the sealer's side, as well as its returning trip lengthened by the continual recession of the goal.

The advancing speck was observed by the blacks. Their shouts attracted the attention of Don Benito, who, with a return of courtesy, approaching Captain Delano, expressed satisfaction at the coming of some supplies, slight and temporary as they must necessarily prove.

Captain Delano responded; but while doing so, his attention was drawn to something passing on the deck below: among the crowd climbing the landward bulwarks, anxiously watching the coming boat, two blacks, to all appearances accidentally incommoded by one of the sailors, flew out against him with horrible curses, which the sailor someway resenting, the two blacks dashed him to the deck and jumped upon him, despite the earnest cries of the oakum-pickers.

"Don Benito," said Captain Delano quickly, "do you see what is going on there? Look!"

But, seized by his cough, the Spaniard staggered, with both hands to his face, on the point of falling. Captain Delano would have supported him, but the servant was more alert, who, with one hand sustaining his master, with the other applied the cordial. Don Benito, restored, the black withdrew his support, slipping aside a little, but dutifully remaining within call of a whisper. Such discretion was here evinced as quite wiped away, in the visitor's eyes, any blemish of impropriety which might have attached to the attendant, from the indecorous conferences before mentioned; showing, too, that if the servant were to blame, it might be more the master's fault than his own, since when left to himself he could conduct thus well.

His glance thus called away from the spectacle of disorder to the more pleasing one before him, Captain Delano could not avoid again congratulating Don Benito upon possessing such a servant, who, though perhaps a little too forward now and then, must upon the whole be invaluable to one in the invalid's situation.

"Tell me, Don Benito," he added, with a smile — "I should like to have your man here myself — what will you take for him? Would fifty doubloons be any object?"

"Master wouldn't part with Babo for a thousand doubloons," murmured the black, overhearing the offer, and taking it in earnest, and, with the strange vanity of a faithful slave appreciated by his master, scorning to hear so paltry a valuation put upon him by a stranger. But

Don Benito, apparently hardly yet completely restored, and again interrupted by his cough, made but some broken reply.

Soon his physical distress became so great, affecting his mind, too, apparently, that, as if to screen the sad spectacle, the servant gently conducted his master below.

Left to himself, the American, to while away the time till his boat should arrive, would have pleasantly accosted some one of the few Spanish seamen he saw; but recalling something that Don Benito had said touching their ill conduct, he refrained, as a ship-master indisposed to countenance cowardice or unfaithfulness in seamen.

While, with these thoughts, standing with eye directed forward toward that handful of sailors — suddenly he thought that some of them returned the glance and with a sort of meaning. He rubbed his eyes, and looked again; but again seemed to see the same thing. Under a new form, but more obscure than any previous one, the old suspicions recurred, but, in the absence of Don Benito, with less of panic than before. Despite the bad account given of the sailors, Captain Delano resolved forthwith to accost one of them. Descending the poop, he made his way through the blacks, his movement drawing a queer cry from the oakum-pickers, prompted by whom the negroes, twitching each other aside, divided before him; but, as if curious to see what was the object of this deliberate visit to their Ghetto, closing in behind, in tolerable order, followed the white stranger up. His progress thus proclaimed as by mounted kings-at-arms, and escorted as by a Caffre guard of honour, Captain Delano, assuming a good-humoured, offhand air, continued to advance; now and then saying a blithe word to the negroes, and his eye curiously surveying the white faces, here and there sparsely mixed in with the blacks, like stray white pawns venturously involved in the ranks of the chessmen opposed.

While thinking which of them to select for his purpose, he chanced to observe a sailor seated on the deck engaged in tarring the strap of a large block, with a circle of blacks squatted round him inquisitively eyeing the process.

The mean employment of the man was in contrast with something superior in his figure. His hand, black with continually thrusting it into the tar-pot held for him by a negro, seemed not naturally allied to his face, a face which would have been a very fine one but for its haggardness. Whether this haggardness had aught to do with criminality could not be determined; since, as intense heat and cold, though unlike, produce like sensations, so innocence and guilt, when, through casual association with mental pain, stamping any visible impress, use one seal — a hacked one.

Not again that this reflection occurred to Captain Delano at the time, charitable man as he was. Rather another idea. Because observing so singular a haggardness to be combined with a dark eye, averted as in trouble and shame, and then, however illogically, uniting in his mind his own private suspicions of the crew with the confessed ill-opinion on the part of their captain, he was insensibly operated upon by certain general notions, which, while disconnecting pain and abashment from virtue, as invariably link them with vice.

If, indeed, there be any wickedness on board this ship, thought Captain Delano, be sure that man there has fouled his hand in it, even as now he fouls it in the pitch. I don't like to accost him. I will speak to this other, this old Jack here on the windlass.

He advanced to an old Barcelona tar, in ragged red breeches and dirty night-cap, cheeks trenched and bronzed, whiskers dense as thorn hedges. Seated between two sleepy-looking Africans, this mariner, like his younger shipmate, was employed upon some rigging — splicing a cable — the sleepy-looking blacks performing the inferior function of holding the outer parts of the ropes for him.

Upon Captain Delano's approach, the man at once hung his head below its previous level; the one necessary for business. It appeared as if he desired to be thought absorbed, with more than common fidelity, in his task. Being addressed, he glanced up, but with what seemed a furtive, diffident air, which sat strangely enough on his weatherbeaten visage, much as if a grizzly bear, instead of growling and biting, should simper and cast sheep's eyes. He was asked several questions concerning the voyage — questions purposely referring to several particulars in Don Benito's narrative — not previously corroborated by those impulsive cries greeting the visitor on first coming on board. The questions were briefly answered, confirming all that remained to be confirmed of the story. The negroes about the windlass joined in with the old sailor, but, as they became talkative, he by degrees became mute, and at length quite glum, seemed morosely unwilling to answer more questions, and yet, all the while, this ursine air was somehow mixed with his sheepish one.

Despairing of getting into unembarrassed talk with such a centaur, Captain Delano, after glancing round for a more promising countenance, but seeing none, spoke pleasantly to the blacks to make way for him; and so, amid various grins and grimaces, returned to the poop, feeling a little strange at first, he could hardly tell why, but upon the whole with regained confidence in Benito Cereno.

How plainly, thought he, did that old whiskerando yonder betray a consciousness of ill-desert. No doubt, when he saw me coming, he dreaded lest I, apprised by his captain of the crew's general misbehaviour, came with sharp words for him, and so down with his head. And yet — and yet, now that I think of it, that very old fellow, if I err not, was one of those who seemed so earnestly eyeing me here awhile since. Ah, these currents spin one's head round almost as much as they do the ship. Ha, there now's a pleasant sort of sunny sight; quite sociable, too.

His attention had been drawn to a slumbering negress, partly disclosed through the lace-work of some rigging, lying, with youthful limbs carelessly disposed, under the lee of the bulwarks, like a doe in the shade of a woodland rock. Sprawling at her lapped breasts was her wide-awake fawn, stark naked, its black little body half lifted from the deck, crosswise with its dam's; its hands, like two paws, clambering upon her; its mouth and nose ineffectually rooting to get at the mark; and meantime giving a vexatious half-grunt, blending with the composed snore of the negress.

The uncommon vigour of the child at length roused the mother. She started up, at distance facing Captain Delano. But, as if not at all concerned at the attitude in which she had been caught, delightedly she caught the child up, with maternal transports, covering it with kisses.

There's naked nature, now; pure tenderness and love, thought Captain Delano, well pleased.

This incident prompted him to remark the other negresses more particularly than before. He was gratified with their manners; like most uncivilized women, they seemed at once tender of heart and tough of constitution; equally ready to die for their infants or fight for them. Unsophisticated as leopardesses; loving as doves. Ah! thought Captain Delano, these perhaps are some of the very women whom Mungo Park saw in Africa, and gave such a noble account of.

These natural sights somehow insensibly deepened his confidence and ease. At last he looked to see how his boat was getting on; but it was still pretty remote. He turned to see if Don Benito had returned; but he had not.

To change the scene, as well as to please himself with a leisurely observation of the coming boat, stepping over into the mizzen-chains he clambered his way into the starboard quarter-gallery; one of those abandoned Venetian-looking water-balconies previously mentioned; retreats cut off from the deck. As his foot pressed the half-damp, half-dry seamosses matting the place, and a chance phantom cat's-paw — an islet of breeze, unheralded, unfollowed — as this ghostly cat's-paw came fanning his cheek, as his glance fell upon the row of small, round dead-lights — all closed like coppered eyes of the coffined — and the state-cabin door, once connecting with the gallery, even as the dead-lights had once looked out upon it, but now caulked fast like a sarcophagus lid; and to a purple-black, tarred-over panel, threshold, and post; and he bethought him of the time, when that state-cabin and this state-balcony had heard the voices of the Spanish king's officers, and the forms of the Lima viceroy's daughters had perhaps leaned where he stood — as these and other images flitted through his mind, as the cat's-paw through the calm, gradually he felt rising a dreamy inquietude, like that of one who alone on the prairie feels unrest from the repose of the noon.

He leaned against the carved balustrade, again looking off toward his boat; but found his eye falling upon the ribboned grass, trailing along the ship's water-line, straight as a border of green box; and parterres of sea-weed, broad ovals and crescents, floating nigh and far, with what seemed long formal alleys between, crossing the terraces of swells, and sweeping round as if leading to the grottoes below. And overhanging all was the balustrade by his arm, which, partly stained with pitch and partly embossed with moss, seemed the charred ruin of some summer-house in a grand garden long running to waste.

Trying to break one charm, he was but becharmed anew. Though upon the wide sea, he seemed in some far inland country; prisoner in some deserted château, left to stare at empty grounds, and peer out at vague roads, where never wagon or wayfarer passed.

But these enchantments were a little disenchanted as his eye fell on the corroded main-chains. Of an ancient style, massy and rusty in link, shackle and bolt, they seemed even more fit for the ship's present business than the one for which probably she had been built.

Presently he thought something moved nigh the chains. He rubbed his eyes, and looked hard. Groves of rigging were about the chains; and there, peering from behind a great stay, like an Indian from behind a hemlock, a Spanish sailor, a marlingspike in his hand, was seen, who made what seemed an imperfect gesture toward the balcony — but immediately, as if alarmed by some advancing step along the deck within, vanished into the recesses of the hempen forest, like a poacher.

What meant this? Something the man had sought to communicate unbeknown to any one, even to his captain. Did the secret involve aught unfavourable to his captain? Were those previous misgivings of Captain Delano's about to be verified? Or, in his haunted mood at the moment, had some random, unintentional motion of the man, while busy with the stay, as if repairing it, been mistaken for a significant beckoning?

Not unbewildered, again he gazed off for his boat. But it was temporarily hidden by a rocky spur of the isle. As with some eagerness he bent forward, watching for the first shooting view of its beak, the balustrade gave way before him like charcoal. Had he not clutched an outreaching rope he would have fallen into the sea. The crash, though feeble, and the fall, though hollow, of the rotten fragments, must have been overheard. He glanced up. With sober curiosity peering down upon him was one of the old oakum-pickers, slipped from his perch to an outside boom; while below the old negro — and, invisible to him, reconnoitring from a port-hole like a fox from the mouth of its den — crouched the Spanish sailor again. From something suddenly suggested by the man's air, the mad idea now darted into Captain Delano's mind; that Don Benito's plea of indisposition, in withdrawing below, was but a pretence: that he was engaged there maturing some plot, of which the sailor, by some means gaining an inkling, had a mind to warn the stranger against; incited, it may be, by gratitude for a kind word on first boarding the ship. Was it from foreseeing some possible interference like this, that Don Benito had, beforehand, given such a bad character of his sailors, while praising the negroes; though, indeed, the former seemed as docile as the latter the contrary? The whites, too, by nature, were the shrewder race. A man with some evil design, would not he be likely to speak well of that stupidity which was blind to his depravity, and malign that intelligence from which it might not be hidden? Not unlikely, perhaps. But if the whites had dark secrets concerning Don Benito, could then Don Benito be any way in complicity with the blacks? But they were too stupid. Besides, who ever heard of a white so far a renegade as to apostatize from his very species almost, by leaguing in against it with negroes? These difficulties recalled former ones. Lost in their mazes, Captain Delano, who had now regained the deck, was uneasily advancing along it, when he observed a new face; an aged sailor seated cross-legged near the main hatchway.

His skin was shrunk up with wrinkles like a pelican's empty pouch; his hair frosted; his countenance grave and composed. His hands were full of ropes, which he was working into a large knot. Some blacks were about him obligingly dipping the strands for him, here and there, as the exigencies of the operation demanded.

Captain Delano crossed over to him, and stood in silence surveying the knot; his mind, by a not uncongenial transition, passing from its own entanglements to those of the hemp. For intricacy such a knot he had never seen in an American ship, or indeed any other. The old man looked like an Egyptian priest, making gordian knots for the temple of Ammon. The knot seemed a combination of double-bow-line-knot,   treble-crown-knot,   back-handed-well-knot, knot-in-and-out-knot, and jamming-knot.

At last, puzzled to comprehend the meaning of such a knot, Captain Delano, addressed the knotter: —

"What are you knotting there, my man?"

"The knot," was the brief reply, without looking up.

"So it seems; but what is it for?"

"For some one else to undo," muttered back the old man, plying his fingers harder than ever, the knot being now nearly completed.

While Captain Delano stood watching him, suddenly the old man threw the knot toward him, and said in broken English, — the first heard in the ship, — something to this effect — "Undo it, cut it, quick." It was said lowly, but with such condensation of rapidity, that the long, slow words in Spanish, which had preceded and followed, almost operated as covers to the brief English between.

For a moment, knot in hand, and knot in head, Captain Delano stood mute; while, without further heeding him, the old man was now intent upon other ropes. Presently there was a slight stir behind Captain Delano. Turning, he saw the chained negro, Atufal, standing quietly there. The next moment the old sailor rose, muttering, and, followed by his subordinate negroes, removed to the forward part of the ship, where in the crowd he disappeared.

An elderly negro, in a clout like an infant's, and with a pepper and salt head, and a kind of attorney air, now approached Captain Delano. In tolerable Spanish, and with a good-natured, knowing wink, he informed him that the old knotter was simple-witted, but harmless; often playing his old tricks. The negro concluded by begging the knot, for of course the stranger would not care to be troubled with it. Unconsciously, it was handed to him. With a sort of congé, the negro received it, and turning his back ferreted into it like a detective Custom House officer after smuggled laces. Soon, with some African word, equivalent to pshaw, he tossed the knot overboard.

All this is very queer now, thought Captain Delano, with a qualmish sort of emotion; but as one feeling incipient seasickness, he strove, by ignoring the symptoms, to get rid of the malady. Once more he looked off for his boat. To his delight, it was now again in view, leaving the rocky spur astern.

The sensation here experienced, after at first relieving his uneasiness, with unforeseen efficiency, soon began to remove it. The less distant sight of that well-known boat — showing it, not as before, half blended with the haze, but with outline defined, so that its individuality, like a man's, was manifest; that boat, *Rover* by name, which, though now in strange seas, had often pressed the beach of Captain Delano's home, and, brought to its threshold for repairs, had familiarly lain there, as a Newfoundland dog; the sight of that household boat evoked a thousand trustful associations, which, contrasted with previous suspicions, filled him not only with lightsome confidence, but somehow with half humorous self-reproaches at his former lack of it.

"What, I, Amasa Delano — Jack of the Beach, as they called me when a lad — I, Amasa; the same that, duck-satchel in hand, used to paddle along the waterside to the schoolhouse made from the old hulk; — I, little Jack of the Beach, that used to go berrying with cousin Nat and the rest; I to be murdered here at the ends of the earth, on board a haunted pirate-ship by a horrible Spaniard? — Too nonsensical to think of! Who would murder Amasa Delano? His conscience is clean. There is some one above. Fie, fie, Jack of the Beach! you are a child indeed; a child of the second childhood, old boy; you are beginning to dote and drule, I'm afraid."

Light of heart and foot, he stepped aft, and there was met by Don Benito's servant, who, with a pleasing expression, responsive to his own present feelings, informed him that his master had recovered from the effects of his coughing fit, and had just ordered him to go present his compliments to his good guest, Don Amasa, and say that he (Don Benito) would soon have the happiness to rejoin him.

There now, do you mark that? again thought Captain Delano, walking the poop. What a donkey I was. This kind gentleman who here sends me his kind compliments, he, but ten minutes ago, dark-lantern in hand, was dodging round some old grind-stone in the hold, sharpening a hatchet for me, I thought. Well, well; these long calms have a morbid effect on the mind, I've often heard, though I never believed it before. Ha! glancing toward the boat; there's *Rover*; a good dog; a white bone in her mouth. A pretty big bone though, seems to me. — What? Yes, she has fallen afoul of the bubbling tide-rip there. It sets her the other way, too, for the time. Patience.

It was now about noon, though, from the greyness of everything, it seemed to be getting toward dusk.

The calm was confirmed. In the far distance, away from the influence of land, the leaden ocean seemed laid out and leaded up, its course finished, soul gone, defunct. But the current from landward, where the ship was, increased; silently sweeping her further and further toward the tranced waters beyond.

Still, from his knowledge of those latitudes, cherishing hopes of a breeze, and a fair and fresh one, at any moment, Captain Delano, despite present prospects, buoyantly counted upon bringing the *San Dominick* safely to anchor ere night. The distance swept over was nothing; since, with a good wind, ten minutes' sailing would retrace more than sixty minutes' drifting. Meantime, one moment turning to mark "Rover" fighting the tide-rip, and the next to see Don Benito approaching, he continued walking the poop.

Gradually he felt a vexation arising from the delay of his boat; this soon merged into uneasiness; and at last, his eye falling continually, as from a stage-box into the pit, upon the strange crowd before and below him, and by-and-by recognizing there the face — now composed to indifference — of the Spanish sailor who had seemed to beckon from the main chains, something of his old trepidations returned.

Ah, thought he — gravely enough — this is like the ague: because it went off, it follows not that it won't come back.

Though ashamed of the relapse, he could not altogether subdue it; and so, exerting his good nature to the utmost, insensibly he came to a compromise.

Yes, this is a strange craft; a strange history, too, and strange folks on board. But — nothing more.

By way of keeping his mind out of mischief till the boat should arrive, he tried to occupy it with turning over and over, in a purely speculative sort of way, some lesser peculiarities of the captain and crew. Among others, four curious points recurred.

First, the affair of the Spanish lad assailed with a knife by the slave boy; an act winked at by Don Benito. Second, the tyranny in Don Benito's treatment of Atufal, the black; as if a child should lead a bull of the Nile by the ring in his nose. Third, the trampling of the sailor by the two negroes; a piece of insolence passed over without so much as a reprimand. Fourth, the cringing submission to their master of all the ship's underlings, mostly blacks; as if by the least inadvertence they feared to draw down his despotic displeasure.

Coupling these points, they seemed somewhat contradictory. But what then, thought Captain Delano, glancing toward his now nearing boat, — what then? Why, this Don Benito is a very capricious commander. But he is not the first of the sort I have seen; though it's true he rather exceeds any other. But as a nation — continued he in his reveries — these Spaniards are all an odd set; the very word Spaniard has a curious, conspirator, Guy-Fawkish twang to it. And yet, I dare say, Spaniards in the main are as good folks as any in Duxbury, Massachusetts. Ah, good! At last "Rover" has come.

As, with its welcome freight, the boat touched the side, the oakumpickers, with venerable gestures, sought to restrain the blacks, who, at the sight of three gurried water-casks in its bottom, and a pile of wilted pumpkins in its bow, hung over the bulwarks in disorderly raptures.

Don Benito with his servant now appeared; his coming, perhaps, hastened by hearing the noise. Of him Captain Delano sought permission to serve out the water, so that all might share alike, and none injure themselves by unfair excess. But sensible, and, on Don Benito's account, kind as this offer was, it was received with what seemed impatience; as if aware that he lacked energy as a commander, Don Benito, with the true jealousy of weakness, resented as an affront any interference. So, at least, Captain Delano inferred.

In another moment the casks were being hoisted in, when some of the eager negroes accidentally jostled Captain Delano, where he stood by the gangway; so that, unmindful of Don Benito, yielding to the impulse of the moment, with good-natured authority he bade the blacks stand back; to enforce his words making use of a half-mirthful, halfmenacing gesture. Instantly the blacks paused, just where they were, each negro and negress suspended in his or her posture, exactly as the word had found them — for a few seconds continuing so — while, as between the responsive posts of a telegraph, an unknown syllable ran from man to man among the perched oakum-pickers. While Captain Delano's attention was fixed by this scene, suddenly the hatchetpolishers half rose, and a rapid cry came from Don Benito.

Thinking that at the signal of the Spaniard he was about to be massacred, Captain Delano would have sprung for his boat, but paused, a; the oakum-pickers, dropping down into the crowd with earnest exclamations, forced every white and every negro back, at the same moment, with gestures friendly and familiar, almost jocose, bidding him, in substance, not be a fool. Simultaneously the hatchet-polishers resumed their seats, quietly as so many tailors, and at once, as if nothing had happened, the work of hoisting in the casks was resumed, whites and blacks singing at the tackle.

Captain Delano glanced toward Don Benito. As he saw his meagre form in the act of recovering itself from reclining in the servant's arms, into which the agitated invalid had fallen, he could not but marvel at the panic by which himself had been surprised on the darting supposition that such a commander, who upon a legitimate occasion, so trivial, too, as it now appeared, could lose all self-command, was, with energetic iniquity, going to bring about his murder.

The casks being on deck, Captain Delano was handed a number of jars and cups by one of the steward's aides, who, in the name of Don Benito, entreated him to do as he had proposed: dole out the water. He complied, with republican impartiality as to this republican element, which always seeks one level, serving the oldest white no better than the youngest black; excepting, indeed, poor Don Benito, whose condition, if not rank, demanded an extra allowance. To him, in the first place, Captain Delano presented a fair pitcher of the fluid; but, thirsting as he was for fresh water, Don Benito quaffed not a drop until after several grave bows and salutes: a reciprocation of courtesies which the sight-loving Africans hailed with clapping of hands.

Two of the less wilted pumpkins being reserved for the cabin table, the residue were minced up on the spot for the general regalement. But the soft bread, sugar, and bottled cider, Captain Delano would have given the Spaniards alone, and in chief Don Benito; but the latter objected; which disinterestedness, on his part, not a little pleased the American; and so mouthfuls all around were given alike to whites and blacks; excepting one bottle of cider, which Babo insisted upon setting aside for his master.

Here it may be observed that as, on the first visit of the boat, the American had not permitted his men to board the ship, neither did he now; being unwilling to add to the confusion of the decks.

Not uninfluenced by the peculiar good humour at present prevailing, and for the time oblivious of any but benevolent thoughts, Captain Delano, who from recent indications counted upon a breeze within an hour or two at furthest, despatched the boat back to the sealer with orders for all the hands that could be spared immediately to set about rafting casks to the watering-place and filling them. Likewise he bade word be carried to his chief officer, that if against present expectation the ship was not brought to anchor by sunset, he need be under no concern, for as there was to be a full moon that night, he (Captain Delano) would remain on board ready to play the pilot, should the wind come soon or late.

As the two captains stood together, observing the departing boat — the servant as it happened having just spied a spot on his master's velvet sleeve, and silently engaged rubbing it out — the American expressed his regrets that the *San Dominick* had no boats; none, at least, but the unseaworthy old hulk of the long-boat, which, warped as a camel's skeleton in the desert, and almost as bleached, lay potwise inverted amidships, one side a little tipped, furnishing a subterraneous sort of den for family groups of the blacks, mostly women and small children; who, squatting on old mats below, or perched above in the dark dome, on the elevated seats, were descried, some distance within, like a social circle of bats, sheltering in some friendly cave; at intervals, ebon flights of naked boys and girls, three or four years old, darting in and out of the den's mouth.

"Had you three or four boats now, Don Benito," said Captain Delano, "I think that, by tugging at the oars, your negroes here might help along matters some. — Did you sail from port without boats, Don Benito?"

"They were stove in the gales, Señor."

"That was bad. Many men, too, you lost then. Boats and men. — Those must have been hard gales, Don Benito."

"Past all speech," cringed the Spaniard.

"Tell me, Don Benito," continued his companion with increased interest, "tell me, were these gales immediately off the pitch of Cape Horn?"

"Cape Horn? — who spoke of Cape Horn?"

"Yourself did, when giving me an account of your voyage," answered Captain Delano with almost equal astonishment at this eating of his own words, even as he ever seemed eating his own heart, on the part of the Spaniard. "You yourself, Don Benito, spoke of Cape Horn," he emphatically repeated.

The Spaniard turned, in a sort of stooping posture, pausing an instant, as one about to make a plunging exchange of elements, as from air to water.

At this moment a messenger-boy, a white, hurried by, in the regular performance of his function carrying the last expired half-hour forward to the forecastle, from the cabin time-piece, to have it struck at the ship's large bell.

"Master," said the servant, discontinuing his work on the coat sleeve, and addressing the rapt Spaniard with a sort of timid apprehensiveness, as one charged with a duty, the discharge of which, it was foreseen, would prove irksome to the very person who had imposed it, and for whose benefit it was intended, "master told me never mind where he was, or how engaged, always to remind him, to a minute, when shaving-time comes. Miguel has gone to strike the half-hour afternoon. It is *now*, master. Will master go into the cuddy?"

"Ah — yes," answered the Spaniard, starting, somewhat as from dreams into realities; then turning upon Captain Delano, he said that ere long he would resume the conversation.

"Then if master means to talk more to Don Amasa," said the servant, "why not let Don Amasa sit by master in the cuddy, and master can talk, and Don Amasa can listen, while Babo here lathers and strops."

"Yes," said Captain Delano, not unpleased with this sociable plan, "yes, Don Benito, unless you had rather not, I will go with you."

"Be it so, Señor."

As the three passed aft, the American could not but think it another strange instance of his host's capriciousness, this being shaved with such uncommon punctuality in the middle of the day. But he deemed it more than likely that the servant's anxious fidelity had something to do with the matter; inasmuch as the timely interruption served to rally his master from the mood which had evidently been coming upon him.

The place called the cuddy was a light deck-cabin formed by the poop, a sort of attic to the large cabin below. Part of it had formerly been the quarters of the officers; but since their death all the partitionings had been thrown down, and the whole interior converted into one spacious and airy marine hall; for absence of fine furniture and picturesque disarray, of odd appurtenances, somewhat answering to the wide, cluttered hall of some eccentric bachelor-squire in the country, who hangs his shooting-jacket and tobacco-pouch on deer antlers, and keeps his fishing-rod, tongs, and walking-stick in the same corner.

The similitude was heightened, if not originally suggested, by glimpses of the surrounding sea; since, in one aspect, the country and the ocean seem cousins-german.

The floor of the cuddy was matted. Overhead, four or five old muskets were stuck into horizontal holes along the beams. On one side was a claw-footed old table lashed to the deck; a thumbed missal on it, and over it a small, meagre crucifix attached to the bulkhead. Under the table lay a dented cutlass or two, with a hacked harpoon, among some melancholy old rigging, like a heap of poor friar's girdles. There were also two long, sharp-ribbed settees of malacca cane, black with age, and uncomfortable to look at as inquisitors' racks, with a large, misshapen arm-chair, which, furnished with a rude barber's crutch at the back, working with a screw, seemed some grotesque Middle Age engine of torment. A flag locker was in one corner, exposing various coloured bunting, some rolled up, others half unrolled, still others tumbled. Opposite was a cumbrous washstand, of black mahogany, all of one block, with a pedestal, like a font, and over it a railed shelf, containing combs, brushes, and other implements of the toilet. A torn hammock of stained grass swung near; the sheets tossed, and the pillow wrinkled up like a brow, as if whoever slept here slept but illy, with alternate visitations of sad thoughts and bad dreams.

The further extremity of the cuddy, overhanging the ship's stern, was pierced with three openings, windows or port holes, according as men or cannon might peer, socially or unsocially, out of them. At present neither men nor cannon were seen, though huge ring-bolts and other rusty iron fixtures of the wood-work hinted of twenty-four-pounders.

Glancing toward the hammock as he entered, Captain Delano said, "You sleep here, Don Benito?"

"Yes, Señor, since we got into mild weather."

"This seems a sort of dormitory, sitting-room, sail-loft, chapel, armoury, and private closet together, Don Benito," added Captain Delano, looking round.

"Yes, Señor; events have not been favourable to much order in my arrangements."

Here the servant, napkin on arm, made a motion as if waiting his master's good pleasure. Don Benito signified his readiness, when, seating him in the malacca arm-chair, and for the guest's convenience drawing opposite it one of the settees, the servant commenced operations by throwing back his master's collar and loosening his cravat.

There is something in the negro which, in a peculiar way, fits him for avocations about one's person. Most negroes are natural valets and hair-dressers; taking to the comb and brush congenially as to the castanets, and flourishing them apparently with almost equal satisfaction. There is, too, a smooth tact about them in this employment, with a marvelous, noiseless, gliding briskness, not ungraceful in its way, singularly pleasing to behold, and still more so to be the manipulated subject of. And above all is the great gift of good humour. Not the mere grin or laugh is here meant. Those were unsuitable. But a certain easy cheerfulness, harmonious in every glance and gesture; as though God had set the whole negro to some pleasant tune.

When to all this is added the docility arising from the unaspiring contentment of a limited mind, and that susceptibility of blind attachment sometimes inhering in indisputable inferiors, one readily perceives why those hypochondriacs, Johnson and Byron — it may be something like the hypochondriac, Benito Cereno — took to their hearts, almost to the exclusion of the entire white race, their serving men, the negroes, Barber and Fletcher. But if there be that in the negro which exempts him from the inflicted sourness of the morbid or cynical mind, how, in his most prepossessing aspects, must he appear to a benevolent one? When at ease with respect to exterior things, Captain Delano's nature was not only benign, but familiarly and humourously so. At home, he had often taken rare satisfaction in sitting in his door, watching some free man of colour at his work or play. If on a voyage he chanced to have a black sailor, invariably he was on chatty, and half-gamesome terms with him. In fact, like most men of a good, blithe heart, Captain Delano took to negroes, not philanthropically, but genially, just as other men to Newfoundland dogs.

Hitherto the circumstances in which he found the *San Dominick* had repressed the tendency. But in the cuddy, relieved from his former uneasiness, and, for various reasons, more sociably inclined than at any previous period of the day, and seeing the coloured servant, napkin on arm, so debonair about his master, in a business so familiar as that of shaving, too, all his old weakness for negroes returned.

Among other things, he was amused with an odd instance of the African love of bright colours and fine shows, in the black's informally taking from the flag-locker a great piece of bunting of all hues, and lavishly tucking it under his master's chin for an apron.

The mode of shaving among the Spaniards is a little different from what it is with other nations. They have a basin, specially called a barber's basin, which on one side is scooped out, so as accurately to receive the chin, against which it is closely held in lathering; which is done, not with a brush, but with soap dipped in the water of the basin and rubbed on the face.

In the present instance salt-water was used for lack of better; and the parts lathered were only the upper lip, and low down under the throat, all the rest being cultivated beard.

These preliminaries being somewhat novel to Captain Delano he sat curiously eyeing them, so that no conversation took place, nor for the present did Don Benito appear disposed to renew any.

Setting down his basin, the negro searched among the razors, as for the sharpest, and having found it, gave it an additional edge by expertly stropping it on the firm, smooth, oily skin of his open palm; he then made a gesture as if to begin, but midway stood suspended for an instant, one hand elevating the razor, the other professionally dabbling among the bubbling suds on the Spaniard's lank neck. Not unaffected by the close sight of the gleaming steel, Don Benito nervously shuddered, his usual ghastliness was heightened by the lather, which lather, again, was intensified in its hue by the contrasting sootiness of the negro's body. Altogether the scene was somewhat peculiar, at least to Captain Delano, nor, as he saw the two thus postured, could he resist the vagary, that in the black he saw a headsman, and in the white, a man at the block. But this was one of those antic conceits, appearing and vanishing in a breath, from which, perhaps, the best regulated mind is not free.

Meantime the agitation of the Spaniard had a little loosened the bunting from around him, so that one broad fold swept curtain-like over the chair-arm to the floor, revealing, amid a profusion of armorial bars and ground-colours — black, blue and yellow — a closed castle in a blood-red field diagonal with a lion rampant in a white.

"The castle and the lion," exclaimed Captain Delano — "why, Don Benito, this is the flag of Spain you use here. It's well it's only I and not the King, that sees this," he added with a smile, "but" — turning toward the black, — "it's all one, I suppose, so the colours be gay," which playful remark did not fail somewhat to tickle the negro.

"Now, master," he said, readjusting the flag, and pressing the head gently further back into the crotch of the chair; "now master," and the steel glanced nigh the throat.

Again Don Benito faintly shuddered.

"You must not shake so, master. — See, Don Amasa, master always shakes when I shave him. And yet master knows I never yet have drawn blood, though it's true, if master will shake so, I may some of these times. Now, master," he continued. "And now, Don Amasa, please go on with your talk about the gale, and all that, master can hear, and between times master can answer."

"Ah yes, these gales," said Captain Delano; "but the more I think of your voyage, Don Benito, the more I wonder, not at the gales, terrible as they must have been, but at the disastrous interval following them. For here, by your account, have you been these two months and more getting from Cape Horn to St. Maria, a distance which I myself, with a good wind, have sailed in a few days. True, you had calms, and long ones, but to be becalmed for two months, that is, at least, unusual. Why, Don Benito, had almost any other gentleman told me such a story, I should have been half disposed to a little incredulity."

Here an involuntary expression came over the Spaniard, similar to that just before on the deck, and whether it was the start he gave, or a sudden gawky roll of the hull in the calm, or a momentary unsteadiness of the servant's hand; however it was, just then the razor drew blood, spots of which stained the creamy lather under the throat; immediately the black barber drew back his steel, and remaining in his professional attitude, back to Captain Delano, and face to Don Benito, held up the trickling razor, saying, with a sort of half humorous sorrow, "See, master, — you shook so — here's Babo's first blood."

No sword drawn before James the First of England, no assassination in that timid King's presence, could have produced a more terrified aspect than was now presented by Don Benito.

Poor fellow, thought Captain Delano, so nervous he can't even bear the sight of barber's blood; and this unstrung, sick man, is it credible that I should have imagined he meant to spill all my blood, who can't endure the sight of one little drop of his own? Surely, Amasa Delano, you have been beside yourself this day. Tell it not when you get home, sappy Amasa. Well, well, he looks like a murderer, doesn't he? More like as if himself were to be done for. Well, well, this day's experience shall be a good lesson.

Meantime, while these things were running through the honest seaman's mind, the servant had taken the napkin from his arm, and to Don Benito had said: "But answer Don Amasa, please, master, while I wipe this ugly stuff off the razor, and strop it again."

As he said the words, his face was turned half round, so as to be alike visible to the Spaniard and the American, and seemed by its expression to hint, that he was desirous, by getting his master to go on with the conversation, considerably to withdraw his attention from the recent annoying accident. As if glad to snatch the offered relief, Don Benito resumed, rehearsing to Captain Delano, that not only were the calms of unusual duration, but the ship had fallen in with obstinate currents and other things he added, some of which were but repetitions of former statements, to explain how it came to pass that the passage from Cape Horn to St. Maria had been so exceedingly long, now and then mingling with his words, incidental praises, less qualified than before, to the blacks for their general good conduct.

These particulars were not given consecutively, the servant now and then using his razor, and so, between the intervals of shaving, the story and panegyric went on with more than usual huskiness.

To Captain Delano's imagination, now again not wholly at rest, there was something so hollow in the Spaniard's manner, with apparently some reciprocal hollowness in the servant's dusky comment of silence, that the idea flashed across him. that possibly master and man, for some unknown purpose, were acting out, both in word and deed, nay, to the very tremor of Don Benito's limbs, some juggling play before him. Neither did the suspicion of collusion lack apparent support, from the fact of those whispered conferences before mentioned. But then, what could be the object of enacting this play of the barber before him? At last, regarding the motion as a whimsy, insensibly suggested, perhaps, by the theatrical aspect of Don Benito in his harlequin ensign, Captain Delano speedily banished it.

The shaving over, the servant bestirred himself with a small bottle of scented waters, pouring a few drops on the head, and then diligently rubbing; the vehemence of the exercise causing the muscles of his face to twitch rather strangely.

His next operation was with comb, scissors and brush; going round and round, smoothing a curl here, clipping an unruly whisker-hair there, giving a graceful sweep to the temple-lock, with other impromptu touches evincing the hand of a master; while, like any resigned gentleman in barber's hands, Don Benito bore all, much less uneasily, at least, than he had done the razoring; indeed, he sat so pale and rigid now, that the negro seemed a Nubian sculptor finishing off a white statue-head.

All being over at last, the standard of Spain removed, tumbled up, and tossed back into the flag-locker, the negro's warm breath blowing away any stray hair which might have lodged down his master's neck; collar and cravat readjusted; a speck of lint whisked off the velvet lapel; all this being done; backing off a little space, and pausing with an expression of subdued self-complacency, the servant for a moment surveyed his master, as, in toilet at least, the creature of his own tasteful hands.

Captain Delano playfully complimented him upon his achievement; at the same time congratulating Don Benito.

But neither sweet waters, nor shampooing, nor fidelity, nor sociality, delighted the Spaniard. Seeing him relapsing into forbidding gloom, and still remaining seated, Captain Delano, thinking that his presence was undesired just then, withdrew, on pretence of seeing whether, as he had prophesied, any signs of a breeze were visible.

Walking forward to the mainmast, he stood awhile thinking over the scene, and not without some undefined misgivings, when he heard a noise near the cuddy, and turning, saw the negro, his hand to his cheek. Advancing, Captain Delano perceived that the cheek was bleeding. He was about to ask the cause, when the negro's wailing soliloquy enlightened him.

"Ah, when will master get better from his sickness; only the sour heart that sour sickness breeds made him serve Babo so; cutting Babo with the razor, because, only by accident, Babo had given master one little scratch; and for the first time in so many a day, too. Ah, ah, ah," holding his hand to his face.

Is it possible, thought Captain Delano; was it to wreak in private his Spanish spite against this poor friend of his, that Don Benito, by his sullen manner, impelled me to withdraw? Ah, this slavery breeds ugly passions in man! Poor fellow!

He was about to speak in sympathy to the negro, but with a timid reluctance he now re-entered the cuddy.

Presently master and man came forth; Don Benito leaning on his servant as if nothing had happened.

But a sort of love-quarrel, after all, thought Captain Delano.

He accosted Don Benito, and they slowly walked together. They had gone but a few paces, when the steward — a tall, rajah-looking mulatto, orientally set off with a pagoda turban formed by three or four Madras handkerchiefs wound about his head, tier on tier — approaching with a salaam, announced lunch in the cabin.

On their way thither, the two captains were preceded by the mulatto, who, turning round as he advanced, with continual smiles and bows, ushered them in, a display of elegance which quite completed the insignificance of the small bare-headed Babo, who, as if not unconscious of inferiority, eyed askance the graceful steward. But in part,

Captain Delano imputed his jealous watchfulness to that peculiar feeling which the full-blooded African entertains for the adulterated one. As for the steward, his manner, if not bespeaking much dignity of self-respect, yet evidenced his extreme desire to please; which is doubly meritorious, as at once Christian and Chesterfieldian.

Captain Delano observed with interest that while the complexion of the mulatto was hybrid, his physiognomy was European; classically so.

"Don Benito," whispered he, "I am glad to see this usher-of-the-golden-rod of yours; the sight refutes an ugly remark once made to me by a Barbados planter that when a mulatto has a regular European face, look out for him; he is a devil. But see, your steward here has features more regular than King George's of England; and yet there he nods, and bows, and smiles; a king, indeed — the king of kind hearts and polite fellows. What a pleasant voice he has, too?"

"He has, Señor."

"But, tell me, has he not, so far as you have known him, always proved a good, worthy fellow?" said Captain Delano, pausing, while with a final genuflexion the steward disappeared into the cabin; "come, for the reason just mentioned, I am curious to know."

"Francesco is a good man," rather sluggishly responded Don Benito, like a phlegmatic appreciator, who would neither find fault nor flatter.

"Ah, I thought so. For it were strange indeed, and not very creditable to us white-skins, if a little of our blood mixed with the African's, should, far from improving the latter's quality, have the sad effect of pouring vitriolic acid into black broth; improving the hue, perhaps, but not the wholesomeness."

"Doubtless, doubtless, Señor, but" — glancing at Babo — "not to speak of negroes, your planter's remark I have heard applied to the Spanish and Indian intermixtures in our provinces. But I know nothing about the matter," he listlessly added.

And here they entered the cabin.

The lunch was a frugal one. Some of Captain Delano's fresh fish and pumpkins, biscuit and salt beef, the reserved bottle of cider, and the *San Dominick's* last bottle of Canary.

As they entered, Francesco, with two or three coloured aids, was hovering over the table giving the last adjustments. Upon perceiving their master they withdrew, Francesco making a smiling congé, and the Spaniard, without condescending to notice it, fastidiously remarking to his companion that he relished not superfluous attendance.

Without companions, host and guest sat down, like a childless married couple, at opposite ends of the table, Don Benito waving Captain Delano to his place, and, weak as he was, insisting upon that gentleman being seated before himself.

The negro placed a rug under Don Benito's feet, and a cushion behind his back, and then stood behind, not his master's chair, but Captain Delano's. At first, this a little surprised the latter. But it was soon evident that, in taking his position, the black was still true to his master; since by facing him he could the more readily anticipate his slightest want.

"This is an uncommonly intelligent fellow of yours, Don Benito," whispered Captain Delano across the table.

"You say true, Señor."

During the repast, the guest again reverted to parts of Don Benito's story, begging further particulars here and there. He inquired how it was that the scurvy and fever should have committed such wholesale havoc upon the whites, while destroying less than half of the blacks. As if this question reproduced the whole scene of plague before the Spaniard's eyes, miserably reminding him of his solitude in a cabin where before he had had so many friends and officers round him, his hand shook, his face became hueless, broken words escaped; but directly the sane memory of the past seemed replaced by insane terrors of the present. With starting eyes he stared before him at vacancy. For nothing was to be seen but the hand of his servant pushing the Canary over toward him. At length a few sips served partially to restore him. He made random reference to the different constitutions of races, enabling one to offer more resistance to certain maladies than another. The thought was new to his companion.

Presently Captain Delano, intending to say something to his host concerning the pecuniary part of the business he had undertaken for him, especially — since he was strictly accountable to his owners — with reference to the new suit of sails, and other things of that sort; and naturally preferring to conduct such affairs in private, was desirous that the servant should withdraw; imagining that Don Benito for a few minutes could dispense with his attendance. He, however, waited awhile; thinking that, as the conversation proceeded, Don Benito, without being prompted, would perceive the propriety of the step.

But it was otherwise. At last catching his host's eye, Captain Delano, with a slight backward gesture of his thumb, whispered, "Don Benito, pardon me, but there is an interference with the full expression of what I have to say to you."

Upon this the Spaniard changed countenance; which was imputed to his resenting the hint, as in some way a reflection upon his servant. After a moment's pause, he assured his guest that the black's remaining with him could be of no disservice; because since losing his officers he had made Babo (whose original office, it now appeared, had been captain of the slaves) not only his constant attendant and companion, but in all things his confidant.

After this, nothing more could be said; though, indeed, Captain Delano could hardly avoid some little tinge of irritation upon being left ungratified in so inconsiderable a wish, by one, too, for whom he intended such solid services. But it is only his querulousness, thought he; and so filling his glass he proceeded to business.

The price of the sails and other matters was fixed upon. But while this was being done, the American observed that, though his original offer of assistance had been hailed with hectic animation, yet now when it was reduced to a business transaction, indifference and apathy were betrayed. Don Benito, in fact, appeared to submit to hearing the details more out of regard to common propriety, than from any impression that weighty benefit to himself and his voyage was involved.

Soon, this manner became still more reserved. The effort was vain to seek to draw him into social talk. Gnawed by his splenetic mood, he sat twitching his beard, while to little purpose the hand of his servant, mute as that on the wall, slowly pushed over the Canary.

Lunch being over, they sat down on the cushioned transom; the servant placing a pillow behind his master. The long continuance of the calm had now affected the atmosphere. Don Benito sighed heavily, as if for breath.

"Why not adjourn to the cuddy," said Captain Delano; "there is more air there." But the host sat silent and motionless.

Meantime his servant knelt before him, with a large fan of feathers. And Francesco, coming in on tiptoes, handed the negro a little cup of aromatic waters, with which at intervals he chafed his master's brow, smoothing the hair along the temples as a nurse does a child's. He spoke no word. He only rested his eye on his master's, as if, amid all Don Benito's distress, a little to refresh his spirit by the silent sight of fidelity.

Presently the ship's bell sounded two o'clock; and through the cabin-windows a slight rippling of the sea was discerned; and from the desired direction.

"There," exclaimed Captain Delano, "I told you so, Don Benito, look!"

He had risen to his feet, speaking in a very animated tone, with a view the more to rouse his companion. But though the crimson curtain of the stern-window near him that moment fluttered against his pale cheek, Don Benito seemed to have even less welcome for the breeze than the calm.

Poor fellow, thought Captain Delano, bitter experience has taught him that one ripple does not make a wind, any more than one swallow a summer. But he is mistaken for once. I will get his ship in for him, and prove it.

Briefly alluding to his weak condition, he urged his host to remain quietly where he was, since he (Captain Delano) would with pleasure take upon himself the responsibility of making the best use of the wind.

Upon gaining the deck, Captain Delano started at the unexpected figure of Atufal, monumentally fixed at the threshold, like one of those sculptured porters of black marble guarding the porches of Egyptian tombs.

But this time the start was, perhaps, purely physical. Atufal's presence, singularly attesting docility even in sullenness, was contrasted with that of the hatchet-polishers, who in patience evinced their industry; while both spectacles showed, that lax as Don Benito's general authority might be, still, whenever he chose to exert it, no man so savage or colossal but must, more or less, bow.

Snatching a trumpet which hung from the bulwarks, with a free step Captain Delano advanced to the forward edge of the poop, issuing his orders in his best Spanish. The few sailors and many negroes, all equally pleased, obediently set about heading the ship toward the harbour.

While giving some directions about setting a lower stu'n'-sail, suddenly Captain Delano heard a voice faithfully repeating his orders. Turning, he saw Babo, now for the time acting, under the pilot, his original part of captain of the slaves. This assistance proved valuable. Tattered sails and warped yards were soon brought into some trim. And no brace or halyard was pulled but to the blithe songs of the inspirited negroes.

Good fellows, thought Captain Delano, a little training would make fine sailors of them. Why see, the very women pull and sing, too. These must be some of those Ashantee negresses that make such capital soldiers, I've heard. But who's at the helm? I must have a good hand there.

He went to see.

The *San Dominick* steered with a cumbrous tiller, with large horizontal pullies attached. At each pulley-end stood a subordinate black, and between them, at the tiller-head, the responsible post, a Spanish seaman, whose countenance evinced his due share in the general hopefulness and confidence at the coming of the breeze.

He proved the same man who had behaved with so shamefaced an air on the windlass.

"Ah, — it is you, my man," exclaimed Captain Delano — "well, no more sheep's-eyes now; — look straightforward and keep the ship so. Good hand, I trust? And want to get into the harbour, don't you?"

"Sí Señor," assented the man with an inward chuckle, grasping the tiller-head firmly. Upon this, unperceived by the American, the two blacks eyed the sailor askance.

Finding all right at the helm, the pilot went forward to the forecastle, to see how matters stood there.

The ship now had way enough to breast the current. With the approach of evening, the breeze would be sure to freshen.

Having done all that was needed for the present, Captain Delano, giving his last orders to the sailors, turned aft to report affairs to Don Benito in the cabin; perhaps additionally incited to rejoin him by the hope of snatching a moment's private chat while his servant was engaged upon deck.

From opposite sides, there were, beneath the poop, two approaches to the cabin; one further forward than the other, and consequently communicating with a longer passage. Marking the servant still above, Captain Delano, taking the nighest entrance — the one last named, and at whose porch Atufal still stood — hurried on his way, till, arrived at the cabin threshold, he paused an instant, a little to recover from his eagerness. Then, with the words of his intended business upon his lips, he entered. As he advanced toward the Spaniard, on the transom, he heard another footstep, keeping time with his. From the opposite door, a salver in hand, the servant was likewise advancing.

"Confound the faithful fellow," thought Captain Delano; "what a vexatious coincidence."

Possibly, the vexation might have been something different, were it not for the buoyant confidence inspired by the breeze. But even as it was, he felt a slight twinge, from a sudden involuntary association in his mind of Babo with Atufal.

"Don Benito," said he, "I give you joy; the breeze will hold, and will increase. By the way, your tall man and time-piece, Atufal, stands without. By your order, of course?"

Don Benito recoiled, as if at some bland satirical touch, delivered with such adroit garnish of apparent good-breeding as to present no handle for retort.

He is like one flayed alive, thought Captain Delano; where may one touch him without causing a shrink?

The servant moved before his master, adjusting a cushion; recalled to civility, the Spaniard stiffly replied: "You are right. The slave appears where you saw him, according to my command; which is, that if at the given hour I am below, he must take his stand and abide my coming."

"Ah now, pardon me, but that is treating the poor fellow like an ex-king denied. Ah, Don Benito," smiling, "for all the license you permit in some things, I fear lest, at bottom, you are a bitter hard master."

Again Don Benito shrank; and this time, as the good sailor thought, from a genuine twinge of his conscience.

Conversation now became constrained. In vain Captain Delano called attention to the now perceptible motion of the keel gently cleaving the sea; with lack-lustre eye, Don Benito returned words few and reserved.

By-and-by, the wind having steadily risen, and still blowing right into the harbour, bore the *San Dominick* swiftly on. Rounding a point of land, the sealer at distance came into open view.

Meantime Captain Delano had again repaired to the deck, remaining there some time. Having at last altered the ship's course, so as to give the reef a wide berth, he returned for a few moments below.

I will cheer up my poor friend, this time, thought he.

"Better and better, Don Benito," he cried as he blithely reentered; "there will soon be an end to your cares, at least for awhile. For when, after a long, sad voyage, you know, the anchor drops into the haven, all its vast weight seems lifted from the captain's heart. We are getting on famously, Don Benito. My ship is in sight. Look through this side-light here; there she is; all a-taunt-o! The *Bachelor's Delight*, my good friend. Ah, how this wind braces one up. Come, you must take a cup of coffee with me this evening. My old steward will give you as fine a cup as ever any sultan tasted. What say you, Don Benito, will you?"

At first, the Spaniard glanced feverishly up, casting a longing look toward the sealer, while with mute concern his servant gazed into his face. Suddenly the old ague of coldness returned, and dropping back to his cushions he was silent.

"You do not answer. Come, all day you have been my host; would you have hospitality all on one side?"

"I cannot go," was the response.

"What? it will not fatigue you. The ships will lie together as near as they can, without swinging foul. It will be little more than stepping from deck to deck; which is but as from room to room. Come, come, you must not refuse me."

"I cannot go," decisively and repulsively repeated Don Benito.

Renouncing all but the last appearance of courtesy, with a sort of cadaverous sullenness, and biting his thin nails to the quick, he glanced, almost glared, at his guest; as if impatient that a stranger's presence should interfere with the full indulgence of his morbid hour. Meantime the sound of the parted waters came more and more gurglingly and merrily in at the windows; as reproaching him for his dark spleen; as telling him that, sulk as he might, and go mad with it, nature cared not a jot; since, whose fault was it, pray?

But the foul mood was now at its depth, as the fair wind at its height.

There was something in the man so far beyond any mere unsociality or sourness previously evinced, that even the forbearing good-nature of his guest could no longer endure it. Wholly at a loss to account for such demeanour, and deeming sickness with eccentricity, however extreme, no adequate excuse, well satisfied, too, that nothing in his own conduct could justify it, Captain Delano's pride began to be roused. Himself became reserved. But all seemed one to the Spaniard. Quitting him, therefore, Captain Delano once more went to the deck.

The ship was now within less than two miles of the sealer. The whale-boat was seen darting over the interval.

To be brief, the two vessels, thanks to the pilot's skill, ere long in neighborly style lay anchored together.

Before returning to his own vessel, Captain Delano had intended communicating to Don Benito the practical details of the proposed services to be rendered. But, as it was, unwilling anew to subject himself to rebuffs, he resolved, now that he had seen the *San Dominick* safely moored, immediately to quit her, without further allusion to hospitality or business. Indefinitely postponing his ulterior plans, he would regulate his future actions according to future circumstances. His boat was ready to receive him; but his host still tarried below.

Well, thought Captain Delano, if he has little breeding, the more need to show mine. He descended to the cabin to bid a ceremonious, and, it may be, tacitly rebukeful adieu. But to his great satisfaction, Don Benito, as if he began to feel the weight of that treatment with which his slighted guest had, not indecorously, retaliated upon him, now supported by his servant, rose to his feet, and grasping Captain Delano's hand, stood tremulous; too much agitated to speak. But the good augury hence drawn was suddenly dashed, by his resuming all his previous reserve, with augmented gloom, as, with half-averted eyes, he silently reseated himself on his cushions. With a corresponding return to his own chilled feelings, Captain Delano bowed and withdrew.

He was hardly midway in the narrow corridor, dim as a tunnel, leading from the cabin to the stairs, when a sound, as of the tolling for execution in some jail-yard, fell on his ears. It was the echo of the ship's flawed bell, striking the hour, drearily reverberated in this subterranean vault. Instantly, by a fatality not to be withstood, his mind, responsive to the portent, swarmed with superstitious suspicions. He paused. In images far swifter than these sentences, the minutest details of all his former distrusts swept through him.

Hitherto, credulous good-nature had been too ready to furnish excuses for reasonable fears. Why was the Spaniard, so superfluously punctilious at times, now heedless of common propriety in not accompanying to the side his departing guest? Did indisposition forbid? Indisposition had not forbidden more irksome exertion that day. His last equivocal demeanour recurred. He had risen to his feet, grasped his guest's hand, motioned toward his hat; then, in an instant, all was eclipsed in sinister muteness and gloom. Did this imply one brief, repentant relenting at the final moment, from some iniquitous plot, followed by remorseless return to it? His last glance seemed to express a calamitous, yet acquiescent farewell to Captain Delano for ever. Why decline the invitation to visit the sealer that evening? Or was the Spaniard less hardened than the Jew, who refrained not from supping at the board of Him whom the same night he meant to betray? What imported all those day-long enigmas and contradictions, except they were intended to mystify, preliminary to some stealthy blow? Atufal, the pretended rebel, but punctual shadow, that moment lurked by the threshold without. He seemed a sentry, and more. Who, by his own confession, had stationed him there? Was the negro now lying in wait?

The Spaniard behind — his creature before: to rush from darkness to light was the involuntary choice.

The next moment, with clenched jaw and hand, he passed Atufal, and stood unarmed in the light. As he saw his trim ship lying peacefully at her anchor, and almost within ordinary call; as he saw his household boat, with familiar faces in it, patiently rising and falling on the short waves by the *San Dominick's* side; and then, glancing about the decks where he stood, saw the oakum-pickers still gravely plying their fingers; and heard the low, buzzing whistle and industrious hum of the hatchet-polishers, still bestirring themselves over their endless occupation; and more than all, as he saw the benign aspect of Nature, taking her innocent repose in the evening; the screened sun in the quiet camp of the west shining out like the mild light from Abraham's tent; as his charmed eye and ear took in all these, with the chained figure of the black, the clenched jaw and hand relaxed. Once again he smiled at the phantoms which had mocked him, and felt something like a tinge of remorse, that, by indulging them even for a moment, he should, by implication, have betrayed an almost atheist doubt of the everwatchful Providence above.

There was a few minutes' delay, while, in obedience to his orders, the boat was being hooked along to the gangway. During this interval, a sort of saddened satisfaction stole over Captain Delano, at thinking of the kindly offices he had that day discharged for a stranger. Ah, thought he, after good actions one's conscience is never ungrateful, however much so the benefited party may be.

Presently, his foot, in the first act of descent into the boat, pressed the first round of the side-ladder, his face presented inward upon the deck. In the same moment, he heard his name courteously sounded; and, to his pleased surprise, saw Don Benito advancing — an unwonted energy in his air, as if, at the last moment, intent upon making amends for his recent discourtesy. With instinctive good feeling, Captain Delano, revoking his foot, turned and reciprocally advanced. As he did so, the Spaniard's nervous eagerness increased, but his vital energy failed; so that, the better to support him, the servant, placing his master's hand on his naked shoulder, and gently holding it there, formed himself into a sort of crutch.

When the two captains met, the Spaniard again fervently took the hand of the American, at the same time casting an earnest glance into his eyes, but, as before, too much overcome to speak.

I have done him wrong, self-reproachfully thought Captain Delano; his apparent coldness has deceived me; in no instance has he meant to offend.

Meantime, as if fearful that the continuance of the scene might too much unstring his master, the servant seemed anxious to terminate it. And so, still presenting himself as a crutch, and walking between the two captains, he advanced with them toward the gangway; while still, as if full of kindly contrition, Don Benito would not let go the hand of Captain Delano, but retained it in his, across the black's body.

Soon they were standing by the side, looking over into the boat, whose crew turned up their curious eyes. Waiting a moment for the Spaniard to relinquish his hold, the now embarrassed Captain Delano lifted his foot, to overstep the threshold of the open gangway; but still, Don Benito would not let go his hand. And yet, with an agitated tone, he said, "I can go no further; here I must bid you adieu. Adieu, my dear, dear Don Amasa. Go — go!" suddenly tearing his hand loose, "go, and God guard you better than me, my best friend."

Not unaffected, Captain Delano would now have lingered; but catching the meekly admonitory eye of the servant, with a hasty farewell he descended into his boat, followed by the continual adieus of Don Benito, standing rooted in the gangway.

Seating himself in the stern, Captain Delano, making a last salute, ordered the boat shoved off. The crew had their oars on end. The bowsman pushed the boat a sufficient distance for the oars to be lengthwise dropped. The instant that was done, Don Benito sprang over the bulwarks, falling at the feet of Captain Delano; at the same time, calling towards his ship, but in tones so frenzied, that none in the boat could understand him. But, as if not equally obtuse, three Spanish sailors, from three different and distant parts of the ship, splashed into the sea, swimming after their captain, as if intent upon his rescue.

The dismayed officer of the boat eagerly asked what this meant. To which, Captain Delano, turning a disdainful smile upon the unaccountable Benito Cereno, answered that, for his part, he neither knew nor cared; but it seemed as if the Spaniard had taken it into his head to produce the impression among his people that the boat wanted to kidnap him. "Or else — give way for your lives," he wildly added, starting at a clattering hubbub in the ship, above which rang the tocsin of the hatchet-polishers; and seizing Don Benito by the throat he added, "this plotting pirate means murder!" Here, in apparent verification of the words, the servant, a dagger in his hand, was seen on the rail overhead, poised, in the act of leaping, as if with desperate fidelity to befriend his master to the last; while, seemingly to aid the black, the three Spanish sailors were trying to clamber into the hampered bow.

Meantime, the whole host of negroes, as if inflamed at the sight of their jeopardized captain, impended in one sooty avalanche over the bulwarks.

All this, with what preceded, and what followed, occurred with such involutions of rapidity, that past, present, and future seemed one.

Seeing the negro coming, Captain Delano had flung the Spaniard aside, almost in the very act of clutching him, and, by the unconscious recoil, shifting his place, with arms thrown up, so promptly grappled the servant in his descent, that with dagger presented at Captain Delano's heart, the black seemed of purpose to have leaped there as to his mark. But the weapon was wrenched away, and the assailant dashed down into the bottom of the boat, which now, with disentangled oars, began to speed through the sea.

At this juncture, the left hand of Captain Delano, on one side, again clutched the half-reclined Don Benito, heedless that he was in a speechless faint, while his right foot, on the other side, ground the prostrate negro; and his right arm pressed for added speed on the after oar, his eye bent forward, encouraging his men to their utmost.

But here, the officer of the boat, who had at last succeeded in beating off the towing Spanish sailors, and was now, with face turned aft, assisting the bowsman at his oar, suddenly called to Captain Delano, to see what the black was about; while a Portuguese oarsman shouted to him to give heed to what the Spaniard was saying.

Glancing down at his feet, Captain Delano saw the freed hand of the servant aiming with a second dagger — a small one, before concealed in his wool — with this he was snakishly writhing up from the boat's bottom, at the heart of his master, his countenance lividly vindictive, expressing the centred purpose of his soul; while the Spaniard, half-choked, was vainly shrinking away, with husky words, incoherent to all but the Portuguese.

That moment, across the long benighted mind of Captain Delano, a flash of revelation swept, illuminating in unanticipated clearness Benito Cereno's whole mysterious demeanour, with every enigmatic event of the day, as well as the entire past voyage of the *San Dominick*. He smote Babo's hand down, but his own heart smote him harder. With infinite pity he withdrew his hold from Don Benito. Not Captain Delano, but Don Benito, the black, in leaping into the boat, had intended to stab.

Both the black's hands were held, as, glancing up toward the *San Dominick*, Captain Delano, now with the scales dropped from his eyes, saw the negroes, not in misrule, not in tumult, not as if frantically concerned for Don Benito, but with mask torn away, flourishing hatchets and knives, in ferocious piratical revolt. Like delirious black dervishes, the six Ashantees danced on the poop. Prevented by their foes from springing into the water, the Spanish boys were hurrying up to the topmost spars, while such of the few Spanish sailors, not already in the sea, less alert, were descried, helplessly mixed in, on deck, with the blacks.

Meantime Captain Delano hailed his own vessel, ordering the ports up, and the guns run out. But by this time the cable of the *San Dominick* had been cut; and the fag-end, in lashing out, whipped away the canvas shroud about the beak, suddenly revealing, as the bleached hull swung round toward the open ocean, death for the figurehead, in a human skeleton; chalky comment on the chalked words below, "*Follow your leader.*"

At the sight, Don Benito, covering his face, wailed out: "'Tis he, Aranda! my murdered, unburied friend!"

Upon reaching the sealer, calling for ropes, Captain Delano bound the negro, who made no resistance, and had him hoisted to the deck. He would then have assisted the now almost helpless Don Benito up the side; but Don Benito, wan as he was, refused to move, or be moved, until the negro should have been first put below out of view. When, presently assured that it was done, he no more shrank from the ascent.

The boat was immediately despatched back to pick up the three swimming sailors. Meantime, the guns were in readiness, though, owing to the *San Dominick* having glided somewhat astern of the sealer, only the aftermost one could be brought to bear. With this, they fired six times; thinking to cripple the fugitive ship by bringing down her spars. But only a few inconsiderable ropes were shot away. Soon the ship was beyond the guns' range, steering broad out of the bay; the blacks thickly clustering round the bowsprit, one moment with taunting cries toward the whites, the next with upthrown gestures hailing the now dusky expanse of ocean — cawing crows escaped from the hand of the fowler.

The first impulse was to slip the cables and give chase. But, upon second thought, to pursue with whale-boat and yawl seemed more promising.

Upon inquiring of Don Benito what firearms they had on board the *San Dominick*, Captain Delano was answered that they had none that could be used; because, in the earlier stages of the mutiny, a cabin-passenger, since dead, had secretly put out of order the locks of what few muskets there were. But with all his remaining strength, Don Benito entreated the American not to give chase, either with ship or boat; for the negroes had already proved themselves such desperadoes, that, in case of a present assault, nothing but a total massacre of the whites could be looked for. But, regarding this warning as coming from one whose spirit had been crushed by misery, the American did not give up his design.

The boats were got ready and armed. Captain Delano ordered twenty-five men into them. He was going himself when Don Benito grasped his arm.

"What! have you saved my life, Señor, and are you now going to throw away your own?"

The officers also, for reasons connected with their interests and those of the voyage, and a duty owing to the owners, strongly objected against their commander's going. Weighing their remonstrances a moment, Captain Delano felt bound to remain; appointing his chief mate — an athletic and resolute man, who had been a privateer's man, and, as his enemies whispered, a pirate — to head the party. The more to encourage the sailors, they were told, that the Spanish captain considered his ship as good as lost; that she and her cargo, including some gold and silver, were worth upwards of ten thousand doubloons. Take her, and no small part should be theirs. The sailors replied with a shout.

The fugitives had now almost gained an offing. It was nearly night; but the moon was rising. After hard, prolonged pulling, the boats came up on the ship's quarters, at a suitable distance laying upon their oars to discharge their muskets. Having no bullets to return, the negroes sent their yells. But, upon the second volley, Indian-like, they hurtled their hatchets. One took off a sailor's fingers. Another struck the whale-boat's bow, cutting off the rope there, and remaining stuck in the gunwale, like a woodman's axe. Snatching it, quivering from its lodgment, the mate hurled it back. The returned gauntlet now stuck in the ship's broken quarter-gallery, and so remained.

The negroes giving too hot a reception, the whites kept a more respectful distance. Hovering now just out of reach of the hurtling hatchets, they, with a view to the close encounter which must soon come, sought to decoy the blacks into entirely disarming themselves of their most murderous weapons in a hand-to-hand fight, by foolishly flinging them, as missiles, short of the mark, into the sea. But ere long perceiving the stratagem, the negroes desisted, though not before many of them had to replace their lost hatchets with handspikes; an exchange which, as counted upon, proved in the end favourable to the assailants.

Meantime, with a strong wind, the ship still clove the water; the boats alternately falling behind, and pulling up, to discharge fresh volleys.

The fire was mostly directed toward the stern, since there, chiefly, the negroes, at present, were clustering. But to kill or maim the negroes was not the object. To take them, with the ship, was the object. To do it, the ship must be boarded; which could not be done by boats while she was sailing so fast.

A thought now struck the mate. Observing the Spanish boys still aloft, high as they could get, he called to them to descend to the yards, and cut adrift the sails. It was done. About this time, owing to causes hereafter to be shown, two Spaniards, in the dress of sailors and conspicuously showing themselves, were killed; not by volleys, but by deliberate marksman's shots; while, as it afterwards appeared, during one of the general discharges, Atufal, the black, and the Spaniard at the helm likewise were killed. What now, with the loss of the sails, and loss of leaders, the ship became unmanageable to the negroes.

With creaking masts she came heavily round to the wind; the prow slowly swinging into view of the boats, its skeleton gleaming in the horizontal moonlight, and casting a gigantic ribbed shadow upon the water. One extended arm of the ghost seemed beckoning the whites to avenge it.

"Follow your leader!" cried the mate; and, one on each bow, the boats boarded. Scaling-spears and cutlasses crossed hatchets and handspikes. Huddled upon the long-boat amidships, the negresses raised a wailing chant, whose chorus was the clash of the steel.

For a time, the attack wavered; the negroes wedging themselves to beat it back; the half-repelled sailors, as yet unable to gain a footing, fighting as troopers in the saddle, one leg sideways flung over the bulwarks, and one without, plying their cutlasses like carters' whips. But in vain. They were almost overborne, when, rallying themselves into a squad as one man, with a huzza, they sprang inboard; where, entangled, they involuntarily separated again. For a few breaths' space there was a vague, muffled, inner sound as of submerged sword-fish rushing hither and thither through shoals of black-fish. Soon, in a re-united band, and joined by the Spanish seamen, the whites came to the surface, irresistibly driving the negroes toward the stern. But a barricade of casks and sacks, from side to side, had been thrown up by the mainmast. Here the negroes faced about, and though scorning peace or truce, yet fain would have had a respite. But, without pause, overleaping the barrier, the unflagging sailors again closed. Exhausted, the blacks now fought in despair. Their red tongues lolled, wolf-like, from their black mouths. But the pale sailors' teeth were set; not a word was spoken; and, in five minutes more, the ship was won.

Nearly a score of the negroes were killed. Exclusive of those by the balls, many were mangled; their wounds — mostly inflicted by the long-edged scaling-spears — resembling those shaven ones of the English at Preston Pans, made by the poled scythes of the Highlanders. On the other side, none were killed, though several were wounded; some severely, including the mate. The surviving negroes were temporarily secured, and the ship, towed back into the harbour at midnight, once more lay anchored.

Omitting the incidents and arrangements ensuing, suffice it that, after two days spent in refitting, the two ships sailed in company for Concepcion in Chili, and thence for Lima in Peru; where, before the vice-regal courts, the whole affair, from the beginning, underwent investigation.

Though, midway on the passage, the ill-fated Spaniard, relaxed from constraint, showed some signs of regaining health with free-will; yet, agreeably to his own foreboding, shortly before arriving at Lima, he relapsed, finally becoming so reduced as to be carried ashore in arms. Hearing of his story and plight, one of the many religious institutions of the City of Kings opened an hospitable refuge to him, where both physician and priest were his nurses, and a member of the order volunteered to be his one special guardian and consoler, by night and by day.

The following extracts, translated from one of the official Spanish documents, will, it is hoped, shed light on the preceding narrative, as well as, in the first place, reveal the true port of departure and true history of the *San Dominick's* voyage, down to the time of her touching at the island of Santa Maria.

But, ere the extracts come, it may be well to preface them with a remark.

The document selected, from among many others, for partial translation, contains the deposition of Benito Cereno; the first taken in the case. Some disclosures therein were, at the time, held dubious for both learned and natural reasons. The tribunal inclined to the opinion that the deponent, not undisturbed in his mind by recent events, raved of some things which could never have happened.   But subsequent depositions of the surviving sailors, bearing out the revelations of their captain in several of the strangest particulars, gave credence to the rest.   So that the tribunal, in its final decision, rested its capital sentences upon statements which, had they lacked confirmation, it would have deemed it but duty to reject.

. . . .

I, DON JOSÉ DE ABOS AND PADILLA, His Majesty's Notary for the Royal Revenue, and Register of this Province, and Notary Public of the Holy Crusade of this Bishopric, etc.

Do certify and declare, as much as is requisite in law, that, in the criminal cause commenced the twenty-fourth of the month of September, in the year seventeen hundred and ninety-nine, against the Senegal negroes of the ship *San Dominick*, the following declaration before me was made.

Declaration of the first witness, DON BENITO CERENO.

The same day, and month, and year, His Honour Doctor Juan Martinez de Dozas, Councillor of the Royal Audience of this Kingdom, and learned in the law of this Intendancy, ordered the captain of the ship *San Dominick*, Don Benito Cereno, to appear; which he did in his litter, attended by the monk Infelez; of whom he received, before Don José de Abos and Padilla, Notary Public of the Holy Crusade, the oath, which he took by God, our Lord, and a sign of the Cross; under which he promised to tell the truth of whatever he should know and should be asked; — and being interrogated agreeably to the tenor of the act commencing the process, he said, that on the twentieth of May last, he set sail with his ship from the port of Valparaiso, bound to that of Callao; loaded with the produce of the country and one hundred and sixty blacks, of both sexes, mostly belonging to Don Alexandro Aranda, gentleman, of the city of Mendoza; that the crew of the ship consisted of thirty-six men, beside the persons who went as passengers; that the negroes were in part as follows:

[*Here, in the original, follows a list of some fifty names, descriptions, and ages, compiled from certain recovered documents of Aranda's, and also from recollections of the deponent, from which portions only are extracted.*]

— One, from about eighteen to nineteen years, named José, and this was the man that waited upon his master, Don Alexandro, and who speaks well the Spanish, having served him four or five years; . . . a mulatto, named Francesco, the cabin steward, of a good person and voice, having sung in the Valparaiso churches, native of the province of Buenos Ayres, aged about thirty-five years. . . . A smart negro, named Dago, who had been for many years a grave-digger among the Spaniards, aged forty-six years. . . . Four old negroes, born in Africa, from sixty to seventy, but sound, caulkers by trade, whose names are as follows: — the first was named Muri, and he was killed (as was also his son named Diamelo); the second, Nacta; the third, Yola, likewise killed; the fourth, Ghofan; and six full-grown negroes, aged from thirty to forty-five, all raw, and born among the Ashantees — Martiniqui, Yan, Lecbe, Hapenda, Yambaio, Akim; four of whom were killed; . . . a powerful negro named Atufal, who, being supposed to have been a chief in Africa, his owners set great store by him. . . . And a small negro of Senegal, but some years among the Spaniards, aged about thirty, which negro's name was Babo; . . . that he does not remember the names of the others, but that still expecting the residue of Don Alexandro's papers will be found, will then take due account of them all, and remit to the court; . . . and thirty-nine women and children of all ages.

[*After the catalogue, the deposition goes on as follows:*]

. . . That all the negroes slept upon deck, as is customary in this navigation, and none wore fetters, because the owner, his friend Aranda, told him that they were all tractable; . . . that on the seventh day after leaving port, at three o'clock in the morning, all the Spaniards being asleep except the two officers on the watch, who were the boatswain, Juan Robles, and the carpenter, Juan Bautista Gayete, and the helmsman and his boy, the negroes revolted suddenly, wounded dangerously the boatswain and the carpenter, and successively killed eighteen men of those who were sleeping upon deck, some with handspikes and hatchets, and others by throwing them alive overboard, after tying them; that of the Spaniards upon deck, they left about seven, as he thinks, alive and tied, to manœuvre the ship and three or four more who hid themselves, remained also alive. Although in the act of revolt the negroes made themselves masters of the hatchway, six or seven wounded went through it to the cockpit, without any hindrance on their part; that in the act of revolt, the mate and another person,

whose name he does not recollect, attempted to come up through the
hatchway, but having been wounded at the onset, they were obliged
to return to the cabin; that the deponent resolved at break of day to
come up the companionway, where the negro Babo was, being the
ringleader, and Atufal, who assisted him, and having spoken to them,
exhorted them to cease committing such atrocities, asking them, at
the same time, what they wanted and intended to do, offering, himself, to obey their commands; that, notwithstanding this, they threw,
in his presence, three men, alive and tied, overboard; that they told
the deponent to come up, and that they would not kill him; which
having done, the negro Babo asked him whether there were in those
seas any negro countries where they might be carried, and he answered
them, no; that the negro Babo afterwards told him to carry them to
Senegal, or to the neighbouring islands of St. Nicholas; and he answered, that this was impossible, on account of the great distance, the
necessity involved of rounding Cape Horn, the bad condition of the
vessel, the want of provisions, sails, and water; but that the negro
Babo replied to him he must carry them in any way; that they would
do and conform themselves to everything the deponent should require
as to eating and drinking; that after a long conference, being absolutely compelled to please them, for they threatened him to kill all the
whites if they were not, at all events, carried to Senegal, he told them
that what was most wanting for the voyage was water; that they would
go near the coast to take it, and hence they would proceed on their
course; that the negro Babo agreed to it; and the deponent steered
toward the intermediate ports, hoping to meet some Spanish or foreign
vessel that would save them; that within ten or eleven days they saw
the land, and continued their course by it in the vicinity of Nasca;
that the deponent observed that the negroes were now restless and
mutinous, because he did not effect the taking in of water, the negro
Babo having required, with threats, that it should be done, without
fail, the following day; he told him he saw plainly that the coast was
steep, and the rivers designated in the maps were not to be found, with
other reasons suitable to the circumstances; that the best way would
be to go to the island of Santa Maria, where they might water and
victual easily, it being a desert island, as the foreigners did; that the
deponent did not go to Pisco, that was near, nor make any other port
of the coast, because the negro Babo had intimated to him several
times, that he would kill all the whites the very moment he should perceive any city, town, or settlement of any kind on the shores to which

they should be carried: that having determined to go to the island of Santa Maria, as the deponent had planned, for the purpose of trying whether, in the passage or in the island itself, they could find any vessel that should favour them, or whether he could escape from it in a boat to the neighbouring coast of Arruco; to adopt the necessary means he immediately changed his course, steering for the island; that the negroes Babo and Atufal held daily conferences, in which they discussed what was necessary for their design of returning to Senegal, whether they were to kill all the Spaniards, and particularly the deponent; that eight days after parting from the coast of Nasca, the deponent being on the watch a little after day-break, and soon after the negroes had their meeting, the negro Babo came to the place where the deponent was, and told him that he had determined to kill his master, Don Alexandro Aranda, both because he and his companions could not otherwise be sure of their liberty, and that, to keep the seamen in subjection, he wanted to prepare a warning of what road they should be made to take did they or any of them oppose him; and that, by means of the death of Don Alexandro, that warning would best be given; but, that what this last meant, the deponent did not at the time comprehend, nor could not, further than that the death of Don Alexandro was intended; and moreover, the negro Babo proposed to the deponent to call the mate Raneds, who was sleeping in the cabin, before the thing was done, for fear, as the deponent understood it, that the mate, who was a good navigator, should be killed with Don Alexandro and the rest; that the deponent, who was the friend, from youth of Don Alexandro, prayed and conjured, but all was useless; for the negro Babo answered him that the thing could not be prevented, and that all the Spaniards risked their death if they should attempt to frustrate his will in this matter, or any other; that, in this conflict, the deponent called the mate, Raneds, who was forced to go apart, and immediately the negro Babo commanded the Ashantee Martinqui and the Ashantee Lecbe to go and commit the murder; that those two went down with hatchets to the berth of Don Alexandro; that, yet half alive and mangled, they dragged him on deck; that they were going to throw him overboard in that state, but the negro Babo stopped them, bidding the murder be completed on the deck before him, which was done, when, by his orders, the body was carried below, forward; that nothing more was seen of it by the deponent for three days; . . . that Don Alonzo Sidonia, an old man, long resident at Valparaiso, and lately appointed to a civil office in Peru, whither he had taken passage, was at the time sleeping in the berth opposite Don Alexandro's; that, awakening at his cries, surprised by them, and at the sight of the negroes with their bloody hatchets in their hands, he threw himself into the sea through a window which was near him, and was drowned, without it being in the power of the deponent to assist to take him up; ... that, a short time after killing Aranda, they brought upon deck his german-cousin, of middle-age, Don Francisco Masa, of Mendoza, and the young Don Joaquin, Marques de Aramboalaza, then lately from Spain, with his Spanish servant Ponce, and the three young clerks of Aranda, José Mozairi, Lorenzo Bargas, and Hermenegildo Gandix, all of Cadiz; that Don Joaquin and Hermenegildo Gandix, the negro Babo for purposes hereafter to appear, preserved alive; but Don Francisco Masa, José Mozairi, and Lorenzo Bargas, with Ponce, the servant, beside the boatswain, Juan Robles, the boatswain's mates, Manuel Viscaya and Roderigo Hurta, and four of the sailors, the negro Babo ordered to be thrown alive into the sea, although they made no resistance, nor begged for anything else but mercy; that the boatswain, Juan Robles, who knew how to swim, kept the longest above water, making acts of contrition, and, in the last words he uttered, charged this deponent to cause mass to be said for his soul to our Lady of Succour: ... that, during the three days which followed, the deponent, uncertain what fate had befallen the remains of Don Alexandro, frequently asked the negro Babo where they were, and, if still on board, whether they were to be preserved for interment ashore, entreating him so to order it; that the negro Babo answered nothing till the fourth day, when at sunrise, the deponent coming on deck, the negro Babo showed him a skeleton, which had been substituted for the ship's proper figure-head, the image of Christopher Colon, the discoverer of the New World; that the negro Babo asked him whose skeleton that was, and whether, from its whiteness, he should not think it a white's; that, upon his covering his face, the negro Babo, coming close, said words to this effect: "Keep faith with the blacks from here to Senegal, or you shall in spirit, as now in body, follow your leader," pointing to the prow; ... that the same morning the negro Babo took by succession each Spaniard forward, and asked him whose skeleton that was, and whether, from its whiteness, he should not think it a white's; that each Spaniard covered his face; that then to each the negro Babo repeated the words in the first place said to the deponent; ... that they (the Spaniards), being then assembled aft, the negro Babo harangued them, saying that he had now done all; that the deponent (as navigator for the negroes) might pursue his course, warning him and all of them that they should, soul and body, go the way of Don Alexandro if he saw them (the Spaniards) speak or plot anything against them (the negroes) — a threat which was repeated every day; that, before the events last mentioned, they had tied the cook to throw him overboard, for it is not known what thing they heard him speak, but finally the negro Babo spared his life, at the request of the deponent; that a few days after, the deponent, endeavouring not to omit any means to preserve the lives of the remaining whites, spoke to the negroes peace and tranquillity, and agreed to draw up a paper, signed by the deponent and the sailors who could write, as also by the negro Babo, for himself and all the blacks, in which the deponent obliged himself to carry them to Senegal, and they not to kill any more, and he formally to make over to them the ship, with the cargo, with which they were for that time satisfied and quieted. . . . But the next day, the more surely to guard against the sailors' escape, the negro Babo commanded all the boats to be destroyed but the long-boat, which was unseaworthy, and another, a cutter in good condition, which, knowing it would yet be wanted for lowering the water casks, he had it lowered down into the hold.

.   .   .   .   .

[*Various particulars of the prolonged and perplexed navigation ensuing here follow, with incidents of a calamitous calm, from which portion one passage is extracted, to wit:*]

— That on the fifth day of the calm, all on board suffering much from the heat, and want of water, and five having died in fits, and mad, the negroes became irritable, and for a chance gesture, which they deemed suspicious — though it was harmless — made by the mate, Raneds, to the deponent, in the act of handing a quadrant, they killed him; but that for this they afterwards were sorry, the mate being the only remaining navigator on board, except the deponent.

.   .   .   .   .

— That omitting other events, which daily happened, and which can only serve uselessly to recall past misfortunes and conflicts, after seventy-three days' navigation, reckoned from the time they sailed from Nasca, during which they navigated under a scanty allowance of water, and were afflicted with the calms before mentioned, they at last arrived at the island of Santa Maria, on the seventeenth of the month of August, at about six o'clock in the afternoon, at which hour they cast anchor very near the American ship, *Bachelor's Delight*, which lay in the same bay, commanded by the generous Captain Amasa Delano; but at six o'clock in the morning, they had already descried the port, and the negroes became uneasy, as soon as at distance they saw the ship, not having expected to see one there; that the negro Babo pacified them, assuring them that no fear need be had; that straightway he ordered the figure on the bow to be covered with canvas, as for repairs, and had the decks a little set in order; that for a time the negro Babo and the negro Atufal conferred; that the negro Atufal was for sailing away, but the negro Babo would not, and, by himself, cast about what to do; that at last he came to the deponent, proposing to him to say and do all that the deponent declares to have said and done to the American captain; . . . that the negro Babo warned him that if he varied in the least, or uttered any word, or gave any look that should give the least intimation of the past events or present state, he would instantly kill him, with all his companions, showing a dagger, which he carried hid, saying something which, as he understood it, meant that that dagger would be alert as his eye; that the negro Babo then announced the plan to all his companions, which pleased them; that he then, the better to disguise the truth, devised many expedients, in some of them uniting deceit and defence; that of this sort was the device of the six Ashantees before named, who were his bravos; that them he stationed on the break of the poop, as if to clean certain hatchets (in cases, which were part of the cargo), but in reality to use them, and distribute them at need, and at a given word he told them that, among other devices, was the device of presenting Atufal, his righthand man, as chained, though in a moment the chains could be dropped; that in every particular he informed the deponent what part he was expected to enact in every device, and what story he was to tell on every occasion, always threatening him with instant death if he varied in the least: that, conscious that many of the negroes would be turbulent, the negro Babo appointed the four aged negroes, who were caulkers, to keep what domestic order they could on the decks; that again and again he harangued the Spaniards and his companions, informing them of his intent, and of his devices, and of the invented story that this deponent was to tell, charging them lest any of them varied from that story; that these arrangements were made and matured during the interval of two or three hours, between their first sighting the ship and the arrival on board of Captain Amasa Delano; that this happened at about half-past seven in the morning, Captain Amasa Delano coming in his boat, and all gladly receiving him; that the deponent, as well as he could force himself, acting then the part of principal owner, and a free captain of the ship, told Captain Amasa Delano, when called upon, that he came from Buenos Ayres, bound to Lima, with three hundred negroes; that off Cape Horn, and in a subsequent fever, many negroes had died; that also, by similar casualties, all the sea officers and the greatest part of the crew had died.

. . . .

[*And so the deposition goes on, circumstantially recounting the fictitious story dictated to the deponent by Babo, and through the deponent imposed upon Captain Delano; and also recounting the friendly offers of Captain Delano, with other things, but all of which is here omitted. After the fictitious, strange story, etc., the deposition proceeds:*]

— That the generous Captain Amasa Delano remained on board all the day, till he left the ship anchored at six o'clock in the evening, deponent speaking to him always of his pretended misfortunes, under the fore-mentioned principles, without having had it in his power to tell a single word, or give him the least hint, that he might know the truth and state of things; because the negro Babo, performing the office of an officious servant with all the appearance of submission of the humble slave, did not leave the deponent one moment; that this was in order to observe the deponent's actions and words, for the negro Babo understands well the Spanish; and besides, there were thereabout some others who were constantly on the watch, and likewise understood the Spanish; . . . that upon one occasion, while deponent was standing on the deck conversing with Amasa Delano, by a secret sign the negro Babo drew him (the deponent) aside, the act appearing as if originating with the deponent; that then, he being drawn aside, the negro Babo proposed to him to gain from Amasa Delano full particulars about his ship, and crew, and arms; that the deponent asked "For what?" that the negro Babo answered he might conceive; that, grieved at the prospect of what might overtake the generous Captain Amasa Delano, the deponent at first refused to ask the desired questions, and used every argument to induce the negro Babo to give up this new design; that the negro Babo showed the point of his dagger; that, after the information had been obtained, the negro Babo again drew him aside, telling him that that very night he (the deponent) would be captain of two ships instead of one, for that, great part of the American's ship's crew going to be absent fishing, the six Ashantees. without any one else, would easily take it; that at this time he said other things to the same purpose; that no entreaties availed; that before Amasa Delano's coming on board, no hint had been given touching the capture of the American ship: that to prevent this project the deponent was powerless; ... — that in some things his memory is confused, he cannot distinctly recall every event; ... — that as soon as they had cast anchor at six of the clock in the evening, as has before been stated, the American captain took leave to return to his vessel; that upon a sudden impulse, which the deponent believes to have come from God and his angels, he, after the farewell had been said, followed the generous Captain Amasa Delano as far as the gunwale, where he stayed, under the pretence of taking leave, until Amasa Delano should have been seated in his boat; that on shoving off, the deponent sprang from the gunwale, into the boat, and fell into it, he knows not how, God guarding him; that —

.   .   .   .

[*Here, in the original, follows the account of what further happened at the escape, and how the "San Dominick" was retaken, and of the passage to the coast; including in the recital many expressions of "eternal gratitude" to the "generous Captain Amasa Delano." The deposition then proceeds with recapitulatory remarks, and a partial renumeration of the negroes, making record of their individual part in the past events, with a view to furnishing, according to command of the court, the data whereon to found the criminal sentences to be pronounced. From this portion is the following:*]

— That he believes that all the negroes, though not in the first place knowing to the design of revolt, when it was accomplished, approved it. ... That the negro, José, eighteen years old, and in the personal service of Don Alexandro, was the one who communicated the information to the negro Babo, about the state of things in the cabin, before the revolt; that this is known, because, in the preceding midnight, he used to come from his berth, which was under his master's, in the cabin, to the deck where the ringleader and his associates were, and had secret conversations with the negro Babo, in which he was several times seen by the mate; that, one night, the mate drove him away twice; ... that this same negro José, was the one who, without being commanded to do so by the negro Babo, as Lecbe and Martinqui were, stabbed his master, Don Alexandro, after he had been dragged half-lifeless to the deck; ... that the mulatto steward, Francesco, was of the first band of revolters, that he was, in all things, the creature and tool of the negro Babo; that, to make his court, he, just before a repast in the cabin, proposed, to the negro Babo, poisoning a dish for the generous Captain Amasa Delano; this is known and believed, because the negroes have said it; but that the negro Babo, having another design, forbade Francesco; ... that the Ashantee Lecbe was one of the worst of them; for that, on the day the ship was retaken, he assisted in the defence of her, with a hatchet in each hand, with one of which he wounded, in the breast, the chief mate of Amasa Delano, in the first act of boarding; this all knew; that, in sight of the deponent, Lecbe struck, with a hatchet, Don Francisco Masa when, by the negro Babo's orders, he was carrying him to throw him overboard, alive; beside participating in the murder, before mentioned, of Don Alexandro Aranda, and others of the cabin-passengers; that, owing to the fury with which the Ashantees fought in the engagement with the boats, but this Lecbe and Yan survived; that Yan was bad as Lecbe; that Yan was the man who, by Babo's command, willingly prepared the skeleton of Don Alexandro, in a way the negroes afterwards told the deponent, but which he, so long as reason is left him, can never divulge; that Yan and Lecbe were the two who, in a calm by night, riveted the skeleton to the bow; this also the negroes told him; that the negro Babo was he who traced the inscription below it; that the negro Babo was the plotter from first to last; he ordered every murder, and was the helm and keel of the revolt; that Atufal was his lieutenant in all; but Atufal, with his own hand, committed no murder; nor did the negro Babo; ... that Atufal was shot, being killed in the fight with the boats, ere boarding; ... that the negresses, of age, were knowing to the revolt, and testified themselves satisfied at the death of their master, Don Alexandro; that, had the negroes not restrained them, they would have tortured to death, instead of simply killing, the Spaniards slain by command of the negro Babo; that the negresses used their utmost influence to have the deponent made away with; that, in the various acts of murder, they sang songs and danced — not gaily, but solemnly; and before the engagement with the boats, as well as during the action, they sang melancholy songs to the negroes, and that this melancholy tone was more inflaming than a different one would have been, and was so intended; that all this is believed, because the negroes have said it. — That of the thirty-six men of the crew — exclusive of the passengers (all of whom are now dead), which the deponent had knowledge of — six only remained alive, with four cabin-boys and ship-boys, not included with the crew; ... — that the negroes broke an arm of one of the cabin-boys and gave him strokes with hatchets.

[*Then follow various random disclosures referring to various periods of time. The following are extracted:*]

— That during the presence of Captain Amasa Delano on board, some attempts were made by the sailors, and one by Hermenegildo Gandix, to convey hints to him of the true state of affairs; but that these attempts were ineffectual, owing to fear of incurring death, and furthermore owing to the devices which offered contradictions to the true state of affairs; as well as owing to the generosity and piety of Amasa Delano, incapable of sounding such wickedness; ... that Luys Galgo, a sailor about sixty years of age, and formerly of the king's navy, was one of those who sought to convey tokens to Captain Amasa Delano; but his intent, though undiscovered, being suspected, he was, on a pretence, made to retire out of sight, and at last into the hold, and there was made away with. This the negroes have since said; ... that one of the ship-boys feeling, from Captain Amasa Delano's presence, some hopes of release, and not having enough prudence, dropped some chance-word respecting his expectations, which being overheard and understood by a slave-boy with whom he was eating at the time, the latter struck him on the head with a knife, inflicting a bad wound, but of which the boy is now healing; that likewise, not long before the ship was brought to anchor, one of the seamen, steering at the time, endangered himself by letting the blacks remark a certain unconscious hopeful expression in his countenance, arising from some cause similar to the above; but this sailor, by his heedful after conduct, escaped; ... that these statements are made to show the court that from the beginning to the end of the revolt, it was impossible for the deponent and his men to act otherwise than they did; ... — that the third clerk, Hermenegildo Gandix, who before had been forced to live among the seamen, wearing a seaman's habit, and in all respects appearing to be one for the time; he, Gandix, was killed by a musket-ball fired through a mistake from the American boats before boarding; having in his fright ran up the mizzen-rigging, calling to the boats — "don't board," lest upon their boarding the negroes should kill him; that this inducing the Americans to believe he some way favoured the cause of the negroes, they fired two balls at him, so that he fell wounded from the rigging, and was drowned in the sea; ... — that the young Don Joaquin, Marques de Arambaolaza, like Hermenegildo Gandix, the third clerk, was degraded to the office and appearance of a common seaman; that upon one occasion, when Don Joaquin shrank, the negro Babo commanded the Ashantee Lecbe to take tar and heat it, and pour it upon Don Joaquin's hands; ... — that Don Joaquin was killed owing to another mistake of the Americans, but one impossible to be avoided, as upon the approach of the boats, Don Joaquin, with a hatchet tied edge out and upright to his hand, was made by the negroes to appear on the bulwarks; whereupon, seen with arms in his hands and in a questionable attitude, he was shot for a renegade seaman; ... — that on the person of Don Joaquin was found secreted a jewel, which, by papers that were discovered, proved to have been meant for the shrine of our Lady of Mercy in Lima; a votive offering, beforehand prepared and guarded, to attest his gratitude, when he should have landed in Peru, his last destination, for the safe conclusion of his entire voyage from Spain; ... — that the jewel, with the other effects of the late Don Joaquin, is in the custody of the brethren of the Hospital de Sacerdotes, awaiting the decision of the honourable court; ... — that, owing to the condition of the deponent, as well as the haste in which the boats departed for the attack, the Americans were not forewarned that there were, among the apparent crew, a passenger and one of the clerks disguised by the negro Babo; ... — that, beside the negroes killed in the action, some were killed after the capture and reanchoring at night, when shackled to the ring-bolts on deck; that these deaths were committed by the sailors, ere they could be prevented. That so soon as informed of it, Captain Amasa Delano used all his authority, and, in particular with his own hand, struck down Martinez Gola, who, having found a razor in the pocket of an old jacket of his, which one of the shackled negroes had on, was aiming it at the negro's throat; that the noble Captain Amasa Delano also wrenched from the hand of Bartholomew Barlo, a dagger secreted at the time of the massacre of the whites, with which he was in the act of stabbing a shackled negro, who, the same day, with another negro, had thrown him down and jumped upon him; ... — that, for all the events, befalling through so long a time, during which the ship was in the hands of the negro Babo, he cannot here give account; but that, what he has said is the most substantial of what occurs to him at present, and is the truth under the oath which he has taken; which declaration he affirmed and ratified, after hearing it read to him.

He said that he is twenty-nine years of age, and broken in body and mind; that when finally dismissed by the court, he shall not return home to Chili, but betake himself to the monastery on Mount Agonia without; and signed with his honour, and crossed himself, and, for the time, departed as he came, in his litter, with the monk Infelez, to the Hospital de Sacerdotes.

BENITO CERENO.

DOCTOR ROZAS.

If the deposition of Benito Cereno has served as the key to fit into the lock of the complications which preceded it, then, as a vault whose door has been flung back, the *San Dominick's* hull lies open to-day.

Hitherto the nature of this narrative, besides rendering the intricacies in the beginning unavoidable, has more or less required that many things, instead of being set down in the order of occurrence, should be retrospectively, or irregularly given; this last is the case with the following passages, which will conclude the account:

During the long, mild voyage to Lima, there was, as before hinted, a period during which Don Benito, a little recovered his health, or, at least in some degree, his tranquillity. Ere the decided relapse which came, the two captains had many cordial conversations — their fraternal unreserve in singular contrast with former withdrawments.

Again and again, it was repeated, how hard it had been to enact the part forced on the Spaniard by Babo.

"Ah, my dear Don Amasa," Don Benito once said, "at those very times when you thought me so morose and ungrateful — nay when, as you now admit, you half thought me plotting your murder — at those very times my heart was frozen; I could not look at you, thinking of what, both on board this ship and your own, hung, from other hands, over my kind benefactor. And as God lives, Don Amasa, I know not whether desire for my own safety alone could have nerved me to that leap into your boat, had it not been for the thought that, did you, unenlightened, return to your ship, you, my best friend, with all who might be with you, stolen upon, that night, in your hammocks, would never in this world have wakened again. Do but think how you walked this deck, how you sat in this cabin, every inch of ground mined into honey-combs under you. Had I dropped the least hint, made the least advance toward an understanding between us, death, explosive death — yours as mine — would have ended the scene."

"True, true," cried Captain Delano, starting, "you saved my life, Don Benito, more than I yours; saved it, too, against my knowledge and will."

"Nay, my friend," rejoined the Spaniard, courteous even to the point of religion, "God charmed your life, but you saved mine. To think of some things you did — those smilings and chattings, rash pointings and gesturings. For less than these, they slew my mate, Raneds; but you had the Prince of Heaven's safe conduct through all ambuscades."

"Yes, all is owing to Providence, I know; but the temper of my mind that morning was more than commonly pleasant, while the sight of so much suffering — more apparent than real — added to my good nature, compassion, and charity, happily interweaving the three. Had it been otherwise, doubtless, as you hint, some of my interferences with the blacks might have ended unhappily enough. Besides that, those feelings I spoke of enabled me to get the better of momentary distrust, at times when acuteness might have cost me my life, without saving another's. Only at the end did my suspicions get the better of me, and you know how wide of the mark they then proved."

"Wide, indeed," said Don Benito, sadly; "you were with me all day; stood with me, sat with me, talked with me, looked at me, ate with me, drank with me; and yet, your last act was to clutch for a villain, not only an innocent man, but the most pitiable of all men. To such degree may malign machinations and deceptions impose. So far may even the best men err, in judging the conduct of one with the recesses of whose condition he is not acquainted. But you were forced to it; and you were in time undeceived. Would that, in both respects, it was so ever, and with all men."

"I think I understand you; you generalize, Don Benito; and mournfully enough. But the past is passed: why moralize upon it? Forget it. See, yon bright sun has forgotten it all, and the blue sea, and the blue sky; these have turned over new leaves."

"Because they have no memory," he dejectedly replied; "because they are not human."

"But these mild trades that now fan your cheek, Don Benito, do they not come with a human-like healing to you? Warm friends, steadfast friends are the trades."

"With their steadfastness they but waft me to my tomb, Señor," was the foreboding response.

"You are saved, Don Benito," cried Captain Delano, more and more astonished and pained; "you are saved; what has cast such a shadow upon you?"

"The negro."

There was silence, while the moody man sat, slowly and unconsciously gathering his mantle about him, as if it were a pall.

There was no more conversation that day.

But if the Spaniard's melancholy sometimes ended in muteness upon topics like the above, there were others upon which he never spoke at all; on which, indeed, all his old reserves were piled. Pass over the worst and, only to elucidate, let an item or two of these be cited. The dress so precise and costly, worn by him on the day whose events have been narrated, had not willingly been put on. And that silver-mounted sword, apparent symbol of despotic command, was not, indeed, a sword, but the ghost of one. The scabbard, artificially stiffened, was empty.

As for the black — whose brain, not body, had schemed and led the revolt, with the plot — his slight frame, inadequate to that which it held, had at once yielded to the superior muscular strength of his captor, in the boat. Seeing all was over, he uttered no sound, and could not be forced to. His aspect seemed to say: since I cannot do deeds, I will not speak words. Put in irons in the hold, with the rest, he was carried to Lima. During the passage Don Benito did not visit him. Nor then, nor at any time after, would he look at him. Before the tribunal he refused. When pressed by the judges he fainted. On the testimony of the sailors alone rested the legal identity of Babo. And yet the Spaniard would, upon occasion, verbally refer to the negro, as has been shown; but look on him he would not, or could not.

Some months after, dragged to the gibbet at the tail of a mule, the black met his voiceless end. The body was burned to ashes; but for many days, the head, that hive of subtlety, fixed on a pole in the Plaza, met, unabashed, the gaze of the whites; and across the Plaza looked toward St. Bartholomew's church, in whose vaults slept then, as now, the recovered bones of Aranda; and across the Rimac bridge looked toward the monastery, on Mount Agonia without; where, three months after being dismissed by the court, Benito Cereno, borne on the bier, did, indeed, follow his leader.

Feodor Mikhailovich Dostoyevsky

NOTES FROM UNDERGROUND [1]

1 8 6 4

❧

Part I — Underground

I

I AM a sick man. I am a spiteful man. I am an unattractive man. I believe my liver is diseased. However, I know nothing at all about my disease and do not know for certain what ails me. I don't consult a doctor for it, and never have, though I have a respect for medicine and doctors. Besides, I am extremely superstitious, sufficiently so to respect medicine, at any rate (I am well-educated enough not to be superstitious, even though I am). No, I refuse to consult a doctor out of spite. That is something you probably will not understand. Well, I do. Of course, I can't explain whom precisely I am mortifying in this case by my spite: I am perfectly well aware that I cannot "get even" with the doctors by not consulting them; I know better than anyone that by all this I am only injuring myself and no one else. But still, if I don't consult a doctor it is out of spite. My liver is bad, well — let it get worse!

I have been going on like that for a long time — twenty years. Now I am forty. I used to be in the government service, but am no longer. I was a spiteful official. I was rude and took pleasure in being so. I did not take bribes, you see, so I was bound to find a recompense in that, at least. (A poor jest, but I will not cross it out. I wrote it thinking

---

[1] The author of the diary and the diary itself are, of course, imaginary. Nevertheless it is clear that such persons as the writer of these notes not only may, but positively must, exist in our society, when we consider the circumstances in the midst of which our society is formed. I have tried to expose to the view of the public, more distinctly than is commonly done, one of the characters of the recent past. He is one of the representatives of a generation still living. In this fragment, entitled *Underground*, this person introduces himself and his views and, as it were, tries to explain the causes owing to which he has made his appearance and was bound to make his appearance in our midst. In the second fragment there are added the actual notes of this person concerning certain events in his life.--*Author's Note.*

125

it would sound very witty; but now that I have perceived myself that I was merely trying to show off in a despicable way, I will purposely refrain from crossing it out!)

When petitioners would come to my desk for information, I would grind my teeth at them and feel intense enjoyment whenever I succeeded in making anybody unhappy. I almost always did succeed. For the most part they were all timid people — of course, since they were petitioners. But of the uppity ones there was one officer in particular I could not endure. He simply would not be humble, and kept clanking his sword in a disgusting way. I carried on a feud with him for eighteen months over that sword. At last I got the better of him. He left off clanking it. That happened in my youth, though.

But do you know, gentlemen, what was the chief point about my spite? Why, the whole point, the real sting of it lay in the fact that continually, even in the moment of the acutest spleen, I was inwardly conscious with shame that I was not only not a spiteful man but not even an embittered one, that I was simply scaring sparrows at random and amusing myself by it. I might foam at the mouth, but bring me a doll to play with, give me a cup of tea with sugar in it, and I could be appeased. I might even be genuinely touched, though probably I should grind my teeth at myself afterward and lie awake at night from shame for months after. That was my way.

I was lying when I said just now that I was a spiteful official. I was lying from spite. I was simply amusing myself with the petitioners and with the officer, and in reality I never could become spiteful. I was conscious every moment in myself of many, very many elements absolutely opposite to that. I felt them positively swarming in me, these opposed elements. I knew that they had been swarming in me all my life and craving some outlet from me, but let them out I would not. I would not let them, I purposely would not let them come out. They tormented me till I was ashamed; they drove me to convulsions and at last sickened me — how they sickened me! Now, aren't you imagining, gentlemen, that I am expressing remorse over something, that I am asking your forgiveness for something? I am sure you are. However, I assure you I don't care about that.

It was not only that I could not become spiteful; I did not know how to become anything: either spiteful or kind, either a rascal or an honest man, either a hero or an insect. Now I am living out my life in my corner, taunting myself with the spiteful and useless consolation that an intelligent man cannot seriously become anything and it is only the fool who becomes something. Yes, a man in the nineteenth century must and morally ought to be pre-eminently a characterless creature; a man of character, an active man is pre-eminently a limited creature. That is my conviction of forty years. I am forty years old now, and you know forty years is a whole lifetime; you know it is extreme old age. To live longer than forty years is bad manners, it's vulgar, immoral. Who lives beyond forty? Answer that, sincerely and honestly. I will tell you who: fools and good-for-nothings. I tell all old men that to their faces, all these venerable old men, all these silver-haired and reverend ancients! I tell the whole world that to its face! I have a right to say so, for I'll go on living to sixty myself. To seventy! To eighty! Hold on, let me catch my breath.

No doubt, gentlemen, you imagine that I wish to amuse you. You are mistaken in that, too. I am by no means such a mirthful person as you imagine, or may imagine; however, irritated by all this babble (and I feel that you are irritated), you think fit to ask me who am I; my answer is, I am a Collegiate Assessor. I went into Civil Service so as to have something to eat (that and nothing else), and when last year a distant relation left me six thousand rubles in his will I immediately retired from the Service and settled down in my hole. I used to live in this hole before, but now I have settled down in it. My room is a wretched, horrid one on the outskirts of the town. My servant is an old countrywoman, ill-natured from stupidity, and, moreover, there is always a nasty smell about her. I am told that the Petersburg climate is bad for me, and that with my small means it is very expensive to live there. I know all that better than all these sage and experienced counselors and preceptors. But I am remaining in Petersburg; I am not going away from Petersburg! I am not going away because — eh, it absolutely doesn't matter whether I am going away or not going away.

But what can a decent man speak of with most pleasure?
Answer: Of himself.
Well, then, I will talk about myself.

II

And now, gentlemen, whether you care to hear it or not, I want to tell you why I could not become even an insect. I tell you solemnly that I have tried to become an insect, many's the time. But I was not equal even to that. I swear, gentlemen, that to be too conscious is an illness — a real out-and-out illness. For man's everyday needs it would have been quite enough to have the ordinary human consciousness, that is, half or a quarter of the amount which falls to the lot of a cultivated man of our unhappy nineteenth century, especially one who has the fatal ill-luck to inhabit Petersburg, the most theoretical and intentional town on the whole terrestrial globe. (There are intentional and unintentional towns.) It would have been quite enough, for instance, to have the consciousness by which all so-called straightforward persons and men of action live. I'll bet you think I am writing all this from affectation, to be witty at the expense of men of action; and what is more, that from ill-bred affectation I am clanking a sword, like my officer. But, gentlemen, whoever can pride himself on his diseases and even swagger over them?

Although, after all, everyone does do just that; people do pride themselves on their diseases, and I, perhaps, more than anyone else. We will not dispute it; my contention was absurd. And yet I am firmly persuaded that a great deal of consciousness — every sort of consciousness, in fact — is a disease. I stick to that. But let's leave that, too, for a minute. Tell me this: why does it happen that at the very — yes, at the *very* — moments when I am most capable of feeling every refinement of all that is *good and beautiful* (as they used to say at one time), I would, as though on purpose, happen not only to feel but to do such ugly things that — well, in short, such actions as perhaps all men commit, but which, as though purposely, came at the very time when I was most conscious that they ought not to be committed. The more conscious I was of goodness and of all that was *good and beautiful,* the more deeply I sank into my mire and the more ready I was to sink in it altogether. But the chief point was that all this was not accidental in me, as it were, but apparently had to be so. It was as though it were my most normal condition, and not in the least disease or depravity, so that at last all desire in me to struggle against this depravity passed. It ended by my almost (perhaps actually) believing that this was perhaps my normal condition.

But at first, in the beginning, what agonies I endured in that struggle! I did not believe it was the same with other people, and all my life I hid this fact about myself as a secret. I was ashamed (even now, perhaps, I am ashamed); I got to the point of feeling a sort of secret, abnormal, despicable enjoyment in returning home to my hole on some disgustingly inclement Petersburg night, acutely conscious that that day I had committed a loathsome action again, that what was done could never be undone, and secretly, inwardly gnawing, gnawing at myself for it, rending and consuming myself till at last the bitterness turned into a sort of shameful accursed sweetness, and at last into positive real enjoyment! Yes, into enjoyment — into enjoyment! I insist upon that. I have spoken of this because I keep wanting to know for a fact whether other people feel such enjoyment? I will explain: the enjoyment was just from the too intense consciousness of one's own degradation; it was from feeling that you had reached the last barrier, that it was horrible, but that it could not be otherwise; that there was no escape for you; that you never could become a different man; that even if time and faith were still left you to change into something different you would most likely not wish to change; or if you did wish to, even then you would do nothing, because perhaps in reality there was nothing for you to change into.

And the worst of it, and the root of it all, was that it was all in accord with the normal fundamental laws of overacute consciousness, and with the inertia that was the direct result of those laws, and that consequently one was not only unable to change but could do absolutely nothing. Thus it would follow, as the result of acute consciousness, that one is not to blame in being a scoundrel; as though that were any consolation to the scoundrel once he has come to realize that he actually is a scoundrel. But enough! Eh, I've talked a lot of nonsense, yet what have I explained? How is such enjoyment to be explained? Yet explain it I will. I will get to the bottom of it! That is why I have taken up my pen. . . .

I, for instance, have a great deal of *amour propre.* I am as suspicious and prone to take offense as a hunchback or a dwarf. But, upon my word, I sometimes have had moments when, if I had happened to be slapped in the face, I should, perhaps, have been positively glad of it. I say, in earnest, that I should probably have been able to discover even in that a peculiar sort of enjoyment — the enjoyment, of course, of despair; but in despair there are the most intense enjoyments, especially when one is very acutely conscious of the hopelessness of one's position. And when one is slapped in the face — why, then the consciousness of being rubbed into a pulp would positively overwhelm one. The worst of it is, look at it which way you will, it still turns out that I was always most to blame in everything. And what is most humiliating of all, to blame for no fault of my own but, so to say, through the laws of nature. In the first place, I was to blame because I am cleverer than any of the people surrounding me. (I have always considered myself cleverer than any of the people surrounding me, and sometimes, would you believe it, have been positively ashamed of it. At any rate, I have all my life, as it were, turned my eyes away and never could look people straight in the face.) I was to blame, finally, because even if I had had magnanimity, I should only have had more suffering from the sense of its uselessness. I should certainly have never been able to do anything because of being magnanimous — either to forgive (for my assailant would perhaps have slapped me from the laws of nature, and one cannot forgive the laws of nature) or to forget (for even if the slap were owing to the laws of nature, it is insulting all the same). Finally, even if I had wanted to be anything but magnanimous, had desired on the contrary to avenge myself on my assailant, I could not have avenged myself on anyone for anything, because I should certainly never have made up my mind to do anything, even if I had been able to. Why shouldn't I have made up my mind? I want to say a few words about that in particular.

III

With people who know how to avenge themselves and to stand up for themselves in general, how is it done? Why, when they are possessed, let us suppose, by the feeling of revenge, then for the time being there is nothing else but that feeling left in their whole being. Such a gentleman simply dashes straight for his object like an infuriated bull with its horns down, and nothing but a wall will stop him. (By the way: facing the wall, such gentlemen — that is, the *straightforward* persons and men of action — are genuinely nonplused. For them a wall is not an evasion, as for us who think and consequently do nothing; it is not an excuse for turning aside, an excuse which we always are very glad of, though we scarcely believe in it ourselves, as a rule. No, they are nonplused in all sincerity. The wall has for them something tranquilizing, morally soothing, final — perhaps even something mysterious — but of this wall more later.)

Well, such a straightforward person I regard as the real normal man, as his tender Mother Nature wished to see him when she graciously brought him into being on the earth. I envy such a man till I am green in the face. He is stupid. I am not disputing that, but perhaps, for all we know, the normal man should be stupid. Perhaps it's all very beautiful, in fact. And I am the more persuaded of that suspicion, if one can call it so, by the fact that if you take, for instance, the antithesis of the normal man, that is, the man of acute consciousness, who has come, of course, not out of the lap of nature but out of a retort (this is almost mysticism, gentlemen, but I suspect that this, too, is so), this retort-made man is sometimes so nonplused in the presence of his antithesis that with all his exaggerated consciousness he genuinely thinks of himself as a mouse and not a man. It may be an acutely conscious mouse, yet it is a mouse, while the other is a man, and, therefore, *et cetera, et cetera.* And the worst of it is, he himself, his very own self, looks on himself as a mouse; no one asks him to do so; and that is an important point. Now let us look at this mouse in action. Let us suppose, for instance, that it feels insulted, too (and it almost always does feel insulted), and wants to revenge itself likewise. There may even be a greater accumulation of spite in it than in *l'homme de la nature et de la vérité.* The base and nasty desire to vent that spite on its assailant rankles perhaps even more nastily in it than in *l'homme de la nature et de la vérité.* For through his innate stupidity the latter looks upon his revenge as justice, pure and simple; while in consequence of its acute consciousness the mouse does not believe in the justice of it.

To come at last to the deed itself, to the very act of revenge. Apart from the one fundamental nastiness the luckless mouse succeeds in creating around it, so many other nastinesses in the form of doubts and questions add to the one question so many unsettled questions that there inevitably works up around it a sort of fatal ferment, a stinking mess, made up of its doubts, emotions, and of the contempt spat upon it by the *straightforward* men of action who stand solemnly about it as judges and arbitrators, laughing at it till their healthy sides ache. Of course, the only thing left for it is to dismiss all that with a wave of its paw and, with a smile of assumed contempt in which it does not even itself believe, creep ignominiously into its mousehole. There in its nasty, stinking, underground home our insulted, crushed and ridiculed mouse promptly becomes absorbed in cold, malignant, and, above all, everlasting spite. For forty years together it will remember its injury down to the smallest, most ignominious details, and every time will add, of itself, details still more ignominious, spitefully teasing and tormenting itself with its own imagination. It will itself be ashamed of its imaginings, but yet it will recall everything, it will go over and over every detail, it will invent unheard-of things against itself, pretending that those things might happen, and will forgive nothing. Perhaps it will take to avenging itself, too, but piecemeal, as it were, in trivial ways, from behind the stove, incognito, without believing either in its own right to vengeance or in the success of its revenge, knowing that from all its efforts at revenge it will suffer a hundred times more than he on whom it revenges itself, while the victim, I daresay, will not even know a thing about it. On its deathbed the mouse will recall everything all over again, with interest compounded through all the years, and —

But it is just in that cold, abominable half-despair, half-belief, in that conscious burying of oneself alive for grief in the underworld for forty years, in that acutely recognized and yet partly doubtful hopelessness of one's position, in that hell of unsatisfied, introverted desires, in that fever of oscillations, of resolutions determined for ever and repented of again a minute later — that the savor of that strange enjoyment of which I have spoken lies. It is so subtle, so difficult of analysis, that persons who are a little limited, or even simply persons of strong nerves, will not understand a single atom of it. "Possibly," you will add on your own account with a grin, "people who have never received a slap in the face will not understand it either," and in that way you will politely hint to me that I, too, perhaps, have had the experience of a slap in the face in my life, and therefore speak as one who knows. I'll bet that's what you're thinking. But set your minds at rest, gentlemen, I have not received a slap in the face, though it is absolutely a matter of indifference to me what you may think about it. Possibly I even regret, myself, that I have given so few slaps in the face during my life. But enough — not another word on that subject of such extreme interest to you.

I will continue calmly concerning persons with strong nerves who do not understand a certain refinement of enjoyment. Though in certain circumstances these gentlemen bellow their loudest like bulls, though this, let us suppose, does them the greatest credit, yet, as I have said already, confronted with the impossible they subside at once. The impossible means the stone wall! What stone wall? Why, of course, the laws of nature, the deductions of natural science, mathematics. As soon as they prove to you, for instance, that you are descended from a monkey, there's no use scowling, accept it for a fact. When they prove to you that in reality one drop of your own suet must be dearer to you than a hundred thousand of your fellow creatures, and that this conclusion is the final solution of all the so-called virtues and duties and all such prejudices and fancies, why, you just have to accept it; there's no help for it, for two times two is a law of mathematics. Just try refuting it!

"Upon my word," they will shout at you, "it is no use protesting: it's a case of two times two making four! Nature does not ask your permission, she has nothing to do with your wishes, and whether you like her laws or dislike them, you're bound to accept her as she is, and consequently all her conclusions. A wall, you see, is a wall —" and so on and so on.

Merciful Heavens! But what do I care for the laws of nature and arithmetic, when, for some reason, I dislike those laws and the fact that two times two makes four? Of course I can't break through the wall by battering my head against it if I really haven't the strength to knock it down, but I'm not going to be reconciled to it simply because it is a stone wall and I haven't the strength.

As though such a stone wall really were a consolation and really did contain some word of conciliation, simply because it is as true as that two times two makes four. Oh, absurdity of absurdities! How much better it is to understand all, to recognize all — all the impossibilities and the stone wall; not to be reconciled to one of those impossibilities and stone walls if it disgusts you to be reconciled to it; by the way of the most inevitable, logical combinations to reach the most revolting conclusions on the everlasting theme: that you yourself are somehow to blame even for the stone wall, though again it is as clear as day you are not to blame in the least, and therefore grinding your teeth in silent impotence to sink into luxurious inertia, brooding on the fact that there's no one for you even to feel vindictive against, that you have not, and perhaps never will have, an object for your spite, that it is a sleight of hand, a bit of jugglery, a cardsharper's trick, that it is simply a mess, no knowing what and no knowing who. But in spite of all these uncertainties and juggleries, there is still an ache in you, and the more you do not know, the worse the ache.

IV

"Ha, ha, ha! You'll be finding enjoyment in toothache next," you cry with a laugh.

"Well? There is enjoyment even in toothache," I answer. I had a toothache for a whole month and I know there is. In that case, of course, people aren't silently spiteful but moan; the moans, however, are not candid but malevolent. And it is in their malevolence that the whole point lies. The enjoyment of the sufferer finds expression in those moans; if he did not feel enjoyment in them he would not moan. It is a good example, gentlemen, and I will develop it. Those moans express in the first place all the aimlessness of your pain, which is so humiliating to your consciousness; the whole legal system of nature on which you spit disdainfully, of course, but from which you suffer all the same while nature doesn't. They express the consciousness that you have no enemy to punish, but that you do have pain; the consciousness that in spite of all possible autosuggestionists you are in complete slavery to your teeth; that if someone wishes it, your teeth will leave off aching, and if he does not, they will go on aching another three months; and that, finally, if you are still contumacious and still protest, all that is left you for your own gratification is to beat yourself, or beat your wall with your fists as hard as you can — that, and absolutely nothing more. Well, these mortal insults, these jeers on the part of someone unknown, end at last in an enjoyment which sometimes reaches the highest degree of voluptuousness.

I ask you, gentlemen, listen sometimes to the moans of an educated man of the nineteenth century suffering from toothache on the second or third day of the attack, when he is beginning to moan not as he moaned on the first day — that is, not simply because he has toothache, not just as any coarse peasant, but as a man affected by progress and European civilization, a man who is "divorced from the soil and the national elements," as they express it nowadays. His moans become nasty, disgustingly malevolent, and go on for whole days and nights. And of course he himself knows that he isn't doing himself the least good with his moans; he knows better than anyone that he is only lacerating and harassing himself and others for nothing; he knows that even the audience before whom he is making his efforts, and his whole family, listen to him with loathing, without the least belief in him, and inwardly understand that he might moan differently, more simply, without trills and grace notes, and that he is only amusing himself like that from ill-humor, from malevolency. Well, it is in all these recognitions and disgraces that the voluptuous pleasure lies. As though he would say: "I am worrying you, I am lacerating your hearts, I am keeping everyone in the house awake. Well, stay awake; then you, too, will feel every moment that I have toothache. I am not a hero to you now, as I tried to seem before, but simply a nasty person, an impostor. Well, so be it, then! I am very glad that you see through me. It is nasty for you to hear my despicable moans; well, let it be nasty; there, I'll let you have a nastier quaver in just a moment!" You do not understand even now, gentlemen? No, it seems our development and our consciousness must go further to understand all the intricacies of this pleasure. You laugh? Delighted! My jests, gentlemen, are of course in bad taste, abrupt, involved, lacking in self-confidence. But

of course that is because I do not respect myself.   Can a man of perception respect himself at all?

V

Come, can a man who attempts to find enjoyment in the very feeling
of his own degradation possibly have a spark of respect for himself?
I am not saying this now from any mawkish kind of remorse.   And,
indeed, I could never endure saying: "Forgive me, Papa, I won't do
it again" — not because I am incapable of saying that; on the contrary,
perhaps just because I have been too capable of it, and how, at that!
As though on purpose, I used to get into trouble in cases when I was
not to blame in any way.   That was the nastiest part of it.   At the same
time I was genuinely touched and penitent; I used to shed tears and,
of course, deceived myself, though I was not acting in the least and
there was a sick feeling in my heart at the time.   For that, one could
not blame even the laws of nature, though the laws of nature have
continually all my life offended me more than anything else.   It is
loathsome to remember it all, but it was loathsome even then.   Of
course, a minute or so later I would realize wrathfully that it was all
a lie, a revolting lie, a stilted lie — I mean all this penitence, this emotion, these vows of reform.   You will ask why I upset myself with
such antics: the answer is because it was very dull to sit with one's
hands folded, and so I began cutting capers.   That's it, really.   Observe yourselves more carefully, gentlemen, then you will understand
that it's so.   I invented adventures for myself and made up a life, so as
at least to live in some way.   How many times it has happened to me —
well, for instance, to take offense simply on purpose, for nothing; and
you know yourself, of course, that you're offended at nothing, that
you're putting on an act, and yet you bring yourself at last to the point
of being really offended.   All my life have I had an impulse to play
such pranks, so that in the end I could not control that impulse in
myself.

Another time — twice, in fact — I tried hard to fall in love.   I suffered, too, gentlemen, I assure you.   In the depth of my heart there was
no faith in my suffering, only a faint stir of mockery, yet suffer I did,
and that in the real, orthodox way; I was jealous, beside myself — and
it was all from ennui, gentlemen, all from ennui; inertia overcame me.
You know the direct, legitimate fruit of consciousness is inertia, that
is, conscious sitting-with-your-hands-folded.   I have referred to this
already.   I repeat, I repeat with emphasis: all *straightforward* persons

and men of action are active just because they are stupid and limited. How explain that? I will tell you: in consequence of their limitation they take immediate and secondary causes for primary ones, and in that way persuade themselves more quickly and easily than other people that they have found an infallible basis for their activity, and their minds are at ease and that, you know, is the chief thing. To begin to act, you know, you must first have your mind completely at ease and no trace of doubt left in it. Why, how am I, for example, to set my mind at rest? Where are the primary causes on which I am to build? Where are my bases? Where am I to get them from? I exercise myself in reflection, and consequently with me every primary cause at once draws after itself another still more primary, and so on to infinity. That is just the essence of every sort of consciousness and reflection. It must be a case of the laws of nature again. What is the result of it in the end? Why, the same unvarying one.

Remember I spoke just now of vengeance. (I am sure you did not take it in.) I said that a man avenges himself because he sees justice in it. Therefore he has found a primary cause — that is, justice. And so he is at rest all around, and consequently he carries out his revenge calmly and successfully, being persuaded that he is doing a just and honest thing. But I see no justice in it, I find no sort of virtue in it, either, and consequently if I attempt to avenge myself, it is only out of spite. Spite, of course, might overcome everything, all my doubts and so might serve quite successfully in place of a primary cause, precisely because it is not a cause. But what is to be done if I have not even spite (I began with that just now, you know)? In consequence again of those accursed laws of consciousness, anger in me is subject to chemical disintegration. You look into it, the object flies off into air, your reasons evaporate, the criminal is not to be found, the wrong becomes not a wrong but a phantom, something like the toothache, for which no one is to blame, and consequently there is only the same outlet left again — that is, to pound the wall as hard as you can. So you give it up with a wave of the hand because you have not found a fundamental cause. And you try letting yourself be carried away by your feelings, blindly, without reflection, without a primary cause, repelling consciousness at least for a time; you hate or love, just so as not to sit with your hands folded. The day after tomorrow, at the latest, you will begin despising yourself for having knowingly deceived yourself. Result: a soap bubble and inertia. Oh, gentlemen, do you know, perhaps I consider myself an intelligent man only because all my life I have been able neither to begin nor to finish anything. Granted I am a babbler, a harmless, vexatious babbler, like all of us. But what is to be done if the direct and sole vocation of every intelligent man is babbling — that is, the intentional pouring of water through a sieve?

VI

Oh, if I had done nothing simply from laziness! Heavens, how I should have respected myself then! I should have respected myself because I should at least have been capable of being lazy; there would at least have been one positive quality, as it were, in me, in which I could have believed myself. Question: What is he? Answer: A sluggard. How very pleasant it would have been to hear that of oneself! It would mean that I was positively defined, it would mean that there was something to say about me. "Sluggard" — why, it is a calling and vocation, it is a career. Do not jest — it is so. I should then be a member of the best club, by right, and should find my occupation in continually respecting myself. I knew a gentleman who prided himself all his life on being a connoisseur of Lafitte. He considered this as his positive virtue and never doubted himself. He died not simply with a tranquil but with a triumphant conscience, and he was quite right, too. Then I should have chosen a career for myself, I should have been a sluggard and a glutton, not a simple one, but, for instance, one with sympathies for everything good and beautiful. How do you like that? I have long had visions of it. That *good and beautiful* weighs heavily on my mind at forty. But that is at forty; then — oh, then it would have been different! I should have found for myself a form of activity in keeping with it — to be precise, drinking to the health of everything *good and beautiful*. I should have snatched at every opportunity to drop a tear into my glass and then to drain it to all that is *good and beautiful*. I should then have turned everything into the good and the beautiful; in the nastiest, unquestionable trash, I should have sought out the *good and the beautiful*. I should have exuded tears as a wet sponge exudes water. An artist, for instance, paints a picture worthy of Goya. At once I drink to the health of the artist who painted the picture worthy of Goya, because I love all that is *good and beautiful*. An author has written *As You Like It:* at once I drink to the health of *As You Like It* because I love all that is *good and beautiful*.

I should claim respect for doing so. I should persecute anyone who would not show me respect. I should live at ease, I should die with dignity, why, it's charming, utterly charming! And what a good round belly I'd grow, what a triple chin I'd fit myself out with, what a ruby nose I'd color for myself, so that everyone would say, looking at me: "Here is an asset! Here is something real and solid!"

And, say what you like, it is very agreeable to hear such remarks about oneself in this negative age.

VII

But these are all golden dreams. Oh, tell me, who was it first announced, who was it first proclaimed, that man only does nasty things because he does not know his own interests; and that if he were enlightened, if his eyes were opened to his real normal interests, man would at once cease to do nasty things, would at once become good and noble because, being enlightened and understanding his real advantage, he would see his own advantage in the good and nothing else, and we all know that not one man can, consciously, act against his own interests, consequently, so to say, through necessity, he would begin doing good? Oh, the babe! Oh, the pure, innocent child! Why, in the first place, when in all these thousands of years has there been a time when man has acted only from his own interest? What is to be done with the millions of facts that bear witness that men, *consciously*, that is, fully understanding their real interests, have left them in the background and have rushed headlong on another path, to meet peril and danger, compelled to this course by nobody and by nothing, but, as it were, simply disliking the beaten track, and have obstinately, willfully, beaten another difficult, absurd path, seeking it almost in the darkness? So, I suppose, this obstinacy and perversity were pleasanter to them than any advantage. Advantage! What is advantage? And will you take it upon yourself to define with perfect accuracy of what the advantage of man consists? And what if it so happens that a man's advantage, *sometimes*, not only may, but even must, consist in his desiring in certain cases what is harmful to himself and not advantageous? And if so, if there can be such a case, the whole principle falls into dust. What do you think — are there such cases? You laugh; laugh away, gentlemen, but only answer me: have man's advantages been reckoned up with perfect certainty? Are there not some which not only have not been included but cannot possibly be included under any classification?

You see, you gentlemen have, to the best of my knowledge, taken your whole register of human advantages from the averages of statistical figures and politico-economical formulas. Your advantages are prosperity, wealth, freedom, peace — and so on, and so on. So that the man who should, for instance, go openly and knowingly in opposition to all that list would, to your thinking, and indeed mine, too, of course, be an obscurantist or an absolute madman: wouldn't he? But, you know, this is what is surprising: why does it so happen that all these statisticians, sages and lovers of humanity, when they reckon up human advantages, invariably leave out one? They don't even take it into their reckoning in the form in which it should be taken, yet the whole reckoning depends upon that. It would be no great matter, they would simply have to take it, this advantage, and add it to the list. But the trouble is that this strange advantage does not fall under any classification and is out of place in any list. I have a friend, for instance — Eh, gentleman, but of course he is your friend, too; and indeed there is no one — no one! — to whom he is not a friend! When he prepares for any undertaking this gentleman immediately explains to you, elegantly and clearly, exactly how he must act in accordance with the laws of reason and truth. What is more, he will talk to you with animation and passion of the true normal interests of man; with irony he will upbraid the shortsighted fools who do not understand their own interests, nor the true significance of virtue; and, within a quarter of an hour, without any sudden outside provocation, but simply through something inside him which is stronger than all his interests, he will go off on quite a different tack — that is, act in direct opposition to what he has just been saying about himself, in opposition to the laws of reason, in opposition to his own advantage, in fact, in opposition to everything. I warn you that my friend is a compound personality, and therefore it is difficult to blame him as an individual.

The fact is, gentlemen, there apparently must really exist something that is dearer to almost every man than his greatest advantages, or (not to be illogical) there is a most advantageous advantage (the very one omitted, of which we spoke just now) which is more important and more advantageous than all other advantages, for the sake of which a man if necessary is ready to act in opposition to all laws; that is, in opposition to reason, honor, peace, prosperity — in fact, in opposition to all those excellent and useful things if only he can attain that fundamental, most advantageous advantage which is dearer to him than all.

"Yes, but it's an advantage all the same," you will retort. But excuse me, I'll make the point clear, and it isn't a case of playing upon words, either. What matters is that this advantage is remarkable from the very fact that it breaks down all our classifications and continually shatters every system constructed by lovers of mankind for the benefit of mankind. In fact, it upsets everything. But before mentioning this advantage to you, I want to compromise myself personally, and therefore I boldly declare that all these fine systems — all these theories for explaining to mankind its real normal interests, so that inevitably striving to pursue these interests men may at once become good and noble — are, in my opinion, so far, mere logical exercises! Yes, logical exercises. Why, to maintain this theory of the regeneration of mankind by means of the pursuit of its own advantage is to my mind almost the same thing as — as to affirm, for instance, following Buckle, that through civilization mankind becomes softer, and consequently less bloodthirsty and less fitted for warfare. Logically it does seem to follow from his arguments. But man has such a predilection for systems and abstract deductions that he is ready to distort the truth intentionally, he is ready to deny the evidence of his senses only to justify his logic.

I take this example because it is the most glaring instance of it. Only look about you: blood is being spilt in streams, and in the merriest way, as though it were champagne. Take the whole of the nineteenth century in which Buckle lived. Take Napoleon — the Great, and also the present one. Take North America — the eternal Union. Take the farce of Schleswig-Holstein. And what is it that civilization softens in us? The only gain of civilization for mankind is the greater capacity for variety of sensations — and absolutely nothing more. And through the development of this many-sidedness man may come to finding enjoyment in bloodshed. In fact, this has already happened to him. Have you noticed that it is the most civilized gentlemen who have been the subtlest slaughterers, to whom the Attilas and Stenka Razins could not hold a candle? And if they are not so conspicuous as the Attilas and Stenka Razins, it is simply because they are so often met with, are so ordinary and have become so familiar to us. In any case, civilization has made mankind, if not more bloodthirsty, at least more vilely, more loathsomely bloodthirsty.

In the old days man saw justice in bloodshed, and with his conscience at peace exterminated people as he saw fit. Now we do think bloodshed abominable and yet we engage in this abomination, and with more energy than ever. Which is worse? Decide that for yourselves. They say that Cleopatra (excuse an instance from Roman history) was fond of sticking gold pins into her slave-girls' breasts and derived gratification from their screams and writhings. You will say that that was in the comparatively barbarous times; that these are barbarous times, too, because also, comparatively speaking, pins are stuck in even now; that though man has now learned to see more clearly than in barbarous ages, he is still far from having learned to act as reason and science would dictate.   But yet you are fully convinced that he will be sure to learn when he gets rid of certain old bad habits, and when common sense and science have completely re-educated human nature and turned it in a normal direction.   You are confident that then man will cease from *intentional* error and, so to say, will be compelled not to want to set his will against his normal interests.   That is not all;   then, you say, science itself will teach man (though to my mind it's a superfluous luxury) that he never has really had any caprice or will of his own, and that he himself is something in the nature of a piano-key or the stop of an organ, and that there are, besides, things called the laws of nature;   so that everything he does is not done by his willing it, but is done by itself, by the laws of nature.   Consequently we have only to discover these laws of nature, and man will no longer have to answer for his actions and life will become exceedingly easy for him.   All human actions will then, of course, be tabulated according to these laws, mathematically, like tables of logarithms up to 108,000, and entered in an index;   or, better still, there would be published certain edifying works in the nature of encyclopedic lexicons, in which everything will be so clearly calculated and explained that there will be no more incidents or adventures in the world.

Then — it is you who are saying all this — new economic relations will be established, all ready-made and worked out with mathematical exactitude, so that every possible question will vanish in the twinkling of an eye, simply because every possible answer to it will be provided. Then will the Palace of Crystal be built.   Then . . . in fact, those will be halcyon days.   Of course, there is no guaranteeing (this is my comment) that it will not be, for instance, frightfully dull then (for what will one have to do when everything will be calculated and tabulated?), but on the other hand everything will be extraordinarily rational.   Of course boredom may lead you to anything.   It is boredom that sets one to sticking golden pins into people, but all that would not matter. What is bad (this is my comment again) is that, I dare say, people will be thankful for the gold pins then.   Man is stupid, you know, phenomenally stupid;   or rather he is not at all stupid, but he is so ungrateful that you could not find his like in all creation.

I, for instance, would not be in the least surprised if all of a sudden, *à propos* of nothing, in the midst of general prosperity, a gentleman with an ignoble, or rather with a reactionary and ironical, countenance were to arise and, putting his arms akimbo, say to us all: "I say, gentlemen, hadn't we better kick over the whole show and scatter rationalism to the winds, simply to send these logarithms to the devil, and to enable us to live once more at our own sweet foolish will?"

That, again, would not matter; but what is annoying is that he would be sure to find followers — such is the nature of man. And all that for the most foolish reason, which, one would think, was hardly worth mentioning: that is, that man everywhere and at all times, whoever he may be, has preferred to act as he chose and not in the least as his reason and advantage dictated. And one may choose what is contrary to one's own interests, and sometimes one *positively ought* (that is my idea). One's own free, unfettered choice, one's own caprice, however wild it may be, one's own fancy worked up at times to frenzy — is that very *most advantageous advantage* which we have overlooked, which comes under no classification and against which all systems and theories are continually being shattered to atoms. And how do these wiseacres know that man wants a normal, a virtuous choice? What has made them conceive that man must want a rationally advantageous choice? What man wants is simply *independent* choice, whatever that independence may cost and wherever it may lead. And a choice, of course, whose nature only the devil knows.

VIII

"Ha! ha! ha! But you know there is no such thing as choice in reality, say what you like," you will interpose with a chuckle. "Science has succeeded in so far analyzing man that we know already that choice and what is called freedom of will is nothing else than —"

Hold on, gentlemen, I meant to begin with that myself. I confess I was rather frightened. I was just going to say that the devil only knows what choice depends on, and that perhaps that was a very good thing, but I remembered the teachings of science — and pulled myself up short. And here you have begun upon it. Indeed, if a formula for all our desires and caprices is really discovered some day — that is, an explanation of what they depend upon, by which laws they arise, how they develop, what they are aiming at in this case and that, and so on, that is, a real mathematical formula — then, most likely, man will at once cease to feel desire; indeed, he will be certain to cease feeling desire. For who would want to choose by rule? Besides, he will at once be transformed from a human being into an organ-stop or something of the sort; for what is a man without desires, without free will and without choice, if not a stop in an organ? What do you think? Let us reckon the chances — can such a thing happen or not?

"H'm!" you decide. "Our choice is usually mistaken from a false view of our advantage. We sometimes choose absolute nonsense because in our foolishness we see in that nonsense the easiest means for attaining a supposed advantage. But when all that is explained and worked out on paper (which is perfectly possible, for it is contemptible and senseless to suppose that some laws of nature man will never understand), then certainly so-called desires will no longer exist. For if a desire should come into conflict with reason we shall then reason and not desire, because it will be impossible, retaining our reason, to be *senseless* in our desires, and in that way knowingly act against reason and desire to injure ourselves. And as all choice and reasoning can be really calculated — because there will some day be discovered the laws of our so-called free will — so, joking apart, there may one day be something like a table constructed of them, so that we really shall choose in accordance with it. If, for instance, some day they calculate and prove to me that I thumbed my nose at someone because I could not help thumbing my nose at him and that I had to do it in that particular way, what *freedom* is left me, especially if I am a learned man and have taken my degree somewhere? Then I should be able to calculate my whole life for thirty years beforehand. In short, if this could be arranged there would be nothing left for us to do; anyway, that would have to be our understanding. And, in fact, we ought unwearyingly to repeat to ourselves that at such and such a time and in such and such circumstances nature does not ask our leave; that we have got to take her as she is and not fashion her to suit our fancy, and if we really aspire to formulas and tables of rules, and — well, even to the chemical retort — there's no help for it, we must accept the retort, too, or else it will be accepted without our consent."

Yes, but here I come to a stop! Gentlemen, you must excuse me for being overphilosophical; it's the result of forty years underground! Allow me to indulge my fancy. You see, gentlemen, reason is an excellent thing, there's no disputing that, but reason is nothing but reason and satisfies only the rational side of man's nature, while will is a manifestation of the whole life, that is, of the whole human life including reason and all the impulses. And although our life, in this manifestation of it, is often worthless, yet it is life and not simply extracting square roots. Here I, for instance, quite naturally want to live, in order to satisfy all my capacities for life, and not simply my capacity for reasoning, that is, not simply one-twentieth of my capacity or life. What does reason know? Reason only knows what it has succeeded in learning (some things, perhaps, it will never learn; this is a poor comfort, but why not say so frankly?), and human nature acts as a whole, with everything that is in it, consciously or unconsciously, and, even if it goes wrong, it still lives on. I suspect, gentlemen, that you're looking at me with compassion; you tell me again that an enlightened and developed man, such, in short, as the future man will be, cannot consciously desire anything disadvantageous to himself, that this can be proved mathematically. I thoroughly agree it can — by mathematicians. But I repeat for the hundredth time, there is one case, one only, when man may consciously, purposely, desire what is injurious to himself, what is stupid, very stupid — simply in order to have the right to desire for himself even what is very stupid and not to be bound by an obligation to desire only what is sensible.

Of course, this very stupid thing, this caprice of ours, may be in reality, gentlemen, more advantageous for us than anything else on earth, especially in certain cases. And in particular it may be more advantageous than any advantage even when it does us obvious harm and contradicts the soundest conclusions of our reason concerning our advantage — for it preserves for us, at any rate, what is most precious and most important — that is, our personality, our individuality. Some, you see, maintain that this really is the most precious thing for mankind; choice, of course, if it chooses, can be in agreement with reason; and especially if the choice be not abused but kept within bounds. It is profitable and sometimes even praiseworthy. But very often, and even most often, choice is utterly and stubbornly opposed to reason . . . and . . . and . . . do you know that that, too, is profitable, sometimes even praiseworthy?

Gentlemen, let us suppose that man is not stupid. (Indeed, one cannot refuse to suppose that, if only from the one consideration, that, if man is stupid, then who is wise?) But if he is not stupid, he is monstrously ungrateful! Phenomenally ungrateful. In fact, I believe that the best definition of man is the ungrateful biped. But that is not all, that is not his worst defect; his worst defect is his perpetual moral obliquity, perpetual — from the days of the Flood to the Schleswig-Holstein period. Moral obliquity and consequently lack of good sense; for it has long been accepted that lack of good sense is due to no other

cause than moral obliquity.   Put it to the test and cast your eyes upon
the history of mankind.   What will you see?   Is it a grand spectacle?
Grand, if you like.   Take the Colossus of Rhodes, for instance, that's
worth something.   With good reason Mr. Anaevski testifies of it that
some say that it is the work of man's hands, while others maintain that
it has been created by nature herself.   Is history motley with many
colors?   Maybe it is, at that: if you take the dress uniforms, military and
civilian, of all peoples in all ages — that alone is worth something, and
if you take the undress uniforms you'll never get to the end of the
thing; no historian would be equal to the job.   Is it monotonous?   Maybe it's monotonous, too: it's all fighting and fighting; they are fighting
now, they fought first and they fought last — you will admit that it's
almost too monotonous.

In short, one may say anything about the history of the world —
anything that might enter the most disordered imagination.   The only
thing you can't say is that it's rational.   The very word sticks in your
throat.   And, indeed, this is the odd thing that is continually happening:
there are continually turning up in life moral and rational persons,
sages and lovers of humanity, who make it their object to live all their
lives as morally and rationally as possible, to be, so to speak, a light
to their neighbors simply in order to show them that it is possible to
live morally and rationally in this world.   And yet we all know that
those very people sooner or later have been false to themselves, playing
some queer trick, often a most unseemly one.   Now I ask you: what
can be expected of man since he is a being endowed with such strange
qualities?   Shower upon him every earthly blessing, drown him in a
sea of happiness, so that nothing but bubbles of bliss can be seen on
the surface; give him economic prosperity, such that he should have
nothing else to do but sleep, live on cakes and ale and busy himself
with the continuation of his species, and even then out of sheer ingratitude, sheer spite, man would play you some nasty trick.   He would
even risk his cakes and ale and would deliberately desire the most
fatal rubbish, the most uneconomical absurdity, simply to introduce
into all this positive good sense his fatal fantastic element.   It is just his
fantastic dreams, his vulgar folly, that he will desire to retain, simply
in order to prove to himself — as though that were so necessary — that
men still are men and not the keys of a piano, which the laws of nature
threaten to control so completely that soon one will not be able to
desire anything but by the calendar.   And that is not all: even if man
really were nothing but a piano-key, even if this were proved to him

by natural science and mathematics, even then he would not become reasonable, but would purposely do something perverse out of simple ingratitude, simply to gain his point. And if he does not find means he will contrive destruction and chaos, will contrive sufferings of all sorts, only to gain his point! He will launch a curse upon the world, and as only man can curse (it is his privilege, the primary distinction between him and other animals), maybe by his curse alone he will attain his object — that is, convince himself that he is a man and not a piano-key! If you say that all this, too, can be calculated and tabulated — chaos and darkness and curses, so that the mere possibility of calculating it all beforehand would stop it all, and reason would reassert itself — then man would purposely go mad in order to be rid of reason and gain his point! I believe in it, I answer for it, for the whole work of man really seems to consist in nothing but proving to himself every minute that he is a man and not a piano-key! It may be at the cost of his skin, it may be by cannibalism! And this being so, can one help being tempted to rejoice that it has not yet come off, and that desire still depends on something we don't know?

You will scream at me (that is, if you condescend to do so) that no one is touching my free will, that all they are concerned with is that my will should of itself, of its own free will, coincide with my own normal interests, with the laws of nature and arithmetic.

Good Heavens, gentlemen, what sort of free will is left when we come to tabulation and arithmetic, when it will all be a case of two times two making four? Two times two makes four without my will. As if free will meant that!

IX

Gentlemen, I am joking, and I know myself that my jokes are not brilliant, but you know one can't take everything as a joke. I am, perhaps, jesting against the grain. Gentlemen, I am tormented by questions; answer them for me. You, for instance, want to cure men of their old habits and reform their will in accordance with science and good sense. But how do you know, not only that it is possible, but also that it is *desirable*, to reform man in that way? And what leads you to the conclusion that man's inclinations *need* reforming? In short, how do you know that such a reformation will be a benefit to man? And to go to the root of the matter — why are you so positively convinced that not to act against his real normal interests as guaranteed by the conclusions of reason and arithmetic is certainly always advantageous for man, and must always be a law for mankind? So far, you know, this is only your supposition. It may be the law of logic, but not the law of humanity. You think, gentlemen, perhaps that I am mad? Allow me to defend myself. I agree that man is pre-eminently a creative animal, predestined to strive consciously for an object and to engage in engineering — that is, incessantly and eternally to make new roads, *wherever they may lead.* But the reason why he wants sometimes to go off at a tangent may be precisely because he is *predestined* to make the road, and perhaps, too, that however stupid the straightforward practical man may be, the thought sometimes will occur to him that the road almost always does lead *somewhere,* and that the destination it leads to is less important than the process of making it, and that the chief thing is to save the well-conducted child from despising engineering, and so giving way to fatal idleness, which, as we all know, is the mother of all the vices.

Man likes to make roads and to create, that's a fact beyond dispute. But why has he such a passionate love for destruction and chaos also? Tell me that! But on that point I want to say a couple of words myself. May it not be that he loves chaos and destruction (there can be no disputing that he does sometimes love them) because he is instinctively afraid of attaining his object and completing the edifice he is constructing? Who knows, perhaps he only loves that edifice from a distance, and is by no means in love with it at close quarters; perhaps he only loves building it and does not want to live in it, but will leave it, when completed, for the use of *les animaux domestiques* — such as the ants, the sheep, and so on. Now the ants have quite a different taste. They have a marvelous edifice of that pattern which endures forever — the ant heap.

With the ant heap the respectable race of ants began and with the ant heap it will probably end, which does the greatest credit to the perseverance and good sense of ants. But man is a frivolous and ludicrous creature, and perhaps, like a chess player, loves the process of the game, not the end of it. And who knows (there is no saying this with certainty), perhaps the only goal on earth to which mankind is striving lies in this incessant process of attaining (in other words, in life itself), and not in the thing to be attained, which must always be expressed as a formula, as positive as that two times two makes four, and such positiveness is not life, gentlemen, but is the beginning of death. Anyway, man has always been afraid of this mathematical certainty, and I am afraid of it now. Granted man does nothing but seek that mathematical certainty, he traverses oceans, he sacrifices his life in the quest; but I assure you, he dreads to succeed, really to find it. He feels that when he has found it there will be nothing for him to look for. When workmen have finished their work they do at least receive their pay, they go to the tavern, then they are taken to the police station — and there is occupation for a week. But where can man go? Anyway, one can observe a certain awkwardness about him when he has attained such objects. He loves the process of attaining, but does not quite like to have attained, and that, of course, is very absurd. In fact, man is a comical creature; there seems to be a kind of jest in it all. But yet mathematical certainty is, after all, something insufferable. Two times two making four seems to me simply a piece of insolence. Two times two making four is a pert coxcomb who stands with arms akimbo barring your path and spitting. I admit that two times two making four is an excellent thing, but if we are to give everything its due, two times two making five is sometimes a very charming thing, too.

And why are you so firmly, so triumphantly convinced that only the normal and the positive — in other words, only what is conducive to welfare — is for the advantage of man? Is not reason in error as regards advantage? Does not man, perhaps, love something besides well-being? Perhaps he is just as fond of suffering? Perhaps suffering is just as great a benefit to him as well-being? Man is sometimes extraordinarily, passionately in love with suffering, and that's a fact. There is no need to appeal to universal history to prove that; only ask yourself, if you are a man and have lived at all. As far as my personal opinion is concerned, to care only for well-being seems to me positively ill-bred. Whether it's good or bad, it is sometimes very pleasant, too, to smash things. I hold no brief for suffering nor for well-being either. I am standing for . . . my caprice, and for its being guaranteed to me when necessary. Suffering would be out of place in musical comedies, for instance; I know that. In the Palace of Crystal it is unthinkable; suffering means doubt, negation, and what would be the good of a *palace of crystal* if there could be any doubt about it? And yet I think man will never renounce real suffering, that is, destruction and chaos. Why, suffering is the sole origin of consciousness. Though I did lay it down at the beginning that consciousness is the greatest misfortune for man, yet I know man prizes it and would not give it up for any satisfaction. Consciousness, for instance, is infinitely superior to two times two making four. Once you have mathematical certainty there is nothing left to do or to understand. There will be nothing left but to bottle up your five senses and plunge into contemplation. While if you stick to consciousness, even though the same result is attained, you can at least flog yourself at times, and that will, at any rate, liven you up. Reactionary as it is, corporal punishment is better than nothing.

X

You believe in a *palace of crystal* that can never be destroyed — a palace at which one will not be able to put out one's tongue or thumb one's nose on the sly. And perhaps that is just why I am afraid of this edifice, that it is of crystal, and can never be destroyed, and that one can't put one's tongue out at it even on the sly.

You see, if it were not a palace, but a henhouse, I might creep into it to avoid getting wet, and yet I would not call the henhouse a palace out of gratitude to it for keeping me dry. You laugh and say that in such circumstances a henhouse is as good as a mansion. Yes, I answer, if one had to live simply to keep out of the rain.

But what is to be done if I have taken it into my head that that is not the only object in life, and that if one must live one had better live in a mansion? That is my choice, my desire. You will only eradicate it when you have changed my preference. Well, do change it, allure me with something else, give me another ideal. But meanwhile I will not take a henhouse for a mansion. The *palace of crystal* may be an idle dream, it may be that it is inconsistent with the laws of nature and that I have invented it only through my own stupidity, through the old-fashioned irrational habits of my generation. But what does it matter to me that it is inconsistent? That makes no difference, since it exists in my desires, or rather exists as long as my desires exist. Perhaps you are laughing again? Laugh away; I will put up with any mockery rather than pretend that I am sated when I am hungry. I know, anyway, that I will not be put off with a compromise, with a recurring zero, simply because it is consistent with the laws of nature and actually exists. I will not accept as the crown of my desires a block of slum tenements on a lease of a thousand years, and perhaps with a signboard of a dentist hanging out. Destroy my desires, eradicate my ideals, show me something better, and I will follow you. You will say, perhaps, that it is not worth your trouble; but in that case I can give you the same answer. We are discussing things seriously; but if you won't deign to give me your attention, I'll drop your acquaintance. I can retreat into my underground hole.

But while I am alive and have desires I would rather my hand were withered off than bring one brick to such a building! Don't remind me that I have just rejected the *palace of crystal* for the sole reason that one cannot put out one's tongue at it. I did not say that because I am so fond of putting my tongue out. Perhaps the thing I resented was that of all your edifices there has not been one at which one could not put out one's tongue. On the contrary, I would let my tongue be cut off out of gratitude if things could be so arranged that I should lose all desire to put it out. It's not my fault that things cannot be so arranged, and that one must be satisfied with model flats. Then why am I made with such desires? Can I have been constructed simply in order to come to the conclusion that all my construction is a cheat? Can this be my whole purpose? I do not believe it.

But do you know what? I'm convinced that we underground folk ought to be kept in check. Though we may sit forty years underground without speaking, when we do come out into the light of day and break out we talk and talk *and* talk . . .

XI

The long and the short of it is, gentlemen, that it's better to do nothing! Better conscious inertia! And so hurrah for the underground! Though I have said that I envy the normal man to the last drop of my bile, yet I should not care to be in his place such as he is now (though I shall not cease envying him). No, no; anyway, the underground life is more advantageous. There, at any rate, one can. . . . Oh, but even now I'm lying! I'm lying because I know myself that it is not the underground that is better, but something different, quite different, for which I am thirsting, but which I cannot find. Damn the underground!

I will tell you another thing that would be better, and that is, if I myself believed in anything of what I have just written. I swear to you, gentlemen, there is not one thing, not one word of what I have written that I really believe. That is, I believe it, perhaps, but at the same time I feel and suspect that I am lying like a politician.

"Then why have you written all this?" you will say to me.

"I ought to put you underground for forty years without anything to do and then come to you in your cellar, to find out what stage you have reached! How can a man be left with nothing to do for forty years?"

"Isn't that shameful, isn't that humiliating?" You will say, perhaps, wagging your heads contemptuously. "You thirst for life and try to settle the problems of life by a logical tangle. And how persistent, how insolent are your sallies, and at the same time what a fright you are in! You spout nonsense and are pleased with it; you say impudent things and are in continual alarm and apologizing for them. You declare that you are afraid of nothing and at the same time try to ingratiate yourself in our good opinion. You declare that you are gnashing your teeth and at the same time you try to be witty so as to amuse us. You know that your witticisms are not witty, but you are evidently well satisfied with their literary value. You may, perhaps, have really suffered, but you have no respect for your own suffering. You may have sincerity, but you have no modesty; out of the pettiest vanity you expose your sincerity to publicity and ignominy. You doubtless mean to say something but hide your last word through fear, because you haven't the resolution to utter it and have only a cowardly impudence. You boast of consciousness, but you are not sure of your ground, for though your mind works, yet your heart is darkened and corrupt, and you cannot have a full, genuine consciousness without a pure heart. And how intrusive you are, how you insist and grimace! Lies, lies, lies!"

Of course I have myself made up all the things you say. That, too, is of the underground. I have been for forty years listening to you through a crack under the floor. I have invented them myself, there was nothing else I could invent. It is no wonder that I have learned it all by heart and it has taken a literary form.

But can you really be so credulous as to think that I will print all this and give it to you to read, too? And another problem: Why do I call you "gentlemen," why do I address you as though you really were my readers? Such confessions as I intend to make are never printed nor given to other people to read. Anyway, I am not strong-minded enough for that, and I don't see why I should be. But, you see, a fancy has struck me and I want to realize it at all costs. Let me explain.

Every man has reminiscences which he would not tell to everyone, but only to his friends. He has other matters in his mind which he would not reveal even to his friends, but only to himself, and that in secret. But there are other things which a man is afraid to tell even to himself, and every decent man has a number of such things stored away in his mind. The more decent he is, the greater the number of such things in his mind. Anyway, I have only lately determined to remember some of my early adventures. Till now I have always avoided them, even with a certain uneasiness. Now, when I am not only recalling them, but have actually decided to write an account of them,

I want to try the experiment whether one can, even with oneself, be perfectly open and not take fright at the whole truth. I will observe, in parenthesis, that Heine says that a true autobiography is almost an impossibility, and that man is bound to lie about himself. He considers that Rousseau certainly told lies about himself in his *Confessions*, and even intentionally lied, out of vanity. I am convinced that Heine is right; I quite understand how sometimes one may, out of sheer vanity, attribute regular crimes to oneself, and indeed I can very well conceive that kind of vanity. But Heine judged of people who made their confessions to the public. I write only for myself, and I wish to declare once and for all that if I write as though I were addressing readers, that is simply because it is easier for me to write in that form. It is a form, an empty form — I'll never have readers. I have made this plain already.

I don't wish to be hampered by any restrictions in the compilation of my notes. I shall not attempt any system or method. I will jot things down as I remember them.

But here, perhaps, someone will catch at the word and ask me: "If you really don't reckon on readers, why do you make such compacts with yourself — and on paper, too — as that you won't attempt any system or method, that you'll jot things down as you remember them, and so on, and so on? Why the explanations? Why the apologies?"

"There, now!" I answer.

There is a whole psychology in all this, though. Perhaps it is simply that I am a coward. And perhaps that I purposely imagine an audience before me in order that I may be more dignified while I write. There are perhaps thousands of reasons. Again, what precisely is my object in writing? If it is not for the benefit of the public why should I not simply recall these incidents in my own mind without putting them on paper?

Quite so; but yet it is more imposing on paper. There's something more impressive about it; I'll be better able to criticize myself and improve my style. Besides, I may obtain actual relief from writing. Today, for instance, I'm particularly oppressed by one memory of a distant past. It came back vividly to my mind a few days ago, and has remained haunting me like an annoying tune that one cannot get rid of. And yet get rid of it I must, somehow. I have hundreds of such reminiscences; but at times some one of them stands out from a hundred others and oppresses me. For some reason I believe that if I wrote it down I'd get rid of it. Why not try?

Besides, I'm bored, and I never have anything to do. Writing will be a sort of work.   They say work makes man kindhearted and honest. Well, here is a chance for me, anyway.

Snow is falling today, yellow and dingy.   It fell yesterday, too, as well as a few days ago.   I fancy it is the wet snow that has reminded me of that incident which I cannot shake off now.   And so let it be a story *à propos* of the falling snow.

Part II — A propos of the Wet Snow

From out dark error's subjugation
My words of passionate exhortation
　　Had wrenched thy fainting spirit free;
And writhing prone in thine affliction
Thou didst recall with malediction
　　The vice that had encompassed thee:
And then, thy slumbering conscience fretting
　　From recollection's torturing flame,
Thou didst reveal the hideous setting
　　Of thy life's current ere I came;
And suddenly I saw thee sicken,
　　And weeping, hide thine anguished face,
Revolted, maddened, horror-stricken,
　　At memories of foul disgrace.

　　　　　　　　　　　　　　NECRASSOV

I

AT that time I was only twenty-four.   My life was even then gloomy, ill-regulated, and as solitary as that of a savage.   I made friends with no one and positively avoided speech, burying myself more and more in my hole.   At work in the office I never looked at anyone, and I was perfectly well aware that my companions looked upon me not only as a queer fellow, but even — I always fancied this — with a sort of loathing.   I sometimes wondered why it was that nobody else fancied that he was looked upon with aversion.   One of the clerks had a most repulsive, pock-marked face, which looked positively villainous.   I believe I should not have dared to look at anyone with such an unsightly countenance.   Another had such a very dirty old uniform that there was an unpleasant odor in his proximity.   Yet neither of these gentlemen showed in any way the slightest self-consciousness, either about his clothes or his countenance or his character.   Neither of them ever imagined that he was looked at with disgust; if they had imagined it they would not have minded — so long as their superiors did not look at them in that way.

It is clear to me now that, owing to my unbounded vanity and to the high standard I set for myself, I often looked at myself with furious discontent, which verged on loathing, and so I inwardly attributed the same feeling to everyone. I hated my face, for instance: I thought it disgusting, and even suspected that there was something base in my expression, and so every day when I turned up at the office I tried to behave as independently as possible and to assume a lofty expression, so that I might not be suspected of being abject. "My face may be ugly," I thought, "but let it be lofty, expressive, and, above all, *extremely* intelligent." But I was positively and painfully certain that it was impossible for my countenance ever to express those qualities. And what was worst of all, I thought it actually stupid-looking, and I would have been quite satisfied if I could have looked intelligent. In fact, I would even have put up with looking base if, at the same time, my face could have been thought strikingly intelligent.

Of course, I hated my fellow clerks one and all, and I despised them all, yet at the same time I was, as it were, afraid of them. In fact, it happened at times that I thought more highly of them than of myself. It somehow happened quite suddenly that I alternated between despising them and thinking them superior to myself. A cultivated and decent man cannot be vain without setting a fearfully high standard for himself, and without despising and almost hating himself at certain moments. But whether I despised them or thought them superior, I dropped my eyes almost every time I met anyone. I even made experiments whether I could face so-and-so's looking at me, and I was always the first to drop my eyes. This worried me to distraction. I had a sickly dread, too, of being ridiculous, and so had a slavish passion for the conventional in everything external. I loved to fall into the common rut and had a wholehearted terror of any kind of eccentricity in myself. But how could I live up to it? I was morbidly sensitive, as a man of our age should be. They were all stupid and as like one another as so many sheep. Perhaps I was the only one in the office who fancied that I was a coward and a slave, and I fancied it just because I was more highly developed. But it was not only that I fancied it, it really was so. I *was* a coward and a slave. I say this without the slightest embarrassment. Every decent man of our age must be a coward and a slave. That is his normal condition. Of that I am firmly convinced. He is made and constructed to that very end. And not only at the present time, owing to certain casual circumstances, but always, at all times, a decent man is bound to be a coward and a slave. It is the law of nature for all decent people all over the earth. If any one of them happens to be valiant about something, he need not be comforted nor carried away by that; he would show the white feather just the same before something else. That's how it invariably and inevitably ends. Only donkeys and mules are valiant, and then only till they are up against the wall. It's not worth while to pay attention to them, for they really don't count.

Another circumstance, too, worried me in those days: that there was no one like me and that I was not like anyone else. "I am unique, but they are like all," I thought — and pondered.

From which it's evident that I was still a youngster.

Sometimes the very opposite would happen. It was loathsome sometimes to go to the office; things reached such a point that I often came home ill. But all at once, *à propos* of nothing, there would come a phase of skepticism and indifference (everything happened in phases to me), and I myself would laugh at my intolerance and fastidiousness, I would reproach myself with being *romantic*. At one time I was unwilling to speak to anyone, while at other times I would not merely talk with people but go to the extent of contemplating friendship with them. All my fastidiousness would suddenly, without rhyme or reason, vanish. Who knows, perhaps I never had really had it, and it had simply been affected and gotten out of books. I haven't decided that question even up to now. Once I actually made friends with them, visited their homes, played cards, drank vodka, talked of promotions. But here let me make a digression.

We Russians, speaking generally, have never had those foolish transcendental *romantics* (German, and still more, French) on whom nothing produces any effect; if there were an earthquake, if all France perished at the barricades, the French *romantics* would still be the same, they would not even have the decency to affect a change, but would still go on singing their transcendental songs to the hour of their death, because they are fools. We, in Russia, have no fools; that's something everybody knows well. That's what distinguishes our land from others. Consequently these transcendental natures are not found amongst us in their pure form. The idea that they are so found is due to our *realistic* journalists and critics of the day, always on the lookout for Kostanzhoglos and Uncle Peter Ivanichs and foolishly accepting them as our ideal; they have slandered our *romantics*, taking them for the same transcendental sort as in Germany or France. On the contrary, the characteristics of our *romantics* are absolutely and directly opposed to the transcendental European type, and no European standard can be applied to them. (Allow me to make use of this word *romantic* — an old-fashioned and much-respected word which has done good service and is familiar to all.) The characteristics of our *romantic* are to understand everything, *to see everything and to see it often incomparably more clearly than our most realistic minds see it;* to refuse to accept anyone or anything, but at the same time not to despise anything; to give way, to yield, from policy; never to lose sight of a useful practical object (such as rent-free quarters at the government expense, pensions, decorations), to keep an eye on that object through all the enthusiasms and volumes of lyrical poems, and at the same time to preserve *the good and the beautiful* inviolate within them to the hour of their death, and to preserve themselves also, incidentally, like some precious jewel wrapped in cotton wool, if only for the benefit of *the good and the beautiful.* Our *romantic* is a man of great breadth and the greatest rogue of all our rogues, I assure you. I can assure you of that from experience, indeed. Of course, that is, if he is intelligent. But what am I saying? The *romantic* is always intelligent, and I only meant to observe that although we have had foolish romantics they don't count, and they were foolish only because in the flower of their youth they degenerated into Germans and, to preserve their precious jewel more comfortably, settled somewhere out there — by preference in Weimar or the Black Forest.

I, for instance, genuinely despised my official work and did not openly abuse it simply because I was in it myself and got a salary out of it. Anyway, take note, I did not openly abuse it. Our *romantic* would rather go out of his mind — a thing, however, which very rarely happens — than take to open abuse, unless he had some other career in view; and he is never kicked out. At most, they would take him to the lunatic asylum as "the King of Spain" if he should go very mad. But it is only the slim, fair-haired lads who go out of their minds in Russia. Innumerable *romantics* attain later in life to considerable rank in the Service. Their many-sidedness is remarkable! And what a faculty they have for the most contradictory sensations! I was comforted by this thought even in those days, and I am of the same opinion now. That is why there are so many *broad natures* among us who never lose their ideal even in the depths of degradation; and though they never stir a finger for their ideal, though they are arrant thieves and knaves, yet they tearfully cherish their first ideal and are extraordinarily honest at heart. Yes, it is only among us that the most incorrigible rogue can be absolutely and loftily honest at heart without in the least ceasing to be a rogue. I repeat, our *romantics*, frequently, become such accomplished rascals (I use the term *rascals* affectionately), suddenly display such a sense of reality and practical knowledge, that their bewildered superiors and the public generally can only ejaculate in amazement.

Their many-sidedness is really amazing, and goodness knows what it may develop into later on, and what the future has in store for us. It is not a poor material! I do not say this from any foolish or boastful patriotism. But I feel sure that you are again imagining that I am joking. Or perhaps it's just the contrary, and you are convinced that I really think so. Anyway, gentlemen, I shall welcome both views as an honor and a special favor. And do forgive my digression.

I did not, of course, maintain friendly relations with my comrades and soon was at loggerheads with them, and in my youth and inexperience I even gave up bowing to them, as though I had cut off all relations. That, however, only happened to me once. As a rule, I was always alone.

In the first place I spent most of my time at home, reading. I tried to stifle all that was continually seething within me by means of external impressions. And the only external means I had was reading. Reading, of course, was a great help — stirring me, giving me pleasure and pain. Yet at times it bored me fearfully. One longed for movement in spite of everything, and I plunged all at once into dark, underground, loathsome vice of the pettiest kind. My wretched passions were acute, smarting, from my continual, sickly irritability. I had hysterical impulses, accompanied by tears and convulsions. I had no resource except reading — that is, there was nothing in my surroundings which I could respect and which attracted me. I was overwhelmed with depression, too; I had an hysterical craving for incongruity and for contrast, and so I took to vice. I have not said all this to justify myself. . . . But, no — I'm lying. I did want to justify myself. I made that little observation for my own benefit, gentlemen. I don't want to lie. I vowed to myself I wouldn't.

And so, furtively, timidly, in solitude, at night, I indulged in filthy vice, with a feeling of shame which never deserted me, even at the most loathsome moments, and which at such moments nearly made me curse. Already even then I had my underground world in my soul. I was fearfully afraid of being seen, of being met, of being recognized. I visited various obscure haunts.

One night as I was passing a tavern I saw through a lighted window some gentlemen fighting with billiard cues, and saw one of them thrown out of a window. At other times I should have felt very much disgusted, but I was in such a mood at the time that I actually envied the gentleman thrown out of a window — and I envied him so much that I even went into the tavern and into the billiard room. "Perhaps," I thought, "I'll have a fight, too, and they'll throw me out of a window."

I wasn't drunk — but what is one to do? Depression will drive a man to such a pitch of hysteria! But nothing happened. It seemed that I was not even up to being thrown out of a window, and I went away without having had my fight.

An officer put me in my place from the first moment.

I was standing by the billiard table and in my ignorance blocking up the way, and he wanted to pass; he took me by the shoulders and without a word — without a warning or explanation — thrust me from where I was standing to another spot and passed by as though he had not noticed me. I could have forgiven blows, but I could not forgive his having thrust me aside without noticing me.

The devil knows what I would have given for a real, regular quarrel — a more decent, a more *literary* one, so to speak. I had been treated like a fly. This officer was over six feet, while I was a spindly little fellow. But the quarrel was in my hands. I had only to protest and I certainly would have been thrown out of a window. But I changed my mind and preferred to beat a resentful retreat.

From the tavern I went straight home, confused and troubled, and the next night I went out again with the same lewd intentions, still more furtively, abjectly and miserably than before, as it were, with tears in my eyes — but still I did go out again. Don't imagine, though, it was cowardice which made me slink away from the officer: I never have been a coward at heart, though I have always been a coward in action. Don't be in a hurry to laugh — I assure you I can explain it all.

Oh, if only that officer had been one of the sort who would consent to fight a duel! But no, he was one of those gentlemen (alas, long extinct!) who preferred fighting with cues or, like Gogol's Lieutenant Pirogov, appealing to the police. They did not fight duels and would have thought a duel with a civilian like me an utterly unseemly procedure in any case — and they looked upon the duel altogether as something impossible, something freethinking and French. But they were quite ready to bully, especially when they were over six feet.

I did not slink away through cowardice, but through an unbounded vanity. I was afraid not of his six-foot height, nor of getting a sound

thrashing and being thrown out of a window; I should have had physical courage enough, I assure you; but I hadn't the moral courage.
What I was afraid of was that everyone present, from the insolent marker
down to the lowest little stinking, pimply clerk in a greasy collar, would
jeer at me and fail to understand when I began to protest and to address
them in literary language. For of the point of honor — not of honor,
but of the point of honor (*point d'honneur*) — one cannot speak among
us except in literary language. You can't allude to the *point of honor*
in ordinary language. I was fully convinced (the sense of reality, in
spite of all my romanticism!) that they would all simply split their sides
with laughter, and that the officer would not simply beat me (that is,
without insulting me), but would certainly give me his knee in the back,
kick me round the billiard table, and only then, perhaps, have pity and
drop me out of a window.

Of course, for me this trivial incident could not end in that. I often
met that officer afterward in the street and noticed him very carefully.
I'm not quite sure whether he recognized me; I imagine not. I judge
from certain signs. But I — I stared at him with spite and hatred, and
so it went on — for several years! My resentment grew even deeper with
the years. At first I began making stealthy inquiries about this officer.
It was difficult for me to do so, for I knew no one. But one day I heard
someone shout his last name in the street as I was following him at a
distance, as though I were tied to him — and so I learned his last name.
Another time I followed him to his flat, and for a small silver coin
learned from the janitor where he lived, on which floor, whether he
lived alone or with others, and so on — in fact, everything one could
learn from a janitor. One morning, though I had never tried my hand
with the pen, it suddenly occurred to me to write a satire on this officer
in the form of a novel which would unmask his villainy. I wrote the
novel with relish. I did unmask his villainy, I even exaggerated it; at
first I so altered his last name that it could easily be recognized, but
on second thoughts I changed it and sent the story to *Notes of the
Fatherland*. But at that time such attacks were not the fashion and my
story was not printed. Which was a great vexation to me.

Sometimes I was positively choked with resentment. At last I determined to challenge my enemy to a duel. I composed a splendid,
charming letter to him, imploring him to apologize to me and hinting
rather plainly at a duel in case of refusal. The letter was so composed
that if the officer had had the least understanding of the good and the
beautiful he would certainly have flung himself on my neck and have

offered me his friendship. And how fine that would have been! How we should have got on together! "He could have shielded me with his higher rank, while I could have improved his mind with my culture, and, well . . . my ideas; and all sorts of things might have happened." Just imagine, this was two years after his insult to me, and my challenge would have been a ridiculous anachronism, in spite of all the ingenuity of my letter in disguising and explaining away the anachronism. But, thank God (to this day I thank the Almighty with tears in my eyes), I did not send the letter to him. Cold shivers run down my back when I think of what might have happened if I had sent it.

And all at once I revenged myself in the simplest way, by a stroke of genius! A brilliant thought suddenly dawned upon me. Sometimes on holidays I used to stroll along the sunny side of the Nevski Prospect about four o'clock in the afternoon. Though it was hardly a stroll so much as a series of innumerable miseries, humiliations and resentments; but no doubt that was just what I wanted. I used to squirm along in a most unseemly fashion, like an eel, continually moving aside to make way for generals, for officers of the guards and hussars, or for ladies. At such moments there used to be a convulsive twinge at my heart, and I used to feel hot all down my back at the mere thought of the wretchedness of my attire, of the wretchedness and abjectness of my little scurrying figure. This was a regular martyrdom; a continual, intolerable humiliation at the thought, which passed into an incessant and direct sensation, that I was a mere fly in the eyes of all this world, a nasty, disgusting fly — more intelligent, more highly developed, more refined in feeling than any of them, of course — but a fly that was continually making way for everyone, insulted and injured by everyone. Why I inflicted this torture upon myself, why I went to the Nevski Prospect, I don't know. I felt simply drawn there at every possible opportunity.

Already then I began to experience a rush of the enjoyment of which I spoke in the first chapter. After my affair with the officer I felt even more drawn there than before: it was on the Nevski Prospect that I met him most frequently; there I could admire him. He, too, went there chiefly on holidays. He, too, turned out of his path for generals and persons of high rank, and he, too, squirmed in and out among them like an eel; but people like me, or even those better dressed, yet like me, he simply walked over; he made straight for them as though there was nothing but empty space before him, and never, under any circumstances, turned aside. I gloated over my resentment, watching him and

— always made way for him resentfully.   It exasperated me that even in the street I could not be on an even footing with him.

"Why must you invariably be the first to move aside?"   I kept asking myself in hysterical rage, waking up sometimes at three o'clock in the morning.   "Why you and not he?   There's no regulation about it; there's no written law.   Let there be equality about making way, as there usually is when refined people meet: he moves halfway and you move halfway; you pass with mutual respect."

But that never happened, and I always moved aside, while he didn't as much as notice my making way for him.   And lo and behold, a bright idea dawned upon me!   "What," I thought, "if I meet him and don't move to one side?   What if I don't move aside on purpose, even if I bump against him?   How would that do?"   This audacious idea took such a hold on me that it gave me no peace.   I was dreaming of it continually, horribly, and I purposely went more frequently to the Nevski Prospect in order to picture more vividly how I should do it when I did do it.   I was delighted.   This intention seemed to me more and more practical and feasible.

"Of course I won't really jostle him," I thought, already more good-natured in my joy.   "I simply won't turn aside, will run up against him, not very violently, but merely shouldering him — just as much as decency permits.   I'll jostle against him just as much as he jostles against me."   At last I made up my mind completely.   But my preparations took a great deal of time.   To begin with, when I carried out my plan I'd have to look rather more decent, and so I had to think of my getup. "In case of emergency, if, for instance, there were any sort of public scandal (and the public there is of the most *recherché*: the Countess walks there; Prince D — walks there; all the literary world is there), I must be well dressed; that inspires respect and of itself puts us on an equal footing in the eyes of society."

With this object I asked for some of my salary in advance and bought at Churkin's a pair of black gloves and a decent hat.   Black gloves seemed to me both more dignified and *bon ton* than the lemon-colored ones which I had contemplated at first.   "The color is too gaudy; it looks as though one were trying to be conspicuous," and I did not take the lemon-colored ones.   I had got ready long beforehand a good shirt, with white bone studs; my overcoat was the only thing that held me back. The coat in itself was a very good one, it kept me warm; but it was quilted and it had a raccoon collar, which was the height of vulgarity. I had to change the collar at any sacrifice, and get one of beaver, like an officer's. For this purpose I began visiting the Drapers' Row and after several attempts I decided upon some cheap German beaver. Though German beaver soon grows stagey and looks wretched, yet at first it looks exceedingly well, and I only needed it for one occasion. I asked the price; even so, it was too expensive. After thinking it over thoroughly I decided to sell my raccoon collar; the rest of the sum (a considerable one for me) I decided to borrow from Anton Antonich Syetochkin, my immediate superior, an unassuming person, though grave and judicious. He never lent money to anyone, but I had, on entering the service, been specially recommended to him by an important personage who had got me my job. I was horribly worried. To borrow from Anton Antonich seemed to me monstrous and shameful. I did not sleep for two or three nights. Indeed, I did not sleep well at that time, I was in a fever; I had a vague sinking at my heart or else a sudden throbbing, throbbing, throbbing! Anton Antonich was surprised at first, then he frowned, then he reflected, and after all lent me the money, receiving from me a written authorization to take from my salary a fortnight later the sum that he had lent me.

In this way everything was at last ready. The handsome beaver replaced the mean-looking raccoon, and I began by degrees to get ready for action. It would never have done to act offhand, at random; the plan had to be carried out skillfully, by degrees. But I must confess that after many efforts I began to despair: we simply could not run into each other. I made every preparation, I was quite determined — it seemed as though we should run into one another directly — and before I knew what I was doing I had stepped aside for him again and he had passed without noticing me. I even prayed as I approached him that God would grant me determination. One time I had made up my mind thoroughly, but it ended in my stumbling and falling at his feet because at the very last instant when I was only six inches from him my courage failed me. He very calmly stepped over me, while I flew to one side like a ball. That night I was ill again, feverish and delirious.

And suddenly it ended most happily. The night before I had made up my mind not to carry out my fatal plan and to abandon it all, and with that object I went to the Nevski Prospect for the last time, just to see how I would abandon it all. Suddenly, three paces from my enemy, I unexpectedly made up my mind — I closed my eyes, and we ran full tilt, shoulder to shoulder, against one another! I did not budge an inch and passed him on a perfectly equal footing! He did not even look round and pretended not to notice it; but he was only pretending,

I am convinced of that. I am convinced of that to this day! Of course, I got the worst of it — he was stronger, but that was not the point. The point was that I had attained my object; I had kept up my dignity, I had not yielded a step and had put myself publicly on an equal social footing with him. I returned home feeling that I was fully avenged for everything. I was delighted. I was triumphant and sang Italian arias. Of course, I will not describe to you what happened to me three days later; if you have read my first chapter you can guess that for yourself. The officer was afterwards transferred; I have not seen him now for fourteen years. What is the dear fellow doing now? Whom is he trampling now?

II

But the period of my dissipation would end, and I always felt very sick afterward. It was followed by remorse — I tried to drive it away: I felt too sick. By degrees, however, I grew used to that, too. I grew used to everything, or rather I voluntarily resigned myself to enduring it. But I had a means of escape that reconciled everything — that was to find refuge in *the good and the beautiful* — in dreams, of course. I was a terrible dreamer, I would dream for three months on end, tucked away in my corner, and you may believe me that at those moments I had no resemblance to the gentleman who, in his chickenhearted perturbation, had put a collar of German beaver on his overcoat. I suddenly became a hero. I would not have admitted my six-foot lieutenant even if he had called on me. I could not even picture him before me then. What were my dreams and how could I satisfy myself with them? It is hard to say now, but at the time I was satisfied with them. Though, indeed, even now, I am to some extent satisfied with them.

Dreams were particularly sweet and vivid after a spell of dissipation; they came with remorse and with tears, with curses and transports. There were moments of such positive intoxication, of such happiness, that there was not the faintest trace of irony within me, on my honor. I had faith, hope, love. I believed blindly at such times that by some miracle, by some external circumstance, all this would suddenly open out, expand; that suddenly a vista of suitable activity — beneficent, good, and, above all, *ready-made* (what sort of activity I had no idea, but the great thing was that it should be all ready for me) — would rise up before me — and I should come out into the light of day, well-nigh riding a white horse and crowned with laurel. Anything but the foremost place I could not conceive for myself, and for that very reason, in reality, I quite contentedly occupied the lowest. Either to be a hero or to grovel in the mud — there was nothing between. That was my ruin, for when I was in the mud I comforted myself with the thought that at other times I was a hero, and the hero was a cloak for the mud; for an ordinary man it was shameful to defile himself, but a hero was too lofty to be utterly defiled, and so he might defile himself. It is worth noting that these attacks of *the good and the beautiful* visited me even during the period of dissipation and just at the times when I was touching bottom. They came in separate spurts, as though reminding me of themselves, but did not banish the dissipation by their appearance. On the contrary, they seemed to add a zest to it by contrast, and were only sufficiently present to serve as an appetizing sauce. That sauce was made up of contradictions and sufferings, of agonizing inward analysis, and all these pangs and pinpricks gave a certain piquancy, even a significance, to my dissipation — in fact, completely answered the purpose of an appetizing sauce. There was a certain depth of meaning in it. And I could hardly have resigned myself to the simple, vulgar, direct debauchery of a clerk and have endured all the filthiness of it. What could have allured me about it then and have drawn me at night into the street? No, I had a lofty way of getting out of it all.

And what loving-kindness, O Lord, what loving-kindness I felt at times in those dreams of mine, in those flights into *the good and the beautiful.* Though it was fantastic love, though it was never applied to anything human in reality, yet there was so much of this love that one did not feel afterward even the impulse to apply it in reality — that would have been superfluous. Everything, however, passed satisfactorily by a lazy and fascinating transition into the sphere of art, that is, into the beautiful forms of life, lying ready, largely stolen from the poets and novelists and adapted to all sorts of needs and uses. I, for instance, was triumphant over everyone; everyone, of course, was in dust and ashes, and was forced spontaneously to recognize my superiority, and I forgave them all. I was a poet and a grand gentleman; I fell in love; I came in for countless millions and immediately devoted them to humanity, and at the same time I confessed before all the people my shameful deeds, which, of course, were not merely shameful but had in them much that was *good and beautiful,* something in the style of Manfred. Everyone would kiss me and weep (what idiots they would be if they didn't), while I'd go barefoot and hungry preaching new ideas and fighting a victorious Austerlitz against the obscurantists. Then the band would play a march, an amnesty would be declared, the Pope would agree to retire from Rome to Brazil; then there would be a ball for the whole of Italy at the Villa Borghese on the shores of the Lake of Como (the Lake of Como being for that purpose transferred to the neighborhood of Rome); then would come a scene in the bushes, and so on, and so on — as though you didn't know all about it!

You will say that it is vulgar and contemptible to drag all this out before everybody after all the tears and transports which I have myself confessed. But why is it contemptible? Can you imagine that I am ashamed of it all, and that it was stupider than anything in your life, gentlemen? And I can assure you that some of these fancies were by no means badly composed. It did not all happen on the shores of Lake Como. And yet you are right — it really is vulgar and contemptible. And most contemptible of all is the fact that I am now attempting to justify myself to you. And even more contemptible than that is my making this remark now. But that's enough, or there will be no end to it: each step will be more contemptible than the last. . . .

I could never stand more than three months of dreaming at a time without feeling an irresistible desire to plunge into society. To plunge into society meant to visit my superior at the office, Anton Antonich Syetochkin. He was the only permanent acquaintance I ever had in my life, and I wonder at the fact myself now. But I only went to see him when that phase came over me and when my dreams had reached such a point of bliss that it became essential at once to embrace my fellows and all mankind; and for that purpose I needed, at least, one human being, actually existing. I had to call on Anton Antonich, however, on Tuesday — his at-home day, so I always had to time my passionate desire to embrace humanity so that it might fall on a Tuesday.

This Anton Antonich lived on the fourth floor in a house in Five Corners, in four low-pitched rooms, each smaller than the next, of a particularly frugal and sere appearance. He had two daughters, and the daughters had an aunt, who used to pour out the tea. Of the daughters one was thirteen and the other fourteen; they both had snub noses, and I was awfully shy in their presence because they were always whispering and giggling together. The master of the house usually sat in his study on a leather couch in front of the table with some gray-headed gentleman, usually a colleague from our office or some other department. I never saw more than two or three visitors there, always the same. They talked about the excise duties, about matters in the Senate, about salaries, about promotions, about His Excellency, and the best means of pleasing him, and so on. I had the patience to sit like a fool beside these people for four hours at a stretch, listening to them without knowing what to say to them or venturing to say a word. I became stupefied, several times I felt myself perspiring, I was overcome by a sort of paralysis; but this was pleasant and good for me. On returning home I deferred for a time my desire to embrace all mankind.

I had, however, one other acquaintance of a sort, Simonov, who was an old schoolfellow. In fact, I had a number of schoolfellows in Petersburg, but I did not associate with them and had even given up nodding to them in the street. I believe I had asked to be transferred into the department I was in simply to avoid their company and to cut off all connection with my hateful childhood. Curses on that school and all those terrible years of penal servitude! In short, I parted from my schoolfellows as soon as I got out into the world. There were two or three left to whom I did nod in the street. One of them was Simonov, who had been in no way distinguished at school, and was of a quiet and equable disposition; but I discovered in him a certain independence of character and even honesty. I don't even suppose that he was particularly stupid. I had at one time spent some rather soulful moments with him, but these had not lasted long and had somehow been suddenly clouded over. He was evidently uncomfortable at these recollections and was, I imagine, always afraid that I might take up the same tone again. I suspected that he had an aversion for me, but still I went on going to see him, not being quite certain of it.

And so on one occasion, unable to endure my solitude and knowing that since it was Thursday Anton Antonich's door would be closed, I thought of Simonov. Climbing up to his fourth-floor flat, I was thinking that the man disliked me and that it was a mistake to go and see him. But as it always happened that such reflections impelled me, as though purposely, to put myself into a false position, I went in. It was almost a year since I had last seen Simonov.

III

I found two of my old schoolfellows with him. They seemed to be discussing an important matter. All of them took scarcely any notice of my entrance, which was strange, for I had not met them for years. Evidently they looked upon me as something on the level of a common housefly. I had not been treated like that even at school, though they had all hated me. I knew, of course, that they must despise me now for my lack of success in the Service, and for my having let myself sink so low, going about badly dressed, and so on — which seemed to them a sign of my incapacity and insignificance. But I had not expected such contempt. Simonov was positively surprised at my turning up. Even in the old days he had always seemed surprised at my coming. All this disconcerted me. I sat down, feeling rather miserable, and began listening to what they were saying.

They were engaged in warm and earnest conversation about a farewell dinner which they wanted to arrange for the next day to a comrade of theirs called Zvercov, an officer in the army, who was going away to a distant province. This Zvercov, too, had been at school all the time I was there. I had begun to hate him, particularly in the upper grades. In the lower grades he had simply been a pretty, playful boy whom everybody liked. I had hated him, however, even in the lower grades, just because he was a pretty and playful boy. He was always poor at his lessons and got worse and worse as he went on; however, he left with a good certificate, since he had influential people interested in him. During his last year at school he came in for an estate of two hundred serfs, and as almost all of us were poor he took to swaggering among us. He was vulgar in the extreme, but at the same time he was a good-natured fellow, even in his swaggering. In spite of superficial, fantastic and sham notions of honor and dignity, all but very few of us positively groveled before Zvercov, and the more he swaggered the more they groveled. And it was not from any interested motive that they groveled, but simply because he had been favored by the gifts of nature. Moreover, it was, as it were, an accepted idea among us that Zvercov was a specialist in tact and the social graces. This last fact particularly infuriated me. I hated the abrupt self-confident tone of his voice, his admiration of his own witticisms, which were often frightfully stupid, though he was bold in his language; I hated his handsome but stupid face (for which I would, however, have gladly exchanged my intelligent one), and the free-and-easy military manners in fashion in the forties.

I hated the way in which he used to talk of his future conquests of women (he did not venture to begin his attacks upon women until he had the epaulettes of an officer, and was looking forward to them with impatience), and boasted of the duels he would constantly be fighting. I remember how I, invariably so taciturn, suddenly fastened upon Zvercov, when one day while talking at a leisure moment with his schoolfellows of his future relations with the fair sex, and growing as sportive as a puppy in the sun, he all at once declared that he would not leave a single village girl on his estate unnoticed, that that was his *droit de seigneur,* and that if the peasants dared to protest he would have them all flogged and double the tax on them, the bearded rascals. Our servile rabble applauded, but I attacked him, not from compassion for the girls and their fathers, but simply because they were applauding such an insect. I got the better of him on that occasion, but though Zvercov was stupid he was also lively and impudent, and so laughed it off, and in such a way that my victory was not really complete: the laugh was on his side. He got the better of me on several occasions afterward, but without malice, jestingly, casually. I remained angrily and contemptuously silent and would not answer him.

When we left school he made advances to me; I did not rebuff them, for I was flattered, but we soon parted, and quite naturally. Afterward I heard of his barrack-room success as a lieutenant, and of the fast life he was leading. Then there came other rumors — of his successes in the Service. By then he had taken to cutting me in the street, and I suspected that he was afraid of compromising himself by greeting a personage as insignificant as myself. I saw him once at a theater, in the third tier of boxes. By then he was wearing shoulder straps. He was twisting and turning, ingratiating himself with the daughters of an ancient general. In three years he had become considerably shopworn, though he was still rather handsome and adroit. One could see that by the time he was thirty he would be corpulent.

So it was to this Zvercov that my schoolfellows were going to give a dinner on his departure. They had kept up with him for those three years, though privately they did not consider themselves on an equal footing with him, I am convinced of that.

Of Simonov's two visitors, one was Ferfichkin, a Russianized German — a little fellow with the face of a monkey, a blockhead who was always deriding everyone, a very bitter enemy of mine from our days in the lower grades — a vulgar, impudent, swaggering fellow, who affected a most sensitive feeling of personal honor, though, of course, he was a wretched little coward at heart. He was one of those worshipers of Zvercov who made up to the latter from interested motives, and often borrowed money from him. Simonov's other visitor, Trudolyubov, was a person in no way remarkable — a tall young fellow, in the army, with a cold face, fairly honest, though he worshiped success of every sort, and was capable only of thinking about promotion. He was some sort of distant relation of Zvercov's, and this, foolish as it seems, gave him a certain importance among us. He always thought me of no consequence whatever; his behavior to me, though not quite courteous, was tolerable.

"Well, with seven rubles each," said Trudolyubov, "which is twenty-one rubles for the three of us, we ought to be able to get a good dinner. Zvercov, of course, won't pay."

"Of course not, since we're inviting him," Simonov decided.

"Can you imagine," Ferfichkin interrupted hotly and conceitedly, like some insolent flunky boasting of his master's, the general's, decorations, "can you imagine that Zvercov will let us pay alone? He'll accept from delicacy, but he'll order half a dozen bottles of champagne."

"Do we want half a dozen for the four of us?" observed Trudolyubov, taking notice only of the half dozen.

"It's settled then — the three of us, with Zvercov for the fourth, twenty-one rubles, at the Hôtel de Paris, at five o'clock tomorrow," Simonov, who had been asked to make the arrangements, concluded finally.

"How do you figure twenty-one rubles?" I asked in some agitation, with a show of being offended. "If you count me it won't be twenty-one but twenty-eight rubles."

It seemed to me that to invite myself so suddenly and unexpectedly would be positively graceful, and that they would all be conquered at once and would look upon me with respect.

"Do you want to join, too?" Simonov observed, with no appearance of pleasure, seeming to avoid looking at me. He knew me through and through.

It infuriated me that he knew me so thoroughly.

"Why not? I'm an old schoolfellow of his, too, I believe, and I must own I feel hurt at your having left me out," I said, boiling over again.

"And where were we to find you?" Ferfichkin put in rudely.

"You never were on good terms with Zvercov," Trudolyubov added, frowning.

But I had already grabbed at the idea and would not give it up.

"It seems to me that no one has a right to form an opinion upon that," I retorted in a shaky voice, as though something tremendous had happened. "Perhaps that is just my reason for wishing it now, that I have not always been on good terms with him."

"Oh, there's no making you out — with all these refinements," Trudolyubov jeered.

"We'll put your name down," Simonov decided, addressing me. "Tomorrow at five o'clock, at the Hôtel de Paris."

"What about the money?" Ferfichkin began in an undertone, indicating me to Simonov, but he broke off, for even Simonov was embarrassed

"That will do," said Trudolyubov, getting up. "If he wants to come so much, let him."

"But it's a private affair, among friends," Ferfichkin said crossly as he, too, picked up his hat. "It's not an official gathering."

They went away. Ferfichkin did not greet me in any way as he went out, Trudolyubov barely nodded. Simonov, with whom I was left tête-à-tête, was in a state of vexation and perplexity, and looked at me queerly. He did not sit down nor did he ask me to.

"H'm . . . yes . . . tomorrow, then. Will you pay your share now? I'm merely asking to make sure," he muttered in embarrassment.

I flushed crimson, and as I did so I remembered that I had owed Simonov fifteen rubles for ages — which I had, indeed, never forgotten, though I had not paid it.

"You will understand, Simonov, that I could have no idea of this when I came here. I'm very much embarrassed that I have forgotten —"

"All right, all right, that doesn't matter. You can pay tomorrow after the dinner. I simply wanted to know. Please don't —"

He broke off and began pacing the room, still more vexed. As he walked he began to stamp with his heels.

"Am I keeping you?" I asked after two minutes of silence.

"Oh!" he said, starting, "for — to be truthful — yes. I have to go and see someone — not far from here," he added in an apologetic voice, somewhat abashed.

"My goodness, why didn't you say so?" I cried, seizing my cap, with an astonishing free-and-easy air, which was the last thing I should have expected of myself.

"It's close by — not two steps away," Simonov repeated, accompanying me to the front door with a fussy air which did not suit him at all. "So five o'clock, punctually, tomorrow," he called down the stairs after me. He was very glad to get rid of me. I was furious.

"What possessed me — what possessed me to force myself upon them?" I wondered, grinding my teeth as I strode along the street, "for a scoundrel, a swine like that Zvercov! Of course, I'd better not go; of course, I must just snap my fingers at them. I'm not bound in any way. I'll send Simonov a note by tomorrow's mail —"

But what made me furious was that I knew for certain that I should go, that I should make a point of going; and the more tactless, the more unseemly my going would be, the more certainly I would go.

And there was a positive obstacle to my going: I had no money. All I had was nine rubles. I had to give seven of that to my servant, Apollon, for his monthly wages. That was all I paid him — he had to keep himself.

Not to pay him was impossible, considering his character. But I will talk about that fellow, about that plague of mine, another time.

However, I knew I would go and wouldn't pay him his wages.

That night I had the most hideous dreams. No wonder; all the evening I had been oppressed by memories of my miserable days at school, and I couldn't shake them off. I had been sent to the school by distant relations, upon whom I was dependent and of whom I have heard nothing since; they had sent me there a forlorn, silent boy, already crushed by their reproaches, already troubled by doubt, and looking with savage distrust at everyone. My schoolfellows met me with spiteful and merciless gibes because I was unlike any of them. But I could not endure their taunts; I could not give in to them with the ignoble readiness with which they gave in to one another. I hated them from the first, and shut myself away from everyone in timid, wounded, and disproportionate pride. Their coarseness revolted me. They laughed cynically at my face, at my clumsy figure; and yet what stupid faces they had themselves! In our school the boys' faces seemed in a special way to degenerate and grow stupider. How many fine-looking boys came to us! In a few years they became repulsive. Even at sixteen I wondered at them morosely; even then I was struck by the pettiness of their thoughts, the stupidity of their pursuits, their games, their conversations. They had no understanding of things that were so essential, they took no interest in matters that were so striking, so impressive, that I could not help considering them inferior to myself.

It was not wounded vanity that drove me to this, and for God's sake do not thrust upon me your hackneyed remarks, repeated *ad nauseam*, that "I was only a dreamer," while they even then had an understanding of life. They understood nothing, they had no idea of real life, and I swear that that was what made me most indignant about them. On the contrary, the most obvious, striking reality they accepted with fantastic stupidity and even at that time were accustomed to respect success. Everything that was just, but oppressed and looked down upon, they laughed at heartlessly and shamefully. They took rank for intelligence; even at sixteen they were already talking about a snug berth. Of course, a great deal of it was due to their stupidity, to the bad examples with which they had always been surrounded in their childhood and boyhood. They were monstrously depraved. Of course, a great deal of that, too, was superficial and an assumption of cynicism; of course, there were glimpses of youth and freshness even in their depravity; but even that freshness was not attractive, and showed itself n a certain rakishness.

I hated them horribly, though perhaps I was worse than any of them. They repaid me in the same way, and did not conceal their aversion for me. But by then I did not desire their affection: on the contrary, I continually longed for their humiliation. To escape from their derision I purposely began to make all the progress I could with my studies and forced my way to the very top. This impressed them. Moreover, they all began by degrees to grasp that I had already read books none of them could read, and understood things (not forming part of our school curriculum) of which they had not even heard. They took a savage and sarcastic view of it, but were morally impressed, especially as the teachers began to notice me on those grounds. The mockery ceased, but the hostility remained, and cold and strained relations became permanent between us. In the end I could not put up with it; with years a craving for society, for friends, developed in me. I attempted to get on friendly terms with some of my schoolfellows, but somehow or other my intimacy with them was always strained and soon ended of itself.

Once, indeed, I did have a friend. But I was already a tyrant at heart; I wanted to exercise unbounded sway over him; I tried to instill in him a contempt for his surroundings; I required of him a disdainful and complete break with those surroundings. I frightened him with my passionate affection; I reduced him to tears, to hysterics. He was a simple and devoted soul; but when he devoted himself to me entirely I began to hate him immediately and repulsed him — as though all I needed him for was to win a victory over him, to subjugate him and nothing else. But I could not subjugate all of them; my friend was not at all like them either; he was, in fact, a rare exception. The first thing I did on leaving school was to give up the special job for which I had been destined, so as to break all ties, to curse my past and shake its dust from off my feet. And goodness knows why, after all that, I should go trudging off to Simonov's!

Early next morning I roused myself and jumped out of bed with excitement, as though it were all about to happen at once. But I believed that some radical change in my life was coming, and would come inevitably on that day. Owing to its rarity, perhaps, any external event, however trivial, always made me feel as though some radical change in my life were at hand. I went to the office, however, as usual, but sneaked away home two hours earlier to get ready. The great thing, I thought, was not to be the first to arrive, or they would think me overjoyed at coming. But there were thousands of such great points to consider, and they all agitated and overwhelmed me. I polished my boots a second time with my own hands; nothing in the world would have induced Apollon to clean them twice a day, as he considered that it was more than his duties required of him. I stole the brushes to clean them from the passage, being careful he should not detect it, for fear of his contempt. Then I minutely examined my clothes and thought that everything looked old, worn, and threadbare. I had let myself get too slovenly. My uniform, perhaps, was tidy, but I could hardly go out to dinner in it. The worst of it was that there was a big yellow stain on the knees of my trousers. I had a foreboding that that stain would deprive me of nine-tenths of my personal dignity. I knew, too, that it was very bad to think so. "But this is no time for thinking: now I am in for the real thing," I thought, and my heart sank.

I knew, too, perfectly well even then, that I was monstrously exaggerating the facts. But how could I help it? I could not control myself and was already shaking with fever. With despair I pictured to myself how co!d y and disdainfully that scoundrel Zvercov would meet me; with what dull-witted, invincible contempt that blockhead Trudolyubov would look at me; with what impudent rudeness that insect Ferfichkin would snigger at me in order to curry favor with Zvercov; how completely Simonov would take it all in, and how he would despise me for the abjectedness of my vanity and lack of spirit — and worst of all, how paltry, *unliterary*, commonplace it would all be. Of course, the best thing would be not to go at all. But that was most impossible of all: if I feel impelled to do anything, I seem to be pitchforked into it. I should have jeered at myself ever afterward: "So you fell down, you fell down, you fell down when it came to the *real thing!*" On the contrary, I passionately longed to show all that "rabble" that I was by no means such a spiritless creature as I seemed to myself.

What is more, even in the acutest paroxysm of this cowardly fever, I dreamed of getting the upper hand, of dominating them, carrying them away, making them like me — if only for my "elevation of thought and unmistakable wit." They would abandon Zvercov, he would sit to one side, silent and ashamed, while I would crush him. Then, perhaps, we'd be reconciled and drink to our everlasting friendship; but what was most bitter and most humiliating for me was that I knew even then, knew fully and for certain that I really needed nothing of all this, that I did not really want to crush, to subdue, to attract them, and that I didn't really care a straw for the result, even if I did achieve it. Oh, how I prayed for the day to pass quickly! In unutterable anguish I went to the window, opened the ventilator, and looked out into the troubled darkness of the thickly falling wet snow.

At last my wretched little clock hissed out five. I seized my hat and, trying not to look at Apollon, who had been all day expecting his month's wages, but in his foolishness was unwilling to be the first to speak about it, I slipped out between him and the door and, jumping into a high-class sleigh on which I spent my last half ruble, I drove up in grand style to the Hôtel de Paris.

IV

I had been certain the day before that I should be the first to arrive. But it was not a question of being the first to arrive. Not only were they not there, but I had difficulty in finding our room. The table had not been laid even. What did it mean? After a good many questions I elicited from the waiters that the dinner had been ordered not for five but for six o'clock. This was confirmed at the bar as well. I felt really ashamed to go on questioning them. It was only twenty-five minutes past five. If they had changed the dinner hour they ought at least to have let me know — that's what the mail is for — and not put me in an absurd position in my own eyes and . . . and even before the waiters. I sat down; the servant began laying the table; I felt even more humiliated when he was present. Toward six o'clock they brought in candles, though there were lamps burning in the room. It had not occurred to the waiter, however, to bring them in at once when I arrived. In the next room two gloomy, angry-looking persons were eating their dinners in silence at two different tables. There was a great deal of noise, even shouting, in a room further away; one could hear the laughter of a crowd of people and nasty little shrieks in French: there were ladies at the dinner. It was sickening, in fact. I rarely passed more unpleasant moments, so much so that when they did arrive all together punctually at six I was overjoyed to see them, as though they were my deliverers, and even forgot that I really ought to show resentment.

Zvercov walked in at the head of them; evidently he was the leading spirit. He and all of them were laughing; but, seeing me, Zvercov drew himself up a little and walked up to me deliberately with a slight, rather jaunty bend from the waist. He shook hands with me in a friendly, but not overfriendly, fashion, with a sort of circumspect courtesy like that of a general, as though in giving me his hand he were warding off something. I had imagined, on the contrary, that on coming in he would at once break into his habitual thin, shrill laugh and fall to making his insipid jokes and witticisms. I had been preparing for them ever since the previous day, but I had not expected such condescension, such high-official courtesy. So, then, he felt himself ineffably superior to me in every respect! If he only meant to insult me by that high-official tone it would not matter, I thought — I could pay him back for it one way or another. But what if, in reality, without the least desire to be offensive, that muttonhead had a notion in earnest that he was superior to me and could only look at me in a patronizing way? The very supposition made me gasp.

"I was surprised to hear of your desire to join us," he began, lisping and drawling, which was something new. "You and I seem to have seen nothing of each other. You fight shy of us. You shouldn't. We're not such dreadful people as you think. Well, anyway, I am glad to renew our acquaintance."

And he turned carelessly to put down his hat on the window.

"Have you been waiting long?" Trudolyubov inquired.

"I arrived at five o'clock as you told me yesterday," I answered loudly, with an irritability that threatened an explosion.

"Didn't you let him know that we had changed the hour?" said Trudolyubov to Simonov.

"No, I didn't. I forgot," the latter replied, with no sign of regret, and, without even apologizing to me, he went off to order the hors d'oeuvres.

"So you've been here a whole hour? Oh, you poor fellow!" Zvercov cried out ironically, for to his notion this was bound to be extremely funny. That rascal Ferfichkin chimed in with his nasty little snigger, like a puppy yapping. My position struck him, too, as exquisitely ludicrous and embarrassing.

"It isn't funny at all!" I cried to Ferfichkin, more and more irritated. "It wasn't my fault, but that of others. They neglected to let me know. It was . . . it was . . . it was simply absurd!"

"It's not only absurd, but something else as well," muttered Trudolyubov, naïvely taking my part. "You're too mild about it. It was simply rudeness — unintentional, of course. And how could Simonov — h'm!"

"If a trick like that had been played on me," observed Ferfichkin, "I'd —"

"But you should have ordered something for yourself," Zvercov interrupted, "or simply asked for dinner without waiting for us."

"You'll admit that I might have done that without your permission," I rapped out. "If I waited, it was because—"

"Let us sit down, gentlemen," called out Simonov, coming in. "Everything is ready; I can answer for the champagne; it is capitally iced. You see, I didn't know your address; where was I to look for you?" He suddenly turned to me, but again he seemed to avoid looking at me. Evidently he had something against me. It must have been what had happened yesterday.

All sat down; I did the same. It was a round table. Trudolyubov was on my left, Simonov on my right. Zvercov was sitting opposite, Ferfichkin next to him, between him and Trudolyubov.

"Tell me, are you . . . in a government office?" Zvercov went on being attentive to me. Seeing that I was embarrassed, he seriously thought that he ought to be friendly to me, and, so to speak, cheer me up.

"Does he want me to throw a bottle at his head?" I thought, in a rage. In my novel surroundings I was unnaturally ready to be irritated.

"In the N — office," I answered jerkily, with my eyes on my plate.

"And ha-ave you a goo-ood berth? I say, what ma-a-de you leave your or:ginal job?"

"What ma-a-de me was that I wanted to leave my original job," I drawled more than he, hardly able to control myself. Ferfichkin went off into a guffaw. Simonov looked at me sarcastically. Trudolyubov left off eating and began looking at me with curiosity.

Zvercov winced, but he tried not to notice anything.

"And the remuneration?"

"What remuneration?"

"I mean, your sa-a-lary?"

"Why are you cross-examining me?" However, I told him at once what my salary was. I turned horribly red.

"It's not very handsome," Zvercov observed majestically.

"Yes, you can't afford to dine at cafés on that," Ferfichkin added insolently.

"To my thinking it's very poor," Trudolyubov observed gravely.

"And how thin you have grown! How you have changed!" added

Zvercov, with a shade of venom in his voice, scanning me and my attire with a sort of insolent compassion.

"Oh, spare his blushes," cried Ferfichkin, sniggering.

"My dear Sir, allow me to tell you I am not blushing," I broke out at last: "Do you hear? I am dining here, at this café, at my own expense, not at other people's — note that, Mr. Ferfichkin."

"Wha-at? Isn't everyone here dining at his own expense? You seem to be — " Ferfichkin turned on me, becoming as red as a lobster and looking me in the face with fury.

"We won't go into tha-at," I mimicked in answer, feeling I had gone too far. "And I imagine it would be better to talk of something more intelligent."

"You intend to show off your intelligence, I suppose?"

"Don't upset yourself; that would be quite out of place here."

"Why are you jabbering away like that, my good Sir, eh? Have you gone out of your wits in your office?"

"Enough, gentlemen, enough!" Zvercov cried authoritatively.

"How stupid all this is!" muttered Simonov.

"It really is stupid. We've met here, a party of friends, for a farewell dinner to a comrade, and you carry on a fight," said Trudolyubov, rudely addressing himself to me alone. "You invited yourself to join us, so don't disturb the general harmony."

"Enough, enough!" cried Zvercov. "Quit it, gentlemen, it's out of place. Better let me tell you how I nearly got married the day before yesterday —"

And then followed a burlesque narrative of how this gentleman had almost been married two days before. There was not a word about the marriage, however, but the story was adorned with generals, colonels, and gentlemen-in-waiting, while Zvercov almost took the lead among them. It was greeted with approving laughter; Ferfichkin positively squealed.

No one paid any attention to me, and I sat crushed and humiliated.

"Good Heavens, these are not the people for me!" I thought. "And what a fool I have made of myself before them! I let Ferfichkin go too far, though. The brutes imagine they are doing me an honor in letting me sit down with them. They don't understand that it's an honor to them and not to me! I've grown thinner! My clothes! Oh, damn my trousers! Zvercov noticed the yellow stain on the knee as soon as he came in. But what's the use! I must get up at once, this very minute, take my hat and simply go without a word — with contempt! And tomorrow I can send a challenge. The scoundrels! As though I cared about the seven rubles. They may think . . . Damn it! I don't care about the seven rubles. I'll go this minute!"

Of course I remained. I drank sherry and Lafitte by the glassful in my discomfiture. Being unaccustomed to it, I was quickly affected. My annoyance increased as the wine went to my head. I longed, all of a sudden, to insult them all in a most flagrant manner and then go away. To seize the moment and show what I could do, so that they would say: "He's clever, though he's absurd," and . . . and . . . in fact, damn them all!

I scanned them all insolently with my drowsy eyes. But they seemed to have forgotten me altogether. They were noisy, vociferous, cheerful. Zvercov was talking all the time. I began listening. Zvercov was talking of some exuberant lady whom he had at last led on to declaring her love (of course he was lying like a trooper), and how he had been helped in this affair by an intimate friend of his, a Prince Nicky, an officer in the hussars, who had three thousand serfs.

"And yet this Nicky, who has three thousand serfs, hasn't put in an appearance here tonight to see you off," I cut in suddenly.

For a minute everyone was silent. "You are drunk already." Trudolyubov deigned to notice me at last, glancing contemptuously in my direction. Zvercov, without a word, examined me as though I were an insect. I dropped my eyes. Simonov made haste to fill up the goblets with champagne.

Trudolyubov raised his goblet, as did everyone else but me.

"Your health and good luck on the journey!" he said to Zvercov. "To old times, to our future, hurrah!"

They all tossed off their goblets and crowded around Zvercov to kiss him. I didn't stir; my full goblet stood untouched before me.

"Why, aren't you going to drink the toast?" roared Trudolyubov, losing patience and turning menacingly to me.

"I want to make a speech separately, on my own account —and then I'll drink to it, Mr. Trudolyubov."

"Spiteful brute!" muttered Simonov.

I drew myself up in my chair and feverishly seized my goblet, prepared for something extraordinary, though I did not know myself precisely what I was going to say.

"*S.lence!*" cried Ferfichkin. "Now for a display of wit!"

Zvercov waited very gravely, knowing what was coming.

"Lieutenant Zvercov, Sir," I began, "let me tell you that I hate phrases, phrasemongers, and men who wear corsets — that's the first point, and there's a second one to follow it."

There was a general stir.

"The second point is: I hate loose talk and loose talkers. Especially loose talkers! The third point: I love justice, truth, and honesty." I went on almost mechanically, for I was beginning to shiver with horror myself and had no idea how I had come to be talking like this. "I love thought, Monsieur Zvercov; I love true comradeship, on an equal footing and not — h'm! I love — but, however, why not? I'll drink your health, too, Monsieur Zvercov. Seduce the Circassian girls, shoot the enemies of the fatherland, and — and — here's to your health, Monsieur Zvercov!"

Zvercov got up from his seat, bowed to me, and said:

"I'm very much obliged to you." He was frightfully offended and had turned pale.

"Damn the fellow!" roared Trudolyubov, bringing his fist down on the table.

"Well, he ought to get a punch in the nose for that," squealed Ferfichkin.

"We ought to turn him out," muttered Simonov.

"Not a word, gentlemen, not a move!" cried Zvercov gravely, checking the general indignation. "I thank you all, but I am able to show him myself how much value I attach to his words."

"Mr. Ferfichkin, you will give me satisfaction tomorrow for your words just now!" I said aloud, turning with dignity to Ferfichkin.

"A duel, you mean? Certainly," he answered. But probably I was so ridiculous as I challenged him, and it was so out of keeping with my appearance, that everyone, including Ferfichkin, was prostrate with laughter.

"Yes, let him alone, of course! He's quite drunk," Trudolyubov said with disgust.

"I'll never forgive myself for letting him join us," Simonov muttered again.

"Now is the time to throw a bottle at their heads," I thought to myself. I picked up the bottle — and filled my glass.

"No, I'd better sit on to the end," I went on thinking; "you would be pleased, my friends, if I went away. Nothing will induce me to go. I'll go on sitting here and drinking to the end, on purpose, just to show that I don't think you of the slightest consequence. I'll go on sitting and drinking, because this is a tavern and I paid my entrance money.

I'll sit here and drink, for I look upon you as so many pawns, so many inanimate pawns. I'll sit here and drink — and sing if I want to. Yes, sing, for I have the right to — to sing. H'm!"

But I did not sing. I simply tried not to look at any of them. I assumed various attitudes, ever so unconcerned, and waited with impatience for them to speak *first*. But alas, they did not address me! And oh, how I wished at that moment to be reconciled to them! It struck eight, and nine, at last. They moved from the table to the sofa. Zvercov stretched himself on a lounge and put one foot on a round table. Wine was brought there. He did, as a fact, order three bottles on his own account. I, of course, was not invited to join them. They all sat round him on the sofa. They listened to him, almost with reverence. It was evident that they were fond of him.

"What for? What for?" I wondered. From time to time they were moved to drunken enthusiasm and kissed one another. They talked of the Caucasus, of the nature of true passion, of snug berths in the Service, of the income of an hussar called Podharzhevski, whom none of them knew personally, and rejoiced at the hugeness of it, at the extraordinary grace and beauty of a Princess D ——, whom none of them had ever seen; then it came to Shakespeare's being immortal.

I smiled contemptuously and walked up and down the other side of the room, opposite the sofa, from the table to the stove and back again. I tried my very utmost to show them that I could do without them, and yet I purposely made a noise with my shoes, thumping my heels. But it was all in vain. They paid no attention. I had the patience to walk up and down in front of them from eight o'clock till eleven, in the same place, from the table to the stove and back again. "I walk up and down to please myself, and no one can prevent me." The waiter who came into the room stopped, from time to time, to look at me. I was somewhat giddy from turning round so often; at moments it seemed to me that I was in delirium. During those three hours I was three times soaked with sweat and dry again.

At times, with an intense, acute pang, I was stabbed to the heart by the thought that ten years, twenty years, forty years would pass, and that even in forty years I would remember with loathing and humiliation those filthiest, most ludicrous, and most awful moments of my life No one could have gone out of his way to degrade himself more shamelessly, and I fully realized it, fully, and yet I went on pacing up and down from the table to the stove. "Oh, if you only knew what thoughts and feelings I am capable of, how cultured I am!" I thought at moments, mentally addressing the sofa on which my enemies were sitting. But my enemies behaved as though I were not in the room. Once — only once — they turned toward me, just when Zvercov was talking about Shakespeare, and I suddenly gave a contemptuous laugh. I laughed in such an affected and disgusting way that they all at once broke off their conversation and silently and gravely for two minutes watched me walking up and down from the table to the stove, *taking no notice of them.* But nothing came of it: they said nothing, and two minutes later they ceased to notice me again. It struck eleven.

"Friends," cried Zvercov, getting up from the sofa, "let us all go *there* now!"

"Of course, of course," the others assented. I turned sharply to Zvercov. I was so harassed, so exhausted, that I would have cut my throat to put an end to it. I was in a fever; my hair, soaked with perspiration, stuck to my forehead and temples.

"Zvercov, I beg your pardon," I said abruptly and resolutely. "Ferfichkin, yours, too, and everyone's, everyone's: I have insulted you all!"

"Aha! A duel is not in your line, old man," Ferfichkin got out venomously through clenched teeth.

It sent a sharp pang to my heart.

"No, it's not the duel I'm afraid of, Ferfichkin! I'm ready to fight you tomorrow, after we're reconciled. I insist upon it, in fact, and you cannot refuse. I want to show you that I am not afraid of a duel. You'll fire first and I'll fire into the air."

"He's comforting himself," said Simonov.

"He's simply raving," said Trudolyubov.

"Look, let us pass. Why are you barring our way? What do you want?" Zvercov answered disdainfully.

They were all flushed; their eyes were bright; they had been drinking heavily.

"I ask for your friendship, Zvercov; I insulted you, but — "

"Insulted? *You* insulted *me?* Understand, Sir, that you never, under any circumstances, could possibly insult *me.*"

"And that's enough for you. Out of the way!" concluded Trudolyubov.

"Olympia is mine, friends, that's agreed!" cried Zvercov.

"We won't dispute your right, we won't dispute your right," the others answered, laughing.

I stood there as though they had spat upon me. The party went noisily out of the room. Trudolyubov struck up some stupid song.

Simonov remained behind for a moment to tip the waiters. I suddenly went up to him.

"Simonov, give me six rubles!" I said with desperate resolution.

He looked at me in extreme amazement, with vacant eyes. He, too, was drunk.

"You don't mean you're coming with us?"

"Yes."

"I've no money," he snapped out, and with a scornful laugh he went toward the door.

I clutched at his overcoat. It was a nightmare.

"Simonov, I saw you had money. Why do you refuse me? Am I a scoundrel? Beware of refusing me: if you knew, if you but knew why I'm asking! My whole future, my whole plans depend upon it!"

Simonov pulled out the money and almost flung it at me.

"Take it, if you have no sense of shame!" he uttered pitilessly, and ran to overtake the others.

I was left alone for a moment. Disorder, the remains of dinner, a broken wineglass on the floor, spilt wine, cigarette ends, fumes of drink and delirium in my brain, an agonizing misery in my heart and finally the waiter, who had seen and heard all and was looking inquisitively into my face.

"I'm going there!" I cried. "Either they'll all go down on their knees to beg for my friendship or I'll give Zvercov a slap in the face!"

V

"So this is it, this is it at last — contact with real life," I muttered as I ran headlong down the stairs. "This is very different from the Pope's leaving Rome and going to Brazil, very different from the ball on Lake Como!"

"You're a scoundrel," a thought flashed through my mind, "if you laugh at this now."

"No matter!" I cried, answering myself. "Now everything is lost!"

There was no trace to be seen of them, but that made no difference — I knew where they had gone.

At the steps stood a solitary nighthawk of a sleigh driver in a rough peasant coat, powdered over with the still-falling snow, wet and seemingly warm. It felt hot and steamy. The little shaggy piebald horse was also covered with snow and wheezing — I remember that very well. I made a rush for the ramshackle sleigh, but as soon as I raised my foot to get into it, the recollection of how Simonov had just given me six rubles seemed to double me up and I tumbled into the sledge like a sack.

"No, I must do a great deal to make up for all this!" I cried. "But I will make up for it or perish on the spot this very night. Get going!" I told the driver.

We set off. My head was all in a whirl.

"They won't go down on their knees to beg for my friendship. That's a mirage, a cheap mirage, revolting, romantic, and fantastical — that's another ball on Lake Como. And so I'm bound to slap Zvercov's face! It's my duty to. And so it's settled; I'm rushing to give him a slap in the face. Hurry up!"

The driver tugged at the reins.

"Soon as I go in I'll let him have it. Should I say a few words by way of preface before giving him a slap in the face? No. I'll simply go in and let him have it. They will all be sitting in the drawing room, and he with Olympia on the sofa. That damned Olympia! She laughed at my looks on one occasion and turned me down. I'll pull Olympia's hair, pull Zvercov's ears! No, better one ear, and drag him by it round the room. Maybe they'll all begin beating me and will kick me out. That's most likely, indeed. No matter! Anyway, I'll first slap him; the initiative will be mine; and by the laws of honor that's everything: he'll be branded and unable to wipe off the slap by any blows, by nothing short of a duel. He'll be forced to fight. And let them beat me now. Let them, the ungrateful wretches! Trudolyubov will beat me hardest, he's so strong; Ferfichkin will be sure to edge in and tug at my hair. But no matter, no matter! That's what I'm going for. The blockheads will be forced at last to see the tragedy of it all! When they drag me to the door I'll call out to them that in reality they're not worth my little finger. Hurry, driver, hurry!" I cried. He started and flicked his whip, so savagely had I shouted.

"We'll fight at daybreak, that's settled. I've done with my job. Ferfichkin made fun of it just now. But where can I get pistols? Nonsense! I'll get my salary in advance and buy them. And powder and bullets? That's the second's business. And how can it all be done by daybreak? And where am I to get a second? I have no friends. Nonsense!" I cried, working myself up more and more. "It's of no consequence! The first person I meet in the street is bound to be my second, just as he would be bound to pull a drowning man out of water. The most peculiar things may happen. Even if I were to ask the director himself to be my second tomorrow, he'd be bound to consent, if only from a feeling of chivalry, and to keep the secret! Anton Antonich —"

The fact is that at that very minute the disgusting absurdity of my plan and the other side of the question was clearer and more vivid to my imagination than it could be to anyone else on earth. But —

"Hurry, driver! Hurry, you! Hurry!"

"Yes, Sir!" said the son of toil, and grunted.

Cold shivers suddenly ran down my back. Wouldn't it be better to . . . go straight home? My God, my God! Why did I invite myself to this dinner yesterday? But no, it's impossible. And my pacing up and down for three hours from the table to the stove? No, they, *they* and no one else must pay for that promenade of mine! They must wipe out that dishonor! Drive on!

And what if they give me into custody? They won't dare! They'll be afraid of the scandal. And what if Zvercov is so contemptuous that he refuses to fight a duel? He's sure to; but in that case I'll show them! I'll turn up at the posting station when he is setting off tomorrow, I'll catch him by the leg, I'll pull off his coat when he gets into the carriage. I'll sink my teeth into his hand, I'll bite him. "See what lengths you can drive a desperate man to!" He may hit me on the head and they may belabor me from behind. I'll shout to the assembled multitude: "Look at this puppy who's driving off to captivate the Circassian girls after letting me spit in his face!"

Of course, after that everything will be over! The office will have vanished off the face of the earth. I shall be arrested, I shall be tried, I shall be dismissed from the Service, thrown in prison, sent to Siberia. Never mind! In fifteen years when they let me out of prison I'll trudge off to him, a beggar, in rags. I shall find him in some provincial town. He'll be married and happy. He'll have a grown-up daughter. . . . I'll say to him: "Look, monster, at my hollow cheeks and my rags! I've lost everything — my career, my happiness, art, science, *the woman I loved*, and all through you. Here are pistols. I have come to discharge my pistol in the air and — and — I forgive you. Then I'll fire into the air and he'll hear nothing more of me. . . . "

I was actually on the point of tears, though I knew perfectly well at that moment that all this was out of Pushkin's *Sylvio* and Lermontov's *Masquerade.* And all at once I felt horribly ashamed, so ashamed that I stopped the horse, got out of the sleigh, and stood still in the snow in the middle of the street. The driver gazed at me with a gasping wonder.

What was I to do? I could not go on there — it was evidently stupid, and I could not leave things as they were, because that would seem as though . . . Heavens, how could I leave things just so? And after such insults! "No!" I cried, throwing myself into the sleigh again. "It is ordained! It is fate! Drive on, drive on!"

And in my impatience I hit the back of the driver's neck.

"What are you up to? What are you hitting me for?" the peasant shouted, but he whipped up his nag so that it began kicking.

The snow was falling in big wet flakes; I opened my coat in spite of that. I forgot everything else, for I had finally decided on slapping Zvercov's face, and felt with horror that the thing was going to happen *now, at once*, and that *no force could stop it.* The deserted street lamps gleamed sullenly in the snowy darkness like torches at a funeral. The snow drifted under my greatcoat, under my coat, under my cravat, and melted there. I did not wrap myself up — all was lost, anyway.

At last we arrived. I jumped out, almost unconscious, ran up the steps, and began knocking and kicking at the door. I felt fearfully weak, particularly in my legs and knees. The door was opened quickly as though they knew I was coming. As a fact, Simonov had warned them that perhaps another gentleman would arrive, and this was a place in which one had to give notice and to observe certain precautions. It was one of those *millinery emporia* which the police had closed down some time ago. By day it really was a shop; but at night, if one had an introduction, one might visit it for other purposes.

I walked rapidly through the dark shop into the familiar drawing room, where there was only one candle burning, and stood still in amazement: there was no one there. "Where are they?" I asked somebody. But by now, of course, they had separated. Before me was standing a person with a stupid smile, the *madam* herself, who had seen me before. A minute later a door opened and another person came in.

Taking no notice of anything, I strode about the room and, I believe, I talked to myself. I felt as though I had been saved from death and was conscious of this, joyfully, all over: I should have given that slap, I should certainly, certainly have given it! But now they were not here and . . . everything had vanished and changed! I looked around. I could not realize my condition yet. I looked mechanically at the girl who had come in, and had a glimpse of a fresh, young, rather pale face, with straight, dark eyebrows, and with grave, as it were wondering, eyes that attracted me at once; I should have hated her if she had been smiling. I began looking at her more intently and with something like an effort. I had not fully collected my thoughts. There was something simple and good-natured in her face, yet somehow strangely grave. I am sure that this stood in her way here, and no one of those fools had noticed her. She could not, however, have been called a beauty, though she was tall, strong-looking, and well built. She was very simply dressed. Something loathsome stirred within me. I went straight up to her.

I chanced to look into the glass. My harassed face struck me as revolting in the extreme, pale, wrought-up, abject, with disheveled hair. "No matter, I'm glad of it," I thought: "I'm glad I'll seem repulsive to her; I like that."

VI

Somewhere behind a screen a clock began wheezing, as though oppressed by something, as though someone were strangling it. After an unnaturally prolonged wheezing there followed a shrill, nasty, and, as it were, unexpectedly rapid, chime — as though someone were suddenly leaping forward. It struck two. I woke up, though I hadn't really been asleep but lying half conscious.

It was almost completely dark in the narrow, cramped, low-ceiled room, cumbered up with an enormous wardrobe and piles of cardboard boxes and all sorts of frippery and litter. The candle end that had been burning on the table was going out and gave a faint flicker from time to time. In a few minutes there would be complete darkness.

I was not long in coming to myself; everything came back to my mind at once, without an effort, as though it had been in ambush to pounce out on me again. And, indeed, even while I was unconscious a point seemed continually to remain in my memory unforgotten, and round it my dreams moved drearily. But, strange to say, everything that had happened to me in that day seemed to me now, on waking, to be in the far, faraway past, as though I had long, long since lived all that down.

My head was full of fumes. Something seemed to be hovering over me, rousing me, exciting me, and making me restless. Misery and spite seemed surging up in me again and seeking an outlet. Suddenly I saw beside me two wide-open eyes scrutinizing me curiously and persistently. The look in those eyes was coldly detached, sullen, utterly remote, as it were; it weighed upon me.

A grim idea came into my brain and passed all over my body, as a horrible sensation, such as one feels when one goes into a damp and moldy cellar. There was something unnatural in those two eyes, beginning to look at me only now. I recalled, too, that during those two hours I had not said a single word to this creature, and had, in fact, considered it utterly superfluous; in fact, the silence had for some reason gratified me. Now I suddenly realized vividly the hideous idea — revolting as a spider — of vice, which, without love, grossly and shamelessly begins with that in which true love finds its consummation. For a long time we gazed at each other like that, but she did not drop her eyes before mine and her expression did not change, so that at last I felt uncomfortable.

"What is your name?" I asked abruptly, to put an end to it.

"Liza," she answered almost in a whisper, but somehow far from graciously, and she turned her eyes away.

I was silent.

"What weather! The snow is disgusting!" I said, almost to myself, putting my arm under my head despondently and gazing at the ceiling.

She made no answer. This was horrible.

"Have you always lived in Petersburg?" I asked a minute later, almost angrily, turning my head slightly toward her.

"No."

"Where do you come from?"

"From Riga," she answered reluctantly.

"Are you a German?"

"No, Russian."

"Have you been here long?"

"Where?"

"In this house?"

"A fortnight."

She spoke more and more jerkily. The candle went out; I could no longer distinguish her face.

"Have you a father and mother?"

"Yes . . . no. Yes, I have."

"Where are they?"

"There — in Riga."

"Who are they?"

"Oh, nobody in particular."

"Nobody? Why, what do they do?"

"They're tradespeople."

"Have you always lived with them?"

"Yes."

"How old are you?"

"Twenty."

"Why did you leave them?"

"Oh, for no special reason."

That answer meant "Let me alone; I feel sick, sad."

We were silent.

God knows why I did not go away. I felt myself more and more sick and dreary. The images of the previous day began of themselves, apart from my will, flitting through my memory in confusion. I suddenly recalled something I had seen that morning when, full of anxious thoughts, I was hurrying to the office.

"I saw them carrying a coffin out yesterday and they nearly dropped it," I suddenly said aloud, not that I desired to open the conversation, but by accident, as it were.

"A coffin?"

"Yes, in the Hay Market; they were bringing it up out of a cellar."

"From a cellar?"

"Not from a cellar, but from a basement. Oh, you know — from somewhere underground — from a sporting house. It was all so filthy there. Eggshells, rubbish, stink. It was loathsome."

Silence.

"A nasty day to be buried," I began, simply to avoid being silent.

"Nasty — in what way?"

"The snow, the wet." (I yawned.)

"It makes no difference," she said suddenly, after a brief silence.

"No, it's horrid." (I yawned again.) "The gravediggers must have sworn at getting wet from the snow. And there must have been water in the grave."

"Why should there be water in the grave?" she asked with a sort of curiosity, but speaking even more harshly and abruptly than before.

I suddenly began to feel provoked.

"Why, there must have been water at the bottom a foot deep. You can't dig a dry grave in Volkovo Cemetery."

"Why?"

"Why? Because the place is quaggy. It's a regular marsh. So they bury them in water. I've seen it myself — many times."

(I had never seen it once; as a matter of fact, I'd never been in Volkovo and had only heard stories of it.)

"Do you mean to say, you don't mind how you die?"

"But why should I die?" she answered, as though defending herself.

"Why, some day you'll die, and you'll die just the same as that dead woman. She was a — girl — like you. She died of consumption."

"A tart would have died in a hospital . . ." (She knows all about it already: she said *tart*, not *girl*.)

"She was in debt to her madam," I retorted, more and more provoked by the discussion; "and went on earning money for her up to the end, though she had consumption. The sleigh drivers standing about were talking about her to some soldiers and telling them so. No doubt they knew her. They were laughing. They were going to meet in a pothouse to drink to her memory."

A great deal of this was my own invention. Silence followed, profound silence. She did not stir.

"And is it better to die in a hospital?"

"Isn't it just the same? Besides, why should I die?" she added irritably.

"If not now, a little later."

"Why a little later?"

"Why, indeed? Now you're young, not bad-looking, fresh, you fetch a high price. But after another year of this life you'll be very different — you'll pop off."

"In a year?"

"Anyway, in a year you'll be worth less," I continued maliciously. "You'll go from here to something lower, to some other house; a year later — to a third, lower and lower, and in seven years you will come to a basement around the Hay Market. That is, if you're lucky. But it would be much worse if you got some disease, tuberculosis, say. All you have to do is catch a chill or something. It's not easy to get over an illness in your way of life. If you catch anything you may not get rid of it. And so you'll die."

"Oh, well, then I'll die," she answered quite vindictively, and she made a quick movement.

"Still, one feels sorry."

"Sorry for whom? Or what?"

"Sorry for life."

Silence.

"Were you ever engaged? Eh?"

"What's it to you?"

"Oh, I'm not cross-examining you. It's nothing to me. Why are you so cross? Of course you may have had your own troubles. What's it to me? It's simply that I felt sorry."

"Sorry for whom?"

"Sorry for you."

"No need," she whispered hardly audibly, and again made a faint movement.

That incensed me at once. What! I was so gentle with her, but she —

"Why, do you think that you're on the right path?"

"I don't think anything."

"That's just what's wrong. You don't think. Come to your senses while there's still time. There still *is* time. You are still young, not bad-looking; you might love, be married, be happy —"

"Not all married women are happy," she snapped in the rude, abrupt tone she had used at first.

"Not all, of course, but anyway it's much better than the life here. Infinitely better. Besides, with love one can live even without happiness. Even in sorrow life is sweet; life is sweet however one lives. But here — what is there except . . . filth? Phew!"

I turned away with disgust; I was no longer reasoning coldly. I myself began to feel what I was saying and warmed to the subject. I was already longing to expound the cherished ideas I had brooded over in my cubbyhole. Something suddenly flared up in me. An object had appeared before me.

"Never mind my being here, I'm no example for you. I am, perhaps, worse than you are. I was drunk when I came here, though," I nevertheless hastened to say in self-defense. "Besides, a man is no example for a woman. It's a different thing. I may degrade and defile myself, but I'm not anybody's slave. I come and go, and that's the end of it. I shake it off and I'm a different man. But you are a slave from the start. Yes, a slave! You give up everything, your whole freedom. If you want to break your chains afterward, you won't be able to: you'll get more and more tangled. It's an accursed bondage. I know it. I won't speak of anything else, maybe you won't understand, but tell me: no doubt you're in debt to your madam? There, you see," I added, though she made no answer, but only listened in silence, entirely absorbed, "that's bondage for you! You'll never buy your freedom. They'll see to that. It's like selling your soul to the Devil. And besides, perhaps I, too, am just as unlucky — how do you know — and wallow in the mud on purpose, out of misery? You know, men take to drink from grief; well, maybe I'm here from grief. Come, tell me, what is there good here? Here you and I . . . came together . . . just now and didn't say a single word to each other all the time, and it was only afterward you began staring at me like a wild creature, and I at you. Is that love? Is that how one human being should meet another? It's hideous, that's what it is!"

"Yes!" she assented sharply and quickly.

I was positively astounded by the promptitude of this "Yes." So the same thought may have been straying through her mind when she was staring at me just before. So she, too, was capable of certain thoughts? "Damn it all, this was interesting, this was a point of likeness!" I thought, almost rubbing my hands. And indeed it's easy to turn a young soul like that!

It was the exercise of my power that attracted me most.

She turned her head nearer to me, and it seemed to me in the darkness that she propped herself on her arm. Perhaps she was scrutinizing me. How I regretted that I could not see her eyes. I heard her deep breathing.

"Why have you come here?" I asked her, with a note of authority already in my voice.

"Oh, I don't know."

"But how fine it would be to be living in your father's house! It's warm, and no one bothers you; you have a home of your own."

"But what if it's worse than this?"

"I must take the right tone," flashed through my mind. "I may not get far with sentimentality." But it was only a momentary thought. I swear she really did interest me. Besides, I was exhausted and moody. And cunning so easily goes hand-in-hand with feeling.

"Who denies it!" I hastened to answer. "Anything may happen. I am convinced that someone has wronged you, and that you are more sinned against than sinning. Of course, I know nothing of your story, but it's not likely a girl like you has come here of her own inclination. . . . "

"A girl like me?" she whispered, hardly audibly; but I heard it.

Damn it all, I was flattering her. That was horrid. But perhaps it was a good thing. . . . She was silent.

"Look, Liza, I'll tell you about myself. If I had had a home from childhood, I shouldn't be what I am now. I often think that. However bad it may be at home, anyway they are your father and mother, and not enemies, strangers. Once a year, at least, they'll show their love of you. Anyhow, you know you are at home. I grew up without a home, and perhaps that's why I've turned so — unfeeling."

I waited again. "Perhaps she doesn't understand," I thought, "and, indeed, it's absurd. this moralizing."

"If I were a father and had a daughter, I believe I'd really love my daughter more than my sons," I began indirectly, as though talking of something else, to distract her attention.   I must confess I blushed.

"Why so?" she asked.

Ah! so she was listening!

"I don't know, Liza. I knew a father who was a stern, austere man, but used to go down on his knees to his daughter, used to kiss her hands, her feet, he couldn't make enough of her, really.   When she danced at parties he used to stand for five hours at a stretch, gazing at her. He was mad over her: I understand that! She'd fall asleep tired at night, and he'd wake to kiss her in her sleep and make the sign of the cross over her. He would go about in a dirty old coat, he was stingy to everyone else, but would spend his last penny for her, giving her expensive presents, and it was his greatest delight when she was pleased with what he gave her. Fathers always love their daughters more than the mothers do. Some girls live happily at home! And I believe I'd never let my daughters marry."

"What next?" she asked with a faint smile.

"I'd be jealous, I really should. To think that she should kiss anyone else! That she should love a stranger more than her father! It's painful to imagine it. Of course, that's all nonsense; of course, every father would be reasonable at last. But I believe before I should let her marry I'd worry myself to death; I'd find fault with all her suitors. But I'd end by letting her marry whomever she herself loved. The one whom the daughter loves always seems the worst to the father, you know. That's always so. So many family troubles come from that."

"Some are glad to sell their daughters rather than to marry them off honorably."

Ah, so that was it!

"Such a thing, Liza, happens in those accursed families in which there is neither love nor God," I retorted warmly, "and where there is no love, there is no sense either. There are such families, it's true, but I am not speaking of them. You must have seen wickedness in your own family, if you talk like that. Truly, you must have been unlucky. H'm! That sort of thing mostly comes about through poverty."

"And is it any better with the gentry? Even among the poor, honest people live happily."

"H'm . . . yes. Perhaps. Another thing, Liza, man is fond of reckoning up his troubles, but does not count his joys. If he counted them up as he ought, he'd see that every lot has enough happiness provided for it. And what if all goes well with the family, if the blessing of God is upon it, if the husband is a good one, loves you, cherishes you, never leaves you! There's happiness in such a family! Even sometimes there is happiness in the midst of sorrow; and indeed sorrow is everywhere. If you marry *you will find out for yourself.* But think of the first years of married life with one you love: what happiness, what happiness there sometimes is in it! And indeed it's the usual thing. In those early days even quarrels with one's husband end happily. Some women get up quarrels with their husbands just because they love them. Indeed, I knew a woman like that: she seemed to say that because she loved him she'd torment him and make him feel it. You know that you may torment a man on purpose through love. Women are particularly given to that, thinking to themselves 'I will love him so, I will make so much of him afterward, that it's no sin to torment him a little now.' And all in the house rejoice at the sight of you, and you are happy and gay and peaceful and honored. Then there are some women who are jealous. I knew one such woman; she couldn't restrain herself, but would jump up at night and run off on the sly to find out where he was, if he went off anywhere, whether he was with some other woman. That's a pity. And the woman knows herself it's wrong, and her heart fails her and she suffers, but she loves — it's all through love. And how sweet it is to make up after quarrels, to own herself in the wrong or to forgive him! And they are both suddenly so happy — as though they had met anew, been married over again, as though their love had begun afresh. And no one, no one should know what passes between husband and wife if they love one another. And whatever quarrels there may be between them, they ought not to call in even their own mothers to judge between them and tell tales of one another. They are their own judges. Love is a holy mystery and ought to be hidden from all other eyes, whatever happens. That makes it holier and better. They respect one another more, and much is built on respect. And if once there has been love, if they have been married for love, why should love pass away? Surely one can keep it! It is rare that one can't keep it. And if the husband is kind and straightforward, why should not love last? The first phase of married love will pass, it's true, but then there will come a love that is better still. Then there will be the union of souls, they will have everything in common, there'll be no secrets between them. And once they have children, the most difficult times will seem to them happy, so long as there is love and courage. Even toil will be a joy; you may deny yourself bread for your children and even that will

be a joy. They'll love you for it afterward, so you are putting something away for your future. As the children grow up you feel that you're
an example, a support for them; that even after you die, your children
will always keep your thoughts and feelings, because they have received
them from you; they will take on your semblance and likeness. So you
see this is a great duty. How can it fail to draw the father and mother
nearer? People say it's a trial to have children. Who says that? It is
heavenly happiness! Are you fond of little children, Liza? I'm awfully
fond of them. You know — a little rosy baby boy at your bosom, and
what husband's heart isn't touched, seeing his wife nursing his child!
A plump little rosy baby, sprawling and snuggling, chubby little hands
and feet, clean tiny little nails, so tiny that it makes one laugh to look
at them; eyes that look as if they understand everything. And while
it sucks it clutches at your bosom with its little hand and plays. When
its father comes up, the child tears itself away from the bosom, flings
itself back, looks at its father, laughs, as though it were fearfully funny,
and falls to sucking again. Or it will bite its mother's breast when its
little teeth are coming, while it looks sideways at her, with its little
eyes as though to say, 'Look, I'm biting!' Isn't it happiness when the
three are together, husband, wife, and child? One can forgive a great
deal for the sake of such moments. Yes, Liza, one must first learn to
live oneself before one blames others!"

"It's by pictures, pictures like that one must get at you," I thought
to myself, though I did speak with real feeling, and all at once I flushed
crimson. "What if she were suddenly to burst out laughing, what should
I do then?" That idea drove me to fury. Toward the end of my speech
I really was excited, and now my vanity was somehow wounded. The
silence continued. I almost nudged her.

"Why are you — " she began and stopped. But I understood: there
was a quiver of something different in her voice, not abrupt, harsh,
and unyielding as before, but something soft and shamefaced, so shamefaced that I suddenly felt ashamed and guilty.

"What?" I asked with tender curiosity.

"Why, you —"

"What?"

"Why, you — talk like a book, somehow," she said, and again there
was a note of irony in her voice.

That remark sent a pang through my heart. It wasn't what I had
been expecting.

I did not understand that she was hiding her feelings under irony, that this is usually the last refuge of modest and chaste-souled people when the privacy of their soul is coarsely and unfeelingly invaded, and that their pride makes them refuse to surrender till the last moment and shrink from giving expression to their feelings before you. I ought to have guessed the truth from the timidity with which she had repeatedly approached her sarcasm, only bringing herself to utter it at last with an effort. But I did not guess, and an evil feeling took possession of me.

"Wait a bit!" I thought.

VII

"Oh, hush, Liza! How can you talk about talking like a book, when it makes even me, an outsider, feel sick? Though I don't look at it as an outsider, for, indeed, it touches me to the heart. Is it possible — is it possible that you do not feel sick at being here yourself? Evidently habit does wonders! God knows what habit can do with anyone. Can you seriously think that you'll never grow old, that you'll never lose your looks, and that they'll keep you here for ever and ever? I say nothing of the loathsomeness of the life here. Though let me tell you this about it — about your present life, I mean; here though you are young now, attractive, nice, with soul and feeling, yet you know as soon as I came to myself just now I felt at once sick at being here with you! One can only come here when one is drunk. But if you were anywhere else, living as good people live, I would perhaps be more than attracted by you, fall in love with you, be glad of a look from you, let alone a word; I'd hang about your door, go down on my knees to you, look upon you as my betrothed and think it an honor. I would not dare to have an impure thought about you. But here, you see, I know that I have only to whistle and you have to come with me whether you like it or not. I don't consult your wishes, but you mine. The lowest laborer hires himself as a workman but he doesn't make a slave of himself altogether, besides, he knows that he will be free again presently. But when are you free? Only think what you're giving up here! What are you enslaving? Your soul, together with your body; you're selling your soul, which you have no right to dispose of! You give your love to be outraged by every drunkard! Love! But that's everything, you know, it's a priceless diamond, it's a maiden's treasure; love — why, a man would be ready to give his soul, to face death to gain that love. But how much is your love worth now? You are sold, all of you, body and soul, and there's no need to strive for love when one can have everything without love. And you know there's no greater insult to a girl than that, do you understand? To be sure, I've heard that they comfort you poor fools, they let you have lovers of your own here. But you know that's simply a farce, that's simply a sham, it's just mockery, and you're taken in by it! Why, do you suppose he really loves you, that lover of yours? I don't believe it. How can he love you when he knows you may be called away from him, any minute? He would be a low fellow if he did! Will he have a grain of respect for you? What have you in common with him? He laughs at you and robs you — that's all his love amounts to! You are lucky if he doesn't beat you. Very likely he does beat you, too. Ask him if you have got one, whether he'll marry you. He'll laugh in your face, if he doesn't spit in it or give you a blow — though maybe he isn't worth a damn himself. And for what have you ruined your life, if you come to think of it? For the coffee they give you to drink and the plentiful meals? But with what object are they fattening you? An honest girl couldn't swallow the food, for she'd know what she was being fed for. You're in debt here, and, of course, you'll always be in debt, and you will go on being in debt to the very end, till the visitors here begin to scorn you. And that'll happen soon enough. Don't rely upon your youth — all that flies by express here, you know. You'll be kicked out. And not simply kicked out; long before that the madam will begin nagging at you, scolding you, abusing you, as though you had not sacrificed your health for her, had not thrown away your youth and your soul for her benefit, but as though you had ruined her, beggared her, robbed her. And don't expect anyone to take your part: the others, your companions, will attack you, too, to win her favor, for all are in slavery here, and here they have lost all conscience and pity long ago. They have become utterly vile, and nothing on earth is viler, more loathsome, and more insulting than their abuse. And you're laying down everything here, unconditionally, youth and health and beauty and hope, and at twenty-two you will look like a woman of five-and-thirty, and you'll be lucky if you're not diseased; pray to God to save you from that! No doubt you are thinking now that you have a fine time and no work to do! Yet there is no work harder or more dreadful in the world or ever has been. One would think that the heart alone would be worn out with tears. And you won't dare to say a word, not half a word, when they drive you away from here; you'll go away as though you were to blame. You'll change to another house, then to a third, then somewhere else, till you come down at last to the Hay Market. There you'll be beaten at every turn; that's good manners there, the visitors don't know how to be friendly without beating you. You don't believe that it's so hateful there? Go and look for yourself some time, you can see with your own eyes. Once, one New Year's Day, I saw a woman at a door. They had turned her out as a joke, to give her a taste of the frost because she had been crying so much, and they shut the door behind her. At nine o'clock in the morning she was already quite drunk, disheveled, half naked, covered with bruises, her face was powdered but she had a black eye, blood was trickling from her nose and her teeth; some cabman had just given her a drubbing. She was sitting on the stone steps, a salt fish of some sort in her hand; she was crying, wailing something about her luck and slapping the fish on the steps, and cabmen and drunken soldiers were crowding in the doorway taunting her. You don't believe that you'll ever get to be like that? I'd be sorry to believe it, too, but how do you know — maybe ten years, eight years ago, that very woman with the salt fish came here fresh as a cherub, innocent, pure, knowing no evil, blushing at every word. Perhaps she was like you, proud, ready to take offense, not like the others; perhaps she looked like a queen, and knew what happiness was in store for the man who should love her and whom she should love. Do you see how it ended? And what if at that very moment when she was pounding her salted fish on the filthy steps, drunken and disheveled — what if at that very moment she recalled the early days of her purity in her father's house, when she used to go to school and the neighbor's son watched for her on the way, declaring that he'd love her as long as he lived, that he'd devote his life to her, and when they vowed to love one another for ever and be married as soon as they were grown up! No, Liza, it would be happy for you if you were to die soon of tuberculosis in some corner, in some cellar like that woman just now. In the hospital, do you say? You'll be lucky if they take you, but what if you are still of use to the madam here? Tuberculosis is a queer disease; it's not like fever. The patient goes on hoping till the last minute and says he's all right. He deludes himself. And that just suits your madam. Never doubt it, that's how it is. You've sold your soul, and what is more, you owe money, so you daren't say a word. But when you're dying, everyone will abandon you, everyone will turn away from you, for then there will be nothing to get from you. What's more, they will reproach you for cumbering the place, for being so long over dying. However you beg you won't get a drink of water without abuse: 'Whenever are you going off, you nasty hussy, you won't let us sleep with your moaning, you make the gentlemen sick.' That's true, I've heard such things said myself. They

will thrust you dying into the filthiest corner in the cellar — in the damp
and the darkness; what will your thoughts be, lying there alone? When
you die, strange hands will lay you out, with grumbling and impatience;
no one will bless you, no one will sigh for you, all they want is to get
rid of you as soon as possible; they'll buy a coffin, drag you to the grave
as they did that poor woman today, and celebrate your memory at some
pothouse. There'll be sleet, filth, melting snow in the grave — no need
to put themselves out for you. 'Let her down, Vanuha. It's just like her
luck — even here she's upside down, the hussy. Tauten the rope, you
scalawag.' 'It's all right as it is.' 'All right, is it? Why, she's on her
side! She was a fellow creature, after all! But, never mind, throw the
earth on her.' And they won't care to waste much time quarreling over
you. They'll throw on the wet blue clay as quick as they can and go off to
the pothouse — and there all memory of you on earth will end; other
women have children to go to their graves, fathers, husbands. But for
you there'll be never a tear, nor a sigh, nor any remembrance; no one
in the whole world will ever come to you, your name will vanish from
off the face of the earth — as though you'd never existed, never been
born at all! Nothing but filth and mud, however you knock at your
coffin lid at night, when the dead arise, however you cry: 'Let me out,
kind people, to live in the light of day! My life was no life at all; my
life was thrown away like a dishclout; it was drunk away in the pothouse
at the Hay Market; let me out, kind people, to live in the world again!'"

And I worked myself up to such a pitch that I began to have a lump
in my throat myself, and . . . and all at once I stopped, sat up in
dismay, and, bending over apprehensively, began to listen with a beating heart. I had reason to be worried.

I had felt for some time that I was turning her soul inside out and
rending her heart, and — and the more I was convinced of it, the more
eagerly I desired to gain my object as quickly and as effectually as
possible. It was the exercise of my skill that carried me away; yet it
was more than mere sport.

I knew I was speaking stiffly, artificially, even bookishly; in fact,
I could not speak except "like a book." But that did not trouble me:
I knew, I felt that I should be understood and that this very bookish-
ness might be a help. But now, having attained my effect, I was suddenly panic-stricken. Never before had I witnessed such despair! She
was lying on her face, thrusting her face into the pillow and clutching at
it with both hands. Her heart was being rent. Her youthful body was
shuddering all over as though in convulsions. Suppressed sobs rent her

bosom and suddenly burst out in weeping and wailing, whereupon she buried her face deeper in the pillow: she did not want anyone here, not a living soul, to know of her anguish and her tears.   She bit the pillow, bit her hand till it bled (I saw that afterward), or, plunging her fingers into her disheveled hair, seemed rigid with the effort of restraint, holding her breath and clenching her teeth.   I started to say something, begging her to calm herself, but felt that I did not dare; and all at once, in a sort of cold shiver, almost in terror, began fumbling in the dark, trying hurriedly to get dressed and then go.   It was dark: though I tried my best I could not finish dressing quickly.   Suddenly I felt a box of matches and a candlestick with a whole candle in it. As soon as the room was lighted up, Liza sprang up, sat up in bed, and with a contorted face, with a half-insane smile, looked at me almost senselessly.   I sat down beside her and took her hands; she came to herself, made an impulsive movement toward me, would have caught hold of me, but did not dare, and slowly bowed her head before me.

"Liza, my dear, I was wrong — forgive me, my dear," I began, but she squeezed my hand in her fingers so tightly that I felt I was saying the wrong thing and stopped.

"This is my address, Liza.   Come to me."

"I'll come," she answered resolutely, her head still bowed.

"But now I am going, good-by — till we meet again."

I got up.   She, too, stood up and suddenly flushed all over, gave a shudder, snatched up a shawl that was lying on a chair, and muffled herself in it to her chin.   As she did this she gave another sickly smile, blushed and looked at me strangely.   I felt wretched; I was in haste to get away — to disappear.

"Wait a minute," she said suddenly in the passage just at the doorway, stopping me with her hand on my overcoat.   She put down the candle in hot haste and ran off; evidently she had thought of something or wanted to show me something.   As she ran away she flushed, her eyes shone, and there was a smile on her lips — what was the meaning of it?   Against my will I waited; she came back a minute later with an expression that seemed to ask forgiveness for something.   In fact, it was not the same face, not the same look as the evening before — sullen, mistrustful, and obstinate.   Her eyes now were imploring, soft, and at the same time trustful, caressing, timid.   The expression with which children look at people they are very fond of, of whom they are asking a favor.   Her eyes were a light hazel, they were lovely eyes, full of life, and capable of expressing love as well as sullen hatred.

Making no explanation, as though I, as a sort of higher being, must understand everything without explanations, she held out a piece of paper to me. Her whole face was positively beaming at that instant with naïve, almost childish triumph. I unfolded it. It was a letter to her from a medical student or someone of that sort — a very highflown and flowery, but extremely respectful, love letter. I don't recall the words now, but I remember well that through the highflown phrases there was apparent a genuine feeling, which could not be feigned. When I had finished reading it I met her glowing, questioning, and childishly impatient eyes fixed upon me. She fixed her eyes upon my face and waited impatiently for what I should say. In a few words, hurriedly, but with a sort of joy and pride, she explained to me that she had been to a dance somewhere in a private house, a family of "very nice people, *who knew nothing*, absolutely nothing, for she had only come here so lately, and it was only through chance she'd gotten in here . . . and she hadn't made up her mind to stay and was certainly going away as soon as she'd paid her debt. . . . " And the student had been at that party and had danced with her all evening. He had talked to her, and it turned out that he'd known her in the old days at Riga when he was a child, they had played together, but a very long time ago — and he knew her parents, but *about this* he knew nothing, nothing whatever, and had no suspicion! And the day after the dance (three days ago) he had sent her that letter through the friend with whom she had gone to the party . . . and . . . well, that was all.

She dropped her shining eyes with a sort of bashfulness as she finished.

The poor girl was keeping that student's letter as a precious treasure, and had run to fetch it, her only treasure, because she did not want me to go away without knowing that she, too, was honestly and genuinely loved; that she, too, was addressed respectfully. No doubt that letter was destined to lie in her box and lead to nothing. But none the less I am certain that she would keep it all her life as a precious treasure, as her pride and justification, and now at such a minute she had thought of that letter and brought it with naïve pride to raise herself in my eyes that I might see; that I, too, might think well of her. I said nothing, pressed her hand, and went out. I very much longed to get away. I walked all the way home, in spite of the fact that the snow was still falling in heavy melting flakes. I was exhausted, shattered, in bewilderment. But behind the bewilderment the truth was already glinting. The loathsome truth.

VIII

It was some time, however, before I consented to recognize that truth. Waking up in the morning after some hours of heavy, leaden sleep, and immediately realizing all that had happened on the previous day, I was positively amazed at my last night's *sentimentality* with Liza, at all those "outcries of horror and pity." "To think of having such an attack of womanish hysteria, pah!" I concluded. And what did I thrust my address upon her for? What if she comes? Let her come, though; it doesn't matter. But *obviously*, that was not now the chief and the most important matter: I had to make haste and at all costs save my reputation in the eyes of Zvercov and Simonov as quickly as possible; that was the chief business. And I was so taken up that morning that I actually forgot all about Liza.

First of all I had at once to repay what I had borrowed the day before from Simonov. I resolved on a desperate measure: to borrow fifteen rubles at once from Anton Antonich. As luck would have it, he was in the best of moods that morning and gave me the sum right away, without waiting to be asked twice. I was so delighted at this that, as I signed the I O U with a swaggering air, I told him casually that the night before "I'd been hitting it up with some friends at the Hôtel de Paris; we were giving a farewell party to a comrade, in fact, I might say a friend of my childhood, and you know — a desperate rake, fearfully spoilt — of course, he belongs to a good family, and has considerable means, a brilliant career; he's witty, charming, a regular Don Juan, you understand; we drank an extra half-dozen and — "

And it went off all right; all this was uttered very casually, unconstrainedly, and complacently.

On reaching home I promptly wrote to Simonov.

To this hour I am lost in admiration when I recall the truly gentlemanly, good-humored, candid tone of my letter. With tact and good breeding and, above all, entirely without superfluous words, I blamed myself for all that had happened. I defended myself, "if I really may be allowed to defend myself," by alleging that being utterly unaccustomed to wine, I had been intoxicated with the first glass, which I said I had drunk before they arrived, while waiting for them at the Hôtel de Paris between five and six o'clock. I begged Simonov's pardon in particular. I asked him to convey my explanations to all the others, especially to Zvercov, whom "I seemed to remember insulting as though in a dream." I added that I would have called upon all of them myself, but my head ached, and besides I could not face them. I was particularly pleased with a certain lightness, almost nonchalance (strictly within the bounds of politeness, however), which was apparent in my style, and better than any possible arguments gave them at once to understand that I took rather an independent view of "all that unpleasantness last night," that I was by no means so utterly crushed as you, my friends, probably imagine, but on the contrary looked upon it as a gentleman serenely respecting himself should. "On a young hero's past no censure is cast!"

"There is actually an aristocratic playfulness about it!" I thought admiringly as I read over the letter. And it's all because I am an intellectual and cultured man! Another man in my place would not have known how to extricate himself, but here I have gotten out of it and am again as jolly as ever, and all because I am "a cultured and educated man of our day." And, indeed, perhaps everything was due to the wine yesterday. H'm! No, it wasn't the wine. I hadn't drunk anything at all between five and six when I was waiting for them. I had lied to Simonov; I had lied shamelessly; and indeed I wasn't ashamed now. Hang it all, though, the great thing was that I was rid of the mess.

I put six rubles in the letter, sealed it up, and asked Apollon to take it to Simonov. When he learned that there was money in the letter, Apollon became more respectful and agreed to take it. Toward evening I went out for a walk. My head was still aching and dizzy after yesterday. But as evening came on and the twilight deepened, my impressions and, following them, my thoughts grew more and more different and confused. Something was not dead within me, in the depths of my heart and conscience it would not die, and it evinced itself in acute depression. For the most part I jostled my way through the most crowded business streets, along Meshchanski Street, along Sadovyi Street, and in Yusupov Garden. I always liked particularly sauntering along these streets in the dusk, just when there were crowds of working people of all sorts going home from their daily work, with faces looking cross from worry. What I liked was just that cheap bustle, that bald prose. On this occasion the jostling of the streets irritated me more than ever. I could not make out what was wrong with me, I could not find the clue, something seemed rising up in my soul continually, painfully, and refusing to be appeased. I returned home completely upset. It was just as though some crime were lying on my conscience.

The thought that Liza was coming worried me continually. It seemed queer to me that of all my recollections of yesterday this, seemingly, tormented me especially, quite by itself, as it were. Everything else I had quite succeeded in forgetting by evening; I dismissed it all and was still perfectly satisfied with my letter to Simonov. But on this point I was not satisfied at all. It was as though I were worried only by Liza. "What if she comes?" I thought incessantly. "Well, it doesn't matter, let her come! H'm, it's horrid that she should see how I live, for instance. Yesterday I seemed such a hero to her, while now — h'm! It's horrid, though, that I have let myself go so; my room looks like a beggar's. And I brought myself to go out to dinner in such a suit! And my leatheroid sofa with the stuffing sticking out, and my dressing gown which won't cover me, it's so tattered. And she'll see all this — and Apollon, too. That beast is certain to insult her. He'll fasten upon her in order to be rude to me. And, of course, I'll be panic-stricken as usual; I'll begin bowing and scraping before her and pulling my dressing gown about me; I'll begin smiling, telling lies. Oh, the loathsomeness of it all! And it isn't the loathsomeness that matters most! There's something more important, more loathsome, viler! Yes, viler! And to put on that dishonest lying mask again!"

When I reached that thought I fired up all at once.

"Why dishonest? How dishonest? I was speaking sincerely last night. I remember there was real feeling in me, too. What I wanted was to excite an honorable feeling in her. . . . Her crying was a good thing; it'll have a good effect."

Yet I could not feel at ease. All that evening, even when I had come back home, even after nine o'clock, when I calculated that Liza could not possibly come, she still haunted me, and what was worse she came back to my mind always in the same attitude. One moment out of all that had happened last night stood vividly before my imagination: the moment when I struck a match and saw her pale, distorted face, with its look of torture. And what a pitiful, what an unnatural, what a distorted smile she had at that moment! But I did not know then that fifteen years later I should still see Liza in my imagination, always with the pitiful, distorted, incongruous smile which was on her face at that moment.

Next day I was ready again to look upon it all as nonsense, due to overexcited nerves, and, above all, as *exaggerated*. I was always conscious of that weak point of mine, and sometimes very much afraid of it. "I exaggerate everything; that's where I go wrong," I repeated to myself every hour. But, however, "Liza will very likely come all the same" was the refrain with which all my reflections ended. I was so uneasy that I sometimes flew into a fury: "She'll come, she's certain to come!" I cried, dashing about the room, "if not today then tomorrow; she'll find me out! The damnable romanticism of these pure hearts! Oh, the vileness —oh, the silliness — oh, the stupidity of these "wretched sentimental souls"! Why, how could one fail to understand? How could one?

But at this point I stopped short, and in great confusion, at that.

And how few, how few words, I thought, in passing, were needed; how little of the idyllic (and affectedly, bookishly, artificially idyllic too) had sufficed to turn a whole human life at once according to my will. That's virginity, to be sure! Freshness of soil!

At times a thought occurred to me, to go to her to "tell her all," and beg her not to come to me. But this thought stirred up such wrath in me that I believed I would have crushed that "damned" Liza if she had chanced to be near me at the time. I would have insulted her, have spat at her, have turned her out, have struck her!

One day passed, however, then another and another; she did not come and I began to grow calmer. I felt particularly bold and cheerful after nine o'clock. I even sometimes began dreaming and rather sweetly: I, for instance, became Liza's salvation, simply through her coming to me and my talking to her. I developed her, educated her. Finally, I noticed that she loved me, loved me passionately. I pretended not to understand (I don't know, however, why I pretended — just for effect, perhaps). At last all in confusion, transfigured, trembling and sobbing, she flung herself at my feet and said that I was her savior, and that she loved me better than anything in the world. I was amazed, but — "Liza," I said, "can you imagine that I have not noticed your love? I saw it all, I divined it, but I did not dare to approach you first, because I had an influence over you and was afraid that you would force yourself, from gratitude, to respond to my love, would try to rouse in your heart a feeling which was perhaps absent, and I did not wish that — because it would be tyranny. It would be indelicate [in short, I launched off at that point into Continental, inexplicably lofty subtleties à la George Sand], but now, now you are mine, you are my creation, you are pure, you are good, you are my noble wife.

> 'And into my house, calm and fearless,
> As its full mistress walk thou in.' "

Then we began living together, went abroad, and so on and so on.

In fact, in the end it seemed vulgar to my own self, and I began putting out my tongue at myself.

Besides, they won't let the hussy out, I thought. They don't let them go out very readily, especially in the evening (for some reason I fancied she would come in the evening, and at seven o'clock precisely). Though she did say she was not altogether a slave there yet, and had certain rights, so — h'm! Damn it all, she will come, she's sure to come!

It was a good thing, in fact, that Apòllon distracted my attention at that time by his rudeness. He drove me beyond all patience! He was the bane of my life, the curse laid upon me by Providence. We had been squabbling continually for years, and I hated him. My God, how I hated him! I believe I had never hated anyone in my life as I hated him, especially at certain moments. He was an elderly, dignified man, who worked part of his time as a tailor. But for some unknown reason he despised me beyond all measure, and looked down upon me insufferably. Though, for that matter, he looked down upon everyone. Simply to glance at that flaxen, smoothly brushed head, at the tuft of hair he combed up on his forehead and oiled with sunflower oil, at that dignified mouth, compressed into the shape of the letter B, made one feel one was confronting a man who never had any doubts of himself. He was a pedant, to the utmost degree, the greatest pedant I had met on this earth, and with that had a vanity befitting only Alexander of Macedonia. He was in love with every button on his coat, every nail on his fingers — absolutely in love with them, and he looked it! In his behavior to me he was a perfect tyrant, he spoke very little to me, and if he chanced to glance at me he gave me a firm, majestically self-confident and invariably sarcastic look that sometimes drove me to fury. He did his work with the air of doing me the greatest favor — though he did scarcely anything for me, and did not, indeed, consider himself bound to do anything. There could be no doubt that he looked upon me as the greatest fool on earth, and that he did not "get rid" of me was simply so he could get wages from me every month. He consented to do nothing for me for seven rubles a month. Many sins should be forgiven me for what I suffered from him.

My hatred reached such a point that sometimes his very step almost threw me into convulsions. What I loathed particularly was his lisp. His tongue must have been a little too long or something of that sort, for he continually lisped, and seemed to be very proud of it, imagining that it greatly added to his dignity. He spoke in a slow, measured tone, with his hands behind his back and his eyes fixed on the ground. He maddened me particularly when he read aloud the Psalms to himself behind his partition. Many a battle I waged over that reading! But he was awfully fond of reading aloud in the evenings, in a slow, even, singsong voice, as though over the dead. Interestingly enough, that's just how he wound up his career: he hired himself out to read the Psalms over the dead, and at the same time killed rats and made shoe-blacking. But at that time I could not get rid of him; it was as though he were chemically combined with my existence. Besides, nothing would have induced him to consent to leaving me. I could not live in furnished lodgings: my lodging was my private solitude, my shell, my cave, in which I concealed myself from all mankind, and Apollon seemed to me, for some reason, an integral part of that flat, and for seven years I could not turn him away.

To be two or three days behind with his wages, for instance, was impossible. He would have made such a fuss that I wouldn't have known where to hide my head. But I was so exasperated with everyone during those days that I made up my mind for some reason and with some object to *punish* Apollon and not to pay him for a fortnight the wages that were due him. I had for a long time — for the last two years — been intending to do this, simply in order to teach him not to give himself airs before me, and to show him that if I liked I could withhold his wages. I proposed to say nothing to him about it, and was indeed purposely silent, in order to score off his pride and force him to be the first to speak of his wages. Then I would take the seven rubles out of a drawer, show him I had the money put aside on purpose, but that I wouldn't, I wouldn't, I simply wouldn't pay him his wages; I wouldn't, just because that was "my wish," because "I was master, and it was for me to decide," because he had been disrespectful, because he had been rude; but if he were to ask respectfully I might be softened and give it to him, otherwise he might wait another fortnight, another three weeks, a whole month.

But angry as I was, he nevertheless got the better of me. I could not hold out for four days. He began as he always did in such cases, for there had been such cases already, there had been attempts (and it may be observed I knew all this beforehand, I knew his nasty tactics by heart). He would begin by fixing upon me an exceedingly severe stare, keeping it up for several minutes at a time, particularly on meeting me or seeing me out of the house. If I held out and pretended not to notice these stares he would, still in silence, proceed to further tortures. All at once, *à propos* of nothing, he would glide softly into

my room, when I was pacing up and down or reading, stand at the
door, one hand behind his back and one foot back of the other, and
fix upon me a stare more than severe, utterly contemptuous. If I suddenly asked him what he wanted he would make me no answer but
continue staring at me persistently for some seconds, then, with a
peculiar compression of his lips and a most significant air, deliberately
turn around and deliberately go back to his room. Two hours later he
would come out again, and again present himself before me in the
same way. Sometimes I was so infuriated I did not even ask him what
he wanted but simply raised my head sharply and imperiously and
began staring back at him. We stared at one another for two minutes;
at last he turned with deliberation and dignity and went back again
for two hours.

If I were still not brought to reason by all this but persisted in my
revolt, he would suddenly begin sighing while he looked at me, long,
deep sighs as though measuring by them the depths of my moral
degradation, and, of course, it ended at last by his triumphing completely: I raged and shouted, but still was forced to do what he wanted.

This time the usual staring maneuvers had scarcely begun when I
lost my temper and flew at him in a fury. I was irritated beyond endurance, and not only on his account.

"Wait!" I cried in a frenzy as he was slowly and silently turning,
with one hand behind his back, to go to his room. "Wait! Come back,
come back, I tell you!" and I must have screamed so unnaturally that
he turned around and even looked at me with some wonder. However,
he persisted in saying nothing, and that infuriated me.

"How dare you come and look at me like that without being sent
for? Answer me!"

After looking at me calmly for half a minute, he began turning
round again.

"Wait!" I roared, running up to him. "Don't stir! There. Answer,
now — what did you come to look at?"

"If you have any order to give me it's my duty to carry it out,"
he answered after another silent pause, with a slow, measured lisp,
raising his eyebrows and calmly twisting his head from side to side,
all this with exasperating composure.

"That's not what I'm asking you about, you torturer!" I shouted,
turning crimson with anger. "I'll tell you myself why you came here.
You see, I don't give you your wages, but you are so proud you don't
want to bow down and ask for them, and so you come to punish me

with your stupid stares, to worry me, and you have no sus-pi-cion how stupid it is — stupid, stupid, stupid, stupid!"

He would have turned around again without a word, but I seized him.

"Listen," I shouted to him, "here's the money, do you see, here it is [I took it out of the table drawer], here are the seven rubles, in full, but you're not going to get them. You — are — not — going — to — get — them until you come respectfully with bowed head and beg my pardon. You hear?"

"That cannot be," he answered with the most preternatural self-confidence.

"It shall be so," I said. "I give you my word of honor it shall be!"

"And there's nothing for me to beg your pardon for," he went on, as though he had not noticed my exclamations at all. "And, besides, you called me a 'torturer,' for which I can summon you to the police station at any time, for an insulting action."

"Go, summon me," I roared. "Go at once, this very minute, this very second! You are a torturer all the same! A torturer!"

But he merely looked at me, then turned, and, regardless of my loud calls to him, walked to his room with an even step and without looking around.

"If it had not been for Liza nothing of this would have happened," I decided inwardly. Then, after waiting a minute, I went myself behind his screen with a dignified and solemn air, though my heart was beating slowly and violently.

"Apollon," I said quietly and emphatically, though I was breathless, "go at once without a minute's delay and fetch the police officer."

He had meanwhile settled himself at his table, put on his spectacles, and picked up some garment he was mending. But, hearing my order, he burst into a guffaw.

"At once, go this minute! Go on or else you can't imagine what will happen."

"You are certainly out of your mind," he observed without even raising his head, lisping as deliberately as ever and threading his needle. "Whoever heard of a man sending for the police against himself? And as for being frightened — you are upsetting yourself about nothing, for nothing will come of it."

"Go!" I shrieked, shaking him by the shoulder. I felt I would strike him in a minute.

But I did not notice the door from the passage softly and slowly open at that instant and a figure come in, stop short, and begin staring at us in perplexity. I glanced, nearly swooned with shame, and rushed back to my room. There, clutching at my hair with both hands, I leaned my head against the wall and stood thus motionless.

Two minutes later I heard Apollon's deliberate footsteps.

"There's some woman asking for you," he said, looking at me with peculiar severity. Then he stood aside and let in Liza. He would not go away, but stared at us sarcastically.

"Go away, go away," I commanded in desperation. At that moment my clock began whirring and wheezing and struck seven.

IX

And into my house, calm and fearless,
As its full mistress walk thou in.

I stood before her crushed, crestfallen, revoltingly confused, and I believe I smiled as I did my utmost to wrap myself in the folds of my ragged quilted dressing gown — exactly as, in a fit of depression, ι had imagined the scene not long before. After standing over us for a couple of minutes Apollon went away, but that did not put me any more at ease. What made it worse was that she, too, was overwhelmed with confusion — more so, in fact, than I might have expected. Overwhelmed at the sight of me, of course.

"Sit down," I said mechanically, moving a chair up to the table, and I sat down on the sofa. She obediently seated herself at once and gazed at me open-eyed, evidently expecting something from me at once. This naïveté of expectation drove me to fury, but I restrained myself.

She ought to have tried not to notice, as though everything had been as usual, while instead of that, she. . . . And I dimly felt that I should make her pay dearly for *all this.*

"You have found me in a strange position, Liza," I began, stammering and knowing that this was the wrong way to begin. "No, no, don't imagine anything," I cried, seeing that she had suddenly flushed. "I am not ashamed of my poverty. On the contrary, I regard my poverty with pride. I am poor but honorable. One can be poor and honorable," I mumbled. "However . . . Would you like tea?"

"No" — she was about to refuse.

"Wait a minute."

I leaped up and ran to Apollon. I had to get out of the room somehow.

"Apollon," I whispered in feverish haste, flinging down before him the seven rubles which had remained all the time in my clenched fist, "here are your wages. See, I give them to you; but for that you must come to my rescue: bring me tea and a dozen zwieback from the restaurant. If you won't go, you'll make me a miserable man! You don't know who this woman is. This is — everything! You may be imagining something — but you don't know what that woman is!"

Apollon, who had already sat down to his work and put on his spectacles again, at first glanced askance at the money without speaking or putting down his needle; then, without paying the slightest attention to me or making any answer, he went on busying himself with his needle, which he had not yet threaded. I waited before him for three minutes with my arms crossed à la Napoleon. My temples were dank with sweat. I was pale, I felt. But, thank God, he must have been moved to pity, looking at me. Having threaded his needle he deliberately got up from his seat, deliberately moved back his chair, deliberately took off his spectacles, deliberately counted the money, and, finally asking me over his shoulder: "Shall I get enough for two?", deliberately walked out of the room. As I was going back to Liza the thought occurred to me: Shouldn't I run away just as I was in my dressing gown, no matter where, and then let come what might?

I sat down again. She looked at me uneasily. For some minutes we were silent.

"I will kill him," I shouted suddenly, striking the table with my fist so that the ink spurted out of the inkstand.

"What are you saying!" she cried, starting.

"I will kill him! Kill him!" I shrieked, suddenly striking the table in absolute frenzy and at the same time fully understanding how stupid it was to be so frenzied. "You don't know, Liza, what a torturer he is to me. He is my torturer. He went just now to fetch something; he —"

And suddenly I burst into tears. It was an hysterical attack. How ashamed I felt in the midst of my sobs! But still I could not restrain them.

She was frightened.

"What's the matter? What's wrong?" she cried, fussing about me.

"Water, give me water! Over there!" I muttered faintly, though I was inwardly conscious that I could have got on very well without water and without muttering faintly. But I was what is called *putting on an act*, to save appearances, though the attack was a genuine one.

She gave me water, looking at me in bewilderment. At that moment

Apollon brought in the tea. It suddenly seemed to me that this commonplace, prosaic tea was horribly undignified and paltry after all that had happened, and I blushed crimson. Liza looked at Apollon with positive alarm. He went out without a glance at either of us.

"Liza, do you despise me?" I asked, looking at her fixedly, trembling with impatience to know what she was thinking.

She was confused and did not know what to answer.

"Drink your tea," I said to her angrily. I was angry with myself, but, of course, it was she who would have to pay for it. A horrible spite against her suddenly surged up in my heart; I believe I could have killed her. To revenge myself on her I swore inwardly not to say a word to her all the time. "She is the cause of it all," I thought.

Our silence lasted for five minutes. The tea stood on the table; we did not touch it. I had got to the point of purposely refraining from breaking the silence in order to embarrass her further; it was awkward for her to begin. Several times she glanced at me with mournful perplexity. I was obstinately silent. I was, of course, myself the chief sufferer, because I was fully conscious of the disgusting meanness of my spiteful stupidity, and yet at the same time I could not restrain myself.

"I want to — get away from there altogether," she began, to break the silence in some way, but, poor girl, that was just what she ought not to have spoken about at such a stupid moment to a man as stupid as I was. My heart positively ached with pity for her tactless and unnecessary straightforwardness. But something hideous at once stifled all compassion in me; it even provoked me to greater venom. I did not care what happened. Another five minutes passed.

"Perhaps I am in your way," she began with timidity, hardly audibly, and was getting up.

But as soon as I saw this first impulse of wounded dignity I positively trembled with spite, and at once burst out:

"Why have you come to me? Tell me that, please?" I began, gasping for breath and disregarding all logical connection in my words. I longed to have it all out at once, at one sweep; I did not even trouble how to begin. "Why have you come? Answer me, answer me!" I cried, hardly knowing what I was doing. "I'll tell you, my good girl, why you have come. You've come because I talked sentimental bosh to you that time. So now you are soft as butter and longing for fine sentiments again. But you may as well know that I was laughing at you then. And I'm laughing at you now. Why are you shuddering?

Yes, I was laughing at you! I had been insulted just before, at dinner, by the fellows who came that evening before me. I came to you, meaning to thrash one of them, an officer. But I didn't succeed, I didn't find him; I had to avenge the insult on someone to get even; you turned up, I vented my spleen on you and laughed at you. I had been humiliated, so I wanted to humiliate; I had been treated like a rag, so I wanted to show my power. That's what it was, and you imagined I had come there on purpose to save you. Yes? You imagined that? You imagined that?"

I knew that she would perhaps be muddled and not take it all in exactly, but I knew, too, that she would grasp the gist of it, very well indeed. And so, in fact, she did. She turned white as linen, tried to say something, and her lips worked painfully; but she sank on a chair as though she had been felled by an ax. And all the time afterward she listened to me with her lips parted and her eyes wide open, shuddering in awful terror. The cynicism, the cynicism of my words overwhelmed her.

"Save you!" I went on, jumping up from my chair and dashing up and down the room before her. "Save you from what? But perhaps I myself am worse than you. Why didn't you throw it in my teeth when I was giving you that sermon: 'But what did you yourself come here for? Was it to read me a sermon?' Power, power was what I wanted then, sport was what I wanted; I wanted to wring out your tears, your humiliation, your hysteria — that was what I wanted then! Of course, I couldn't keep it up then, because I'm a foolishly wretched creature, I was frightened, and, the devil knows why, foolishly gave you my address. Afterward, before I got home, I was cursing and swearing at you because of that address; I hated you already because of the lies I had told you. Because I only like playing with words, only dreaming. But, do you know, what I really want is that you should all go to hell. That's what I want. I want peace; yes, I'd sell the whole world for a copper, straight off, if only I'd be left in peace. Is the world to go to pot or am I to go without my tea? I say that the world may go to pot for all I care, so long as I always get my tea. Did you know that or not? Well, anyway, I know that I'm a blackguard, a scoundrel, an egoist, a sluggard. Here I've been shuddering for the last three days at the thought of your coming. And do you know what has worried me particularly for these three days? That I posed as such a hero to you, and now you would see me in a wretched, torn dressing gown, beggarly, loathsome. I told you just now that I was not ashamed of my poverty; well, you may as well know that I am ashamed of it. I am ashamed of it more than of anything, more afraid of it than of being found out if I were a thief, because I am as touchy as though I had been flayed, and the very air blowing on me hurts. Surely by now you must realize that I shall never forgive you for having found me in this wretched dressing gown, just as I was flying at Apollon like a spiteful cur. The savior, the former hero, was flying like a mangy, unkempt sheep dog at his flunky, and the flunky was jeering at him! And I shall never forgive you for the tears I could not help shedding before you just now, like some silly woman put to shame! And for what I am confessing to you now I'll never forgive *you* either! Yes — you must answer for it all because you turned up like this, because I am a blackguard, because I am the nastiest, stupidest, absurdest, and most envious of all the worms on earth, who are not a bit better than I am, but, the devil knows why, are never embarrassed, while I shall always be insulted by every louse. That is my doom! And what is it to me that you don't understand a word of this? And what do I care, what do I care about you, and whether you go to ruin there or not? Do you understand? How I'll hate you now after saying this, for having been here and listening. Why, it's not once in a lifetime a man speaks out like this, and then it is in hysterics! What more do you want? Why do you still stand confronting me, after all this? Why are you upsetting me? Why don't you go?"

But at this point a strange thing happened. I was so accustomed to thinking and imagining everything from books, and to picturing everything in the world to myself just as I had made it up in my dreams beforehand, that I could not all at once take in this strange circumstance. What happened was this: Liza, insulted and crushed by me, understood a great deal more than I imagined. She understood from all this what a woman understands first of all, if she feels genuine love, that is, that I was myself unhappy.

The frightened and wounded expression on her face was followed first by a look of sorrowful perplexity. When I began calling myself a scoundrel and a blackguard and my tears flowed (the tirade was accompanied throughout by tears), her whole face worked convulsively. She was on the point of getting up and stopping me; when I finished she took no notice of my shouting: "Why are you here, why don't you go away?" but realized only that it must have been very bitter for me to say all this. Besides, she was so crushed, poor girl; she considered herself infinitely beneath me; how could she feel anger or resentment? She suddenly leaped up from her chair with an irresistible impulse and held out her hands, yearning toward me, though still timid and not daring to move forward. At this point there was a revulsion in my heart, too. Then she suddenly rushed to me, threw her arms around me, and burst into tears. I, too, could not restrain myself and sobbed as I never had before.

"They won't let me — I can't be good!" I managed to articulate; then I went to the sofa, fell on it face downward, and sobbed on it for a quarter of an hour in genuine hysterics. She came close to me, put her arms around me, and stayed thus, motionless. But the trouble was that the hysterics could not go on forever, and (I am writing the loathsome truth) lying face down on the sofa with my face thrust into my nasty leatheroid cushion, I began by degrees to be aware of a faraway, involuntary but irresistible feeling that it would be awkward now for me to raise my head and look Liza straight in the face. Why was I ashamed? I don't know, but I was ashamed. The thought, too, came into my overwrought brain that our parts now were completely reversed, that she was now the heroine, while I was just such a crushed and humiliated creature as she had been before me that night — four days before. And all this came into my mind during the minutes I was lying on my face on the sofa.

My God! Surely I was not envious of her then.

I don't know, to this day I cannot decide, and at the time, of course, I was still less able than now to understand, what I was feeling. I cannot get on without domineering and tyrannizing over someone, but . . . there is no explaining anything by reasoning and so it is useless to reason.

I mastered myself, however, and raised my head; I had to do so sooner or later. And I am convinced to this day that it was just because I was ashamed to look at her that another feeling was suddenly kindled and flamed up in my heart — a feeling of mastery and possession. My eyes gleamed with passion and I gripped her hands tightly. How I hated her and how I was drawn to her at that minute! The one feeling intensified the other. It was almost like an act of vengeance. At first there was a look of amazement, even of terror on her face, but only for one instant. She warmly and rapturously embraced me.

X

A quarter of an hour later I was rushing up and down the room in frenzied impatience; from minute to minute I went up to the screen and peeped through the crack at Liza. She was sitting on the ground with her head leaning against the bed, and must have been crying. But she did not go away, and that irritated me. This time she understood it all. I had insulted her finally, but . . . there's no need to describe it. She realized that my outburst of passion had been simply revenge, a fresh humiliation, and that to my earlier, almost causeless hatred was added now a *personal hatred*, born of envy. Though I do not maintain positively that she understood all this distinctly; but she certainly did fully understand that I was a despicable man, and, what was worse, incapable of loving her.

I know I shall be told that this is incredible — but it is incredible to be as spiteful and stupid as I was; it may be added that it was strange I should not love her, or, at any rate, appreciate her love. Why is it strange? In the first place, by then I was incapable of love,.for I repeat, with me loving meant tyrannizing and showing my moral superiority. I have never in my life been able to imagine any other sort of love, and have nowadays come to the point of sometimes thinking that love really consists in the right — freely given by the beloved — to tyrannize over her.

Even in my underground dreams I did not imagine love except as a struggle. I began it always with hatred and ended it with moral subjugation, and afterward I never knew what to do with the subjugated object. And what is there to wonder at in that, since I had succeeded in so corrupting myself, since I was so out of touch with "real life," as to have actually thought of reproaching her and putting her to shame for having come to me to hear "fine sentiments"; and did not even guess that she had come, not to hear fine sentiments but to love me, because to a woman all reformation, all salvation from any sort of ruin, and all moral renewal, is contained in love and can only show itself in that form.

I did not hate her so much, however, when I was dashing about the room and peeping through the crack in the screen. I was only insufferably oppressed by her being here. I wanted her to disappear. I wanted "peace," to be left alone in my underground world. Real life oppressed me with its novelty so much that I could hardly breathe.

But several minutes passed and she still remained, without stirring, as though she were unconscious. I had the shamelessness to tap softly on the screen as though to remind her. She started, sprang up, and flew to seek her kerchief, her hat, her coat, as though making her escape from me. Two minutes later she came from behind the screen and, with heavy eyes, looked at me. I gave a spiteful grin, which was forced, however, to *keep up appearances*, and turned away from her eyes.

"Good-by" she said, going toward the door.

I ran up to her, seized her hand, opened it, thrust something in it, and closed it again. Then I turned at once and dashed away in haste to the other corner of the room to avoid seeing her, at any rate.

I did mean a moment ago to tell a lie — to write that I did this accidentally, not knowing through foolishness, through having lost my head, what I was doing. But I don't want to lie, and so I'll say right out that I opened her hand and put the money in it from spite. It came into my head to do this while I was dashing up and down the room and she was sitting behind the screen. But this I can say for certain: though I did that cruel thing purposely, it was not an impulse from the heart, but came from my evil brain. This cruelty was so affected, so purposely made up, so completely a product of the brain, of books, that I could not even keep it up a minute — first I dashed away to avoid seeing Liza, and then in shame and despair rushed after her. I opened the door in the passage and began listening.

"Liza! Liza!" I cried on the stairs, but in a low voice, not boldly.

There was no answer, but I fancied I heard her footsteps, lower down on the stairs.

"Liza!" I cried more loudly.

No answer. But at that minute I heard the unwieldy outer glass door open heavily with a creak and slam violently, the sound echoing up the stairs.

She had gone. I went back to my room hesitatingly. I felt horribly oppressed.

I stood still at the table, beside the chair on which she had sat, and looked aimlessly before me. A minute passed, suddenly I started; straight before me on the table I saw — in short, I saw a crumpled blue five-ruble note, the one I had thrust into her hand a minute before. It was the same note; it could be no other, there was no other in the flat. So she had managed to fling it from her hand on the table at the moment when I had dashed into the corner furthest from her.

Well! I might have expected that she would do that. Might I have expected it? No, I was such an egoist, I was so lacking in respect for my fellow creatures that I could not even imagine she would do so. I could not endure it. A minute later I flew like a madman to dress, flinging on what I could at random and ran headlong after her. She could not have got two hundred paces away when I ran out into the street.

It was a still night, and the snow was coming down thick and falling almost perpendicularly, covering the pavement and the empty street as though with a pillow. There was no one in the street; not a sound was to be heard. The street lamps gave a disconsolate and ineffectual glimmer. I ran two hundred paces to the street intersection and stopped short.

Where had she gone? And why was I running after her?

Why? To fall down before her, to sob with remorse, to kiss her feet, to entreat her forgiveness! I longed for that, my whole breast was being rent to pieces, and never, never shall I recall that moment with indifference. "But — what for?" I thought. Should I not begin to hate her, perhaps, even tomorrow, just because I had kissed her feet today? Should I give her happiness? Had I not recognized that day, for the hundredth time, what I was worth? Should I not torture her?

I stood in the snow, gazing into the troubled darkness, and pondered this.

"And will it not be better," I mused fantastically afterward at home, stifling the living pang of my heart with fantastic dreams — "will it not be better that she should keep the resentment of the insult forever? Resentment — why, it is purification; it is a most stinging and painful consciousness! Tomorrow I should have defiled her soul and have exhausted her heart, while now the feeling of insult will never die in her heart, and however loathsome the filth awaiting her, the feeling of insult will elevate and purify her through hatred. H'm! Perhaps, too, by forgiveness. . . . Will all that make things easier for her, though?"

And, indeed, I will ask an idle question here on my own account: Which is better — cheap happiness or exalted sufferings? Well, which *is* better?

So I dreamed as I sat at home that evening, almost dead with the pain in my soul. Never had I endured such suffering and remorse, yet could there have been the faintest doubt when I ran out from my lodging that I should turn back halfway?

I never met Liza again and I have heard nothing of her. I will add, too, that I remained for a long time afterward pleased with the phrase about the benefit from resentment and hatred in spite of the fact that I almost fell ill from misery.

Even now, so many years later, all this is somehow a very evil memory. I have many evil memories now, but — hadn't I better end my "Notes" here? I believe I made a mistake in beginning to write them;

anyway, I have felt ashamed all the time I've been writing this story. So it's hardly literature as much as a corrective punishment. Why, to tell long stories, showing how I have spoiled my life through morally rotting in my cubbyhole, through lack of fitting environment, through divorce from real life and rankling spite in my underground world, would certainly not be interesting; a novel needs a hero, and all the traits for an antihero are *expressly* gathered together here, and (what matters most) it all produces an unpleasant impression, for we are all divorced from life, we are all cripples, every one of us, more or less.

We are so divorced from it that we feel at once a sort of loathing for real life, and so cannot bear to be reminded of it. Why, we have come almost to look upon real life as an effort, almost as hard work, and we are all privately agreed that it is better in books. And why do we fuss and fume sometimes? Why are we perverse, asking for something else, without ourselves knowing what? It would be the worse for us if our petulant prayers were answered. Come, try, give any one of us, for instance, a little more independence, untie our hands, widen the spheres of our activity, relax the control and we — yes, I assure you — we'd be begging to be under control again at once. I know that you will very likely be angry with me for that, and will begin shouting and stamping. Speak for yourself, you will say, and for your miseries in your underground holes, and don't dare to say "all of us." Excuse me, gentlemen, I'm not justifying myself with that "all of us."

As for what concerns me in particular, I have in my life only carried to an extreme what you have not dared to carry halfway, and what's more, you have taken your cowardice for good sense, and have found comfort in deceiving yourselves. So that perhaps, after all, there is more life in me than in you. Look into it more carefully! Why, we don't even know what living means now, what it is, and what it is called Leave us alone without books and we'll be lost and in confusion at once We'll not know what to join to, what to cling to, what to love and what to hate, what to respect and what to despise. We are oppressed at being men — men with real individual flesh and blood, we are ashamed of it, we think it a disgrace and try to contrive to be some sort of impossible generalized man. We are stillborn, and for generations past have been begotten not by living fathers, and that suits us more and more. We are developing a taste for it. Soon we shall contrive to be born from an idea somehow. But enough; I don't want to write more from *underground.*

[*The notes of this paradoxalist do not end here, however. He could not refrain from going on with them, but it seems to us that we may stop here.*]

[*Translated by* CONSTANCE GARNETT, *revised by* BERNARD GUILBERT GUERNEY.]

Gustave Flaubert

A SIMPLE HEART

1 8 7 7

❦

1

MADAME AUBAIN's servant Félicité was the envy of the ladies of Pont-
l'Évêque for half a century.

She received four pounds a year. For that she was cook and general
servant, and did the sewing, washing, and ironing; she could bridle
a horse, fatten poultry, and churn butter — and she remained faithful
to her mistress, unamiable as the latter was.

Mme. Aubain had married a gay bachelor without money who died
at the beginning of 1809, leaving her with two small children and a
quantity of debts. She then sold all her property except the farms
of Toucques and Geffosses, which brought in two hundred pounds a
year at most, and left her house in Saint-Melaine for a less expensive
one that had belonged to her family and was situated behind the
market.

This house had a slate roof and stood between an alley and a lane
that went down to the river. There was an unevenness in the levels
of the rooms which made you stumble. A narrow hall divided the
kitchen from the "parlour" where Mme. Aubain spent her day,
sitting in a wicker easy chair by the window. Against the panels,
which were painted white, was a row of eight mahogany chairs. On
an old piano under the barometer a heap of wooden and cardboard
boxes rose like a pyramid. A stuffed armchair stood on either side of
the Louis-Quinze chimney-piece, which was in yellow marble with
a clock in the middle of it modelled like a temple of Vesta. The
whole room was a little musty, as the floor was lower than the garden.

The first floor began with "Madame's" room: very large, with a
pale-flowered wallpaper and a portrait of "Monsieur" as a dandy
of the period. It led to a smaller room, where there were two children's
cots without mattresses. Next came the drawing-room, which was

always shut up and full of furniture covered with sheets. Then there was a corridor leading to a study. The shelves of a large bookcase were respectably lined with books and papers, and its three wings surrounded a broad writing-table in darkwood. The two panels at the end of the room were covered with pen-drawings, water-colour landscapes, and engravings by Audran, all relics of better days and vanished splendour. Félicité's room on the top floor got its light from a dormer-window, which looked over the meadows.

She rose at daybreak to be in time for Mass, and worked till evening without stopping. Then, when dinner was over, the plates and dishes in order, and the door shut fast, she thrust the log under the ashes and went to sleep in front of the hearth with her rosary in her hand. Félicité was the stubbornest of all bargainers; and as for cleanness, the polish on her saucepans was the despair of other servants. Thrifty in all things, she ate slowly, gathering off the table in her fingers the crumbs of her loaf — a twelve-pound loaf expressly baked for her, which lasted for three weeks.

At all times of year she wore a print handkerchief fastened with a pin behind, a bonnet that covered her hair, grey stockings, a red skirt, and a bibbed apron — such as hospital nurses wear — over her jacket.

Her face was thin and her voice sharp. At twenty-five she looked like forty. From fifty onwards she seemed of no particular age; and with her silence, straight figure, and precise movements she was like a woman made of wood, and going by clockwork.

II

She had had her love-story like another.

Her father, a mason, had been killed by falling off some scaffolding. Then her mother died, her sisters scattered, and a farmer took her in and employed her, while she was still quite little, to herd the cows at pasture. She shivered in rags and would lie flat on the ground to drink water from the ponds; she was beaten for nothing, and finally turned out for the theft of a shilling which she did not steal. She went to another farm, where she became dairy-maid; and as she was liked by her employers her companions were jealous of her.

One evening in August (she was then eighteen) they took her to the assembly at Colleville. She was dazed and stupefied in an instant by the noise of the fiddlers, the lights in the trees, the gay medley of dresses, the lace, the gold crosses, and the throng of people jigging all together. While she kept shyly apart a young man with a well-to-do air, who was leaning on the shaft of a cart and smoking his pipe, came up to ask her to dance. He treated her to cider, coffee, and cake, and bought her a silk handkerchief; and then, imagining she had guessed his meaning, offered to see her home. At the edge of a field of oats he pushed her roughly down. She was frightened and began to cry out; and he went off.

One evening later she was on the Beaumont road. A big hay-wagon was moving slowly along; she wanted to get in front of it, and as she brushed past the wheels she recognized Theodore. He greeted her quite calmly, saying she must excuse it all because it was "the fault of the drink." She could not think of any answer and wanted to run away.

He began at once to talk about the harvest and the worthies of the commune, for his father had left Colleville for the farm at Les Écots, so that now he and she were neighbours. "Ah!" she said. He added that they thought of settling him in life. Well, he was in no hurry; he was waiting for a wife to his fancy. She dropped her head; and then he asked her if she thought of marrying. She answered with a smile that it was mean to make fun of her.

"But I am not, I swear!" — and he passed his left hand round her waist. She walked in the support of his embrace; their steps grew slower. The wind was soft, the stars glittered, the huge wagon-load of hay swayed in front of them, and dust rose from the dragging steps of the four horses. Then, without a word of command, they turned to the right. He clasped her once more in his arms, and she disappeared into the shadow.

The week after Theodore secured some assignations with her.

They met at the end of farmyards, behind a wall, or under a solitary tree. She was not innocent as young ladies are — she had learned knowledge from the animals — but her reason and the instinct of her honour would not let her fall. Her resistance exasperated Theodore's passion; so much so that to satisfy it — or perhaps quite artlessly — he made her an offer of marriage. She was in doubt whether to trust him, but he swore great oaths of fidelity.

Soon he confessed to something troublesome; the year before his parents had bought him a substitute for the army, but any day he might be taken again, and the idea of serving was a terror to him. Félicité took this cowardice of his as a sign of affection, and it redoubled hers. She stole away at night to see him, and when she reached their meeting-place Theodore racked her with his anxieties and urgings.

At last he declared that he would go himself to the prefecture for information, and would tell her the result on the following Sunday, between eleven and midnight.

When the moment came she sped towards her lover. Instead of him she found one of his friends.

He told her that she would not see Theodore any more. To ensure himself against conscription he had married an old woman, Madame Lehoussais, of Toucques, who was very rich.

There was an uncontrollable burst of grief. She threw herself on the ground, screamed, called to the God of mercy, and moaned by herself in the fields till daylight came. Then she came back to the farm and announced that she was going to leave; and at the end of the month she received her wages, tied all her small belongings with a handkerchief, and went to Pont-l'Évêque.

In front of the inn there she made inquiries of a woman in a widow's cap, who, as it happened, was just looking for a cook. The girl did not know much, but her willingness seemed so great and her demands so small that Mme. Aubain ended by saying:

"Very well, then, I will take you."

A quarter of an hour afterwards Félicité was installed in her house.

She lived there at first in a tremble, as it were, at "the style of the house" and the memory of "Monsieur" floating over it all. Paul and Virginie, the first aged seven and the other hardly four, seemed to her beings of a precious substance; she carried them on her back like a horse; it was a sorrow to her that Mme. Aubain would not let her kiss them every minute. And yet she was happy there. Her grief had melted in the pleasantness of things all round.

Every Thursday regular visitors came in for a game of boston, and Félicité got the cards and foot-warmers ready beforehand. They arrived punctually at eight and left before the stroke of eleven.

On Monday mornings the dealer who lodged in the covered passage spread out all his old iron on the ground. Then a hum of voices began to fill the town, mingled with the neighing of horses, bleating of lambs, grunting of pigs, and the sharp rattle of carts along the street. About noon, when the market was at its height, you might see a tall, hook-nosed old countryman with his cap pushed back making his appearance at the door. It was Robelin, the farmer of Geffosses. A little later came Liébard, the farmer from Toucques — short, red, and corpulent — in a grey jacket and gaiters shod with spurs.

Both had poultry or cheese to offer their landlord. Félicité was invariably a match for their cunning, and they went away filled with respect for her.

At vague intervals Mme. Aubain had a visit from the Marquis de Gremanville, one of her uncles, who had ruined himself by debauchery and now lived at Falaise on his last remaining morsel of land. He invariably came at the luncheon hour, with a dreadful poodle whose paws left all the furniture in a mess. In spite of efforts to show his breeding, which he carried to the point of raising his hat every time he mentioned "my late father," habit was too strong for him; he poured himself out glass after glass and fired off improper remarks. Félicité edged him politely out of the house — "You have had enough, Monsieur de Gremanville! Another time!" — and she shut the door on him.

She opened it with pleasure to M. Bourais, who had been a lawyer. His baldness, his white stock, frilled shirt, and roomy brown coat, his way of rounding the arm as he took snuff — his whole person, in fact, created that disturbance of mind which overtakes us at the sight of extraordinary men.

As he looked after the property of "Madame" he remained shut up with her for hours in "Monsieur's" study, though all the time he was afraid of compromising himself. He respected the magistracy immensely, and had some pretensions to Latin.

To combine instruction and amusement he gave the children a geography book made up of a series of prints. They represented scenes in different parts of the world: cannibals with feathers on their heads, a monkey carrying off a young lady, Bedouins in the desert, the harpooning of a whale, and so on. Paul explained these engravings to Félicité; and that, in fact, was the whole of her literary education. The children's education was undertaken by Guyot, a poor creature employed at the town hall, who was famous for his beautiful hand and sharpened his penknife on his boots.

When the weather was bright the household set off early for a day at Geffosses Farm.

Its courtyard is on a slope, with the farmhouse in the middle, and the sea looks like a grey streak in the distance.

Félicité brought slices of cold meat out of her basket, and they breakfasted in a room adjoining the dairy. It was the only surviving fragment of a country house which was now no more. The wall-paper hung in tatters, and quivered in the draughts. Mme. Aubain sat with bowed head, overcome by her memories; the children became afraid to speak. "Why don't you play, then?" she would say, and off they went.

Paul climbed into the barn, caught birds, played at ducks and drakes over the pond, or hammered with his stick on the big casks which boomed like drums. Virginie fed the rabbits or dashed off to pick cornflowers, her quick legs showing their embroidered little drawers.

One autumn evening they went home by the fields. The moon was in its first quarter, lighting part of the sky; and mist floated like a scarf over the windings of the Toucques. Cattle, lying out in the middle of the grass, looked quietly at the four people as they passed. In the third meadow some of them got up and made a half-circle in front of the walkers. "There's nothing to be afraid of," said Félicité, as she stroked the nearest on the back with a kind of crooning song; he wheeled round and the others did the same. But when they crossed the next pasture there was a formidable bellow. It was a bull, hidden by the mist. Mme. Aubain was about to run. "No! no! don't go so fast!" They mended their pace, however, and heard a loud breathing behind them which came nearer. His hoofs thudded on the meadow grass like hammers; why, he was galloping now! Félicité turned round, and tore up clods of earth with both hands and threw them in his eyes. He lowered his muzzle, waved his horns, and quivered with fury, bellowing terribly. Mme. Aubain, now at the end of the pasture with her two little ones, was looking wildly for a place to get over the high bank. Félicité was retreating, still with her face to the bull, keeping up a shower of clods which blinded him, and crying all the time, "Be quick! be quick!"

Mme. Aubain went down into the ditch, pushed Virginie first and then Paul, fell several times as she tried to climb the bank, and managed it at last by dint of courage.

The bull had driven Félicité to bay against a rail-fence; his slaver was streaming into her face; another second, and he would have gored her. She had just time to slip between two of the rails, and the big animal stopped short in amazement.

This adventure was talked of at Pont-l'Évêque for many a year. Félicité did not pride herself on it in the least, not having the barest suspicion that she had done anything heroic.

Virginie was the sole object of her thoughts, for the child developed a nervous complaint as a result of her fright, and M. Poupart, the doctor, advised sea-bathing at Trouville. It was not a frequented place then. Mme. Aubain collected information, consulted Bourais, and made preparations as though for a long journey.

Her luggage started a day in advance, in Liébard's cart. The next day he brought round two horses, one of which had a lady's saddle with a velvet back to it, while a cloak was rolled up to make a kind of seat on the crupper of the other. Mme. Aubain rode on that, behind the farmer. Félicité took charge of Virginie, and Paul mounted M. Lechaptois' donkey, lent on condition that great care was taken of it.

The road was so bad that its five miles took two hours. The horses sank in the mud up to their pasterns, and their haunches jerked abruptly in the effort to get out; or else they stumbled in the ruts, and at other moments had to jump. In some places Liébard's mare came suddenly to a halt. He waited patiently until she went on again, talking about the people who had properties along the road, and adding moral reflections to their history. So it was that as they were in the middle of Toucques, and passed under some windows bowered with nasturtiums, he shrugged his shoulders and said: "There's a Mme. Lehoussais lives there; instead of taking a young man she . . ." Félicité did not hear the rest; the horses were trotting and the donkey galloping. They all turned down a bypath; a gate swung open and two boys appeared; and the party dismounted in front of a manure-heap at the very threshold of the farmhouse door.

When Mme. Liébard saw her mistress she gave lavish signs of joy. She served her a luncheon with a sirloin of beef, tripe, black-pudding, a fricassee of chicken, sparkling cider, a fruit tart, and brandied plums; seasoning it all with compliments to Madame, who seemed in better health; Mademoiselle, who was "splendid" now; and Monsieur Paul, who had "filled out" wonderfully. Nor did she forget their deceased grandparents, whom the Liébards had known, as they had been in the service of the family for several generations. The farm, like them, had the stamp of antiquity. The beams on the ceiling were worm-eaten, the walls blackened with smoke, and the window-panes grey with dust. There was an oak dresser laden with every sort of useful article — jugs, plates, pewter bowls, wolf-traps, and sheep-shears; and a huge syringe made the children laugh. There was not a tree in the three courtyards without mushrooms growing at the bottom of it or a tuft of mistletoe on its boughs. Several of them had been thrown down by the wind. They had taken root again at the middle; and all were bending under their wealth of apples. The thatched roofs, like brown velvet and of varying thickness, withstood the heaviest squalls. The cart-shed, however, was falling into ruin. Mme. Aubain said she would see about it, and ordered the animals to be saddled again.

It was another half-hour before they reached Trouville. The little caravan dismounted to pass Écores — it was an overhanging cliff with boats below it — and three minutes later they were at the end of the quay and entered the courtyard of the Golden Lamb, kept by good Mme. David.

From the first days of their stay Virginie began to feel less weak, thanks to the change of air and the effect of the sea-baths. These, for want of a bathing-dress, she took in her chemise; and her nurse dressed her afterwards in a coastguard's cabin which was used by the bathers.

In the afternoons they took the donkey and went off beyond the Black Rocks, in the direction of Hennequeville. The path climbed at first through ground with dells in it like the green sward of a park, and then reached a plateau where grass fields and arable lay side by side. Hollies rose stiffly out of the briary tangle at the edge of the road; and here and there a great withered tree made zigzags in the blue air with its branches.

They nearly always rested in a meadow, with Deauville on their left, Havre on their right, and the open sea in front. It glittered in the sunshine, smooth as a mirror and so quiet that its murmur was scarcely to be heard; sparrows chirped in hiding and the immense sky arched over it all. Mme. Aubain sat doing her needlework; Virginie plaited rushes by her side; Félicité pulled up lavender, and Paul was bored and anxious to start home.

Other days they crossed the Toucques in a boat and looked for shells. When the tide went out sea-urchins, starfish, and jelly-fish were left exposed; and the children ran in pursuit of the foam-flakes which scudded in the wind. The sleepy waves broke on the sand and un-rolled all along the beach; it stretched away out of sight, bounded on the land-side by the dunes which parted it from the Marsh, a wide meadow shaped like an arena. As they came home that way, Trouville, on the hill-slope in the background, grew bigger at every step, and its miscellaneous throng of houses seemed to break into a gay disorder.

On days when it was too hot they did not leave their room. From the dazzling brilliance outside light fell in streaks between the laths of the blinds. There were no sounds in the village; and on the pavement below not a soul. This silence round them deepened the quietness of things. In the distance, where men were caulking, there was a tap of hammers as they plugged the hulls, and a sluggish breeze wafted up the smell of tar.

The chief amusement was the return of the fishing-boats. They began to tack as soon as they had passed the buoys. The sails came down on two of the three masts; and they drew on with the foresail swelling like a balloon, glided through the splash of the waves, and when they had reached the middle of the harbour suddenly dropped anchor. Then the boats drew up against the quay. The sailors threw quivering fish over the side; a row of carts was waiting, and women in cotton bonnets darted out to take the baskets and give their men a kiss.

One of them came up to Félicité one day, and she entered the lodgings a little later in a state of delight. She had found a sister again — and then Nastasie Barette, "wife of Leroux," appeared, holding an infant at her breast and another child with her right hand, while on her left was a little cabin boy with his hands on his hips and a cap over his ear.

After a quarter of an hour Mme. Aubain sent them off; but they were always to be found hanging about the kitchen, or encountered in the course of a walk. The husband never appeared.

Félicité was seized with affection for them. She bought them a blanket, some shirts, and a stove; it was clear that they were making a good thing out of her. Mme. Aubain was annoyed by this weakness of hers, and she did not like the liberties taken by the nephew, who said "thee" and "thou" to Paul. So as Virginie was coughing and the fine weather gone, she returned to Pont-l'Évêque.

There M. Bourais enlightened her on the choice of a boys' school. The one at Caen was reputed to be the best, and Paul was sent to it. He said his good-byes bravely, content enough at going to live in a house where he would have companions.

Mme. Aubain resigned herself to her son's absence as a thing that had to be. Virginie thought about it less and less. Félicité missed the noise he made. But she found an occupation to distract her; from Christmas onward she took the little girl to catechism every day.

III

After making a genuflexion at the door she walked up between the double row of chairs under the lofty nave, opened Mme. Aubain's pew, sat down, and began to look about her. The choir stalls were filled with the boys on the right and the girls on the left, and the curé stood by the lectern. On a painted window in the apse the Holy Ghost looked down upon the Virgin. Another window showed her on her knees before the child Jesus, and a group carved in wood behind the altar-shrine represented St. Michael overthrowing the dragon.

The priest began with a sketch of sacred history. The Garden, the Flood, the Tower of Babel, cities in flames, dying nations, and over-turned idols passed like a dream before her eyes; and the dizzying vision left her with reverence for the Most High and fear of his wrath. Then she wept at the story of the Passion. Why had they crucified Him, when He loved the children, fed the multitudes, healed the blind, and had willed, in His meekness, to be born among the poor, on the dungheap of a stable? The sowings, harvests, wine-presses, all the familiar things the Gospel speaks of, were a part of her life. They had been made holy by God's passing; and she loved the lambs more tenderly for her love of the Lamb, and the doves because of the Holy Ghost.

She found it hard to imagine Him in person, for He was not merely a bird, but a flame as well, and a breath at other times. It may be His light, she thought, which flits at night about the edge of the marshes, His breathing which drives on the clouds, His voice which gives har-mony to the bells; and she would sit rapt in adoration, enjoying the cool walls and the quiet of the church.

Of doctrines she understood nothing — did not even try to under-stand. The curé discoursed, the children repeated their lesson, and finally she went to sleep, waking up with a start when their wooden shoes clattered on the flagstones as they went away.

It was thus that Félicité, whose religious education had been neg-lected in her youth, learned the catechism by dint of hearing it; and from that time she copied all Virginie's observances, fasting as she did and confessing with her. On Corpus Christi Day they made a festal altar together.

The first communion loomed distractingly ahead. She fussed over the shoes, the rosary, the book and gloves; and how she trembled as she helped Virginie's mother to dress her!

All through the mass she was racked with anxiety. She could not see one side of the choir because of M. Bourais; but straight in front of her was the flock of maidens, with white crowns above their hanging veils, making the impression of a field of snow; and she knew her dear child at a distance by her dainty neck and thoughtful air. The bell tinkled. The heads bowed, and there was silence. As the organ pealed, singers and congregation took up the "Agnus Dei"; then the procession of the boys began, and after them the girls rose. Step by step, with their hands joined in prayer, they went towards the lighted altar, knelt on the first step, received the sacrament in turn, and came back in the same order to their places. When Virginie's turn came Félicité leaned forward to see her; and with the imaginativeness of deep and tender feeling it seemed to her that she actually was the child; Virginie's face became hers, she was dressed in her clothes, it was her heart beating in her breast. As the moment came to open her mouth she closed her eyes and nearly fainted.

She appeared early in the sacristy next morning for Monsieur the curé to give her the communion. She took it with devotion, but it did not give her the same exquisite delight.

Mme. Aubain wanted to make her daughter into an accomplished person; and as Guyot could not teach her music or English she decided to place her in the Ursuline Convent at Honfleur as a boarder. The child made no objection. Félicité sighed and thought that Madame lacked feeling. Then she reflected that her mistress might be right; matters of this kind were beyond her.

So one day an old spring-van drew up at the door, and out of it stepped a nun to fetch the young lady. Félicité hoisted the luggage on to the top, admonished the driver, and put six pots of preserves, a dozen pears, and a bunch of violets under the seat.

At the last moment Virginie broke into a fit of sobbing; she threw her arms round her mother, who kissed her on the forehead, saying over and over "Come, be brave! be brave!" The step was raised, and the carriage drove off.

Then Mme. Aubain's strength gave way; and in the evening all her friends — the Lormeau family, Mme. Lechaptois, the Rochefeuille ladies, M. de Houppeville, and Bourais — came in to console her.

To be without her daughter was very painful for her at first. But she heard from Virginie three times a week, wrote to her on the other days, walked in the garden, and so filled up the empty hours.

From sheer habit Félicité went into Virginie's room in the mornings and gazed at the walls. It was boredom to her not to have to comb the child's hair now, lace up her boots, tuck her into bed — and not to see her charming face perpetually and hold her hand when they went out together. In this idle condition she tried making lace. But her fingers were too heavy and broke the threads; she could not attend to anything, she had lost her sleep, and was, in her own words, "destroyed."

To "divert herself" she asked leave to have visits from her nephew Victor.

He arrived on Sundays after mass, rosy-cheeked, bare-chested, with the scent of the country he had walked through still about him. She laid her table promptly and they had lunch, sitting opposite each other. She ate as little as possible herself to save expense, but stuffed him with food so generously that at last he went to sleep. At the first stroke of vespers she woke him up, brushed his trousers, fastened his tie, and went to church, leaning on his arm with maternal pride.

Victor was always instructed by his parents to get something out of her — a packet of moist sugar, it might be, a cake of soap, spirits, or even money at times. He brought his things for her to mend and she took over the task, only too glad to have a reason for making him come back.

In August his father took him off on a coasting voyage. It was holiday time, and she was consoled by the arrival of the children. Paul, however, was getting selfish, and Virginie was too old to be called "thou" any longer; this put a constraint and barrier between them.

Victor went to Morlaix, Dunkirk, and Brighton in succession and made Félicité a present on his return from each voyage. It was a box made of shells the first time, a coffee cup the next, and on the third occasion a large gingerbread man. Victor was growing handsome. He was well made, had a hint of a moustache, good honest eyes, and a small leather hat pushed backwards like a pilot's. He entertained her by telling stories embroidered with nautical terms.

On a Monday, July 14, 1819 (she never forgot the date), he told her that he had signed on for the big voyage and next night but one he would take the Honfleur boat and join his schooner, which was to weigh anchor from Havre before long. Perhaps he would be gone two years.

The prospect of this long absence threw Félicité into deep distress; one more good-bye she must have, and on the Wednesday evening, when Madame's dinner was finished, she put on her clogs and made short work of the twelve miles between Pont-l'Évêque and Honfleur.

When she arrived in front of the Calvary she took the turn to the right instead of the left, got lost in the timber-yards, and retraced her steps; some people to whom she spoke advised her to be quick. She went all round the harbour basin, full of ships, and knocked against hawsers; then the ground fell away, lights flashed across each other, and she thought her wits had left her, for she saw horses up in the sky.

Others were neighing by the quay-side, frightened at the sea. They were lifted by a tackle and deposited in a boat, where passengers jostled each other among cider casks, cheese baskets, and sacks of grain; fowls could be heard clucking, the captain swore; and a cabin-boy stood leaning over the bows, indifferent to it all. Félicité, who had not recognized him, called "Victor!" and he raised his head; all at once, as she was darting forwards, the gangway was drawn back.

The Honfleur packet, women singing as they hauled it, passed out of harbour. Its framework creaked and the heavy waves whipped its bows. The canvas had swung round, no one could be seen on board now; and on the moon-silvered sea the boat made a black speck which paled gradually, dipped, and vanished.

As Félicité passed by the Calvary she had a wish to commend to God what she cherished most, and she stood there praying a long time with her face bathed in tears and her eyes towards the clouds. The town was asleep, coastguards were walking to and fro; and water poured without cessation through the holes in the sluice, with the noise of a torrent. The clocks struck two.

The convent parlour would not be open before day. If Félicité were late Madame would most certainly be annoyed; and in spite of her desire to kiss the other child she turned home. The maids at the inn were waking up as she came in to Pont-l'Évêque.

So the poor slip of a boy was going to toss for months and months at sea! She had not been frightened by his previous voyages. From England or Brittany you came back safe enough; but America, the colonies, the islands — these were lost in a dim region at the other end of the world.

Félicité's thoughts from that moment ran entirely on her nephew. On sunny days she was harassed by the idea of thirst; when there was a storm she was afraid of the lightning on his account. As she listened to the wind growling in the chimney or carrying off the slates she pictured him lashed by that same tempest, at the top of a shattered mast, with his body thrown backwards under a sheet of foam; or else (with a reminiscence of the illustrated geography) he was being eaten by savages, captured in a wood by monkeys, or dying on a desert shore. And never did she mention her anxieties.

Mme. Aubain had anxieties of her own, about her daughter. The good sisters found her an affectionate but delicate child. The slightest emotion unnerved her. She had to give up the piano.

Her mother stipulated for regular letters from the convent. She lost patience one morning when the postman did not come, and walked to and fro in the parlour from her armchair to the window. It was really amazing; not a word for four days!

To console Mme. Aubain by her own example Félicité remarked: "As for me, Madame, it's six months since I heard . . ."

"From whom, pray?"

"Why . . . from my nephew," the servant answered gently.

"Oh! your nephew!" And Mme. Aubain resumed her walk with a shrug of the shoulders, as much as to say: "I was not thinking of him! And what is more, it's absurd! A scamp of a cabin-boy — what does he matter? . . . whereas my daughter . . . why, just think!"

Félicité, though she had been brought up on harshness, felt indignant with Madame — and then forgot. It seemed the simplest thing in the world to her to lose one's head over the little girl. For her the two children were equally important; a bond in her heart made them one, and their destinies must be the same.

She heard from the chemist that Victor's ship had arrived at Havana. He had read this piece of news in a gazette.

Cigars — they made her imagine Havana as a place where no one does anything but smoke, and there was Victor moving among the negroes in a cloud of tobacco. Could you, she wondered, "in case you needed," return by land? What was the distance from Pont-l'Évêque? She questioned M. Bourais to find out.

He reached for his atlas and began explaining the longitudes; Félicité's consternation provoked a fine pedantic smile. Finally he marked with his pencil a black, imperceptible point in the indentations of an oval spot, and said as he did so, "Here it is." She bent over the map; the maze of coloured lines wearied her eyes without conveying anything; and on an invitation from Bourais to tell him her difficulty she begged him to show her the house where Victor was living. Bourais threw up his arms, sneezed, and laughed immensely: a simplicity like hers was a positive joy. And Félicité did not understand the reason; how could she when she expected, very likely, to see the actual image of her nephew — so stunted was her mind!

A fortnight afterwards Liébard came into the kitchen at market-time as usual and handed her a letter from her brother-in-law. As neither of them could read she took it to her mistress.

Mme. Aubain, who was counting the stitches in her knitting, put the work down by her side, broke the seal of the letter, started, and said in a low voice, with a look of meaning:

"It is bad news . . . that they have to tell you. Your nephew . . ."

He was dead. The letter said no more.

Félicité fell on to a chair, leaning her head against the wainscot; and she closed her eyelids, which suddenly flushed pink. Then with bent forehead, hands hanging, and fixed eyes, she said at intervals:

"Poor little lad! poor little lad!"

Liébard watched her and heaved sighs. Mme. Aubain trembled a little.

She suggested that Félicité should go to see her sister at Trouville. Félicité answered by a gesture that she had no need.

There was a silence. The worthy Liébard thought it was time for them to withdraw.

Then Félicité said:

"They don't care, not they!"

Her head dropped again; and she took up mechanically, from time to time, the long needles on her work-table.

Women passed in the yard with a barrow of dripping linen.

As she saw them through the window-panes she remembered her washing; she had put it to soak the day before, to-day she must wring it out; and she left the room.

Her plank and tub were at the edge of the Toucques. She threw a pile of linen on the bank, rolled up her sleeves, and taking her wooden beater dealt lusty blows whose sound carried to the neighbouring gardens. The meadows were empty, the river stirred in the wind; and down below long grasses wavered, like the hair of corpses floating in the water. She kept her grief down and was very brave until the evening; but once in her room she surrendered to it utterly, lying stretched on the mattress with her face in the pillow and her hands clenched against her temples.

Much later she heard, from the captain himself, the circumstances of Victor's end. They had bled him too much at the hospital for yellow fever. Four doctors held him at once. He had died instantly, and the chief had said:

"Bah! there goes another!"

His parents had always been brutal to him. She preferred not to see them again; and they made no advances, either because they forgot her or from the callousness of the wretchedly poor.

Virginie began to grow weaker.

Tightness in her chest, coughing, continual fever, and veinings on her cheek-bones betrayed some deep-seated complaint. M. Poupart had advised a stay in Provence. Mme. Aubain determined on it, and would have brought her daughter home at once but for the climate of Pont-l'Évêque.

She made an arrangement with a job-master, and he drove her to the convent every Tuesday. There is a terrace in the garden, with a view over the Seine. Virginie took walks there over the fallen vine-leaves, on her mother's arm. A shaft of sunlight through the clouds made her blink sometimes, as she gazed at the sails in the distance and the whole horizon from the castle of Tancarville to the lighthouses at Havre. Afterwards they rested in the arbour. Her mother had secured a little cask of excellent Malaga; and Virginie, laughing at the idea of getting tipsy, drank a thimble-full of it, no more.

Her strength came back visibly. The autumn glided gently away. Félicité reassured Mme. Aubain. But one evening, when she had been out on a commission in the neighbourhood, she found M. Poupart's gig at the door. He was in the hall, and Mme. Aubain was tying her bonnet.

"Give me my foot-warmer, purse, gloves! Quicker, come!"

Virginie had inflammation of the lungs; perhaps it was hopeless.

"Not yet!" said the doctor, and they both got into the carriage under whirling flakes of snow. Night was coming on and it was very cold.

Félicité rushed into the church to light a taper. Then she ran after the gig, came up with it in an hour, and jumped lightly in behind. As she hung on by the fringes a thought came into her mind: "The courtyard has not been shut up; supposing burglars got in!" And she jumped down.

At dawn next day she presented herself at the doctor's. He had come in and started for the country again. Then she waited in the inn, thinking that a letter would come by some hand or other. Finally, when it was twilight, she took the Lisieux coach.

The convent was at the end of a steep lane. When she was about half-way up it she heard strange sounds — a death-bell tolling. "It is for someone else," thought Félicité, and she pulled the knocker violently.

After some minutes there was a sound of trailing slippers, the door opened ajar, and a nun appeared.

The good sister, with an air of compunction, said that "she had just passed away." On the instant the bell of St. Leonard's tolled twice as fast.

Félicité went up to the second floor.

From the doorway she saw Virginie stretched on her back, with her hands joined, her mouth open, and head thrown back under a black crucifix that leaned towards her, between curtains that hung stiffly, less pale than was her face. Mme. Aubain, at the foot of the bed which she clasped with her arms, was choking with sobs of agony. The mother superior stood on the right. Three candlesticks on the chest of drawers made spots of red, and the mist came whitely through the windows. Nuns came and took Mme. Aubain away.

For two nights Félicité never left the dead child. She repeated the same prayers, sprinkled holy water over the sheets, came and sat down again, and watched her. At the end of the first vigil she noticed that the face had grown yellow, the lips turned blue, the nose was sharper, and the eyes sunk in. She kissed them several times, and would not have been immensely surprised if Virginie had opened them again; to minds like hers the supernatural is quite simple. She made the girl's toilette, wrapped her in her shroud, lifted her down into her bier, put a garland on her head, and spread out her hair. It was fair, and extraordinarily long for her age. Félicité cut off a big lock and slipped half of it into her bosom, determined that she should never part with it.

The body was brought back to Pont-l'Évêque, as Mme. Aubain intended; she followed the hearse in a closed carriage.

It took another three-quarters of an hour after the mass to reach the cemetery. Paul walked in front, sobbing. M. Bourais was behind, and then came the chief residents, the women shrouded in black mantles, and Félicité. She thought of her nephew; and because she had not been able to pay these honours to him her grief was doubled, as though the one were being buried with the other.

Mme. Aubain's despair was boundless. It was against God that she first rebelled, thinking it unjust of Him to have taken her daughter from her — she had never done evil and her conscience was so clear! Ah, no! — she ought to have taken Virginie off to the south. Other doctors would have saved her. She accused herself now, wanted to join her child, and broke into cries of distress in the middle of her dreams. One dream haunted her above all. Her husband, dressed as a sailor, was returning from a long voyage, and shedding tears he told her that he had been ordered to take Virginie away. Then they consulted how to hide her somewhere.

She came in once from the garden quite upset. A moment ago — and she pointed out the place — the father and daughter had appeared to her, standing side by side, and they did nothing, but they looked at her.

For several months after this she stayed inertly in her room. Félicité lectured her gently; she must live for her son's sake, and for the other, in remembrance of "her."

"Her?" answered Mme. Aubain, as though she were just waking up. "Ah, yes! . . . yes! . . . You do not forget her!" This was an allusion to the cemetery, where she was strictly forbidden to go.

Félicité went there every day.

Precisely at four she skirted the houses, climbed the hill, opened the gate, and came to Virginie's grave. It was a little column of pink marble with a stone underneath and a garden plot enclosed by chains. The beds were hidden under a coverlet of flowers. She watered their leaves, freshened the gravel, and knelt down to break up the earth better. When Mme. Aubain was able to come there she felt a relief and a sort of consolation.

Then years slipped away, one like another, and their only episodes were the great festivals as they recurred — Easter, the Assumption, All Saints' Day. Household occurrences marked dates that were referred to afterwards. In 1825, for instance, two glaziers whitewashed the hall; in 1827 a piece of the roof fell into the courtyard and nearly killed a man. In the summer of 1828 it was Madame's turn to offer the consecrated bread; Bourais, about this time, mysteriously absented himself; and one by one the old acquaintances passed away: Guyot, Liébard, Mme. Lechaptois, Robelin, and Uncle Gremanville, who had been paralysed for a long time.

One night the driver of the mail-coach announced the Revolution of July in Pont-l'Évêque. A new sub-prefect was appointed a few days later — Baron de Larsonnière, who had been consul in America, and brought with him, besides his wife, a sister-in-law and three young ladies, already growing up. They were to be seen about on their lawn, in loose blouses, and they had a negro and a parrot. They paid a call on Mme. Aubain which she did not fail to return. The moment they were seen in the distance Félicité ran to let her mistress know. But only one thing could really move her feelings — the letters from her son.

He was swallowed up in a tavern life and could follow no career. She paid his debts, he made new ones; and the sighs that Mme. Aubain uttered as she sat knitting by the window reached Félicité at her spinning-wheel in the kitchen.

They took walks together along the espaliered wall, always talking of Virginie and wondering if such and such a thing would have pleased her and what, on some occasion, she would have been likely to say.

All her small belongings filled a cupboard in the two-bedded room. Mme. Aubain inspected them as seldom as she could. One summer day she made up her mind to it — and some moths flew out of the wardrobe.

Virginie's dresses were in a row underneath a shelf, on which there were three dolls, some hoops, a set of toy pots and pans, and the basin that she used. They took out her petticoats as well, and the stockings and handkerchiefs, and laid them out on the two beds before folding them up again. The sunshine lit up these poor things, bringing out their stains and the creases made by the body's movements. The air was warm and blue, a blackbird warbled, life seemed bathed in a deep sweetness. They found a little plush hat with thick, chestnut-coloured pile; but it was eaten all over by moth. Félicité begged it for her own. Their eyes met fixedly and filled with tears; at last the mistress opened her arms, the servant threw herself into them, and they embraced each other, satisfying their grief in a kiss that made them equal.

It was the first time in their lives, Mme. Aubain's nature not being expansive. Félicité was as grateful as though she had received a favour, and cherished her mistress from that moment with the devotion of an animal and a religious worship.

The kindness of her heart unfolded.

When she heard the drums of a marching regiment in the street she posted herself at the door with a pitcher of cider and asked the soldiers to drink. She nursed cholera patients and protected the Polish refugees; one of these even declared that he wished to marry her. They quarrelled, however; for when she came back from the Angelus one morning she found that he had got into her kitchen and made himself a vinegar salad which he was quietly eating.

After the Poles came father Colmiche, an old man who was supposed to have committed atrocities in '93. He lived by the side of the river in the ruins of a pigsty. The little boys watched him through the cracks in the wall, and threw pebbles at him which fell on the pallet where he lay constantly shaken by a catarrh; his hair was very long, his eyes inflamed, and there was a tumour on his arm bigger than his head. She got him some linen and tried to clean up his miserable hole; her dream was to establish him in the bakehouse, without letting him annoy Madame. When the tumour burst she dressed it every day; sometimes she brought him cake, and would put him in the sunshine on a truss of straw. The poor old man, slobbering and trembling, thanked her in his worn-out voice, was terrified that he might lose her, and stretched out his hands when he saw her go away. He died; and she had a mass said for the repose of his soul.

That very day a great happiness befell her; just at dinner-time appeared Mme. de Larsonnière's negro, carrying the parrot in its cage, with perch, chain, and padlock. A note from the baroness informed Mme. Aubain that her husband had been raised to a prefecture and they were starting that evening; she begged her to accept the bird as a memento and mark of her regard.

For a long time he had absorbed Félicité's imagination, because he came from America; and that name reminded her of Victor, so much so that she made inquiries of the negro. She had once gone so far as to say "How Madame would enjoy having him!"

The negro repeated the remark to his mistress; and as she could not take the bird away with her she chose this way of getting rid of him.

IV

His name was Loulou. His body was green and the tips of his wings rose-pink; his forehead was blue and his throat golden.

But he had the tiresome habits of biting his perch, tearing out his feathers, sprinkling his dirt about, and spattering the water of his tub. He annoyed Mme. Aubain, and she gave him to Félicité for good.

She endeavoured to train him; soon he could repeat "Nice boy! Your servant, sir! Good morning, Marie!" He was placed by the side of the door, and astonished several people by not answering to the name Jacquot, for all parrots are called Jacquot. People compared him to a turkey and a log of wood, and stabbed Félicité to the heart each time. Strange obstinacy on Loulou's part! — directly you looked at him he refused to speak.

None the less he was eager for society; for on Sundays, while the Rochefeuille ladies, M. de Houppeville, and new familiars — Onfroy the apothecary, Monsieur Varin, and Captain Mathieu — were playing their game of cards, he beat the windows with his wings and threw himself about so frantically that they could not hear each other speak.

Bourais' face, undoubtedly, struck him as extremely droll. Directly he saw it he began to laugh — and laugh with all his might. His peals rang through the courtyard and were repeated by the echo; the neighbours came to their windows and laughed too; while M. Bourais, gliding along under the wall to escape the parrot's eye, and hiding his profile with his hat, got to the river and then entered by the garden gate. There was a lack of tenderness in the looks which he darted at the bird.

Loulou had been slapped by the butcher-boy for making so free as to plunge his head into his basket; and since then he was always trying to nip him through his shirt. Fabu threatened to wring his neck, although he was not cruel, for all his tattooed arms and large whiskers. Far from it; he really rather liked the parrot, and in a jovial humour even wanted to teach him to swear. Félicité, who was alarmed by such proceedings, put the bird in the kitchen. His little chain was taken off and he roamed about the house.

His way of going downstairs was to lean on each step with the curve of his beak, raise the right foot, and then the left; and Félicité was afraid that these gymnastics brought on fits of giddiness. He fell ill and could not talk or eat any longer. There was a growth under his tongue, such as fowls have sometimes. She cured him by tearing the pellicle off with her finger-nails. Mr. Paul was thoughtless enough one day to blow some cigar smoke into his nostrils, and another time when Mme. Lormeau was teasing him with the end of her umbrella he snapped at the ferrule. Finally he got lost.

Félicité had put him on the grass to refresh him, and gone away for a minute, and when she came back — no sign of the parrot! She began by looking for him in the shrubs, by the waterside, and over the roofs, without listening to her mistress's cries of "Take care, do! You are out of your wits!" Then she investigated all the gardens in Pont-l'Évêque, and stopped the passers-by. "You don't ever happen to have seen my parrot, by any chance, do you?" And she gave a description of the parrot to those who did not know him. Suddenly, behind the mills at the foot of the hill she thought she could make out something green that fluttered. But on the top of the hill there was nothing. A hawker assured her that he had come across the parrot just before, at Saint-Melaine, in Mère Simon's shop. She rushed there; they had no idea of what she meant. At last she came home exhausted, with her slippers in shreds and despair in her soul; and as she was sitting in the middle of the garden-seat at Madame's side, telling the whole story of her efforts, a light weight dropped on to her shoulder — it was Loulou! What on earth had he been doing? Taking a walk in the neighbourhood, perhaps!

She had some trouble in recovering from this, or rather never did recover. As the result of a chill she had an attack of quinsy, and soon afterwards an earache. Three years later she was deaf; and she spoke very loud, even in church. Though Félicité's sins might have been published in every corner of the diocese without dishonour to her or scandal to anybody, his Reverence the priest thought it right now to hear her confession in the sacristy only.

Imaginary noises in the head completed her upset. Her mistress often said to her, "Heavens! how stupid you are!" "Yes, Madame," she replied, and looked about for something.

Her little circle of ideas grew still narrower; the peal of church-bells and the lowing of cattle ceased to exist for her. All living beings moved as silently as ghosts. One sound only reached her ears now — the parrot's voice.

Loulou, as though to amuse her, reproduced the click-clack of the turn-spit, the shrill call of a man selling fish, and the noise of the saw in the joiner's house opposite; when the bell rang he imitated Mme. Aubain's "Félicité! the door! the door!"

They carried on conversations, he endlessly reciting the three phrases in his repertory, to which she replied with words that were just as disconnected but uttered what was in her heart. Loulou was almost a son and a lover to her in her isolated state. He climbed up her fingers, nibbled at her lips, and clung to her kerchief; and when she bent her forehead and shook her head gently to and fro, as nurses do, the great wings of her bonnet and the bird's wings quivered together.

When the clouds massed and the thunder rumbled Loulou broke into cries, perhaps remembering the downpours in his native forests. The streaming rain made him absolutely mad; he fluttered wildly about, dashed up to the ceiling, upset everything, and went out through the window to dabble in the garden; but he was back quickly to perch on one of the fire-dogs and hopped about to dry himself, exhibiting his tail and his beak in turn.

One morning in the terrible winter of 1837 she had put him in front of the fireplace because of the cold. She found him dead, in the middle of his cage: head downwards, with his claws in the wires.

He had died from congestion, no doubt. But Félicité thought he had been poisoned with parsley, and though there was no proof of any kind her suspicions inclined to Fabu.

She wept so piteously that her mistress said to her, "Well, then, have him stuffed!"

She asked advice from the chemist, who had always been kind to the parrot. He wrote to Havre, and a person called Fellacher undertook the business. But as parcels sometimes got lost in the coach she decided to take the parrot as far as Honfleur herself.

Along the sides of the road were leafless apple-trees, one after the other. Ice covered the ditches. Dogs barked about the farms; and Félicité, with her hands under her cloak, her little black sabots and her basket, walked briskly in the middle of the road.

She crossed the forest, passed High Oak, and reached St. Gatien.

A cloud of dust rose behind her, and in it a mail-coach, carried away by the steep hill, rushed down at full gallop like a hurricane. Seeing this woman who would not get out of the way, the driver stood up in front and the postilion shouted too. He could not hold in his four horses, which increased their pace, and the two leaders were grazing her when he threw them to one side with a jerk of the reins. But he was wild with rage, and lifting his arm as he passed at full speed, gave her such a lash from waist to neck with his big whip that she fell on her back.

Her first act, when she recovered consciousness, was to open her basket. Loulou was happily none the worse. She felt a burn in her right cheek, and when she put her hands against it they were red; the blood was flowing.

She sat down on a heap of stones and bound up her face with her handkerchief. Then she ate a crust of bread which she had put in the basket as a precaution, and found a consolation for her wound in gazing at the bird.

When she reached the crest of Ecquemauville she saw the Honfleur lights sparkling in the night sky like a company of stars; beyond, the sea stretched dimly. Then a faintness overtook her and she stopped; her wretched childhood, the disillusion of her first love, her nephew's going away, and Virginie's death all came back to her at once like the waves of an oncoming tide, rose to her throat, and choked her.

Afterwards, at the boat, she made a point of speaking to the captain, begging him to take care of the parcel, though she did not tell him what was in it.

Fellacher kept the parrot a long time.   He was always promising it for the following week.   After six months he announced that a packing-case had started, and then nothing more was heard of it.   It really seemed as though Loulou was never coming back.   "Ah, they have stolen him!" she thought.

He arrived at last, and looked superb.   There he was, erect upon a branch which screwed into a mahogany socket, with a foot in the air and his head on one side, biting a nut which the bird-stuffer — with a taste for impressiveness — had gilded.

Félicité shut him up in her room.   It was a place to which few people were admitted, and held so many religious objects and miscellaneous things that it looked like a chapel and bazaar in one.

A big cupboard impeded you as you opened the door.   Opposite the window commanding the garden a little round one looked into the court;   there was a table by the folding-bed with a water-jug, two combs, and a cube of blue soap in a chipped plate.   On the walls hung rosaries, medals, several benign Virgins, and a holy water vessel made out of cocoa-nut;   on the chest of drawers, which was covered with a cloth like an altar, was the shell box that Victor had given her, and after that a watering-can, a toy-balloon, exercise-books, the illustrated geography, and a pair of young lady's boots;   and, fastened by its ribbons to the nail of the looking-glass, hung the little plush hat! Félicité carried observances of this kind so far as to keep one of Monsieur's frock-coats.   All the old rubbish which Mme. Aubain did not want any longer she laid hands on for her room.   That was why there were artificial flowers along the edge of the chest of drawers and a portrait of the Comte d'Artois in the little window recess.

With the aid of a bracket Loulou was established over the chimney, which jutted into the room.   Every morning when she woke up she saw him there in the dawning light, and recalled old days and the smallest details of insignificant acts in a deep quietness which knew no pain.

Holding, as she did, no communication with anyone, Félicité lived as insensibly as if she were walking in her sleep.   The Corpus Christi processions roused her to life again.   Then she went round begging mats and candlesticks from the neighbours to decorate the altar they put up in the street.

In church she was always gazing at the Holy Ghost in the window, and observed that there was something of the parrot in him.   The likeness was still clearer, she thought, on a crude colour-print representing the baptism of Our Lord. With his purple wings and emerald body he was the very image of Loulou.

She bought him, and hung him up instead of the Comte d'Artois, so that she could see them both together in one glance. They were linked in her thoughts; and the parrot was consecrated by his association with the Holy Ghost, which became more vivid to her eye and more intelligible. The Father could not have chosen to express Himself through a dove, for such creatures cannot speak; it must have been one of Loulou's ancestors, surely. And though Félicité looked at the picture while she said her prayers she swerved a little from time to time towards the parrot.

She wanted to join the Ladies of the Virgin, but Mme. Aubain dissuaded her.

And then a great event loomed up before them — Paul's marriage.

He had been a solicitor's clerk to begin with, and then tried business, the Customs, the Inland Revenue, and made efforts, even, to get into the Rivers and Forests. By an inspiration from heaven he had suddenly, at thirty-six, discovered his real line — the Registrar's Office. And there he showed such marked capacity that an inspector had offered him his daughter's hand and promised him his influence.

So Paul, grown serious, brought the lady to see his mother.

She sniffed at the ways of Pont-l'Évêque, gave herself great airs, and wounded Félicité's feelings. Mme. Aubain was relieved at her departure.

The week after came news of M. Bourais' death in an inn in Lower Brittany. The rumour of suicide was confirmed, and doubts arose as to his honesty. Mme. Aubain studied his accounts, and soon found out the whole tale of his misdoings — embezzled arrears, secret sales of wood, forged receipts, etc. Besides that he had an illegitimate child, and "relations with a person at Dozulé."

These shameful facts distressed her greatly. In March 1853 she was seized with a pain in the chest; her tongue seemed to be covered with film, and leeches did not ease the difficult breathing. On the ninth evening of her illness she died, just at seventy-two.

She passed as being younger, owing to the bands of brown hair which framed her pale, pock-marked face. There were few friends to regret her, for she had a stiffness of manner which kept people at a distance.

But Félicité mourned for her as one seldom mourns for a master. It upset her ideas and seemed contrary to the order of things, impossible and monstrous, that Madame should die before her.

Ten days afterwards, which was the time it took to hurry there from Besançon, the heirs arrived. The daughter-in-law ransacked the drawers, chose some furniture, and sold the rest; and then they went back to their registering.

Madame's armchair, her small round table, her foot-warmer, and the eight chairs were gone! Yellow patches in the middle of the panels showed where the engravings had hung. They had carried off the two little beds and the mattresses, and all Virginie's belongings had disappeared from the cupboard. Félicité went from floor to floor dazed with sorrow.

The next day there was a notice on the door, and the apothecary shouted in her ear that the house was for sale.

She tottered, and was obliged to sit down. What distressed her most of all was to give up her room, so suitable as it was for poor Loulou. She enveloped him with a look of anguish when she was imploring the Holy Ghost, and formed the idolatrous habit of kneeling in front of the parrot to say her prayers. Sometimes the sun shone in at the attic window and caught his glass eye, and a great luminous ray shot out of it and put her in an ecstasy.

She had a pension of fifteen pounds a year which her mistress had left her. The garden gave her a supply of vegetables. As for clothes, she had enough to last her to the end of her days, and she economized in candles by going to bed at dusk.

She hardly ever went out, as she did not like passing the dealer's shop, where some of the old furniture was exposed for sale. Since her fit of giddiness she dragged one leg; and as her strength was failing Mère Simon, whose grocery business had collapsed, came every morning to split the wood and pump water for her.

Her eyes grew feeble. The shutters ceased to be thrown open. Years and years passed, and the house was neither let nor sold.

Félicité never asked for repairs because she was afraid of being sent away. The boards on the roof rotted; her bolster was wet for a whole winter. After Easter she spat blood.

Then Mère Simon called in a doctor. Félicité wanted to know what was the matter with her. But she was too deaf to hear, and the only word which reached her was "pneumonia." It was a word she knew, and she answered softly "Ah! like Madame," thinking it natural that she should follow her mistress.

The time for the festal shrines was coming near. The first one was always at the bottom of the hill, the second in front of the postoffice, and the third towards the middle of the street. There was some rivalry in the matter of this one, and the women of the parish ended by choosing Mme. Aubain's courtyard.

The hard breathing and fever increased. Félicité was vexed at doing nothing for the altar. If only she could at least have put something there! Then she thought of the parrot. The neighbours objected that it would not be decent. But the priest gave her permission, which so intensely delighted her that she begged him to accept Loulou, her sole possession, when she died.

From Tuesday to Saturday, the eve of the festival, she coughed more often. By the evening her face had shrivelled, her lips stuck to her gums, and she had vomitings; and at twilight next morning, feeling herself very low, she sent for a priest.

Three kindly women were round her during the extreme unction. Then she announced that she must speak to Fabu. He arrived in his Sunday clothes, by no means at his ease in the funereal atmosphere.

"Forgive me," she said, with an effort to stretch out her arm; "I thought it was you who had killed him."

What did she mean by such stories? She suspected him of murder — a man like him! He waxed indignant, and was on the point of making a row.

"There," said the women, "she is no longer in her senses, you can see it well enough!"

Félicité spoke to shadows of her own from time to time. The women went away, and Mère Simon had breakfast. A little later she took Loulou and brought him close to Félicité with the words:

"Come, now, say good-bye to him!"

Loulou was not a corpse, but the worms devoured him; one of his wings was broken, and the tow was coming out of his stomach. But she was blind now; she kissed him on the forehead and kept him close against her cheek. Mère Simon took him back from her to put him on the altar.

V

Summer scents came up from the meadows; flies buzzed; the sun made the river glitter and heated the slates. Mère Simon came back into the room and fell softly asleep.

She woke at the noise of bells; the people were coming out from vespers. Félicité's delirium subsided. She thought of the procession and saw it as if she had been there.

All the school children, the church-singers, and the firemen walked on the pavement, while in the middle of the road the verger armed with his hallebard and the beadle with a large cross advanced in front. Then came the schoolmaster, with an eye on the boys, and the sister, anxious about her little girls; three of the daintiest, with angelic curls, scattered rose-petals in the air; the deacon controlled the band with outstretched arms; and two censer-bearers turned back at every step towards the Holy Sacrament, which was borne by Monsieur the curé, wearing his beautiful chasuble, under a canopy of dark-red velvet held up by four churchwardens. A crowd of people pressed behind, between the white cloths covering the house walls, and they reached the bottom of the hill.

A cold sweat moistened Félicité's temples. Mère Simon sponged her with a piece of linen, saying to herself that one day she would have to go that way.

The hum of the crowd increased, was very loud for an instant, and then went further away.

A fusillade shook the window-panes. It was the postilions saluting the monstrance. Félicité rolled her eyes and said as audibly as she could: "Does he look well?" The parrot was weighing on her mind.

Her agony began. A death-rattle that grew more and more convulsed made her sides heave. Bubbles of froth came at the corners of her mouth and her whole body trembled.

Soon the booming of the ophicleides, the high voices of the children, and the deep voices of the men were distinguishable. At intervals all was silent, and the tread of feet, deadened by the flowers they walked on, sounded like a flock pattering on grass.

The clergy appeared in the courtyard. Mère Simon clambered on to a chair to reach the attic window, and so looked down straight upon the shrine. Green garlands hung over the altar, which was decked with a flounce of English lace. In the middle was a small frame with relics in it; there were two orange-trees at the corners, and all along stood silver candlesticks and china vases, with sunflowers, lilies, peonies, foxgloves, and tufts of hortensia. This heap of blazing colour slanted from the level of the altar to the carpet which went on over the pavement; and some rare objects caught the eye. There was a silver-gilt sugar-basin with a crown of violets; pendants of Alençon stone glittered on the moss, and two Chinese screens displayed their landscapes. Loulou was hidden under roses, and showed nothing but his blue forehead, like a plaque of lapis lazuli.

The churchwardens, singers, and children took their places round the three sides of the court. The priest went slowly up the steps, and placed his great, radiant golden sun upon the lace. Everyone knelt down. There was a deep silence; and the censers glided to and fro on the full swing of their chains.

An azure vapour rose up into Félicité's room. Her nostrils met it; she inhaled it sensuously, mystically; and then closed her eyes. Her lips smiled. The beats of her heart lessened one by one, vaguer each time and softer, as a fountain sinks, an echo disappears; and when she sighed her last breath she thought she saw an opening in the heavens, and a gigantic parrot hovering above her head.

[*Translated by* ARTHUR McDOWALL]

Leo Tolstoy

THE DEATH OF IVÁN ILÝCH

1884

༄

I

DURING AN INTERVAL in the Melvínski trial in the large building of the
Law Courts the members and public prosecutor met in Iván Egórovich
Shébek's private room, where the conversation turned on the celebrated Krasóvski case. Fëdor Vasílievich warmly maintained that
it was not subject to their jurisdiction, Iván Egórovich maintained the
contrary, while Peter Ivánovich, not having entered into the discussion
at the start, took no part in it but looked through the *Gazette* which had
just been handed in.

"Gentlemen," he said, "Iván Ilých has died!"

"You don't say so!"

"Here, read it yourself," replied Peter Ivánovich, handing Fëdor
Vasílievich the paper still damp from the press. Surrounded by a
black border were the words: "Praskóvya Fëdorovna Goloviná, with
profound sorrow, informs relatives and friends of the demise of her
beloved husband Iván Ilých Golovín, Member of the Court of Justice,
which occurred on February the 4th of this year 1882. The funeral
will take place on Friday at one o'clock in the afternoon."

Iván Ilých had been a colleague of the gentlemen present and was
liked by them all. He had been ill for some weeks with an illness said
to be incurable. His post had been kept open for him, but there had
been conjectures that in case of his death Alexéev might receive his
appointment, and that either Vínnikov or Shtábel would succeed
Alexéev. So on receiving the news of Iván Ilých's death the first
thought of each of the gentlemen in that private room was of the
changes and promotions it might occasion among themselves or their
acquaintances.

"I shall be sure to get Shtábel's place or Vínnikov's," thought Fëdor
Vasílievich. "I was promised that long ago, and the promotion means
an extra eight hundred rubles a year for me besides the allowance."

"Now I must apply for my brother-in-law's transfer from Kalúga," thought Peter Ivánovich. "My wife will be very glad, and then she won't be able to say that I never do anything for her relations."

"I thought he would never leave his bed again," said Peter Ivánovich aloud. "It's very sad."

"But what really was the matter with him?"

"The doctors couldn't say — at least they could, but each of them said something different. When last I saw him I thought he was getting better."

"And I haven't been to see him since the holidays. I always meant to go."

"Had he any property?"

"I think his wife had a little — but something quite trifling."

"We shall have to go to see her, but they live so terribly far away."

"Far away from you, you mean. Everything's far away from your place."

"You see, he never can forgive my living on the other side of the river," said Peter Ivánovich, smiling at Shébek. Then, still talking of the distances between different parts of the city, they returned to the Court.

Besides considerations as to the possible transfers and promotions likely to result from Iván Ilých's death, the mere fact of the death of a near acquaintance aroused, as usual, in all who heard of it the complacent feeling that, "it is he who is dead and not I."

Each one thought or felt, "Well, he's dead but I'm alive!" But the more intimate of Iván Ilých's acquaintances, his so-called friends, could not help thinking also that they would now have to fulfil the very tiresome demands of propriety by attending the funeral service and paying a visit of condolence to the widow.

Fëdor Vasílievich and Peter Ivánovich had been his nearest acquaintances. Peter Ivánovich had studied law with Iván Ilých and had considered himself to be under obligations to him.

Having told his wife at dinner-time of Iván Ilých's death, and of his conjecture that it might be possible to get her brother transferred to their circuit, Peter Ivánovich sacrificed his usual nap, put on his evening clothes, and drove to Iván Ilých's house.

At the entrance stood a carriage and two cabs. Leaning against the wall in the hall downstairs near the cloak-stand was a coffin-lid covered with cloth of gold, ornamented with gold cord and tassels, that had been polished up with metal powder. Two ladies in black were taking off their fur cloaks. Peter Ivánovich recognized one of them as Iván Ilých's sister, but the other was a stranger to him. His colleague Schwartz was just coming downstairs, but on seeing Peter Ivánovich enter he stopped and winked at him, as if to say: "Iván Ilých has made a mess of things — not like you and me."

Schwartz's face with his Piccadilly whiskers, and his slim figure in evening dress, had as usual an air of elegant solemnity which contrasted with the playfulness of his character and had a special piquancy here, or so it seemed to Peter Ivánovich.

Peter Ivánovich allowed the ladies to precede him and slowly followed them upstairs. Schwartz did not come down but remained where he was, and Peter Ivánovich understood that he wanted to arrange where they should play bridge that evening. The ladies went upstairs to the widow's room, and Schwartz with seriously compressed lips but a playful look in his eyes, indicated by a twist of his eyebrows the room to the right where the body lay.

Peter Ivánovich, like everyone else on such occasions, entered feeling uncertain what he would have to do. All he knew was that at such times it is always safe to cross oneself. But he was not quite sure whether one should make obeisances while doing so. He therefore adopted a middle course. On entering the room he began crossing himself and made a slight movement resembling a bow. At the same time, as far as the motion of his head and arm allowed, he surveyed the room. Two young men — apparently nephews, one of whom was a high-school pupil — were leaving the room, crossing themselves as they did so. An old woman was standing motionless, and a lady with strangely arched eyebrows was saying something to her in a whisper. A vigorous, resolute Church Reader, in a frock-coat, was reading something in a loud voice with an expression that precluded any contradiction. The butler's assistant, Gerásim, stepping lightly in front of Peter Ivánovich, was strewing something on the floor. Noticing this, Peter Ivánovich was immediately aware of a faint odour of a decomposing body.

The last time he had called on Iván Ilých, Peter Ivánovich had seen Gerásim in the study. Iván Ilých had been particularly fond of him and he was performing the duty of a sick nurse.

Peter Ivánovich continued to make the sign of the cross slightly inclining his head in an intermediate direction between the coffin, the Reader, and the icons on the table in a corner of the room. Afterwards, when it seemed to him that this movement of his arm in crossing himself had gone on too long, he stopped and began to look at the corpse.

The dead man lay, as dead men always lie, in a specially heavy way, his rigid limbs sunk in the soft cushions of the coffin, with the head forever bowed on the pillow. His yellow waxen brow with bald patches over his sunken temples was thrust up in the way peculiar to the dead, the protruding nose seeming to press on the upper lip. He was much changed and had grown even thinner since Peter Ivánovich had last seen him, but, as is always the case with the dead, his face was handsomer and above all more dignified than when he was alive. The expression on the face said that what was necessary had been accomplished, and accomplished rightly. Besides this there was in that expression a reproach and a warning to the living. This warning seemed to Peter Ivánovich out of place, or at least not applicable to him. He felt a certain discomfort and so he hurriedly crossed himself once more and turned and went out of the door — too hurriedly and too regardless of propriety, as he himself was aware.

Schwartz was waiting for him in the adjoining room with legs spread wide apart and both hands toying with his top-hat behind his back. The mere sight of that playful, well-groomed, and elegant figure refreshed Peter Ivánovich. He felt that Schwartz was above all these happenings and would not surrender to any depressing influences. His very look said that this incident of a church service for Iván Ilých could not be a sufficient reason for infringing the order of the session — in other words, that it would certainly not prevent his unwrapping a new pack of cards and shuffling them that evening while a footman placed four fresh candles on the table: in fact, there was no reason for supposing that this incident would hinder their spending the evening agreeably. Indeed he said this in a whisper as Peter Ivánovich passed him, proposing that they should meet for a game at Fëdor Vasílievich's. But apparently Peter Ivánovich was not destined to play bridge that evening. Praskóvya Fëdorovna (a short, fat woman who despite all efforts to the contrary had continued to broaden steadily from her shoulders downwards and who had the same extraordinarily arched eyebrows as the lady who had been standing by the coffin), dressed all in black, her head covered with lace, came out of her own room with some other ladies, conducted them to the room where the dead body lay, and said: "The service will begin immediately. Please go in."

Schwartz, making an indefinite bow, stood still, evidently neither accepting nor declining this invitation. Praskóvya Fëdorovna recognizing Peter Ivánovich, sighed, went close up to him, took his hand, and said: "I know you were a true friend to Iván Ilých . . ." and looked at him awaiting some suitable response. And Peter Ivánovich knew that, just as it had been the right thing to cross himself in that room, so what he had to do here was to press her hand, sigh, and say, "Believe me . . .". So he did all this and as he did it felt that the desired result had been achieved: that both he and she were touched.

"Come with me. I want to speak to you before it begins," said the widow. "Give me your arm."

Peter Ivánovich gave her his arm and they went to the inner rooms, passing Schwartz who winked at Peter Ivánovich compassionately.

"That does for our bridge! Don't object if we find another player. Perhaps you can cut in when you do escape," said his playful look.

Peter Ivánovich sighed still more deeply and despondently, and Praskóvya Fëdorovna pressed his arm gratefully. When they reached the drawing-room, upholstered in pink cretonne and lighted by a dim lamp, they sat down at the table — she on a sofa and Peter Ivánovich on a low pouffe, the springs of which yielded spasmodically under his weight. Praskóvya Fëdorovna had been on the point of warning him to take another seat, but felt that such a warning was out of keeping with her present condition and so changed her mind. As he sat down on the pouffe Peter Ivánovich recalled how Iván Ilých had arranged this room and had consulted him regarding this pink cretonne with green leaves. The whole room was full of furniture and knick-knacks, and on her way to the sofa the lace of the widow's black shawl caught on the carved edge of the table. Peter Ivánovich rose to detach it, and the springs of the pouffe, relieved of his weight, rose also and gave him a push. The widow began detaching her shawl herself, and Peter Ivánovich again sat down, suppressing the rebellious springs of the pouffe under him. But the widow had not quite freed herself and Peter Ivánovich got up again, and again the pouffe rebelled and even creaked. When this was all over she took out a clean cambric handkerchief and began to weep. The episode with the shawl and the struggle with the pouffe had cooled Peter Ivánovich's emotions and he sat there with a sullen look on his face. This awkward situation was interrupted by Sokolóv, Iván Ilých's butler, who came to report that the plot in the cemetery that Praskóvya Fëdorovna had chosen would cost two hundred rubles. She stopped weeping and, looking at Peter Ivánovich with the air of a victim, remarked in French that it was very hard for her.   Peter Ivánovich made a silent gesture signifying his full conviction that it must indeed be so.

"Please smoke," she said in a magnanimous yet crushed voice, and turned to discuss with Sokolóv the price of the plot for the grave.

Peter Ivánovich while lighting his cigarette heard her inquiring very circumstantially into the price of different plots in the cemetery and finally decide which she would take.   When that was done she gave instructions about engaging the choir.   Sokolóv then left the room.

"I look after everything myself," she told Peter Ivánovich, shifting the albums that lay on the table;   and noticing that the table was endangered by his cigarette-ash, she immediately passed him an ash-tray, saying as she did so: "I consider it an affectation to say that my grief prevents my attending to practical affairs.   On the contrary, if anything can — I won't say console me, but — distract me, it is seeing to everything concerning him."   She again took out her hand-kerchief as if preparing to cry, but suddenly, as if mastering her feeling, she shook herself and began to speak calmly.   "But there is something I want to talk to you about."

Peter Ivánovich bowed, keeping control of the springs of the pouffe, which immediately began quivering under him.

"He suffered terribly the last few days."

"Did he?" said Peter Ivánovich.

"Oh, terribly!   He screamed unceasingly, not for minutes but for hours.   For the last three days he screamed incessantly.   It was unendurable.   I cannot understand how I bore it; you could hear him three rooms off.   Oh, what I have suffered!"

"Is it possible that he was conscious all that time?" asked Peter Ivánovich.

"Yes," she whispered.   "To the last moment.   He took leave of us a quarter of an hour before he died, and asked us to take Volódya away."

The thought of the sufferings of this man he had known so intimately, first as a merry little boy, then as a school-mate, and later as a grown-up colleague, suddenly struck Peter Ivánovich with horror, despite an unpleasant consciousness of his own and this woman's dissimulation. He again saw that brow, and that nose pressing down on the lip, and felt afraid for himself.

"Three days of frightful suffering and then death!   Why, that might suddenly, at any time, happen to me," he thought, and for a moment felt terrified.   But — he did not himself know how — the customary reflection at once occurred to him that this had happened to Iván Ilých and not to him, and that it should not and could not happen to him, and that to think that it could would be yielding to depression which he ought not to do, as Schwartz's expression plainly showed. After which reflection Peter Ivánovich felt reassured, and began to ask with interest about the details of Iván Ilých's death, as though death was an accident natural to Iván Ilých but certainly not to himself.

After many details of the really dreadful physical sufferings Iván Ilých had endured (which details he learnt only from the effect those sufferings had produced on Praskóvya Fëdorovna's nerves) the widow apparently found it necessary to get to business.

"Oh, Peter Ivánovich, how hard it is! How terribly, terribly hard!" and she again began to weep.

Peter Ivánovich sighed and waited for her to finish blowing her nose. When she had done so he said, "Believe me . . .", and she again began talking and brought out what was evidently her chief concern with him — namely, to question him as to how she could obtain a grant of money from the government on the occasion of her husband's death. She made it appear that she was asking Peter Ivánovich's advice about her pension, but he soon saw that she already knew about that to the minutest detail, more even than he did himself. She knew how much could be got out of the government in consequence of her husband's death, but wanted to find out whether she could not possibly extract something more. Peter Ivánovich tried to think of some means of doing so, but after reflecting for a while and, out of propriety, condemning the government for its niggardliness, he said he thought that nothing more could be got. Then she sighed and evidently began to devise means of getting rid of her visitor. Noticing this, he put out his cigarette, rose, pressed her hand, and went out into the anteroom.

In the dining-room where the clock stood that Iván Ilých had liked so much and had bought at an antique shop, Peter Ivánovich met a priest and a few acquaintances who had come to attend the service, and he recognized Iván Ilých's daughter, a handsome young woman. She was in black and her slim figure appeared slimmer than ever. She had a gloomy, determined, almost angry expression, and bowed to Peter Ivánovich as though he were in some way to blame. Behind her, with the same offended look, stood a wealthy young man, an examining magistrate, whom Peter Ivánovich also knew and who was her fiancé, as he had heard. He bowed mournfully to them and was about to pass into the death-chamber, when from under the stairs appeared the figure of Iván Ilých's schoolboy son, who was extremely like his father. He seemed a little Iván Ilých, such as Peter Ivánovich remembered when they studied law together. His tear-stained eyes had in them the look that is seen in the eyes of boys of thirteen or fourteen who are not pure-minded. When he saw Peter Ivánovich he scowled morosely and shame-facedly. Peter Ivánovich nodded to him and entered the death-chamber. The service began: candles, groans, incense, tears, and sobs. Peter Ivánovich stood looking gloomily down at his feet. He did not look once at the dead man, did not yield to any depressing influence, and was one of the first to leave the room. There was no one in the anteroom, but Gerásim darted out of the dead man's room, rummaged with his strong hands among the fur coats to find Peter Ivánovich's and helped him on with it.

"Well, friend Gerásim," said Peter Ivánovich, so as to say something. "It's a sad affair, isn't it?"

"It's God's will. We shall all come to it some day," said Gerásim, displaying his teeth — the even, white teeth of a healthy peasant — and, like a man in the thick of urgent work, he briskly opened the front door, called the coachman, helped Peter Ivánovich into the sledge, and sprang back to the porch as if in readiness for what he had to do next.

Peter Ivánovich found the fresh air particularly pleasant after the smell of incense, the dead body, and carbolic acid.

"Where to, sir?" asked the coachman.

"It's not too late even now. . . . I'll call round on Fëdor Vasílievich."

He accordingly drove there and found them just finishing the first rubber, so that it was quite convenient for him to cut in.

II

Iván Ilých's life had been most simple and most ordinary and therefore most terrible.

He had been a member of the Court of Justice, and died at the age of forty-five. His father had been an official who after serving in various ministries and departments in Petersburg had made the sort of career which brings men to positions from which by reason of their long service they cannot be dismissed, though they are obviously unfit to hold any responsible position, and for whom therefore posts are specially created, which though fictitious carry salaries of from six to ten thousand rubles that are not fictitious, and in receipt of which they live on to a great age.

Such was the Privy Councillor and superfluous member of various superfluous institutions, Ilyá Epímovich Golovín.

He had three sons, of whom Iván Ilých was the second. The eldest son was following in his father's footsteps only in another department, and was already approaching that stage in the service at which a similar sinecure would be reached. The third son was a failure. He had ruined his prospects in a number of positions and was now serving in the railway department. His father and brothers, and still more their wives, not merely disliked meeting him, but avoided remembering his existence unless compelled to do so. His sister had married Baron Greff, a Petersburg official of her father's type. Iván Ilých was *le phénix de la famille* as people said. He was neither as cold and formal as his elder brother nor as wild as the younger, but was a happy mean between them — an intelligent, polished, lively and agreeable man. He had studied with his younger brother at the School of Law, but the latter had failed to complete the course and was expelled when he was in the fifth class. Iván Ilých finished the course well. Even when he was at the School of Law he was just what he remained for the rest of his life: a capable, cheerful, good-natured, and sociable man, though strict in the fulfilment of what he considered to be his duty: and he considered his duty to be what was so considered by those in authority. Neither as a boy nor as a man was he a toady, but from early youth was by nature attracted to people of high station as a fly is drawn to the light, assimilating their ways and views of life and establishing friendly relations with them. All the enthusiasms of childhood and youth passed without leaving much trace on him; he succumbed to sensuality, to vanity, and latterly among the highest classes to liberalism, but always within limits which his instinct unfailingly indicated to him as correct.

At school he had done things which had formerly seemed to him very horrid and made him feel disgusted with himself when he did them; but when later on he saw that such actions were done by people of good position and that they did not regard them as wrong, he was able not exactly to regard them as right, but to forget about them entirely or not be at all troubled at remembering them.

Having graduated from the School of Law and qualified for the tenth rank of the civil service, and having received money from his father for his equipment, Iván Ilých ordered himself clothes at

Scharmer's, the fashionable tailor, hung a medallion inscribed *respice finen* on his watch-chain, took leave of his professor and the prince who was patron of the school, had a farewell dinner with his comrades at Donon's first-class restaurant, and with his new and fashionable portmanteau, linen, clothes, shaving and other toilet appliances, and a travelling rug, all purchased at the best shops, he set off for one of the provinces where, through his father's influence, he had been attached to the Governor as an official for special service.

In the province Iván Ilých soon arranged as easy and agreeable a position for himself as he had had at the School of Law. He performed his official tasks, made his career, and at the same time amused himself pleasantly and decorously. Occasionally he paid official visits to country districts, where he behaved with dignity both to his superiors and inferiors, and performed the duties entrusted to him, which related chiefly to the sectarians, with an exactness and incorruptible honesty of which he could not but feel proud.

In official matters, despite his youth and taste for frivolous gaiety, he was exceedingly reserved, punctilious, and even severe; but in society he was often amusing and witty, and always good-natured, correct in his manner, and *bon enfant*, as the governor and his wife — with whom he was like one of the family — used to say of him.

In the provinces he had an affair with a lady who made advances to the elegant young lawyer, and there was also a milliner; and there were carousals with aides-de-camp who visited the district, and after-supper visits to a certain outlying street of doubtful reputation; and there was too some obsequiousness to his chief and even to his chief's wife, but all this was done with such a tone of good breeding that no hard names could be applied to it. It all came under the heading of the French saying: "*Il faut que jeunesse se passe.*" [1] It was all done with clean hands, in clean linen, with French phrases, and above all among people of the best society and consequently with the approval of people of rank.

So Iván Ilých served for five years and then came a change in his official life. The new and reformed judicial institutions were introduced, and new men were needed. Iván Ilých became such a new man. He was offered the post of Examining Magistrate, and he accepted it though the post was in another province and obliged him to give up the connexions he had formed and to make new ones. His friends met to give him a send-off; they had a group-photograph taken and pre-

[1] Youth must have its fling.

sented him with a silver cigarette-case, and he set off to his new post.

As examining magistrate Iván Ilých was just as *comme il faut* and decorous a man, inspiring general respect and capable of separating his official duties from his private life, as he had been when acting as an official on special service. His duties now as examining magistrate were far more interesting and attractive than before. In his former position it had been pleasant to wear an undress uniform made by Scharmer, and to pass through the crowd of petitioners and officials who were timorously awaiting an audience with the governor, and who envied him as with free and easy gait he went straight into his chief's private room to have a cup of tea and a cigarette with him. But not many people had then been directly dependent on him — only police officials and the sectarians when he went on special missions — and he liked to treat them politely, almost as comrades, as if he were letting them feel that he who had the power to crush them was treating them in this simple, friendly way. There were then but few such people. But now, as an examining magistrate, Iván Ilých felt that everyone without exception, even the most important and self-satisfied, was in his power, and that he need only write a few words on a sheet of paper with a certain heading, and this or that important, self-satisfied person would be brought before him in the role of an accused person or a witness, and if he did not choose to allow him to sit down, would have to stand before him and answer his questions. Iván Ilých never abused his power; he tried on the contrary to soften its expression, but the consciousness of it and of the possibility of softening its effect, supplied the chief interest and attraction of his office. In his work itself, especially in his examinations, he very soon acquired a method of eliminating all considerations irrelevant to the legal aspect of the case, and reducing even the most complicated case to a form in which it would be presented on paper only in its externals, completely excluding his personal opinion of the matter, while above all observing every prescribed formality. The work was new and Iván Ilých was one of the first men to apply the new Code of 1864.[2]

On taking up the post of examining magistrate in a new town, he made new acquaintances and connexions, placed himself on a new footing, and assumed a somewhat different tone. He took up an attitude of rather dignified aloofness towards the provincial authori-

[2] The emancipation of the serfs in 1861 was followed by a thorough all-round reform of judicial proceedings. — A.M.

ties, but picked out the best circle of legal gentlemen and wealthy gentry living in the town and assumed a tone of slight dissatisfaction with the government, of moderate liberalism, and of enlightened citizenship. At the same time, without at all altering the elegance of his toilet, he ceased shaving his chin and allowed his beard to grow as it pleased.

Iván Ilých settled down very pleasantly in this new town. The society there, which inclined towards opposition to the Governor, was friendly, his salary was larger, and he began to play *vint* [a form of bridge], which he found added not a little to the pleasure of life, for he had a capacity for cards, played good-humouredly, and calculated rapidly and astutely, so that he usually won.

After living there for two years he met his future wife, Praskóvya Fëdorovna Míkhel, who was the most attractive, clever, and brilliant girl of the set in which he moved, and among other amusements and relaxations from his labours as examining magistrate, Iván Ilých established light and playful relations with her.

While he had been an official on special service he had been accustomed to dance, but now as an examining magistrate it was exceptional for him to do so. If he danced now, he did it as if to show that though he served under the reformed order of things, and had reached the fifth official rank, yet when it came to dancing he could do it better than most people. So at the end of an evening he sometimes danced with Praskóvya Fëdorovna, and it was chiefly during these dances that he captivated her. She fell in love with him. Iván Ilých had at first no definite intention of marrying, but when the girl fell in love with him he said to himself: "Really, why shouldn't I marry?"

Praskóvya Fëdorovna came of a good family, was not bad looking, and had some little property. Iván Ilých might have aspired to a more brilliant match, but even this was good. He had his salary, and she, he hoped, would have an equal income. She was well connected, and was a sweet, pretty, and thoroughly correct young woman. To say that Iván Ilých married because he fell in love with Praskóvya Fëdorovna and found that she sympathized with his views of life would be as incorrect as to say that he married because his social circle approved of the match. He was swayed by both these considerations: the marriage gave him personal satisfaction, and at the same time it was considered the right thing by the most highly placed of his associates.

So Iván Ilých got married.

The preparations for marriage and the beginning of married life, with its conjugal caresses, the new furniture, new crockery, and new linen, were very pleasant until his wife became pregnant — so that Iván Ilých had begun to think that marriage would not impair the easy, agreeable, gay and always decorous character of his life, approved of by society and regarded by himself as natural, but would even improve it. But from the first months of his wife's pregnancy, something new, unpleasant, depressing, and unseemly, and from which there was no way of escape, unexpectedly showed itself.

His wife, without any reason — *de gaieté de cœur* as Iván Ilých expressed it to himself — began to disturb the pleasure and propriety of their life. She began to be jealous without any cause, expected him to devote his whole attention to her, found fault with everything, and made coarse and ill-mannered scenes.

At first Iván Ilých hoped to escape from the unpleasantness of this state of affairs by the same easy and decorous relation to life that had served him heretofore: he tried to ignore his wife's disagreeable moods, continued to live in his usual easy and pleasant way, invited friends to his house for a game of cards, and also tried going out to his club or spending his evenings with friends. But one day his wife began upbraiding him so vigorously, using such coarse words, and continued to abuse him every time he did not fulfil her demands, so resolutely and with such evident determination not to give way till he submitted — that is, till he stayed at home and was bored just as she was — that he became alarmed. He now realized that matrimony — at any rate with Praskóvya Fëdorovna — was not always conducive to the pleasures and amenities of life but on the contrary often infringed both comfort and propriety, and that he must therefore entrench himself against such infringement. And Iván Ilých began to seek for means of doing so. His official duties were the one thing that imposed upon Praskóvya Fëdorovna, and by means of his official work and the duties attached to it he began struggling with his wife to secure his own independence.

With the birth of their child, the attempts to feed it and the various failures in doing so, and with the real and imaginary illnesses of mother and child, in which Iván Ilých's sympathy was demanded but about which he understood nothing, the need of securing for himself an existence outside his family life became still more imperative.

As his wife grew more irritable and exacting and Iván Ilých transferred the centre of gravity of his life more and more to his official work, so did he grow to like his work better and became more ambitious than before

Very soon, within a year of his wedding, Iván Ilých had realized that marriage, though it may add some comforts to life, is in fact a very intricate and difficult affair towards which in order to perform one's duty, that is, to lead a decorous life approved of by society, one must adopt a definite attitude just as towards one's official duties.

And Iván Ilých evolved such an attitude towards married life. He only required of it those conveniences — dinner at home, house-wife, and bed — which it could give him, and above all that propriety of external forms required by public opinion. For the rest he looked for light-hearted pleasure and propriety, and was very thankful when he found them, but if he met with antagonism and querulousness he at once retired into his separate fenced-off world of official duties, where he found satisfaction.

Iván Ilých was esteemed a good official, and after three years was made Assistant Public Prosecutor. His new duties, their importance, the possibility of indicting and imprisoning anyone he chose, the publicity his speeches received, and the success he had in all these things, made his work still more attractive.

More children came. His wife became more and more querulous and ill-tempered, but the attitude Iván Ilých had adopted towards his home life rendered him almost impervious to her grumbling.

After seven years' service in that town he was transferred to another province as Public Prosecutor. They moved, but were short of money and his wife did not like the place they moved to. Though the salary was higher the cost of living was greater, besides which two of their children died and family life became still more unpleasant for him.

Praskóvya Fëdorovna blamed her husband for every inconvenience they encountered in their new home. Most of the conversations be-tween husband and wife, especially as to the children's education, led to topics which recalled former disputes, and those disputes were apt to flare up again at any moment. There remained only those rare periods of amorousness which still came to them at times but did not last long. These were islets at which they anchored for a while and then again set out upon that ocean of veiled hostility which showed itself in their aloofness from one another. This aloofness might have grieved Iván Ilých had he considered that it ought not to exist, but he now regarded the position as normal, and even made it the goal at which he aimed in family life. His aim was to free himself more and more from those unpleasantnesses and to give them a semblance of harmlessness and propriety. He attained this by spending less and less time with his family, and when obliged to be at home he tried to safe-guard his position by the presence of outsiders. The chief thing how-ever was that he had his official duties. The whole interest of his life now centred in the official world and that interest absorbed him. The consciousness of his power, being able to ruin anybody he wished to ruin, the importance, even the external dignity of his entry into court, or meetings with his subordinates, his success with superiors and inferiors, and above all his masterly handling of cases, of which he was conscious — all this gave him pleasure and filled his life, together with chats with his colleagues, dinners, and bridge. So that on the whole Iván Ilých's life continued to flow as he considered it should do — pleasantly and properly.

So things continued for another seven years. His eldest daughter was already sixteen, another child had died, and only one son was left, a schoolboy and a subject of dissension. Iván Ilých wanted to put him in the School of Law, but to spite him Praskóvya Fëdorovna entered him at the High School. The daughter had been educated at home and had turned out well: the boy did not learn badly either.

III

So Iván Ilých lived for seventeen years after his marriage. He was already a Public Prosecutor of long standing, and had declined several proposed transfers while awaiting a more desirable post, when an unanticipated and unpleasant occurrence quite upset the peaceful course of his life. He was expecting to be offered the post of presiding judge in a University town, but Happe somehow came to the front and obtained the appointment instead. Iván Ilých became irritable, reproached Happe, and quarrelled both with him and with his imme-diate superiors — who became colder to him and again passed him over when other appointments were made.

This was in 1880, the hardest year of Iván Ilých's life. It was then that it became evident on the one hand that his salary was insufficient for them to live on, and on the other that he had been forgotten, and not only this, but that what was for him the greatest and most cruel injustice appeared to others a quite ordinary occurrence. Even his father did not consider it his duty to help him. Iván Ilých felt himself abandoned by everyone, and that they regarded his position with a salary of 3,500 rubies [about £350] as quite normal and even fortunate. He alone knew that with the consciousness of the injustices done him, with his wife's incessant nagging, and with the debts he had contracted by living beyond his means, his position was far from normal.

In order to save money that summer he obtained leave of absence and went with his wife to live in the country at her brother's place.

In the country, without his work, he experienced *ennui* for the first time in his life, and not only *ennui* but intolerable depression, and he decided that it was impossible to go on living like that, and that it was necessary to take energetic measures.

Having passed a sleepless night pacing up and down the veranda, he decided to go to Petersburg and bestir himself, in order to punish those who had failed to appreciate him and to get transferred to another ministry.

Next day, despite many protests from his wife and her brother, he started for Petersburg with the sole object of obtaining a post with a salary of five thousand rubles a year. He was no longer bent on any particular department, or tendency, or kind of activity. All he now wanted was an appointment to another post with a salary of five thousand rubles, either in the administration, in the banks, with the railways, in one of the Empress Márya's Institutions, or even in the customs — but it had to carry with it a salary of five thousand rubles and be in a ministry other than that in which they had failed to appreciate him.

And this quest of Iván Ilých's was crowned with remarkable and unexpected success. At Kursk an acquaintance of his, F. I. Ilyín, got into the first-class carriage, sat down beside Iván Ilých, and told him of a telegram just received by the Governor of Kursk announcing that a change was about to take place in the ministry: Peter Ivánovich was to be superseded by Iván Semënovich.

The proposed change, apart from its significance for Russia, had a special significance for Iván Ilých, because by bringing forward a new man, Peter Petróvich, and consequently his friend Zachár Ivánovich, it was highly favourable for Iván Ilých, since Zachár Ivánovich was a friend and colleague of his.

In Moscow this news was confirmed, and on reaching Petersburg Iván Ilých found Zachár Ivánovich and received a definite promise of an appointment in his former department of Justice.

A week later he telegraphed to his wife: "Zachár in Miller's place. I shall receive appointment on presentation of report."

Thanks to this change of personnel, Iván Ilých had unexpectedly obtained an appointment in his former ministry which placed him two stages above his former colleagues besides giving him five thousand rubles salary and three thousand five hundred rubles for expenses connected with his removal.   All his ill humor towards his former enemies and the whole department vanished, and Iván Ilých was completely happy.

He returned to the country more cheerful and contented than he had been for a long time.   Praskóvya Fëdorovna also cheered up and a truce was arranged between them.   Iván Ilých told of how he had been fêted by everybody in Petersburg, how all those who had been his enemies were put to shame and now fawned on him, how envious they were of his appointment, and how much everybody in Petersburg had liked him.

Praskóvya Fëdorovna listened to all this and appeared to believe it. She did not contradict anything, but only made plans for their life in the town to which they were going.   Iván Ilých saw with delight that these plans were his plans, that he and his wife agreed, and that, after a stumble, his life was regaining its due and natural character of pleasant lightheartedness and decorum.

Iván Ilých had come back for a short time only, for he had to take up his new duties on the 10th of September.   Moreover, he needed time to settle into the new place, to move all his belongings from the province, and to buy and order many additional things: in a word, to make such arrangements as he had resolved on, which were almost exactly what Praskóvya Fëdorovna too had decided on.

Now that everything had happened so fortunately, and that he and his wife were at one in their aims and moreover saw so little of one another, they got on together better than they had done since the first years of marriage.   Iván Ilých had thought of taking his family away with him at once, but the insistence of his wife's brother and her sister-in-law, who had suddenly become particularly amiable and friendly to him and his family, induced him to depart alone.

So he departed, and the cheerful state of mind induced by his success and by the harmony between his wife and himself, the one intensifying the other, did not leave him.   He found a delightful house, just the thing both he and his wife had dreamt of.   Spacious, lofty reception rooms in the old style, a convenient and dignified study, rooms for his wife and daughter, a study for his son — it might have been specially built for them.   Iván Ilých himself superintended the arrangements, chose the wall-papers, supplemented the furniture (preferably with antiques which he considered particularly *comme il faut*), and supervised the upholstering. Everything progressed and progressed and approached the ideal he had set himself: even when things were only half completed they exceeded his expectations. He saw what a refined and elegant character, free from vulgarity, it would all have when it was ready. On falling asleep he pictured to himself how the reception-room would look. Looking at the yet unfinished drawing-room he could see the fireplace, the screen, the what-not, the little chairs dotted here and there, the dishes and plates on the walls, and the bronzes, as they would be when everything was in place. He was pleased by the thought of how his wife and daughter, who shared his taste in this matter, would be impressed by it. They were certainly not expecting as much. He had been particularly successful in finding, and buying cheaply, antiques which gave a particularly aristocratic character to the whole place. But in his letters he intentionally understated everything in order to be able to surprise them. All this so absorbed him that his new duties — though he liked his official work — interested him less than he had expected. Sometimes he even had moments of absent-mindedness during the Court Sessions, and would consider whether he should have straight or curved cornices for his curtains. He was so interested in it all that he often did things himself, rearranging the furniture, or rehanging the curtains. Once when mounting a step-ladder to show the upholsterer, who did not understand, how he wanted the hangings draped, he made a false step and slipped, but being a strong and agile man he clung on and only knocked his side against the knob of the window frame. The bruised place was painful but the pain soon passed, and he felt particularly bright and well just then. He wrote: "I feel fifteen years younger." He thought he would have everything ready by September, but it dragged on till mid-October. But the result was charming not only in his eyes but to everyone who saw it.

In reality it was just what is usually seen in the houses of people of moderate means who want to appear rich, and therefore succeed only in resembling others like themselves: there were damasks, dark wood, plants, rugs, and dull and polished bronzes — all the things people of a certain class have in order to resemble other people of that class. His house was so like the others that it would never have been noticed, but to him it all seemed to be quite exceptional. He was very happy when he met his family at the station and brought them to the newly furnished house all lit up, where a footman in a white tie opened the door into the hall decorated with plants, and when they went on into the drawing-room and the study uttering exclamations of delight. He conducted them everywhere, drank in their praises eagerly, and beamed with pleasure. At tea that evening, when Praskóvya Fëdorovna among other things asked him about his fall, he laughed, and showed them how he had gone flying and had frightened the upholsterer.

"It's a good thing I'm a bit of an athlete. Another man might have been killed, but I merely knocked myself, just here; it hurts when it's touched, but it's passing off already — it's only a bruise."

So they began living in their new home — in which, as always happens, when they got thoroughly settled in they found they were just one room short — and with the increased income, which as always was just a little (some five hundred rubles) too little, but it was all very nice.

Things went particularly well at first, before everything was finally arranged and while something had still to be done: this thing bought, that thing ordered, another thing moved, and something else adjusted. Though there were some disputes between husband and wife, they were both so well satisfied and had so much to do that it all passed off without any serious quarrels. When nothing was left to arrange it became rather dull and something seemed to be lacking, but they were then making acquaintances, forming habits, and life was growing fuller.

Iván Ilých spent his mornings at the law court and came home to dinner, and at first he was generally in a good humour, though he occasionally became irritable just on account of his house. (Every spot on the tablecloth or the upholstery, and every broken window-blind string, irritated him. He had devoted so much trouble to arranging it all that every disturbance of it distressed him.) But on the whole his life ran its course as he believed life should do: easily, pleasantly, and decorously.

He got up at nine, drank his coffee, read the paper, and then put on his undress uniform and went to the law courts. There the harness in which he worked had already been stretched to fit him and he donned it without a hitch: petitioners, inquiries at the chancery, the chancery itself, and the sittings public and administrative. In all this the thing was to exclude everything fresh and vital, which always disturbs the regular course of official business, and to admit only official relations with people, and then only on official grounds. A man would come, for instance, wanting some information. Iván Ilých, as one in whose sphere the matter did not lie, would have nothing to do with him: but if the man had some business with him in his official capacity, something that could be expressed on officially stamped paper, he would do everything, positively everything he could within the limits of such relations, and in doing so would maintain the semblance of friendly human relations, that is, would observe the courtesies of life. As soon as the official relations ended, so did everything else. Iván Ilých possessed this capacity to separate his real life from the official side of affairs and not mix the two, in the highest degree, and by long practice and natural aptitude had brought it to such a pitch that sometimes, in the manner of a virtuoso, he would even allow himself to let the human and official relations mingle. He let himself do this just because he felt that he could at any time he chose resume the strictly official attitude again and drop the human relation. And he did it all easily, pleasantly, correctly, and even artistically. In the intervals between the sessions he smoked, drank tea, chatted a little about politics, a little about general topics, a little about cards, but most of all about official appointments. Tired, but with the feelings of a virtuoso — one of the first violins who has played his part in an orchestra with precision — he would return home to find that his wife and daughter had been out paying calls, or had a visitor, and that his son had been to school, had done his homework with his tutor, and was duly learning what is taught at High Schools. Everything was as it should be. After dinner, if they had no visitors, Iván Ilých sometimes read a book that was being much discussed at the time, and in the evening settled down to work, that is, read official papers, compared the depositions of witnesses, and noted paragraphs of the Code applying to them. This was neither dull nor amusing. It was dull when he might have been playing bridge, but if no bridge was available it was at any rate better than doing nothing or sitting with his wife. Iván Ilých's chief pleasure was giving little dinners to which he invited men and women of good social position, and just as his drawing-room resembled all other drawing-rooms so did his enjoyable little parties resemble all other such parties.

Once they even gave a dance. Iván Ilých enjoyed it and everything went off well, except that it led to a violent quarrel with his wife about the cakes and sweets. Praskóvya Fëdorovna had made her own plans, but Iván Ilých insisted on getting everything from an expensive confectioner and ordered too many cakes, and the quarrel occurred because some of those cakes were left over and the confectioner's bill came to forty-five rubles. It was a great and disagreeable quarrel. Praskóvya Fëdorovna called him "a fool and an imbecile", and he clutched at his head and made angry allusions to divorce.

But the dance itself had been enjoyable. The best people were there, and Iván Ilých had danced with Princess Trúfonova, a sister of the distinguished founder of the Society "Bear my Burden".

The pleasures connected with his work were pleasures of ambition; his social pleasures were those of vanity; but Iván Ilých's greatest pleasure was playing bridge. He acknowledged that whatever disagreeable incident happened in his life, the pleasure that beamed like a ray of light above everything else was to sit down to bridge with good players, not noisy partners, and of course to four-handed bridge (with five players it was annoying to have to stand out, though one pretended not to mind), to play a clever and serious game (when the cards allowed it) and then to have supper and drink a glass of wine. After a game of bridge, especially if he had won a little (to win a large sum was unpleasant), Iván Ilých went to bed in specially good humour.

So they lived. They formed a circle of acquaintances among the best people and were visited by people of importance and by young folk. In their views as to their acquaintances, husband, wife and daughter were entirely agreed, and tacitly and unanimously kept at arm's length and shook off the various shabby friends and relations who, with much show of affection, gushed into the drawing-room with its Japanese plates on the walls. Soon these shabby friends ceased to obtrude themselves and only the best people remained in the Golovíns' set.

Young men made up to Lisa, and Petríschhev, an examining magistrate and Dmítri Ivánovich Petríshchev's son and sole heir, began to be so attentive to her that Iván Ilých had already spoken to Praskóvya Fëdorovna about it, and considered whether they should not arrange a party for them, or get up some private theatricals.

So they lived, and all went well, without change, and life flowed pleasantly.

IV

They were all in good health. It could not be called ill health if Iván Ilých sometimes said that he had a queer taste in his mouth and felt some discomfort in his left side.

But this discomfort increased and, though not exactly painful, grew into a sense of pressure in his side accompanied by ill humour. And his irritability became worse and worse and began to mar the agreeable, easy, and correct life that had established itself in the Golovín family. Quarrels between husband and wife became more and more frequent, and soon the ease and amenity disappeared and even the decorum was barely maintained. Scenes again became frequent, and very few of those islets remained on which husband and wife could meet without an explosion. Praskóvya Fëdoróvna now had good reason to say that her husband's temper was trying. With characteristic exaggeration she said he had always had a dreadful temper, and that it had needed all her good nature to put up with it for twenty years. It was true that now the quarrels were started by him. His bursts of temper always came just before dinner, often just as he began to eat his soup. Sometimes he noticed that a plate or dish was chipped, or the food was not right, or his son put his elbow on the table, or his daughter's hair was not done as he liked it, and for all this he blamed Praskóvya Fëdorovna. At first she retorted and said disagreeable things to him, but once or twice he fell into such a rage at the beginning of dinner that she realized it was due to some physical derangement brought on by taking food, and so she restrained herself and did not answer, but only hurried to get the dinner over. She regarded this self-restraint as highly praiseworthy. Having come to the conclusion that her husband had a dreadful temper and made her life miserable, she began to feel sorry for herself, and the more she pitied herself the more she hated her husband. She began to wish he would die; yet she did not want him to die because then his salary would cease. And this irritated her against him still more. She considered herself dreadfully unhappy just because not even his death could save her, and though she concealed her exasperation, that hidden exasperation of hers increased his irritation also.

After one scene in which Iván Ilých had been particularly unfair and after which he had said in explanation that he certainly was irritable but that it was due to his not being well, she said that if he was ill it should be attended to, and insisted on his going to see a celebrated doctor.

He went. Everything took place as he had expected and as it always does. There was the usual waiting and the important air assumed by the doctor, with which he was so familiar (resembling that which he himself assumed in court), and the sounding and listening, and the questions which called for answers that were foregone conclusions and were evidently unnecessary, and the look of importance which implied that "if only you put yourself in our hands we will arrange everything — we know indubitably how it has to be done, always in the same way for everybody alike." It was all just as it was in the law courts. The doctor put on just the same air towards him as he himself put on towards an accused person.

The doctor said that so-and-so indicated that there was so-and-so inside the patient, but if the investigation of so-and-so did not confirm this, then he must assume that and that. If he assumed that and that, then . . . and so on. To Iván Ilých only one question was important: was his case serious or not? But the doctor ignored that inappropriate question. From his point of view it was not the one under consideration, the real question was to decide between a floating kidney, chronic catarrh, or appendicitis. It was not a question of Iván Ilých's life or death, but one between a floating kidney and appendicitis. And that question the doctor solved brilliantly, as it seemed to Iván Ilých, in favour of the appendix, with the reservation that should an examination of the urine give fresh indications the matter would be reconsidered. All this was just what Iván Ilých had himself brilliantly accomplished a thousand times in dealing with men on trial. The doctor summed up just as brilliantly, looking over his spectacles triumphantly and even gaily at the accused. From the doctor's summing up Iván Ilých concluded that things were bad, but that for the doctor, and perhaps for everybody else, it was a matter of indifference, though for him it was bad. And this conclusion struck him painfully, arousing in him a great feeling of pity for himself and of bitterness towards the doctor's indifference to a matter of such importance.

He said nothing of this, but rose, placed the doctor's fee on the table, and remarked with a sigh: "We sick people probably often put inappropriate questions. But tell me, in general, is this complaint dangerous, or not? . . ."

The doctor looked at him sternly over his spectacles with one eye, as if to say: "Prisoner, if you will not keep to the questions put to you, I shall be obliged to have you removed from the court."

"I have already told you what I consider necessary and proper. The analysis may show something more." And the doctor bowed.

Iván Ilých went out slowly, seated himself disconsolately in his sledge, and drove home. All the way home he was going over what the doctor had said, trying to translate those complicated, obscure, scientific phrases into plain language and find in them an answer to the question: "Is my condition bad? Is it very bad? Or is there as yet nothing much wrong?" And it seemed to him that the meaning of what the doctor had said was that it was very bad. Everything in the streets seemed depressing. The cabmen, the houses, the passers-by, and the shops, were dismal. His ache, this dull gnawing ache that never ceased for a moment, seemed to have acquired a new and more serious significance from the doctor's dubious remarks. Iván Ilých now watched it with a new and oppressive feeling.

He reached home and began to tell his wife about it. She listened, but in the middle of his account his daughter came in with her hat on, ready to go out with her mother. She sat down reluctantly to listen to this tedious story, but could not stand it long, and her mother too did not hear him to the end.

"Well, I am very glad," she said. "Mind now to take your medicine regularly. Give me the prescription and I'll send Gerásim to the chemist's." And she went to get ready to go out.

While she was in the room Iván Ilých had hardly taken time to breathe, but he sighed deeply when she left it.

"Well," he thought, "perhaps it isn't so bad after all."

He began taking his medicine and following the doctor's directions, which had been altered after the examination of the urine. But then it happened that there was a contradiction between the indications drawn from the examination of the urine and the symptoms that showed themselves. It turned out that what was happening differed from what the doctor had told him, and that he had either forgotten, or blundered, or hidden something from him. He could not, however, be blamed for that, and Iván Ilých still obeyed his orders implicitly and at first derived some comfort from doing so.

From the time of his visit to the doctor, Iván Ilých's chief occupation was the exact fulfilment of the doctor's instructions regarding hygiene and the taking of medicine, and the observation of his pain and his excretions. His chief interests came to be people's ailments and people's health. When sickness, deaths, or recoveries, were mentioned in his presence, especially when the illness resembled his own, he listened with agitation which he tried to hide, asked questions, and applied what he heard to his own case.

The pain did not grow less, but Iván Ilých made efforts to force himself to think that he was better. And he could do this so long as nothing agitated him. But as soon as he had any unpleasantness with his wife, any lack of success in his official work, or held bad cards at bridge, he was at once acutely sensible of his disease. He had formerly borne such mischances, hoping soon to adjust what was wrong, to master it and attain success, or make a grand slam. But now every mischance upset him and plunged him into despair. He would say to himself: "There now, just as I was beginning to get better and the medicine had begun to take effect, comes this accursed misfortune, or unpleasantness . . ." And he was furious with the mishap, or with the people who were causing the unpleasantness and killing him, for he felt that this fury was killing him but could not restrain it. One would have thought that it should have been clear to him that this exasperation with circumstances and people aggravated his illness, and that he ought therefore to ignore unpleasant occurrences. But he drew the very opposite conclusion: he said that he needed peace, and he watched for everything that might disturb it and became irritable at the slightest infringement of it. His condition was rendered worse by the fact that he read medical books and consulted doctors. The progress of his disease was so gradual that he could deceive himself when comparing one day with another — the difference was so slight. But when he consulted the doctors it seemed to him that he was getting worse, and even very rapidly. Yet despite this he was continually consulting them.

That month he went to see another celebrity, who told him almost the same as the first had done but put his questions rather differently, and the interview with this celebrity only increased Iván Ilých's doubts and fears. A friend of a friend of his, a very good doctor, diagnosed his illness again quite differently from the others, and though he predicted recovery, his questions and suppositions bewildered Iván Ilých still more and increased his doubts. A homoeopathist diagnosed the disease in yet another way, and prescribed medicine which Iván Ilých took secretly for a week. But after a week, not feeling any improvement and having lost confidence both in the former doctor's treatment and in this one's, he became still more despondent. One day a lady acquaintance mentioned a cure effected by a wonder-working icon. Iván Ilých caught himself listening attentively and beginning to believe that it had occurred. This incident alarmed him. "Has my mind really weakened to such an extent?" he asked himself. "Nonsense! It's all rubbish. I mustn't give way to nervous fears but having chosen a doctor must keep strictly to his treatment. That is what I will do. Now it's all settled. I won't think about it, but will follow the treatment seriously till summer, and then we shall see. From now there must be no more of this wavering!" This was easy to say but impossible to carry out. The pain in his side oppressed him and seemed to grow worse and more incessant, while the taste in his mouth grew stranger and stranger. It seemed to him that his breath had a disgusting smell, and he was conscious of a loss of appetite and strength. There was no deceiving himself: something terrible, new, and more important than anything before in his life, was taking place within him of which he alone was aware. Those about him did not understand or would not understand it, but thought everything in the world was going on as usual. That tormented Iván Ilých more than anything. He saw that his household, especially his wife and daughter who were in a perfect whirl of visiting, did not understand anything of it and were annoyed that he was so depressed and so exacting, as if he were to blame for it. Though they tried to disguise it he saw that he was an obstacle in their path, and that his wife had adopted a definite line in regard to his illness and kept to it regardless of anything he said or did. Her attitude was this: "You know," she would say to her friends, "Iván Ilých can't do as other people do, and keep to the treatment prescribed for him. One day he'll take his drops and keep strictly to his diet and go to bed in good time, but the next day unless I watch him he'll suddenly forget his medicine, eat sturgeon — which is forbidden — and sit up playing cards till one o'clock in the morning."

"Oh, come, when was that?" Iván Ilých would ask in vexation. "Only once at Peter Ivánovich's."

"And yesterday with Shébek."

"Well, even if I hadn't stayed up, this pain would have kept me awake."

"Be that as it may you'll never get well like that, but will always make us wretched."

Praskóvya Fëdorovna's attitude to Iván Ilých's illness, as she expressed it both to others and to him, was that it was his own fault and was another of the annoyances he caused her. Iván Ilých felt that this opinion escaped her involuntarily — but that did not make it easier for him.

At the law courts too, Iván Ilých noticed, or thought he noticed, a strange attitude towards himself. It sometimes seemed to him that people were watching him inquisitively as a man whose place might soon be vacant. Then again, his friends would suddenly begin to chaff him in a friendly way about his low spirits, as if the awful, horrible, and unheard-of thing that was going on within him, incessantly gnawing at him and irresistibly drawing him away, was a very agreeable subject for jests. Schwartz in particular irritated him by his jocularity, vivacity, and *savoir-faire*, which reminded him of what he himself had been ten years ago.

Friends came to make up a set and they sat down to cards. They dealt, bending the new cards to soften them, and he sorted the diamonds in his hand and found he had seven. His partner said "No trumps" and supported him with two diamonds. What more could be wished for? It ought to be jolly and lively. They would make a grand slam. But suddenly Iván Ilých was conscious of that gnawing pain, that taste in his mouth, and it seemed ridiculous that in such circumstances he should be pleased to make a grand slam.

He looked at his partner Mikháil Mikháylovich, who rapped the table with his strong hand and instead of snatching up the tricks pushed the cards courteously and indulgently towards Iván Ilých that he might have the pleasure of gathering them up without the trouble of stretching out his hand for them. "Does he think I am too weak to stretch out my arm?" thought Iván Ilých, and forgetting what he was doing he over-trumped his partner, missing the grand slam by three tricks. And what was most awful of all was that he saw how upset Mikháil Mikháylovich was about it but did not himself care. And it was dreadful to realize why he did not care.

They all saw that he was suffering, and said: "We can stop if you are tired. Take a rest." Lie down? No, he was not at all tired, and he finished the rubber. All were gloomy and silent. Iván Ilých felt that he had diffused this gloom over them and could not dispel it. They had supper and went away, and Iván Ilých was left alone with the consciousness that his life was poisoned and was poisoning the lives of others, and that this poison did not weaken but penetrated more and more deeply into his whole being.

With this consciousness, and with physical pain besides the terror, he must go to bed, often to lie awake the greater part of the night. Next morning he had to get up again, dress, go to the law courts, speak, and write; or if he did not go out, spend at home those twenty-four hours a day each of which was a torture. And he had to live thus all alone on the brink of an abyss, with no one who understood or pitied him.

V

So one month passed and then another. Just before the New Year his brother-in-law came to town and stayed at their house. Iván Ilych was at the law courts and Praskóvya Fëdorovna had gone shopping. When Iván Ilých came home and entered his study he found his brother-in-law there — a healthy, florid man — unpacking his portmanteau himself. He raised his head on hearing Iván Ilých's footsteps and looked up at him for a moment without a word. That stare told Iván Ilých everything. His brother-in-law opened his mouth to utter an exclamation of surprise but checked himself, and that action confirmed it all.

"I have changed, eh?"

"Yes, there is a change."

And after that, try as he would to get his brother-in-law to return to the subject of his looks, the latter would say nothing about it. Praskóvya Fëdorovna came home and her brother went out to her. Iván Ilých locked the door and began to examine himself in the glass, first full face, then in profile. He took up a portrait of himself taken with his wife, and compared it with what he saw in the glass. The change in him was immense. Then he bared his arms to the elbow, looked at them, drew the sleeves down again, sat down on an ottoman, and grew blacker than night.

"No, no, this won't do!" he said to himself, and jumped up, went to the table, took up some law papers and began to read them, but could not continue. He unlocked the door and went into the reception-room. The door leading to the drawing-room was shut. He approached it on tiptoe and listened.

"No, you are exaggerating!" Praskóvya Fëdorovna was saying.

"Exaggerating! Don't you see it? Why, he's a dead man! Look at his eyes — there's no light in them. But what is it that is wrong with him?"

"No one knows. Nikoláevich [that was another doctor] said something, but I don't know what. And Leshchetítsky [this was the celebrated specialist] said quite the contrary . . ."

Iván Ilých walked away, went to his own room, lay down, and began musing: "The kidney, a floating kidney." He recalled all the doctors had told him of how it detached itself and swayed about. And by an effort of imagination he tried to catch that kidney and arrest it and support it. So little was needed for this, it seemed to him. "No, I'll go to see Peter Ivánovich again." [That was the friend whose friend was a doctor.] He rang, ordered the carriage, and got ready to go.

"Where are you going, Jean?" asked his wife, with a specially sad and exceptionally kind look.

This exceptionally kind look irritated him. He looked morosely at her.

"I must go to see Peter Ivánovich."

He went to see Peter Ivánovich, and together they went to see his friend, the doctor. He was in, and Iván Ilých had a long talk with him.

Reviewing the anatomical and physiological details of what in the doctor's opinion was going on inside him, he understood it all.

There was something, a small thing, in the vermiform appendix. It might all come right. Only stimulate the energy of one organ and check the activity of another, then absorption would take place and everything would come right. He got home rather late for dinner, ate his dinner, and conversed cheerfully, but could not for a long time bring himself to go back to work in his room. At last, however, he went to his study and did what was necessary, but the consciousness that he had put something aside — an important, intimate matter which he would revert to when his work was done — never left him. When he had finished his work he remembered that this intimate matter was the thought of his vermiform appendix. But he did not give himself up to it, and went to the drawing-room for tea. There were callers there, including the examining magistrate who was a desirable match for his daughter, and they were conversing, playing the piano, and singing. Iván Ilých, as Praskóvya Fёdorovna remarked, spent that evening more cheerfully than usual, but he never for a moment forgot that he had postponed the important matter of the appendix. At eleven o'clock he said good-night and went to his bedroom. Since his illness he had slept alone in a small room next to his study. He undressed and took up a novel by Zola, but instead of reading it he fell into thought, and in his imagination that desired improvement in the vermiform appendix occurred. There was the absorption and evacuation and the re-establishment of normal activity. "Yes, that's it!" he said to himself. "One need only assist nature, that's all." He remembered his medicine, rose, took it, and lay down on his back watching for the beneficent action of the medicine and for it to lessen the pain. "I need only take it regularly and avoid all injurious influences. I am already feeling better, much better." He began touching his side: it was not painful to the touch. "There, I really don't feel it. It's much better already." He put out the light and turned on his side . . . "The appendix is getting better, absorption is occurring." Suddenly he felt the old, familiar, dull, gnawing pain, stubborn and serious. There was the same familiar loathsome taste in his mouth. His heart sank and he felt dazed. "My God! My God!" he muttered. "Again, again! And it will never cease." And suddenly the matter presented itself in a quite different aspect. "Vermiform appendix! Kidney!" he said to himself. "It's not a question of appendix or kidney, but of life and . . . death. Yes, life was there and now it is going, going and I cannot stop it. Yes. Why deceive myself? Isn't it obvious to everyone but me that I'm dying, and that it's only a question of weeks, days . . . it may happen this moment. There was light and now there is darkness. I was here and now I'm going there! Where?" A chill came over him, his breathing ceased, and he felt only the throbbing of his heart.

"When I am not, what will there be? There will be nothing. Then where shall I be when I am no more? Can this be dying? No, I don't want to!" He jumped up and tried to light the candle, felt for it with trembling hands, dropped candle and candlestick on the floor, and fell back on his pillow.

"What's the use? It makes no difference," he said to himself, staring with wide-open eyes into the darkness. "Death. Yes, death. And none of them know or wish to know it, and they have no pity for me. Now they are playing." (He heard through the door the distant sound of a song and its accompaniment.) "It's all the same to them, but they will die too! Fools! I first, and they later, but it will be the same for them. And now they are merry . . . the beasts!"

Anger choked him and he was agonizingly, unbearably miserable. "It is impossible that all men have been doomed to suffer this awful horror!" He raised himself.

"Something must be wrong. I must calm myself — must think it all over from the beginning." And he again began thinking. "Yes, the beginning of my illness: I knocked my side, but I was still quite well that day and the next. It hurt a little, then rather more. I saw the doctors, then followed despondency and anguish, more doctors, and I drew nearer to the abyss. My strength grew less and I kept coming nearer and nearer, and now I have wasted away and there is no light in my eyes. I think of the appendix — but this is death! I think of mending the appendix, and all the while here is death! Can it really be death?" Again terror seized him and he gasped for breath. He leant down and began feeling for the matches, pressing with his elbow on the stand beside the bed. It was in his way and hurt him, he grew furious with it, pressed on it still harder, and upset it. Breathless and in despair he fell on his back, expecting death to come immediately.

Meanwhile the visitors were leaving. Praskóvya Fëdorovna was seeing them off. She heard something fall and came in.

"What has happened?"

"Nothing. I knocked it over accidentally."

She went out and returned with a candle. He lay there panting heavily, like a man who has run a thousand yards, and stared upwards at her with a fixed look.

"What is it, Jean?"

"No . . . o . . . thing. I upset it." ("Why speak of it? She won't understand," he thought.)

And in truth she did not understand. She picked up the stand, lit his candle, and hurried away to see another visitor off. When she came back he still lay on his back, looking upwards.

"What is it? Do you feel worse?"

"Yes."

She shook her head and sat down.

"Do you know, Jean, I think we must ask Leshchetítsky to come and see you here."

This meant calling in the famous specialist, regardless of expense. He smiled malignantly and said "No." She remained a little longer and then went up to him and kissed his forehead.

While she was kissing him he hated her from the bottom of his soul and with difficulty refrained from pushing her away.

"Good-night. Please God you'll sleep."

"Yes."

VI

Iván Ilých saw that he was dying, and he was in continual despair.

In the depth of his heart he knew he was dying, but not only was he not accustomed to the thought, he simply did not and could not grasp it.

The syllogism he had learnt from Kiezewetter's Logic: "Caius is a man, men are mortal, therefore Caius is mortal", had always seemed to him correct as applied to Caius, but certainly not as applied to himself. That Caius — man in the abstract — was mortal, was perfectly correct, but he was not Caius, not an abstract man, but a creature quite quite separate from all others. He had been little Ványa, with a

mamma and a papa, with Mitya and Volódya, with the toys, a coachman and a nurse, afterwards with Kátenka and with all the joys,
griefs, and delights of childhood, boyhood, and youth. What did
Caius know of the smell of that striped leather ball Ványa had been
so fond of? Had Caius kissed his mother's hand like that, and did
the silk of her dress rustle so for Caius? Had he rioted like that at
school when the pastry was bad? Had Caius been in love like that?
Could Caius preside at a session as he did? "Caius really was mortal,
and it was right for him to die; but for me, little Ványa, Iván Ilých,
with all my thoughts and emotions, it's altogether a different matter.
It cannot be that I ought to die. That would be too terrible."

Such was his feeling.

"If I had to die like Caius I should have known it was so. An inner
voice would have told me so, but there was nothing of the sort in me
and I and all my friends felt that our case was quite different from that
of Caius. And now here it is!" he said to himself. "It can't be.
It's impossible! But here it is. How is this? How is one to understand it?"

He could not understand it, and tried to drive this false, incorrect,
morbid thought away and to replace it by other proper and healthy
thoughts. But that thought, and not the thought only but the reality
itself, seemed to come and confront him.

And to replace that thought he called up a succession of others,
hoping to find in them some support. He tried to get back into the
former current of thoughts that had once screened the thought of
death from him. But strange to say, all that had formerly shut off,
hidden, and destroyed, his consciousness of death, no longer had that
effect. Iván Ilých now spent most of his time in attempting to re-
establish that old current. He would say to himself: "I will take up
my duties again — after all I used to live by them." And banishing
all doubts he would go to the law courts, enter into conversation with
his colleagues, and sit carelessly as was his wont, scanning the crowd
with a thoughtful look and leaning both his emaciated arms on the
arms of his oak chair; bending over as usual to a colleague and drawing
his papers nearer he would interchange whispers with him, and then
suddenly raising his eyes and sitting erect would pronounce certain
words and open the proceedings. But suddenly in the midst of those
proceedings the pain in his side, regardless of the stage the proceedings
had reached, would begin its own gnawing work. Iván Ilých would
turn his attention to it and try to drive the thought of it away, but

without success. *It* would come and stand before him and look at him, and he would be petrified and the light would die out of his eyes, and he would again begin asking himself whether *It* alone was true. And his colleagues and subordinates would see with surprise and distress that he, the brilliant and subtle judge, was becoming confused and making mistakes. He would shake himself, try to pull himself together, manage somehow to bring the sitting to a close, and return home with the sorrowful consciousness that his judicial labours could not as formerly hide from him what he wanted them to hide, and could not deliver him from *It*. And what was worst of all was that *It* drew his attention to itself not in order to make him take some action but only that he should look at *It*, look it straight in the face: look at it and without doing anything, suffer inexpressibly.

And to save himself from this condition Iván Ilých looked for consolations — new screens — and new screens were found and for a while seemed to save him, but then they immediately fell to pieces or rather became transparent, as if *It* penetrated them and nothing could veil *It*.

In these latter days he would go into the drawing-room he had arranged — that drawing-room where he had fallen and for the sake of which (how bitterly ridiculous it seemed) he had sacrificed his life — for he knew that his illness originated with that knock. He would enter and see that something had scratched the polished table. He would look for the cause of this and find that it was the bronze ornamentation of an album, that had got bent. He would take up the expensive album which he had lovingly arranged, and feel vexed with his daughter and her friends for their untidiness — for the album was torn here and there and some of the photographs turned upside down. He would put it carefully in order and bend the ornamentation back into position. Then it would occur to him to place all those things in another corner of the room, near the plants. He would call the footman, but his daughter or wife would come to help him. They would not agree, and his wife would contradict him, and he would dispute and grow angry. But that was all right, for then he did not think about *It*. *It* was invisible.

But then, when he was moving something himself, his wife would say: "Let the servants do it. You will hurt yourself again." And suddenly *It* would flash through the screen and he would see it. It was just a flash, and he hoped it would disappear, but he would involuntarily pay attention to his side. "It sits there as before, gnawing

just the same!" And he could no longer forget *It*, but could distinctly
see it looking at him from behind the flowers. "What is it all for?"

"It really is so I lost my life over that curtain as I might have done
when storming a fort. It that possible? How terrible and how stupid.
It can't be true! It can't, but it is."

He would go to his study, lie down, and again be alone with *It:*
face to face with *It*. And nothing could be done with *It* except to
look at it and shudder.

VII

How it happened it is impossible to say because it came about step
by step, unnoticed, but in the third month of Iván Ilých's illness, his
wife, his daughter, his son, his acquaintances, the doctors, the servants,
and above all he himself, were aware that the whole interest he had for
other people was whether he would soon vacate his place, and at last
release the living from the discomfort caused by his presence and be
himself released from his sufferings.

He slept less and less. He was given opium and hypodermic injec-
tions of morphine, but this did not relieve him. The dull depression
he experienced in a somnolent condition at first gave him a little relief,
but only as something new, afterwards it became as distressing as the
pain itself or even more so.

Special foods were prepared for him by the doctors' orders, but all
those foods became increasingly distasteful and disgusting to him.

For his excretions also special arrangements had to be made, and
this was a torment to him every time — a torment from the uncleanliness, the unseemliness, and the smell, and from knowing that another
person had to take part in it.

But just through this most unpleasant matter, Iván Ilých obtained
comfort. Gerásim, the butler's young assistant, always came in to carry
the things out. Gerásim was a clean, fresh peasant lad, grown stout
on town food and always cheerful and bright. At first the sight of him,
in his clean Russian peasant costume, engaged on that disgusting task
embarrassed Iván Ilých.

Once when he got up from the commode too weak to draw up his
trousers, he dropped into a soft armchair and looked with horror at
his bare, enfeebled thighs with the muscles so sharply marked on
them.

Gerásim with a firm light tread, his heavy boots emitting a pleasant
smell of tar and fresh winter air, came in wearing a clean Hessian apron,

the sleeves of his print shirt tucked up over his strong bare young arms; and refraining from looking at his sick master out of consideration for his feelings, and restraining the joy of life that beamed from his face, went up to the commode.

"Gerásim!" said Iván Ilých in a weak voice.

Gerásim started, evidently afraid he might have committed some blunder, and with a rapid movement turned his fresh, kind, simple young face which just showed the first downy signs of a beard.

"Yes, sir?"

"That must be very unpleasant for you. You must forgive me. I am helpless."

"Oh, why, sir," and Gerásim's eyes beamed and he showed his glistening white teeth, "what's a little trouble? It's a case of illness with you, sir."

And his deft strong hands did their accustomed task, and he went out of the room stepping lightly. Five minutes later he as lightly returned.

Iván Ilých was still sitting in the same position in the armchair.

"Gerásim," he said when the latter had replaced the freshly-washed utensil. "Please come here and help me." Gerásim went up to him. "Lift me up. It is hard for me to get up, and I have sent Dmítri away."

Gerásim went up to him, grasped his master with his strong arms deftly but gently, in the same way that he stepped — lifted him, supported him with one hand, and with the other drew up his trousers and would have set him down again, but Iván Ilých asked to be led to the sofa. Gerásim, without an effort and without apparent pressure, led him, almost lifting him, to the sofa and placed him on it.

"Thank you. How easily and well you do it all!"

Gerásim smiled again and turned to leave the room. But Iván Ilých felt his presence such a comfort that he did not want to let him go.

"One thing more, please move up that chair. No, the other one — under my feet. It is easier for me when my feet are raised."

Gerásim brought the chair, set it down gently in place, and raised Iván Ilých's legs on to it. It seemed to Iván Ilých that he felt better while Gerásim was holding up his legs.

"It's better when my legs are higher," he said. "Place that cushion under them."

Gerásim did so. He again lifted the legs and placed them, and again Iván Ilých felt better while Gerásim held his legs. When he set them down Iván Ilých fancied he felt worse.

"Gerásim," he said. "Are you busy now?"

"Not at all, sir," said Gerásim, who had learnt from the townsfolk how to speak to gentlefolk.

"What have you still to do?"

"What have I to do? I've done everything except chopping the logs for to-morrow."

"Then hold my legs up a bit higher, can you?"

"Of course I can. Why not?" And Gerásim raised his master's legs higher and Iván Ilých thought that in that position he did not feel any pain at all.

"And how about the logs?"

"Don't trouble about that, sir. There's plenty of time."

Iván Ilých told Gerásim to sit down and hold his legs, and began to talk to him. And strange to say it seemed to him that he felt better while Gerásim held his legs up.

After that Iván Ilých would sometimes call Gerásim and get him to hold his legs on his shoulders, and he liked talking to him. Gerásim did it all easily, willingly, simply, and with a good nature that touched Iván Ilých. Health, strength, and vitality in other people were offensive to him, but Gerásim's strength and vitality did not mortify but soothed him.

What tormented Iván Ilých most was the deception, the lie, which for some reason they all accepted, that he was not dying but was simply ill, and that he only need keep quiet and undergo a treatment and then something very good would result. He however knew that do what they would nothing would come of it, only still more agonizing suffering and death. This deception tortured him — their not wishing to admit what they all knew and what he knew, but wanting to lie to him concerning his terrible condition, and wishing and forcing him to participate in that lie. Those lies — lies enacted over him on the eve of his death and destined to degrade this awful, solemn act to the level of their visitings, their curtains, their sturgeon for dinner — were a terrible agony for Iván Ilých. And strangely enough, many times when they were going through their antics over him he had been within a hairbreadth of calling out to them: "Stop lying! You know and I know that I am dying. Then at least stop lying about it!" But he had never had the spirit to do it. The awful, terrible act of his dying was, he could see, reduced by those about him to the level of a casual, unpleasant, and almost indecorous incident (as if someone entered a drawing-room diffusing an unpleasant odour) and this was done by that very decorum which he had served all his life long. He saw that no one felt for him, because no one even wished to grasp his position. Only Gerásim recognized it and pitied him. And so Iván Ilých felt at ease only with him. He felt comforted when Gerásim supported his legs (sometimes all night long) and refused to go to bed, saying: "Don't you worry, Iván Ilých. I'll get sleep enough later on," or when he suddenly became familiar and exclaimed: "If you weren't sick it would be another matter, but as it is, why should I grudge a little trouble?" Gerásim alone did not lie; everything showed that he alone understood the facts of the case and did not consider it necessary to disguise them, but simply felt sorry for his emaciated and enfeebled master. Once when Iván Ilých was sending him away he even said straight out: "We shall all of us die, so why should I grudge a little trouble?" — expressing the fact that he did not think his work burdensome, because he was doing it for a dying man and hoped someone would do the same for him when his time came.

Apart from this lying, or because of it, what most tormented Iván Ilých was that no one pitied him as he wished to be pitied. At certain moments after prolonged suffering he wished most of all (though he would have been ashamed to confess it) for someone to pity him as a sick child is pitied. He longed to be petted and comforted. He knew he was an important functionary, that he had a beard turning grey, and that therefore what he longed for was impossible, but still he longed for it. And in Gerásim's attitude towards him there was something akin to what he wished for, and so that attitude comforted him. Iván Ilých wanted to weep, wanted to be petted and cried over, and then his colleague Shébek would come, and instead of weeping and being petted, Iván Ilých would assume a serious, severe, and profound air, and by force of habit would express his opinion on a decision of the Court of Cassation and would stubbornly insist on that view. This falsity around him and within him did more than anything else to poison his last days.

VIII

It was morning. He knew it was morning because Gerásim had gone, and Peter the footman had come and put out the candles, drawn back one of the curtains, and begun quietly to tidy up. Whether it was morning or evening, Friday or Sunday, made no difference, it was all just the same: the gnawing, unmitigated, agonizing pain, never ceasing for an instant, the consciousness of life inexorably waning but not yet extinguished, that approach of that ever dreaded and hateful Death which was the only reality, and always the same falsity. What were days, weeks, hours, in such a case?

"Will you have some tea, sir?"

"He wants things to be regular, and wishes the gentlefolk to drink tea in the morning," thought Iván Ilých, and only said "No".

"Wouldn't you like to move onto the sofa, sir?"

"He wants to tidy up the room, and I'm in the way. I am uncleanliness and disorder," he thought, and said only:

"No, leave me alone."

The man went on bustling about. Iván Ilých stretched out his hand. Peter came up, ready to help.

"What is it, sir?"

"My watch."

Peter took the watch which was close at hand and gave it to his master.

"Half-past eight. Are they up?"

"No sir, except Vladímir Ivánich" (the son) "who has gone to school. Praskóvya Fëdorovna ordered me to wake her if you asked for her. Shall I do so?"

"No, there's no need to." "Perhaps I'd better have some tea," he thought, and added aloud: "Yes, bring me some tea."

Peter went to the door but Iván Ilých dreaded being left alone. "How can I keep him here? Oh yes, my medicine." "Peter, give me my medicine." "Why not? Perhaps it may still do me some good." He took a spoonful and swallowed it. "No, it won't help. It's all tomfoolery, all deception," he decided as soon as he became aware of the familiar, sickly, hopeless taste. "No, I can't believe in it any longer. But the pain, why this pain? If it would only cease just for a moment!" And he moaned. Peter turned towards him. "It's all right. Go and fetch me some tea."

Peter went out. Left alone Iván Ilých groaned not so much with pain, terrible though that was, as from mental anguish. Always and for ever the same, always these endless days and nights. If only it would come quicker! If only *what* would come quicker? Death, darkness? . . . No, no! Anything rather than death!

When Peter returned with the tea on a tray, Iván Ilých stared at him for a time in perplexity, not realizing who and what he was. Peter was disconcerted by that look and his embarrassment brought Iván Ilých to himself.

"Oh, tea! All right, put it down. Only help me to wash and put on a clean shirt."

And Iván Ilých began to wash. With pauses for rest, he washed his hands and then his face, cleaned his teeth, brushed his hair, and looked in the glass. He was terrified by what he saw, especially by the limp way in which his hair clung to his pallid forehead.

While his shirt was being changed he knew that he would be still more frightened at the sight of his body, so he avoided looking at it. Finally he was ready. He drew on a dressing-gown, wrapped himself in a plaid, and sat down in the armchair to take his tea. For a moment he felt refreshed, but as soon as he began to drink the tea he was again aware of the same taste, and the pain also returned. He finished it with an effort, and then lay down stretching out his legs, and dismissed Peter.

Always the same. Now a spark of hope flashes up, then a sea of despair rages, and always pain; always pain, always despair, and always the same. When alone he had a dreadful and distressing desire to call someone, but he knew beforehand that with others present it would be still worse. "Another dose of morphine — to lose consciousness. I will tell him, the doctor, that he must think of something else. It's impossible, impossible, to go on like this."

An hour and another pass like that. But now there is a ring at the door bell. Perhaps it's the doctor? It is. He comes in fresh, hearty, plump, and cheerful, with that look on his face that seems to say: "There now, you're in a panic about something, but we'll arrange it all for you directly!" The doctor knows this expression is out of place here, but he has put it on once for all and can't take it off — like a man who has put on a frock-coat in the morning to pay a round of calls.

The doctor rubs his hands vigorously and reassuringly.

"Brr! How cold it is! There's such a sharp frost; just let me warm myself!" he says, as if it were only a matter of waiting till he was warm, and then he would put everything right.

"Well now, how are you?"

Iván Ilých feels that the doctor would like to say: "Well, how are our affairs?" but that even he feels that this would not do, and says instead: "What sort of a night have you had?"

Iván Ilých looks at him as much as to say: "Are you really never ashamed of lying?" But the doctor does not wish to understand this question, and Iván Ilých says: "Just as terrible as ever. The pain never leaves me and never subsides. If only something . . ."

"Yes, you sick people are always like that. . . . There, now I think I am warm enough. Even Praskóvya Fëdorovna, who is so particular, could find no fault with my temperature. Well, now I can say good-morning," and the doctor presses his patient's hand.

Then, dropping his former playfulness, he begins with a most serious face to examine the patient, feeling his pulse and taking his temperature, and then begins the sounding and auscultation.

Iván Ilých knows quite well and definitely that all this is nonsense and pure deception, but when the doctor, getting down on his knee, leans over him, putting his ear first higher then lower, and performs various gymnastic movements over him with a significant expression on his face, Iván Ilých submits to it all as he used to submit to the speeches of the lawyers, though he knew very well that they were all lying and why they were lying.

The doctor, kneeling on the sofa, is still sounding him when Praskóvya Fëdorovna's silk dress rustles at the door and she is heard scolding Peter for not having let her know of the doctor's arrival.

She comes in, kisses her husband, and at once proceeds to prove that she has been up a long time already, and only owing to a misunderstanding failed to be there when the doctor arrived.

Iván Ilých looks at her, scans her all over, sets against her the whiteness and plumpness and cleanness of her hands and neck, the gloss of her hair, and the sparkle of her vivacious eyes. He hates her with his whole soul. And the thrill of hatred he feels for her makes him suffer from her touch.

Her attitude towards him and his disease is still the same. Just as the doctor had adopted a certain relation to his patient which he could not abandon, so had she formed one towards him — that he was not doing something he ought to do and was himself to blame, and that she reproached him lovingly for this — and she could not now change that attitude.

"You see he doesn't listen to me and doesn't take his medicine at the proper time. And above all he lies in a position that is no doubt bad for him — with his legs up."

She described how he made Gerásim hold his legs up.

The doctor smiled with a contemptuous affability that said: "What's to be done? These sick people do have foolish fancies of that kind, but we must forgive them."

When the examination was over the doctor looked at his watch, and then Praskóvya Fëdorovna announced to Iván Ilých that it was of course as he pleased, but she had sent to-day for a celebrated specialist who would examine him and have a consultation with Michael Danílovich (their regular doctor).

"Please don't raise any objections. I am doing this for my own sake," she said ironically, letting it be felt that she was doing it all for his sake and only said this to leave him no right to refuse. He remained silent, knitting his brows. He felt that he was so surrounded and involved in a mesh of falsity that it was hard to unravel anything.

Everything she did for him was entirely for her own sake, and she told him she was doing for herself what she actually was doing for herself, as if that was so incredible that he must understand the opposite.

At half-past eleven the celebrated specialist arrived. Again the sounding began and the significant conversations in his presence and in another room, about the kidneys and the appendix, and the questions and answers, with such an air of importance that again, instead of the real question of life and death which now alone confronted him, the question arose of the kidney and appendix which were not behaving as they ought to and would now be attacked by Michael Danílovich and the specialist and forced to amend their ways.

The celebrated specialist took leave of him with a serious though not hopeless look, and in reply to the timid question Iván Ilých, with eyes glistening with fear and hope, put to him as to whether there was a chance of recovery, said that he could not vouch for it but there was a possibility. The look of hope with which Iván Ilých watched the doctor out was so pathetic that Praskóvya Fëdorovna, seeing it, even wept as she left the room to hand the doctor his fee.

The gleam of hope kindled by the doctor's encouragement did not last long. The same room, the same pictures, curtains, wall-paper, medicine bottles, were all there, and the same aching suffering body, and Iván Ilých began to moan. They gave him a subcutaneous injection and he sank into oblivion.

It was twilight when he came to. They brought him his dinner and he swallowed some beef tea with difficulty, and then everything was the same again and night was coming on.

After dinner, at seven o'clock, Praskóvya Fëdorovna came into the room in evening dress, her full bosom pushed up by her corset, and with traces of powder on her face. She had reminded him in the morning that they were going to the theatre. Sarah Bernhardt was visiting the town and they had a box, which he had insisted on their taking. Now he had forgotten about it and her toilet offended him, but he concealed his vexation when he remembered that he had himself insisted on their securing a box and going because it would be an instructive and aesthetic pleasure for the children.

Praskóvya Fëdorovna came in, self-satisfied but yet with a rather guilty air. She sat down and asked how he was but, as he saw, only for the sake of asking and not in order to learn about it, knowing that there was nothing to learn — and then went on to what she really wanted to say: that she would not on any account have gone but that the box had been taken and Helen and their daughter were going, as well as Petríshchev (the examining magistrate, their daughter's fiancé) and that it was out of the question to let them go alone; but that she would have much preferred to sit with him for a while; and he must be sure to follow the doctor's orders while she was away.

"Oh, and Fëdor Petróvich" (the fiancé) "would like to come in. May he? And Lisa?"

"All right."

Their daughter came in in full evening dress, her fresh young flesh exposed (making a show of that very flesh which in his own case caused so much suffering), strong, healthy, evidently in love, and impatient with illness, suffering, and death, because they interfered with her happiness.

Fëdor Petróvich came in too, in evening dress, his hair curled *à la Capoul*, a tight stiff collar round his long sinewy neck, an enormous white shirt-front and narrow black trousers tightly stretched over his strong thighs. He had one white glove tightly drawn on, and was holding his opera hat in his hand.

Following him the schoolboy crept in unnoticed, in a new uniform, poor little fellow, and wearing gloves. Terribly dark shadows showed under his eyes, the meaning of which Iván Ilých knew well.

His son had always seemed pathetic to him, and now it was dreadful to see the boy's frightened look of pity. It seemed to Iván Ilých that Vásya was the only one besides Gerásim who understood and pitied him.

They all sat down and again asked how he was. A silence followed. Lisa asked her mother about the opera-glasses, and there was an altercation between mother and daughter as to who had taken them and where they had been put. This occasioned some unpleasantness.

Fëdor Petróvich inquired of Iván Ilých whether he had ever seen Sarah Bernhardt. Iván Ilých did not at first catch the question, but then replied: "No, have you seen her before?"

"Yes, in *Adrienne Lecouvreur.*"

Praskóvya Fëdorovna mentioned some roles in which Sarah Bernhardt was particularly good. Her daughter disagreed. Conversation sprang up as to the elegance and realism of her acting — the sort of conversation that is always repeated and is always the same.

In the midst of the conversation Fëdor Petróvich glanced at Iván Ilých and became silent. The others also looked at him and grew silent. Iván Ilých was staring with glittering eyes straight before him, evidently indignant with them This had to be rectified, but it was impossible to do so. The silence had to be broken, but for a time no one dared to break it and they all became afraid that the conventional deception would suddenly become obvious and the truth become plain to all. Lisa was the first to pluck up courage and break that silence, but by trying to hide what everybody was feeling, she betrayed it.

"Well, if we are going it's time to start," she said, looking at her watch, a present from her father, and with a faint and significant smile at Fëdor Petróvich relating to something known only to them. She got up with a rustle of her dress.

They all rose, said good-night, and went away.

When they had gone it seemed to Iván Ilých that he felt better; the falsity had gone with them. But the pain remained — that same pain and that same fear that made everything monotonously alike, nothing harder and nothing easier. Everything was worse.

Again minute followed minute and hour followed hour. Everything remained the same and there was no cessation. And the inevitable end of it all became more and more terrible.

"Yes, send Gerásim here," he replied to a question Peter asked.

IX

His wife returned late at night. She came in on tiptoe, but he heard her, opened his eyes, and made haste to close them again. She wished to send Gerásim away and to sit with him herself, but he opened his eyes and said: "No, go away."

"Are you in great pain?"

"Always the same."

"Take some opium."

He agreed and took some. She went away.

Till about three in the morning he was in a state of stupefied misery. It seemed to him that he and his pain were being thrust into a narrow, deep black sack, but though they were pushed further and further in they could not be pushed to the bottom. And this, terrible enough in itself, was accompanied by suffering. He was frightened yet wanted to fall through the sack, he struggled but yet co-operated. And sud denly he broke through, fell, and regained consciousness. Gerásim was sitting at the foot of the bed dozing quietly and patiently, while he himself lay with his emaciated stockinged legs resting on Gerásim's shoulders; the same shaded candle was there and the same unceasing pain.

"Go away, Gerásim," he whispered.

"It's all right, sir. I'll stay a while."

"No. Go away."

He removed his legs from Gerásim's shoulders, turned sideways onto his arm, and felt sorry for himself. He only waited till Gerásim had gone into the next room and then restrained himself no longer but wept like a child. He wept on account of his helplessness, his terrible loneliness, the cruelty of man, the cruelty of God, and the absence of God.

"Why hast Thou done all this? Why hast Thou brought me here? Why, why dost Thou torment me so terribly?"

He did not expect an answer and yet wept because there was no answer and could be none. The pain again grew more acute, but he did not stir and did not call. He said to himself: "Go on! Strike me! But what is it for? What have I done to Thee? What is it for?"

Then he grew quiet and not only ceased weeping but even held his breath and became all attention. It was as though he were listening not to an audible voice but to the voice of his soul, to the current of thoughts arising within him.

"What is it you want?" was the first clear conception capable of expression in words, that he heard.

"What do you want? What do you want?" he repeated to himself.

"What do I want? To live and not to suffer," he answered.

And again he listened with such concentrated attention that even his pain did not distract him.

"To live? How?" asked his inner voice.

"Why, to live as I used to — well and pleasantly."

"As you lived before, well and pleasantly?" the voice repeated.

And in imagination he began to recall the best moments of his pleasant life. But strange to say none of these best moments of his pleasant life now seemed at all what they had then seemed — none

of them except the first recollections of childhood. There, in childhood, there had been something really pleasant with which it would
be possible to live if it could return. But the child who had experienced that happiness existed no longer, it was like a reminiscence of
somebody else.

As soon as the period began which had produced the present Iván
Ilých, all that had then seemed joys now melted before his sight and
turned into something trivial and often nasty.

And the further he departed from childhood and the nearer he came
to the present the more worthless and doubtful were the joys. This
began with the School of Law. A little that was really good was still
found there — there was light-heartedness, friendship, and hope.
But in the upper classes there had already been fewer of such good
moments. Then during the first years of his official career, when he
was in the service of the Governor, some pleasant moments again
occurred: they were the memories of love for a woman. Then all
became confused and there was still less of what was good; later on
again there was still less that was good, and the further he went the
less there was. His marriage, a mere accident, then the disenchant-
ment that followed it, his wife's bad breath and the sensuality and
hypocrisy: then that deadly official life and those preoccupations
about money, a year of it, and two, and ten, and twenty, and always
the same thing. And the longer it lasted the more deadly it became.
"It is as if I had been going downhill while I imagined I was going up.
And that is really what it was. I was going up in public opinion, but
to the same extent life was ebbing away from me. And now it is all
done and there is only death."

"Then what does it mean? Why? It can't be that life is so senseless
and horrible. But if it really has been so horrible and senseless, why
must I die and die in agony? There is something wrong!"

"Maybe I did not live as I ought to have done," it suddenly occurred
to him. "But how could that be, when I did everything properly?" he
replied, and immediately dismissed from his mind this, the sole solution of all the riddles of life and death, as something quite impossible.

"Then what do you want now? To live? Live how? Live as you
lived in the law courts when the usher proclaimed "The judge is
coming!" The judge is coming, the judge!" he repeated to himself.
"Here he is, the judge. But I am not guilty!" he exclaimed angrily.
"What is it for?" And he ceased crying, but turning his face to the
wall continued to ponder on the same question: Why, and for what

purpose, is there all this horror?   But however much he pondered he found no answer.   And whenever the thought occurred to him, as it often did, that it all resulted from his not having lived as he ought to have done, he at once recalled the correctness of his whole life and dismissed so strange an idea.

X

Another fortnight passed.   Iván Ilých now no longer left his sofa. He would not lie in bed but lay on the sofa, facing the wall nearly all the time.   He suffered ever the same unceasing agonies and in his loneliness pondered always on the same insoluble question: "What is this? Can it be that it is Death?"   And the inner voice answered: "Yes, it is Death."

"Why these sufferings?"   And the voice answered, "For no reason — they just are so."   Beyond and besides this there was nothing.

From the very beginning of his illness, ever since he had first been to see the doctor, Iván Ilých's life had been divided between two contrary and alternating moods: now it was despair and the expectation of this uncomprehended and terrible death, and now hope and an intently interested observation of the functioning of his organs.   Now before his eyes there was only a kidney or an intestine that temporarily evaded its duty, and now only that incomprehensible and dreadful death from which it was impossible to escape.

These two states of mind had alternated from the very beginning of his illness, but the further it progressed the more doubtful and fantastic became the conception of the kidney, and the more real the sense of impending death.

He had but to call to mind what he had been three months before and what he was now, to call to mind with what regularity he had been going downhill, for every possibility of hope to be shattered.

Latterly during that loneliness in which he found himself as he lay facing the back of the sofa, a loneliness in the midst of a populous town and surrounded by numerous acquaintances and relations but that yet could not have been more complete anywhere — either at the bottom of the sea or under the earth — during that terrible loneliness Iván Ilých had lived only in memories of the past.   Pictures of his past rose before him one after another.   They always began with what was nearest in time and then went back to what was most remote — to his childhood — and rested there.   If he thought of the stewed prunes that had been offered him that day, his mind went back to the raw shrivelled French plums of his childhood, their peculiar flavour and the flow of saliva when he sucked their stones, and along with the memory of that taste came a whole series of memories of those days: his nurse, his brother, and their toys. "No, I mustn't think of that. . . . It is too painful," Iván Ilých said to himself, and brought himself back to the present — to the button on the back of the sofa and the creases in its morocco. "Morocco is expensive, but it does not wear well: there had been a quarrel about it. It was a different kind of quarrel and a different kind of morocco that time when we tore father's portfolio and were punished, and mamma brought us some tarts. . . ." And again his thoughts dwelt on his childhood, and again it was painful and he tried to banish them and fix his mind on something else.

Then again together with that chain of memories another series passed through his mind — of how his illness had progressed and grown worse. There also the further back he looked the more life there had been. There had been more of what was good in life and more of life itself. The two merged together. "Just as the pain went on getting worse and worse so my life grew worse and worse," he thought. "There is one bright spot there at the back, at the beginning of life, and afterwards all becomes blacker and blacker and proceeds more and more rapidly — in inverse ratio to the square of the distance from death," thought Iván Ilých. And the example of a stone falling downwards with increasing velocity entered his mind. Life, a series of increasing sufferings, flies further and further towards its end — the most terrible suffering. "I am flying. . . ." He shuddered, shifted himself, and tried to resist, but was already aware that resistance was impossible, and again with eyes weary of gazing but unable to cease seeing what was before them, he stared at the back of the sofa and waited — awaiting that dreadful fall and shock and destruction.

"Resistance is impossible!" he said to himself. "If I could only understand what it is all for! But that too is impossible. An explanation would be possible if it could be said that I have not lived as I ought to. But it is impossible to say that," and he remembered all the legality, correctitude, and propriety of his life. "That at any rate can certainly not be admitted," he thought, and his lips smiled ironically as if someone could see that smile and be taken in by it. "There is no explanation! Agony, death. . . . What for?"

XI

Another two weeks went by in this way and during that fortnight an event occurred that Iván Ilých and his wife had desired. Petríshchev formally proposed. It happened in the evening. The next day Praskóvya Fëdorovna came into her husband's room considering how best to inform him of it, but that very night there had been a fresh change for the worse in his condition. She found him still lying on the sofa but in a different position. He lay on his back, groaning and staring fixedly straight in front of him.

She began to remind him of his medicines, but he turned his eyes towards her with such a look that she did not finish what she was saying; so great an animosity, to her in particular, did that look express.

"For Christ's sake let me die in peace!" he said.

She would have gone away, but just then their daughter came in and went up to say good morning. He looked at her as he had done at his wife, and in reply to her inquiry about his health said dryly that he would soon free them all of himself. They were both silent and after sitting with him for a while went away.

"Is it our fault?" Lisa said to her mother. "It's as if we were to blame! I am sorry for papa, but why should we be tortured?"

The doctor came at his usual time. Iván Ilých answered "Yes" and "No", never taking his angry eyes from him, and at last said: "You know you can do nothing for me, so leave me alone."

"We can ease your sufferings."

"You can't even do that. Let me be."

The doctor went into the drawing-room and told Praskóvya Fëdorovna that the case was very serious and that the only resource left was opium to allay her husband's sufferings, which must be terrible.

It was true, as the doctor said, that Iván Ilých's physical sufferings were terrible, but worse than the physical sufferings were his mental sufferings which were his chief torture.

His mental sufferings were due to the fact that that night, as he looked at Gerásim's sleepy, good-natured face with its prominent cheek-bones, the question suddenly occurred to him: "What if my whole life has really been wrong?"

It occurred to him that what had appeared perfectly impossible before, namely that he had not spent his life as he should have done, might after all be true. It occurred to him that his scarcely perceptible attempts to struggle against what was considered good by the most highly placed people, those scarcely noticeable impulses which he had immediately suppressed, might have been the real thing, and all the rest false. And his professional duties and the whole arrangement of his life and of his family, and all his social and official interests, might all have been false. He tried to defend all those things to himself and suddenly felt the weakness of what he was defending. There was nothing to defend.

"But if that is so," he said to himself, "and I am leaving this life with the consciousness that I have lost all that was given me and it is impossible to rectify it — what then?"

He lay on his back and began to pass his life in review in quite a new way. In the morning when he saw first his footman, then his wife, then his daughter, and then the doctor, their every word and movement confirmed to him the awful truth that had been revealed to him during the night. In them he saw himself — all that for which he had lived — and saw clearly that it was not real at all, but a terrible and huge deception which had hidden both life and death. This consciousness intensified his physical suffering tenfold. He groaned and tossed about, and pulled at his clothing which choked and stifled him. And he hated them on that account.

He was given a large dose of opium and became unconscious, but at noon his sufferings began again. He drove everybody away and tossed from side to side.

His wife came to him and said:

"Jean, my dear, do this for me. It can't do any harm and often helps. Healthy people often do it."

He opened his eyes wide.

"What? Take communion? Why? It's unnecessary! However. . . ."

She began to cry.

"Yes, do, my dear. I'll send for our priest. He is such a nice man."

"All right. Very well," he muttered.

When the priest came and heard his confession, Iván Ilých was softened and seemed to feel a relief from his doubts and consequently from his sufferings, and for a moment there came a ray of hope. He again began to think of the vermiform appendix and the possibility of correcting it. He received the sacrament with tears in his eyes.

When they laid him down again afterwards he felt a moment's ease, and the hope that he might live awoke in him again. He began to think of the operation that had been suggested to him. "To live! I want to live!" he said to himself.

His wife came in to congratulate him after his communion, and when uttering the usual conventional words she added:

"You feel better, don't you?"

Without looking at her he said "Yes".

Her dress, her figure, the expression of her face, the tone of her voice, all revealed the same thing. "This is wrong, it is not as it should be. All you have lived for and still live for is falsehood and deception, hiding life and death from you." And as soon as he admitted that thought, his hatred and his agonizing physical suffering again sprang up, and with that suffering a consciousness of the unavoidable, approaching end. And to this was added a new sensation of grinding shooting pain and a feeling of suffocation.

The expression of his face when he uttered that "yes" was dreadful. Having uttered it, he looked her straight in the eyes, turned on his face with a rapidity extraordinary in his weak state and shouted:

"Go away! Go away and leave me alone!"

XII

From that moment the screaming began that continued for three days, and was so terrible that one could not hear it through two closed doors without horror. At the moment he answered his wife he realized that he was lost, that there was no return, that the end had come, the very end, and his doubts were still unsolved and remained doubts.

"Oh! Oh! Oh!" he cried in various intonations. He had begun by screaming "I won't!" and continued screaming on the letter "o".

For three whole days, during which time did not exist for him, he struggled in that black sack into which he was being thrust by an invisible, resistless force. He struggled as a man condemned to death struggles in the hands of the executioner, knowing that he cannot save himself. And every moment he felt that despite all his efforts he was drawing nearer and nearer to what terrified him. He felt that his agony was due to his being thrust into that black hole and still more to his not being able to get right into it. He was hindered from getting into it by his conviction that his life had been a good one. That very justification of his life held him fast and prevented his moving forward, and it caused him most torment of all.

Suddenly some force struck him in the chest and side, making it still harder to breathe, and he fell through the hole and there at the bottom was a light. What had happened to him was like the sensa-tion one sometimes experiences in a railway carriage when one thinks one is going backwards while one is really going forwards and suddenly becomes aware of the real direction.

"Yes, it was all not the right thing," he said to himself, "but that's no matter. It can be done. But what *is* the right thing?" he asked himself, and suddenly grew quiet.

This occurred at the end of the third day, two hours before his death. Just then his schoolboy son had crept softly in and gone up to the bed-side. The dying man was still screaming desperately and waving his arms. His hand fell on the boy's head, and the boy caught it, pressed it to his lips, and began to cry.

At that very moment Iván Ilých fell through and caught sight of the light, and it was revealed to him that though his life had not been what it should have been, this could still be rectified. He asked himself, "What *is* the right thing?" and grew still, listening. Then he felt that someone was kissing his hand. He opened his eyes, looked at his son, and felt sorry for him. His wife came up to him and he glanced at her. She was gazing at him open-mouthed, with undried tears on her nose and cheek and a despairing look on her face. He felt sorry for her too.

"Yes, I am making them wretched," he thought. "They are sorry, but it will be better for them when I die." He wished to say this but had not the strength to utter it. "Besides, why speak? I must act," he thought. With a look at his wife he indicated his son and said: "Take him away . . . sorry for him . . . sorry for you too. . . ." He tried to add, "forgive me", but said "forego" and waved his hand, knowing that He whose understanding mattered would understand.

And suddenly it grew clear to him that what had been oppressing him and would not leave him was all dropping away at once from two sides, from ten sides, and from all sides. He was sorry for them, he must act so as not to hurt them: release them and free himself from these sufferings. "How good and how simple!" he thought. "And the pain?" he asked himself. "What has become of it? Where are you, pain?"

He turned his attention to it.

"Yes, here it is. Well, what of it? Let the pain be."

"And death . . . where is it?"

He sought his former accustomed fear of death and did not find it. "Where is it? What death?" There was no fear because there was no death.

In place of death there was light.

"So that's what it is!" he suddenly exclaimed aloud. "What joy!"

To him all this happened in a single instant, and the meaning of that instant did not change. For those present his agony continued for another two hours. Something rattled in his throat, his emaciated body twitched, then the gasping and rattle became less and less frequent.

"It is finished!" said someone near him.

He heard these words and repeated them in his soul.

"Death is finished," he said to himself. "It is no more!"

He drew in a breath, stopped in the midst of a sigh, stretched out, and died.

[*Translated by* AYLMER MAUDE]

Henry James

THE ASPERN PAPERS

1 8 8 8

෧

I

I HAD taken Mrs. Prest into my confidence; without her in truth I should have made but little advance, for the fruitful idea in the whole business dropped from her friendly lips. It was she who found the short cut and loosed the Gordian knot. It is not supposed easy for women to rise to the large free view of anything, anything to be done; but they sometimes throw off a bold conception — such as a man wouldn't have risen to — with singular serenity. "Simply make them take you in on the footing of a lodger" — I don't think that unaided I should have risen to that. I was beating about the bush, trying to be ingenious, wondering by what combination of arts I might become an acquaintance, when she offered this happy suggestion that the way to become an acquaintance was first to become an intimate. Her actual knowledge of the Misses Bordereau was scarcely larger than mine, and indeed I had brought with me from England some definite facts that were new to her. Their name had been mixed up ages before with one of the greatest names of the century, and they now lived obscurely in Venice, lived on very small means, unvisited, unapproachable, in a sequestered and dilapidated old palace: this was the substance of my friend's impression of them. She herself had been established in Venice some fifteen years and had done a great deal of good there; but the circle of her benevolence had never embraced the two shy, mysterious and, as was somehow supposed, scarcely respectable Americans — they were believed to have lost in their long exile all national quality, besides being as their name implied of some remoter French affilia- tion — who asked no favours and desired no attention. In the early years of her residence she had made an attempt to see them, but this had been successful only as regards the little one, as Mrs. Prest called the niece; though in fact I afterwards found her the bigger of the two in inches. She had heard Miss Bordereau was ill and had a suspicion she was in want, and had gone to the house to offer aid, so that if there were suffering, American suffering in particular, she shouldn't have it on her conscience. The "little one" had received her in the great cold tarnished Venetian *sala*, the central hall of the house, paved with marble and roofed with dim cross-beams, and hadn't even asked her to sit down. This was not encouraging for me, who wished to sit so fast, and I remarked as much to Mrs. Prest. She replied, however, with profundity "Ah, but there's all the difference: I went to confer a favour and you'll go to ask one. If they're proud you'll be on the right side." And she offered to show me their house to begin with — to row me thither in her gondola. I let her know I had already been to look at it half a dozen times; but I accepted her invitation, for it charmed me to hover about the place. I had made my way to it the day after my arrival in Venice — it had been described to me in advance by the friend in England to whom I owed definite information as to their possession of the papers — laying siege to it with my eyes while I considered my plan of campaign. Jeffrey Aspern had never been in it that I knew of, but some note of his voice seemed to abide there by a roundabout implication and in a "dying fall."

Mrs. Prest knew nothing about the papers, but was interested in my curiosity, as always in the joys and sorrows of her friends. As we went, however, in her gondola, gliding there under the sociable hood with the bright Venetian picture framed on either side by the moveable window, I saw how my eagerness amused her and that she found my interest in my possible spoil a fine case of monomania. "One would think you expected from it the answer to the riddle of the universe," she said; and I denied the impeachment only by replying that if I had to choose between that precious solution and a bundle of Jeffrey Aspern's letters I knew indeed which would appear to me the greater boon. She pretended to make light of his genius and I took no pains to defend him. One doesn't defend one's god: one's god is in himself a defence. Besides, to-day, after his long comparative obscuration, he hangs high in the heaven of our literature for all the world to see; he's a part of the light by which we walk. The most I said was that he was no doubt not a woman's poet: to which she rejoined aptly enough that he had been at least Miss Bordereau's. The strange thing had been for me to discover in England that she was still alive: it was as if I had been told Mrs. Siddons was, or Queen Caroline, or the famous Lady Hamilton, for it seemed to me that she belonged to a generation as extinct. "Why she must be tremendously old — at least a hundred,"

I had said; but on coming to consider dates I saw it not strictly involved that she should have far exceeded the common span. None the less she was of venerable age and her relations with Jeffrey Aspern had occurred in her early womanhood. "That's her excuse," said Mrs. Prest half sententiously and yet also somewhat as if she were ashamed of making a speech so little in the real tone of Venice. As if a woman needed an excuse for having loved the divine poet! He had been not only one of the most brilliant minds of his day — and in those years, when the century was young, there were, as every one knows, many — but one of the most genial men and one of the handsomest.

The niece, according to Mrs. Prest, was of minor antiquity, and the conjecture was risked that she was only a grand-niece. This was possible; I had nothing but my share in the very limited knowledge of my English fellow-worshipper John Cumnor, who had never seen the couple. The world, as I say, had recognised Jeffrey Aspern, but Cumnor and I had recognised him most. The multitude to-day flocked to his temple, but of that temple he and I regarded ourselves as the appointed ministers. We held, justly, as I think, that we had done more for his memory than any one else, and had done it simply by opening lights into his life. He had nothing to fear from us because he had nothing to fear from the truth, which alone at such a distance of time we could be interested in establishing. His early death had been the only dark spot, as it were, on his fame, unless the papers in Miss Bordereau's hands should perversely bring out others. There had been an impression about 1825 that he had "treated her badly," just as there had been an impression that he had "served," as the London populace says, several other ladies in the same masterful way. Each of these cases Cumnor and I had been able to investigate, and we had never failed to acquit him conscientiously of any grossness. I judged him perhaps more indulgently than my friend; certainly, at any rate, it appeared to me that no man could have walked straighter in the given circumstances. These had been almost always difficult and dangerous. Half the women of his time, to speak liberally, had flung themselves at his head, and while the fury raged — the more that it was very catching — accidents, some of them grave, had not failed to occur. He was not a woman's poet, as I had said to Mrs. Prest, in the modern phase of his reputation; but the situation had been different when the man's own voice was mingled with his song. That voice, by every testimony, was one of the most charming ever heard.

"Orpheus and the Mænads!" had been of course my foreseen judgement when first I turned over his correspondence. Almost all the Mænads were unreasonable and many of them unbearable; it struck me that he had been kinder and more considerate than in his place — if I could imagine myself in any such box — I should have found the trick of.

It was certainly strange beyond all strangeness, and I shall not take up space with attempting to explain it, that whereas among all these other relations and in these other directions of research we had to deal with phantoms and dust, the mere echoes of echoes, the one living source of information that had lingered on into our time had been unheeded by us. Every one of Aspern's contemporaries had, according to our belief, passed away; we had not been able to look into a single pair of eyes into which his had looked or to feel a transmitted contact in any aged hand that his had touched. Most dead of all did poor Miss Bordereau appear, and yet she alone had survived. We exhausted in the course of months our wonder that we had not found her out sooner, and the substance of our explanation was that she had kept so quiet. The poor lady on the whole had had reason for doing so. But it was a revelation to us that self-effacement on such a scale had been possible in the latter half of the nineteenth century — the age of newspapers and telegrams and photographs and interviewers. She had taken no great trouble for it either — hadn't hidden herself away in an undiscoverable hole, had boldly settled down in a city of exhibition. The one apparent secret of her safety had been that Venice contained so many much greater curiosities. And then accident had somehow favoured her, as was shown for example in the fact that Mrs. Prest had never happened to name her to me, though I had spent three weeks in Venice — under her nose, as it were — five years before. My friend indeed had not named her much to anyone; she appeared almost to have forgotten the fact of her continuance. Of course Mrs. Prest hadn't the nerves of an editor. It was meanwhile no explanation of the old woman's having eluded us to say that she lived abroad, for our researches had again and again taken us — not only by correspondence but by personal enquiry — to France, to Germany, to Italy, in which countries, not counting his important stay in England, so many of the too few years of Aspern's career had been spent. We were glad to think at least that in all our promulgations — some people now consider I believe that we have overdone them — we had only touched in passing and in the most discreet manner on Miss Bordereau's connexion. Oddly enough, even if we had had the material — and we had often wondered what could have become of it — this would have been the most difficult episode to handle.

The gondola stopped, the old palace was there; it was a house of the class which in Venice carries even in extreme dilapidation the dignified name. "How charming! It's gray and pink!" my companion exclaimed; and that is the most comprehensive description of it. It was not particularly old, only two or three centuries; and it had an air not so much of decay as of quiet discouragement, as if it had rather missed its career. But its wide front, with a stone balcony from end to end of the *piano nobile* or most important floor, was architectural enough, with the aid of various pilasters and arches; and the stucco with which in the intervals it had long ago been endued was rosy in the April afternoon. It overlooked a clean melancholy rather lonely canal, which had a narrow *riva* or convenient footway on either side. "I don't know why — there are no brick gables," said Mrs. Prest, "but this corner has seemed to me before more Dutch than Italian, more like Amsterdam than like Venice. It's eccentrically neat, for reasons of its own; and though you may pass on foot scarcely any one ever thinks of doing so. It's as negative — considering *where* it is — as a Protestant Sunday. Perhaps the people are afraid of the Misses Bordereau. I dare say they have the reputation of witches."

I forget what answer I made to this — I was given up to two other reflections. The first of these was that if the old lady lived in such a big and imposing house she couldn't be in any sort of misery and therefore wouldn't be tempted by a chance to let a couple of rooms. I expressed this fear to Mrs. Prest, who gave me a very straight answer. "If she didn't live in a big house how could it be a question of her having rooms to spare? If she were not amply lodged you'd lack ground to approach her. Besides, a big house here, and especially in this *quartier perdu*, proves nothing at all: it's perfectly consistent with a state of penury. Dilapidated old palazzi, if you'll go out of the way for them, are to be had for five shillings a year. And as for the people who live in them — no, until you've explored Venice socially as much as I have, you can form no idea of their domestic desolation. They live on nothing, for they've nothing to live on." The other idea that had come into my head was connected with a high blank wall which appeared to confine an expanse of ground on one side of the house. Blank I call it, but it was figured over with the patches that please a painter, repaired breaches, crumblings of plaster, extrusions of brick that had turned pink with time; while a few thin trees, with the poles of certain rickety trellises, were visible over the top. The place was a garden and apparently attached to the house. I suddenly felt that so attached it gave me my pretext.

I sat looking out on all this with Mrs. Prest (it was covered with the golden glow of Venice) from the shade of our *felze*, and she asked me if I would go in then, while she waited for me, or come back another time. At first I couldn't decide — it was doubtless very weak of me. I wanted still to think I *might* get a footing, and was afraid to meet failure, for it would leave me, as I remarked to my companion, without another arrow for my bow. "Why not another?" she enquired as I sat there hesitating and thinking it over; and she wished to know why even now and before taking the trouble of becoming an inmate — which might be wretchedly uncomfortable after all, even if it succeeded — I hadn't the resource of simply offering them a sum of money down. In that way I might get what I wanted without bad nights.

"Dearest lady," I exclaimed, "excuse the impatience of my tone when I suggest that you must have forgotten the very fact — surely I communicated it to you — which threw me on your ingenuity. The old woman won't have her relics and tokens so much as spoken of; they're personal, delicate, intimate, and she hasn't the feelings of the day, God bless her! If I should sound that note first I should certainly spoil the game. I can arrive at my spoils only by putting her off her guard, and I can put her off her guard only by ingratiating diplomatic arts. Hypocrisy, duplicity are my only chance. I'm sorry for it, but there's no baseness I wouldn't commit for Jeffrey Aspern's sake. First I must take tea with her — then tackle the main job." And I told over what had happened to John Cumnor on his respectfully writing to her. No notice whatever had been taken of his first letter, and the second had been answered very sharply, in six lines, by the niece. "Miss Bordereau requested her to say that she couldn't imagine what he meant by troubling them. They had none of Mr. Aspern's 'literary remains,' and if they *had* had wouldn't have dreamed of showing them to any one on any account whatever. She couldn't imagine what he was talking about and begged he would let her alone." I certainly didn't want to be met that way.

"Well," said Mrs. Prest after a moment and all provokingly, "perhaps they really haven't anything. If they deny it flat how are you sure?"

"John Cumnor's sure, and it would take me long to tell you how his conviction, or his very strong presumption — strong enough to stand against the old lady's not unnatural fib — has built itself up. Besides, he makes much of the internal evidence of the niece's letter."

"The internal evidence?"

"Her calling him 'Mr. Aspern.' "

"I don't see what that proves."

"It proves familiarity, and familiarity implies the possession of mementoes, of tangible objects. I can't tell you how that 'Mr.' affects me — how it bridges over the gulf of time and brings our hero near to me — nor what an edge it gives to my desire to see Juliana. You don't say 'Mr.' Shakespeare."

"Would I, any more, if I had a box full of his letters?"

"Yes, if he had been your lover and some one wanted them!" And I added that John Cumnor was so convinced, and so all the more convinced by Miss Bordereau's tone, that he would have come himself to Venice on the undertaking were it not for the obstacle of his having, for any confidence, to disprove his identity with the person who had written to them, which the old ladies would be sure to suspect in spite of dissimulation and a change of name. If they were to ask him point-blank if he were not their snubbed correspondent it would be too awkward for him to lie; whereas I was fortunately not tied in that way. I was a fresh hand — I could protest without lying.

"But you'll have to take a false name," said Mrs. Prest. "Juliana lives out of the world as much as it is possible to live, but she has none the less probably heard of Mr. Aspern's editors. She perhaps possesses what you've published."

"I've thought of that," I returned; and I drew out of my pocket-book a visiting card neatly engraved with a well-chosen *nom de guerre*.

"You're very extravagant — it adds to your immorality. You might have done it in pencil or ink," said my companion.

"This looks more genuine."

"Certainly you've the courage of your curiosity. But it will be awkward about your letters; they won't come to you in that mask."

"My banker will take them in and I shall go every day to get them. It will give me a little walk."

"Shall you depend all on that?" asked Mrs. Prest. "Aren't you coming to see me?"

"Oh you'll have left Venice for the hot months long before there are any results. I'm prepared to roast all summer — as well as through the long hereafter perhaps you'll say! Meanwhile John Cumnor will bombard me with letters addressed, in my feigned name, to the care of the padrona."

"She'll recognise his hand," my companion suggested.

"On the envelope he can disguise it."

"Well, you're a precious pair! Doesn't it occur to you that even if you're able to say you're not Mr. Cumnor in person they may still suspect you of being his emissary?"

"Certainly, and I see only one way to parry that."

"And what may that be?"

I hesitated a moment. "To make love to the niece."

"Ah," cried my friend, "wait till you see her!"

II

"I must work the garden — I must work the garden," I said to myself five minutes later and while I waited, upstairs, in the long, dusky sala, where the bare scagliola floor gleamed vaguely in a chink of the closed shutters. The place was impressive, yet looked somehow cold and cautious. Mrs. Prest had floated away, giving me a rendezvous at the end of half an hour by some neighbouring water-steps; and I had been let into the house, after pulling the rusty bell-wire, by a small red-headed and white-faced maidservant, who was very young and not ugly and wore clicking pattens and a shawl in the fashion of a hood. She had not contented herself with opening the door from above by the usual arrangement of a creaking pulley, though she had looked down at me first from an upper window, dropping the cautious challenge which in Italy precedes the act of admission. I was irritated as a general thing by this survival of mediæval manners, though as so fond, if yet so special, an antiquarian I suppose I ought to have liked it; but, with my resolve to be genial from the threshold at any price, I took my false card out of my pocket and held it up to her, smiling as if it were a magic token. It had the effect of one indeed, for it brought her, as I say, all the way down. I begged her to hand it to her mistress, having first written on it in Italian the words: "Could you very kindly see a gentleman, a travelling American, for a moment?" The little maid wasn't hostile — even that was perhaps something gained. She coloured, she smiled and looked both frightened and pleased. I could see that my arrival was a great affair, that visits in such a house were rare and that she was a person who would have liked a bustling place. When she pushed forward the heavy door behind me I felt my foot in the citadel and promised myself ever so firmly to keep it there. She pattered across the damp stony lower hall and I followed her up the high staircase — stonier still, as it seemed — without an invitation. I think she had meant I should wait for her below, but such was not my idea, and I took up my station in the sala. She flitted, at the far end of it, into impenetrable regions, and I looked at the place with my heart beating as I had known it to do in dentists' parlours. It had a gloomy grandeur, but owed its character almost all to its noble shape and to the fine architectural doors, as high as those of grand frontages, which, leading into the various rooms, repeated themselves on either side at intervals. They were surmounted with old faded painted escutcheons, and here and there in the spaces between them hung brown pictures, which I noted as speciously bad, in battered and tarnished frames that were yet more desirable than the canvases themselves. With the exception of several straw-bottomed chairs that kept their backs to the wall the grand obscure vista contained little else to minister to effect. It was evidently never used save as a passage, and scantly even as that. I may add that by the time the door through which the maid-servant had escaped opened again my eyes had grown used to the want of light.

I hadn't meanwhile meant by my private ejaculation that I must myself cultivate the soil of the tangled enclosure which lay beneath the windows, but the lady who came toward me from the distance over the hard shining floor might have supposed as much from the way in which, as I went rapidly to meet her, I exclaimed, taking care to speak Italian: "The garden, the garden — do me the pleasure to tell me if it's yours!"

She stopped short, looking at me with wonder; and then, "Nothing here is mine," she answered in English, coldly and sadly.

"Oh you're English; how delightful!" I ingenuously cried. "But surely the garden belongs to the house?"

"Yes, but the house doesn't belong to me." She was a long lean pale person, habited apparently in a dull-coloured dressing-gown, and she spoke very simply and mildly. She didn't ask me to sit down, any more than years before — if she were the niece — she had asked Mrs. Prest, and we stood face to face in the empty pompous hall.

"Well then, would you kindly tell me to whom I must address myself? I'm afraid you will think me horribly intrusive, but you know I *must* have a garden — upon my honour I must!"

Her face was not young, but it was candid; it was not fresh, but it was clear. She had large eyes which were not bright, and a great deal of hair which was not "dressed," and long fine hands which were — possibly — not clean. She clasped these members almost convulsively as, with a confused alarmed look, she broke out: "Oh, don't take it away from us; we like it ourselves!"

"You have the use of it then?"

"Oh yes. If it wasn't for that — !" And she gave a wan vague smile.

"Isn't it a luxury, precisely? That's why intending to be in Venice some weeks, possibly all summer, and having some literary work, some reading and writing to do, so that I must be quiet and yet if possible a great deal in the open air — that's why I've felt a garden to be really indispensable. I appeal to your own experience," I went on with as sociable a smile as I could risk. "Now can't I look at yours?"

"I don't know, I don't understand," the poor woman murmured, planted there and letting her weak wonder deal — helplessly enough, as I felt — with my strangeness.

"I mean only from one of those windows — such grand ones as you have here — if you'll let me open the shutters." And I walked toward the back of the house. When I had advanced halfway I stopped and waited as in the belief she would accompany me. I had been of necessity quite abrupt, but I strove at the same time to give her the impression of extreme courtesy. "I've looked at furnished rooms all over the place, and it seems impossible to find any with a garden attached. Naturally in a place like Venice gardens are rare. It's absurd if you like, for a man, but I can't live without flowers."

"There are none to speak of down there." She came nearer, as if, though she mistrusted me, I had drawn her by an invisible thread. I went on again, and she continued as she followed me: "We've a few, but they're very common. It costs too much to cultivate them; one has to have a man."

"Why shouldn't I be the man?" I asked. "I'll work without wages; or rather I'll put in a gardener. You shall have the sweetest flowers in Venice."

She protested against this with a small quaver of sound that might have been at the same time a gush of rapture for my free sketch. Then she gasped: "We don't know you — we don't know you."

"You know me as much as I know you, or rather much more, because you know my name.   And if you're English I'm almost a countryman."

"We're not English," said my companion, watching me in practical submission while I threw open the shutters of one of the divisions of the wide high window.

"You speak the language so beautifully: might I ask what you are?"   Seen from above the garden was in truth shabby, yet I felt at a glance that it had great capabilities.   She made no rejoinder, she was so lost in her blankness and gentleness, and I exclaimed, "You don't mean to say you're also by chance American?"

"I don't know.   We used to be."

"Used to be?   Surely you haven't changed?"

"It's so many years ago.   We don't seem to be anything now."

"So many years that you've been living here?   Well, I don't wonder at that; it's a grand old house.   I suppose you all use the garden," I went on, "but I assure you I shouldn't be in your way.   I'd be very quiet and stay quite in one corner."

"We all use it?" she repeated after me vaguely, not coming close to the window but looking at my shoes.   She appeared to think me capable of throwing her out.

"I mean all your family — as many as you are."

"There's only one other than me.   She's very old.   She never goes down."

I feel again my thrill at this close identification of Juliana; in spite of which, however, I kept my head.   "Only one other in all this great house!"   I feigned to be not only amazed but almost scandalized.   "Dear lady, you must have space then to spare!"

"To spare?" she repeated — almost as for the rich unwonted joy to her of spoken words.

"Why you surely don't live (two quiet women — I see *you* are quiet, at any rate) in fifty rooms!"   Then with a burst of hope and cheer I put the question straight: "Couldn't you for a good rent *let* me two or three?   That would set me up!"

I had now struck the note that translated my purpose, and I needn't reproduce the whole of the tune I played.   I ended by making my entertainer believe me an undesigning person, though of course I didn't even attempt to persuade her I was not an eccentric one.   I repeated that I had studies to pursue; that I wanted quiet; that I delighted in a garden and had vainly sought one up and down the city; that I would undertake that before another month was over the dear old house should be smothered in flowers. I think it was the flowers that won my suit, for I afterwards found that Miss Tina — for such the name of this high tremulous spinster proved somewhat incongruously to be — had an insatiable appetite for them. When I speak of my suit as won I mean that before I left her she had promised me she would refer the question to her aunt. I invited information as to who her aunt might be and she answered "Why Miss Bordereau!" with an air of surprise, as if I might have been expected to know. There were contradictions like this in Miss Tina which, as I observed later, contributed to make her rather pleasingly incalculable and interesting. It was the study of the two ladies to live so that the world shouldn't talk of them or touch them, and yet they had never altogether accepted the idea that it didn't hear of them. In Miss Tina at any rate a grateful susceptibility to human contact had not died out, and contact of a limited order there would be if I should come to live in the house.

"We've never done anything of the sort; we've never had a lodger or any kind of inmate." So much as this she made a point of saying to me. "We're very poor, we live very badly — almost on nothing. The rooms are very bare — those you might take; they've nothing at all in them. I don't know how you'd sleep, how you'd eat."

"With your permission I could easily put in a bed and a few tables and chairs. *C'est la moindre des choses* and the affair of an hour or two. I know a little man from whom I can hire for a trifle what I should so briefly want, what I should use; my gondolier can bring the things round in his boat. Of course in this great house you must have a second kitchen, and my servant who's a wonderfully handy fellow" — this personage was an evocation of the moment — "can easily cook me a chop there. My tastes and habits are of the simplest; I live on flowers!" And then I ventured to add that if they were very poor it was all the more reason they should let their rooms. They were bad economists — I had never heard of such a waste of material.

I saw in a moment my good lady had never before been spoken to in any such fashion — with a humorous firmness that didn't exclude sympathy, that was quite founded on it. She might easily have told me that my sympathy was impertinent, but this by good fortune didn't occur to her. I left her with the understanding that she would submit the question to her aunt and that I might come back the next day for their decision.

"The aunt will refuse; she'll think the whole proceeding very *louche!*" Mrs. Prest declared shortly after this, when I had resumed my place in her gondola. She had put the idea into my head and now — so little are women to be counted on — she appeared to take a despondent view of it. Her pessimism provoked me and I pretended to have the best hopes; I went so far as to boast of a distinct pre-vision of success. Upon this Mrs. Prest broke out, "Oh I see what's in your head! You fancy you've made such an impression in five minutes that she's dying for you to come and can be depended on to bring the old one round. If you do get in you'll count it as a triumph."

I did count it as a triumph, but only for the commentator — in the last analysis — not for the man, who had not the tradition of personal conquest. When I went back on the morrow the little maid-servant conducted me straight through the long sala — it opened there as before in large perspective and was lighter now, which I thought a good omen — into the apartment from which the recipient of my former visit had emerged on that occasion. It was a spacious shabby parlour with a fine old painted ceiling under which a strange figure sat alone at one of the windows. They come back to me now almost with the palpitation they caused, the suc-cessive states marking my consciousness that as the door of the room closed behind me I was really face to face with the Juliana of some of Aspern's most exquisite and most renowned lyrics. I grew used to her afterwards, though never completely; but as she sat there before me my heart beat as fast as if the miracle of resurrection had taken place for my benefit. Her presence seemed somehow to contain and express his own, and I felt nearer to him at that first moment of seeing her than I ever had been before or ever have been since. Yes, I remember my emotions in their order, even including a curious little tremor that took me when I saw the niece not to be there. With her, the day before, I had become sufficiently familiar, but it almost exceeded my courage — much as I had longed for the event — to be left alone with so terrible a relic as the aunt. She was too strange, too literally resurgent. Then came a check from the perception that we weren't really face to face, inasmuch as she had over her eyes a horrible green shade which served for her almost as a mask. I believed for the instant that she had put it on expressly, so that from under-neath it she might take me all in without my getting at herself. At the same time it created a presumption of some ghastly death's head lurking behind it.   The divine Juliana as a grinning skull — the vision hung there until it passed.   Then it came to me that she *was* tremendously old — so old that death might take her at any moment, before I should have time to compass my end.   The next thought was a correction to that; it lighted up the situation.   She would die next week, she would die to-morrow — then I could pounce on her possessions and ransack her drawers.   Meanwhile she sat there neither moving nor speaking.   She was very small and shrunken, bent forward with her hands in her lap.   She was dressed in black and her head was wrapped in a piece of old black lace which showed no hair.

My emotion keeping me silent she spoke first, and the remark she made was exactly the most unexpected.

III

"Our house is very far from the centre, but the little canal is very *comme il faut.*"

"It's the sweetest corner of Venice and I can imagine nothing more charming," I hastened to reply.   The old lady's voice was very thin and weak, but it had an agreeable, cultivated murmur and there was wonder in the thought that that individual note had been in Jeffrey Aspern's ear.

"Please to sit down there.   I hear very well," she said quietly, as if perhaps I had been shouting;   and the chair she pointed to was at a certain distance.   I took possession of it, assuring her I was perfectly aware of my intrusion and of my not having been properly introduced, and that I could but throw myself on her indulgence. Perhaps the other lady, the one I had had the honor of seeing the day before, would have explained to her about the garden.   That was literally what had given me courage to take a step so unconventional. I had fallen in love at sight with the whole place — she herself was probably so used to it that she didn't know the impression it was capable of making on a stranger — and I had felt it really a case to risk something.   Was her own kindness in receiving me a sign that I was not wholly out in my calculation?   It would make me extremely happy to think so.   I could give her my word of honour that I was a most respectable inoffensive person and that as a co-tenant of the palace, so to speak, they would be barely conscious of my existence.   I would conform to any regulations, any restrictions, if they would only let me enjoy the garden.   Moreover I should be delighted to give her references, guarantees; they would be of the very best, both in Venice and in England, as well as in America.

She listened to me in perfect stillness and I felt her look at me with great penetration, though I could see only the lower part of her bleached and shrivelled face. Independently of the refining process of old age it had a delicacy which once must have been great. She had been very fair, she had had a wonderful complexion. She was silent a little after I had ceased speaking; then she began: "If you're so fond of a garden why don't you go to *terra firma*, where there are so many far better than this?"

"Oh it's the combination!" I answered, smiling; and then with rather a flight of fancy; "It's the idea of a garden in the middle of the sea."

"This isn't the middle of the sea; you can't so much as see the water."

I stared a moment, wondering if she wished to convict me of fraud. "Can't see the water? Why, dear madam, I can come up to the very gate in my boat."

She appeared inconsequent, for she said vaguely in reply to this: "Yes, if you've got a boat. I haven't any; it's many years since I have been in one of the *gondole*." She uttered these words as if they designed a curious far-away craft known to her only by hearsay.

"Let me assure you of the pleasure with which I would put mine at your service!" I returned. I had scarcely said this however before I became aware that the speech was in questionable taste and might also do me the injury of making me appear too eager, too possessed of a hidden motive. But the old woman remained impenetrable and her attitude worried me by suggesting that she had a fuller vision of me than I had of her. She gave me no thanks for my somewhat extravagant offer, but remarked that the lady I had seen the day before was her niece; she would presently come in. She had asked her to stay away a little on purpose — had had her reasons for seeing me first alone. She relapsed into silence and I turned over the fact of these unmentioned reasons and the question of what might come yet; also that of whether I might venture on some judicious remark in praise of her companion. I went so far as to say I should be delighted to see our absent friend again: she had been so very patient with me, considering how odd she must have thought me — a declaration which drew from Miss Bordereau another of her whimsical speeches.

"She has very good manners; I bred her up myself!" I was on the point of saying that that accounted for the easy grace of the niece, but I arrested myself in time, and the next moment the old woman went on: "I don't care who you may be — I don't want to know; it signifies very little to-day." This had all the air of being a formula of dismissal, as if her next words would be that I might take myself off now that she had had the amusement of looking on the face of such a monster of indiscretion. Therefore I was all the more surprised when she added in her soft venerable quaver: "You may have as many rooms as you like — if you'll pay me a good deal of money."

I hesitated but an instant, long enough to measure what she meant in particular by this condition. First it struck me that she must have really a large sum in her mind; then I reasoned quickly that her idea of a large sum would probably not correspond to my own. My deliberation, I think, was not so visible as to diminish the promptitude with which I replied: "I will pay with pleasure and of course in advance whatever you may think it proper to ask me."

"Well then, a thousand francs a month," she said instantly, while her baffling green shade continued to cover her attitude.

The figure, as they say, was startling and my logic had been at fault. The sum she had mentioned was, by the Venetian measure of such matters, exceedingly large; there was many an old palace in an out-of-the-way corner that I might on such terms have enjoyed the whole of by the year. But so far as my resources allowed I was prepared to spend money, and my decision was quickly taken. I would pay her with a smiling face what she asked, but in that case I would make it up by getting hold of my "spoils" for nothing. Moreover if she had asked five times as much I should have risen to the occasion, so odious would it have seemed to me to stand chaffering with Aspern's Juliana. It was queer enough to have a question of money with her at all. I assured her that her views perfectly met my own and that on the morrow I should have the pleasure of putting three months' rent into her hand. She received this announcement with apparent complacency and with no discoverable sense that after all it would become her to say that I ought to see the rooms first. This didn't occur to her, and indeed her serenity was mainly what I wanted. Our little agreement was just concluded when the door opened and the younger lady appeared on the threshold. As soon as Miss Bordereau saw her niece she cried out almost gaily: "He'll give three thousand — three thousand to-morrow!"

Miss Tina stood still, her patient eyes turning from one of us to the other; then she brought out, scarcely above her breath: "Do you mean francs?"

"Did you mean francs or dollars?" the old woman asked of me at this.

"I think francs were what you said," I sturdily smiled.

"That's very good," said Miss Tina, as if she had felt how over-reaching her own question might have looked.

"What do *you* know? You're ignorant," Miss Bordereau remarked; not with acerbity but with a strange soft coldness.

"Yes, of money — certainly of money!" Miss Tina hastened to concede.

"I'm sure you've your own fine branches of knowledge," I took the liberty of saying genially. There was something painful to me, somehow, in the turn the conversation had taken, in the discussion of dollars and francs.

"She had a very good education when she was young. I looked into that myself," said Miss Bordereau. Then she added: "But she has learned nothing since."

"I have always been with *you*," Miss Tina rejoined very mildly, and of a certainty with no intention of an epigram.

"Yes, but for that —!" her aunt declared with more satirical force. She evidently meant that but for this her niece would never have got on at all; the point of the observation however being lost on Miss Tina, though she blushed at hearing her history revealed to a stranger. Miss Bordereau went on, addressing herself to me: "And what time will you come tomorrow with the money?"

"The sooner the better. If is suits you I'll come at noon."

"I am always here, but I have my hours," said the old woman as if her convenience were not to be taken for granted.

"You mean the times when you receive?"

"I never receive. But I'll see you at noon when you come with the money."

"Very good, I shall be punctual." To which I added: "May I shake hands with you on our contract?" I thought there ought to be some little form; it would make me really feel easier, for I was sure there would be no other. Besides, though Miss Bordereau couldn't to-day be called personally attractive and there was something even in her wasted antiquity that bade one stand at one's distance, I felt an irresistible desire to hold in my own for a moment the hand Jeffrey Aspern had pressed.

For a minute she made no answer, and I saw that my proposal failed to meet with her approbation. She indulged in no movement of withdrawal, which I half expected; she only said coldly: "I belong to a time when that was not the custom."

I felt rather snubbed but I exclaimed good-humouredly to Miss Tina, "Oh you'll do as well!" I shook hands with her while she assented with a small flutter. "Yes, yes, to show it's all arranged!"

"Shall you bring the money in gold?" Miss Bordereau demanded as I was turning to the door.

I looked at her a moment. "Aren't you a little afraid, after all, of keeping such a sum as that in the house?" It was not that I was annoyed at her avidity, but was truly struck with the disparity between such a treasure and such scanty means of guarding it.

"Whom should I be afraid of if I'm not afraid of you?" she asked with her shrunken grimness.

"Ah well," I laughed, "I shall be in point of fact a protector and I'll bring gold if you prefer."

"Thank you," the old woman returned with dignity and with an inclination of her head which evidently signified my dismissal. I passed out of the room, thinking how hard it would be to circumvent her. As I stood in the sala again I saw that Miss Tina had followed me, and I supposed that as her aunt had neglected to suggest I should take a look at my quarters it was her purpose to repair the omission. But she made no such overture; she only stood there with a dim, though not a languid smile, and with an effect of irresponsible incompetent youth almost comically at variance with the faded facts of her person. She was not infirm, like her aunt, but she struck me as more deeply futile, because her inefficiency was inward, which was not the case with Miss Bordereau's. I waited to see if she would offer to show me the rest of the house but I didn't precipitate the question, inasmuch as my plan was from this moment to spend as much of my time as possible in her society. A minute indeed elapsed before I committed myself.

"I've had better fortune than I hoped. It was very kind of her to see me. Perhaps you said a good word for me."

"It was the idea of the money," said Miss Tina.

"And did you suggest that?"

"I told her you'd perhaps pay largely."

"What made you think that?"

"I told her I thought you were rich."

"And what put that into your head?"

"I don't know; the way you talked."

"Dear me, I must talk differently now," I returned. "I'm sorry to say it's not the case."

"Well," said Miss Tina, "I think that in Venice the *forestieri* in general often give a great deal for something that after all isn't much." She appeared to make this remark with a comforting intention, to wish to remind me that if I had been extravagant I wasn't foolishly singular. We walked together along the sala, and as I took its magnificent measure I said that I was afraid it wouldn't form a part of my *quartiere*. Were my rooms by chance to be among those that opened into it? "Not if you go above — to the second floor," she answered as if she had rather taken for granted I would know my proper place.

"And I infer that that's where your aunt would like me to be."

"She said your apartments ought to be very distinct."

"That certainly would be best." And I listened with respect while she told me that above I should be free to take whatever I might like; that there was another staircase, but only from the floor on which we stood, and that to pass from it to the garden-level or to come up to my lodging I should have in effect to cross the great hall. This was an immense point gained; I foresaw that it would constitute my whole leverage in my relations with the two ladies. When I asked Miss Tina how I was to manage at present to find my way up she replied with an access of that sociable shyness which constantly marked her manner:

"Perhaps you can't. I don't see — unless I should go with you." She evidently hadn't thought of this before.

We ascended to the upper floor and visited a long succession of empty rooms. The best of them looked over the garden; some of the others had above the opposite rough-tiled house-tops a view of the blue lagoon. They were all dusty and even a little disfigured with long neglect, but I saw that by spending a few hundred francs I should be able to make three or four of them habitable enough. My experiment was turning out costly, yet now that I had all but taken possession I ceased to allow this to trouble me. I mentioned to my companion a few of the things I should put in, but she replied rather more precipitately than usual that I might do exactly what I liked: she seemed to wish to notify me that the Misses Bordereau would take none but the most veiled interest in my proceedings.

I guessed that her aunt had instructed her to adopt this tone, and I may as well say now that I came afterwards to distinguish perfectly (as I believed) between the speeches she made on her own responsibility and those the old woman imposed upon her. She took no notice of the unswept condition of the rooms and indulged neither in explanations nor in apologies. I said to myself that this was a sign Juliana and her niece — disenchanting idea! — were untidy persons with a low Italian standard; but I afterwards recognised that a lodger who had forced an entrance had no *locus standi* as a critic. We looked out of a good many windows, for there was nothing within the rooms to look at, and still I wanted to linger. I asked her what several different objects in the prospect might be, but in no case did she appear to know. She was evidently not familiar with the view — it was as if she had not looked at it for years — and I presently saw that she was too preoccupied with something else to pretend to care for it. Suddenly she said — the remark was not suggested:

"I don't know whether it will make any difference to you, but the money is for me."

"The money —?"

"The money you're going to bring."

"Why you'll make me wish to stay here two or three years!" I spoke as benevolently as possible, though it had begun to act on my nerves that these women so associated with Aspern should so constantly bring the pecuniary question back.

"That would be very good for me," she answered almost gaily.

"You put me on my honour!"

She looked as if she failed to understand this, but went on: "She wants me to have more. She thinks she's going to die."

"Ah not soon I hope!" I cried with genuine feeling. I had perfectly considered the possibility of her destroying her documents on the day she should feel her end at hand. I believed that she would cling to them till then, and I was as convinced of her reading Aspern's letters over every night or at least pressing them to her withered lips. I would have given a good deal for some view of those solemnities. I asked Miss Tina if her venerable relative were seriously ill, and she replied that she was only very tired — she had lived so extraordinarily long. That was what she said herself — she wanted to die for a change. Besides, all her friends had been dead for ages; either they ought to have remained or she ought to have gone. That

was another thing her aunt often said: she was not at all resigned —
resigned, that is, to life.

"But people don't die when they like, do they?" Miss Tina inquired.
I took the liberty of asking why, if there was actually enough money
to maintain both of them, there would not be more than enough in
case of her being left alone. She considered this difficult problem a
moment and then said: "Oh well, you know, she takes care of me.
She thinks that when I'm alone I shall be a great fool and shan't
know how to manage."

"I should have supposed rather that you took care of *her*. I'm
afraid she's very proud."

"Why, have you discovered that already?" Miss Tina cried with a
dimness of glad surprise.

"I was shut up with her there for a considerable time and she struck
me, she interested me extremely. It didn't take me long to make
my discovery. She won't have much to say to me while I'm here."

"No, I don't think she will," my companion averred.

"Do you suppose she has some suspicion of me?"

Miss Tina's honest eyes gave me no sign I had touched a mark.
"I shouldn't think so — letting you in after all so easily."

"You call it easily? She has covered her risk," I said. "But where
is it one could take an advantage of her?"

"I oughtn't to tell you if I knew, ought I?" And Miss Tina added,
before I had time to reply to this, smiling dolefully: "Do you think
we've any weak points?"

"That's exactly what I'm asking. You'd only have to mention
them for me to respect them religiously."

She looked at me hereupon with that air of timid but candid and
even gratified curiosity with which she had confronted me from the
first; after which she said: "There's nothing to tell. We're terribly
quiet. I don't know how the days pass. We've no life."

"I wish I might think I should bring you a little."

"Oh we know what we want," she went on. "It's all right."

There were twenty things I desired to ask her: how in the world
they did live; whether they had any friends or visitors, any relations
in America or in other countries. But I judged such probings pre-
mature; I must leave it to a later chance. "Well, don't *you* be
proud," I contented myself with saying. "Don't hide from me altogether."

"Oh I must stay with my aunt," she returned without looking

at me. And at the same moment, abruptly, without any ceremony of parting, she quitted me and disappeared, leaving me to make my own way downstairs. I stayed a while longer, wandering about the bright desert — the sun was pouring in — of the old house, thinking the situation over on the spot. Not even the pattering little *serva* came to look after me, and I reflected that after all this treatment showed confidence.

IV

Perhaps it did, but all the same, six weeks later, towards the middle of June, the moment when Mrs. Prest undertook her annual migration, I had made no measurable advance. I was obliged to confess to her that I had no results to speak of. My first step had been unexpectedly rapid, but there was no appearance it would be followed by a second. I was a thousand miles from taking tea with my hostesses — that privilege of which, as I reminded my good friend, we both had had a vision. She reproached me with lacking boldness and I answered that even to be bold you must have an opportunity: you may push on through a breach, but you can't batter down a dead wall. She returned that the breach I had already made was big enough to admit an army and accused me of wasting precious hours in whimpering in her salon when I ought to have been carrying on the struggle in the field. It is true that I went to see her very often — all on the theory that it would console me (I freely expressed my discouragement) for my want of success on my own premises. But I began to feel that it didn't console me to be perpetually chaffed for my scruples, especially since I was really so vigilant; and I was rather glad when my ironic friend closed her house for the summer. She had expected to gather amusement from the drama of my intercourse with the Misses Bordereau, and was disappointed that the intercourse, and consequently the drama, had not come off. "They'll lead you on to your ruin," she said before she left Venice. "They'll get all your money without showing you a scrap." I think I settled down to my business with more concentration after her departure.

It was a fact that up to that time I had not, save on a single brief occasion, had even a moment's contact with my queer hostesses. The exception had occurred when I carried them according to my promise the terrible three thousand francs. Then I found Miss Tina awaiting me in the hall, and she took the money from my hand with a promptitude that prevented my seeing her aunt. The old lady had promised to receive me, yet apparently thought nothing of breaking that vow. The money was contained in a bag of chamois leather, of respectable dimensions, which my banker had given me, and Miss Tina had to make a big fist to receive it. This she did with extreme solemnity though I tried to treat the affair a little as a joke. It was in no jocular strain, yet it was with a clearness akin to a brightness that she enquired, weighing the money in her two palms: "Don't you think it's too much?" To which I replied that this would depend on the amount of pleasure I should get for it. Hereupon she turned away from me quickly, as she had done the day before, murmuring in a tone different from any she had used hitherto: "Oh pleasure, pleasure — there's no pleasure in this house!"

After that, for a long time, I never saw her, and I wondered the common chances of the day shouldn't have helped us to meet. It could only be evident that she was immensely on her guard against them; and in addition to this the house was so big that for each other we were lost in it. I used to look out for her hopefully as I crossed the sala in my comings and goings, but I was not rewarded with a glimpse of the tail of her dress. It was as if she never peeped out of her aunt's apartment. I used to wonder what she did there week after week and year after year. I had never met so stiff a policy of seclusion; it was more than keeping quiet — it was like hunted creatures feigning death. The two ladies appeared to have no visitors whatever and no sort of contact with the world. I judged at least that people couldn't have come to the house and that Miss Tina couldn't have gone out without my catching some view of it. I did what I disliked myself for doing — considering it but as once in a way: I questioned my servant about their habits and let him infer that I should be interested in any information he might glean. But he gleaned amazingly little for a knowing Venetian: it must be added that where there is a perpetual fast there are very few crumbs on the floor. His ability in other ways was sufficient, if not quite all I had attributed to him on the occasion of my first interview with Miss Tina. He had helped my gondolier to bring me round a boatload of furniture; and when these articles had been carried to the top of the palace and distributed according to our associated wisdom he organized my household with such dignity as answered to its being composed exclusively of himself. He made me in short as comfortable as I could be with my indifferent prospects. I should have been glad if he had fallen in love with Miss Bordereau's maid or, failing this, had taken her in aversion; either event might have brought about some catastrophe, and a catastrophe might have led to some parley. It was my idea that she would have been sociable, and I myself on various occasions saw her flit to and fro on domestic errands, so that I was sure she was accessible. But I tasted of no gossip from that fountain, and I afterwards learned that Pasquale's affections were fixed upon an object that made him heedless of other women. This was a young lady with a powdered face, a yellow cotton gown and much leisure, who used often to come to see him. She practised, at her convenience, the art of a stringer of beads — these ornaments are made in Venice to profusion; she had her pocket full of them and I used to find them on the floor of my apartment — and kept an eye on the possible rival in the house. It was not for me of course to make the domestics tattle, and I never said a word to Miss Bordereau's cook.

It struck me as a proof of the old woman's resolve to have nothing to do with me that she should never have sent me a receipt for my three months' rent. For some days I looked out for it and then, when I had given it up, wasted a good deal of time in wondering what her reason had been for neglecting so indispensable and familiar a form. At first I was tempted to send her a reminder; after which I put by the idea — against my judgement as to what was right in the particular case — on the general ground of wishing to keep quiet. If Miss Bordereau suspected me of ulterior aims she would suspect me less if I should be businesslike, and yet I consented not to be. It was possible she intended her omission as an impertinence, a visible irony, to show how she could overreach people who attempted to overreach her. On that hypothesis it was well to let her see that one didn't notice her little tricks. The real reading of the matter, I afterwards gathered, was simply the poor lady's desire to emphasise the fact that I was in the enjoyment of a favour as rigidly limited as it had been liberally bestowed. She had given me part of her house, but she wouldn't add to that so much as a morsel of paper with her name on it. Let me say that even at first this didn't make me too miserable, for the whole situation had the charm of its oddity. I foresaw that I should have a summer after my own literary heart, and the sense of playing with my opportunity was much greater after all than any sense of being played with. There could be no Venetian business without patience, and since I adored the place I was much more in the spirit of it for having laid in a large provision. That spirit kept me perpetual company and seemed to look out at me from the revived immortal face — in which all his genius shone — of the great poet who was my prompter. I had invoked him and he had come; he hovered before me half the time; it was as if his bright ghost had returned to earth to assure me he regarded the affair as his own no less than as mine and that we should see it fraternally and fondly to a conclusion. It was as if he had said: "Poor dear, be easy with her; she has some natural prejudices; only give her time. Strange as it may appear to you she was very attractive in 1820. Meanwhile aren't we in Venice together, and what better place is there for the meeting of dear friends? See how it glows with the advancing summer; how the sky and the sea and the rosy air and the marble of the palaces all shimmer and melt together." My eccentric private errand became a part of the general romance and the general glory — I felt even a mystic companionship, a moral fraternity with all those who in the past had been in the service of art. They had worked for beauty, for a devotion; and what else was I doing? That element was in everything that Jeffrey Aspern had written, and I was only bringing it to light.

I lingered in the sala when I went to and fro; I used to watch — as long as I thought decent — the door that led to Miss Bordereau's part of the house. A person observing me might have supposed I was trying to cast a spell on it or attempting some odd experiment in hypnotism. But I was only praying it might open or thinking what treasure probably lurked behind it. I hold it singular, as I look back, that I should never have doubted for a moment that the sacred relics were there; never have failed to know the joy of being beneath the same roof with them. After all they were under my hand — they had not escaped me yet; and they made my life continuous, in a fashion, with the illustrious life they had touched at the other end. I lost myself in this satisfaction to the point of assuming — in my quiet extravagance — that poor Miss Tina also went back, and still went back, as I used to phrase it. She did indeed, the gentle spinster, but not quite so far as Jeffrey Aspern, who was simple hearsay to her quite as he was to me. Only she had lived for years with Juliana, she had seen and handled all mementoes and — even though she was stupid — some esoteric knowledge had rubbed off on her. That was what the old woman represented — esoteric knowledge; and this was the idea with which my critical heart used to thrill. It literally beat faster often, of an evening when I had been out, as I stopped with my candle in the re-echoing hall on my way up to bed. It was as if at such a moment as that, in the stillness and after the long contradiction of the day, Miss Bordereau's secrets were in the air, the wonder of her survival more vivid. These were the acute impressions. I had them in another form, with more of a certain shade of reciprocity, during the hours I sat in the garden looking up over the top of my book at the closed windows of my hostess. In these windows no sign of life ever appeared; it was as if, for fear of my catching a glimpse of them, the two ladies passed their days in the dark. But this only emphasised their having matters to conceal; which was what I had wished to prove. Their motionless shutters became as expressive as eyes consciously closed, and I took comfort in the probability that, though invisible themselves, they kept me in view between the lashes.

I made a point of spending as much time as possible in the garden, to justify the picture I had originally given of my horticultural passion. And I not only spent time, but (hang it! as I said) spent precious money. As soon as I had got my rooms arranged and could give the question proper thought I surveyed the place with a clever expert and made terms for having it put in order. I was sorry to do this, for personally I liked it better as it was, with its weeds and its wild rich tangle, its sweet characteristic Venetian shabbiness. I had to be consistent, to keep my promise that I would smother the house in flowers. Moreover I clung to the fond fancy that by flowers I should make my way — I should succeed by big nosegays. I would batter the old women with lilies — I would bombard their citadel with roses. Their door would have to yield to the pressure when a mound of fragrance should be heaped against it. The place in truth had been brutally neglected. The Venetian capacity for dawdling is of the largest, and for a good many days unlimited litter was all my gardener had to show for his ministrations. There was a great digging of holes and carting about of earth, and after a while I grew so impatient that I had thoughts of sending for my "results" to the nearest stand. But I felt sure my friends would see through the chinks of their shutters where such tribute *couldn't* have been gathered, and might so make up their minds against my veracity. I possessed my soul and finally, though the delay was long, perceived some appearances of bloom. This encouraged me and I waited serenely enough till they multiplied. Meanwhile the real summer days arrived and began to pass, and as I look back upon them they seem to me almost the happiest of my life. I took more and more care to be in the garden whenever it was not too hot. I had an arbour arranged and a low table and an armchair put into it; and I carried out books and portfolios — I had always some business of writing in hand — and worked and waited and mused and hoped, while the golden hours elapsed and the plants drank in the light and the inscrutable old palace turned pale and then, as the day waned, began to recover and flush and my papers rustled in the wandering breeze of the Adriatic.

Considering how little satisfaction I got from it at first it is wonderful I shouldn't have grown more tired of trying to guess what mystic rites of ennui the Misses Bordereau celebrated in their darkened rooms; whether this had always been the tenor of their life and how in previous years they had escaped elbowing their neighbours. It was supposable they had then had other habits, forms and resources; that they must once have been young or at least middle-aged. There was no end to the questions it was possible to ask about them and no end to the answers it was not possible to frame. I had known many of my country-people in Europe and was familiar with the strange ways they were liable to take up there; but the Misses Bordereau formed altogether a new type of the American absentee. Indeed it was clear the American name had ceased to have any application to them — I had seen this in the ten minutes I spent in the old woman's room. You could never have said whence they came from the appearance of either of them; wherever it was they had long ago shed and unlearned all native marks and notes. There was nothing in them one recognised or fitted, and, putting the question of speech aside, they might have been Norwegians or Spaniards. Miss Bordereau, after all, had been in Europe nearly three-quarters of a century; it appeared by some verses addressed to her by Aspern on the occasion of his own second absence from America — verses of which Cumnor and I had after infinite conjecture established solidly enough the date — that she was even then, as a girl of twenty, on the foreign side of the sea. There was a profession in the poem — I hope not just for the phrase — that he had come back for her sake. We had no real light on her circumstances at that moment, any more than we had upon her origin, which we believed to be of the sort usually spoken of as modest. Cumnor had a theory that she had been a governess in some family in which the poet visited and that, in consequence of her position, there was from the first something unavowed, or rather something quite clandestine, in their relations. I on the other hand had hatched a little romance according to which she was the daughter of an artist, a painter or a sculptor, who had left the Western world, when the century was fresh, to study in the ancient schools. It wa essential to my hypothesis that this amiable man should have lost his wife, should have been poor and unsuccessful and should have had a second daughter of a disposition quite different from Juliana's. It was also indispensable that he should have been accompanied to Europe by these young ladies and should have established himself there for the remainder of a struggling saddened life. There was a further implication that Miss Bordereau had had in her youth a perverse and reckless, albeit a generous and fascinating character, and that she had braved some wondrous chances. By what passions had she been ravaged, by what adventures and sufferings had she been blanched, what store of memories had she laid away for the monotonous future?

I asked myself these things as I sat spinning theories about her in my arbour and the bees droned in the flowers. It was incontestable that, whether for right or for wrong, most readers of certain of Aspern's poems (poems not as ambiguous as the sonnets — scarcely more divine, I think — of Shakespeare) had taken for granted that Juliana had not always adhered to the steep footway of renunciation. There hovered about her name a perfume of impenitent passion, an intimation that she had not been exactly as the respectable young person in general. Was this a sign that her singer had betrayed her, had given her away, as we say nowadays, to posterity? Certain it is that it would have been difficult to put one's finger on the passage in which her fair fame suffered injury. Moreover was not any fame fair enough that was so sure of duration and was associated with works immortal through their beauty? It was a part of my idea that the young lady had had a foreign lover — and say an unedifying tragical rupture — before her meeting with Jeffrey Aspern. She had lived with her father and sister in a queer old-fashioned expatriated artistic Bohemia of the days when the æsthetic was only the academic and the painters who knew the best models for *contadina* and *pifferaro* wore peaked hats and long hair. It was a society less awake than the coteries of to-day — in its ignorance of the wonderful chances, the opportunities of the early bird, with which its path was strewn — to tatters of old stuff and fragments of old crockery; so that Miss Bordereau appeared not to have picked up or have inherited many objects of importance. There was no enviable *bric-à-brac*, with its provoking legend of cheapness, in the room in which I had seen her. Such a fact as that

suggested bareness, but none the less it worked happily into the sentimental interest I had always taken in the early movements of my
countrymen as visitors to Europe. When Americans went abroad in
1820 there was something romantic, almost heroic in it, as compared
with the perpetual ferryings of the present hour, the hour at which
photography and other conveniences have annihilated surprise.
Miss Bordereau had sailed with her family on a tossing brig in the days
of long voyages and sharp differences; she had had her emotions on
the top of yellow diligences, passed the night at inns where she dreamed
of travellers' tales, and was most struck, on reaching the Eternal City,
with the elegance of Roman pearls and scarfs and mosaic brooches.
There was something touching to me in all that, and my imagination
frequently went back to the period. If Miss Bordereau carried it there
of course Jeffrey Aspern had at other times done so with greater
force. It was a much more important fact, if one was looking at his
genius critically, that he had lived in the days before the general
transfusion. It had happened to me to regret that he had known
Europe at all; I should have liked to see what he would have written
without that experience, by which he had incontestably been enriched.
But as his fate had ruled otherwise I went with him — I tried to
judge how the general old order would have struck him. It was not
only there, however, I watched him; the relations he had entertained
with the special new had even a livelier interest. His own country
after all had had most of his life, and his muse, as they said at that
time, was essentially American. That was originally what I had
prized him for: that at a period when our native land was nude and
crude and provincial, when the famous "atmosphere" it is supposed
to lack was not even missed, when literature was lonely there and
art and form almost impossible, he had found means to live and write
like one of the first; to be free and general and not at all afraid; to
feel, understand and express everything.

V

I was seldom at home in the evening, for when I attempted to
occupy myself in my apartments the lamplight brought in a swarm
of noxious insects, and it was too hot for closed windows. Accordingly I spent the late hours either on the water — the moonlights of
Venice are famous — or in the splendid square which serves as a vast
forecourt to the strange old church of Saint Mark. I sat in front of
Florian's café eating ices, listening to music, talking with acquaint-

ances: the traveller will remember how the immense cluster of tables and little chairs stretches like a promontory into the smooth lake of the Piazza. The whole place, of a summer's evening, under the stars and with all the lamps, all the voices and light footsteps on marble — the only sounds of the immense arcade that encloses it — is an open-air saloon dedicated to cooling drinks and to a still finer degustation, that of the splendid impressions received during the day. When I didn't prefer to keep mine to myself there was always a stray tourist, disencumbered of his Bädeker, to discuss them with, or some domesticated painter rejoicing in the return of the season of strong effects. The great basilica, with its low domes and bristling embroideries, the mystery of its mosaic and sculpture, looked ghostly in the tempered gloom, and the sea-breeze passed between the twin columns of the Piazzetta, the lintels of a door no longer guarded, as gently as if a rich curtain swayed there. I used sometimes on these occasions to think of the Misses Bordereau and of the pity of their being shut up in apartments which in the Venetian July even Venetian vastness couldn't relieve of some stuffiness. Their life seemed miles away from the life of the Piazza, and no doubt it was really too late to make the austere Juliana change her habits. But poor Miss Tina would have enjoyed one of Florian's ices, I was sure; sometimes I even had thoughts of carrying one home to her. Fortunately my patience bore fruit and I was not obliged to do anything so ridiculous.

One evening about the middle of July I came in earlier than usual — I forgot what chance had led to this — and instead of going up to my quarters made my way into the garden. The temperature was very high; it was such a night as one would gladly have spent in the open air, and I was in no hurry to go to bed. I had floated home in my gondola, listening to the slow splash of the oar in the dark narrow canals, and now the only thought that occupied me was that it would be good to recline at one's length in the fragrant darkness on a garden bench. The odour of the canal was doubtless at the bottom of that aspiration, and the breath of the garden, as I entered it, gave consistency to my purpose. It was delicious — just such an air as must have trembled with Romeo's vows when he stood among the thick flowers and raised his arms to his mistress's balcony. I looked at the windows of the palace to see if by chance the example of Verona — Verona being not far off — had been followed; but everything was dim, as usual, and everything was still. Juliana might on the summer nights of her youth have murmured down from open

windows at Jeffrey Aspern, but Miss Tina was not a poet's mistress
any more than I was a poet. This however didn't prevent my gratification from being great as I became aware on reaching the end of
the garden that my younger padrona was seated in one of the bowers.
At first I made out but an indistinct figure, not in the least counting
on such an overture from one of my hostesses; it even occurred to
me that some enamoured maidservant had stolen in to keep a tryst
with her sweetheart. I was going to turn away, not to frighten her,
when the figure rose to its height and I recognised Miss Bordereau's
niece. I must do myself the justice that I didn't wish to frighten her
either, and much as I had longed for some such accident I should
have been capable of retreating. It was as if I had laid a trap for her
by coming home earlier than usual and by adding to that oddity my
invasion of the garden. As she rose she spoke to me, and then I
guessed that perhaps, secure in my almost inveterate absence, it was
her nightly practice to take a lonely airing. There was no trap in
truth, because I had had no suspicion. At first I took the words she
uttered for an impatience of my arrival; but as she repeated them —
I hadn't caught them clearly — I had the surprise of hearing her say:
"Oh dear, I'm so glad you've come!" She and her aunt had in common the property of unexpected speeches. She came out of the
arbour almost as if to throw herself in my arms.

I hasten to add that I escaped this ordeal and that she didn't even
then shake hands with me. It was an ease to her to see me and presently she told me why — because she was nervous when out-of-doors
at night alone. The plants and shrubs looked so strange in the dark,
and there were all sorts of queer sounds — she couldn't tell what they
were — like the noises of animals. She stood close to me, looking about
her with an air of greater security but without any demonstration of
interest in me as an individual. Then I felt how little nocturnal
prowlings could have been her habit, and I was also reminded — I
had been afflicted by the same in talking with her before I took possession — that it was impossible to allow too much for her simplicity.

"You speak as if you were lost in the backwoods," I cheeringly
laughed. "How you manage to keep out of this charming place when
you've only three steps to take to get into it is more than I've yet
been able to discover. You hide away amazingly so long as I'm on
the premises, I know; but I had a hope you peeped out a little at
other times. You and your poor aunt are worse off than Carmelite
nuns in their cells. Should you mind telling me how you exist with-

out air, without exercise, without any sort of human contact? I don't see how you carry on the common business of life."

She looked at me as if I had spoken a strange tongue, and her answer was so little of one that I felt it make for irritation. "We go to bed very early — earlier than you'd believe." I was on the point of saying that this only deepened the mystery, but she gave me some relief by adding: "Before you came we weren't so private. But I've never been out at night."

"Never in these fragrant alleys, blooming here under your nose?"

"Ah," said Miss Tina, "they were never nice till now!" There was a finer sense in this and a flattering comparison, so that it seemed to me I had gained some advantage. As I might follow that further by establishing a good grievance I asked her why, since she thought my garden nice, she had never thanked me in any way for the flowers I had been sending up in such quantities for the previous three weeks. I had not been discouraged — there had been, as she would have observed, a daily armful; but I had been brought up in the common forms and a word of recognition now and then would have touched me in the right place.

"Why I didn't know they were for me!"

"They were for both of you. Why should I make a difference?"

Miss Tina reflected as if she might be thinking of a reason for that, but she failed to produce one. Instead of this she asked abruptly: "Why in the world do you want so much to know us?"

"I ought after all to make a difference," I replied. "That question's your aunt's; it isn't yours. You wouldn't ask it if you hadn't been put up to it."

"She didn't tell me to ask you," Miss Tina replied without confusion. She was indeed the oddest mixture of shyness and straightness.

"Well, she has often wondered about it herself and expressed her wonder to you. She has insisted on it, so that she has put the idea into your head that I'm insufferably pushing. Upon my word I think I've been very discreet. And how completely your aunt must have lost every tradition of sociability, to see anything out of the way in the idea that respectable intelligent people, living as we do under the same roof, should occasionally exchange a remark! What could be more natural? We are of the same country and have at least some of the same tastes, since, like you, I'm intensely fond of Venice."

My friend seemed incapable of grasping more than one clause in any proposition, and she now spoke quickly, eagerly, as if she were answering my whole speech: "I'm not in the least fond of Venice. I should like to go far away!"

"Has she always kept you back so?" I went on, to show her I could be as irrelevant as herself.

"She told me to come out to-night; she has told me very often," said Miss Tina. "It is I who wouldn't come. I don't like to leave her."

"Is she too weak, is she really failing?" I demanded, with more emotion, I think, than I meant to betray. I measured this by the way her eyes rested on me in the darkness. It embarrassed me a little, and to turn the matter off I continued genially: "Do let us sit down together comfortably somewhere — while you tell me all about her."

Miss Tina made no resistance to this. We found a bench less secluded, less confidential, as it were, than the one in the arbour; and we were still sitting there when I heard midnight ring out from those clear bells of Venice which vibrate with a solemnity of their own over the lagoon and hold the air so much more than the chimes of other places. We were together more than an hour and our interview gave, as it struck me, a great lift to my undertaking. Miss Tina accepted the situation without a protest; she had avoided me for three months, yet now she treated me almost as if these three months had made me an old friend. If I had chosen I might have gathered from this that though she had avoided me she had given a good deal of consideration to doing so. She paid no attention to the flight of time — never worried at my keeping her so long away from her aunt. She talked freely, answering questions and asking them and not even taking advantage of certain longish pauses by which they were naturally broken to say she thought she had better go in. It was almost as if she were waiting for something — something I might say to her — and intended to give me my opportunity. I was the more struck by this as she told me how much less well her aunt had been for a good many days, and in a way that was rather new. She was markedly weaker; at moments she showed no strength at all; yet more than ever before she wished to be left alone. That was why she had told her to come out — not even to remain in her own room, which was alongside; she pronounced poor Miss Tina "a worry, a bore and a source of aggravation." She sat still for hours together, as if for long sleep; she had always done that, musing and dozing; but at such times formerly she gave, in breaks, some small sign of life, of interest, liking her companion to be near her with her work. This sad personage confided to me that at present her aunt was so motionless as to create the fear she was dead; moreover she scarce ate or drank — one couldn't see what she lived on. The great thing was that she still on most days got up; the serious job was to dress her, to wheel her out of her bedroom. She clung to as many of her old habits as possible and had always, little company as they had received for years, made a point of sitting in the great parlour.

I scarce knew what to think of all this — of Miss Tina's sudden conversion to sociability and of the strange fact that the more the old woman appeared to decline to her end the less she should desire to be looked after. The story hung indifferently together, and I even asked myself if it mightn't be a trap laid for me, the result of a design to make me show my hand. I couldn't have told why my companions (as they could only by courtesy be called) should have this purpose — why they should try to trip up so lucrative a lodger. But at any hazard I kept on my guard, so that Miss Tina shouldn't have occasion again to ask me what I might really be "up to." Poor woman, before we parted for the night my mind was at rest as to what *she* might be. She was up to nothing at all.

She told me more about their affairs than I had hoped; there was no need to be prying, for it evidently drew her out simply to feel me listen and care. She ceased wondering why I *should*, and at last while describing the brilliant life they had led years before, she almost chattered. It was Miss Tina who judged it brilliant; she said that when they first came to live in Venice, years and years back — I found her essentially vague about dates and the order in which events had occurred — there was never a week they hadn't some visitor or didn't make some pleasant *passeggio* in the town. They had seen all the curiosities; they had even been to the Lido in a boat — she spoke as if I might think there was a way on foot; they had had a collation there, brought in three baskets and spread out on the grass. I asked her what people they had known and she said Oh very nice ones — the Cavaliere Bombicci and the Contessa Altemura, with whom they had had a great friendship! Also English people — the Churtons and the Goldies and Mrs. Stock-Stock, whom they had loved dearly; she was dead and gone, poor dear. That was the case with most of their kind circle — this expression was Miss Tina's own; though a few were left, which was a wonder considering how they had neglected them She mentioned the names of two or three Venetian old women;

of a certain doctor, very clever, who was so attentive — he came as a friend, he had really given up practice; of the *avvocato* Pochintesta, who wrote beautiful poems and had addressed one to her aunt. These people came to see them without fail every year, usually at the *capo d'anno*, and of old her aunt used to make them some little present — her aunt and she together: small things that she, Miss Tina, turned out with her own hand, paper lamp-shades, or mats for the decanters of wine at dinner, or those woollen things that in cold weather are worn on the wrists. The last few years there hadn't been many presents; she couldn't think what to make and her aunt had lost interest and never suggested. But the people came all the same; if the good Venetians liked you once they liked you for ever.

There was affecting matter enough in the good faith of this sketch of former social glories; the picnic at the Lido had remained vivid through the ages and poor Miss Tina evidently was of the impression that she had had a dashing youth. She had in fact had a glimpse of the Venetian world in its gossiping home-keeping parsimonious professional walks; for I noted for the first time how nearly she had acquired by contact the trick of the familiar soft-sounding almost infantile prattle of the place. I judged her to have imbibed this invertebrate dialect from the natural way the names of things and people — mostly purely local — rose to her lips. If she knew little of what they represented she knew still less of anything else. Her aunt had drawn in — the failure of interest in the table-mats and lamp-shades was a sign of that — and she hadn't been able to mingle in society or to entertain it alone; so that her range of reminiscence struck one as an old world altogether. Her tone, hadn't it been so decent, would have seemed to carry one back to the queer rococo Venice of Goldoni and Casanova. I found myself mistakenly think of her too as one of Jeffrey Aspern's contemporaries; this came from her having so little in common with my own. It was possible, I indeed reasoned, that she hadn't even heard of him; it might very well be that Juliana had forborne to lift for innocent eyes the veil that covered the temple of her glory. In this case she perhaps wouldn't know of the existence of the papers, and I welcomed that presumption — it made me feel more safe with her — till I remembered we had believed the letter of disavowal received by Cumnor to be in the handwriting of the niece. If it had been dictated to her she had of course to know what it was about; though the effect of it withal was to repudiate the idea of any connexion with the poet. I held it probable at

all events that Miss Tina hadn't read a word of his poetry. Moreover if, with her companion, she had always escaped invasion and
research, there was little occasion for her having got it into her head
that people were "after" the letters. People had not been after them,
for people hadn't heard of them. Cumnor's fruitless feeler would
have been a solitary accident.

When midnight sounded Miss Tina got up; but she stopped at the
door of the house only after she had wandered two or three times
with me round the garden. "When shall I see you again?" I asked
before she went in; to which she replied with promptness that she
should like to come out the next night. She added, however, that
she shouldn't come — she was so far from doing everything she liked.

"You might do a few things *I* like," I quite sincerely sighed.

"Oh you — I don't believe you!" she murmured at this, facing me
with her simple solemnity.

"Why don't you believe me?"

"Because I don't understand you."

"That's just the sort of occasion to have faith." I couldn't say
more, though I should have liked to, as I saw I only mystified her;
for I had no wish to have it on my conscience that I might pass for
having made love to her. Nothing less should I have seemed to do
had I continued to beg a lady to "believe in me" in an Italian garden
on a midsummer night. There was some merit in my scruples, for
Miss Tina lingered and lingered: I made out in her conviction that
she shouldn't really soon come down again and the wish therefore
to protract the present. She insisted too on making the talk between
us personal to ourselves; and altogether her behaviour was such as
would have been possible only to a perfectly artless and a considerably
witless woman.

"I shall like the flowers better now that I know them also meant
for me."

"How could you have doubted it? If you'll tell me the kind you
like best I'll send a double lot."

"Oh I like them all best!" Then she went on familiarly: "Shall
you study — shall you read and write — when you go up to your
rooms?"

"I don't do that at night — at this season. The lamplight brings in
the animals."

"You might have known that when you came."

"I did know it!"

"And in winter do you work at night?"

"I read a good deal, but I don't often write." She listened as if these details had a rare interest, and suddenly a temptation quite at odds with all the prudence I had been teaching myself glimmered at me in her plain mild face. Ah yes, she was safe and I could make her safer! It seemed to me from one moment to another that I couldn't wait longer — that I really must take a sounding. So I went on: "In general before I go to sleep (very often in bed; it's a bad habit, but I confess to it) I read some great poet. In nine cases out of ten it's a volume of Jeffrey Aspern."

I watched her well as I pronounced that name, but I saw nothing wonderful. Why should I indeed? Wasn't Jeffrey Aspern the property of the human race?

"Oh *we* read him — we *have* read him," she quietly replied.

"He's my poet of poets — I know him almost by heart."

For an instant Miss Tina hesitated; then her sociability was too much for her. "Oh by heart — that's nothing;" and, though dimly, she quite lighted. "My aunt used to know him — to know him" — she paused an instant and I wondered what she was going to say — "to know him as a visitor."

"As a visitor?" I guarded my tone.

"He used to call on her and take her out."

I continued to stare. "My dear lady, he died a hundred years ago!"

"Well," she said amusingly, "my aunt's a hundred and fifty."

"Mercy on us!" I cried; "why didn't you tell me before? I should like so to ask her about him."

"She wouldn't care for that — she wouldn't tell you," Miss Tina returned.

"I don't care what she cares for! She *must* tell me — it's not a chance to be lost."

"Oh you should have come twenty years ago. Then she still talked about him."

"And what did she say?" I eagerly asked.

"I don't know — that he liked her immensely."

"And she — didn't she like *him*?"

"She said he was a god." Miss Tina gave me this information flatly, without expression; her tone might have made it a piece of trivial gossip. But it stirred me deeply as she dropped the words into the summer night; their sound might have been the light rustle of an old unfolded love-letter.

"Fancy, fancy!" I murmured. And then, "Tell me this, please — has she got a portrait of him? They're distressingly rare."

"A portrait? I don't know," said Miss Tina; and now there was discomfiture in her face. "Well, good-night!" she added; and she turned into the house.

I accompanied her into the wide dusky stone-paved passage that corresponded on the ground floor with our grand sala. It opened at one end into the garden, at the other upon the canal, and was lighted now only by the small lamp always left for me to take up as I went to bed. An extinguished candle which Miss Tina apparently had brought down with her stood on the same table with it. "Good-night, good-night!" I replied, keeping beside her as she went to get her light. "Surely you'd know, shouldn't you, if she had one?"

"If she had what?" the poor lady asked, looking at me queerly over the flame of her candle.

"A portrait of the god. I don't know what I wouldn't give to see it."

"I don't know what she has got. She keeps her things locked up." And Miss Tina went away toward the staircase with the sense evidently of having said too much.

I let her go — I wished not to frighten her — and I contented myself with remarking that Miss Bordereau wouldn't have locked up such a glorious possession as that: a thing a person would be proud of and hang up in a prominent place on the parlour-wall. Therefore of course she hadn't any portrait. Miss Tina made no direct answer to this and, candle in hand, with her back to me, mounted two or three degrees. Then she stopped short and turned round, looking at me across the dusky space.

"Do you write — do you write?" There was a shake in her voice — she could scarcely bring it out.

"Do I write? Oh don't speak of my writing on the same day with Aspern's!"

"Do you write about *him* — do you pry into his life?"

"Ah that's your aunt's question; it can't be yours!" I said in a tone of slightly wounded sensibility.

"All the more reason then that you should answer it. Do you, please?"

I thought I had allowed for the falsehoods I should have to tell, but I found that in fact when it came to the point I hadn't. Besides, now that I had an opening there was a kind of relief in being frank.

Lastly — it was perhaps fanciful, even fatuous — I guessed that Miss Tina personally wouldn't in the last resort be less my friend. So after a moment's hesitation I answered: "Yes, I've written about him and I'm looking for more material. In heaven's name have you got any?"

"*Santo Dio!*" she exclaimed without heeding my question; and she hurried upstairs and out of sight. I might count upon her in the last resort, but for the present she was visibly alarmed. The proof of it was that she began to hide again, so that for a fortnight I kept missing her. I found my patience ebbing and after four or five days of this I told the gardener to stop the "floral tributes."

VI

One afternoon, at last, however, as I came down from my quarters to go out, I found her in the sala: it was our first encounter on that ground since I had come to the house. She put on no air of being there by accident; there was an ignorance of such arts in her honest angular diffidence. That I might be quite sure she was waiting for me she mentioned it at once, but telling me with it that Miss Bordereau wished to see me: she would take me into the room at that moment if I had time. If I had been late for a love-tryst I would have stayed for this, and I quickly signified that I should be delighted to wait on my benefactress. "She wants to talk with you — to know you," Miss Tina said, smiling as if she herself appreciated that idea; and she led me to the door of her aunt's apartment. I stopped her a moment before she had opened it, looking at her with some curiosity. I told her that this was a great satisfaction to me and a great honour; but all the same I should like to ask what had made Miss Bordereau so markedly and suddenly change. It had been only the other day that she wouldn't suffer me near her. Miss Tina was not embarrassed by my question; she had as many little unexpected serenities, plausibilities almost, as if she told fibs, but the odd part of them was that they had on the contrary their source in her truthfulness. "Oh my aunt varies," she answered; "it's so terribly dull — I suppose she's tired."

"But you told me she wanted more and more to be alone."

Poor Miss Tina coloured as if she found me too pushing. "Well, if you don't believe she wants to see you, I haven't invented it! I think people often are capricious when they're very old."

"That's perfectly true. I only wanted to be clear as to whether you've repeated to her what I told you the other night."

"What you told me?"

"About Jeffrey Aspern — that I'm looking for materials."

"If I had told her do you think she'd have sent for you?"

"That's exactly what I want to know. If she wants to keep him to herself she might have sent for me to tell me so."

"She won't speak of him," said Miss Tina. Then as she opened the door she added in a lower tone: "I told her nothing."

The old woman was sitting in the same place in which I had seen her last, in the same position, with the same mystifying bandage over her eyes. Her welcome was to turn her almost invisible face to me and show me that while she sat silent she saw me clearly. I made no motion to shake hands with her; I now felt too well that this was out of place for ever. It had been sufficiently enjoined on me that she was too sacred for trivial modernisms — too venerable to touch. There was something so grim in her aspect — it was partly the accident of her green shade — as I stood there to be measured, that I ceased on the spot to doubt her suspecting me, though I didn't in the least myself suspect that Miss Tina hadn't just spoken the truth. She hadn't betrayed me, but the old woman's brooding instinct had served her; she had turned me over and over in the long still hours and had guessed. The worst of it was that she looked terribly like an old woman who at a pinch would, even like Sardanapalus, burn her treasure. Miss Tina pushed a chair forward, saying to me: "This will be a good place for you to sit." As I took possession of it I asked after Miss Bordereau's health; expressed the hope that in spite of the very hot weather it was satisfactory. She answered that it was good enough — good enough; that it was a great thing to be alive.

"Oh as to that, it depends upon what you compare it with!" I returned with a laugh.

"I don't compare — I don't compare. If I did that I should have given everything up long ago."

I liked to take this for a subtle allusion to the rapture she had known in the society of Jeffrey Aspern — though it was true that such an allusion would have accorded ill with the wish I imputed to her to keep him buried in her soul. What it accorded with was my constant conviction that no human being had ever had a happier social gift than his, and what it seemed to convey was that nothing in the world was worth speaking of if one pretended to speak of that. But one didn't pretend! Miss Tina sat down beside her aunt, looking as if she had reason to believe some wonderful talk would come off between us.

"It's about the beautiful flowers," said the old lady; "you sent us so many — I ought to have thanked you for them before. But I don't write letters and I receive company but at long intervals."

She hadn't thanked me while the flowers continued to come, but she departed from her custom so far as to send for me as soon as she began to fear they wouldn't come any more. I noted this; I remembered what an acquisitive propensity she had shown when it was a question of extracting gold from me, and I privately rejoiced at the happy thought I had had in suspending my tribute. She had missed it and was willing to make a concession to bring it back. At the first sign of this concession I could only go to meet her. "I'm afraid you haven't had many, of late, but they shall begin again immediately — to-morrow, to-night."

"Oh do send us some to-night!" Miss Tina cried as if it were a great affair.

"What else should you do with them? It isn't a manly taste to make a bower of your room," the old woman remarked.

"I don't make a bower of my room, but I'm exceedingly fond of growing flowers, of watching their ways. There's nothing unmanly in that: it has been the amusement of philosophers, of statesmen in retirement; even I think of great captains."

"I suppose you know you can sell them — those you don't use," Miss Bordereau went on. "I dare say they wouldn't give you much for them; still, you could make a bargain."

"Oh I've never in my life made a bargain, as you ought pretty well to have gathered. My gardener disposes of them and I ask no questions."

"I'd ask a few, I can promise you!" said Miss Bordereau; and it was so I first heard the strange sound of her laugh, which was as if the faint "walking" ghost of her old-time tone had suddenly cut a caper. I couldn't get used to the idea that this vision of pecuniary profit was most what drew out the divine Juliana.

"Come into the garden yourself and pick them; come as often as you like; come every day. The flowers are all for you," I pursued, addressing Miss Tina and carrying off this veracious statement by treating it as an innocent joke. "I can't imagine why she doesn't come down," I added for Miss Bordereau's benefit.

"You must make her come; you must come up and fetch her," the old woman said to my stupefaction. "That odd thing you've made in the corner will do very well for her to sit in."

The allusion to the most elaborate of my shady coverts, a sketchy "summer-house," was irreverent; it confirmed the impression I had already received that there was a flicker of impertinence in Miss Bordereau's talk, a vague echo of the boldness or the archness of her adventurous youth and which had somehow automatically outlived passions and faculties. None the less I asked: "Wouldn't it be possible for you to come down there yourself? Wouldn't it do you good to sit there in the shade and the sweet air?"

"Oh, sir, when I move out of this it won't be to sit in the air, and I'm afraid that any that may be stirring around me won't be particularly sweet! It will be a very dark shade indeed. But that won't be just yet," Miss Bordereau continued cannily, as if to correct any hopes this free glance at the last receptacle of her mortality might lead me to entertain. "I've sat here many a day and have had enough of arbours in my time. But I'm not afraid to wait till I'm called."

Miss Tina had expected, as I felt, rare conversation, but perhaps she found it less gracious on her aunt's side — considering I had been sent for with a civil intention — than she had hoped. As to give the position a turn that would put our companion in a light more favourable she said to me: "Didn't I tell you the other night that she had sent me out? You see I can do what I like!"

"Do you pity her — do you teach her to pity herself?" Miss Bordereau demanded, before I had time to answer this appeal. "She has a much easier life than I had at her age."

"You must remember it has been quite open to me," I said, "to think you rather inhuman."

"Inhuman? That's what the poets used to call the women a hundred years ago. Don't try that; you won't do as well as they!" Juliana went on. "There's no more poetry in the world — that *I* know of at least. But I won't bandy words with you," she said, and I well remember the old-fashioned artificial sound she gave the speech. "You make me talk, talk, talk! It isn't good for me at all." I got up at this and told her I would take no more of her time; but she detained me to put a question, "Do you remember, the day I saw you about the rooms, that you offered us the use of your gondola?" And when I assented promptly, struck again with her disposition to make a "good thing" of my being there and wondering what she now had in her eye, she produced: "Why don't you take that girl out in it and show her the place?"

"Oh dear aunt, what do you want to do with me?" cried the "girl" with a piteous quaver. "I know all about the place!"

"Well then go with him and explain!" said Miss Bordereau, who gave an effect of cruelty to her implacable power of retort. This showed her as a sarcastic profane cynical old woman. "Haven't we heard that there have been all sorts of changes in all these years? You ought to see them, and at your age — I don't mean because you're so young — you ought to take the chances that come. You're old enough, my dear, and this gentleman won't hurt you. He'll show you the famous sunsets, if they still go on — *do* they go on? The sun set for me so long ago. But that's not a reason. Besides, I shall never miss you; you think you're too important. Take her to the Piazza; it used to be very pretty," Miss Bordereau continued, addressing herself to me. "What have they done with the funny old church? I hope it hasn't tumbled down. Let her look at the shops; she may take some money, she may buy what she likes."

Poor Miss Tina had got up, discountenanced and helpless, and as we stood there before her aunt it would certainly have struck a spectator of the scene that our venerable friend was making rare sport of us. Miss Tina protested in a confusion of exclamations and murmurs; but I lost no time in saying that if she would do me the honour to accept the hospitality of my boat I would engage she really shouldn't be bored. Or if she didn't want so much of my company, the boat itself, with the gondolier, was at her service; he was a capital oar and she might have every confidence. Miss Tina, without definitely answering this speech, looked away from me and out of the window, quite as if about to weep, and I remarked that once we had Miss Bordereau's approval we could easily come to an understanding. We would take an hour, whichever she liked, one of the very next days. As I made my obeisance to the old lady I asked her if she would kindly permit me to see her again.

For a moment she kept me; then she said: "Is it very necessary to your happiness?"

"It diverts me more than I can say."

"You're wonderfully civil. Don't you know it almost kills *me?*"

"How can I believe that when I see you more animated, more brilliant than when I came in?"

"That's very true, aunt," said Miss Tina. "I think it does you good."

"Isn't it touching, the solicitude we each have that the other shall enjoy herself?" sneered Miss Bordereau. "If you think me brilliant to-day you don't know what you are talking about; you've never seen an agreeable woman. What do you people know about good society?" she cried; but before I could tell her, "Don't try to pay me a complment; I've been spoiled," she went on. "My door's shut, but you may sometimes knock."

With this she dismissed me and I left the room. The latch closed behind me, but Miss Tina, contrary to my hope, had remained within. I passed slowly across the hall and before taking my way downstairs waited a little. My hope was answered; after a minute my conductress followed me. "That's a delightful idea about the Piazza," I said. "When will you go — to-night, to-morrow?"

She had been disconcerted, as I have mentioned, but I had already perceived, and I was to observe again, that when Miss Tina was embarrassed she didn't — as most women would have in like case — turn away, floundering and hedging, but came closer, as it were, with a deprecating, a clinging appeal to be spared, to be protected. Her attitude was a constant prayer for aid and explanation, and yet no woman in the world could have been less of a comedian. From the moment you were kind to her she depended on you absolutely; her self-consciousness dropped and she took the greatest intimacy, the innocent intimacy that was all she could conceive, for granted. She didn't know, she now declared, what possessed her aunt, who had changed so quickly, who had got some idea. I replied that she must catch the idea and let me have it: we would go and take an ice together at Florian's and she should report while we listened to the band.

"Oh, it will take me a long time to be able to 'report'!" she said rather ruefully; and she could promise me this satisfaction neither for that night nor for the next. I was patient now, however, for I felt I had only to wait; and in fact at the end of the week, one lovely evening after dinner, she stepped into my gondola, to which in honour of the occasion I had attached a second oar.

We swept in the course of five minutes into the Grand Canal; whereupon she uttered a murmur of ecstasy as fresh as if she had been a tourist just arrived. She had forgotten the splendour of the great water-way on a clear summer evening, and how the sense of floating between marble palaces and reflected lights disposed the mind to freedom and ease. We floated long and far, and though my friend gave no high-pitched voice to her glee I was sure of her full surrender. She was more than pleased, she was transported; the whole thing was an immense liberation. The gondola moved with slow strokes, to give her time to enjoy it, and she listened to the plash of the oars, which grew louder and more musically liquid as we passed into narrow canals, as if it were a revelation of Venice. When I asked her how long it was since she had thus floated, she answered: "Oh I don't know; a long time — not since my aunt began to be ill." This was not the only show of her extreme vagueness about the previous years and the line marking off the period of Miss Bordereau's eminence. I was not at liberty to keep her out long, but we took a considerable *giro* before going to the Piazza. I asked her no questions, holding off by design from her life at home and the things I wanted to know; I poured, rather, treasures of information about the objects before and around us into her ears, describing also Florence and Rome, discoursing on the charms and advantages of travel. She reclined, receptive, on the deep leather cushions, turned her eyes conscientiously to every-thing I noted and never mentioned to me till some time afterwards that she might be supposed to know Florence better than I, as she had lived there for years with her kinswoman. At last she said with the shy impatience of a child: "Are we not really going to the Piazza? That's what I want to see!" I immediately gave the order that we should go straight, after which we sat silent with the expectation of arrival. As some time still passed, however, she broke out of her own movement: "I've found out what's the matter with my aunt: she's afraid you'll go!"

I quite gasped. "What has put that into her head?"

"She has had an idea you've not been happy. That's why she is different now."

"You mean she wants to make me happier?"

"Well, she wants you not to go. She wants you to stay."

"I suppose you mean on account of the rent," I remarked candidly.

Miss Tina's candour but profited. "Yes, you know; so that I shall have more."

"How much does she want you to have?" I asked with all the gaiety I now felt. "She ought to fix the sum, so that I may stay till it's made up."

"Oh that wouldn't please me," said Miss Tina. "It would be unheard of, your taking that trouble."

"But suppose I should have my own reasons for staying in Venice?"

"Then it would be better for you to stay in some other house."

"And what would your aunt say to that?"

"She wouldn't like it at all. But I should think you'd do well to give up your reasons and go away altogether."

"Dear Miss Tina," I said, "it's not so easy to give up my reasons!"

She made no immediate answer to this, but after a moment broke out afresh: "I think I know what your reasons are!"

"I dare say, because the other night I almost told you how I wished you'd help me to make them good."

"I can't do that without being false to my aunt."

"What do you mean by being false to her?"

"Why she would never consent to what you want. She has been asked, she has been written to. It makes her fearfully angry."

"Then she *has* papers of value" I precipitately cried.

"Oh she has everything!" sighed Miss Tina, with a curious weariness, a sudden lapse into gloom.

These words caused all my pulses to throb, for I regarded them as precious evidence. I felt them too deeply to speak, and in the interval the gondola approached the Piazzetta. After we had disembarked I asked my companion if she would rather walk round the square or go and sit before the great café; to which she replied that she would do whichever I liked best — I must only remember again how little time she had. I assured her there was plenty to do both, and we made the circuit of the long arcades. Her spirits revived at the sight of the bright shop-windows, and she lingered and stopped, admiring or disapproving of their contents, asking me what I thought of things, theorizing about prices. My attention wandered from her; her words of a while before "Oh she has everything!" echoed so in my consciousness. We sat down at last in the crowded circle at Florian's, finding an unoccupied table among those that were ranged in the square. It was a splendid night and all the world out-of-doors; Miss Tina couldn't have wished the elements more auspicious for her return to society. I saw she felt it all even more than she told, but her impressions were well-nigh too many for her. She had forgotten the attraction of the world and was learning that she had for the best years of her life been rather mercilessly cheated of it. This didn't make her angry; but as she took in the charming scene her face had, in spite of its smile of appreciation, the flush of a wounded surprise. She didn't speak, sunk in the sense of opportunities, for ever lost, that ought to have been easy; and this gave me a chance to say to her: "Did you mean a while ago that your aunt has a plan of keeping me on by admitting me occasionally to her presence?"

"She thinks it will make a difference with you if you sometimes see her. She wants you so much to stay that she's willing to make that concession."

"And what good does she consider I think it will do me to see her?"

"I don't know; it must be interesting," said Miss Tina simply. "You told her you found it so."

"So I did; but every one doesn't think that."

"No, of course not, or more people would try."

"Well, if she's capable of making that reflexion she's capable also of making this further one," I went on: "that I must have a particular reason for not doing as others do, in spite of the interest she offers — for not leaving her alone." Miss Tina looked as if she failed to grasp this rather complicated proposition; so I continued: "If you've not told her what I said to you the other night may she not at least have guessed it?"

"I don't know — she's very suspicious."

"But she hasn't been made so by indiscreet curiosity, by persecution?"

"No, no; it isn't that," said Miss Tina, turning on me a troubled face. "I don't know how to say it; it's on account of something — ages ago, before I was born — in her life."

"Something? What sort of thing?" — and I asked it as if I could have no idea.

"Oh she has never told me." And I was sure my friend spoke the truth.

Her extreme limpidity was almost provoking, and I felt for the moment that she would have been more satisfactory if she had been less ingenuous. "Do you suppose it's something to which Jeffrey Aspern's letters and papers — I mean the things in her possession — have reference?"

"I dare say it is!" my companion exclaimed as if this were a very happy suggestion. "I've never looked at any of those things."

"None of them? Then how do you know what they are?"

"I don't," said Miss Tina placidly. "I've never had them in my hands. But I've seen them when she has had them out."

"Does she have them out often?"

"Not now, but she used to. She's very fond of them."

"In spite of their being compromising?"

"Compromising?" Miss Tina repeated as if vague as to what that meant. I felt almost as one who corrupts the innocence of youth.

"I allude to their containing painful memories."

"Oh I don't think anything's painful."

"You mean there's nothing to affect her reputation?"

An odder look even than usual came at this into the face of Miss Bordereau's niece — a confession, it seemed, of helplessness, an appeal to me to deal fairly, generously with her. I had brought her to the Piazza, placed her among charming influences, paid her an attention she appreciated, and now I appeared to show it all as a bribe — a bribe to make her turn in some way against her aunt. She was of a yielding nature and capable of doing almost anything to please a person markedly kind to her; but the greatest kindness of all would be not to presume too much on this. It was strange enough, as I afterwards thought, that she had not the least air of resenting my want of consideration for her aunt's character, which would have been in the worst possible taste if anything less vital — from my point of view — had been at stake. I don't think she really measured it. "Do you mean she ever did something bad?" she asked in a moment.

"Heaven forbid I should say so, and it's none of my business. Besides, if she did," I agreeably put it, "that was in other ages, in another world. But why shouldn't she destroy her papers?"

"Oh she loves them too much."

"Even now, when she may be near her end?"

"Perhaps when she's sure of that she will."

"Well, Miss Tina," I said, "that's just what I should like you to prevent."

"How can I prevent it?"

"Couldn't you get them away from her?"

"And give them to you?"

This put the case, superficially, with sharp irony, but I was sure of her not intending that. "Oh I mean that you might let me see them and look them over. It isn't for myself, or that I should want them at any cost to anyone else. It's simply that they would be of such immense interest to the public, such immeasurable importance as a contribution to Jeffrey Aspern's history."

She listened to me in her usual way, as if I abounded in matters she had never heard of, and I felt almost as base as the reporter of a newspaper who forces his way into a house of mourning. This was marked when she presently said: "There was a gentleman who some time ago wrote to her in very much those words. He also wanted her papers."

"And did she answer him?" I asked, rather ashamed of not having my friend's rectitude.

"Only when he had written two or three times. He made her very angry."

"And what did she say?"

"She said he was a devil," Miss Tina replied categorically.

"She used that expression in her letter?"

"Oh no; she said it to me. She made me write to him."

"And what did you say?"

"I told him there were no papers at all."

"Ah poor gentleman!" I groaned.

"I knew there were, but I wrote what she bade me."

"Of course you had to do that. But I hope I shan't pass for a devil."

"It will depend upon what you ask me to do for you," my companion smiled.

"Oh if there's a chance of *your* thinking so my affair's in a bad way! I shan't ask you to steal for me, nor even to fib — for you *can't* fib, unless on paper. But the principal thing is this — to prevent her destroying the papers."

"Why I've no control of her," said Miss Tina. "It's she who controls me."

"But she doesn't control her own arms and legs, does she? The way she would naturally destroy her letters would be to burn them. Now she can't burn them without fire, and she can't get fire unless you give it to her."

"I've always done everything she has asked," my poor friend pleaded. "Besides, there's Olimpia."

I was on the point of saying that Olimpia was probably corruptible, but I thought it best not to sound that note. So I simply put it that this frail creature might perhaps be managed.

"Every one can be managed by my aunt," said Miss Tina. And then she remembered that her holiday was over; she must go home.

I laid my hand on her arm, across the table, to stay her a moment. "What I want of you is a general promise to help me."

"Oh how *can* I, how *can* I?" she asked, wondering and troubled.

She was half-surprised, half-frightened at my attaching that importance to her, at my calling on her for action.

"This is the main thing: to watch our friend carefully and warn me in time, before she commits that dreadful sacrilege."

"I can't watch her when she makes me go out."

"That's very true."

"And when you do too."

"Mercy on us — do you think she'll have done anything to-night?"

"I don't know. She's very cunning."

"Are you trying to frighten me?" I asked.

I felt this question sufficiently answered when my companion murmured in a musing, almost envious way: "Oh but she loves them — she loves them!"

This reflexion, repeated with such emphasis, gave me great comfort; but to obtain more of that balm I said: "If she shouldn't intend to destroy the objects we speak of before her death she'll probably have made some disposition by will."

"By will?"

"Hasn't she made a will for your benefit?"

"Ah she has so little to leave. That's why she likes money," said Miss Tina.

"Might I ask, since we're really talking things over, what you and she live on?"

"On some money that comes from America, from a gentleman — I think a lawyer — in New York. He sends it every quarter. It isn't much!"

"And won't she have disposed of that?"

My companion hesitated — I saw she was blushing. "I believe it's mine," she said; and the look and tone which accompanied these words betrayed so the absence of the habit of thinking of herself that I almost thought her charming. The next instant she added: "But she had in an *avvocato* here once, ever so long ago. And some people came and signed something."

"They were probably witnesses. And you weren't asked to sign? Well then," I argued, rapidly and hopefully, "it's because you're the legatee. She must have left all her documents to you!"

"If she has it's with very strict conditions," Miss Tina responded, rising quickly, while the movement gave the words a small character of decision. They seemed to imply that the bequest would be accompanied with a proviso that the articles bequeathed should remain concealed from every inquisitive eye, and that I was very much mistaken if I thought her the person to depart from an injunction so absolute.

"Oh of course you'll have to abide by the terms," I said; and she uttered nothing to mitigate the rigour of this conclusion. None the less, later on, just before we disembarked at her own door after a return which had taken place almost in silence, she said to me abruptly: "I'll do what I can to help you." I was grateful for this — it was very well so far as it went; but it didn't keep me from remembering that night in a worried waking hour that I now had her word for it to re-enforce my own impression that the old woman was full of craft.

VII

The fear of what this side of her character might have led her to do made me nervous for days afterwards. I waited for an intimation from Miss Tina; I almost read it as her duty to keep me informed, to let me know definitely whether or no Miss Bordereau had sacrificed her treasures. But as she gave no sign I lost patience and determined to put the case to the very touch of my own senses. I sent late one afternoon to ask if I might pay the ladies a visit, and my servant came back with surprising news. Miss Bordereau could be approached without the least difficulty; she had been moved out into the sala and was sitting by the window that overlooked the garden. I descended and found this picture correct; the old lady had been wheeled forth into the world and had a certain air, which came mainly perhaps from some brighter element in her dress, of being prepared again to have converse with it. It had not yet, however, begun to flock about her; she was perfectly alone and, though the door leading to her own quarters stood open, I had at first no glimpse of Miss Tina. The window at which she sat had the afternoon shade and, one of the shutters having been pushed back, she could see the pleasant garden, where the summer sun had by this time dried up too many of the plants — she could see the yellow light and the long shadows.

"Have you come to tell me you'll take the rooms for six months more?" she asked as I approached her, startling me by something coarse in her cupidity almost as much as if she hadn't already given me a specimen of it. Juliana's desire to make our acquaintance lucrative had been, as I have sufficiently indicated, a false note in my image of the woman who had inspired a great poet with immortal lines; but I may say here definitely that I after all recognised large allowance to be made for her. It was I who had kindled the unholy flame; it was I who had put into her head that she had the means of making money. She appeared never to have thought of that; she had been living wastefully for years, in a house five times too big for her, on a footing that I could explain only by the presumption that, excessive as it was, the space she enjoyed cost her next to nothing and that, small as were her revenues, they left her, for Venice, an appreciable margin. I had descended on her one day and taught her to calculate, and my almost extravagant comedy on the subject of the garden had presented me irresistibly in the light of a victim. Like all persons who achieve the miracle of changing their point of view late in life, she had been intensely converted; she had seized my hint with a desperate tremulous clutch.

I invited myself to go and get one of the chairs that stood, at a distance, against the wall — she had given herself no concern as to whether I should sit or stand; and while I placed it near her I began gaily: "Oh dear madam, what an imagination you have, what an intellectual sweep! I'm a poor devil of a man of letters who lives from day to day. How can I take palaces by the year? My existence is precarious. I don't know whether six months hence I shall have bread to put in my mouth. I've treated myself for once; it has been an immense luxury. But when it comes to going on ——!"

"Are your rooms too dear? If they are you can have more for the same money," Juliana responded. "We can arrange, we can *combinare*, as they say here."

"Well yes, since you ask me, they're too dear, much too dear," I said. "Evidently you suppose me richer than I am."

She looked at me as from the mouth of her cave. "If you write books don't you sell them?"

"Do you mean don't people buy them? A little, a very little — not so much as I could wish. Writing books, unless one be a great genius — and even then! — is the last road to fortune. I think there's no more money to be made by good letters."

"Perhaps you don't choose nice subjects. What do you write about?" Miss Bordereau implacably pursued.

"About the books of other people. I'm a critic, a commentator, an historian, in a small way." I wondered what she was coming to.

"And what other people now?"

"Oh better ones than myself: the great writers mainly — the great philosophers and poets of the past; those who are dead and gone and can't, poor darlings, speak for themselves."

"And what do you say about them?"

"I say they sometimes attached themselves to very clever women!" I replied as for pleasantness. I had measured, as I thought, my risk, but as my words fell upon the air they were to strike me as imprudent. However, I had launched them and I wasn't sorry, for perhaps after all the old woman would be willing to treat. It seemed tolerably obvious that she knew my secret; why therefore drag the process out? But she didn't take what I had said as a confession; she only asked:

"Do you think it's right to rake up the past?"

"I don't feel that I know what you mean by raking it up. How can we get at it unless we dig a little? The present has such a rough way of treading it down."

"Oh I like the past, but I don't like critics," my hostess declared with her hard complacency.

"Neither do I, but I like their discoveries."

"Aren't they mostly lies?"

"The lies are what they sometimes discover," I said, smiling at the quiet impertinence of this. "They often lay bare the truth."

"The truth is God's, it isn't man's; we had better leave it alone. Who can judge of it? — who can say?"

"We're terribly in the dark, I know," I admitted; "but if we give up trying what becomes of all the fine things? What becomes of the work I just mentioned, that of the great philosophers and poets? It's all vain words if there's nothing to measure it by."

"You talk as if you were a tailor," said Miss Bordereau whimsically; and then she added quickly and in a different manner: "This house is very fine; the proportions are magnificent. To-day I wanted to look at this part again. I made them bring me out here. When your man came just now to learn if I would see you I was on the point of sending for you to ask if you didn't mean to go on. I wanted to judge what I'm letting you have. This sala is very grand," she pursued like an auctioneer, moving a little, as I guessed, her invisible eyes. "I don't believe you often have lived in such a house, eh?"

"I can't often afford to!" I said.

"Well then how much will you give me for six months?"

I was on the point of exclaiming — and the air of excrucation in my face would have denoted a moral fact — "Don't, Juliana; for *his* sake, don't!" But I controlled myself and asked less passionately: "Why should I remain so long as that?"

"I thought you liked it," said Miss Bordereau with her shrivelled dignity.

"So I thought I should."

For a moment she said nothing more, and I left my own words to suggest to her what they might. I half-expected her to say, coldly enough, that if I had been disappointed we needn't continue the discussion, and this in spite of the fact that I believed her now to have in her mind — however it had come there — what would have told her that my disappointment was natural. But to my extreme surprise she ended by observing: "If you don't think we've treated you well enough perhaps we can discover some way of treating you better." This speech was somehow so incongruous that it made me laugh again, and I excused myself by saying that she talked as if I were a sulky boy pouting in the corner and having to be "brought round." I hadn't a grain of complaint to make; and could anything have exceeded Miss Tina's graciousness in accompanying me a few nights before to the Piazza? At this the old woman went on: "Well, you brought it on yourself!" And then in a different tone: "She's a very fine girl." I assented cordially to this proposition, and she expressed the hope that I did so not merely to be obliging, but that I really liked her. Meanwhile I wondered still more what Miss Bordereau was coming to. "Except for me, to-day," she said, "she hasn't a relation in the world." Did she by describing her niece as amiable and unencumbered wish to represent her as a *parti?*

It was perfectly true that I couldn't afford to go on with my rooms at a fancy price and that I had already devoted to my undertaking almost all the hard cash I had set apart for it. My patience and my time were by no means exhausted, but I should be able to draw upon them only on a more usual Venetian basis. I was willing to pay the precious personage with whom my pecuniary dealings were such a discord twice as much as any other *padrona di casa* would have asked, but I wasn't willing to pay her twenty times as much. I told her so plainly, and my plainness appeared to have some success, for she exclaimed: "Very good; you've done what I asked — you've made an offer!"

"Yes, but not for half a year. Only by the month."

"Oh I must think of that then." She seemed disappointed that I wouldn't tie myself to a period, and I guessed that she wished both to secure me and to discourage me; to say severely: "Do you dream that you can get off with less than six months? Do you dream that even by the end of that time you'll be appreciably nearer your victory?" What was most in my mind was that she had a fancy to play me the trick of making me engage myself when in fact she had sacrificed her treasure. There was a moment when my suspense on this point was so acute that I all but broke out with the question, and what kept it back was but an instinctive recoil — lest it should be a mistake — from the last violence of self-exposure. She was such a subtle old witch that one could never tell where one stood with her. You may imagine whether it cleared up the puzzle when, just after she had said she would think of my proposal and without any formal transition, she drew out of her pocket with an embarrassed hand a small object wrapped in crumpled white paper. She held it there a moment and then resumed: "Do you know much about curiosities?"

"About curiosities?"

"About antiquities, the old gimcracks that people pay so much for to-day. Do you know the kind of price they bring?"

I thought I saw what was coming, but I said ingenuously: "Do you want to buy something?"

"No, I want to sell. What would an amateur give me for that?" She unfolded the white paper and made a motion for me to take from her a small oval portrait. I possessed myself of it with fingers of which I could only hope that they didn't betray the intensity of their clutch, and she added: "I would part with it only for a good price."

At the first glance I recognized Jeffrey Aspern, and was well aware that I flushed with the act. As she was watching me however I had the consistency to exclaim: "What a striking face! Do tell me who it is."

"He's an old friend of mine, a very distinguished man in his day. He gave it me himself, but I'm afraid to mention his name, lest you never should have heard of him, critic and historian as you are. I know the world goes fast and one generation forgets another. He was all the fashion when I was young."

She was perhaps amazed at my assurance, but I was surprised at hers; at her having the energy, in her state of health and at her time of life, to wish to sport with me to that tune simply for her private entertainment — the humour to test me and practise on me and befool me. This at least was the interpretation that I put upon her production of the relic, for I couldn't believe she really desired to sell it or cared for any information I might give her. What she wished was to dangle it before my eyes and put a prohibitive price on it. "The face comes back to me, it torments me," I said, turning the object this way and that and looking at it very critically. It was a careful but not a supreme work of art, larger than the ordinary miniature and representing a young man with a remarkably handsome face, in a high-collared green coat and a buff waistcoat. I felt in the little work a virtue of likeness and judged it to have been painted when the model was about twenty-five. There are, as all the world knows, three other portraits of the poet in existence, but none of so early a date as this elegant image. "I've never seen the original, clearly a man of a past age, but I've seen other reproductions of this face," I went on. "You expressed doubt of this generation's having heard of the gentleman, but he strikes me for all the world as a celebrity. Now who is he? I can't put my finger on him — I can't give him a label. Wasn't he a writer? Surely he's a poet." I was determined that it should be she, not I, who should first pronounce Jeffrey Aspern's name.

My resolution was taken in ignorance of Miss Bordereau's extremely resolute character, and her lips never formed in my hearing the syllables that meant so much for her. She neglected to answer my question, but raised her hand to take back the picture, using a gesture which though impotent was in a high degree peremptory. "It's only a person who should know for himself that would give me my price," she said with a certain dryness.

"Oh then you have a price?" I didn't restore the charming thing; not from any vindictive purpose, but because I instinctively clung to it. We looked at each other hard while I retained it.

"I know the least I would take. What it occurred to me to ask you about is the most I shall be able to get."

She made a movement, drawing herself together as if, in a spasm of dread at having lost her prize she had been impelled to the immense effort of rising to snatch it from me. I instantly placed it in her hand again, saying as I did so: "I should like to have it myself, but with your ideas it would be quite beyond my mark."

She turned the small oval plate over in her lap, with its face down, and I heard her catch her breath as after a strain or an escape. This however did not prevent her saying in a moment: "You'd buy a likeness of a person you don't know by an artist who has no reputation?"

"The artist may have no reputation, but that thing's wonderfully well painted," I replied, to give myself a reason.

"It's lucky you thought of saying that, because the painter was my father."

"That makes the picture indeed precious!" I returned with gaiety; and I may add that a part of my cheer came from this proof I had been right in my theory of Miss Bordereau's origin. Aspern had of course met the young lady on his going to her father's studio as a sitter. I observed to Miss Bordereau that if she would entrust me with her property for twenty-four hours I should be happy to take advice on it; but she made no other reply than to slip it in silence into her pocket. This convinced me still more that she had no sincere intention of selling it during her lifetime, though she may have desired to satisfy herself as to the sum her niece, should she leave it to her, might expect eventually to obtain for it. "Well, at any rate, I hope you won't offer it without giving me notice," I said as she remained irresponsive. "Remember me as a possible purchaser."

"I should want your money first!" she returned with unexpected rudeness; and then, as if she bethought herself that I might well complain of such a tone and wished to turn the matter off, asked abruptly what I talked about with her niece when I went out with her that way of an evening.

"You speak as if we had set up the habit," I replied. "Certainly I should be very glad if it were to become our pleasant custom. But in that case I should feel a still greater scruple at betraying a lady's confidence."

"Her confidence? Has my niece confidence?"

"Here she is — she can tell you herself," I said; for Miss Tina now appeared on the threshold of the old woman's parlour. "Have you confidence, Miss Tina? Your aunt wants very much to know."

"Not in her, not in her!" the younger lady declared, shaking her head with a dolefulness that was neither jocular nor affected. "I don't know what to do with her; she has fits of horrid imprudence. She's so easily tired — and yet she has begun to roam, to drag herself about the house." And she looked down at her yoke-fellow of long years with a vacancy of wonder, as if all their contact and custom hadn't made her perversities, on occasion, any more easy to follow.

"I know what I'm about. I'm not losing my mind. I dare say you'd like to think so," said Miss Bordereau with a crudity of cynicism.

"I don't suppose you came out here yourself. Miss Tina must have had to lend you a hand," I interposed for conciliation.

"Oh she insisted we should push her; and when she insists!" said Miss Tina, in the same tone of apprehension; as if there were no knowing what service she disapproved of her aunt might force her next to render.

"I've always got most things done I wanted, thank God! The people I've lived with have humoured me," the old woman continued, speaking out of the white ashes of her vanity.

I took it pleasantly up. "I suppose you mean they've obeyed you."

"Well, whatever it is — when they like one."

"It's just because I like you that I want to resist," said Miss Tina with a nervous laugh.

"Oh I suspect you'll bring Miss Bordereau upstairs next to pay me a visit," I went on; to which the old lady replied:

"Oh no; I can keep an eye on you from here!"

"You're very tired; you'll certainly be ill to-night!" cried Miss Tina.

"Nonsense, dear; I feel better at this moment than I've done for a month. To-morrow I shall come out again. I want to be where I can see this clever gentleman."

"Shouldn't you perhaps see me better in your sitting-room?" I asked.

"Don't you mean shouldn't you have a better chance at *me?*" she returned, fixing me a moment with her green shade.

"Ah I haven't that anywhere! I look at you but don't see you."

"You agitate her dreadfully — and that's not good," said Miss Tina, giving me a reproachful deterrent headshake.

"I want to watch you — I want to watch you!" Miss Bordereau went on.

"Well then let us spend as much of our time together as possible — I don't care where. That will give you every facility."

"Oh I've seen you enough for to-day. I'm satisfied. Now I'll go home," Juliana said. Miss Tina laid her hands on the back of the wheeled chair and began to push, but I begged her to let me take her place. "Oh yes, you may move me this way — you shan't in any other!" the old woman cried as she felt herself propelled firmly and easily over the smooth hard floor. Before we reached the door of her own apartment she bade me stop, and she took a long last look up and down the noble sala. "Oh it's a prodigious house!" she murmured; after which I pushed her forward. When we had entered the parlour Miss Tina let me know she should now be able to manage, and at the same moment the little red-haired *donna* came to meet her mistress. Miss Tina's idea was evidently to get her aunt immediately back to bed. I confess that in spite of this urgency I was guilty of the indiscretion of lingering; it held me there to feel myself so close to the objects I coveted — which would be probably put away somewhere in the faded unsociable room. The place had indeed a bareness that suggested no hidden values; there were neither dusky nooks nor curtained corners, neither massive cabinets nor chests with iron bands. Moreover it was possible, it was perhaps even likely, that the old lady had consigned her relics to her bedroom, to some battered box that was shoved under the bed, to the drawer of some lame dressing-table, where they would be in the range of vision by the dim night-lamp. None the less I turned an eye on every article of furniture, on every conceivable cover for a hoard, and noticed that there were half a dozen things with drawers, and in particular a tall old secretary with brass ornaments of the style of the Empire — a receptacle somewhat infirm but still capable of keeping rare secrets. I don't know why this article so engaged me, small purpose as I had of breaking into it; but I stared at it so hard that Miss Tina noticed me and changed colour. Her doing this made me think I was right and that, wherever they might have been before, the Aspern papers at that moment languished behind the peevish little lock of the secretary. It was hard to turn my attention from the dull mahogany front when I reflected that a plain panel divided me from the goal of my hopes; but I gathered up my slightly scattered prudence and with an effort took leave of my hostess. To make the effort graceful I said to her that I should certainly bring her an opinion about the little picture.

"The little picture?" Miss Tina asked in surprise.

"What do *you* know about it, my dear?" the old woman demanded. "You needn't mind. I've fixed my price."

"And what may that be?"

"A thousand pounds."

"Oh Lord!" cried poor Miss Tina irrepressibly.

"Is that what she talks to you about?" said Miss Bordereau.

"Imagine your aunt's wanting to know!" I had to separate from my younger friend with only those words, though I should have liked immensely to add: "For heaven's sake meet me to-night in the garden!"

VIII

As it turned out the precaution had not been needed, for three hours later, just as I had finished my dinner, Miss Tina appeared, unannounced, in the open doorway of the room in which my simple repasts were served. I remember well that I felt no surprise at seeing her; which is not a proof of my not believing in her timidity. It was immense, but in a case in which there was a particular reason for boldness it never would have prevented her from running up to my floor. I saw that she was now quite full of a particular reason; it threw her forward — made her seize me, as I rose to meet her, by the arm.

"My aunt's very ill; I think she's dying!"

"Never in the world," I answered bitterly. "Don't you be afraid!"

"Do go for a doctor — do, do! Olimpia's gone for the one we always have, but she doesn't come back; I don't know what has happened to her. I told her that if he wasn't at home she was to follow him where he had gone; but apparently she's following him all over Venice. I don't know what to do — she looks so as if she were sinking."

"May I see her, may I judge?" I asked. "Of course I shall be delighted to bring some one; but hadn't we better send my man instead, so that I may stay with you?"

Miss Tina assented to this and I dispatched my servant for the best doctor in the neighbourhood. I hurried downstairs with her, and on the way she told me that an hour after I quitted them in the afternoon Miss Bordereau had had an attack of "oppression," a terrible difficulty in breathing. This had subsided, but had left her so exhausted that she didn't come up: she seemed all spent and gone. I repeated that she wasn't gone, that she wouldn't go yet; whereupon Miss Tina gave me a sharper sidelong glance than she had ever favoured me withal and said: "Really, what do you mean? I suppose you don't accuse her of making-believe!" I forget what reply I made to this, but I fear that in my heart I thought the old woman capable of any weird manœuvre. Miss Tina wanted to know what I had done to her; her aunt had told her I had made her so angry. I declared I had done nothing whatever — I had been exceedingly careful; to which my companion rejoined that our friend had assured her she had had a scene with me — a scene that had upset her. I answered with some resentment that the scene had been of *her* making

— that I couldn't think what she was angry with me for unless for not seeing my way to give a thousand pounds for the portrait of Jeffrey Aspern. "And did she show you that? Oh gracious — oh deary me!" groaned Miss Tina, who seemed to feel the situation pass out of her control and the elements of her fate thicken round her. I answered her I'd give anything to possess it, yet that I had no thousand pounds; but I stopped when we came to the door of Miss Bordereau's room. I had an immense curiosity to pass it, but I thought it my duty to represent to Miss Tina that if I made the invalid angry she ought perhaps to be spared the sight of me. "The sight of you? Do you think she can *see?*" my companion demanded, almost with indignation. I did think so but forebore to say it, and I softly followed my conductress.

I remember that what I said to her as I stood for a moment beside the old woman's bed was: "Does she never show you her eyes then? Have you never seen them?" Miss Bordereau had been divested of her green shade, but — it was not my fortune to behold Juliana in her nightcap — the upper half of her face was covered by the fall of a piece of dingy lacelike muslin, a sort of extemporised hood which, wound round her head, descended to the end of her nose, leaving nothing visible but her white withered cheeks and puckered mouth, closed tightly and, as it were, consciously. Miss Tina gave me a glance of surprise, evidently not seeing a reason for my impatience. "You mean she always wears something? She does it to preserve them."

"Because they're so fine?"

"Oh to-day, to-day!" And Miss Tina shook her head speaking very low. "But they used to be magnificent!"

"Yes indeed — we've Aspern's word for that." And as I looked again at the old woman's wrappings I could imagine her not having wished to allow any supposition that the great poet had overdone it. But I didn't waste my time in considering Juliana, in whom the appearance of respiration was so slight as to suggest that no human attention could ever help her more. I turned my eyes once more all over the room, rummaging with them the closets, the chests of drawers, the tables. Miss Tina at once noted their direction and read, I think, what was in them; but she didn't answer it, turning away restlessly, anxiously, so that I felt rebuked, with reason, for an appetite well-nigh indecent in the presence of our dying companion. All the same I took another view, endeavouring to pick out mentally the receptacle to try first, for a person who should wish to put his hand on Miss Bordereau's papers directly after her death. The place was a dire confusion; it looked like the dressing-room of an old actress. There were clothes hanging over chairs, odd-looking shabby bundles here and there, and various pasteboard boxes piled together, battered, bulging and discoloured, which might have been fifty years old. Miss Tina after a moment noticed the direction of my eyes again, and, as if she guessed how I judged such appearances — forgetting I had no business to judge them at all — said, perhaps to defend herself from the imputation of complicity in the disorder:

"She likes it this way; we can't move things. There are old band-boxes she has had most of her life." Then she added, half-taking pity on my real thought: "Those things were *there.*" And she pointed to a small low trunk which stood under a sofa that just allowed room for it. It struck me as a queer superannuated coffer, of painted wood, with elaborate handles and shrivelled straps and with the colour — it had last been endued with a coat of light green — much rubbed off. It evidently had travelled with Juliana in the olden time — in the days of her adventures, which it had shared. It would have made a strange figure arriving at a modern hotel.

"*Were* there — they aren't now?" I asked, startled by Miss Tina's implication.

She was going to answer, but at that moment the doctor came in — the doctor whom the little maid had been sent to fetch and whom she had at last overtaken. My servant, going on his own errand, had met her with her companion in tow, and in the sociable Venetian spirit, retracing his steps with them, had also come up to the threshold of the padrona's room, where I saw him peep over the doctor's shoulder. I motioned him away the more instantly that the sight of his prying face reminded me how little I myself had to do there — an admonition confirmed by the sharp way the little doctor eyed me, his air of taking me for a rival who had the field before him. He was a short fat brisk gentleman who wore the tall hat of his profession and seemed to look at everything but his patient. He kept me still in range, as if it struck him I too should be better for a dose, so that I bowed to him and left him with the women, going down to smoke a cigar in the garden. I was nervous; I couldn't go further; I couldn't leave the place. I don't know exactly what I thought might happen, but I felt it important to be there. I wandered about the alleys — the warm night had come on — smoking cigar after cigar and studying the light in Miss Bordereau's windows. They were open now, I could see; the situation was different. Sometimes the light moved, but not quickly; it didn't suggest the hurry of a crisis. Was the old woman dying or was she already dead? Had the doctor said that there was nothing to be done at her tremendous age but to let her quietly pass away? or had he simply announced with a look a little more conventional that the end of the end had come? Were the other two women just going and coming over the offices that follow in such a case? It made me uneasy not to be nearer, as if I thought the doctor himself might carry away the papers with him. I bit my cigar hard while it assailed me again that perhaps there were now no papers to carry!

I wandered about an hour and more. I looked out for Miss Tina at one of the windows, having a vague idea that she might come there to give me some sign. Wouldn't she see the red tip of my cigar in the dark and feel sure I was hanging on to know what the doctor had said? I'm afraid it's a proof of the grossness of my anxieties that I should have taken in some degree for granted at such an hour, in the midst of the greatest change that could fall on her, poor Miss Tina's having also a free mind for them. My servant came down and spoke to me; he knew nothing save that the doctor had gone after a visit of half an hour. If he had stayed half an hour then Miss Bordereau was still alive: it couldn't have taken so long to attest her decease. I sent the man out of the house; there were moments when the sense of his curiosity annoyed me, and this was one of them. *He* had been watching my cigar-tip from an upper window, if Miss Tina hadn't; he couldn't know what I was after and I couldn't tell him, though I suspected in him fantastic private theories about me which he thought fine and which, had I more exactly known them, I should have thought offensive.

I went upstairs at last, but I mounted no higher than the sala. The door of Miss Bordereau's apartment was open, showing from the parlour the dimness of a poor candle. I went toward it with a light tread, and at the same moment Miss Tina appeared and stood looking at me as I approached. "She's better, she's better," she said even before I had asked. "The doctor has given her something; she woke up, came back to life while he was there. He says there's no immediate danger."

"No immediate danger? Surely he thinks her condition serious!"

"Yes, because she had been excited. That affects her dreadfully."

"It will do so again then, because she works herself up. She did so this afternoon."

"Yes, she mustn't come out any more," said Miss Tina with one of her lapses into a deeper detachment.

"What's the use of making such a remark as that," I permitted myself to ask, "if you begin to rattle her about again the first time she bids you?"

"I won't — I won't do it any more."

"You must learn to resist her," I went on.

"Oh yes, I shall; I shall do so better if you tell me it's right."

"You mustn't do it for me — you must do it for yourself. It all comes back to you, if you're scared and upset."

"Well, I'm not upset now," said Miss Tina placidly enough. "She's very quiet."

"Is she conscious again — does she speak?"

"No, she doesn't speak, but she takes my hand. She holds it fast."

"Yes," I returned, "I can see what force she still has by the way she grabbed that picture this afternoon. But if she holds you fast how comes it that you're here?"

Miss Tina waited a little; though her face was in deep shadow — she had her back to the light in the parlour and I had put down my own candle far off, near the door of the sala — I thought I saw her smile ingenuously. "I came on purpose — I had heard your step."

"Why I came on tiptoe, as soundlessly as possible."

"Well, I had heard you," said Miss Tina.

"And is your aunt alone now?"

"Oh no — Olimpia sits there."

On my side I debated. "Shall we then pass in there?" And I nodded at the parlour; I wanted more and more to be on the spot.

"We can't talk there — she'll hear us."

I was on the point of replying that in that case we'd sit silent, but I felt too much this wouldn't do, there was something I desired so immensely to ask her. Thus I hinted we might walk a little in the sala, keeping more at the other end, where we shouldn't disturb our friend. Miss Tina assented unconditionally; the doctor was coming again, she said, and she would be there to meet him at the door. We strolled through the fine superfluous hall, where on the marble floor — particularly as at first we said nothing — our footsteps were more audible than I had expected. When we reached the other end — the wide window, inveterately closed, connecting with the balcony that overhung the canal — I submitted that we had best remain there, as she would see the doctor arrive the sooner. I opened the window and we passed out on the balcony. The air of the canal seemed even heavier, hotter than that of the sala. The place was hushed and void; the quiet neighborhood had gone to sleep. A lamp, here and there, over the narrow black water, glimmered in double; the voice of a man going homeward singing, his jacket on his shoulder and his hat on his ear, came to us from a distance. This didn't prevent the scene from being very *comme il faut*, as Miss Bordereau had called it the first time I saw her. Presently a gondola passed along the canal with its slow rhythmical plash, and as we listened we watched it in silence. It didn't stop, it didn't carry the doctor; and after it had gone on I said to Miss Tina:

"And where are they now — the things that were in the trunk?"

"In the trunk?"

"That green box you pointed out to me in her room. You said her papers had been there; you seemed to mean she had transferred them."

"Oh yes; they're not in the trunk," said Miss Tina.

"May I ask if you've looked?"

"Yes, I've looked — for you."

"How for me, dear Miss Tina? Do you mean you'd have given them to me if you had found them?" — and I fairly trembled with the question.

She delayed to reply and I waited. Suddenly she broke out: "I don't know what I'd do — what I wouldn't!"

"Would you look again — somewhere else?"

She had spoken with a strange unexpected emotion, and she went on in the same tone: "I can't — I can't — while she lies there. It isn't decent."

"No, it isn't decent," I replied gravely. "Let the poor lady rest in peace." And the words, on my lips, were not hypocritical, for I felt reprimanded and shamed.

Miss Tina added in a moment, as if she had guessed this and were sorry for me, but at the same time wished to explain that I did push her, or at least harp on the chord, too much: "I can't deceive her that way. I can't deceive her — perhaps on her deathbed."

"Heaven forbid I should ask you, though I've been guilty myself!"

"You've been guilty?"

"I've sailed under false colours." I felt now I must make a clean breast of it, must tell her I had given her an invented name on account of my fear her aunt would have heard of me and so refuse to take me in. I explained this as well as that I had really been a party to the letter addressed them by John Cumnor months before.

She listened with great attention, almost in fact gaping for wonder, and when I had made my confession she said: "Then your real name — what is it?" She repeated it over twice when I had told her, accompanying it with the exclamation "Gracious, gracious!" Then she added: "I like your own best."

"So do I," — and I felt my laugh rueful. "Ouf! it's a relief to get rid of the other."

"So it was a regular plot — a kind of conspiracy?"

"Oh a conspiracy — we were only two," I replied, leaving out of course Mrs. Prest.

She considered; I thought she was perhaps going to pronounce us very base. But this was not her way, and she remarked after a moment, as in candid impartial contemplation: "How much you must want them!"

"Oh I do, passionately!" I grinned, I fear to admit. And this chance made me go on, forgetting my compunction of a moment before. "How can she possibly have changed their place herself? How can she walk? How can she arrive at that sort of muscular exertion? How can she lift and carry things?"

"Oh when one wants and when one has so much will!" said Miss Tina as if she had thought over my question already herself and had simply had no choice but that answer — the idea that in the dead of night, or at some moment when the coast was clear, the old woman had been capable of a miraculous effort.

"Have you questioned Olimpia? Hasn't she helped her — hasn't she done it for her?" I asked; to which my friend replied promptly and positively that their servant had had nothing to do with the matter, though without admitting definitely that she had spoken to her. It was as if she were a little shy, a little ashamed now, of letting me see how much she had entered into my uneasiness and had me on her mind. Suddenly she said to me without any immediate relevance:

"I rather feel you a new person, you know, now that you've a new name."

"It isn't a new one; it's a very good old one, thank fortune!"

She looked at me a moment. "Well, I do like it better."

"Oh if you didn't I would almost go on with the other!"

"Would you really?"

I laughed again, but I returned for all answer: "Of course if she can rummage about that way she can perfectly have burnt them."

"You must wait — you must wait," Miss Tina mournfully moralised; and her tone ministered little to my patience, for it seemed after all to accept that wretched possibility. I would teach myself to wait, I declared nevertheless; because in the first place I couldn't do otherwise and in the second I had her promise, given me the other night, that she would help me.

"Of course if the papers are gone that's no use," she said; not as if she wished to recede, but only to be conscientious.

"Naturally. But if you could only find out!" I groaned, quivering again.

"I thought you promised you'd wait."

"Oh you mean wait even for that?"

"For what then?"

"Ah, nothing," I answered rather foolishly, being ashamed to tell her what had been implied in my acceptance of delay — the idea that she would perhaps do more for me than merely find out.

I know not if she guessed this; at all events she seemed to bethink herself of some propriety of showing me more rigour. "I didn't promise to deceive, did I? I don't think I did."

"It doesn't much matter whether you did or not, for you couldn't!"

Nothing is more possible than that she wouldn't have contested this even hadn't she been diverted by our seeing the doctor's gondola shoot into the little canal and approach the house. I noted that he came as fast as if he believed our proprietress still in danger. We looked down at him while he disembarked and then went back into the sala to meet him. When he came up, however, I naturally left Miss Tina to go off with him alone, only asking her leave to come back later for news.

I went out of the house and walked far, as far as the Piazza, where my restlessness declined to quit me. I was unable to sit down; it was very late now though there were people still at the little tables in front of the cafés: I could but uneasily revolve, and I did so half a dozen times. The only comfort, none the less, was in my having told Miss Tina who I really was. At last I took my way home again, getting gradually and all but inextricably lost, as I did whenever I went out in Venice: so that it was considerably past midnight when I reached my door. The sala, upstairs, was as dark as usual and my lamp as I crossed it found nothing satisfactory to show me. I was disappointed, for I had notified Miss Tina that I would come back for a report, and I thought she might have left a light there as a sign. The door of the ladies' apartment was closed; which seemed a hint that my faltering friend had gone to bed in impatience of waiting for me. I stood in the middle of the place, considering, hoping she would hear me and perhaps peep out, saying to myself too that she would never go to bed with her aunt in a state so critical; she would sit up and watch — she would be in a chair, in her dressing-gown. I went nearer the door; I stopped there and listened. I heard nothing at all and at last I tapped gently. No answer came and after another minute I turned the handle. There was no light in the room; this ought to have prevented my entrance, but it had no such effect. If I have frankly stated the importunities, the indelicacies of which my desire to possess myself of Jeffrey Aspern's papers had made me capable I needn't shrink, it seems to me, from confessing this last indiscretion. I regard it as the worst thing I did, yet there were extenuating circumstances. I was deeply though doubtless not dis-interestedly anxious for more news of Juliana, and Miss Tina had accepted from me, as it were, a rendezvous which it might have been a point of honour with me to keep. It may be objected that her leav-ing the place dark was a positive sign that she released me, and to this I can only reply that I wished not to be released.

The door to Miss Bordereau's room was open and I could see be-yond it the faintness of a taper. There was no sound — my footstep caused no one to stir. I came further into the room; I lingered there lamp in hand. I wanted to give Miss Tina a chance to come to me if, as I couldn't doubt, she were still with her aunt. I made no noise to call her; I only waited to see if she wouldn't notice my light. She didn't, and I explained this — I found afterwards I was right — by the idea that she had fallen asleep. If she had fallen asleep her aunt was not on her mind, and my explanation ought to have led me to go out as I had come. I must repeat again that it didn't, for I found myself at the same moment given up to something else. I had no definite purpose, no bad intention, but felt myself held to the spot by an acute, though absurd, sense of opportunity. Oppor-tunity for what I couldn't have said, inasmuch as it wasn't in my mind that I might proceed to thievery. Even had this tempted me I was confronted with the evident fact that Miss Bordereau didn't leave her secretary, her cupboard and the drawers of her tables gaping. I had no keys, no tools and no ambition to smash her furniture. None the less it came to me that I was now, perhaps alone, unmolested, at the hour of freedom and safety, nearer to the source of my hopes than I had ever been. I held up my lamp, let the light play on the different objects as if it could tell me something. Still there came no movement from the other room. If Miss Tina was sleeping she was sleeping sound. Was she doing so — generous creature — on purpose to leave me the field? Did she know I was there and was she just keeping quiet to see what I would do — what I *could* do? Yet might I, when it came to that? She herself knew even better than I how little.

I stopped in front of the secretary, gaping at it vainly and no doubt grotesquely; for what had it to say to me after all? In the first place it was locked, and in the second it almost surely contained nothing in which I was interested. Ten to one the papers had been destroyed, and even if they hadn't the keen old woman wouldn't have put them in such a place as that after removing them from the green trunk — wouldn't have transferred them, with the idea of their safety on her brain, for the better hiding-place to the worse. The secretary was more conspicuous, more exposed in a room in which she could no longer mount guard. It opened with a key, but there was a small brass handle, like a button as well; I saw this as I played my lamp over it. I did something more, for the climax of my crisis; I caught a glimpse of the possibility that Miss Tina wished me really to understand. If she didn't so wish me, if she wished me to keep away, why hadn't she locked the door of communication between the sitting-room and the sala? That would have been a definite sign that I was to leave them alone. If I didn't leave them alone she meant me to come for a purpose — a purpose now represented by the super-subtle inference that to oblige me she had unlocked the secretary. She hadn't left the key, but the lid would probably move if I touched the button. This possibility pressed me hard and I bent very close to judge. I didn't propose to do anything, not even — not in the least — to let down the lid; I only wanted to test my theory, to see if the cover *would* move. I touched the button with my hand — a mere touch would tell me; and as I did so — it is embarrassing for me to relate it — I looked over my shoulder. It was a chance, an instinct, for I had really heard nothing. I almost let my luminary drop and certainly I stepped back, straightening myself up at what I saw. Juliana stood there in her nightdress, by the doorway of her room, watching me; her hands were raised, she had lifted the everlasting curtain that covered half her face, and for the first, the last, the only time I beheld her extraordinary eyes. They glared at me; they were like the sudden drench, for a caught burglar, of a flood of gaslight; they made me horribly ashamed. I never shall forget her strange little bent white tottering figure, with its lifted head, her attitude, her expression; neither shall I forget the tone in which as I turned, looking at her, she hissed out passionately, furiously:

"Ah you publishing scoundrel!"

I can't now say what I stammered to excuse myself, to explain, but I went toward her to tell her I meant no harm. She waved me off with her old hands, retreating before me in horror; and the next thing I knew she had fallen back with a quick spasm, as if death had descended on her, into Miss Tina's arms.

IX

I left Venice the next morning, directly on learning that my hostess had not succumbed, as I feared at the moment, to the shock I had given her — the shock I may also say she had given me. How in the world could I have supposed her capable of getting out of bed by herself? I failed to see Miss Tina before going; I only saw the *donna*, whom I entrusted with a note for her younger mistress. In this note I mentioned that I should be absent but a few days. I went to Treviso, to Bassano, to Castelfranco; I took walks and drives and looked at musty old churches with ill-lighted pictures; I spent hours seated smoking at the doors of cafés, where there were flies and yellow curtains, on the shady side of sleepy little squares. In spite of these pasttimes, which were mechanical and perfunctory, I scantly enjoyed my travels: I had had to gulp down a bitter draught and couldn't get rid of the taste. It had been devilish awkward, as the young men say, to be found by Juliana in the dead of night examining the attachment of her bureau; and it had not been less so to have to believe for a good many hours after that it was highly probable I had killed her. My humiliation galled me, but I had to make the best of it, had, in writing to Miss Tina to minimise it, as well as account for the posture in which I had been discovered. As she gave me no word of answer I couldn't know what impression I made on her. It rankled for me that I had been called a publishing scoundrel, since certainly I did publish and no less certainly hadn't been very delicate. There was a moment when I stood convinced that the only way to purge my dishonour was to take myself straight away on the instant; to sacrifice my hopes and relieve the two poor women for ever of the oppression of my intercourse. Then I reflected that I had better try a short absence first, for I must already have had a sense (unexpressed and dim) that in disappearing completely it wouldn't be merely my own hopes I should condemn to extinction. It would perhaps answer if I kept dark long enough to give the elder lady time to believe herself rid of me. That she would wish to be rid of me after this — if I wasn't rid of her — was now not to be doubted: that midnight monstrosity would have cured her of the disposition to put up with my company for the sake of my dollars. I said to myself that after all I couldn't abandon Miss Tina, and I continued to say this even while I noted that she quite ignored my earnest request — I had given her two or three addresses, at little towns, *poste restante* — for some sign of her actual state. I would have made my servant write me news but that he was unable to manage a pen. Couldn't I measure the scorn of Miss Tina's silence — little disdainful as she had ever been? Really the soreness pressed; yet if I had scruples about going back I had others about not doing so, and I wanted to put myself on a better footing. The end of it was that I did return to Venice on the twelfth day; and as my gondola gently bumped against our palace steps a fine palpitation of suspense showed me the violence my absence had done me.

I had faced about so abruptly that I hadn't even telegraphed to my servant. He was therefore not at the station to meet me, but he poked out his head from an upper window when I reached the house. "They have put her into earth, *quella vecchia*," he said to me in the lower hall while he shouldered my valise; and he grinned and almost winked as if he knew I should be pleased with his news.

"She's dead!" I cried, giving him a very different look.

"So it appears, since they've buried her."

"It's all over then? When was the funeral?"

"The other yesterday. But a funeral you could scarcely call it, signore: *roba da niente — un piccolo passeggio brutto* of two gondolas. Poveretta!" the man continued, referring apparently to Miss Tina. His conception of funerals was that they were mainly to amuse the living.

I wanted to know about Miss Tina, how she might be and generally where; but I asked him no more questions till we had got upstairs. Now that the fact had met me I took a bad view of it, especially of the idea that poor Miss Tina had had to manage by herself after the end. What did she know about arrangements, about the steps to take in such a case? Poveretta indeed! I could only hope the doctor had given her support and that she hadn't been neglected by the old friends of whom she had told me, the little band of the faithful whose fidelity consisted in coming to the house once a year. I elicited from my servant that two old ladies and an old gentleman had in fact rallied round Miss Tina and had supported her — they had come for her in a gondola of their own — during the journey to the cemetery, the little red-walled island of tombs which lies to the north of the town and on the way to Murano. It appeared from these signs that the Misses Bordereau were Catholics, a discovery I had never made, as the old woman couldn't go to church and her niece, so far as I perceived, either didn't, or went only to early mass in the parish before I was stirring. Certainly even the priests respected their seclusion; I had never caught the whisk of the curato's skirt. That evening, an hour later, I sent my servant down with five words on a card to ask if Miss Tina would see me for a few moments. She was not in the house, where he had sought her, he told me when he came back, but in the garden walking about to refresh herself and picking the flowers quite as if they belonged to her. He had found her there and she would be happy to see me.

I went down and passed half an hour with poor Miss Tina. She had always had a look of musty mourning, as if she were wearing out old robes of sorrow that wouldn't come to an end; and in this particular she made no different show. But she clearly had been crying, crying a great deal — simply, satisfyingly, refreshingly, with a primitive retarded sense of solitude and violence. But she had none of the airs or graces of grief, and I was almost surprised to see her stand there in the first dusk with her hands full of admirable roses and smile at me with reddened eyes. Her white face, in the frame of her mantilla, looked longer, leaner than usual. I hadn't doubted her being irreconcilably disgusted with me, her considering I ought to have been on the spot to advise her, to help her; and, though I believed there was no rancour in her composition and no great conviction of the importance of her affairs, I had prepared myself for a change in her manner, for some air of injury and estrangement, which should say to my conscience: "Well, you're a nice person to have professed things!" But historic truth compels me to declare that this poor lady's dull face ceased to be dull, almost ceased to be plain, as she turned it gladly to her late aunt's lodger. That touched

him extremely and he thought it simplified his situation until he found
it didn't. I was as kind to her that evening as I knew how to be, and
I walked about the garden with her as long as seemed good. There
was no explanation of any sort between us; I didn't ask her why she
hadn't answered my letter. Still less did I repeat what I had said to
her in that communication; if she chose to let me suppose she had
forgotten the position in which Miss Bordereau had surprised me and
the effect of the discovery on the old woman, I was quite willing to
take it that way: I was grateful to her for not treating me as if I had
killed her aunt.

We strolled and strolled, though really not much passed between
us save the recognition of her bereavement, conveyed in my manner
and in the expression she had of depending on me now, since I let
her see I still took an interest in her. Miss Tina's was no breast for
the pride or the pretense of independence; she didn't in the least
suggest that she knew at present what would become of her. I for-
bore to press on that question, however, for I certainly was not prepared to say that I would take charge of her. I was cautious; not
ignobly, I think, for I felt her knowledge of life to be so small that
in her unsophisticated vision there would be no reason why — since
I seemed to pity her — I shouldn't somehow look after her. She told
me how her aunt had died, very peacefully at the last, and how everything had been done afterwards by the care of her good friends —
fortunately, thanks to me, she said, smiling, there was money in
the house. She repeated that when once the "nice" Italians like
you they are your friends for life, and when we had gone into this
she asked me about my *giro*, my impressions, my adventures, the
places I had seen. I told her what I could, making it up partly,
I'm afraid, as in my disconcerted state I had taken little in; and
after she had heard me she exclaimed, quite as if she had forgotten her aunt and her sorrow, "Dear, dear, how much I should like
to do such things — to take an amusing little journey!" It came over
me for the moment that I ought to propose some enterprise, say I
would accompany her anywhere she liked; and I remarked at any
rate that a pleasant excursion — to give her a change — might be
managed; we would think of it, talk it over. I spoke never a word of
the Aspern documents, asked no question as to what she had ascer-
tained or what had otherwise happened with regard to them before
Juliana's death. It wasn't that I wasn't on pins and needles to know,
but that I thought it more decent not to show greed again so soon

after the catastrophe. I hoped she herself would say something, but she never glanced that way, and I thought this natural at the time. Later on, however, that night, it occurred to me that her silence was matter for suspicion; since if she had talked of my movements, of anything so detached as the Giorgione at Castelfranco, she might have alluded to what she could easily remember was in my mind. It was not to be supposed that the emotion produced by her aunt's death had blotted out the recollection that I was interested in that lady's relics, and I fidgeted afterwards as it came to me that her reticence might very possibly just mean that no relics survived. We separated in the garden — it was she who said she must go in; now that she was alone on the *piano nobile* I felt that (judged at any rate by Venetian ideas) I was on rather a different footing in regard to the invasion of it. As I shook hands with her for good-night I asked her if she had some general plan, had thought over what she had best do. "Oh yes, oh yes, but I haven't settled anything yet," she replied quite cheerfully. Was her cheerfulness explained by the impression that I would settle for her?

I was glad the next morning that we had neglected practical questions, as this gave me a pretext for seeing her again immediately. There was a practical enough question now to be touched on. I owed it to her to let her know formally that of course I didn't expect her to keep me on as a lodger, as also to show some interest in her own tenure, what she might have on her hands in the way of a lease. But I was not destined, as befell, to converse with her for more than an instant on either of these points. I sent her no message; I simply went down to the sala and walked to and fro there. I knew she would come out; she would promptly see me accessible. Somehow I preferred not to be shut up with her; gardens and big halls seemed better places to talk. It was a splendid morning, with something in the air that told of the waning of the long Venetian summer; a freshness from the sea that stirred the flowers in the garden and made a pleasant draught in the house, less shuttered and darkened now than when the old woman was alive. It was the beginning of autumn, of the end of the golden months. With this it was the end of my experiment — or would be in the course of half an hour, when I should really have learned that my dream had been reduced to ashes. After that there would be nothing left for me but to go to the station; for seriously — and as it struck me in the morning light — I couldn't linger there to act as guardian to a piece of middle-aged female helplessness. If she hadn't saved the papers wherein should I be indebted to her? I think I winced a little as I asked myself how much, if she *had* saved them, I should have to recognise and, as it were, reward such a courtesy. Mightn't that service after all saddle me with a guardianship? If this idea didn't make me more uncomfortable as I walked up and down it was because I was convinced I had nothing to look to. If the old woman hadn't destroyed everything before she pounced on me in the parlour she had done so the next day.

It took Miss Tina rather longer than I had expected to act on my calculation; but when at last she came out she looked at me without surprise. I mentioned I had been waiting for her and she asked why I hadn't let her know. I was glad a few hours later on that I had checked myself before remarking that a friendly intuition might have told her: it turned to comfort for me that I hadn't played even to that mild extent on her sensibility. What I did say was virtually the truth — that I was too nervous, since I expected her now to settle my fate.

"Your fate?" said Miss Tina, giving me a queer look; and as she spoke I noticed a rare change in her. Yes, she was other than she had been the evening before — less natural and less easy. She had been crying the day before and was not crying now, yet she struck me as less confident. It was as if something had happened to her during the night, or at least as if she had thought of something that troubled her — something in particular that affected her relations with me, made them more embarrassing and more complicated. Had she simply begun to feel that her aunt's not being there now altered my position?

"I mean about our papers. *Are* there any? You must know now."

"Yes, there are a great many; more than I supposed." I was struck with the way her voice trembled as she told me this.

"Do you mean you've got them in there — and that I may see them?"

"I don't think you can see them," said Miss Tina, with an extraordinary expression of entreaty in her eyes, as if the dearest hope she had in the world now was that I wouldn't take them from her. But how could she expect me to make such a sacrifice as that after all that had passed between us? What had I come back to Venice for but to see them, to take them? My joy at learning they were still in existence was such that if the poor woman had gone down on her knees to beseech me never to mention them again I would have treated the proceeding as a bad joke. "I've got them but I can't show them," she lamentably added.

"Not even to me? Ah Miss Tina!" I broke into a tone of infinite remonstrance and reproach.

She colored and the tears came back to her eyes; I measured the anguish it cost her to take such a stand which a dreadful sense of duty had imposed on her. It made me quite sick to find myself confronted with that particular obstacle; all the more that it seemed to me I had been distinctly encouraged to leave it out of account. I quite held Miss Tina to have assured me that if she had no greater hindrance than that —! "You don't mean to say you made her a death-bed promise? It was precisely against your doing anything of that sort that I thought I was safe. Oh I would rather she had burnt the papers outright than have to reckon with such a treachery as that."

"No, it isn't a promise," said Miss Tina.

"Pray what is it then?"

She hung fire, but finally said: "She tried to burn them, but I prevented it. She had hid them in her bed."

"In her bed —?"

"Between the mattresses. That's where she put them when she took them out of the trunk. I can't understand how she did it, because Olimpia didn't help her. She tells me so and I believe her. My aunt only told her afterwards, so that she shouldn't undo the bed — anything but the sheets. So it was very badly made," added Miss Tina simply.

"I should think so! And how did she try to burn them?"

"She didn't try much; she was too weak those last days. But she told me — she charged me. Oh it was terrible! She couldn't speak after that night. She could only make signs."

"And what did you do?"

"I took them away. I locked them up."

"In the secretary?"

"Yes, in the secretary," said Miss Tina, reddening again

"Did you tell her you'd burn them?"

"No, I didn't — on purpose."

"On purpose to gratify me?"

"Yes, only for that."

"And what good will you have done me if after all you won't show them?"

"Oh none. I know that — I know that," she dismally sounded.

"And did she believe you had destroyed them?"

"I don't know what she believed at the last. I couldn't tell — she was too far gone."

"Then if there was no promise and no assurance I can't see what ties you."

"Oh she hated it so — she hated it so! She was so jealous. But here's the portrait — you may have that," the poor woman announced, taking the little picture, wrapped up in the same manner in which her aunt had wrapped it, out of her pocket.

"I may have it — do you mean you give it to me?" I gasped as it passed into my hand.

"Oh yes."

"But it's worth money — a large sum."

"Well!" said Miss Tina, still with her strange look.

I didn't know what to make of it, for it could scarcely mean that she wanted to bargain like her aunt. She spoke as for making me a present. "I can't take it from you as a gift," I said, "and yet I can't afford to pay you for it according to the idea Miss Bordereau had of its value. She rated it at a thousand pounds."

"Couldn't we sell it?" my friend threw off.

"God forbid! I prefer the picture to the money."

"Well then keep it."

"You're very generous."

"So are you."

"I don't know why you should think so," I returned; and this was true enough, for the good creature appeared to have in her mind some rich reference that I didn't in the least seize.

"Well, you've made a great difference for me," she said.

I looked at Jeffrey Aspern's face in the little picture, partly in order not to look at that of my companion, which had begun to trouble me, even to frighten me a little — it had taken so very odd, so strained and unnatural a cast. I made no answer to this last declaration; I but privately consulted Jeffrey Aspern's delightful eyes with my own — they were so young and brilliant yet so wise and so deep; I asked him what on earth was the matter with Miss Tina. He seemed to smile at me with mild mockery; he might have been amused at my case. I had got into a pickle for him — as if he needed it! He was unsatisfactory for the only moment since I had known him. Nevertheless, now that I held the little picture in my hand I felt it would be a

precious possession. "Is this a bribe to make me give up the papers?"
I presently and all perversely asked. "Much as I value this, you
know, if I were to be obliged to choose, the papers are what I should
prefer. Ah but ever so much!"

"How can you choose — how can you choose?" Miss Tina returned slowly and woefully.

"I see! Of course there's nothing to be said if you regard the inter-
diction that rules on you as quite insurmountable. In this case it
must seem to you that to part with them would be an impiety of
the worst kind, a simple sacrilege!"

She shook her head, only lost in the queerness of her case. "You'd
understand if you had known her. I'm afraid," she quavered suddenly — "I'm afraid! She was terrible when she was angry."

"Yes, I saw something of that, that night. She was terrible. Then
I saw her eyes. Lord, they were fine!"

"I see them — they stare at me in the dark!" said Miss Tina.

"You've grown nervous with all you've been through."

"Oh yes, very — very!"

"You mustn't mind; that will pass away," I said kindly. Then
I added resignedly, for it really seemed to me that I must accept
the situation: "Well, so it is, and it can't be helped. I must renounce." My friend, at this, with her eyes on me, gave a low soft
moan, and I went on: "I only wish to goodness she had destroyed
them; then there would be nothing more to say. And I can't understand why, with her ideas, she didn't."

"Oh she lived on them!" said Miss Tina.

"You can imagine whether that makes me want less to see them,"
I returned not quite so desperately. "But don't let me stand here as
if I had it in my soul to tempt you to anything base. Naturally,
you understand, I give up my rooms. I leave Venice immediately."
And I took up my hat, which I had placed on a chair. We were still
rather awkwardly on our feet in the middle of the sala. She had
left the door of the apartments open behind her, but had not led me
that way.

A strange spasm came into her face as she saw me take my hat.
"Immediately — do you mean to-day?" The tone of the words was
tragic — they were a cry of desolation.

"Oh no; not so long as I can be of the least service to you."

"Well, just a day or two more — just two or three days," she panted.
Then controlling herself she added in another manner: "She wanted

to say something to me — the last day — something very particular. But she couldn't."

"Something very particular?"

"Something more about the papers."

"And did you guess — have you any idea?"

"No, I've tried to think — but I don't know. I've thought all kinds of things."

"As for instance?"

"Well, that if you were a relation it would be different."

I wondered. "If I were a relation —?"

"If you weren't a stranger. Then it would be the same for you as for me. Anything that's mine would be yours, and you could do what you like. I shouldn't be able to prevent you — and you'd have no responsibility."

She brought out this droll explanation with a nervous rush and as if speaking words got by heart. They gave me an impression of a subtlety which at first I failed to follow. But after a moment her face helped me to see further, and then the queerest of light came to me. It was embarrassing, and I bent my head over Jeffrey Aspern's portrait. What an odd expression was in his face! "Get out of it as you can, my dear fellow!" I put the picture into the pocket of my coat and said to Miss Tina: "Yes, I'll sell it for you. I shan't get a thousand pounds by any means, but I shall get something good."

She looked at me through pitiful tears, but seemed to try to smile as she returned: "We can divide the money."

"No, no, it shall be all yours." Then I went on: "I think I know what your poor aunt wanted to say. She wanted to give directions that the papers should be buried with her."

Miss Tina appeared to weigh this suggestion; after which she answered with striking decision, "Oh no, she wouldn't have thought that safe!"

"It seems to me nothing could be safer."

"She had an idea that when people want to publish they're capable —!" And she paused, very red.

"Of violating a tomb? Mercy on us, what must she have thought of me!"

"She wasn't just, she wasn't generous!" my companion cried with sudden passion.

The light that had come into my mind a moment before spread

further. "Ah don't say that, for we *are* a dreadful race." Then I pursued: "If she left a will that may give you some idea."

"I've found nothing of the sort — she destroyed it. She was very fond of me," Miss Tina added with an effect of extreme inconsequence. "She wanted me to be happy. And if any person should be kind to me — she wanted to speak of that."

I was almost awestricken by the astuteness with which the good lady found herself inspired, transparent astuteness as it was and stitching, as the phrase is, with white thread. "Depend upon it she didn't want to make any provision that would be agreeable to *me*."

"No, not to you, but quite to me. She knew I should like it if you could carry out your idea. Not because she cared for you, but because she did think of me," Miss Tina went on with her unexpected persuasive volubility. "You could see the things — you could use them." She stopped, seeing I grasped the sense of her conditional — stopped long enough for me to give some sign that I didn't give. She must have been conscious, however, that though my face showed the greatest embarrassment ever painted on a human countenance it was not set as a stone, it was also full of compassion. It was a comfort to me a long time afterwards to consider that she couldn't have seen in me the smallest symptom of disrespect. "I don't know what to do; I'm too tormented, I'm too ashamed!" she continued with vehemence. Then turning away from me and burying her face in her hands she burst into a flood of tears. If she didn't know what to do it may be imagined whether I knew better. I stood there dumb, matching her while her sobs resounded in the great empty hall. In a moment she was up at me again with her streaming eyes. "I'd give you everything, and she'd understand, where she is — she'd forgive me!"

"Ah Miss Tina — ah Miss Tina," I stammered for all reply. I didn't know what to do, as I say, but at a venture I made a wild vague movement in consequence of which I found myself at the door. I remember standing there and saying, "It wouldn't do, it wouldn't do!" — saying it pensively, awkwardly, grotesquely, while I looked away to the opposite end of the sala as at something very interesting. The next thing I remembered is that I was downstairs and out of the house. My gondola was there and my gondolier, reclining on the cushions, sprang up as soon as he saw me. I jumped in and to his usual "*Dove commanda?*" replied, in a tone that made him stare: "Anywhere, anywhere; out into the lagoon!"

He rowed me away and I sat there prostrate, groaning softly to myself, my hat pulled over my brow. What in the name of the preposterous did she mean if she didn't mean to offer me her hand? That was the price — that was the price! And did she think I wanted it, poor deluded infatuated extravagant lady? My gondolier, behind me, must have seen my ears red as I wondered, motionless there under the fluttering *tenda* with my hidden face, noticing nothing as we passed — wondered whether her delusion, her infatuation had been my own reckless work. Did she think I had made love to her even to get the papers? I hadn't, I hadn't; I repeated that over to myself for an hour, for two hours, till I was wearied if not convinced. I don't know where, on the lagoon, my gondolier took me; we floated aimlessly and with slow rare strokes. At last I became conscious that we were near the Lido, far up, on the right hand, as you turn your back to Venice, and I made him put me ashore. I wanted to walk, to move, to shed some of my bewilderment. I crossed the narrow strip and got to the sea-beach — I took my way toward Malamocco. But presently I flung myself down again on the warm sand, in the breeze, on the coarse dry grass. It took it out of me to think I had been so much at fault, that I had unwittingly but none the less deplorably trifled. But I hadn't given her cause — distinctly I hadn't. I had said to Mrs. Prest that I would make love to her; but it had been a joke without consequences and I had never said it to my victim. I had been as kind as possible because I really liked her; but since when had that become a crime where a woman of such an age and such an appearance was concerned? I am far from remembering clearly the succession of events and feelings during this long day of confusion, which I spent entirely in wandering about, without going home, until late at night; it only comes back to me that there were moments when I pacified my conscience and others when I lashed it into pain. I didn't laugh all day — that I do recollect; the case, however it might have struck others, seemed to me so little amusing. I should have been better employed perhaps in taking in the comic side of it. At any rate, whether I have given cause or not, there was no doubt whatever that I couldn't pay the price. I couldn't accept the proposal. I couldn't, for a bundle of tattered papers, marry a ridiculous pathetic provincial old woman. It was a proof of how little she supposed the idea would come to me that she should have decided to suggest it herself in that practical argumentative heroic way — with the timidity, however, so much more striking than the boldness, that her reasons appeared to come first and her feelings afterward.

As the day went on I grew to wish I had never heard of Aspern's relics, and I cursed the extravagant curiosity that had put John Cumnor on the scent of them. We had more than enough material without them, and my predicament was the just punishment of that most fatal of human follies, our not having known when to stop. It was very well to say it was no predicament, that the way out was simple, that I had only to leave Venice by the first train in the morning, after addressing Miss Tina a note which should be placed in her hand as soon as I got clear of the house; for it was strong proof of my quandary that when I tried to make up the note to my taste in advance — I would put it on paper as soon as I got home, before going to bed — I couldn't think of anything but "How can I thank you for the rare confidence you've placed in me?" That would never do; it sounded exactly as if an acceptance were to follow. Of course I might get off without writing at all, but that would be brutal, and my idea was still to exclude brutal solutions. As my confusion cooled I lost myself in wonder at the importance I had attached to Juliana's crumpled scraps; the thought of them became odious to me and I was as vexed with the old witch for the superstition that had prevented her from destroying them as I was with myself for having already spent more money than I could afford in attempting to control their fate. I forget what I did, where I went after leaving the Lido, and at what hour or with what recovery of composure I made my way back to my boat. I only know that in the afternoon, when the air was aglow with the sunset, I was standing before the church of Saints John and Paul and looking up at the small square-jawed face of Bartolommeo Colleoni, the terrible *condottiere* who sits so sturdily astride of his huge bronze horse on the high pedestal on which Venetian gratitude maintains him. The statue is incomparable, the finest of all mounted figures, unless that of Marcus Aurelius, who rides benignant before the Roman Capitol, be finer: but I was not thinking of that; I only found myself staring at the triumphant captain as if he had had an oracle on his lips. The western light shines into all his grimness at that hour and makes it wonderfully personal. But he continued to look far over my head, at the red immersion of another day — he had seen so many go down into the lagoon through the centuries — and if he were thinking of battles and stratagems they were of a different quality from any I had to tell him of. He couldn't direct me what to do, gaze up at him as I might. Was it before this or after that I wandered about for an hour in the small canals, to the continued stupefaction of my gondolier, who had never seen me so restless and yet so void of a purpose and could extract from me no order but "Go anywhere — everywhere — all over the place?" He reminded me that I had not lunched and expressed therefore respectfully the hope that I would dine earlier. He had had long periods of leisure during the day, when I had left the boat and rambled, so that I was not obliged to consider him, and I told him that till the morrow, for reasons, I should touch no meat. It was an effect of poor Miss Tina's proposal, not altogether auspicious, that I had quite lost my appetite. I don't know why it happened that on this occasion I was more than ever struck with that queer air of sociability, of cousinship and family life, which makes up half the expression of Venice. Without streets and vehicles, the uproar of wheels, the brutality of horses, and with its little winding ways where people crowd together, where voices sound as in the corridors of a house, where the human step circulates as if it skirted the angles of furniture and shoes never wear out, the place has the character of an immense collective apartment, in which Piazza San Marco is the most ornamented corner and palaces and churches, for the rest, play the part of great divans of repose, tables of entertainment, expanses of decoration. And somehow the splendid common domicile, familiar, domestic and resonant, also resembles a theatre with its actors clicking over bridges and, in straggling processions, tripping along fondamentas. As you sit in your gondola the footways that in certain parts edge the canals assume to the eye the importance of a stage, meeting it at the same angle, and the Venetian figures, moving to and fro against the battered scenery of their little houses of comedy, strike you as members of an endless dramatic troupe.

I went to bed that night very tired and without being able to compose an address to Miss Tina. Was this failure the reason why I became conscious the next morning as soon as I awoke of a determination to see the poor lady again the first moment she would receive me? That had something to do with it, but what had still more was the fact that during my sleep the oddest revulsion had taken place in my spirit. I found myself aware of this almost as soon as I opened my eyes: it made me jump out of my bed with the movement of a man who remembers that he has left the house-door ajar or a candle burning under a shelf. Was I still in time to save my goods? That question was in my heart; for what had now come to pass was that in the unconscious cerebration of sleep I had swung back to a passionate appreciation of Juliana's treasure. The pieces composing it were now more precious than ever and a positive ferocity had come into my need to acquire them. The condition Miss Tina had attached to that act no longer appeared an obstacle worth thinking of, and for an hour this morning my repentant imagination brushed it aside. It was absurd I should be able to invent nothing; absurd to renounce so easily and turn away helpless from the idea that the only way to become possessed was to unite myself to her for life. I mightn't unite myself, yet I might still have what she had. I must add that by the time I sent down to ask if she would see me I had invented no alternative, though in fact I drew out my dressing in the interest of my wit. This failure was humiliating, yet what could the alternative be? Miss Tina sent back word I might come; and as I descended the stairs and crossed the sala to her door — this time she received me in her aunt's forlorn parlour — I hoped she wouldn't think my announcement was to be "favourable." She certainly would have understood my recoil of the day before.

As soon as I came into the room I saw that she had done so, but I also saw something which had not been in my forecast. Poor Miss Tina's sense of her failure had produced a rare alteration in her, but I had been too full of stratagems and spoils to think of that. Now I took it in; I can scarcely tell how it startled me. She stood in the middle of the room with a face of mildness bent upon me, and her look of forgiveness, of absolution, made her angelic. It beautified her; she was younger; she was not a ridiculous old woman. This trick of her expression, this magic of her spirit, transfigured her, and while I still noted it I heard a whisper somewhere in the depths of my conscience: "Why not, after all — why not?" It seemed to me I *could* pay the price. Still more distinctly however than the whisper I heard Miss Tina's own voice. I was so struck with the different effect she made on me that at first I wasn't clearly aware of what she was saying; then I recognised she had bade me good-bye — she said something about hoping I should be very happy.

"Good-bye — good-bye?" I repeated with an inflection interrogative and probably foolish.

I saw she didn't feel the interrogation, she only heard the words; she had strung herself up to accepting our separation and they fell upon her ear as a proof. "Are you going to-day?" she asked. "But it doesn't matter, for whenever you go I shall not see you again. I don't want to." And she smiled strangely, with an infinite gentleness. She had never doubted my having left her the day before in horror. How *could* she, since I hadn't come back before night to contradict, even as a simple form, even as an act of common humanity, such an idea? And now she had the force of soul — Miss Tina with force of soul was a new conception — to smile at me in her abjection.

"What shall you do — where shall you go?" I asked.

"Oh I don't know. I've done the great thing. I've destroyed the papers."

"Destroyed them?" I waited.

"Yes; what was I to keep them for? I burnt them last night, one by one, in the kitchen."

"One by one?" I coldly echoed it.

"It took a long time — there were so many." The room seemed to go round me as she said this and a real darkness for a moment descended on my eyes. When it passed, Miss Tina was there still, but the transfiguration was over and she had changed back to a plain dingy elderly person. It was in this character she spoke as she said "I can't stay with you longer, I can't;" and it was in this character she turned her back upon me, as I had turned mine upon her twenty-four hours before, and moved to the door of her room. Here she did what I hadn't done when I quitted her — she paused long enough to give me one look. I have never forgotten it and I sometimes still suffer from it, though it was not resentful. No, there was no resentment, nothing hard or vindictive in poor Miss Tina; for when, later, I sent her, as the price of the portrait of Jeffrey Aspern, a larger sum of money than I had hoped to be able to gather for her, writing to her that I had sold the picture, she kept it with thanks; she never sent it back. I wrote her that I had sold the picture, but I admitted to Mrs. Prest at the time — I met this other friend in London that autumn — that it hangs above my writing-table. When I look at it I can scarcely bear my loss — I mean of the precious papers.

Anton Pavlovich Chekhov

WARD NO. 6

1 8 9 2

9

I

THE small wing, surrounded by a whole forest of nettles, burdocks, and marijuana, is out in the courtyard of the hospital. The roof of this wing is rusted, its chimney half-fallen, its front steps are rotted and grown over with grass; as for the whitewash, there are only traces of it left. Its façade is toward the hospital, its rear looks out upon a field, from which it is divided by the gray hospital fence with its coping of nails. These nails, their sharp points up, and the fence, and the wing itself, all have that peculiar, dismal, hopelessly accursed air which is to be found only in our hospital and prison buildings.

If you are not afraid of being stung by the nettles, let us take the narrow little path leading to the wing and have a peek at what is going on within. The front door admits us into the entry. Here, along the walls and near the stove, are piled up whole mountains of hospital odds and ends. Mattresses, old tattered robes, trousers, shirts with narrow stripes of blue, utterly useless worn out footgear — all this rag-fair has been dumped in piles, has become rumpled, tangled; it is rotting and giving off a stifling odor.

Nikita the keeper, an old retired soldier whose service stripes have turned rusty from time, is lolling upon these odds and ends, his eternal pipe clenched between his teeth. His face is morose, drink-ravaged; his eyebrows are beetling, bestowing on his face the look of a steppe sheepdog, and his nose is red; he is not tall, rather spare to look at, and sinewy, but his bearing is impressive and his fists are huge, hard. He belongs to the number of those simple-hearted, positive, reliable, and stolid persons who love order above all things on earth, and are therefore convinced that people must be beaten. When he beats somebody he beats him about the face, the chest, the back — wherever his blows may fall — and is convinced that without this there would be no order in this place.

386

Next you enter a large, spacious room which takes up the whole wing — that is, if the entry is not taken into consideration. The walls here are daubed over with a dirty light-blue paint; the ceiling is covered with soot, as in a smoke-house: it is evident that the furnaces here smoke in winter and give off asphyxiating fumes. The windows are made hideous by iron bars on the inside. The floor is gray and splintery. There is a stench of sauerkraut, of charred lamp-wicks, of bedbugs and ammonia, and from the very first this stench gives you the impression that you are entering a menagerie.

Beds, screwed down to the floor, are placed about this room. Men in blue hospital bathrobes and in antiquated nightcaps are sitting or lying on them. These are the madmen.

There are altogether five of them here. Only one of them is of high birth; all the others are mere burghers. The man nearest the door, a tall, gaunt burgher with a red, shiny mustache and tearstained eyes, is sitting with his head propped up and his eyes fixed on one point. Day and night does he grieve, shaking his head, sighing and smiling a bitter smile; rarely does he take any part in the conversations and usually does not answer when questions are put to him. He eats and drinks mechanically, if food and drink are given him. Judging by his excruciating, hacking cough, his thinness and the flush on his cheeks, he has incipient consumption.

The next is a small, lively, exceedingly spry old man, with a little pointed beard, and black, kinky hair, like a Negro's. In the daytime he strolls about the ward, from window to window, or sits on his bed with his legs tucked in under him, Turkish fashion, and with never a let-up, like a bullfinch, whistles, hums, and snickers. He evinces his childish and lively character at night as well, when he gets up to pray to God — that is, to thump his breast and scrape at a doorpost with his finger. This is the Jew Moisseika, an innocent, who lost his mind twenty years ago, when his hat factory burned down.

Of all the inmates of Ward No. 6 he is the only one who is allowed to go out of the wing — and even out of the hospital, into the street. He has enjoyed this privilege for a long, long time, probably because he is one of the time-honored hospital inmates and a quiet, harmless innocent, the butt of the town, whom the people have long since grown used to seeing upon the streets, surrounded by urchins and dogs. In his miserable little bathrobe, his funny nightcap, and in slippers (at times barefooted and even without his trousers) he goes about the streets, stopping at gateways and shops and begging for coppers. In one place they may give him some bread-cider, in another bread, in a third a copper, so that he usually returns to the wing sated and rich. All that he may bring back with him Nikita takes away from him for his own benefit. The soldier does this roughly, with great heat, turning out the idiot's pockets and calling upon God to be his witness that he's never going to let the sheeny go out into the street again, and that such irregularities are to him the most hateful things in the world.

Moisseika loves to make himself useful. He brings water to his fellows, tucks them in when they are asleep, promises each one to bring him back a copper from his street expeditions, and to sew a new hat for him; it is he, too, who feeds with a spoon his neighbor to the left, a paralytic. He acts thus not out of any commiseration, or because of any considerations of a humane nature, but in imitation of and involuntary submission to his neighbor on the right, one Gromov.

Ivan Dmitrich Gromov, a man of thirty-three, nobly born, at one time a court clerk and the secretary of the district, suffers from a persecution mania. He spends his time either lying in bed, curled up in a ball, or else paces from corner to corner, as if he were taking his constitutional; as for sitting, he indulges in that only very rarely. He is always agitated, excited, and tense because of some vague, undefined expectation. The least rustle in the entry, or a shout in the yard, will suffice to make him raise his head and prick up his ears: are they coming to fetch him, perhaps? Is it him, by any chance, they are looking for? And his face at such a time bears an expression of extreme disquiet and revulsion.

I like his broad face with its high cheekbones, a face always pale and unhappy which reflects in itself, as in a mirror, his soul, tortured almost to death by struggling and long continued fear. His grimaces are queer and sickly, but the fine lineaments put on his face by profound, sincere suffering are discerning and intelligent, and his eyes have a warm, wholesome gleam. I like him for himself: polite, accommodating, and unusually delicate in his treatment of all save Nikita. When anyone happens to drop a button or a spoon he is quick to jump off his bed and pick up the fallen object. Every morning he greets his companions with a good morning; when he lies down to sleep he wishes them good night.

Besides his constant state of tension and his grimacing, his madness is also evinced by the following. At times, of evenings, he will muffle himself up in his miserable bathrobe and, with his whole body shaking, his teeth chattering, will take to striding rapidly from corner to corner and between the beds. It looks as if he were in the throes of a severe fit of the ague. One can see by the way he stops abruptly, and glances at his fellows that he wants to say something of the utmost importance but, evidently surmising that no one will listen to him or understand him, he impatiently tosses his head and resumes his pacing. But the desire to speak shortly gets the upper hand over all and any considerations and, letting himself go. he speaks warmly and passionately. His speech is disorderly, feverish, like delirium, impulsive and not always intelligible, yet at the same time one can hear in it (both in the words and the voice) something exceedingly fine. When he speaks, you recognize in him a madman — and a human being. It is difficult to convey his insane speech on paper. He speaks of human baseness, of oppression trampling upon truth, of a splendid life which will in time prevail upon earth, of the window bars which at every moment remind him of the stupidity and cruelty of the oppressors. The result is a disordered, inchoate potpourri of songs that are old yet which thus far have never been sung to the end.

II

Some twelve or fifteen years ago a civil servant by the name of Gromov used to live in this town, in his own house, situated on the most important street. He had two sons, Serghei and Ivan. Serghei, when he was already a student in his fourth semester, contracted galloping consumption and died, and this death seemed to serve as the beginning of a whole series of misfortunes which suddenly fell upon the Gromov family. A week after Serghei's funeral the patriarchal head of the family was brought to trial for forgeries and embezzlements, and died shortly from typhus in the prison hospital. The house and all his personal property were sold under the hammer, and Ivan Dmitrich and his mother were left without any means.

Formerly, when his father had been alive, Ivan Dmitrich, who was living in St. Petersburg, where he was studying at the University, had been getting from sixty to seventy rubles a month and had had no conception of what need was, but now he had to change his life abruptly. He had to tutor from morning to night for coppers, to work at transcribing, yet go hungry just the same, since he sent all his earnings to his mother for her support. Ivan Dmitrich had not been able to stand such a life; his spirits sank, he began to ail and, leaving the University, he came back home. Here, in this little town, he obtained through influential friends a teaching position in the district school; however, he did not find his fellow-teachers congenial, was not liked by the pupils, and soon left the post. His mother died. For half a year or so he went without a position, living on nothing but bread and water; then he became a court clerk. This post he filled until he was dismissed because of his derangement.

Never, even during the years of his youth as a student, did he give the impression of a healthy man. He had always been pale, thin and subject to colds; he ate but little and slept poorly. One glass of wine sufficed to make his head swim and to bring on hysterics. He had always been drawn to people but, thanks to his irritable temper and his self-consciousness, he had never gotten on an intimate footing with anybody and had no friends. Of the people in the town he always spoke with contempt, saying that their boorish ignorance and drowsy, animal life seemed to him abominable and revolting. He spoke in a tenor, loudly, heatedly, and never otherwise than indignantly and wrathfully, or else with rapture and wonder, and always sincerely. No matter what one might begin a conversation with him about, he always brought it around to one thing: life in this town was stifling and tedious; its society had none of the higher interests; it was leading a drab, senseless life, diversifying it with oppression, coarse depravity, and hypocrisy; the scoundrels went well-fed and well-clad, while honest men subsisted on crumbs; there was need for schools, for a local newspaper with an honest policy, a theater, public readings, a consolidation of intellectual forces; there was need for society to recognize itself, and to be horrified by that recognition. In his judgments of people he laid the colors on thick, using only black and white, without admitting any shadings; he divided mankind into honest men and scoundrels — as for any middle ground, there was none. Of women and love he always spoke passionately, with rapture, yet he had not been in love even once.

In the town, despite the harshness of his judgments, he was liked and, behind his back, they called him Vanya. His innate delicacy, his obliging nature, decency, moral purity, and his threadbare, wretched little frock-coat, his ailing appearance and his family misfortunes, inspired people with a fine, warm and melancholy feeling; besides that, he was well educated and widely read; in the opinion of the townsmen he knew everything and, in this town, constituted something in the nature of a walking encyclopedic dictionary.

He read a very great deal. He was forever sitting in the club, nervously tugging at his little beard and turning the leaves of periodicals and books, and one could see by his face that he was not so much reading as swallowing everything, having barely masticated it. It must be supposed that reading was one of his unwholesome habits, since he fell with equal avidity upon everything that came to hand, even newspapers and almanacs years old.

III

One autumn morning, his coat-collar turned up and his feet squelching in the mud, Ivan Dmitrich was making his way through lanes and backlots to the house of a certain burgher, to collect on a writ of execution. His mood was a somber one, the usual thing with him of mornings. In one of the lanes he came upon two convicts in leg-irons, convoyed by four soldiers with guns. Ivan Dmitrich had very often come upon convicts before, and every time they had aroused within him feelings of commiseration and ill-ease, but now this encounter made some sort of a peculiar, strange impression. For some reason or other it suddenly struck him that he, too, could be put in leg-irons and, in the same way, be led off through the mud to prison. On his way home after calling on the burgher he met, near the post office, a police inspector whom he knew, who greeted him and went a few steps with him along the street — and for some reason this struck him as suspicious.

At home, all that day, he could not get those convicts and the soldiers with their guns out of his head, and an incomprehensible psychic disquiet hindered him from reading and concentrating. When evening came he did not light the lamp, while at night he could not sleep and kept on thinking incessantly of the possibility of his being arrested, put in irons and planted in prison. He knew himself to be utterly innocent of anything culpable and could vouch that in the future as well he would not commit murder, or arson, or theft; but then, is it hard to commit a crime accidentally, involuntarily? And being slandered — was that an impossibility? And, finally, what about a miscarriage of justice? It is not in vain that age-old folk-experience teaches that no man is certain of escaping the beggar's sack or prison. As for a miscarriage of justice: that, under present-day judicial procedure was very possible — nothing out of the way about that. Men whose duties, whose business had to do with the sufferings of others — for instance judges, policemen, physicians — became, in the course of time and through the force of habit, inured to such a degree that they could not, even if they wanted to, regard their clients otherwise than formally; in this respect they are in no way different from the muzhik who butchers sheep and calves in his backlot and does not even notice the blood. And where the attitude to the individual is formal, soulless the judge needs, in order to deprive a man of all his property rights and to condemn him to penal servitude, only one thing: time. Only time, for the observance of certain formalities — which is just what the judge receives his salary for — and then it's all over! After that, go and seek justice and protection in this miserable, filthy little town, a hundred and twenty-five miles away from any railroad! Yes, and wasn't it amusing even to think of justice, when every oppression was hailed by society as a sane and salutary necessity, whereas every act of mercy, such as an acquittal, for instance, evoked nothing less than an explosion of unsatisfied, vindictive passion?

In the morning Ivan Dmitrich got up in a state of terror, with sweat beading his forehead, by now altogether convinced that he might be arrested at any minute. Since the oppressive thoughts of yesterday would not leave him in all that time (he reflected), it meant that there must be a modicum of truth in them. Really, they could not have come into his head for no reason at all.

A policeman leisurely passed by under his window; it was not for nothing. There, two men had stopped near the house, and just stood there, in silence. Why were they keeping silent?

And tormenting days and nights set in for Ivan Dmitrich. All the people who passed by his windows and all who entered the courtyard seemed to him spies and detectives. The captain of police usually drove a two-horse carriage through the street about noon; he was merely on his way from his suburban estate to the police station, yet every time it struck Ivan Dmitrich that he was driving much too fast and that his expression was somehow peculiar: evidently he was in a hurry to make known the appearance in the town of a very important criminal. Ivan Dmitrich started at every ring and at every knock on the gate; he was on tenterhooks whenever he encountered a new face at his landlady's; each time he came across policemen and gendarmes he smiled and whistled, so as to appear nonchalant. He stayed awake whole nights through in expectation of an arrest, but snored loudly and breathed deeply, like one sleeping, to make his landlady think he was asleep — for, if he was not sleeping, it would mean he was tormented by the pangs of his conscience: what a piece of circumstantial evidence! Facts and sane logic strove to convince him that all these fears were nonsense and psychopathy; that, if one were to take a broad view of the matter, there was really nothing frightful about arrest and prison — provided one's conscience were clear; however, the more intelligently and logically he reasoned, the more powerful and tormenting did his psychic disquiet become. His was something like the case of a certain anchorite in a wilderness, who wanted to make a tiny clearing for himself in a virgin forest; but, the more assiduously he wielded his ax, the thicker and greater did the forest grow. At the very last Ivan Dmitrich, seeing how useless it was, abandoned reasoning and gave himself up wholly to despair and fear.

He began to isolate himself and to avoid people. Even before this he had found his work repellent, but now it became unbearable to him. He was afraid somebody would trip him up somehow or other, that someone would slip a bribe in his pocket unperceived and then expose him, or that he himself would inadvertently make some error in his official papers, tantamount to a forgery, or that he would lose money in his keeping for others. Strangely enough, at no other time had his mind been as flexible and inventive as now, when every day he was thinking up thousands of reasons for being seriously apprehensive about his liberty and honor. But then his interest in the external world grew markedly weaker, as was also the case, to some extent, with his interest in books, and his memory became very treacherous.

In the spring, when the snow was gone, two half-putrefied corpses were found in a ditch near the graveyard — those of an old woman and a boy, with indications of their having met a violent death. Nothing else was talked of in the town save these two corpses and their unknown slayers. Ivan Dmitrich, in order that people might not think that it was he who had killed these two, went about the streets with a smile; but whenever he met any acquaintances he paled, then turned red, and asserted that there was no crime more vile than the killing of the weak and the defenseless. However, this lie soon wearied him and, after some reflection, he decided that the best thing to do in his position would be to hide in his landlady's cellar. He sat there for a whole day, then through the night and another day, caught a great chill and, after waiting until it was growing dark, made his way to his room stealthily, as if he were a thief. Until the day broke he stood in the middle of his room without stirring and on the alert for every sound.

Early in the morning, before the sun was up, some bricklayers came to his landlady. Ivan Dmitrich knew well enough that they had come to make over the oven, but his fear prompted him that these were policemen disguised as bricklayers. Even so he left his room, ever so quietly and, gripped by terror, without his hat and coat, started running down the street. Dogs, barking, ran after him; somewhere behind him a muzhik was shouting; the wind whistled in his ears, and it seemed to Ivan Dmitrich that all the oppression throughout the world had gathered behind his back and was pursuing him.

They caught him, led him home, and sent his landlady for a doctor. Andrew Ephimich, the doctor (of whom more will be said further on) prescribed cold packs for his head and bay-rum drops, shook his head sadly and took his departure, after telling the landlady that he would not call again, because it was not right to hinder people from going out of their minds. Since Ivan Dmitrich had no means to live on at home and to take treatment, he was shortly sent off to the hospital, and there they placed him in the ward for venereal patients. He did not sleep of nights, was capricious and disturbed the patients, and in a short while by orders of Andrew Ephimich, he was transferred to Ward No. 6.

In a year the town had already completely forgotten Ivan Dmitrich, and his books, which his landlady had dumped in a sleigh out in the shed, were dragged off by little boys.

IV

The patient to the left of Ivan Dmitrich's bed is, as I have already said, the Jew Moisseika, while the patient on his right is a muzhik with a dull, utterly imbecilic face; he is bloated with fat and is almost globular. This is a motionless, gluttonous, and uncleanly animal that has long since lost the ability to think and feel. There is constantly a pungent, stifling odor coming from him.

Nikita, who cleans up after him, beats him frightfully, swinging back with all his might, without sparing his fists — and the frightful thing is not that he is beaten (one can get used to that): what is frightful is that this stupefied animal does not respond to these beatings by either sound, or any move, or the expression of his eyes, but merely keeps teetering slightly, like a heavy cask.

The fifth and last inmate of Ward No. 6 is a townsman who had at one time sorted letters in the post office — a small, rather spare blond fellow with a kindly but somewhat sly face. To judge by his intelligent, calm eyes, with their clear and cheerful look, he is out for Number One, and is harboring some exceedingly important and pleasant secret. He keeps under his pillow and his mattress something or other which he will not show to anybody — not out of any fear that it may be taken away or stolen, however, but out of bashfulness. Occasionally he will walk up to a window and, turning his back on his companions, pin something on his breast and, bending his head, contemplate it;

if one approaches him at such a time he becomes confused and plucks that something off his breast. But it is not hard to fathom his secret.

"Congratulate me!" he often says to Ivan Dmitrich. "I have been presented with the Order of Stanislaus, of the Second Class — with a star. The Second Class — with a star — is given only to foreigners but, for some reason, they want to make an exception in my case." He smiles, shrugging his shoulders in a puzzled way. "There, now, I must confess I never expected that!"

"I don't understand anything about such things," Ivan Dmitrich declares glumly.

"But do you know what I'm going to win, sooner or later?" the one-time sorter continues, puckering up his eyes slyly. "I am absolutely bound to receive the Swedish Polar Star. Now *that* is a decoration which is really worth going to a lot of trouble for. A white cross and a black ribbon. Ever so beautiful."

Probably nowhere else is life as monotonous as in this wing. In the morning the patients (with the exception of the paralytic and the blubbery muzhik) wash themselves in the entry at a big tub, using the skirts of their robes for towels; after this they drink tea out of pewter mugs; the tea is brought to them from the main building by Nikita. Each one is supposed to get just one mug. At noon they eat soup made with sauerkraut and, with it, buckwheat grits; in the evening they sup on the grits left over from dinner. In between they lie on their beds, sleep, look out of the windows, and pace from corner to corner. And thus every day. Even the one-time sorter speaks always of the very same decorations.

Fresh faces are rarely seen in Ward No. 6. The doctor has long ago stopped admitting new mental cases, and there are but few people in this world who like to visit madhouses. Once every two months Semën Lazarich, the barber, calls at the wing. Of how he clips the insane, and how Nikita assists him, and into what confusion the patients are thrown at every appearance of the intoxicated, smiling barber — of that we will not speak.

Save for the barber no one looks in at the wing. The patients are condemned to see no one but Nikita, day in and day out.

However, a rather strange rumor has recently spread through the hospital building.

Someone has started a rumor that, apparently, the doctor has taken to visiting Ward No. 6.

V

A strange rumor!

Doctor Andrew Ephimich Raghin is, after his own fashion, a remarkable man. They say that in his early youth he was exceedingly pious and had been preparing himself for a career in the church, and that, after he had finished studying in the gymnasium in 1863, he had intended to enter a seminary; but his father, a doctor of medicine and a surgeon, had apparently jeered at him caustically and had declared categorically that he would not consider him his son if he joined the psalm-snufflers. How true that is I do not know, but Andrew Ephimich has confessed more than once that he had never felt any call for medicine and, in general, for the applied sciences.

Be that as it may, after finishing his medical courses he did not become a long-haired priest. He did not evince any piety, and at the beginning of his healing career resembled a person of the spiritual calling as little as he did now.

In outward looks he is ponderous, coarse, like a muzhik; his face, his beard, his flat hair and his strong, unwieldy physique make one think of someone who keeps a tavern along some main road, who has overindulged himself in food, is intemperate and hard-headed. His face is stern and criss-crossed with small blue veins, his eyes are small, his nose is red. In keeping with his great height and broad shoulders he has enormous feet and hands — it seems that, were he to swing his fist at you, you would be done for. Yet his step is soft and his walk cautious, stealthy; when you meet him in a narrow corridor he is always the first to stop and give you the right of way, and says "Excuse me!" — not in the bass you expect, however, but in a high, soft little tenor. He has a small swelling on his neck which keeps him from wearing hard, starched collars, and so he always walks about in a soft shirt of linen or calico; in general, he does not dress the way doctors do. He wears the self-same old suit for ten years at a stretch, while his new clothes (which he usually buys at some cheap place) look just as worn and wrinkled on him as his old ones; he will wear the very same coat when receiving patients, or dining, or paying social calls — this is not out of stinginess, however, but from a complete disregard for his appearance.

When Andrew Ephimich came to this town to take his post, the "eleemosynary institution" was in a dreadful state. It was hard to breathe in the wards, the corridors, and the hospital courtyard because of the stench. The hospital orderlies, the nurses, and their children, all used to sleep in the same wards with the sick. Everybody complained there was no living on account of the cockroaches, the bedbugs, and mice. There was never a shortage of erysipelas in the surgical division. For the whole hospital there were but two scalpels and not a single thermometer; the bathtubs were used as storage bins for potatoes. The superintendent, the woman who had full charge of the linen and so forth, and the assistant doctor — they all robbed the sick; while it was told of the old doctor, Andrew Ephimich's predecessor, that he boot-legged the hospital alcohol and had set up for himself a whole harem of nurses and female patients. The people in the town were very familiar with these irregularities and even exaggerated them, yet regarded them with equanimity; some justified them by the fact that the only ones who filled the hospital beds were burghers and muzhiks, who could not possibly be dissatisfied, since they lived far worse at home than they did at the hospital: no use pampering them with delicacies, you know! Others said, in justification, that the town found it beyond its means to maintain a good hospital without any aid from the county: thank God there was even a bad one. As for the county, it would not open a hos-pital either in the city or near it, giving the excuse that the town already had a hospital of its own.

After an inspection of the hospital Andrew Ephimich came to the conclusion that this institution was immoral and in the highest degree harmful to the health of the inhabitants. The most intelligent thing to do, in his opinion, would be to turn the patients loose and close the hospital. But he reasoned that his will alone was not enough for this, and that it would be useless: were the physical and moral uncleanli-ness driven from one place it would pass on to some other; one had to wait until the thing had thoroughly aired itself. In addition to that, if the people opened a hospital and tolerated it in their midst, it meant that they found it necessary; the prejudices and all those everyday vilenesses and abominations were necessary, since in the course of time they become worked over into something useful, even as manure is worked over into black loam. There is nothing on this earth so good that it had not some vileness at its prime source.

After accepting the post Andrew Ephimich evidently took a rather indifferent attitude toward the irregularities. He merely requested the orderlies and the nurses not to pass their nights in the wards, and put in two wall-cases of surgical instruments; as for the superintendent, the woman in charge of linen, the assistant doctor, and the surgical erysipelas, they all stayed put.

Andrew Ephimich is exceedingly fond of intelligence and honesty, yet he has not sufficient character and belief in his rights to establish an intelligent and honest life about him. To order, to forbid, to insist — these things he is utterly unable to do. It seems as if he had taken a vow never to raise his voice and never to use the imperative mood. To say "Let me have this," or "Bring me that," is for him a difficult matter; when he wants to eat he coughs irresolutely and says to the cook: "What about some tea, now?" — or: "What about dinner?" As for telling the superintendent to stop stealing, or driving him out, or doing away altogether with this needless, parasitical post — that is something altogether beyond his strength. Whenever Andrew Ephimich is being taken in or flattered, or a palpably and vilely doctored account is submitted for his signature, he turns as red as a boiled lobster and feels himself guilty, yet he signs the account just the same; whenever the patients complain to him about being starved or about the boorish nurses he becomes confused and mumbles guiltily: "Very well, very well — I'll look into that later. . . . Probably there's some misunderstanding here —"

At first Andrew Ephimich had worked very assiduously. He received patients from morning until dinner-time, performed operations, and even practiced obstetrics. The ladies said of him that he was conscientious and diagnosed complaints excellently — especially those of women and children. But as time went on the work markedly bored him with its monotonousness and obvious futility. Today you received thirty patients; on the morrow, before you knew it, they ran up to thirty-five; the day after there would be forty, and so on from day to day, from year to year, yet the death-rate in the town did not decrease and the sick never ceased coming. It was a physical impossibility, in the time between morning and noon, to extend any real aid to the forty patients who came; therefore, willy-nilly, the result was plain humbug. During the fiscal year twelve thousand out-patients had been received; therefore, it simply stood to reason that twelve thousand people had been humbugged. As for placing those seriously ill into the wards, and treating them in accordance with all the rules of science, that also was impossible — for although there were rules there was no science; on the other hand, were one to abandon philosophy and follow the rules pedantically, as other physicians did, you would need for that, first and foremost, cleanliness and ventilation instead of filth, wholesome food instead of soup cooked out of stinking sauerkraut, and decent assistants instead of thieves.

And besides, why hinder people from dying, since death is the normal and ordained end of every being?   What did it matter if some haggling shopkeeper or petty government clerk did live five or ten years extra? But if one saw the aim of medicine as the alleviation of suffering through drugs then, involuntarily, the question bobbed up: Wherefore should sufferings be alleviated?   In the first place, they say that sufferings lead man to perfection and, in the second, should mankind really learn to alleviate its sufferings through pills and drops, it would abandon altogether religion and philosophy, in which it has found up to now not only a defense against all tribulations but even happiness.   Pushkin, just before death, experienced dreadful tortures; that poor fellow Heine, lay for several years stricken by paralysis — why, then, shouldn't some Andrew Ephimich or Matrëna Savishna ail for a bit, since their lives are devoid of all content and would be altogether vacuous and like the life of an amoeba, were it not for their sufferings?

Crushed by such reflections Andrew Ephimich let his spirits sink and became irregular in his attendance at the hospital.

VI

Here is the way his life goes on. Usually he gets up about eight in the morning, dresses, and has his tea. Then he sits down in his study to read, or goes to the hospital. Here, in the hospital, in a narrow, dark little corridor, sit the ambulatory patients, waiting to be received. Orderlies, their boots clattering on the brick floor, and nurses hurry past them; gaunt patients walk by in their robes; dead bodies and filled bed-pans are carried by; the children are crying; there is a windy draft.   Andrew Ephimich knows that for the ague-stricken, for the consumptives, and, in general, for all the susceptible patients such a setting is excruciating, but what can one do?

In the reception room he is met by Serghei Sergheich, the assistant doctor, a small, stout man with a clean-shaven, well-groomed puffy face, with soft, stately manners and wearing a new, roomy suit: he looks more like a senator than an assistant doctor. He has an enormous practice in town, wears a white cravat and considers himself better informed than the doctor, who has no practice whatsoever. Placed in one corner of the reception room is an icon, in a case, with a ponderous lampad glowing before it; standing near it is a lectern in a white slip-cover; hanging upon the walls are portraits of arch-priests, a view of Holy Mount Monastery and wreaths of dried corn-flowers. Serghei Sergheich is religious and loves churchly pomp. The holy image has been placed here at his expense; of Sundays, in this reception room, one patient or another reads an acathistus at his orders, at which all stand, while after the reading Serghei Sergheich makes the round of all the wards with a censer and thurifies them with frankincense.

The patients are many but the time is short, and therefore the whole business is limited to putting a few brief questions and issuing some medicine or other, such as volatile ointment or castor oil. Andrew Ephimich sits with cheek propped up on his fist, in deep thought, and puts his questions mechanically. Serghei Sergheich is also sitting, rubbing his little hands from time to time and putting in his oar every now and then.

"We ail and endure need," he will say, "because we pray but poorly to the merciful Lord. Yea, verily!"

At these clinical sessions Andrew Ephimich does not perform any operations whatsoever; he has long since grown disused to them and the sight of blood agitates him unpleasantly. When he has to open a baby's mouth to look down its throat, and the baby squalls and defends itself with its tiny hands, his head swims from the noise in his ears and tears appear in his eyes. He hastens to prescribe some medicine and waves his hands at the peasant woman to take the baby away in a hurry.

During such a session he soon becomes bored with the timidity of the patients and their lack of sense, with the proximity of the pompous Serghei Sergheich, with the portraits on the walls and with his own questions which he has been putting, without ever varying them, for more than twenty years by now. And, after having received five or six patients, he leaves. The assistant doctor receives the rest without him.

With the pleasant reflection that, thank God, he has had no private practice for a long, long time now, and that no one will interrupt him, Andrew Ephimich upon getting home immediately sits down at the desk in his study and falls to reading. He reads a very great deal, and always with great pleasure. Half his salary goes for the purchase of books, and out of the six rooms in his quarters three are piled up with books and old periodicals. Most of all he loves works on history and philosophy; in medicine, however, he subscribes only to *The Physician,* which he always begins reading from the end. Each time his reading goes on for several hours without a break and never tires him. He does not read as rapidly and fitfully as Ivan Dmitrich used to do at one time, but slowly, with penetration, frequently pausing at passages which are to his liking or which he cannot grasp. Always standing near his book is a small decanter of vodka, while lying right on the cloth, without any plate, is a pickled cucumber or a pickled apple. Every half hour, without taking his eyes off the book, he pours out a pony of vodka and drinks it down, then, without looking, he gropes for the cucumber and takes a small bite.

At three o'clock he cautiously approaches the kitchen door, coughs and says:

"Dariushka, what about some dinner?"

After dinner, rather badly cooked and sloppily served, Andrew Ephimich paces through his rooms, with his arms crossed on his breast, and meditates. Four o'clock chimes, then five, but he is still pacing and meditating. At rare intervals the kitchen door creaks and Dariushka's red, sleepy face peeks out:

"Isn't it time for your beer, Andrew Ephimich?" she asks solicitously.

"No, not yet," he answers. "I'll wait . . . I'll wait a while —"

In the evening Michael Averianich, the postmaster, usually drops in — the only man in town whose society does not oppress Andrew Ephimich. At one time Michael Averianich had been an exceedingly rich landed proprietor and had served in the cavalry, but he had become ruined and, out of necessity, had in his old age entered the post-office department. He has a wide-awake, hale appearance, luxurious gray side-whiskers, manners that show his fine upbringing, and a booming, pleasant voice. He is kind and responsive but quick-tempered. When, at the post office, any patron protests, disagrees, or simply starts an argument, Michael Averianich turns purple, quivers all over and shouts "Quiet, you!" in a thunderous voice, so that the post office has long since gotten a deep-rooted reputation of an institution a call at which is a frightening experience. Michael Averianich respects and loves Andrew Ephimich for his culture and the nobility of his soul; all the other inhabitants of the town he looks down upon, however, as if they were his subordinates.

"Well, here I am!" he says as he enters Andrew Ephimich's place. "How are you, my dear fellow! Guess you must be tired of me by now -— eh?"

"On the contrary, I am very glad," the doctor answers him. "I am always glad to see you."

The friends seat themselves on the divan in the study and for some time smoke in silence.

"If we could only have some beer now, Dariushka!" says Andrew Ephimich.

The first bottle they drink in the same silence: the doctor in a pensive mood, and Michael Averianich with a gay, animated air, like a man who has something interesting to tell.   It is the doctor who always begins the conversation.

"What a pity it is," he says slowly and softly, without looking into the eyes of his companion (he never looks anyone in the eye), "what a profound pity it is, my dear Michael Averianich, that there are absolutely no people in our town who can, and like to, carry on an intelligent and interesting conversation.   That is an enormous deprivation for us.   Even the intelligents aren't above vulgarity; the level of their development, I assure you, is not in the least above that of the lower masses."

"You're absolutely correct.   I agree with you."

"You yourself know," the doctor continues softly, and with frequent pauses, "that everything in this world is insignificant and uninteresting except the higher spiritual manifestations of the human mind.   The mind draws a sharp dividing line between animal and man, hints at the divinity of the latter and, to a certain degree, even replaces for him immortality, which is non-existent.   Hence it follows that the mind serves as the sole possible source of enjoyment.   True, we have books, but that's not at all the same as animated conversation and sociability. If you will allow me to make a not altogether apt analogy, books are notes, while conversation is singing."

"Absolutely correct!"

A silence ensues.   Dariushka emerges from the kitchen and, with an air of stolid sorrow, propping up her chin on her fist, stops in the doorway to listen.

"Eh!" sighs Michael Averianich.   "The very idea of expecting anybody nowadays to have a mind!"

And he tells how full of zest, and gaiety, and interest life used to be; what clever intelligents there had been in Russia, and how highly they held the concepts of honor and friendship.   Money was loaned without any promissory notes, and it was considered a disgrace not to extend a helping hand to a comrade in need.   And what campaigns there had been, what adventures and set-tos — what comrades, what women! Take the Caucasus — what an astonishing region!   Then there was the wife of a certain battalion commander — a strange woman, who used to put on the uniform of an officer and go off into the mountains of evenings, all by herself, without any guide.   They said she had a romantic affair in one of the eyrie-settlements with some native princeling or other.

"Queen of Heaven, Our Mother —" Dariushka would sigh.

"And how we drank! How we ate! And what reckless liberals there were!"

Andrew Ephimich listens and does not hear; he is meditating upon something and from time to time sips his beer.

"I frequently dream of clever people and of conversations with them," he says unexpectedly, interrupting Michael Averianich. "My father gave me a splendid education but, under the influence of the ideas of the 'sixties, compelled me to become a physician. It seems to me that if I had not heeded him then I would now be in the very center of the intellectual movement. Most probably I would be a member of some faculty or other. Of course, the mind is also not eternal but transitory; however, you already know why I cherish an inclination to it. Life is merely an irritating snare. When a thinking man attains the prime of his manhood and arrives at a mature consciousness of life, he involuntarily feels as if he were in a snare from which there is no escape. Really, now, against his own will, through certain accidental circumstances, he has been summoned from non-being into life. Wherefore? Should he desire to learn the significance and purpose of his existence he is either told nothing or he is told absurdities — he knocks, but it will not be opened unto him; then death comes to him — likewise against his will. And so, even as people in prison, bound by a common misfortune, feel themselves more at ease when they get together, even so in life one does not feel the snare one is in when people inclined to analysis and generalizations get together and pass the time in exchanging lofty, free ideas. In that sense the mind is a delight for which there is no substitute."

"Absolutely correct!"

Without looking into his companion's eyes, softly and with pauses, Andrew Ephimich goes on speaking of clever people and of conversations with them, while Michael Averianich listens to him attentively and concurs:

"Absolutely correct!"

"But don't you believe in the immortality of the soul?" the postmaster suddenly asks.

"No, my esteemed Michael Averianich, I do not believe in it, nor have I any basis for believing."

"I must confess that I, too, have my doubts. But then, I have a feeling as if I'll never die. Come, I think, you old curmudgeon, it's time for you to die. But in my soul there is some sort of a tiny voice: 'Don't you believe it — you won't die!'"

Just a little after ten Michael Averianich leaves. As he is putting on his fur-lined coat out in the entry he says with a sigh:

"But what a wilderness fate has cast us into! And the most vexing thing of all is that we'll even have to die here. Eh!"

VII

After seeing his friend off Andrew Ephimich sits down at his desk and starts reading again. The quietness of the evening, and then of the night, is not disturbed by a single sound, and time seems to stand still and to be rooted to the spot together with the doctor poring over his book, and it seems that nothing exists save this book and the lamp with its green shade. The doctor's coarse, peasant face becomes little by little illuminated by a smile of touched delight and rapture before the courses of the human mind. "O, why is not man immortal?" he thinks. Why has he been given cerebral centers and convolutions, why his sight, speech, consciousness of self, genius, if all these things are fated to go back into the soil and, in the very end, turn cold together with the earth's core and then go careering with the earth for millions of years around the sun, senselessly and aimlessly? Just to have him turn cold and then go off careering there is altogether no need to draw man with his lofty, almost divine mind out of non-being and then, as if in mockery, to turn him into clay.

Transubstantiation! But what cowardice it is to console one's self with this surrogate of immortality! The inanimate processes taking place in nature are beneath even human stupidity, inasmuch as in stupidity there are present, after all, consciousness and will, whereas in these processes there is just nothing at all. Only a coward who has more of the fear of death in him than of dignity is capable of consoling himself with the idea that his body will, in time, live again as grass, as stone, as toad. . . . To see one's immortality in transubstantiation is just as queer as to prophesy a brilliant future to a violin case after the priceless Stradivarius it once held has been shattered and become useless.

Whenever the clock strikes Andrew Ephimich throws himself back in his armchair and closes his eyes for a little thought. And unintentionally, under the influence of the fine thoughts he had read out of his books, he casts a glance over his past and his present. The past is execrable: better not recall it. As for the present, it is filled with the same sort of thing as the past. He knows that even as his thoughts go careering with the cooled earth around the sun, in the great barrack-like structure of the hospital, alongside of the quarters he occupies, people are languishing amid diseases and physical uncleanliness; someone is perhaps not sleeping but warring with insects; someone is being infected with erysipelas or moaning because of a bandage too tightly applied; the patients are, perhaps, playing cards with the nurses and drinking vodka. During the fiscal year twelve thousand people had been humbugged; this whole hospital business, just as the case was twenty years ago, is built upon thievery, squabbles, slanders, nepotism, and upon crass charlatanry, and the hospital, just as hitherto, represents an institution immoral and in the highest degree harmful to the inhabitants. He knows that behind the barred windows of Ward No. 6 Nikita is beating the patients, and that Moisseika goes through the town every day and collects alms.

On the other hand, he knows exceedingly well that a fairy-tale change has taken place in medicine during the last twenty-five years. When he had been studying at the university it had seemed to him that medicine would shortly be overtaken by the same fate as alchemy and metaphysics; but now, when he reads of nights, medicine amazes him and arouses wonder and even rapture in him. And really, what unexpected brilliancy there is here, and what a revolution! Thanks to antiseptics, surgeons perform such operations as the great Pirogov had deemed impossible even *in spe.* Ordinary country doctors have the courage to perform resections of the knee-joint; out of a hundred Caesarian sections one case only ends in mortality; as for gallstones, they are considered such a trifle that no one even writes about them. Syphilis can be radically cured. And what about the theory of heredity, and hypnotism, the discoveries of Pasteur and Koch, hygiene and its statistics? What about the county medical centers in Russia? Psychiatry, with its present classification of derangements, its methods of investigation and treatment — why, by comparison with what used to be, it towers nothing short of the Elbruz. The heads of the insane are no longer doused with cold water, nor are they strapped into straitjackets; they are maintained humanely and, actually (so the newspapers write), theatrical entertainments and balls are arranged for them. Andrew Ephimich knows that, judged by present-day views and tastes, such an abomination as Ward No. 6 is possible only a hundred and twenty-five miles from any railroad, in a miserable little town where the mayor and all the councilmen are semiliterate burghers who regard a physician as a high priest who must be believed without any criticism, even though he were to pour molten lead into your mouth; in any other place the public and the newspapers would long since have left not one stone of this little Bastille standing upon another.

"But what of it?" Andrew Ephimich asks himself, opening his eyes. "What of all this? There are antiseptics, and Koch, and Pasteur, yet in substance the business hasn't changed in the least. Ill-health and mortality are still the same. Balls and theatrical entertainments are arranged for the insane — but, just the same, they're not allowed to go free. Therefore, everything is bosh and pother and, substantially, there's no difference between the best clinic in Vienna and my lazar-house."

However, sorrow and a feeling resembling envy hinder him from being indifferent. This, probably, is due to fatigue. His ponderous head droops toward the book; he places his hands under his face, to make it more comfortable, and reflects:

"I am serving an evil cause, and receive my salary from people whom I dupe: I am not honest. But then I, by myself, am nothing; I am but a particle of a necessary social evil: all the district bureaucrats are harmful and receive their salaries for nothing. Therefore, it is not I who am to blame for my dishonesty but the times. . . . Were I to be born two hundred or so years from now, I would be an honest man."

When three o'clock strikes he puts out the lamp and goes to his bedroom. He does not feel sleepy.

VIII

Two years before the county administration had had a fit of generosity and had voted a yearly appropriation of three hundred rubles as a subsidy for the enlargement of the medical personnel in the town hospital, until such time as the county hospital would be opened, and so the district doctor, Eugene Fedorich Hobotov, was invited to the town to assist Andrew Ephimich. Eugene Fedorich is still a young man, not even thirty yet; he is tall, dark-haired, with broad cheekbones and tiny eyes: probably his ancestors were aliens. He arrived in town without a copper, with a wretched little handbag and a young, homely woman, whom he calls his cook. This woman has a breast baby. Eugene Fedorich walks about in high boots and a round cap with a stiff brim and, in winter, in a short fur-lined coat. He has become very chummy with Serghei Serghéich, the assistant doctor, and with the treasurer; but as for the other officials, he for some reason or other calls them aristocrats and steers clear of them. In his entire flat he has exactly one book: *The Latest Prescriptions of the Vienna Clinic for 1881.* Whenever he goes to call on a patient he infallibly takes this book along with the rest of his equipment. Of evenings, at the club, he plays billiards, but he does not like cards. He is very fond of interlarding his conversation with such phrases as "Long drawn out mess," "Poppycock oil," "That'll do you, trying to pull the wool over my eyes," and so forth.

He visits the hospital twice a week, makes the round of the wards and receives the patients. The complete absence of antiseptics and the presence of cupping-glasses arouse his indignation, but he does not introduce any new ways, being afraid of offending Andrew Ephimich thereby. He considers his colleague Andrew Ephimich an old knave, suspects him of having large means and, in secret, envies him. He would be willing enough to step into his place.

IX

On a certain evening in spring, when there was no longer any snow on the ground and the starlings were singing in the hospital garden, the doctor stepped out to see his friend the postmaster to the gate. Precisely at that moment the Jew Moisseika was entering the yard, returning from his foraging. He was hatless and had shallow galoshes on his bare feet, and was holding a small sack with the alms.

"Gimme a copper!" He turned to the doctor; he was shivering from the cold and smiling.

Andrew Ephimich, who never refused anybody, gave him a ten-kopeck silver coin.

"How bad that is," he thought, glancing at the bare legs, with red, bony ankles. "Why, it's wet out."

And, moved by a feeling which resembled both pity and squeamishness, he set out for the hospital wing after the Jew, glancing now at his bald spot, now at his ankles. At the doctor's entrance Nikita jumped up from his mound of rubbish and drew himself up at attention.

"How do, Nikita," Andrew Ephimich said softly. "What about issuing a pair of boots to this Jew, or something of that sort — for he's likely to catch cold."

"Right, Your Honor. I'll report it to the superintendent."

"Please do. Ask him in my name. Say I asked him to do it."

The entry door was open into the ward. Ivan Dmitrich, lying on his bed and propped up on an elbow, was listening uneasily to the unfamiliar voice, and suddenly recognized the doctor. His whole body began to quiver with wrath; he sprang up and, with a red, angry face, his eyes bulging, ran out into the middle of the ward.

"The doctor has come!" he cried out, and burst into laughter. "At last! Gentlemen, I felicitate you — the doctor is honoring you by his visit! You damned vermin!" he screeched, and stamped his foot in such fury as no one in the ward had ever seen before. "This vermin ought to be killed! No, killing him is not enough! He ought to be drowned in the privy!"

Andrew Ephimich, who had heard this, peeped out into the ward from the entry and asked gently:

"For what?"

"For what?" cried out Ivan Dmitrich, walking up to him with a threatening air and convulsively drawing his robe about him. "For what? You thief!" he uttered with revulsion and shaping his lips as if he wanted to spit. "Quack! Hangman!"

"Calm yourself," said Andrew Ephimich with a guilty smile. "I assure you I have never stolen anything; as for the rest, you probably exaggerate greatly. I can see that you are angry at me. Calm down if you can, I beg of you, and tell me without any heat what you are angry at me for."

"Well, why do you keep me here?"

"Because you are unwell."

"Yes — unwell. But then scores, hundreds of madmen are going about in full freedom, because your ignorance is incapable of distinguishing them from normal people. Why then must I, and all these unfortunates sit here, like so many scapegoats for everybody? You, your assistant doctor, the superintendent, and all your hospital riff-raff are, as far as morals are concerned, immeasurably beneath each one of us: why, then, are we sitting here and not the whole lot of you? Where's the logic in that?"

"A moral attitude and logic have nothing to do with all this. Everything depends on chance. He who has been placed in here stays here, while he who hasn't been placed here goes about in full freedom: that's all there is to it. In the fact that I am a doctor and you are a psychopathic case there is neither morality nor logic, but only trivial chance."

Moisseika, whom Nikita had been too bashful to search in the doctor's presence, had spread out on his bed pieces of bread, scraps of paper and little bones and, still shivering from the cold, began saying something in Hebrew, rapidly and in sing-song. Probably he had gotten the idea that he had opened a shop.

"Let me out," said Ivan Dmitrich, and his voice quavered.

"I can't."

"But why? Why?"

"Because that isn't in my power. Judge for yourself: what good would it do you if I were to let you out? Go ahead. The people in town and the police will detain you and send you back."

"Yes, yes, that's true enough," Ivan Dmitrich managed to say, and rubbed his forehead. "This is horrible! But what am I to do? What?"

The voice of Ivan Dmitrich, and his youthful, clever face with its grimaces proved to the doctor's liking. He felt an impulse to be kind to him and to calm him. He sat down next to him on the bed, thought a while, and said:

"You ask, what's to be done? The best thing to do in your situation is to escape from here. But, regrettably, that is useless. You would be detained. When society fences itself off from criminals, psychopaths, and people who are generally embarrassing, it is insuperable. There is but one thing left for you: to find reassurance in the thought that your staying here is necessary."

"It isn't necessary to anybody."

"Since prisons and madhouses exist, why, somebody is bound to sit in them. If not you, then I; if not I, then some third person. Bide your time; when in the distant future prisons and madhouses will have gone out of existence, there will be no more bars on windows, nor hospital robes. Of course, sooner or later, such a time will come."

Ivan Dmitrich smiled mockingly.

"You jest," said he, puckering his eyes. "Such gentry as you and your helper, Nikita, have nothing to do with the future; but you may rest assured, my dear sir, that better times will come! I may be expressing myself in a banal way — laugh, if you like — but the dawn of a new life will shine forth, truth will rise triumphant — and then it will be our turn to rejoice. I will not live to see the day, I will have perished even as animals perish — but then somebody's grandchildren will live to see it. I hail them with all my soul, and I rejoice — I rejoice for them! Onward! God be with us and help us, my friends!"

Ivan Dmitrich, his eyes shining, stood up and, stretching his arms out toward a window, continued with excitement in his voice:

"From behind these window-bars I bless you! May truth prevail! I rejoice!"

"I can't find any particular cause for rejoicing," said Andrew Ephimich, whom Ivan Dmitrich's gesture had struck as theatrical while, at the same time, it had been very much to his liking. "There will be a time when jails and madhouses will no longer exist and truth, as you were pleased to put it, will rise triumphant; but then, the substance of things will not have changed; the laws of nature will still remain the same. Men will ail, will grow old, and die, even as they do now. No matter how magnificent a dawn may be illuminating your life, after all is said and done you will be nailed up in a coffin just the same and then pitched into a hole in the ground."

"But what of immortality?"

"Oh, come, now!"

"You do not believe; but then I do. Dostoyevsky or Voltaire makes somebody say that if there were no God, men would have to invent Him. And I believe profoundly that if there is no immortality, some great human mind will, sooner or later, invent it."

"Well put," Andrew Ephimich let drop, with a smile of pleasure. "It's a good thing, your having faith. With such a faith one can live as snug as a bug in a rug even bricked up in a wall. Did you receive your education anywhere in particular?"

"Yes; I attended a university, but did not graduate."

"You are a thinking and meditative person. You are capable of finding tranquility within your own self, in any environment. Free and profound reasoning, which strives toward a rationalization of life, and a complete contempt for the foolish vanities of this world: there you have two blessings, higher than which no man has known. And you can possess them, even though you live behind triple bars. Diogenes lived in a tun — yet he was happier than all the princes of this earth."

"Your Diogenes was a blockhead," Ivan Dmitrich said morosely. "Why do you talk to me of Diogenes and of some rationalization or other?" he suddenly became angry and sprang up. "I love life — love it passionately! I have a persecution mania, a constant, excruciating fear; yet there are moments when I am overwhelmed by a thirst for life, and then I am afraid of going out of my mind. I want to live — I want to terribly, terribly!"

In his agitation he took a turn about the ward and then said, lowering his voice:

"When I am in a reverie, I am visited by phantoms. Some people or other come to me; I hear voices, music, and it seems to me that I am strolling through some sort of woods, or along the shore of a sea, and I feel such a passionate yearning for worldly vanity, for striving. . . .

Tell me, now, what's new there?" asked Ivan Dmitrich. "What's going on there?"

"Do you want to know about the town, or about things in general?"

"Well, tell me about the town first, and then about things in general."

"What can I tell you, then? It is oppressively dreary in the town. There's nobody to exchange a word with, nobody one can listen to. There are no new faces. However, a young physician arrived recently — a certain Hobotov."

"He arrived even in my time. What sort of a fellow is he — a lout?"

"Yes, he is not a man of culture. It's odd, don't you know . . . judging by all things, there is no mental stagnation in our capital cities, everything is in motion there; consequently, there also must be real people there — but for some reason or other they always send to us such men as one would rather not even look at. What an unfortunate town!"

"Yes, what an unfortunate town!" Ivan Dmitrich sighed, and began to laugh. "But how are things in general? What do they write in the newspapers and magazines?"

It was dark by now in the ward. The doctor got up and, standing, began telling the madman what was being written abroad and in Russia, and what trend of thought was to be noticed now. Ivan Dmitrich listened attentively and put questions, but suddenly, as though having recalled something horrible, clutched his head and lay down on his bed, with his back to the doctor.

"What is the matter with you?" asked Andrew Ephimich.

"You won't hear another word out of me!" Ivan Dmitrich said rudely. "Leave me alone!"

"But why?"

"Leave me, I tell you! What the devil!"

Andrew Ephimich shrugged his shoulders, sighed, and walked out. On his way through the entry he said:

"What about cleaning up a bit, Nikita? There's a terribly oppressive odor here."

"Right, Your Honor."

"What an agreeable young man!" reflected Andrew Ephimich, as he was going to his quarters. "All the time I've been living here this would seem to be the first man with whom one could chat. He knows how to talk about things, and is interested in precisely the right ones."

While he was reading and later, as he was going to bed, he kept thinking all the time of Ivan Dmitrich, and on awaking the next morning he recalled that he had made the acquaintance of an intelligent and interesting man yesterday, and decided to drop in on him once more at the first opportunity.

X

Ivan Dmitrich was lying in the same pose as yesterday, his hands clutching his head and with his legs tucked up. One could not see his face.

"Good day, my friend," said Andrew Ephimich. "You aren't sleeping?"

"In the first place I am not your friend," Ivan Dmitrich spoke into his pillow, "and, in the second, you are putting yourself out for nothing: you won't get a single word out of me."

"How odd —" Andrew Ephimich muttered in embarrassment. "Yesterday we were conversing so peacefully, but suddenly you took offense for some reason and at once cut our conversation short. Probably I must have expressed myself clumsily, somehow, or perhaps have come out with some idea incompatible with your convictions —"

"Oh, yes — catch me believing you, just like that!" said Ivan Dmitrich, raising himself and regarding the doctor mockingly and in disquiet; his eyes were red. "You can go and do your spying and interrogating somewhere else, but there's nothing for you to do here. I understood even yesterday what you had come here for."

"What a strange fancy!" smiled the doctor. "That means you take me for a spy?"

"Yes, I do. Either a spy or a doctor assigned to testing me — it's all one."

"Oh, come, you must excuse me for saying so, but really — what an odd fellow you are!"

The doctor seated himself on a tabouret next to the madman's bed and shook his head reproachfully.

"Well, let's suppose you are right," he said. "Let's suppose that I am treacherously trying to trip you up on something you say, so as to betray you to the police. You are arrested and then brought to trial. But then, will you be any worse off in the courtroom and in prison than you are here? And even if they send you away to live in some remote part of Siberia, or to penal servitude — would that be worse than sitting here, in this hospital wing? I don't think it would be. What, then, is there to fear?"

Evidently these words had an effect on Ivan Dmitrich. He sat up, reassured.

It was five in the afternoon — the time when Andrew Ephimich, as a rule, was pacing through his rooms, and Dariushka was asking him if it weren't time for his beer. It was calm, clear out of doors.

"I happened to go out for a walk after dinner, and just dropped in on you, as you see," said the doctor. "It's actually spring out."

"What month is it now? March?" asked Ivan Dmitrich.

"Yes — the end of March."

"Is it muddy out?"

"No, it's not so bad. You can see the paths in the garden."

"It would be fine to drive a carriage now, somewhere outside the town," said Ivan Dmitrich, rubbing his red eyes, just as though he were coming out of his sleep, "then to come home to a warm, cozy study and . . . to take treatments for headaches from a decent doctor. . . . It's a long while since I have lived like a human being. But everything here is abominable! Unbearably abominable!"

After the excitement of yesterday he was fatigued and listless, and spoke unwillingly. His fingers were shaky, and one could see by his face that his head ached badly.

"Between a warm, cozy study and this ward there is no difference whatsoever," said Andrew Ephimich. "A man's tranquility and contentment lie not outside of him but within his own self."

"Just how do you mean that?"

"The ordinary man expects that which is good or bad from without — from a carriage and a study, that is; whereas a thinking man expects it from his own self."

"Go and preach that philosophy in Greece, where it is warm and the air is filled with the fragrance of oranges, but here it is not in keeping with the climate. Whom was I speaking with about Diogenes? Was it you, by any chance?"

"Yes, it was with me — yesterday."

"Diogenes had no need of a study and of warm quarters — it's hot enough there as it is. Just lie in your tub and eat oranges and olives. But had he chanced to live in Russia he would be begging his head off for a room not only in December but even in May. Never fear, he would be perishing from the cold."

"No. It is possible not to feel the cold, as well as every pain in general. Marcus Aurelius has said: 'Pain is a living conception of pain; exert thy will, in order to change this conception; put it away from thee, cease complaining, and the pain shall vanish,' which is true enough. A sage, or simply a thinking, meditative man, is distinguished precisely by his holding suffering in contempt; likewise, he is always content, and is not astonished by anything."

"That means I am an idiot, since I suffer, feel discontent, and am astonished at human baseness."

"You are wrong in saying so. If you will think deeply and often, you will comprehend how insignificant are all these matters which perturb you. One must strive toward a rationalization of life; therein lies the true good."

"Rationalization —" Ivan Dmitrich made a wry face. "The inward, the outward.... Pardon me, I don't understand it. All I know," he said, getting up and regarding the doctor angrily, "is that God created me out of warm blood and nerves — yes! And organic tissue, if it be imbued with life, must react to every irritant. And I do react! To pain I respond by screaming and tears; to baseness, by indignation; to vileness, by revulsion. According to me that, precisely, is what they call life. The lower the organism the less sensitive it is, and the more weakly does it respond to irritation, and the higher it is the more receptively and energetically does it react to reality. How can one be ignorant of that? You are a doctor — and yet you don't know such trifles! In order to despise sufferings, to be always content and never astonished at anything, one must reach such a state as this —" and Ivan Dmitrich indicated the obese muzhik, bloated with fat — "or else one must harden one's self through sufferings to such a degree as to lose all sensitivity to them: that is, in other words, cease to live. Pardon me, I am no sage and no philosopher," Ivan Dmitrich went on with irritation, "and I understand nothing of all this. I am in no condition to reason."

"On the contrary, you reason splendidly."

"The Stoics, whom you parody, were remarkable men; but their teaching had congealed even two thousand years ago and hasn't advanced by a jot, nor will it advance, since it is not practical and does not pertain to life. It succeeded only with a minority, with those who spend their time in dabbling in and smacking their lips over all sorts of teachings; as for the majority, it never did understand it. A teaching which preaches indifference to riches, to the comforts of life, a contempt for sufferings and death, is altogether incomprehensible to the vast majority, since this majority has never known either riches or the comforts of life; and as for despising sufferings, that would mean for it to despise life itself, since all of man's nature consists of sensations of hunger, cold, affronts, losses and a Hamletian trepidation in the face of death. All life consists of these sensations: one may find it burdensome, may hate it, but never despise it. Yes. And so I repeat: the teaching of the Stoics can never have a future; but, as you can see, the things that have been progressing from the start of time to this day are struggle, a keen sensitivity to pain, the ability to respond to irritation —"

Ivan Dmitrich suddenly lost the thread of his thought, stopped, and rubbed his forehead in vexation.

"I wanted to say something important but got off the track," he said. "What was I talking about? Oh, yes! And so I say: one of the Stoics had sold himself into bondage in order to redeem a fellow-man. There, you see: it means that even a Stoic reacted to an irritant, since for such a magnanimous act as self-abnegation for a fellow-man one must have a soul that has been aroused to indignation, that is compassionate. Here, in this prison, I have forgotten everything I learned, or else I would have recalled a thing or two besides. And what about Christ? Christ responded to reality by weeping, smiling, grieving, raging — even yearning; He went to meet sufferings with a smile and did not despise death, but prayed in the Garden of Gethsemane that *this cup* might pass from Him!"

Ivan Dmitrich laughed and sat down.

"Let us suppose that man's tranquility and contentment are not outside of him but within his own self," he said. "Let us suppose that one ought to despise sufferings and be astonished at nothing. However, on what basis do *you* preach that? Are you a sage? A philosopher?"

"No, I am not a philosopher; but every man should preach this, because it is reasonable."

"No — what I want to know is why, in these matters of rationalization, contempt for pain, and so forth, you deem yourself competent? Why, have you ever suffered? Have you any conception of sufferings? Pardon me — but were you ever whipped as a child?"

"No; my parents had a deep aversion for corporal punishment."

"Well, my father beat me cruelly. My father was a willful, hemorrhoidal bureaucrat, with a long nose and a yellow neck. However, let's speak about yourself. In all your life no one has ever laid a finger on you, no one frightened you or repressed you with beatings; you are as healthy as a bull. You grew up sheltered under your father's wing and studied at his expense and then, right off, grabbed this sinecure. You have, for more than twenty years, been living in free quarters, with heat and light and servants thrown in, having at the same time the right of working as you liked and only as much as you liked — even to the extent of not working at all. You are, by nature, a lazy, flabby fellow, and therefore you tried to arrange your life so that nothing might perturb you or dislodge you from your place. Your work you turned over to the assistant doctor and the other riff-raff, while you yourself sat in warmth and in quiet, saving up money, reading your books, finding delectation in reflections concerning all sorts of elevated twaddle and [here Ivan Dmitrich glanced at the doctor's rubicund nose] tippling. In a word, you haven't seen life, don't know it perfectly, and when it comes to reality you have only a theoretical acquaintance with it. And as for your contempt of sufferings and your being astonished at nothing, that's all due to a very simple cause: vanity of vanities, internality and externality, contempt for life and death, rationalization, the true good — all these form the most suitable philosophy for the Russian sluggard.

"You may, for example, see a muzhik beating his wife. Why intervene? Let him beat her: both are bound to die anyway, sooner or later, and besides, he who is doing the beating is wronging by his beatings not the one whom he is beating but himself. To be a drunkard is stupid, indecent — yet if one drinks one dies and if one does not drink one dies. A countrywoman comes to you — her teeth are aching. . . . Well, what of it? Pain is but a concept of pain and, on top of that, in this world one can't go through life without illnesses, we've all got to die, and so get you gone, woman, don't interfere with my cogitating and drinking vodka. A young man comes seeking advice as to what he is to do, how he is to live; before answering him another man would go off into deep thought, but you already have an answer all pat: Strive toward rationalization, or toward the true good. But just what is this fantastic *true good?* There is no answer, of course. We are kept here behind iron bars; we are forced to rot, we are mocked and tortured — but that is all splendid and reasonable, inasmuch as, between this ward and a warm, cozy study, there is no difference whatsoever. A handy philosophy: there's not a thing to be done, and one's conscience is clear, and one feels he is a sage. No, my dear sir, this is not philosophy, not reflection, not breadth of view but laziness, fakirism, a somnolent daze. . . . Yes!" Ivan Dmitrich again became angry, "You despise sufferings — but if someone happened to pinch your finger in a door you would yell your head off!"

"And then, again, perhaps I wouldn't yell," said Andrew Ephimich, smiling meekly.

"Oh, yes, to be sure! But, were you to be struck all of a heap by paralysis or, let's say, if some brazen fool, taking advantage of his position and rank, were to insult you publicly, and you knew that he would get away with it — why, you would understand then what it means to refer others to rationalization and the true good."

"That is original," said Andrew Ephimich, laughing from pleasure and rubbing his hands. "I am agreeably struck by your inclination toward generalizations, while the character sketch of me which you were kind enough to make just now is simply brilliant. I must confess that conversing with you affords me enormous pleasure. Well, I have heard you out to the end; I hope you will now be inclined to hear me out —"

XI

This conversation went on for about an hour more and, evidently, made a profound impression on Andrew Ephimich. He took to dropping in at the hospital wing every day. He went there of mornings and after dinner, and often the dusk of evening would find him still conversing with Ivan Dmitrich. At first Ivan Dmitrich had fought shy of him; he suspected him of some evil design and frankly expressed his hostility; later on, however, he became used to him and changed his harsh attitude to a condescendingly ironical one.

It was not long before a rumor spread all through the hospital that Doctor Andrew Ephimich had taken to frequenting Ward No. 6. Nobody — neither the assistant doctor, nor Nikita, nor the nurses — could understand why he went there, why he sat there for hours on end, what he spoke about, and why he did not write out any prescriptions. His actions seemed queer. Many times Michael Averianich failed to find him at home, something that had never happened before, and Dariushka was very much put out because the doctor drank his beer no longer at the designated time, and occasionally was actually late for dinner.

Once (this was already toward the end of June) Doctor Hobotov dropped in at Andrew Ephimich's about something; not finding him at home, he set out to look for him in the courtyard; there he was told that the old doctor had gone to see the psychopathic cases. As he entered the wing and paused in the entry, Hobotov heard the following conversation:

"We shall never sing the same tune, and you won't succeed in converting me to your belief," Ivan Dmitrich was saying in irritation. "You are absolutely unfamiliar with reality and you have never suffered but, like a leech, have merely found your food in the proximity of the sufferings of others, whereas I have suffered ceaselessly from my birth to this very day. Therefore I say frankly: I consider myself superior to you and more competent in all respects. It isn't up to you to teach me."

"I do not at all presume to convert you to my belief," Andrew Ephimich let drop quietly and with regret because the other did not want to understand him. "And that's not where the gist of the matter lies, my friend. It does not lie in that you have suffered, whereas I have not. Sufferings and joys are transitory; let's drop them — God be with them. But the gist of the matter does lie in that you and I do reason; we see in each other someone who can think and reason, and this makes for unity between us, no matter how divergent our views may be. If you only knew how fed up I have become with the general insanity, mediocrity, stolidity, and what a joy it is each time I converse with you! You are an intelligent man, and I find you delightful."

Hobotov opened the door an inch or so and peered into the ward: Ivan Dmitrich in his nightcap and Doctor Andrew Ephimich were sitting side by side on the bed. The madman was grimacing, shuddering and convulsively muffling himself in his bathrobe, while the doctor sat motionless, with his head sunk on his chest, and his face was red, helpless and sad. Hobotov shrugged his shoulders, smiled sneeringly and exchanged glances with Nikita. Nikita, too, shrugged his shoulders.

The next day Hobotov came to the wing with the assistant doctor. Both stood in the entry and eavesdropped.

"Why, it looks as if our grandpa has gone off his nut completely!" Hobotov remarked as they were leaving the wing.

"The Lord have mercy upon us sinners!" sighed the benign-visaged Serghei Sergheich, painstakingly skirting the small puddles so as not to soil his brightly polished shoes. "I must confess, my dear Eugene Fedorovich, I have been long anticipating this!"

XII

After this Andrew Ephimich began to notice a certain atmosphere of mysteriousness all around him. The orderlies, the nurses, and the patients, whenever they came across him, glanced at him questioningly and then fell to whispering among themselves. Masha, the superintendent's little daughter, whom he liked to come upon in the garden, whenever he approached her now with a smile to pat her little head, would run away from him for some reason or other. Michael Averianich, the postmaster, whenever he was listening to the doctor no longer said "Absolutely correct!" but kept mumbling "Yes, yes, yes . . ." in incomprehensible confusion and regarded him thoughtfully and sadly; for some reason he took to advising his friend to leave vodka and beer alone, but in doing so did not speak directly, since he was a man of delicacy, but in hints, telling him now about a certain battalion commander, a splendid person, now about a regimental chaplain, a fine fellow, both of whom had been hard drinkers and had fallen ill; after leaving off drink, however, they had gotten perfectly well. Andrew Ephimich's colleague, Hobotov, dropped in on him two or three times; he, too, advised him to leave spirituous drinks alone and, without any apparent reason, recommended him to take potassium bromid.

In August Andrew Ephimich received a letter from the mayor, requesting the doctor to call on him concerning a very important matter. On arriving at the appointed time in the city offices Andrew Ephimich found there the head of the military, the civilian inspector of the county school, a member of the city council, Hobotov, and also some gentleman or other, stout and flaxen-fair, who was introduced to him as a doctor. This doctor, with a Polish name very hard to pronounce, lived some twenty miles out of town, on a stud-farm, and happened to be passing through the town just then.

"There's a little report here, dealing with your department," said the member of the city council to Andrew Ephimich, after they had all exchanged greetings and seated themselves around a table. "Eugene Fedorovich here tells us the pharmacy is in rather cramped quarters in the main building, and that it ought to be transferred into one of the wings. Of course, that's nothing — one can transfer it, right enough; but the main thing is, the wing will require alterations."

"Yes, it can't be done without alterations," said Andrew Ephimich, after a little thought. "If the corner wing, for instance, were to be fitted out as a pharmacy, it would, I suppose, require five hundred rubles, at a minimum. An unproductive expenditure."

They were all silent for a little while.

"I have already had the honor of submitting a report ten years ago," Andrew Ephimich went on in a quiet voice, "that this hospital, in its present state, appears to be a luxury for this town beyond its resources. It was built in the forties — but at that time the resources were different from what they are now. The town is spending too much on unnecessary buildings and superfluous posts. I think that, under different conditions, two model hospitals could be maintained for the same money."

"There, you just try and set up different conditions!" the member of the city council said with animation.

"I have already had the honor of submitting a report: transfer the medical department to the supervision of the county."

"Yes: transfer the money to the county — and the county will steal it," the flaxen-fair doctor broke into laughter.

"Which is the way of things," concurred the member of the city council, and laughed in his turn.

Andrew Ephimich threw a listless and dull glance at the flaxen-fair doctor and said:

"We must be just."

They were again silent for a little while. Tea was served. The head of the military, who for some reason was very much embarrassed, touched Andrew Ephimich's hand across the table and said:

"You have forgotten us altogether, Doctor. However, you are a monk; you don't play cards, you don't like women. You must feel bored with us fellows."

They all began speaking of how boresome life was for a decent person in this town. No theater, no music, while at the last evening dance given at the club there had been about twenty ladies and only two gentlemen. The young people did not dance but were clustered around the buffet all the time or playing cards. Andrew Ephimich slowly and quietly, without looking at anybody, began saying what a pity, what a profound pity it was that the people in town were expending their life energy, their hearts and their minds, on cards and gossiping, but neither could nor would pass their time in interesting conversation and in reading, they would not avail themselves of the pleasures which the mind affords. The mind alone is interesting and remarkable; as for everything else, it is petty and base. Hobotov was listening attentively to his colleague and suddenly asked:

"Andrew Ephimich, what's today's date?"

Having received his answer he and the flaxen-fair doctor proceeded, in the tone of examiners conscious of their lack of skill, to ask Andrew Ephimich what day it was, how many days there were in the year, and whether it was true that there was a remarkable prophet living in Ward No. 6.

In answering the last question Andrew Ephimich turned red and said:

"Yes, he is ill, but he is an interesting young man."

No further questions were put to him.

As the doctor was putting on his overcoat in the foyer, the head of the military put his hand on his shoulder and said with a sigh:

"It's time we old fellows were given our rest!"

When he had come out of the city offices Andrew Ephimich grasped that this had been a commission appointed to examine his mental faculties. He recalled the questions that had been put to him, turned red and for some reason felt, for the first time now, bitterly sorry for medicine.

"My God!" he reflected, recalling how the physicians had been putting him through a test just now. "Why, they were attending lectures on psychiatry not so long ago, they had to pass examinations — whence, then, comes this all-around ignorance? They haven't the least conception of psychiatry!"

And, for the first time in his life, he felt himself insulted and angered.

That same day, in the evening, Michael Averianich dropped in on him. Without exchanging greetings, the postmaster walked up to him, took both of his hands, and said in an agitated voice:

"My dear friend, prove to me that you believe in my good intentions and consider me your friend.... My friend!" And, preventing Andrew Ephimich from saying anything, he went on, still agitated: "I love you because of your culture and the nobility of your soul. Do listen to me, my dear fellow. The ethics of science obligate doctors to conceal the truth from you but, military fashion, I tell the truth and shame the devil — you are not well! Excuse me, my dear fellow, but that's the truth: all those around you have noticed it long ago. Just now Doctor Eugene Fedorovich was telling me that for the sake of your health you absolutely must take a rest and have some diversion. Absolutely correct! Excellent! In a few days I'll take a leave of absence and go away for a change of air. Prove to me that you are my friend — let's go somewhere together! Let's go — and recall the good old days!"

"I feel myself perfectly well," Andrew Ephimich said, after thinking a while. "But as for going somewhere, that's something I can't do. Do let me prove my friendship for you in some other way."

To be going off somewhere, for some unknown reason, without books, without Dariushka, without beer, breaking off sharply the order of life established through twenty years — the very idea struck him, at the first moment, as wild and fantastic. But he recalled the conversation that had taken place in the city offices and the oppressive mood which he had experienced on his way home from there, and the thought of going away for a short time from the town where stupid people considered him mad appealed to him.

"But where, in particular, do you intend going?" he asked.

"To Moscow, to Petersburg, to Warsaw! I spent five of the happiest years of my life in Warsaw. What an amazing city! Let's go, my dear fellow!"

XIII

A week later it was suggested to Andrew Ephimich that he take a rest — that is, that he hand in his resignation, something which he regarded apathetically — and after another week he and Michael Averianich were already seated in a posting tarantass, bound for the nearest railroad station. The days were cool, clear, with blue skies and a transparent vista. The one hundred and twenty-five miles to the station they covered in two days, and on the way stopped over twice for the night. When, at the posting stations, their tea was served in badly washed tumblers, or too much time was spent in harnessing the horses, Michael Averianich turned purple, his whole body shook, and he shouted "Quiet, you! Don't you dare to argue!" And when he was seated in the tarantass he kept talking without a minute's rest about his journeys through the Caucasus and the Kingdom of Poland. How many adventures there had been, and what encounters! He spoke loudly and, as he spoke, such an astonished look came into his eyes that one might have thought he was lying. To top it off, in the heat of his story-telling he breathed right in Andrew Ephimich's face and laughed in his very ear. This embarrassed the doctor and hindered him from thinking and concentrating.

For reasons of economy they went by third class on the train, in a car where smoking was not permitted. The passengers were halfway decent. Michael Averianich in a short while became well acquainted with all of them and, passing from seat to seat, declared loudly that such exasperating roads ought not to be patronized. All-around knavery! Riding horseback, now, was an altogether different matter: you could cover sixty-five miles in a single day and still feel yourself hale and hearty. As for the poor crops we've been having, that was due to the Pinsk swamps having been drained. As a general thing, everything was at sixes and at sevens — frightfully so. He grew heated, spoke loudly, and gave no chance to the others to say anything. This endless chatter, alternating with loud laughter and expressive gestures, wearied Andrew Ephimich.

"Which one of us two is the madman?" he reflected with vexation. "Is it I, who am trying not to disturb the passengers in any way, or is it this egoist, who thinks he is more intelligent and interesting than all those here, and therefore will not give anybody any rest?"

In Moscow Michael Averianich donned a military frockcoat without any shoulder-straps and trousers with red piping. He went through the streets in a military cap and a uniform overcoat, and the soldiers saluted him. To Andrew Ephimich he now seemed a man who out of all the seigniorial ways that had been his had squandered all that was good and had retained only that which was bad. He loved to be waited on, even when it was unnecessary. Matches might be lying on the table right in front of him, and he saw them, yet he would shout to a waiter to bring him some; he was not at all embarrassed about walking around in nothing but his underwear before a chambermaid; he addressed all waiters indiscriminately — even the old men — as patent inferiors and, if angered, called them blockheads and fools. This, as it seemed to Andrew Ephimich, was seigniorial, yet vile.

First of all Michael Averianich led his friend off to the Iverskaya Church. He prayed ardently, bowing to the very ground and shedding tears and, having done, sighed profoundly and said:

"Even though you may not believe, yet you feel more at peace, somehow, after praying. Kiss the image, my dear friend."

Andrew Ephimich became embarrassed and kissed the holy image, while Michael Averianich puckered up his lips and, shaking his head, offered up a whispered prayer, and tears again welled up in his eyes.

Next they went to the Kremlin and had a look at the Czar-Cannon and the Czar-Bell and even touched them; they admired the view of Moscow-beyond-the-River, visited the Temple of the Saviour and the Rumyantzev Museum.

They dined at Testov's. Michael Averianich studied the menu for a long spell, and said to the waiter in the tone of a gourmet used to feeling himself at home in restaurants:

"Let's see what you will feed us with today, my angel!"

XIV

The doctor went about, saw the sights, ate and drank, yet he had but one feeling: that of vexation at Michael Averianich. He longed for a rest from his friend, to get away from him, to hide himself, whereas his friend considered it his duty not to let the doctor go a step from his side and to provide him with as many diversions as possible. When there were no sights to see he diverted him with conversations. Andrew Ephimich stood this for two days, but on the third he informed his friend that he was ill and wanted to stay in all day. His friend said that in that case he, too, would stay. Really, one had to rest up, otherwise you would run your legs off. Andrew Ephimich lay down on the divan, with his face toward its back and, with clenched teeth, listened to his friend, who assured him ardently that France was inevitably bound to smash Germany, sooner or later, that there were ever so many swindlers in Moscow, and that you can't judge the good points of a horse just by its looks. The doctor's ears began to buzz and his heart to pound but, out of delicacy, he could not find the resolution to ask his friend to go away or to keep still. Fortunately, Michael Averianich grew bored with being cooped up in the hotel room and, after dinner, he went out for a stroll.

Left alone, Andrew Ephimich gave himself up to a feeling of repose. How pleasant to lie motionless on a divan and realize that you were alone in the room! True happiness is impossible without solitude. The Fallen Angel must have betrayed God probably because he had felt a desire for solitude, which the angels know naught of. Andrew Ephimich wanted to think over that which he had seen and heard during the last few days, yet he could not get Michael Averianich out of his head.

"And yet he took a leave of absence and went on this trip with me out of friendship, out of magnanimity," the doctor reflected with vexation. "There's nothing worse than this friendly guardianship. There, now, it would seem he is kindhearted and magnanimous and a merry fellow, and yet he's a bore. An unbearable bore. In precisely the same way there are people whose words are always intelligent and meritorious, yet one feels that they are dull people."

During the days that followed Andrew Ephimich claimed he was ill and did not leave the hotel room. He lay with his face toward the back of the divan and was on tenter-hooks whenever his friend was diverting him with conversations, or rested when his friend was absent. He was vexed with himself for having gone on this trip, and he was vexed with his friend, who was becoming more garrulous and familiar with every day. No matter how hard the doctor tried he could not succeed in attuning his thoughts to a serious, exalted vein.

"This is that reality Ivan Dmitrich spoke of, which is getting me down so," he mused, angry at his own pettiness. "However, that's nonsense. I'll come home, and then things will go on in their old way again."

In St. Petersburg as well he acted the same way; he did not leave the room for days at a time, lying on the divan and getting up only to drink his beer.

Michael Averianich was rushing him all the time to go to Warsaw.

"My dear fellow, why should I go there?" Andrew Ephimich said time and again in an imploring voice. "Go alone, and do let me go home! I beg you!"

"Under no circumstances!" Michael Averianich protested. "It's an amazing city. I spent five of the happiest years of my life there!"

Andrew Ephimich had not enough firmness of character to insist on having his way and, with what heart he could, went to Warsaw. Here he did not leave his room, lay on the divan, and fumed at himself, at his friend, and at the waiters, who stubbornly refused to understand anything but Polish; Michael Averianich, on the other hand, as hale, sprightly and gay as usual, gallivanted all over the city from morning till night, seeking out his old acquaintances. Several times he passed the night away from the hotel. After one such night he came back early in the morning, in a state of great excitement, red and unkempt. For a long while he kept pacing from corner to corner, muttering something to himself; then he halted and said:

"Honor above all!"

After pacing a little longer, he clutched his head and uttered in a tragic voice:

"Yes — honor above all! May that moment be accursed when it first entered my head to come to this Babylon! My dear friend," he turned to the doctor, "despise me! I have lost — gambling! Let me have five hundred rubles!"

Andrew Ephimich counted off five hundred rubles and handed them without a word to his friend. The latter, still purple from shame and wrath, incoherently uttered some uncalled-for vow, put on his cap and went out. Returning some two hours later, he slumped in an armchair, sighed loudly, and said:

"My honor has been saved! Let us go, my friend! I do not wish to remain another minute in this accursed city. Swindlers! Austrian spies!"

When the friends got back to their town it was already November and its streets were deep in snow. Andrew Ephimich's place had been taken by Hobotov, who was still living in his old rooms while waiting for Andrew Ephimich to come and clear out of the hospital quarters. The homely woman whom he called his cook was already living in one of the hospital wings.

New gossip concerning the hospital was floating through the town. It was said that the homely woman had quarreled with the superintendent and that the latter, it would seem, had crawled on his knees before her, begging forgiveness.

On the very first day of his arrival Andrew Ephimich had to look for rooms for himself.

"My friend," the postmaster said to him timidly, "pardon my indiscreet question: what means have you at your disposal?"

Andrew Ephimich counted his money in silence, and said:

"Eighty-six rubles."

"That's not what I am asking you about," Michael Averianich got out in confusion, without having understood the doctor. "I am asking you, what means you have in general?"

"Why, that's just what I'm telling you: eighty-six rubles. Outside of that I have nothing."

Michael Averianich considered the doctor an honest and noble man, but just the same suspected him of having a capital of twenty thousand at the least. But now, having learned that Andrew Ephimich was a pauper, that he had nothing to live on, he for some reason burst into tears and embraced his friend.

XV

Andrew Ephimich was living in a small house with only three windows, belonging to Belova, a burgher's widow. There were just three rooms in this little house, without counting the kitchen. Two of them, with the windows facing the street, were occupied by the doctor, while Dariushka and the burgher's widow with her three children lived in the third room and the kitchen. Occasionally the landlady's lover, a hard-drinking muzhik, would come to pass the night with her; he was tempestuous of nights and inspired the children and Dariushka with terror. Whenever he came and, planting himself on a chair in the kitchen, started demanding vodka, they would all feel very cramped and, out of pity, the doctor would take the crying children to his rooms, making their beds for them on the floor, and this gave him great satisfaction.

He got up at eight, as before, and after tea would sit down to read his old books and periodicals. By now he had no money for new ones.

Either because the books were old, or perhaps because of the change in his environment, reading no longer had as profound a hold on him and tired him out. In order not to spend his time in idleness he was compiling a catalogue *raisonné* of his books and pasting small labels on their backs, and this mechanical, finicky work seemed to him more interesting than reading. The monotonous, finicky work in some incomprehensible fashion lulled his thoughts; he did not think of anything, and the time passed rapidly. Even sitting in the kitchen and cleaning potatoes with Dariushka, or picking the buckwheat grits clean, seemed interesting to him. On Saturdays and Sundays he went to church. Standing close to the wall, with his eyes almost shut, he listened to the chanting and thought of his father, of his mother, of his university, of different religions; he felt at ease and pensive and later, as he left the church, he regretted that the service had ended so soon.

He went twice to the hospital to call on Ivan Dmitrich, to have a chat with him. But on both occasions Ivan Dmitrich had been unusually excited and bad-tempered; he begged to be left in peace, since he had long since wearied of empty chatter, and said that he begged from accursed, vile men but one reward for all his sufferings: solitary confinement. Was it possible that he was being denied even that? On both occasions as Andrew Ephimich was wishing him good night in parting, the madman had snarled back and said:

"Go to the devil!"

And now Andrew Ephimich did not know whether to go to him a third time or not. And yet the wish to go was there.

Formerly, in the interval after dinner, Andrew Ephimich used to pace his rooms and ponder; but now, from dinner until evening tea, he lay on the divan with his face turned to its back, and gave himself up to trivial thoughts, which he could not in any way overcome. He felt aggrieved because he had been given neither a pension nor temporary financial assistance for his service of twenty years. True, he had not served honestly, but then all civil servants receive a pension without any distinction, whether they are honest or not. For contemporary justice consisted precisely in that ranks, decorations and pensions were awarded not for moral qualities or for abilities but for service in general, of whatever sort. Why, then, should he constitute the lone exception? He had no money whatsoever. He felt ashamed whenever he had to pass the general store and see the woman who kept it. By now there were thirty-two rubles owing for the beer. He also owed Belova, the burgher's widow. Dariushka was selling his old clothes and books on the quiet and lying to the landlady that the doctor would be coming into very big money soon.

He was very angry at himself for having spent on the trip the thousand rubles he had hoarded. How handy that thousand would come in now! He felt vexed because people would not leave him in peace. Hobotov considered it his duty to visit his ailing colleague at infrequent intervals. Everything about him aroused aversion in Andrew Ephimich: his well-fed face, and his vile, condescending tone, and the word "colleague," and his high boots; but the most repulsive thing was that he considered himself obliged to treat Andrew Ephimich, and thought that he really was giving him treatment. At his every visit he brought a vial of potassium bromid and some rhubarb pills.

And Michael Averianich, too, considered it his duty to drop in on his friend and divert him. On each occasion he came into Andrew Ephimich's place with an assumed insouciance, laughed boisterously but constrainedly, and fell to assuring him that he looked splendid today and that matters, thanks be to God, were on the mend, and from this one could have concluded that he considered his friend's situation hopeless. He had not yet paid back the debt he had contracted in Warsaw and was crushed by profound shame, on edge, and consequently strove to laugh more loudly and to tell things as amusingly as he could. His anecdotes and stories now seemed endless and were torture both to Andrew Ephimich and to himself.

When he was present Andrew Ephimich would usually lie down on the divan, with his face to the wall, and listen with his teeth clenched; he felt the slag gathering over his soul, layer upon layer, and after his friend's every visit he felt that this slag was rising ever higher and seemed to be reaching his very throat.

In order to drown out these trivial emotions he made haste to reflect that he himself, and Hobotov, and Michael Averianich were bound to perish sooner or later, without leaving as much as an impress upon nature. If one were to imagine some spirit flying through space past the earth a million years hence, that spirit would behold only clay and bare crags. Everything — culture as well as moral law — would perish, and there would not be even a burdock growing over the spot where they had perished. What, then, did shame before the shopkeepers matter, or the insignificant Hobotov, or the oppressive friendship of a Michael Averianich? It was all stuff and nonsense.

But such reflections were no longer of any help. He would no sooner imagine the terrestrial globe a million years hence when, from behind a bare crag, Hobotov would appear in his high boots, or Michael Averianich, guffawing with constraint, and one could even catch his shamefaced whisper: "As for that Warsaw debt, my dear fellow — I'll pay you back one of these days. . . . Without fail!"

XVI

One day Michael Averianich came after dinner, when Andrew Ephimich was lying on the divan. It so happened that Hobotov with his potassium bromid put in his appearance at the same time. Andrew Ephimich rose heavily, sat up, and propped both his hands against the divan.

"Why, my dear fellow," Michael Averianich began, "your complexion is much better than it was yesterday. Yes, you're looking fine! Fine, by God!"

"It's high time you were getting better, colleague — high time," said Hobotov, yawning. "No doubt you yourself must be fed up with this long drawn out mess."

"And get better we will!" Michael Averianich said gaily. "We'll live for another hundred years! We will that!"

"Well, not a hundred, maybe, but he's still good for another twenty," Hobotov remarked consolingly. "Never mind, never mind, colleague, don't despond. That'll do you, trying to pull the wool over my eyes."

"We'll show them what stuff we're made of!" Michael Averianich broke into loud laughter, and patted his friend's knee. "We'll show them yet! Next summer, God willing, we'll dash off to the Caucasus and ride all through it on horseback — *hup, hup, hup!* And when we get back from the Caucasus first thing you know, like as not, we'll be celebrating a wedding." Here Michael Averianich winked slyly. "We'll marry you off, my dear friend . . . we'll marry you off —"

Andrew Ephimich suddenly felt the slag reaching his throat; his heart began to pound frightfully.

"That's vulgar!" he said, getting up quickly and going toward the window. "Is it possible you don't understand that you're saying vulgar things?"

He wanted to go on suavely and politely but, against his will, suddenly clenched his fists and raised them above his head.

"Leave me alone!" he cried out in a voice that was not his own, turning purple and with his whole body quivering. "Get out! Get out, both of you! Both of you!"

Michael Averianich and Hobotov got up and stared at him, in perplexity at first, and then in fear.

"Get out, both of you!" Andrew Ephimich kept shouting. "You dolts! You nincompoops! I don't need either friendship — or your drugs, you dolts! What vulgarity! What vileness!"

Hobotov and Michael Averianich, exchanging bewildered looks, backed toward the door and stepped out into the entry. Andrew Ephimich seized the vial with the potassium bromid and hurled it after them; tinkling, the vial smashed against the threshold.

"Take yourselves off to the devil!" he cried out in a tearful voice, running out into the entry. ."To the devil!"

When his visitors had left Andrew Ephimich, shivering as if in fever, lay down on the divan and for a long time thereafter kept repeating: "Dolts! Nincompoops!"

When he had quieted down, the first thought that came to him was how frightfully ashamed Michael Averianich must feel now and how heavy at heart, and that all this was horrible. Nothing of the sort had ever happened before. What, then, had become of the mind and of tact? What had become of rationalization and philosophic equanimity?

The doctor could not fall asleep all night from shame and vexation at himself and in the morning, about ten, he went to the post office and apologized to the postmaster.

"Let's not recall what has happened," said the touched Michael Averianich with a sigh, squeezing the doctor's hand hard. "Let bygones be bygones. Liubavkin!" he suddenly shouted, so loudly that all the clerks and patrons were startled. "Fetch a chair. And you wait!" he shouted at the countrywoman who was shoving a letter at him through the grilled window for registration. "Can't you see I'm busy? Let's not recall bygones," he went on tenderly, turning to Andrew Ephimich. "Sit down, I entreat you, my dear fellow."

For a minute or so he stroked his knees in silence, and then said:

"It didn't even occur to me to be offended at you. Illness is no sweet bedmate, I understand that. Your fit frightened the doctor and myself yesterday, and we spoke about you for a long time afterwards. My dear fellow, why don't you tackle your illness in earnest? How can one act like that? Pardon my friendly candor," Michael Averianich sank his voice to a whisper, "but you are living in a most unfavorable environment: there isn't room enough, the place isn't clean enough, there's no one to look after you, you have no money for treatment. . . . My dear friend, the doctor and I implore you with all our hearts: heed our advice, go to the hospital! There the food is wholesome, and you'll be looked after, and will receive treatment. Even though Eugene Fedorovich — speaking just between you and me — has atrocious manners, he is nevertheless competent; he can be fully relied on. He gave me his word that he would take you under his care."

Andrew Ephimich was touched by this sincere interest and by the tears which suddenly began to glitter on the postmaster's cheeks.

"My worthiest friend, don't you believe them!" the doctor began whispering, placing his hand on his heart. "Don't you believe them! My illness consists solely of my having found, in twenty years, only one intelligent person in this whole town — and even that one a madman. There's no illness of any sort — but I have simply fallen into a be-witched circle, from which there is no way out. Nothing matters to me; I am ready for everything."

"Go to the hospital, my dear friend."

"Nothing matters to me — I'd even go into a hole in the ground."

"Give me your word, old fellow, that you will obey Eugene Fedoro-vich in everything."

"If you like: I give you my word. But I repeat, my worthiest friend, that I have fallen into a bewitched circle. Everything, even the sincere concern of my friends, now tends toward one thing: my perdition. I am perishing, and I have the fortitude to realize it."

"You will get well, old fellow."

"Why should you say that?" Andrew Ephimich asked with irritation. "There are few men who, toward the close of their lives, do not go through the same experience as mine right now. When you're told that you've got something in the nature of bad kidneys and an enlarged heart, and you start taking treatments, or you're told that you are a madman or a criminal — that is, in short, when people suddenly turn their attention upon you — know, then, that you have fallen into a be-witched circle out of which you will nevermore escape. You will strive to escape — and will go still further astray. Yield, for no human exer-tions will any longer save you. That's how it looks to me."

In the meanwhile people were crowding around the grilled window. So as not to be in the way, Andrew Ephimich got up and started to say good-by. Michael Averianich again secured his word of honor and saw him to the outer door.

That same day, before evening, Hobotov in his short fur-lined coat and his high boots appeared unexpectedly at Andrew Ephimich's and said, in such a tone as if nothing at all had happened yesterday:

"Well, I have come to you on a professional matter, colleague. I have come to invite you: would you care to go to a consultation with me? Eh?"

Thinking that Hobotov wanted to divert him by a stroll, or that he really wanted to give him an opportunity of earning a fee, Andrew Ephimich put on his things and went out with him into the street. He was glad to have this chance to smooth things over after having been at fault yesterday and of effecting a reconciliation, and at heart was thankful to Hobotov, who had not even hinted at yesterday's incident and, evidently, was sparing him. It was difficult to expect such delicacy from this uncultured man.

"But where is your patient?" asked Andrew Ephimich.

"In my hospital. I have been wanting to show him to you for a long while. . . . A most interesting case."

They entered the hospital yard and, skirting the main building, headed for the wing where the demented patients were housed. And all this, for some reason, in silence. When they entered the wing Nikita, as usual, sprang up and stood at attention.

"One of the patients here had a sudden pulmonary complication," Hobotov said in a low voice, entering the ward with Andrew Ephimich. "You wait here a little; I'll be right back. I'm going after my stethoscope."

And he walked out.

XVII

It was already twilight. Ivan Dmitrich was lying on his bed, his face thrust into the pillow; the paralytic was sitting motionlessly, softly crying and moving his lips. The obese muzhik and the one-time mail sorter were sleeping. Everything was quiet.

Andrew Ephimich sat on Ivan Dmitrich's bed and waited. But half an hour passed, and instead of Hobotov it was Nikita who entered the ward, holding in his arms a bathrobe, somebody's underwear, and slippers.

"Please dress yourself, Your Honor," said he quietly. "Here's your little bed — please to come over here," he added, indicating a vacant bed, evidently brought in recently. "Never mind; you'll get well, God willing."

Andrew Ephimich grasped everything. Without uttering a word he went over to the bed Nikita had indicated and sat down; perceiving that Nikita was standing and waiting, he stripped to the skin, and a feeling of shame came over him.   Then he put on the hospital under-wear; the drawers were very short, the shirt was long, while the bath-robe smelt of smoked fish.

"You'll get well, God willing," Nikita repeated.

He picked up Andrew Ephimich's clothes in his arms, went out, and shut the door after him.

"It doesn't matter. . . ." Andrew Ephimich reflected, shamefacedly drawing the bathrobe closely about him, and feeling that in his new outfit he looked like a convict.   "It doesn't matter. . . . It doesn't matter whether it's a frockcoat, or a uniform, or this hospital bathrobe —"

But what about his watch?   And the notebook in his side-pocket?   And his cigarettes?   Where had Nikita carried off his clothes to?   Now, likely as not, he would have no occasion until his very death to put on trousers, vest, and boots.   All this was odd, somehow, and even incom-prehensible, at first.   Andrew Ephimich was convinced, even now, that between the widow Belova's house and Ward No. 6 there was no differ-ence whatsoever; that everything in this world was nonsense and vanity of vanities, yet at the same time his hands were trembling, his feet were turning cold, and he felt eerie at the thought that Ivan Dmitrich would awake soon and see him in a hospital bathrobe.   He stood up, took a turn about the room, and sat down again.

There, he had sat through half an hour, an hour, by now, and he had become deadly wearied.   Could one possibly live through a day here, through a week, and even years, like these people?   There, now, he had been sitting, had taken a turn about the room, and had sat down again; one could go and take a look out of the window, and again traverse the room from one corner to the other.   But, after that, what? Sit just like that, all the time, like an image carved of wood, and medi-tate?   No, that was hardly possible.

Andrew Ephimich lay down, but immediately got up, mopped the cold sweat off his forehead with the sleeve of his bathrobe — and felt that his whole face had begun to reek of smoked fish.   He took another turn about the room.

"This must be some sort of misunderstanding —" he let drop, spread-ing his hands in perplexity.   "I must have an explanation — there's some misunderstanding here —"

At this point Ivan Dmitrich awoke.   He sat up and propped his cheeks on his fists.   He spat.   Then he glanced lazily at the doctor and, evidently, did not grasp anything at the first moment; shortly, how-ever, his sleepy face became rancorous and mocking.

"Aha — so they've planted you here as well, my fine fellow!" he got out in a voice still hoarse from sleep, puckering up one eye. "Very glad of it! There was a time when you drank men's blood, but now they'll drink yours. Splendid!"

"This must be some sort of misunderstanding —" Andrew Ephimich got out, frightened at Ivan Dmitrich's words; he shrugged his shoulders and repeated: "Some sort of misunderstanding —"

Ivan Dmitrich spat again and lay down.

"An accursed life!" he grumbled out. "And the thing that's so bitter about it and that hurts so, is that this life will end neither in a reward for one's sufferings, nor any apotheosis, as in an opera, but in death; the muzhik orderlies will come and haul the dead man off by his hands and feet into the basement. Brrr. . . . Well, no matter. But then, in the other world, it will be our turn to celebrate. I'll appear here from the other world as a shade and will frighten all these vermin. I'll make them sit here a while."

Moisseika came back and, catching sight of the doctor, held out his cupped hand:

"Give us one little copper!" said he.

XVIII

Andrew Ephimich walked away to the window and looked out at the field. It was getting dark by now and on the horizon, to the right, a chill, purple moon was rising. Not far from the hospital fence, seven hundred feet away at the most, stood a tall white building surrounded by a stone wall. This was the prison.

"Reality — there it is!" Andrew Ephimich reflected, and he became frightened.

Frightening was the moon, too, and the prison, and the nails, points up, on the fence, and the distant flare of a bone-burning yard. He heard a sigh behind him. He looked over his shoulder and saw a man with glittering stars and decorations on his breast, who was smiling and slyly winking. And this, too, seemed frightening.

Andrew Ephimich was assuring himself that there was nothing peculiar about the moon and the prison, that even those people who were psychically sound wore decorations, and that everything would rot in time and turn into clay, but despair suddenly took possession of him: he seized the window-bars with both hands and shook them with all his strength. The sturdy bars did not yield.

Then, so that things might not be so frightening, he went to Ivan Dmitrich's bed and sat down.

"I've fallen in spirits, my dear fellow," he muttered, trembling and wiping his cold sweat. "I've fallen in spirits."

"Why, just go ahead and philosophize a bit," Ivan Dmitrich remarked mockingly.

"My God, my God. . . . Yes, yes. . . . You were pleased to say some time ago that there is no philosophy in Russia but that everybody philosophizes — even the small fry. But then, no harm can befall anybody from the philosophizing of the small fry," said Andrew Ephimich, in such a tone as if he wanted to break into tears and stir the other's pity. "Why, then, my dear fellow, this spiteful laughter? And how can the small fry help but philosophize since it is not satisfied? An intelligent, educated, proud, freedom-loving man, in the image of God, has no other way out save to go as a medico into a filthy, stupid, miserable hole of a town — and all his life consists of cupping glasses, leeches, mustard-plasters! Quackery, bigotry, vulgarity! Oh, my God!"

"You're spouting bosh. If you detested being a medico, you should have become a prime minister."

"One can't get anywhere, anywhere. We are weak, my dear fellow. I was equanimous, my reasoning was wide-awake and filled with common sense — yet it sufficed for life merely to touch me roughly to have me fall in spirits. Prostration. . . . We are weak, we are made of shoddy. And you too, my dear fellow. You are intelligent, noble, you have imbibed noble impulses with your mother's milk; yet you had hardly entered upon life when you became wearied and fell ill. We are weak, weak!"

Some other thing, which he was unable to shake off, outside of fear and a sense of having been wronged, had been constantly tormenting Andrew Ephimich ever since nightfall. Finally he realized that he wanted to drink some beer and have a smoke.

"I'm going out of here, my dear fellow," he said. "I'll tell them to let us have some light. I can't stand it this way — I'm in no condition —"

Andrew Ephimich went to the door and opened it, but Nikita immediately sprang up and blocked his way.

"Where you going? You mustn't, you mustn't!" he said. "Time to go to sleep!"

"But I want to go for just a minute, to take a walk in the yard!" Andrew Ephimich was taken aback.

"Mustn't, mustn't — those are orders. You know that yourself."
Nikita slammed the door shut and put his back against it.

"But suppose I were to go out of here, what harm would that do anybody?" asked Andrew Ephimich, shrugging his shoulders. "I can't understand this! Nikita, I must go out!" — and there was a catch in his voice. "I've got to!"

"Don't start any disorders — it's not right!" Nikita admonished him.

"This is the devil and all!" Ivan Dmitrich suddenly cried out and sprang up. "What right has he got not to let us out? How dare they keep us here? The law, it seems, says plainly that no man may be deprived of liberty without a trial! This is oppression! Tyranny!"

"Of course it's tyranny!" said Andrew Ephimich, heartened by Ivan Dmitrich's outcry. "I've got to, I must go out! He has no right to do this! Let me out, I tell you!"

"Do you hear, you stupid brute?" Ivan Dmitrich shouted, and pounded on the door with his fist. "Open up, or else I'll break the door down! You butcher!"

"Open up!" Andrew Ephimich shouted, his whole body quivering. "I demand it!"

"Just keep on talking a little more!" Nikita answered from the other side of the door. "Keep it up!"

"At least go and ask Eugene Fedorovich to come here! Tell him I beg of him to be so kind as to come — for just a minute —"

"He'll come of his own self tomorrow."

"They'll never let us out!" Ivan Dmitrich went on in the meantime. "They'll make us rot here! Oh Lord, is there really no hell in the other world, and these scoundrels will be forgiven? Where is justice, then? Open up, you scoundrel — I'm suffocating!" he cried out in a hoarse voice and threw his weight against the door. "I'll smash my head! You murderers!"

Nikita flung the door open, shoved Andrew Ephimich aside roughly, using both his hands and one knee, then swung back and smashed his fist into the doctor's face. It seemed to Andrew Ephimich that an enormous salty wave had gone over his head and dragged him off toward his bed; there really was a salty taste in his mouth: probably his teeth had begun to bleed. He began to thresh his arms, just as if he were trying to come to the surface, and grabbed at somebody's bed, and at that point felt Nikita strike him twice in the back.

Ivan Dmitrich let out a yell. Probably he, too, was being beaten.

After that everything quieted down. The tenuous moonlight streamed in through the barred windows, and lying on the floor was a shadow that looked like a net. Everything was frightening. Andrew Ephimich lay down and held his breath; he anticipated with horror that he would be struck again. Just as though someone had taken a sickle, had driven it into him and then twisted it several times in his breast and guts. From pain he bit his pillow and clenched his teeth and suddenly, amid all the chaos, a fearful, unbearable thought flashed clearly in his head: that exactly the same pain must have been experienced throughout the years, day in and day out, by these people who now, in the light of the moon, seemed to be black shadows. How could it have come about, during the course of twenty years, that he had not known, and had not wanted to know, all this? He did not know pain, he had had no conception of it — therefore he was not to blame, yet conscience, just as intractable and harsh as Nikita, made him turn cold from the nape of his neck to his heels. He sprang up, wanted to cry out with all his might and to run as fast as he could to kill Nikita, then Hobotov, and the superintendent, and the assistant doctor, and then himself; but never a sound escaped from his breast and his legs would not obey him; suffocating, he yanked at the breast of his bathrobe and shirt, tore them and crashed down unconscious on his bed.

XIX

On the morning of the next day his head ached, his ears hummed, and his whole body felt broken up. He did not blush at the recollection of his weakness of yesterday. Yesterday he had been pusillanimous, had been afraid even of the moon, had given sincere utterance to feelings and thoughts which he had not formerly even suspected of having within him. The thought, for instance, about the dissatisfaction of the small fry. But now nothing mattered to him.

He did not eat, did not drink; he lay without moving and kept silent.

"Nothing matters to me," he thought when questions were put to him. "I'm not going to bother answering. . . . Nothing matters to me."

Michael Averianich came after dinner and brought him a quarter-pound packet of tea and a pound of marmalade candy. Dariushka also came and stood for a whole hour by his bed with an expression of stolid sorrow on her face. Doctor Hobotov, too, paid him a visit. He brought a vial of potassium bromid and ordered Nikita to fumigate the place with something.

Toward evening Andrew Ephimich died from an apoplectic stroke. At first he had felt a staggering ague-fit and nausea; something disgusting (so it seemed), penetrating his whole body, even into his fingers, started pulling from the stomach toward his head, and flooded his eyes and ears. Everything turned green before his eyes. Andrew Ephimich realized that his end had come, and recalled that Ivan Dmitrich, Michael Averianich and millions of men believe in immortality. And what if it should suddenly prove actual? But he felt no desire for immortality, and he thought of it only for an instant. A herd of reindeer, extraordinarily beautiful and graceful (he had read about them yesterday), ran past him; then a countrywoman stretched out her hand to him, holding a letter for registration. . . . Michael Averianich said something. Then everything vanished, and Andrew Ephimich forgot everything for all eternity.

The muzhik orderlies came, took him by his hands and feet, and carried him off into the chapel. There he lay on a table with his eyes open, and, through the night, the moon threw its light upon him. In the morning Serghei Sergheich came, piously prayed before Christ on the Cross, and closed the eyes of his quondam chief.

The day after that they buried Andrew Ephimich. Only Michael Averianich and Dariushka attended the burial.

[*Translated by* BERNARD GUILBERT GUERNEY]

Thomas Mann

DEATH IN VENICE

1 9 1 2

GUSTAVE ASCHENBACH — or von Aschenbach, as he had been known officially since his fiftieth birthday — had set out alone from his house in Prince Regent Street, Munich, for an extended walk. It was a spring afternoon in that year of grace 19—, when Europe sat upon the anxious seat beneath a menace that hung over its head for months. Aschenbach had sought the open soon after tea. He was overwrought by a morning of hard, nerve-taxing work, work which had not ceased to exact his uttermost in the way of sustained concentration, conscientiousness, and tact; and after the noon meal found himself powerless to check the onward sweep of the productive mechanism within him, that *motus animi continuus* in which, according to Cicero, eloquence resides. He had sought but not found relaxation in sleep — though the wear and tear upon his system had come to make a daily nap more and more imperative — and now undertook a walk, in the hope that air and exercise might send him back refreshed to a good evening's work.

May had begun, and after weeks of cold and wet a mock summer had set in. The English Gardens, though in tenderest leaf, felt as sultry as in August and were full of vehicles and pedestrians near the city. But towards Aumeister the paths were solitary and still, and Aschenbach strolled thither, stopping awhile to watch the lively crowds in the restaurant garden with its fringe of carriages and cabs. Thence he took his homeward way outside the park and across the sunset fields. By the time he reached the North Cemetery, however, he felt tired, and a storm was brewing above Föhring; so he waited at the stopping-place for a tram to carry him back to the city.

He found the neighbourhood quite empty. Not a wagon in sight, either on the paved Ungererstrasse, with its gleaming tram-lines stretching off towards Schwabing, nor on the Föhring highway. Nothing stirred behind the hedge in the stone-mason's yard, where crosses, monuments, and commemorative tablets made a supernumerary

439

and untenanted graveyard opposite the real one. The mortuary chapel, a structure in Byzantine style, stood facing it, silent in the gleam of the ebbing day. Its façade was adorned with Greek crosses and tinted hieratic designs, and displayed a symmetrically arranged selection of scriptural texts in gilded letters, all of them with a bearing upon the future life, such as: "They are entering into the House of the Lord" and "May the Light Everlasting shine upon them." Aschenbach beguiled some minutes of his waiting with reading these formulas and letting his mind's eye lose itself in their mystical meaning. He was brought back to reality by the sight of a man standing in the portico, above the two apocalyptic beasts that guarded the staircase, and something not quite usual in this man's appearance gave his thoughts a fresh turn.

Whether he had come out of the hall through the bronze doors or mounted unnoticed from outside, it was impossible to tell. Aschenbach casually inclined to the first idea. He was of medium height, thin, beardless, and strikingly snub-nosed; he belonged to the red-haired type and possessed its milky, freckled skin. He was obviously not Bavarian; and the broad, straight-brimmed straw hat he had on even made him look distinctly exotic. True, he had the indigenous rucksack buckled on his back, wore a belted suit of yellowish woollen stuff, apparently frieze, and carried a grey mackintosh cape across his left forearm, which was propped against his waist. In his right hand, slantwise to the ground, he held an iron-shod stick, and braced himself against its crook, with his legs crossed. His chin was up, so that the Adam's apple looked very bald in the lean neck rising from the loose shirt; and he stood there sharply peering up into space out of colourless, red-lashed eyes, while two pronounced perpendicular furrows showed on his forehead in curious contrast to his little turned-up nose. Perhaps his heightened and heightening position helped out the impression Aschenbach received. At any rate, standing there as though at survey, the man had a bold and domineering, even a ruthless, air, and his lips completed the picture by seeming to curl back, either by reason of some deformity or else because he grimaced, being blinded by the sun in his face; they laid bare the long, white, glistening teeth to the gums.

Aschenbach's gaze, though unawares, had very likely been inquisitive and tactless; for he became suddenly conscious that the stranger was returning it, and indeed so directly, with such hostility, such plain intent to force the withdrawal of the other's eyes, that Aschenbach felt an unpleasant twinge and, turning his back, began to walk along the hedge, hastily resolving to give the man no further heed. He had forgotten him the next minute. Yet whether the pilgrim air the stranger wore kindled his fantasy or whether some other physical or psychical influence came in play, he could not tell; but he felt the most surprising consciousness of a widening of inward barriers, a kind of vaulting unrest, a youthfully ardent thirst for distant scenes — a feeling so lively and so new, or at least so long ago outgrown and forgot, that he stood there rooted to the spot, his eyes on the ground and his hands clasped behind him, exploring these sentiments of his, their bearing and scope.

True, what he felt was no more than a longing to travel; yet coming upon him with such suddenness and passion as to resemble a seizure, almost a hallucination. Desire projected itself visually: his fancy, not quite yet lulled since morning, imaged the marvels and terrors of the manifold earth. He saw. He beheld a landscape, a tropical marshland, beneath a reeking sky, steaming, monstrous, rank — a kind of primeval wilderness-world of islands, morasses, and alluvial channels. Hairy palm-trunks rose near and far out of lush brakes of fern, out of bottoms of crass vegetation, fat, swollen, thick with incredible bloom. There were trees, misshapen as a dream, that dropped their naked roots straight through the air into the ground or into water that was stagnant and shadowy and glassy-green, where mammoth milk-white blossoms floated, and strange high-shouldered birds with curious bills stood gazing sidewise without sound or stir. Among the knotted joints of a bamboo thicket the eyes of a crouching tiger gleamed — and he felt his heart throb with terror, yet with a longing inexplicable. Then the vision vanished. Aschenbach, shaking his head, took up his march once more along the hedge of the stone-mason's yard.

He had, at least ever since he commanded means to get about the world at will, regarded travel as a necessary evil, to be endured now and again willy-nilly for the sake of one's health. Too busy with the tasks imposed upon him by his own ego and the European soul, too laden with the care and duty to create, too preoccupied to be an amateur of the gay outer world, he had been content to know as much of the earth's surface as he could without stirring far outside his own sphere — had, indeed, never even been tempted to leave Europe. Now more than ever, since his life was on the wane, since he could no longer brush aside as fanciful his artist fear of not having done, of not being finished before the works ran down, he had confined himself to close range, had hardly stepped outside the charming city which he had made his home and the rude country house he had built in the mountains, whither he went to spend the rainy summers.

And so the new impulse which thus late and suddenly swept over him was speedily made to conform to the pattern of self-discipline he had followed from his youth up. He had meant to bring his work, for which he lived, to a certain point before leaving for the country, and the thought of a leisurely ramble across the globe, which should take him away from his desk for months, was too fantastic and upsetting to be seriously entertained. Yet the source of the unexpected contagion was known to him only too well. This yearning for new and distant scenes, this craving for freedom, release, forgetfulness — they were, he admitted to himself, an impulse towards flight, flight from the spot which was the daily theatre of a rigid, cold, and passionate service. That service he loved, had even almost come to love the enervating daily struggle between a proud, tenacious, well-tried will and this growing fatigue, which no one must suspect, nor the finished product betray by any faintest sign that his inspiration could ever flag or miss fire. On the other hand, it seemed the part of common sense not to span the bow too far, not to suppress summarily a need that so unequivocally asserted itself. He thought of his work, and the place where yesterday and again today he had been forced to lay it down, since it would not yield either to patient effort or a swift *coup de main*. Again and again he had tried to break or untie the knot — only to retire at last from the attack with a shiver of repugnance. Yet the difficulty was actually not a great one; what sapped his strength was distaste for the task, betrayed by a fastidiousness he could no longer satisfy. In his youth, indeed, the nature and inmost essence of the literary gift had been, to him, this very scrupulosity; for it he had bridled and tempered his sensibilities, knowing full well that feeling is prone to be content with easy gains and blithe half-perfection. So now, perhaps, feeling, thus tyrannized, avenged itself by leaving him, refusing from now on to carry and wing his art and taking away with it all the ecstasy he had known in form and expression. Not that he was doing bad work. So much, at least, the years had brought him, that at any moment he might feel tranquilly assured of mastery. But he got no joy of it — not though a nation paid it homage. To him it seemed his work had ceased to be marked by that fiery play of fancy which is the product of joy, and more, and more potently, than any intrinsic content, forms in turn the joy of the receiving world. He dreaded the summer in the country, alone with the maid who prepared his food and the man who served him; dreaded to see the familiar mountain peaks and walls that would shut him up again with his heavy discontent. What he needed was a break, an interim existence, a means of passing time, other air and a new stock of blood, to make the summer tolerable and productive. Good, then, he would go a journey. Not far — not all the way to the tigers. A night in a *wagon-lit,* three or four weeks of lotus-eating at some one of the gay world's playgrounds in the lovely south. . . .

So ran his thoughts, while the clang of the electric tram drew nearer down the Ungererstrasse; and as he mounted the platform he decided to devote the evening to a study of maps and railway guides. Once in, he bethought him to look back after the man in the straw hat, the companion of this brief interval which had after all been so fruitful. But he was not in his former place, nor in the tram itself, nor yet at the next stop; in short, his whereabouts remained a mystery.

Gustave Aschenbach was born at L—, a country town in the province of Silesia. He was the son of an upper official in the judicature, and his forbears had all been officers, judges, departmental functionaries — men who lived their strict, decent, sparing lives in the service of king and state. Only once before had a livelier mentality — in the quality of a clergyman — turned up among them; but swifter, more perceptive blood had in the generation before the poet's flowed into the stock from the mother's side, she being the daughter of a Bohemian musical conductor. It was from her he had the foreign traits that betrayed themselves in his appearance. The union of dry, conscientious officialdom and ardent, obscure impulse, produced an artist — and this particular artist: author of the lucid and vigorous prose epic on the life of Frederick the Great; careful, tireless weaver of the richly patterned tapestry entitled *Maia,* a novel that gathers up the threads of many human destinies in the warp of a single idea; creator of that powerful narrative *The Abject,* which taught a whole grateful generation that a man can still be capable of moral resolution even after he has plumbed the depths of knowledge; and lastly — to complete the tale of works of his mature period — the writer of that impassioned discourse on the theme of Mind and Art whose ordered force and antithetic eloquence led serious critics to rank it with Schiller's *Simple and Sentimental Poetry.*

Aschenbach's whole soul, from the very beginning, was bent on fame — and thus, while not precisely precocious, yet thanks to the unmistakable trenchancy of his personal accent he was early ripe and ready for a career. Almost before he was out of high school he had a name. Ten years later he had learned to sit at his desk and sustain and live up to his growing reputation, to write gracious and pregnant phrases in letters that must needs be brief, for many claims press upon the solid and successful man. At forty, worn down by the strains and stresses of his actual task, he had to deal with a daily post heavy with tributes from his own and foreign countries.

Remote on one hand from the banal, on the other from the eccentric, his genius was calculated to win at once the adhesion of the general public and the admiration, both sympathetic and stimulating, of the connoisseur. From childhood up he was pushed on every side to achievement, and achievement of no ordinary kind; and so his young days never knew the sweet idleness and blithe *laissez aller* that belong to youth. A nice observer once said of him in company — it was at the time when he fell ill in Vienna in his thirty-fifth year: "You see, Aschenbach has always lived like this" — here the speaker closed the fingers of his left hand to a fist — "never like this" — and he let his open hand hang relaxed from the back of his chair. It was apt. And this attitude was the more morally valiant in that Aschenbach was not by nature robust — he was only called to the constant tension of his career, not actually born to it.

By medical advice he had been kept from school and educated at home. He had grown up solitary, without comradeship; yet had early been driven to see that he belonged to those whose talent is not so much out of the common as is the physical basis on which talent relies for its fulfilment. It is a seed that gives early of its fruit, whose powers seldom reach a ripe old age. But his favourite motto was "Hold fast"; indeed, in his novel on the life of Frederick the Great he envisaged nothing else than the apotheosis of the old hero's word of command, "*Durchhalten*," which seemed to him the epitome of fortitude under suffering. Besides, he deeply desired to live to a good old age, for it was his conviction that only the artist to whom it has been granted to be fruitful on all stages of our human scene can be truly great, or universal, or worthy of honour.

Bearing the burden of his genius, then, upon such slender shoulders and resolved to go so far, he had the more need of discipline — and discipline, fortunately, was his native inheritance from the father's side. At forty, at fifty, he was still living as he had commenced to live in the years when others are prone to waste and revel, dream high thoughts and postpone fulfilment. He began his day with a cold shower over chest and back; then, setting a pair of tall wax candles in silver holders at the head of his manuscript, he sacrificed to art, in two or three hours of almost religious fervour, the powers he had assembled in sleep. Outsiders might be pardoned for believing that his *Maia* world and the epic amplitude revealed by the life of Frederick were a manifestation of great power working under high pressure, that they came forth, as it were, all in one breath. It was the more triumph for his morale; for the truth was that they were heaped up to greatness in layer after layer, in long days of work, out of hundreds and hundreds of single inspirations; they owed their excellence, both of mass and detail, to one thing and one alone: that their creator could hold out for years under the strain of the same piece of work, with an endurance and a tenacity of purpose like that which had conquered his native province of Silesia, devoting to actual composition none but his best and freshest hours.

For an intellectual product of any value to exert an immediate influence which shall also be deep and lasting, it must rest on an inner harmony, yes, an affinity, between the personal destiny of its author and that of his contemporaries in general. Men do not know why they award fame to one work of art rather than another. Without being in the faintest connoisseurs, they think to justify the warmth of their commendations by discovering in it a hundred virtues, whereas the real ground of their applause is inexplicable — it is sympathy. Aschenbach had once given direct expression — though in an unobtrusive place — to the idea that almost everything conspicuously great is great in despite: has come into being in defiance of affliction and pain, poverty, destitution, bodily weakness, vice, passion, and a thousand other obstructions. And that was more than observation — it was the fruit of experience, it was precisely the formula of his life and fame, it was the key to his work. What wonder, then, if it was also the fixed character, the outward gesture, of his most individual figures?

The new type of hero favoured by Aschenbach, and recurring many times in his works, had early been analysed by a shrewd critic: "The conception of an intellectual and virginal manliness, which clenches its teeth and stands in modest defiance of the swords and spears that pierce its side." That was beautiful, it was *spirituel*, it was exact, despite the suggestion of too great passivity it held. Forbearance in the face of fate, beauty constant under torture, are not merely passive. They are a positive achievement, an explicit triumph; and the figure of Sebastian is the most beautiful symbol, if not of art as a whole, yet certainly of the art we speak of here. Within that world of Aschenbach's creation were exhibited many phases of this theme: there was the aristocratic self-command that is eaten out within and for as long as it can conceals its biologic decline from the eyes of the world; the sere and ugly outside, hiding the embers of smouldering fire — and having power to fan them to so pure a flame as to challenge supremacy in the domain of beauty itself; the pallid languors of the flesh, contrasted with the fiery ardours of the spirit within, which can fling a whole proud people down at the foot of the Cross, at the feet of its own sheer self-abnegation; the gracious bearing preserved in the stern, stark service of form; the unreal, precarious existence of the born intrigant with its swiftly enervating alternation of schemes and desires — all these human fates and many more of their like one read in Aschenbach's pages, and reading them might doubt the existence of any other kind of heroism than the heroism born of weakness. And, after all, what kind could be truer to the spirit of the times? Gustave Aschenbach was the poet-spokesman of all those who labour at the edge of exhaustion; of the overburdened, of those who are already worn out but still hold themselves upright; of all our modern moralizers of accomplishment, with stunted growth and scanty resources, who yet contrive by skilful husbanding and prodigious spasms of will to produce, at least for a while, the effect of greatness. There are many such, they are the heroes of the age. And in Aschenbach's pages they saw themselves; he justified, he exalted them, he sang their praise — and they, they were grateful, they heralded his fame.

He had been young and crude with the times and by them badly counselled. He had taken false steps, blundered, exposed himself, offended in speech and writing against tact and good sense. But he had attained to honour, and honour, he used to say, is the natural goal towards which every considerable talent presses with whip and spur. Yes, one might put it that his whole career had been one conscious and overweening ascent to honour, which left in the rear all the misgivings or self-derogation which might have hampered him.

What pleases the public is lively and vivid delineation which makes no demands on the intellect; but passionate and absolutist youth can only be enthralled by a problem. And Aschenbach was as absolute, as problematist, as any youth of them all. He had done homage to intellect, had overworked the soil of knowledge and ground up her seed-corn; had turned his back on the "mysteries," called genius itself in question, held up art to scorn — yes, even while his faithful follow-

ing revelled in the characters he created, he, the young artist, was
taking away the breath of the twenty-year-olds with his cynic utter-
ances on the nature of art and the artist life.

But it seems that a noble and active mind blunts itself against nothing
so quickly as the sharp and bitter irritant of knowledge. And certain
it is that the youth's constancy of purpose, no matter how painfully
conscientious, was shallow beside the mature resolution of the master
of his craft, who made a right-about-face, turned his back on the realm
of knowledge, and passed it by with averted face, lest it lame his will
or power of action, paralyse his feelings or his passions, deprive any of
these of their conviction or utility. How else interpret the oft-cited
story of *The Abject* than as a rebuke to the excesses of a psychology-
ridden age, embodied in the delineation of the weak and silly fool who
manages to lead fate by the nose; driving his wife, out of sheer innate
pusillanimity, into the arms of a beardless youth, and making this disaster an excuse for trifling away the rest of his life?

With rage the author here rejects the rejected, casts out the outcast
— and the measure of his fury is the measure of his condemnation of
all moral shilly-shallying. Explicitly he renounces sympathy with the
abyss, explicitly he refutes the flabby humanitarianism of the phrase:
"*Tout comprendre c'est tout pardonner.*" What was here unfolding, or
rather was already in full bloom, was the "miracle of regained detachment," which a little later became the theme of one of the author's
dialogues, dwelt upon not without a certain oracular emphasis. Strange
sequence of thought! Was it perhaps an intellectual consequence of
this rebirth, this new austerity, that from now on his style showed an
almost exaggerated sense of beauty, a lofty purity, symmetry, and simplicity, which gave his productions a stamp of the classic, of conscious
and deliberate mastery? And yet: this moral fibre, surviving the ham-
pering and disintegrating effect of knowledge, does it not result in its
turn in a dangerous simplification, in a tendency to equate the world
and the human soul, and thus to strengthen the hold of the evil, the
forbidden, and the ethically impossible? And has not form two aspects?
Is it not moral and immoral at once: moral in so far as it is the expression and result of discipline, immoral — yes, actually hostile to morality — in that of its very essence it is indifferent to good and evil, and
deliberately concerned to make the moral world stoop beneath its
proud and undivided sceptre?

Be that as it may. Development is destiny; and why should a career
attended by the applause and adulation of the masses necessarily take

the same course as one which does not share the glamour and the obligations of fame? Only the incorrigible bohemian smiles or scoffs when a man of transcendent gifts outgrows his carefree prentice stage, recognizes his own worth and forces the world to recognize it too and pay it homage, though he puts on a courtly bearing to hide his bitter struggles and his loneliness. Again, the play of a developing talent must give its possessor joy, if of a wilful, defiant kind. With time, an official note, something almost expository, crept into Gustave Aschenbach's method. His later style gave up the old sheer audacities, the fresh and subtle nuances — it became fixed and exemplary, conservative, formal, even formulated. Like Louis XIV — or as tradition has it of him — Aschenbach, as he went on in years, banished from his style every common word. It was at this time that the school authorities adopted selections from his works into their text-books. And he found it inly fitting — and had no thought but to accept — when a German prince signalized his accession to the throne by conferring upon the poet-author of the life of Frederick the Great on his fiftieth birthday the letters-patent of nobility.

He had roved about for a few years, trying this place and that as a place of residence, before choosing, as he soon did, the city of Munich for his permanent home. And there he lived, enjoying among his fellow-citizens the honour which is in rare cases the reward of intellectual eminence. He married young, the daughter of a university family; but after a brief term of wedded happiness his wife had died. A daughter, already married, remained to him. A son he never had.

Gustave von Aschenbach was somewhat below middle height, dark and smooth-shaven, with a head that looked rather too large for his almost delicate figure. He wore his hair brushed back; it was thin at the parting, bushy and grey on the temples, framing a lofty, rugged, knotty brow — if one may so characterize it. The nose-piece of his rimless gold spectacles cut into the base of his thick, aristocratically hooked nose. The mouth was large, often lax, often suddenly narrow and tense; the cheeks lean and furrowed, the pronounced chin slightly cleft. The vicissitudes of fate, it seemed, must have passed over this head, for he held it, plaintively, rather on one side; yet it was art, not the stern discipline of an active career, that had taken over the office of modelling these features. Behind this brow were born the flashing thrust and parry of the dialogue between Frederick and Voltaire on the theme of war; these eyes, weary and sunken, gazing through their glasses, had beheld the blood-stained inferno of the hospitals in the

Seven Years' War. Yes, personally speaking too, art heightens life. She gives deeper joy, she consumes more swiftly. She engraves adventures of the spirit and the mind in the faces of her votaries; let them lead outwardly a life of the most cloistered calm, she will in the end produce in them a fastidiousness, an over-refinement, a nervous fever and exhaustion, such as a career of extravagant passions and pleasures can hardly show.

Eager though he was to be off, Aschenbach was kept in Munich by affairs both literary and practical for some two weeks after that walk of his. But at length he ordered his country home put ready against his return within the next few weeks, and on a day between the middle and the end of May took the evening train for Trieste, where he stopped only twenty-four hours, embarking for Pola the next morning but one.

What he sought was a fresh scene, without associations, which should yet be not too out-of-the-way; and accordingly he chose an island in the Adriatic, not far off the Istrian coast. It had been well known some years, for its splendidly rugged cliff formations on the side next the open sea, and its population, clad in a bright flutter of rags and speaking an outlandish tongue. But there was rain and heavy air; the society at the hotel was provincial Austrian, and limited; besides, it annoyed him not to be able to get at the sea — he missed the close and soothing contact which only a gentle sandy slope affords. He could not feel this was the place he sought; an inner impulse made him wretched, urging him on he knew not whither; he racked his brains, he looked up boats, then all at once his goal stood plain before his eyes. But of course! When one wanted to arrive overnight at the incomparable, the fabulous, the like-nothing-else-in-the-world, where was it one went? Why, obviously; he had intended to go there, what ever was he doing here? A blunder. He made all haste to correct it, announcing his departure at once. Ten days after his arrival on the island a swift motor-boat bore him and his luggage in the misty dawning back across the water to the naval station, where he landed only to pass over the landing-stage and on to the wet decks of a ship lying there with steam up for the passage to Venice.

It was an ancient hulk belonging to an Italian line, obsolete, dingy, grimed with soot. A dirty hunchbacked sailor, smirkingly polite, conducted him at once belowships to a cavernous, lamplit cabin. There behind a table sat a man with a beard like a goat's; he had his hat on the back of his head, a cigar-stump in the corner of his mouth; he reminded Aschenbach of an old-fashioned circus-director. This person put the usual questions and wrote out a ticket to Venice, which he issued to the traveller with many commercial flourishes.

"A ticket for Venice," repeated he, stretching out his arm to dip the pen into the thick ink in a tilted ink-stand. "One first-class to Venice! Here you are, *signore mio.*" He made some scrawls on the paper, strewed bluish sand on it out of a box, thereafter letting the sand run off into an earthen vessel, folded the paper with bony yellow fingers, and wrote on the outside. "An excellent choice," he rattled on. "Ah, Venice! What a glorious city! Irresistibly attractive to the cultured man for her past history as well as her present charm." His copious gesturings and empty phrases gave the odd impression that he feared the traveller might alter his mind. He changed Aschenbach's note, laying the money on the spotted table-cover with the glibness of a croupier. "A pleasant visit to you, signore," he said, with a melodramatic bow. "Delighted to serve you." Then he beckoned and called out: "Next" as though a stream of passengers stood waiting to be served, though in point of fact there was not one. Aschenbach returned to the upper deck.

He leaned an arm on the railing and looked at the idlers lounging along the quay to watch the boat go out. Then he turned his attention to his fellow-passengers. Those of the second class, both men and women, were squatted on their bundles of luggage on the forward deck. The first cabin consisted of a group of lively youths, clerks from Pola, evidently, who had made up a pleasure excursion to Italy and were not a little thrilled at the prospect, bustling about and laughing with satisfaction at the stir they made. They leaned over the railings and shouted, with a glib command of epithet, derisory remarks at such of their fellow-clerks as they saw going to business along the quay; and these in turn shook their sticks and shouted as good back again. One of the party, in a dandified buff suit, a rakish panama with a coloured scarf, and a red cravat, was loudest of the loud: he outcrowed all the rest. Aschenbach's eye dwelt on him, and he was shocked to see that the apparent youth was no youth at all. He was an old man, beyond a doubt, with wrinkles and crow's-feet round eyes and mouth; the dull carmine of the cheeks was rouge, the brown hair a wig. His neck was shrunken and sinewy, his turned-up moustaches and small imperial were dyed, and the unbroken double row of yellow teeth he showed when he laughed were but too obviously a cheapish false set. He wore a seal ring on each forefinger. but the hands were those of an old man.

Aschenbach was moved to shudder as he watched the creature and his association with the rest of the group. Could they not see he was old, that he had no right to wear the clothes they wore or pretend to be one of them? But they were used to him, it seemed; they suffered him among them, they paid back his jokes in kind and the playful pokes in the ribs he gave them. How could they? Aschenbach put his hand to his brow, he covered his eyes, for he had slept little, and they smarted. He felt not quite canny, as though the world were suffering a dream-like distortion of perspective which he might arrest by shutting it all out for a few minutes and then looking at it afresh. But instead he felt a floating sensation, and opened his eyes with unreasoning alarm to find that the ship's dark sluggish bulk was slowly leaving the jetty. Inch by inch, with the to-and-fro motion of her machinery, the strip of iridescent dirty water widened, the boat manœuvred clumsily and turned her bow to the open sea. Aschenbach moved over to the starboard side, where the hunchbacked sailor had set up a deck-chair for him, and a steward in a greasy dress-coat asked for orders.

The sky was grey, the wind humid. Harbour and island dropped behind, all sight of land soon vanished in mist. Flakes of sodden, clammy soot fell upon the still undried deck. Before the boat was an hour out a canvas had to be spread as a shelter from the rain.

Wrapped in his cloak, a book in his lap, our traveller rested; the hours slipped by unawares. It stopped raining, the canvas was taken down. The horizon was visible right round: beneath the sombre dome of the sky stretched the vast plain of empty sea. But immeasurable unarticulated space weakens our power to measure time as well: the time-sense falters and grows dim. Strange, shadowy figures passed and repassed — the elderly coxcomb, the goat-bearded man from the bowels of the ship — with vague gesturings and mutterings through the traveller's mind as he lay. He fell asleep.

At midday he was summoned to luncheon in a corridor-like saloon with the sleeping-cabins giving off it. He ate at the head of the long table; the party of clerks, including the old man, sat with the jolly captain at the other end, where they had been carousing since ten o'clock. The meal was wretched, and soon done. Aschenbach was driven to seek the open and look at the sky — perhaps it would lighten presently above Venice.

He had not dreamed it could be otherwise, for the city had ever given him a brilliant welcome. But sky and sea remained leaden, with spurts of fine, mistlike rain; he reconciled himself to the idea of seeing a different Venice from that he had always approached on the landward side. He stood by the foremast, his gaze on the distance, alert for the first glimpse of the coast. And he thought of the melancholy and susceptible poet who had once seen the towers and turrets of his dreams rise out of these waves; repeated the rhythms born of his awe, his mingled emotions of joy and suffering — and easily susceptible to a prescience already shaped within him, he asked his own sober, weary heart if a new enthusiasm, a new preoccupation, some late adventure of the feelings could still be in store for the idle traveller.

The flat coast showed on the right, the sea was soon populous with fishing-boats. The Lido appeared and was left behind as the ship glided at half speed through the narrow harbour of the same name, coming to a full stop on the lagoon in sight of garish, badly built houses. Here it waited for the boat bringing the sanitary inspector.

An hour passed. One had arrived — and yet not. There was no conceivable haste — yet one felt harried. The youths from Pola were on deck, drawn hither by the martial sound of horns coming across the water from the direction of the Public Gardens. They had drunk a good deal of Asti and were moved to shout and hurrah at the drilling *bersaglieri.* But the young-old man was a truly repulsive sight in the condition to which his company with youth had brought him. He could not carry his wine like them: he was pitiably drunk. He swayed as he stood — watery-eyed, a cigarette between his shaking fingers, keeping upright with difficulty. He could not have taken a step without falling and knew better than to stir, but his spirits were deplorably high. He buttonholed anyone who came within reach, he stuttered, he giggled, he leered, he fatuously shook his beringed old forefinger; his tongue kept seeking the corner of his mouth in a suggestive motion ugly to behold. Aschenbach's brow darkened as he looked, and there came over him once more a dazed sense, as though things about him were just slightly losing their ordinary perspective, beginning to show a distortion that might merge into the grotesque. He was prevented from dwelling on the feeling, for now the machinery began to thud again, and the ship took up its passage through the Canale di San Marco which had been interrupted so near the goal.

He saw it once more, that landing-place that takes the breath away, that amazing group of incredible structures the Republic set up to meet the awe-struck eye of the approaching seafarer: the airy splendour of the palace and Bridge of Sighs, the columns of lion and saint on the shore, the glory of the projecting flank of the fairy temple, the vista of gateway and clock. Looking, he thought that to come to Venice by the station is like entering a palace by the back door. No one should approach, save by the high seas as he was doing now, this most improbable of cities.

The engines stopped. Gondolas pressed alongside, the landing-stairs were let down, customs officials came on board and did their office, people began to go ashore. Aschenbach ordered a gondola. He meant to take up his abode by the sea and needed to be conveyed with his luggage to the landing-stage of the little steamers that ply between the city and the Lido. They called down his order to the surface of the water where the gondoliers were quarrelling in dialect. Then came another delay while his trunk was worried down the ladder-like stairs. Thus he was forced to endure the importunities of the ghastly young-old man, whose drunken state obscurely urged him to pay the stranger the honour of a formal farewell. "We wish you a very pleasant sojourn," he babbled, bowing and scraping. "Pray keep us in mind. *Au revoir, excusez et bon jour, votre Excellence.*" He drooled, he blinked, he licked the corner of his mouth, the little imperial bristled on his elderly chin. He put the tips of two fingers to his mouth and said thickly: "Give her our love, will you, the p-pretty little dear" — here his upper plate came away and fell down on the lower one. . . . Aschenbach escaped. "Little sweety-sweety-sweetheart" he heard behind him, gurgled and stuttered, as he climbed down the rope stair into the boat.

Is there anyone but must repress a secret thrill, on arriving in Venice for the first time — or returning thither after long absence — and stepping into a Venetian gondola? That singular conveyance, come down unchanged from ballad times, black as nothing else on earth except a coffin — what pictures it calls up of lawless, silent adventures in the plashing night; or even more, what visions of death itself, the bier and solemn rites and last soundless voyage! And has anyone remarked that the seat in such a bark, the armchair lacquered in coffin-black and dully black-upholstered, is the softest, most luxurious, most relaxing seat in the world? Aschenbach realized it when he had let himself down at the gondolier's feet, opposite his luggage, which lay neatly composed on the vessel's beak. The rowers still gestured fiercely; he heard their harsh, incoherent tones. But the strange stillness of the water-city seemed to take up their voices gently, to disembody and scatter them over the sea. It was warm here in the harbour. The lukewarm air of the sirocco breathed upon him, he leaned back among his cushions and gave himself to the yielding element, closing his eyes for very pleasure in an indolence as unaccustomed as sweet. "The trip will be short," he thought, and wished it might last forever. They gently swayed away from the boat with its bustle and clamour of voices.

It grew still and stiller all about. No sound but the splash of the oars, the hollow slap of the wave against the steep, black, halbert-shaped beak of the vessel, and one sound more — a muttering by fits and starts, expressed as it were by the motion of his arms, from the lips of the gondolier. He was talking to himself, between his teeth. Aschenbach glanced up and saw with surprise that the lagoon was widening, his vessel was headed for the open sea. Evidently it would not do to give himself up to sweet *far niente;* he must see his wishes carried out.

"You are to take me to the steamboat landing, you know," he said, half turning round towards it. The muttering stopped. There was no reply.

"Take me to the steamboat landing," he repeated, and this time turned quite round and looked up into the face of the gondolier as he stood there on his little elevated deck, high against the pale grey sky. The man had an unpleasing, even brutish face, and wore blue clothes like a sailor's, with a yellow sash; a shapeless straw hat with the braid torn at the brim perched rakishly on his head. His facial structure, as well as the curling blond moustache under the short snub nose, showed him to be of non-Italian stock. Physically rather undersized, so that one would not have expected him to be very muscular, he pulled vigorously at the oar, putting all his body-weight behind each stroke. Now and then the effort he made curled back his lips and bared his white teeth to the gums. He spoke in a decided, almost curt voice, looking out to sea over his fare's head: "The signore is going to the Lido."

Aschenbach answered: "Yes, I am. But I only took the gondola to cross over to San Marco. I am using the *vaporetto* from there."

"But the signore cannot use the *vaporetto.*"

"And why not?"

"Because the *vaporetto* does not take luggage."

It was true. Aschenbach remembered it. He made no answer. But the man's gruff, overbearing manner, so unlike the usual courtesy of his countrymen towards the stranger, was intolerable. Aschenbach spoke again: "That is my own affair. I may want to give my luggage in deposit. You will turn round."

No answer. The oar splashed, the wave struck dull against the prow. And the muttering began anew, the gondolier talked to himself, between his teeth.

What should the traveller do? Alone on the water with this tongue-tied, obstinate, uncanny man, he saw no way of enforcing his will. And if only he did not excite himself, how pleasantly he might rest! Had he not wished the voyage might last forever? The wisest thing — and how much the pleasantest! — was to let matters take their own course. A spell of indolence was upon him; it came from the chair he sat in — this low, black-upholstered arm-chair, so gently rocked at the hands of the despotic boatman in his rear. The thought passed dreamily through Aschenbach's brain that perhaps he had fallen into the clutches of a criminal; it had not power to rouse him to action. More annoying was the simpler explanation: that the man was only trying to extort money. A sense of duty, a recollection, as it were, that this ought to be prevented, made him collect himself to say:

"How much do you ask for the trip?"

And the gondolier, gazing out over his head, replied: "The signore will pay."

There was an established reply to this; Aschenbach made it, mechanically:

"I will pay nothing whatever if you do not take me where I want to go."

"The signore wants to go to the Lido."

"But not with you."

"I am a good rower, signore. I will row you well."

"So much is true," thought Aschenbach, and again he relaxed. "That is true, you row me well. Even if you mean to rob me, even if you hit me in the back with your oar and send me down to the kingdom of Hades, even then you will have rowed me well."

But nothing of the sort happened. Instead, they fell in with company: a boat came alongside and waylaid them, full of men and women singing to guitar and mandolin. They rowed persistently bow for bow with the gondola and filled the silence that had rested on the waters with their lyric love of gain. Aschenbach tossed money into the hat they held out. The music stopped at once, they rowed away. And once more the gondolier's mutter became audible as he talked to himself in fits and snatches.

Thus they rowed on, rocked by the wash of a steamer returning citywards. At the landing two municipal officials were walking up and down with their hands behind their backs and their faces turned towards the lagoon. Aschenbach was helped on shore by the old man with a boat-hook who is the permanent feature of every landing-stage in Venice; and having no small change to pay the boatman, crossed over into the hotel opposite. His wants were supplied in the lobby; but when he came back his possessions were already on a hand-car on the quay, and gondola and gondolier were gone.

"He ran away, signore," said the old boatman. "A bad lot, a man without a licence. He is the only gondolier without one. The others telephoned over, and he knew we were on the look-out, so he made off."

Aschenbach shrugged.

"The signore has had a ride for nothing," said the old man, and held out his hat. Aschenbach dropped some coins. He directed that his luggage be taken to the Hotel des Bains and followed the hand-car through the avenue, that white-blossoming avenue with taverns, booths, and pensions on either side it, which runs across the island diagonally to the beach.

He entered the hotel from the garden terrace at the back and passed through the vestibule and hall into the office. His arrival was expected, and he was served with courtesy and dispatch. The manager, a small, soft, dapper man with a black moustache and a caressing way with him, wearing a French frock-coat, himself took him up in the lift and showed him his room. It was a pleasant chamber, furnished in cherry-wood, with lofty windows looking out to sea. It was decorated with strong-scented flowers. Aschenbach, as soon as he was alone, and while they brought in his trunk and bags and disposed them in the room, went up to one of the windows and stood looking out upon the beach in its afternoon emptiness, and at the sunless sea, now full and sending long, low waves with rhythmic beat upon the sand.

A solitary, unused to speaking of what he sees and feels, has mental experiences which are at once more intense and less articulate than those of a gregarious man. They are sluggish, yet more wayward, and never without a melancholy tinge. Sights and impressions which others brush aside with a glance, a light comment, a smile, occupy him more than their due; they sink silently in, they take on meaning, they become experience, emotion, adventure. Solitude gives birth to the original in us, to beauty unfamiliar and perilous — to poetry. But also, it gives birth to the opposite: to the perverse, the illicit, the absurd. Thus the traveller's mind still dwelt with disquiet on the episodes of his journey hither: on the horrible old fop with his drivel about a mistress, on the outlaw boatman and his lost tip. They did not offend his reason, they hardly afforded food for thought; yet they seemed by their very nature fundamentally strange, and thereby vaguely disquieting. Yet here was the sea; even in the midst of such thoughts he saluted it with his eyes, exulting that Venice was near and accessible. At length he turned round, disposed his personal belongings and made certain arrangements with the chambermaid for his comfort, washed up, and was conveyed to the ground floor by the green-uniformed Swiss who ran the lift.

He took tea on the terrace facing the sea and afterwards went down and walked some distance along the shore promenade in the direction of Hôtel Excelsior. When he came back it seemed to be time to change for dinner. He did so, slowly and methodically as his way was, for he was accustomed to work while he dressed; but even so found himself a little early when he entered the hall, where a large number of guests had collected — strangers to each other and affecting mutual indifference, yet united in expectancy of the meal. He picked up a paper, sat down in a leather arm-chair, and took stock of the company, which compared most favourably with that he had just left.

This was a broad and tolerant atmosphere, of wide horizons. Subdued voices were speaking most of the principal European tongues. That uniform of civilization, the conventional evening dress, gave outward conformity to the varied types. There were long, dry Americans, large-familied Russians, English ladies, German children with French *bonnes.* The Slavic element predominated, it seemed. In Aschenbach's neighbourhood Polish was being spoken.

Round a wicker table next him was gathered a group of young folk in charge of a governess or companion — three young girls, perhaps fifteen to seventeen years old, and a long-haired boy of about fourteen. Aschenbach noticed with astonishment the lad's perfect beauty. His face recalled the noblest moment of Greek sculpture — pale, with a sweet reserve, with clustering honey-coloured ringlets, the brow and nose descending in one line, the winning mouth, the expression of pure and godlike serenity. Yet with all this chaste perfection of form it was of such unique personal charm that the observer thought he had never seen, either in nature or art, anything so utterly happy and consummate. What struck him further was the strange contrast the group afforded, a difference in educational method, so to speak, shown in the way the brother and sisters were clothed and treated. The girls, the eldest of whom was practically grown up, were dressed with an almost disfiguring austerity. All three wore half-length slate-coloured frocks of cloister-like plainness, arbitrarily unbecoming in cut, with white turn-over collars as their only adornment. Every grace of out-line was wilfully suppressed; their hair lay smoothly plastered to their heads, giving them a vacant expression, like a nun's. All this could only be by the mother's orders; but there was no trace of the same pedagogic severity in the case of the boy. Tenderness and softness, it was plain, conditioned his existence. No scissors had been put to the lovely hair that (like the Spinnario's) curled about his brows, above his ears, longer still in the neck. He wore an English sailor suit, with quilted sleeves that narrowed round the delicate wrists of his long and slender though still childish hands. And this suit, with its breast-knot, lacings, and embroideries, lent the slight figure something "rich and strange," a spoilt, exquisite air. The observer saw him in half profile, with one foot in its black patent leather advanced, one elbow resting on the arm of his basket-chair, the cheek nestled into the closed hand in a pose of easy grace, quite unlike the stiff subservient mien which was evidently habitual to his sisters. Was he delicate? His facial tint was ivory-white against the golden darkness of his clustering locks. Or was he simply a pampered darling, the object of a self-willed and partial love? Aschenbach inclined to think the latter. For in almost every artist nature is inborn a wanton and treacherous proneness to side with the beauty that breaks hearts, to single out aristocratic pretensions and pay them homage.

A waiter announced, in English, that dinner was served. Gradually the company dispersed through the glass doors into the dining-room. Late-comers entered from the vestibule or the lifts. Inside, dinner was being served; but the young Poles still sat and waited about their wicker table. Aschenbach felt comfortable in his deep arm-chair, he enjoyed the beauty before his eyes, he waited with them.

The governess, a short, stout, red-faced person, at length gave the signal. With lifted brows she pushed back her chair and made a bow to the tall woman, dressed in palest grey, who now entered the hall. This lady's abundant jewels were pearls, her manner was cool and measured; the fashion of her gown and the arrangement of her lightly powdered hair had the simplicity prescribed in certain circles whose piety and aristocracy are equally marked. She might have been, in Germany, the wife of some high official. But there was something faintly fabulous, after all, in her appearance, though lent it solely by the pearls she wore: they were well-nigh priceless, and consisted of ear-rings and a three-stranded necklace, very long, with gems the size of cherries.

The brother and sisters had risen briskly. They bowed over their mother's hand to kiss it, she turning away from them, with a slight smile on her face, which was carefully preserved but rather sharp-nosed and worn. She addressed a few words in French to the governess, then moved towards the glass door. The children followed, the girls in order of age, then the governess, and last the boy. He chanced to turn before he crossed the threshold, and as there was no one else in the room, his strange, twilit grey eyes met Aschenbach's, as our traveller sat there with the paper on his knee, absorbed in looking after the group.

There was nothing singular, of course, in what he had seen. They had not gone in to dinner before their mother, they had waited, given her a respectful salute, and but observed the right and proper forms on entering the room. Yet they had done all this so expressly, with such self-respecting dignity, discipline, and sense of duty that Aschenbach was impressed. He lingered still a few minutes, then he, too, went into the dining-room, where he was shown a table far off the Polish family, as he noted at once, with a stirring of regret.

Tired, yet mentally alert, he beguiled the long, tedious meal with abstract, even with transcendent matters: pondered the mysterious harmony that must come to subsist between the individual human being and the universal law, in order that human beauty may result; passed on to general problems of form and art, and came at length to the conclusion that what seemed to him fresh and happy thoughts were like the flattering inventions of a dream, which the waking sense proves worthless and insubstantial. He spent the evening in the park, that was sweet with the odours of evening — sitting, smoking, wandering about; went to bed betimes, and passed the night in deep, unbroken sleep, visited, however, by varied and lively dreams.

The weather next day was no more promising. A land breeze blew. Beneath a colourless, overcast sky the sea lay sluggish, and as it were shrunken, so far withdrawn as to leave bare several rows of long sand-banks. The horizon looked close and prosaic. When Aschenbach opened his window he thought he smelt the stagnant odour of the lagoons.

He felt suddenly out of sorts and already began to think of leaving. Once, years before, after weeks of bright spring weather, this wind had found him out; it had been so bad as to force him to flee from the city like a fugitive. And now it seemed beginning again — the same fever-ish distaste, the pressure on his temples, the heavy eyelids. It would be a nuisance to change again; but if the wind did not turn, this was no place for him. To be on the safe side, he did not entirely unpack. At nine o'clock he went down to the buffet, which lay between the hall and the dining-room and served as breakfast-room.

A solemn stillness reigned here, such as it is the ambition of all large hotels to achieve. The waiters moved on noiseless feet. A rattling of tea-things, a whispered word — and no other sounds. In a corner diagonally to the door, two tables off his own, Aschenbach saw the Polish girls with their governess. They sat there very straight, in their stiff blue linen frocks with little turn-over collars and cuffs, their ash-blond hair newly brushed flat, their eyelids red from sleep; and handed each other the marmalade. They had nearly finished their meal. The boy was not there.

Aschenbach smiled. "Aha, little Phæax," he thought. "It seems you are privileged to sleep yourself out." With sudden gaiety he quoted:

> "*Oft veränderten Schmuck und warme Bäder und Ruhe.*"

He took a leisurely breakfast. The porter came up with his braided cap in his hand, to deliver some letters that had been sent on. Aschenbach lighted a cigarette and opened a few letters and thus was still seated to witness the arrival of the sluggard.

He entered through the glass doors and passed diagonally across the room to his sisters at their table. He walked with extraordinary grace — the carriage of the body, the action of the knee, the way he set down his foot in its white shoe — it was all so light, it was at once dainty and proud, it wore an added charm in the childish shyness which made him twice turn his head as he crossed the room, made him give a quick glance and then drop his eyes. He took his seat, with a smile and a murmured word in his soft and blurry tongue; and Aschenbach, sitting so that he could see him in profile, was astonished anew, yes, startled, at the godlike beauty of the human being. The lad had on a light sailor suit of blue and white striped cotton, with a red silk breast-knot and a simple white standing collar round the neck — a not very elegant effect — yet above this collar the head was poised like a flower, in incomparable loveliness. It was the head of Eros, with the yellowish bloom of Parian marble, with fine serious brows, and dusky clustering ringlets standing out in soft plenteousness over temples and ears.

"Good, oh, very good indeed!" thought Aschenbach, assuming the patronizing air of the connoisseur to hide, as artists will, their ravishment over a masterpiece. "Yes," he went on to himself, "if it were not that sea and beach were waiting for me, I should sit here as long as you do." But he went out on that, passing through the hall, beneath the watchful eye of the functionaries, down the steps and directly across the board walk to the section of the beach reserved for the guests of the hotel. The bathing-master, a barefoot old man in linen trousers and sailor blouse, with a straw hat, showed him the cabin that had been rented for him, and Aschenbach had him set up table and chair on the sandy platform before it. Then he dragged the reclining-chair through the pale yellow sand, closer to the sea, sat down, and composed himself.

He delighted, as always, in the scene on the beach, the sight of so-phisticated society giving itself over to a simple life at the edge of the element. The shallow grey sea was already gay with children wading, with swimmers, with figures in bright colours lying on the sand-banks with arms behind their heads. Some were rowing in little keelless boats painted red and blue, and laughing when they capsized. A long row of *capanne* ran down the beach, with platforms, where people sat as on verandas, and there was social life, with bustle and with indolent repose; visits were paid, amid much chatter, punctilious morning toilettes hob-nobbed with comfortable and privileged dishabille. On the hard wet sand close to the sea figures in white bath-robes or loose wrappings in garish colours strolled up and down. A mammoth sand-hill had been built up on Aschenbach's right, the work of children, who had stuck it full of tiny flags. Vendors of sea-shells, fruit, and cakes knelt beside their wares spread out on the sand. A row of cabins on the left stood obliquely to the others and to the sea, thus forming the boundary of the enclosure on this side; and on the little veranda in front of one of these a Russian family was encamped; bearded men with strong white teeth, ripe, indolent women, a Fräulein from the Baltic provinces, who sat at an easel painting the sea and tearing her hair in despair; two ugly but good-natured children and an old maid-servant in a head-cloth, with the caressing, servile manner of the born dependent. There they sat together in grateful enjoyment of their blessings: constantly shouting at their romping children, who paid not the slightest heed; making jokes in broken Italian to the funny old man who sold them sweetmeats, kissing each other on the cheeks — no jot concerned that their domesticity was overlooked.

"I'll stop," thought Aschenbach. "Where could it be better than here?" With his hands clasped in his lap he let his eyes swim in the wideness of the sea, his gaze lose focus, blur, and grow vague in the misty immensity of space. His love of the ocean had profound sources:

the hard-worked artist's longing for rest, his yearning to seek refuge from the thronging manifold shapes of his fancy in the bosom of the simple and vast; and another yearning, opposed to his art and perhaps for that very reason a lure, for the unorganized, the immeasurable, the eternal — in short, for nothingness. He whose preoccupation is with excellence longs fervently to find rest in perfection; and is not nothingness a form of perfection? As he sat there dreaming thus, deep, deep into the void, suddenly the margin line of the shore was cut by a human form. He gathered up his gaze and withdrew it from the illimitable, and lo, it was the lovely boy who crossed his vision coming from the left along the sand. He was barefoot, ready for wading, the slender legs uncovered above the knee, and moved slowly, yet with such a proud, light tread as to make it seem he had never worn shoes. He looked towards the diagonal row of cabins; and the sight of the Russian family, leading their lives there in joyous simplicity, distorted his features in a spasm of angry disgust. His brow darkened, his lips curled, one corner of the mouth was drawn down in a harsh line that marred the curve of the cheek, his frown was so heavy that the eyes seemed to sink in as they uttered beneath the black and vicious language of hate. He looked down, looked threateningly back once more; then giving it up with a violent and contemptuous shoulder-shrug, he left his enemies in the rear.

A feeling of delicacy, a qualm, almost like a sense of shame, made Aschenbach turn away as though he had not seen; he felt unwilling to take advantage of having been, by chance, privy to this passionate reaction. But he was in truth both moved and exhilarated — that is to say, he was delighted. This childish exhibition of fanaticism, directed against the good-naturedest simplicity in the world — it gave to the godlike and inexpressive the final human touch. The figure of the half-grown lad, a masterpiece from nature's own hand, had been significant enough when it gratified the eye alone; and now it evoked sympathy as well — the little episode had set it off, lent it a dignity in the onlooker's eyes that was beyond its years.

Aschenbach listened with still averted head to the boy's voice announcing his coming to his companions at the sand-heap. The voice was clear, though a little weak, but they answered, shouting his name — or his nickname — again and again. Aschenbach was not without curiosity to learn it, but could make out nothing more exact than two musical syllables, something like Adgio — or, oftener still, Adjiu, with a long-drawn-out *u* at the end. He liked the melodious sound, and found it fitting; said it over to himself a few times and turned back with satisfaction to his papers.

Holding his travelling-pad on his knees, he took his fountain-pen and began to answer various items of his correspondence. But presently he felt it too great a pity to turn his back, and the eyes of his mind, for the sake of mere commonplace correspondence, to this scene which was, after all, the most rewarding one he knew. He put aside his papers and swung round to the sea; in no long time, beguiled by the voices of the children at play, he had turned his head and sat resting it against the chair-back, while he gave himself up to contemplating the activities of the exquisite Adgio.

His eye found him out at once, the red breast-knot was unmistakable. With some nine or ten companions, boys and girls of his own age and younger, he was busy putting in place an old plank to serve as a bridge across the ditches between the sand-piles. He directed the work by shouting and motioning with his head, and they were all chattering in many tongues — French, Polish, and even some of the Balkan languages. But his was the name oftenest on their lips, he was plainly sought after, wooed, admired. One lad in particular, a Pole like himself, with a name that sounded something like Jaschiu, a sturdy lad with brilliantined black hair, in a belted linen suit, was his particular liegeman and friend. Operations at the sand-pile being ended for the time, they two walked away along the beach, with their arms round each other's waists, and once the lad Jaschiu gave Adgio a kiss.

Aschenbach felt like shaking a finger at him. "But you, Critobulus," he thought with a smile, "you I advise to take a year's leave. That long, at least, you will need for complete recovery." A vendor came by with strawberries, and Aschenbach made his second breakfast of the great luscious, dead-ripe fruit. It had grown very warm, although the sun had not availed to pierce the heavy layer of mist. His mind felt relaxed, his senses revelled in this vast and soothing communion with the silence of the sea. The grave and serious man found sufficient occupation in speculating what name it could be that sounded like Adgio. And with the help of a few Polish memories he at length fixed on Tadzio, a shortened form of Thaddeus, which sounded, when called, like Tadziu or Adziu.

Tadzio was bathing. Aschenbach had lost sight of him for a moment, then descried him far out in the water, which was shallow a very long way — saw his head, and his arm striking out like an oar. But his watchful family were already on the alert; the mother and governess called from the veranda in front of their bathing-cabin, until the lad's name, with its softened consonants and long-drawn *u*-sound, seemed to possess the beach like a rallying-cry; the cadence had something sweet and wild: "Tadziu! Tadziu!" He turned and ran back against the water, churning the waves to a foam, his head flung high. The sight of this living figure, virginally pure and austere, with dripping locks, beautiful as a tender young god, emerging from the depths of sea and sky, outrunning the element — it conjured up mythologies, it was like a primeval legend, handed down from the beginning of time, of the birth of form, of the origin of the gods. With closed lids Aschenbach listened to this poesy hymning itself silently within him, and anon he thought it was good to be here and that he would stop awhile.

Afterwards Tadzio lay on the sand and rested from his bathe, wrapped in his white sheet, which he wore drawn underneath the right shoulder, so that his head was cradled on his bare right arm. And even when Aschenbach read, without looking up, he was conscious that the lad was there; that it would cost him but the slightest turn of the head to have the rewarding vision once more in his purview. Indeed, it was almost as though he sat there to guard the youth's repose; occupied, of course, with his own affairs, yet alive to the presence of that noble human creature close at hand. And his heart was stirred, it felt a father's kindness: such an emotion as the possessor of beauty can inspire in one who has offered himself up in spirit to create beauty.

At midday he left the beach, returned to the hotel, and was carried up in the lift to his room. There he lingered a little time before the glass and looked at his own grey hair, his keen and weary face. And he thought of his fame, and how people gazed respectfully at him in the streets, on account of his unerring gift of words and their power to charm. He called up all the worldly successes his genius had reaped, all he could remember, even his patent of nobility. Then went to luncheon down in the dining-room, sat at his little table and ate. Afterwards he mounted again in the lift, and a group of young folk, Tadzio among them, pressed with him into the little compartment. It was the first time Aschenbach had seen him close at hand, not merely in perspective, and could see and take account of the details of his humanity. Someone spoke to the lad, and he, answering, with indescribably lovely smile, stepped out again, as they had come to the first floor, backwards, with his eyes cast down. "Beauty makes people self-conscious," Aschenbach thought, and considered within himself imperatively why this should be. He had noted, further, that Tadzio's teeth were imperfect, rather jagged and bluish, without a healthy glaze, and of that peculiar brittle transparency which the teeth of chlorotic people often show. "He is delicate, he is sickly," Aschenbach thought. "He will most likely not live to grow old." He did not try to account for the pleasure the idea gave him.

In the afternoon he spent two hours in his room, then took the *vaporetto* to Venice, across the foul-smelling lagoon. He got out at San Marco, had his tea in the Piazza, and then, as his custom was, took a walk through the streets. But this walk of his brought about nothing less than a revolution in his mood and an entire change in all his plans.

There was a hateful sultriness in the narrow streets. The air was so heavy that all the manifold smells wafted out of houses, shops, and cook-shops — smells of oil, perfumery, and so forth — hung low, like exhalations, not dissipating. Cigarette smoke seemed to stand in the air, it drifted so slowly away. Today the crowd in these narrow lanes oppressed the stroller instead of diverting him. The longer he walked, the more was he in tortures under that state, which is the product of the sea air and the sirocco and which excites and enervates at once. He perspired painfully. His eyes rebelled, his chest was heavy, he felt feverish, the blood throbbed in his temples. He fled from the huddled, narrow streets of the commercial city, crossed many bridges, and came into the poor quarter of Venice. Beggars waylaid him, the canals sickened him with their evil exhalations. He reached a quiet square, one of those that exist at the city's heart, forsaken of God and man; there he rested awhile on the margin of a fountain, wiped his brow, and admitted to himself that he must be gone.

For the second time, and now quite definitely, the city proved that in certain weathers it could be directly inimical to his health. Nothing but sheer unreasoning obstinacy would linger on, hoping for an unprophesiable change in the wind. A quick decision was in place. He could not go home at this stage, neither summer nor winter quarters would be ready. But Venice had not a monopoly of sea and shore: there were other spots where these were to be had without the evil concomitants of lagoon and fever-breeding vapours. He remembered a little bathing-place not far from Trieste of which he had had a good report. Why not go thither? At once, of course, in order that this second change might be worth the making. He resolved, he rose to his feet and sought the nearest gondola-landing, where he took a boat and was conveyed to San Marco through the gloomy windings of many canals, beneath balconies of delicate marble traceries flanked by carven lions; round slippery corners of wall, past melancholy façades with ancient business shields reflected in the rocking water.   It was not too easy to arrive at his destination, for his gondolier, being in league with various lace-makers and glass-blowers, did his best to persuade his fare to pause, look, and be tempted to buy.   Thus the charm of this bizarre passage through the heart of Venice, even while it played upon his spirit, yet was sensibly cooled by the predatory commercial spirit of the fallen queen of the seas.

Once back in his hotel, he announced at the office, even before dinner, that circumstances unforeseen obliged him to leave early next morning.   The management expressed its regret, it changed his money and receipted his bill.   He dined, and spent the lukewarm evening in a rocking-chair on the rear terrace, reading the newspapers.   Before he went to bed, he made his luggage ready against the morning.

His sleep was not of the best, for the prospect of another journey made him restless.   When he opened his window next morning, the sky was still overcast, but the air seemed fresher — and there and then his rue began.   Had he not given notice too soon?   Had he not let himself be swayed by a slight and momentary indisposition?   If he had only been patient, not lost heart so quickly, tried to adapt himself to the climate, or even waited for a change in the weather before deciding!   Then, instead of the hurry and flurry of departure, he would have before him now a morning like yesterday's on the beach.   Too late!   He must go on wanting what he had wanted yesterday.   He dressed and at eight o'clock went down to breakfast.

When he entered the breakfast-room it was empty.   Guests came in while he sat waiting for his order to be filled.   As he sipped his tea he saw the Polish girls enter with their governess, chaste and morning-fresh, with sleep-reddened eyelids.   They crossed the room and sat down at their table in the window.   Behind them came the porter, cap in hand, to announce that it was time for him to go.   The car was waiting to convey him and other travellers to the Hôtel Excelsior, whence they would go by motor-boat through the company's private canal to the station.   Time pressed.   But Aschenbach found it did nothing of the sort.   There still lacked more than an hour of train-time.   He felt irritated at the hotel habit of getting the guests out of the house earlier than necessary; and requested the porter to let him breakfast in peace.   The man hesitated and withdrew, only to come back again five minutes later.   The car could wait no longer.   Good, then it might go, and take his trunk with it, Aschenbach answered with some heat. He would use the public conveyance, in his own time; he begged them to leave the choice of it to him. The functionary bowed. Aschenbach, pleased to be rid of him, made a leisurely meal, and even had a newspaper of the waiter. When at length he rose, the time was grown very short. And it so happened that at that moment Tadzio came through the glass doors into the room.

To reach his own table he crossed the traveller's path, and modestly cast down his eyes before the grey-haired man of the lofty brows — only to lift them again in that sweet way he had and direct his full soft gaze upon Aschenbach's face. Then he was past. "For the last time, Tadzio," thought the elder man. "It was all too brief!" Quite unusually for him, he shaped a farewell with his lips, he actually uttered it, and added: "May God bless you!" Then he went out, distributed tips, exchanged farewells with the mild little manager in the frock-coat, and, followed by the porter with his hand-luggage, left the hotel. On foot as he had come, he passed through the white-blossoming avenue, diagonally across the island to the boat-landing. He went on board at once — but the tale of his journey across the lagoon was a tale of woe, a passage through the very valley of regrets.

It was the well-known route: through the lagoon, past San Marco, up the Grand Canal. Aschenbach sat on the circular bench in the bows, with his elbow on the railing, one hand shading his eyes. They passed the Public Gardens, once more the princely charm of the Piazzetta rose up before him and then dropped behind, next came the great row of palaces, the canal curved, and the splendid marble arches of the Rialto came in sight. The traveller gazed — and his bosom was torn. The atmosphere of the city, the faintly rotten scent of swamp and sea, which had driven him to leave — in what deep, tender, almost painful draughts he breathed it in! How was it he had not known, had not thought, how much his heart was set upon it all! What this morning had been slight regret, some little doubt of his own wisdom, turned now to grief, to actual wretchedness, a mental agony so sharp that it repeatedly brought tears to his eyes, while he questioned himself how he could have foreseen it. The hardest part, the part that more than once it seemed he could not bear, was the thought that he should never more see Venice again. Since now for the second time the place had made him ill, since for the second time he had had to flee for his life, he must henceforth regard it as a forbidden spot, to be forever shunned; senseless to try it again, after he had proved himself unfit.

Yes, if he fled it now, he felt that wounded pride must prevent his return to this spot where twice he had made actual bodily surrender. And this conflict between inclination and capacity all at once assumed, in this middle-aged man's mind, immense weight and importance; the physical defeat seemed a shameful thing, to be avoided at whatever cost; and he stood amazed at the ease with which on the day before he had yielded to it.

Meanwhile the steamer neared the station landing; his anguish of irresolution amounted almost to panic. To leave seemed to the sufferer impossible, to remain not less so. Torn thus between two alternatives, he entered the station. It was very late, he had not a moment to lose. Time pressed, it scourged him onward. He hastened to buy his ticket and looked round in the crowd to find the hotel porter. The man appeared and said that the trunk had already gone off. "Gone already?" "Yes, it has gone to Como." "To Como?" A hasty exchange of words — angry questions from Aschenbach, and puzzled replies from the porter — at length made it clear that the trunk had been put with the wrong luggage even before leaving the hotel, and in company with other trunks was now well on its way in precisely the wrong direction.

Aschenbach found it hard to wear the right expression as he heard this news. A reckless joy, a deep incredible mirthfulness shook him almost as with a spasm. The porter dashed off after the lost trunk, returning very soon, of course, to announce that his efforts were unavailing. Aschenbach said he would not travel without his luggage; that he would go back and wait at the Hôtel des Bains until it turned up. Was the company's motor-boat still outside? The man said yes, it was at the door. With his native eloquence he prevailed upon the ticket-agent to take back the ticket already purchased; he swore that he would wire, that no pains should be spared, that the trunk would be restored in the twinkling of an eye. And the unbelievable thing came to pass: the traveller, twenty minutes after he had reached the station, found himself once more on the Grand Canal on his way back to the Lido.

What a strange adventure indeed, this right-about face of destiny — incredible, humiliating, whimsical as any dream! To be passing again, within the hour, these scenes from which in profoundest grief he had but now taken leave forever! The little swift-moving vessel, a furrow of foam at its prow, tacking with droll agility between steamboats and gondolas, went like a shot to its goal; and he, its sole passenger, sat hiding the panic and thrills of a truant schoolboy beneath a mask of forced resignation. His breast still heaved from time to time with a burst of laughter over the contretemps. Things could not, he told himself, have fallen out more luckily. There would be the necessary explanations, a few astonished faces — then all would be well once more, a mischance prevented, a grievous error set right; and all he had thought to have left forever was his own once more, his for as long as he liked. . . . And did the boat's swift motion deceive him, or was the wind now coming from the sea?

The waves struck against the tiled sides of the narrow canal. At Hôtel Excelsior the automobile omnibus awaited the returned traveller and bore him along by the crisping waves back to the Hôtel des Bains. The little mustachioed manager in the frock-coat came down the steps to greet him.

In dulcet tones he deplored the mistake, said how painful it was to the management and himself; applauded Aschenbach's resolve to stop on until the errant trunk came back; his former room, alas, was already taken, but another as good awaited his approval. "*Pas de chance, monsieur,*" said the Swiss lift-porter, with a smile, as he conveyed him upstairs. And the fugitive was soon quartered in another room which in situation and furnishings almost precisely resembled the first.

He laid out the contents of his hand-bag in their wonted places; then, tired out, dazed by the whirl of the extraordinary forenoon, subsided into the arm-chair by the open window. The sea wore a pale-green cast, the air felt thinner and purer, the beach with its cabins and boats had more colour, notwithstanding the sky was still grey. Aschenbach, his hands folded in his lap, looked out. He felt rejoiced to be back, yet displeased with his vacillating moods, his ignorance of his own real desires. Thus for nearly an hour he sat, dreaming, resting, barely thinking. At midday he saw Tadzio, in his striped sailor suit with red breast-knot, coming up from the sea, across the barrier and along the board walk to the hotel. Aschenbach recognized him, even at this height, knew it was he before he actually saw him, had it in mind to say to himself: "Well, Tadzio, so here you are again too!" But the casual greeting died away before it reached his lips, slain by the truth in his heart. He felt the rapture of his blood, the poignant pleasure, and realized that it was for Tadzio's sake the leavetaking had been so hard.

He sat quite still, unseen at his high post, and looked within himself. His features were lively, he lifted his brows; a smile, alert, inquiring, vivid, widened the mouth. Then he raised his head, and with both hands, hanging limp over the chair-arms, he described a slow motion, palms outward, a lifting and turning movement, as though to indicate a wide embrace. It was a gesture of welcome, a calm and deliberate acceptance of what might come.

Now daily the naked god with cheeks aflame drove his four fire-breathing steeds through heaven's spaces; and with him streamed the strong east wind that fluttered his yellow locks. A sheen, like white satin, lay over all the idly rolling sea's expanse. The sand was burning hot. Awnings of rust-coloured canvas were spanned before the bathing-huts, under the ether's quivering silver-blue; one spent the morning hours within the small, sharp square of shadow they purveyed. But evening too was rarely lovely: balsamic with the breath of flowers and shrubs from the near-by park, while overhead the constellations circled in their spheres, and the murmuring of the night-girted sea swelled softly up and whispered to the soul. Such nights as these contained the joyful promise of a sunlit morrow, brim-full of sweetly ordered idleness, studded thick with countless precious possibilities.

The guest detained here by so happy a mischance was far from finding the return of his luggage a ground for setting out anew. For two days he had suffered slight inconvenience and had to dine in the large salon in his travelling-clothes. Then the lost trunk was set down in his room, and he hastened to unpack, filling presses and drawers with his possessions. He meant to stay on — and on; he rejoiced in the prospect of wearing a silk suit for the hot morning hours on the beach and appearing in acceptable evening dress at dinner.

He was quick to fall in with the pleasing monotony of this manner of life, readily enchanted by its mild soft brilliance and ease. And what a spot it is, indeed! — uniting the charms of a luxurious bathing-resort by a southern sea with the immediate nearness of a unique and marvellous city. Aschenbach was not pleasure-loving. Always, wherever and whenever it was the order of the day to be merry, to refrain from labour and make glad the heart, he would soon be conscious of the imperative summons — and especially was this so in his youth — back to the high fatigues, the sacred and fasting service that consumed his days. This spot and this alone had power to beguile him, to relax his resolution, to make him glad. At times — of a forenoon perhaps, as he lay in the shadow of his awning, gazing out dreamily over the blue of the southern sea, or in the mildness of the night, beneath the wide starry sky, ensconced among the cushions of the gondola that bore him Lido-wards after an evening on the Piazza, while the gay lights faded and the melting music of the serenades died away on his ear — he would think of his mountain home, the theatre of his summer labours. There clouds hung low and trailed through the garden, violent storms extinguished the lights of the house at night, and the ravens he fed swung in the tops of the fir trees. And he would feel transported to Elysium, to the ends of the earth, to a spot most carefree for the sons of men, where no snow is, and no winter, no storms or downpours of rain; where Oceanus sends a mild and cooling breath, and days flow on in blissful idleness, without effort or struggle, entirely dedicate to the sun and the feasts of the sun.

Aschenbach saw the boy Tadzio almost constantly. The narrow confines of their world of hotel and beach, the daily round followed by all alike, brought him in close, almost uninterrupted touch with the beautiful lad. He encountered him everywhere — in the salons of the hotel, on the cooling rides to the city and back, among the splendours of the Piazza, and besides all this in many another going and coming as chance vouchsafed. But it was the regular morning hours on the beach which gave him his happiest opportunity to study and admire the lovely apparition. Yes, this immediate happiness, this daily recurring boon at the hand of circumstance, this it was that filled him with content, with joy in life, enriched his stay, and lingered out the row of sunny days that fell into place so pleasantly one behind the other.

He rose early — as early as though he had a panting press of work — and was among the first on the beach, when the sun was still benign and the sea lay dazzling white in its morning slumber. He gave the watchman a friendly good-morning and chatted with the barefoot, white-haired old man who prepared his place, spread the awning, trundled out the chair and table onto the little platform. Then he settled down; he had three or four hours before the sun reached its height and the fearful climax of its power; three or four hours while the sea went deeper and deeper blue; three or four hours in which to watch Tadzio.

He would see him come up, on the left, along the margin of the sea; or from behind, between the cabins; or, with a start of joyful surprise, would discover that he himself was late, and Tadzio already down, in the blue and white bathing-suit that was now his only wear on the beach; there and engrossed in his usual activities in the sand, beneath the sun. It was a sweetly idle, trifling, fitful life, of play and rest, of strolling, wading, digging, fishing, swimming, lying on the sand. Often the women sitting on the platform would call out to him in their high voices: "Tadziu! Tadziu!" and he would come running and waving his arms, eager to tell them what he had done, show them what he had found, what caught — shells, seahorses, jelly-fish, and sidewards-running crabs. Aschenbach understood not a word he said; it might be the sheerest commonplace, in his ear it became mingled harmonies. Thus the lad's foreign birth raised his speech to music; a wanton sun showered splendour on him, and the noble distances of the sea formed the background which set off his figure.

Soon the observer knew every line and pose of this form that limned itself so freely against sea and sky; its every loveliness, though conned by heart, yet thrilled him each day afresh; his admiration knew no bounds, the delight of his eye was unending. Once the lad was summoned to speak to a guest who was waiting for his mother at their cabin. He ran up, ran dripping wet out of the sea, tossing his curls, and put out his hand, standing with his weight on one leg, resting the other foot on the toes; as he stood there in a posture of suspense the turn of his body was enchanting, while his features wore a look half shamefaced, half conscious of the duty breeding laid upon him to please. Or he would lie at full length, with his bath-robe around him, one slender young arm resting on the sand, his chin in the hollow of his hand; the lad they called Jaschiu squatting beside him, paying him court. There could be nothing lovelier on earth than the smile and look with which the playmate thus singled out rewarded his humble friend and vassal. Again, he might be at the water's edge, alone, removed from his family, quite close to Aschenbach; standing erect, his hands clasped at the back of his neck, rocking slowly on the balls of his feet, day-dreaming away into blue space, while little waves ran up and bathed his toes. The ringlets of honey-coloured hair clung to his temples and neck, the fine down along the upper vertebrae was yellow in the sunlight; the thin envelope of flesh covering the torso betrayed the delicate outlines of the ribs and the symmetry of the breast-structure. His armpits were still as smooth as a statue's, smooth the glistening hollows behind the knees, where the blue network of veins suggested that the body was formed of some stuff more transparent than mere flesh. What discipline, what precision of thought were expressed by the tense youthful perfection of this form! And yet the pure, strong will which had laboured in darkness and succeeded in bringing this godlike work of art to the light of day — was it not known and familiar to him, the artist? Was not the same force at work in himself when he strove in cold fury to liberate from the marble mass of language the slender forms of his art which he saw with the eye of his mind and would body forth to men as the mirror and image of spiritual beauty?

Mirror and image! His eyes took in the proud bearing of that figure there at the blue water's edge; with an outburst of rapture he told himself that what he saw was beauty's very essence; form as divine thought, the single and pure perfection which resides in the mind, of which an image and likeness, rare and holy, was here raised up for adoration. This was very frenzy — and without a scruple, nay, eagerly, the aging artist bade it come. His mind was in travail, his whole mental background in a state of flux. Memory flung up in him the primitive thoughts which are youth's inheritance, but which with him had remained latent, never leaping up into a blaze. Has it not been written that the sun beguiles our attention from things of the intellect to fix it on things of the sense? The sun, they say, dazzles; so bewitching reason and memory that the soul for very pleasure forgets its actual state, to cling with doting on the loveliest of all the objects she shines on. Yes, and then it is only through the medium of some corporeal being that it can raise itself again to contemplation of higher things. Amor, in sooth, is like the mathematician who in order to give children a knowledge of pure form must do so in the language of pictures; so, too, the god, in order to make visible the spirit, avails himself of the forms and colours of human youth, gilding it with all imaginable beauty that it may serve memory as a tool, the very sight of which then sets us afire with pain and longing.

Such were the devotee's thoughts, such the power of his emotions. And the sea, so bright with glancing sunbeams, wove in his mind a spell and summoned up a lovely picture: there was the ancient plane-tree outside the walls of Athens, a hallowed, shady spot, fragrant with willow-blossom and adorned with images and votive offerings in honour of the nymphs and Achelous. Clear ran the smooth-pebbled stream at the foot of the spreading tree. Crickets were fiddling. But on the gentle grassy slope, where one could lie yet hold the head erect, and shelter from the scorching heat, two men reclined, an elder with a younger, ugliness paired with beauty and wisdom with grace. Here Socrates held forth to youthful Phædrus upon the nature of virtue and desire, wooing him with insinuating wit and charming turns of phrase. He told him of the shuddering and unwonted heat that come upon him whose heart is open, when his eye beholds an image of eternal beauty;

spoke of the impious and corrupt, who cannot conceive beauty though they see its image, and are incapable of awe; and of the fear and reverence felt by the noble soul when he beholds a godlike face or a form which is a good image of beauty: how as he gazes he worships the beautiful one and scarcely dares to look upon him, but would offer sacrifice as to an idol or a god, did he not fear to be thought stark mad. "For beauty, my Phædrus, beauty alone, is lovely and visible at once. For, mark you, it is the sole aspect of the spiritual which we can perceive through our senses, or bear so to perceive. Else what should become of us, if the divine, if reason and virtue and truth, were to speak to us through the senses? Should we not perish and be consumed by love, as Semele aforetime was by Zeus? So beauty, then, is the beauty-lover's way to the spirit — but only the way, only the means, my little Phædrus." . . . And then, sly arch-lover that he was, he said the subtlest thing of all: that the lover was nearer the divine than the beloved; for the god was in the one but not in the other — perhaps the tenderest, most mocking thought that ever was thought, and source of all the guile and secret bliss the lover knows.

Thought that can merge wholly into feeling, feeling that can merge wholly into thought — these are the artist's highest joy. And our solitary felt in himself at this moment power to command and wield a thought that thrilled with emotion, an emotion as precise and concentrated as thought: namely, that nature herself shivers with ecstasy when the mind bows down in homage before beauty. He felt a sudden desire to write. Eros, indeed, we are told, loves idleness, and for idle hours alone was he created. But in this crisis the violence of our sufferer's seizure was directed almost wholly towards production, its occasion almost a matter of indifference. News had reached him on his travels that a certain problem had been raised, the intellectual world challenged for its opinion on a great and burning question of art and taste. By nature and experience the theme was his own; and he could not resist the temptation to set it off in the glistering foil of his words. He would write, and moreover he would write in Tadzio's presence. This lad should be in a sense his model, his style should follow the lines of this figure that seemed to him divine; he would snatch up this beauty into the realms of the mind, as once the eagle bore the Trojan shepherd aloft. Never had the pride of the word been so sweet to him, never had he known so well that Eros is in the word, as in those perilous and precious hours when he sat at his rude table, within the shade of his awning, his idol full in his view and the music of his voice in his ears, and fashioned his little essay after the model Tadzio's beauty set: that page and a half of choicest prose, so chaste, so lofty, so poignant with feeling, which would shortly be the wonder and admiration of the multitude. Verily it is well for the world that it sees only the beauty of the completed work and not its origins nor the conditions whence it sprang; since knowledge of the artist's inspiration might often but confuse and alarm and so prevent the full effect of its excellence. Strange hours, indeed, these were, and strangely unnerving the labour that filled them! Strangely fruitful intercourse this, between one body and another mind! When Aschenbach put aside his work and left the beach he felt exhausted, he felt broken — conscience reproached him, as it were after a debauch.

Next morning on leaving the hotel he stood at the top of the stairs leading down from the terrace and saw Tadzio in front of him on his way to the beach. The lad had just reached the gate in the railings, and he was alone. Aschenbach felt, quite simply, a wish to overtake him, to address him and have the pleasure of his reply and answering look; to put upon a blithe and friendly footing his relation with this being who all unconsciously had so greatly heightened and quickened his emotions. The lovely youth moved at a loitering pace — he might easily be overtaken; and Aschenbach hastened his own step. He reached him on the board walk that ran behind the bathing-cabins, and all but put out his hand to lay it on shoulder or head, while his lips parted to utter a friendly salutation in French. But — perhaps from the swift pace of his last few steps — he found his heart throbbing un-pleasantly fast, while his breath came in such quick pants that he could only have gasped had he tried to speak. He hesitated, sought after self-control, was suddenly panic-stricken lest the boy notice him hanging there behind him and look round. Then he gave up, abandoned his plan, and passed him with bent head and hurried step.

"Too late! Too late!" he thought as he went by. But was it too late? This step he had delayed to take might so easily have put everything in a lighter key, have led to a sane recovery from his folly. But the truth may have been that the aging man did not want to be cured, that his illusion was far too dear to him. Who shall unriddle the puzzle of the artist nature? Who understands that mingling of discipline and licence in which it stands so deeply rooted? For not to be able to want sobriety is licentious folly. Aschenbach was no longer disposed to self-analysis. He had no taste for it; his self-esteem, the attitude of mind proper to his years, his maturity and single-mindedness, disinclined him to look within himself and decide whether it was constraint or puerile sensuality that had prevented him from carrying out his project. He felt confused, he was afraid someone, if only the watchman, might have been observing his behaviour and final surrender — very much he feared being ridiculous. And all the time he was laughing at himself for his serio-comic seizure. "Quite crestfallen," he thought. "I was like the gamecock that lets his wings droop in the battle. That must be the Love-God himself, that makes us hang our heads at sight of beauty and weighs our proud spirits low as the ground." Thus he played with the idea — he embroidered upon it, and was too arrogant to admit fear of an emotion.

The term he had set for his holiday passed by unheeded; he had no thought of going home. Ample funds had been sent him. His sole concern was that the Polish family might leave, and a chance question put to the hotel barber elicited the information that they had come only very shortly before himself. The sun browned his face and hands, the invigorating salty air heightened his emotional energies. Heretofore he had been wont to give out at once, in some new effort, the powers accumulated by sleep or food or outdoor air; but now the strength that flowed in upon him with each day of sun and sea and idleness he let go up in one extravagant gush of emotional intoxication.

His sleep was fitful; the priceless, equable days were divided one from the next by brief nights filled with happy unrest. He went, indeed, early to bed, for at nine o'clock, with the departure of Tadzio from the scene, the day was over for him. But in the faint greyness of the morning a tender pang would go through him as his heart was minded of its adventure; he could no longer bear his pillow and, rising, would wrap himself against the early chill and sit down by the window to await the sunrise. Awe of the miracle filled his soul new-risen from its sleep. Heaven, earth, and its waters yet lay enfolded in the ghostly, glassy pallor of dawn; one paling star still swam in the shadowy vast. But there came a breath, a winged word from far and inaccessible abodes, that Eos was rising from the side of her spouse; and there was that first sweet reddening of the farthest strip of sea and sky that manifests creation to man's sense. She neared, the goddess, ravisher of youth, who stole away Cleitos and Cephalus and, defying all the envious Olympians, tasted beautiful Orion's love. At the world's edge began a strewing of roses, a shining and a blooming ineffably pure; baby cloudlets hung illumined, like attendant amoretti, in the blue and

blushful haze; purple effulgence fell upon the sea, that seemed to
heave it forward on its welling waves; from horizon to zenith went
great quivering thrusts like golden lances, the gleam became a glare;
without a sound, with godlike violence, glow and glare and rolling
flames streamed upwards, and with flying hoof-beats the steeds of the
sun-god mounted the sky. The lonely watcher sat, the splendour of
the god shone on him, he closed his eyes and let the glory kiss his lids.
Forgotten feelings, precious pangs of his youth, quenched long since by
the stern service that had been his life and now returned so strangely
metamorphosed — he recognized them with a puzzled, wondering
smile. He mused, he dreamed, his lips slowly shaped a name; still
smiling, his face turned seawards and his hands lying folded in his lap,
he fell asleep once more as he sat.

But that day, which began so fierily and festally, was not like other
days; it was transmuted and gilded with mythical significance. For
whence could come the breath, so mild and meaningful, like a whisper
from higher spheres, that played about temple and ear? Troops of
small feathery white clouds ranged over the sky, like grazing herds of
the gods. A stronger wind arose, and Poseidon's horses ran up, arching
their manes, among them too the steers of him with the purpled locks,
who lowered their horns and bellowed as they came on; while like
prancing goats the waves on the farther strand leaped among the craggy
rocks. It was a world possessed, peopled by Pan, that closed round the
spellbound man, and his doting heart conceived the most delicate
fancies. When the sun was going down behind Venice, he would
sometimes sit on a bench in the park and watch Tadzio, white-clad,
with gay-coloured sash, at play there on the rolled gravel with his ball;
and at such times it was not Tadzio whom he saw, but Hyacinthus,
doomed to die because two gods were rivals for his love. Ah, yes, he
tasted the envious pangs that Zephyr knew when his rival, bow and
cithara, oracle and all forgot, played with the beauteous youth; he
watched the discus, guided by torturing jealousy, strike the beloved
head; paled as he received the broken body in his arms, and saw the
flower spring up, watered by that sweet blood and signed forevermore
with his lament.

There can be no relation more strange, more critical, than that between two beings who know each other only with their eyes, who meet
daily, yes, even hourly, eye each other with a fixed regard, and yet by
some whim or freak of convention feel constrained to act like strangers.
Uneasiness rules between them, unslaked curiosity, a hysterical desire

to give rein to their suppressed impulse to recognize and address each other; even, actually, a sort of strained but mutual regard. For one human being instinctively feels respect and love for another human being so long as he does not know him well enough to judge him; and that he does not, the craving he feels is evidence.

Some sort of relation and acquaintanceship was perforce set up between Aschenbach and the youthful Tadzio; it was with a thrill of joy the older man perceived that the lad was not entirely unresponsive to all the tender notice lavished on him. For instance, what should move the lovely youth, nowadays when he descended to the beach, always to avoid the board walk behind the bathing-huts and saunter along the sand, passing Aschenbach's tent in front, sometimes so unnecessarily close as almost to graze his table or chair? Could the power of an emotion so beyond his own so draw, so fascinate its innocent object? Daily Aschenbach would wait for Tadzio. Then sometimes, on his approach, he would pretend to be preoccupied and let the charmer pass unregarded by. But sometimes he looked up, and their glances met; when that happened both were profoundly serious. The elder's dignified and cultured mien let nothing appear of his inward state; but in Tadzio's eyes a question lay — he faltered in his step, gazed on the ground, then up again with that ineffably sweet look he had; and when he was past, something in his bearing seemed to say that only good breeding hindered him from turning round.

But once, one evening, it fell out differently. The Polish brother and sisters, with their governess, had missed the evening meal, and Aschenbach had noted the fact with concern. He was restive over their absence, and after dinner walked up and down in front of the hotel, in evening dress and a straw hat; when suddenly he saw the nunlike sisters with their companion appear in the light of the arc-lamps, and four paces behind them Tadzio. Evidently they came from the steamer-landing, having dined for some reason in Venice. It had been chilly on the lagoon, for Tadzio wore a dark-blue reefer-jacket with gilt buttons, and a cap to match. Sun and sea air could not burn his skin, it was the same creamy marble hue as at first — though he did look a little pale, either from the cold or in the bluish moonlight of the arc-lamps. The shapely brows were so delicately drawn, the eyes so deeply dark — lovelier he was than words could say, and as often the thought visited Aschenbach, and brought its own pang, that language could but extol, not reproduce, the beauties of the sense.

The sight of that dear form was unexpected, it had appeared un-hoped-for, without giving him time to compose his features. Joy, surprise, and admiration might have painted themselves quite openly upon his face — and just at this second it happened that Tadzio smiled. Smiled at Aschenbach, unabashed and friendly, a speaking, winning, captivating smile, with slowly parting lips. With such a smile it might be that Narcissus bent over the mirroring pool, a smile profound, infatuated, lingering, as he put out his arms to the reflection of his own beauty; the lips just slightly pursed, perhaps half-realizing his own folly in trying to kiss the cold lips of his shadow — with a mingling of coquetry and curiosity and a faint unease, enthralling and enthralled.

Aschenbach received that smile and turned away with it as though entrusted with a fatal gift. So shaken was he that he had to flee from the lighted terrace and front gardens and seek out with hurried steps the darkness of the park at the rear. Reproaches strangely mixed of tenderness and remonstrance burst from him: "How dare you smile like that! No one is allowed to smile like that!" He flung himself on a bench, his composure gone to the winds, and breathed in the nocturnal fragrance of the garden. He leaned back, with hanging arms, quivering from head to foot, and quite unmanned he whispered the hackneyed phrase of love and longing — impossible in these circumstances, absurd, abject, ridiculous enough, yet sacred too, and not unworthy of honour even here: "I love you!"

In the fourth week of his stay on the Lido, Gustave von Aschenbach made certain singular observations touching the world about him. He noticed, in the first place, that though the season was approaching its height, yet the number of guests declined and, in particular, that the German tongue had suffered a rout, being scarcely or never heard in the land. At table and on the beach he caught nothing but foreign words. One day at the barber's — where he was now a frequent visitor — he heard something rather startling. The barber mentioned a German family who had just left the Lido after a brief stay, and rattled on in his obsequious way: "The signore is not leaving — he has no fear of the sickness, has he?" Aschenbach looked at him. "The sickness?" he repeated. Whereat the prattler fell silent, became very busy all at once, affected not to hear. When Aschenbach persisted he said he really knew nothing at all about it, and tried in a fresh burst of eloquence to drown the embarrassing subject.

That was one forenoon. After luncheon Aschenbach had himself ferried across to Venice, in a dead calm, under a burning sun; driven by his mania, he was following the Polish young folk, whom he had seen with their companion, taking the way to the landing-stage. He did not find his idol on the Piazza. But as he sat there at tea, at a little round table on the shady side, suddenly he noticed a peculiar odour, which, it seemed to him now, had been in the air for days without his being aware: a sweetish, medicinal smell, associated with wounds and disease and suspect cleanliness. He sniffed and pondered and at length recognized it; finished his tea and left the square at the end facing the cathedral. In the narrow space the stench grew stronger. At the street corners placards were stuck up, in which the city authorities warned the population against the danger of certain infections of the gastric system, prevalent during the heated season; advising them not to eat oysters or other shell-fish and not to use the canal waters. The ordinance showed every sign of minimizing an existing situation. Little groups of people stood about silently in the squares and on the bridges; the traveller moved among them, watched and listened and thought.

He spoke to a shopkeeper lounging at his door among dangling coral necklaces and trinkets of artificial amethyst, and asked him about the disagreeable odour. The man looked at him, heavy-eyed, and hastily pulled himself together. "Just a formal precaution, signore," he said, with a gesture. "A police regulation we have to put up with. The air is sultry — the sirocco is not wholesome, as the signore knows. Just a precautionary measure, you understand — probably unnecessary...." Aschenbach thanked him and passed on. And on the boat that bore him back to the Lido he smelt the germicide again.

On reaching his hotel he sought the table in the lobby and buried himself in the newspapers. The foreign-language sheets had nothing. But in the German papers certain rumours were mentioned, statistics given, then officially denied, then the good faith of the denials called in question. The departure of the German and Austrian contingent was thus made plain. As for other nationals, they knew or suspected nothing — they were still undisturbed. Aschenbach tossed the newspapers back on the table. "It ought to be kept quiet," he thought, aroused. "It should not be talked about." And he felt in his heart a curious elation at these events impending in the world about him. Passion is like crime: it does not thrive on the established order and the common round; it welcomes every blow dealt the bourgeois structure, every weakening of the social fabric, because therein it feels a sure hope of its own advantage. These things that were going on in the unclean alleys of Venice, under cover of an official hushing-up policy — they gave

Aschenbach a dark satisfaction. The city's evil secret mingled with the one in the depths of his heart — and he would have staked all he possessed to keep it, since in his infatuation he cared for nothing but to keep Tadzio here, and owned to himself, not without horror, that he could not exist were the lad to pass from his sight.

He was no longer satisfied to owe his communion with his charmer to chance and the routine of hotel life; he had begun to follow and waylay him. On Sundays, for example, the Polish family never appeared on the beach. Aschenbach guessed they went to mass at San Marco and pursued them thither. He passed from the glare of the Piazza into the golden twilight of the holy place and found him he sought bowed in worship over a prie-dieu. He kept in the background, standing on the fissured mosaic pavement among the devout populace, that knelt and muttered and made the sign of the cross; and the crowded splendour of the oriental temple weighed voluptuously on his sense. A heavily ornate priest intoned and gesticulated before the altar, where little candle-flames flickered helplessly in the reek of incense-breathing smoke; and with that cloying sacrificial smell another seemed to mingle — the odour of the sickened city. But through all the glamour and glitter Aschenbach saw the exquisite creature there in front turn his head, seek out and meet his lover's eye.

The crowd streamed out through the portals into the brilliant square thick with fluttering doves, and the fond fool stood aside in the vestibule on the watch. He saw the Polish family leave the church. The children took ceremonial leave of their mother, and she turned towards the Piazzetta on her way home, while his charmer and the cloistered sisters, with their governess, passed beneath the clock tower into the Merceria. When they were a few paces on, he followed — he stole behind them on their walk through the city. When they paused, he did so too; when they turned round, he fled into inns and courtyards to let them pass. Once he lost them from view, hunted feverishly over bridges and in filthy *culs-de-sac*, only to confront them suddenly in a narrow passage whence there was no escape, and experience a moment of panic fear. Yet it would be untrue to say he suffered. Mind and heart were drunk with passion, his footsteps guided by the dæmonic power whose pastime it is to trample on human reason and dignity.

Tadzio and his sisters at length took a gondola. Aschenbach hid behind a portico or fountain while they embarked, and directly they pushed off did the same. In a furtive whisper he told the boatman he would tip him well to follow at a little distance the other gondola, just rounding a corner, and fairly sickened at the man's quick, sly grasp and ready acceptance of the go-between's rôle.

Leaning back among soft, black cushions he swayed gently in the wake of the other black-snouted bark, to which the strength of his passion chained him. Sometimes it passed from his view, and then he was assailed by an anguish of unrest. But his guide appeared to have long practice in affairs like these; always, by dint of short cuts or deft manœuvres, he contrived to overtake the coveted sight. The air was heavy and foul, the sun burnt down through a slate-coloured haze. Water slapped gurgling against wood and stone. The gondolier's cry, half warning, half salute, was answered with singular accord from far within the silence of the labyrinth. They passed little gardens, high up the crumbling wall, hung with clustering white and purple flowers that sent down an odour of almonds. Moorish lattices showed shadowy in the gloom. The marble steps of a church descended into the canal, and on them a beggar squatted, displaying his misery to view, showing the whites of his eyes, holding out his hat for alms. Farther on a dealer in antiquities cringed before his lair, inviting the passer-by to enter and be duped. Yes, this was Venice, this the fair frailty that fawned and that betrayed, half fairy-tale, half snare; the city in whose stagnating air the art of painting once put forth so lusty a growth, and where musicians were moved to accords so weirdly lulling and lascivious. Our adventurer felt his senses wooed by this voluptuousness of sight and sound, tasted his secret knowledge that the city sickened and hid its sickness for love of gain, and bent an ever more unbridled leer on the gondola that glided on before him.

It came at last to this — that his frenzy left him capacity for nothing else but to pursue his flame; to dream of him absent, to lavish, lover-like, endearing terms on his mere shadow. He was alone, he was a foreigner, he was sunk deep in this belated bliss of his — all which enabled him to pass unblushing through experiences well-nigh unbelievable. One night, returning late from Venice, he paused by his beloved's chamber door in the second storey, leaned his head against the panel, and remained there long, in utter drunkenness, powerless to tear himself away, blind to the danger of being caught in so mad an attitude.

And yet there were not wholly lacking moments when he paused and reflected, when in consternation he asked himself what path was this on which he had set his foot. Like most other men of parts and attainments, he had an aristocratic interest in his forbears, and when he achieved a success he liked to think he had gratified them, compelled their admiration and regard.   He thought of them now, involved as he was in this illicit adventure, seized of these exotic excesses of feeling; thought of their stern self-command and decent manliness, and gave a melancholy smile.   What would they have said?   What, indeed, would they have said to his entire life, that varied to the point of degeneracy from theirs?   This life in the bonds of art, had not he himself, in the days of his youth and in the very spirit of those bourgeois forefathers, pronounced mocking judgment upon it?   And yet, at bottom, it had been so like their own!   It had been a service, and he a soldier, like some of them; and art was war — a grilling, exhausting struggle that nowadays wore one out before one could grow old.   It had been a life of self-conquest, a life against odds, dour, steadfast, abstinent; he had made it symbolical of the kind of overstrained heroism the time admired, and he was entitled to call it manly, even courageous.   He wondered if such a life might not be somehow specially pleasing in the eyes of the god who had him in his power.   For Eros had received most countenance among the most valiant nations — yes, were we not told that in their cities prowess made him flourish exceedingly?   And many heroes of olden time had willingly borne his yoke, not counting any humiliation such if it happened by the god's decree; vows, prostrations, self-abasements, these were no source of shame to the lover; rather they reaped him praise and honour.

Thus did the fond man's folly condition his thoughts; thus did he seek to hold his dignity upright in his own eyes.   And all the while he kept doggedly on the traces of the disreputable secret the city kept hidden at its heart, just as he kept his own — and all that he learned fed his passion with vague, lawless hopes.   He turned over newspapers at cafés, bent on finding a report on the progress of the disease; and in the German sheets, which had ceased to appear on the hotel table, he found a series of contradictory statements.   The deaths, it was variously asserted, ran to twenty, to forty, to a hundred or more; yet in the next day's issue the existence of the pestilence was, if not roundly denied, reported as a matter of a few sporadic cases such as might be brought into a seaport town.   After that the warnings would break out again, and the protests against the unscrupulous game the authorities were playing.   No definite information was to be had.

And yet our solitary felt he had a sort of first claim on a share in the unwholesome secret; he took a fantastic satisfaction in putting leading questions to such persons as were interested to conceal it, and forcing them to explicit untruths by way of denial.   One day he attacked the manager, that small, soft-stepping man in the French frock-coat, who was moving about among the guests at luncheon, supervising the service and making himself socially agreeable.   He paused at Aschenbach's table to exchange a greeting, and the guest put a question, with a negligent, casual air: "Why in the world are they forever disinfecting the city of Venice?"   "A police regulation," the adroit one replied; "a precautionary measure, intended to protect the health of the public during this unseasonably warm and sultry weather."   "Very praiseworthy of the police," Aschenbach gravely responded.   After a further exchange of meteorological commonplaces the manager passed on.

It happened that a band of street musicians came to perform in the hotel gardens that evening after dinner.   They grouped themselves beneath an iron stanchion supporting an arc-light, two women and two men, and turned their faces, that shone white in the glare, up towards the guests who sat on the hotel terrace enjoying this popular entertainment along with their coffee and iced drinks.   The hotel lift-boys, waiters, and office staff stood in the doorway and listened; the Russian family displayed the usual Russian absorption in their enjoyment — they had their chairs put down into the garden to be nearer the singers and sat there in a half-circle with gratitude painted on their features, the old serf in her turban erect behind their chairs.

These strolling players were adepts at mandolin, guitar, harmonica, even compassing a reedy violin.   Vocal numbers alternated with instrumental, the younger woman, who had a high shrill voice, joining in a love-duet with the sweetly falsettoing tenor.   The actual head of the company, however, and incontestably its most gifted member, was the other man, who played the guitar.   He was a sort of baritone buffo; with no voice to speak of, but possessed of a pantomimic gift and remarkable burlesque *élan*.   Often he stepped out of the group and advanced towards the terrace, guitar in hand, and his audience rewarded his sallies with bursts of laughter.   The Russians in their parterre seats were beside themselves with delight over this display of southern vivacity; their shouts and screams of applause encouraged him to bolder and bolder flights.

Aschenbach sat near the balustrade, a glass of pomegranate-juice and soda-water sparkling ruby-red before him, with which he now and then moistened his lips.   His nerves drank in thirstily the unlovely sounds, the vulgar and sentimental tunes, for passion paralyses good taste and makes its victim accept with rapture what a man in his senses would either laugh at or turn from with disgust. Idly he sat and watched the antics of the buffoon with his face set in a fixed and painful smile, while inwardly his whole being was rigid with the intensity of the regard he bent on Tadzio, leaning over the railing six paces off.

He lounged there, in the white belted suit he sometimes wore at dinner, in all his innate, inevitable grace, with his left arm on the balustrade, his legs crossed, the right hand on the supporting hip; and looked down on the strolling singers with an expression that was hardly a smile, but rather a distant curiosity and polite toleration. Now and then he straightened himself and with a charming movement of both arms drew down his white blouse through his leather belt, throwing out his chest. And sometimes — Aschenbach saw it with triumph, with horror, and a sense that his reason was tottering — the lad would cast a glance, that might be slow and cautious, or might be sudden and swift, as though to take him by surprise, to the place where his lover sat. Aschenbach did not meet the glance. An ignoble caution made him keep his eyes in leash. For in the rear of the terrace sat Tadzio's mother and governess; and matters had gone so far that he feared to make himself conspicuous. Several times, on the beach, in the hotel lobby, on the Piazza, he had seen, with a stealing numbness, that they called Tadzio away from his neighbourhood. And his pride revolted at the affront, even while conscience told him it was deserved.

The performer below presently began a solo, with guitar accompaniment, a street song in several stanzas, just then the rage all over Italy. He delivered it in a striking and dramatic recitative, and his company joined in the refrain. He was a man of slight build, with a thin, undernourished face; his shabby felt hat rested on the back of his neck, a great mop of red hair sticking out in front; and he stood there on the gravel in advance of his troupe, in an impudent, swaggering posture, twanging the strings of his instrument and flinging a witty and rollicking recitative up to the terrace, while the veins on his forehead swelled with the violence of his effort. He was scarcely a Venetian type, belonging rather to the race of Neapolitan jesters, half bully, half comedian, brutal, blustering, an unpleasant customer, and entertaining to the last degree. The words of his song were trivial and silly, but on his lips, accompanied with gestures of head, hands, arms, and body, with leers and winks and the loose play of the tongue in the corner of his mouth, they took on meaning; an equivocal meaning, yet vaguely offensive. He wore a white sports shirt with a suit of ordinary clothes, and a strikingly large and naked-looking Adam's apple rose out of the open collar.

From that pale, snub-nosed face it was hard to judge of his age; vice sat on it, it was furrowed with grimacing, and two deep wrinkles of defiance and self-will, almost of desperation, stood oddly between the red brows, above the grinning, mobile mouth. But what more than all drew upon him the profound scrutiny of our solitary watcher was that this suspicious figure seemed to carry with it its own suspicious odour. For whenever the refrain occurred and the singer, with waving arms and antic gestures, passed in his grotesque march immediately beneath Aschenbach's seat, a strong smell of carbolic was wafted up to the terrace.

After the song he began to take up money, beginning with the Russian family, who gave liberally, and then mounting the steps to the terrace. But here he became as cringing as he had before been forward. He glided between the tables, bowing and scraping, showing his strong white teeth in a servile smile, though the two deep furrows on the brow were still very marked. His audience looked at the strange creature as he went about collecting his livelihood, and their curiosity was not unmixed with disfavour. They tossed coins with their fingertips into his hat and took care not to touch it. Let the enjoyment be never so great, a sort of embarrassment always comes when the comedian oversteps the physical distance between himself and respectable people. This man felt it and sought to make his peace by fawning. He came along the railing to Aschenbach, and with him came that smell no one else seemed to notice.

"Listen!" said the solitary, in a low voice, almost mechanically; "they are disinfecting Venice — why?" The mountebank answered hoarsely: "Because of the police. Orders, signore. On account of the heat and the sirocco. The sirocco is oppressive. Not good for the health." He spoke as though surprised that anyone could ask, and with the flat of his hand he demonstrated how oppressive the sirocco was. "So there is no plague in Venice?" Aschenbach asked the question between his teeth, very low. The man's expressive face fell, he put on a look of comical innocence. "A plague? What sort of plague? Is the sirocco a plague? Or perhaps our police are a plague! You are making fun of us, signore! A plague! Why should there be? The police make regulations on account of the heat and the weather. . . ." He gestured. "Quite," said Aschenbach, once more, soft and low; and dropping an unduly large coin into the man's hat dismissed him with a sign. He bowed very low and left. But he had not reached the steps when two of the hotel servants flung themselves on him and began to whisper, their faces close to his. He shrugged, seemed to be giving assurances, to be swearing he had said nothing. It was not hard to guess the import of his words. They let him go at last and he went back into the garden, where he conferred briefly with his troupe and then stepped forward for a farewell song.

It was one Aschenbach had never to his knowledge heard before, a rowdy air, with words in impossible dialect. It had a laughing-refrain in which the other three artists joined at the top of their lungs. The refrain had neither words nor accompaniment, it was nothing but rhythmical, modulated, natural laughter, which the soloist in particular knew how to render with most deceptive realism. Now that he was farther off his audience, his self-assurance had come back, and this laughter of his rang with a mocking note. He would be overtaken, before he reached the end of the last line of each stanza; he would catch his breath, lay his hand over his mouth, his voice would quaver and his shoulders shake, he would lose power to contain himself longer. Just at the right moment each time, it came whooping, bawling, crashing out of him, with a verisimilitude that never failed to set his audience off in profuse and unpremeditated mirth that seemed to add gusto to his own. He bent his knees, he clapped his thigh, he held his sides, he looked ripe for bursting. He no longer laughed, but yelled, pointing his finger at the company there above as though there could be in all the world nothing so comic as they; until at last they laughed in hotel, terrace, and garden, down to the waiters, lift-boys, and servants — laughed as though possessed.

Aschenbach could no longer rest in his chair, he sat poised for flight. But the combined effect of the laughing, the hospital odour in his nostrils, and the nearness of the beloved was to hold him in a spell; he felt unable to stir. Under cover of the general commotion he looked across at Tadzio and saw that the lovely boy returned his gaze with a seriousness that seemed the copy of his own; the general hilarity, it seemed to say, had no power over him, he kept aloof. The grey-haired man was overpowered, disarmed by this docile, childlike deference; with difficulty he refrained from hiding his face in his hands. Tadzio's habit, too, of drawing himself up and taking a deep sighing breath struck him as being due to an oppression of the chest. "He is sickly, he will never live to grow up," he thought once again, with that dispassionate vision to which his madness of desire sometimes so strangely gave way. And compassion struggled with the reckless exultation of his heart.

The players, meanwhile, had finished and gone; their leader bowing and scraping, kissing his hands and adorning his leave-taking with antics that grew madder with the applause they evoked. After all the others were outside, he pretended to run backwards full tilt against a lamp-post and slunk to the gate apparently doubled over with pain. But there he threw off his buffoon's mask, stood erect, with an elastic straightening of his whole figure, ran out his tongue impudently at the guests on the terrace, and vanished in the night. The company dispersed. Tadzio had long since left the balustrade. But he, the lonely man, sat for long, to the waiters' great annoyance, before the dregs of pomegranate-juice in his glass. Time passed, the night went on. Long ago, in his parental home, he had watched the sand filter through an hour-glass — he could still see, as though it stood before him, the fragile, pregnant little toy. Soundless and fine the rust-red streamlet ran through the narrow neck, and made, as it declined in the upper cavity, an exquisite little vortex.

The very next afternoon the solitary took another step in pursuit of his fixed policy of baiting the outer world. This time he had all possible success. He went, that is, into the English travel bureau in the Piazza, changed some money at the desk, and posing as the suspicious foreigner, put his fateful question. The clerk was a tweed-clad young Britisher, with his eyes set close together, his hair parted in the middle, and radiating that steady reliability which makes his like so strange a phenomenon in the *gamin*, agile-witted south. He began: "No ground for alarm, sir. A mere formality. Quite regular in view of the unhealthy climatic conditions." But then, looking up, he chanced to meet with his own blue eyes the stranger's weary, melancholy gaze, fixed on his face. The Englishman coloured. He continued in a lower voice, rather confused: "At least, that is the official explanation, which they see fit to stick to. I may tell you there's a bit more to it than that." And then, in his good, straightforward way, he told the truth.

For the past several years Asiatic cholera had shown a strong tendency to spread. Its source was the hot, moist swamps of the delta of the Ganges, where it bred in the mephitic air of that primeval island-jungle, among whose bamboo thickets the tiger crouches, where life of every sort flourishes in rankest abundance, and only man avoids the spot. Thence the pestilence had spread throughout Hindustan, raging with great violence; moved eastwards to China, westward to Afghanistan and Persia; following the great caravan routes, it brought terror to Astrakhan, terror to Moscow. Even while Europe trembled lest the

spectre be seen striding westward across country, it was carried by sea
from Syrian ports and appeared simultaneously at several points on the
Mediterranean littoral; raised its head in Toulon and Malaga, Pa-
lermo and Naples, and soon got a firm hold in Calabria and Apulia.
Northern Italy had been spared — so far. But in May the horrible
vibrions were found on the same day in two bodies: the emaciated,
blackened corpses of a bargee and a woman who kept a green-grocer's
shop. Both cases were hushed up. But in a week there were ten more
— twenty, thirty in different quarters of the town. An Austrian provincial, having come to Venice on a few days' pleasure trip, went home
and died with all the symptoms of the plague. Thus was explained the
fact that the German-language papers were the first to print the news
of the Venetian outbreak. The Venetian authorities published in reply
a statement to the effect that the state of the city's health had never
been better; at the same time instituting the most necessary precautions. But by that time the food supplies — milk, meat, or vegetables
— had probably been contaminated, for death unseen and unacknowledged was devouring and laying waste in the narrow streets, while a
brooding, unseasonable heat warmed the waters of the canals and encouraged the spread of the pestilence. Yes, the disease seemed to
flourish and wax strong, to redouble its generative powers. Recoveries
were rare. Eighty out of every hundred died, and horribly, for the
onslaught was of the extremest violence, and not infrequently of the
"dry" type, the most malignant form of the contagion. In this form
the victim's body loses power to expel the water secreted by the blood-
vessels, it shrivels up, he passes with hoarse cries from convulsion to
convulsion, his blood grows thick like pitch, and he suffocates in a few
hours. He is fortunate indeed, if, as sometimes happens, the disease,
after a slight *malaise*, takes the form of a profound unconsciousness, from
which the sufferer seldom or never rouses. By the beginning of June
the quarantine buildings of the *ospedale civico* had quietly filled up, the
two orphan asylums were entirely occupied, and there was a hideously
brisk traffic between the *Nuovo Fundamento* and the island of San Michele,
where the cemetery was. But the city was not swayed by high-minded
motives or regard for international agreements. The authorities were
more actuated by fear of being out of pocket, by regard for the new exhibition of paintings just opened in the Public Gardens, or by apprehension of the large losses the hotels and the shops that catered to foreigners would suffer in case of panic and blockade. And the fears of
the people supported the persistent official policy of silence and denial.

The city's first medical officer, an honest and competent man, had indignantly resigned his office and been privily replaced by a more compliant person. The fact was known; and this corruption in high places played its part, together with the suspense as to where the walking terror might strike next, to demoralize the baser elements in the city and encourage those antisocial forces which shun the light of day. There was intemperance, indecency, increase of crime. Evenings one saw many drunken people, which was unusual. Gangs of men in surly mood made the streets unsafe, theft and assault were said to be frequent, even murder; for in two cases persons supposedly victims of the plague were proved to have been poisoned by their own families. And professional vice was rampant, displaying excesses heretofore unknown and only at home much farther south and in the east.

Such was the substance of the Englishman's tale. "You would do well," he concluded, "to leave today instead of tomorrow. The blockade cannot be more than a few days off."

"Thank you," said Aschenbach, and left the office.

The Piazza lay in sweltering sunshine. Innocent foreigners sat before the cafés or stood in front of the cathedral, the centre of clouds of doves that, with fluttering wings, tried to shoulder each other away and pick the kernels of maize from the extended hand. Aschenbach strode up and down the spacious flags, feverishly excited, triumphant in possession of the truth at last, but with a sickening taste in his mouth and a fantastic horror at his heart. One decent, expiatory course lay open to him; he considered it. Tonight, after dinner, he might approach the lady of the pearls and address her in words which he precisely formulated in his mind: "Madame, will you permit an entire stranger to serve you with a word of advice and warning which self-interest prevents others from uttering? Go away. Leave here at once, without delay, with Tadzio and your daughters. Venice is in the grip of pestilence." Then might he lay his hand in farewell upon the head of that instrument of a mocking deity; and thereafter himself flee the accursed morass. But he knew that he was far indeed from any serious desire to take such a step. It would restore him, would give him back himself once more; but he who is beside himself revolts at the idea of self-possession. There crossed his mind the vision of a white building with inscriptions on it, glittering in the sinking sun — he recalled how his mind had dreamed away into their transparent mysticism; recalled the strange pilgrim apparition that had wakened in the aging man a lust for strange countries and fresh sights. And these memories, again, brought in their train the thought of returning home, returning to reason, self-mastery, an ordered existence, to the old life of effort. Alas! the bare thought made him wince with a revulsion that was like physical nausea. "It must be kept quiet," he whispered fiercely. "I will not speak!" The knowledge that he shared the city's secret, the city's guilt — it put him beside himself, intoxicated him as a small quantity of wine will a man suffering from brain-fag. His thoughts dwelt upon the image of the desolate and calamitous city, and he was giddy with fugitive, mad, unreasoning hopes and visions of a monstrous sweetness. That tender sentiment he had a moment ago evoked, what was it compared with such images as these? His art, his moral sense, what were they in the balance beside the boons that chaos might confer? He kept silence, he stopped on.

That night he had a fearful dream — if dream be the right word for a mental and physical experience which did indeed befall him in deep sleep, as a thing quite apart and real to his senses, yet without his seeing himself as present in it. Rather its theatre seemed to be his own soul, and the events burst in from outside, violently overcoming the profound resistance of his spirit; passed him through and left him, left the whole cultural structure of a lifetime trampled on, ravaged, and destroyed.

The beginning was fear; fear and desire, with a shuddering curiosity. Night reigned, and his senses were on the alert; he heard loud, confused noises from far away, clamour and hubbub. There was a rattling, a crashing, a low dull thunder; shrill halloos and a kind of howl with a long-drawn *u*-sound at the end. And with all these, dominating them all, flute-notes of the cruellest sweetness, deep and cooing, keeping shamelessly on until the listener felt his very entrails bewitched. He heard a voice, naming, though darkly, that which was to come: "The stranger god!" A glow lighted up the surrounding mist and by it he recognized a mountain scene like that about his country home. From the wooded heights, from among the tree-trunks and crumbling moss-covered rocks, a troop came tumbling and raging down, a whirling rout of men and animals, and overflowed the hillside with flames and human forms, with clamour and the reeling dance. The females stumbled over the long, hairy pelts that dangled from their girdles; with heads flung back they uttered loud hoarse cries and shook their tambourines high in air; brandished naked daggers or torches vomiting trails of sparks. They shrieked, holding their breasts in both hands; coiling snakes with quivering tongues they clutched about their waists.

Horned and hairy males, girt about the loins with hides, drooped heads and lifted arms and thighs in unison, as they beat on brazen vessels that gave out droning thunder, or thumped madly on drums. There were troops of beardless youths armed with garlanded staves; these ran after goats and thrust their staves against the creatures' flanks, then clung to the plunging horns and let themselves be borne off with triumphant shouts. And one and all the mad rout yelled that cry, composed of soft consonants with a long-drawn *u*-sound at the end, so sweet and wild it was together, and like nothing ever heard before! It would ring through the air like the bellow of a challenging stag, and be given back many-tongued; or they would use it to goad each other on to dance with wild excess of tossing limbs — they never let it die. But the deep, beguiling notes of the flute wove in and out and over all. Beguiling too it was to him who struggled in the grip of these sights and sounds, shamelessly awaiting the coming feast and the uttermost surrender. He trembled, he shrank, his will was steadfast to preserve and uphold his own god against this stranger who was sworn enemy to dignity and self-control. But the mountain wall took up the noise and howling and gave it back manifold; it rose high, swelled to a madness that carried him away. His senses reeled in the steam of panting bodies, the acrid stench from the goats, the odour as of stagnant waters — and another, too familiar smell — of wounds, uncleanness, and disease. His heart throbbed to the drums, his brain reeled, a blind rage seized him, a whirling lust, he craved with all his soul to join the ring that formed about the obscene symbol of the godhead, which they were unveiling and elevating, monstrous and wooden, while from full throats they yelled their rallying-cry. Foam dripped from their lips, they drove each other on with lewd gesturings and beckoning hands. They laughed, they howled, they thrust their pointed staves into each other's flesh and licked the blood as it ran down. But now the dreamer was in them and of them, the stranger god was his own. Yes, it was he who was flinging himself upon the animals, who bit and tore and swallowed smoking gobbets of flesh — while on the trampled moss there now began the rites in honour of the god, an orgy of promiscuous embraces — and in his very soul he tasted the bestial degradation of his fall.

The unhappy man woke from this dream shattered, unhinged, powerless in the demon's grip. He no longer avoided men's eyes nor cared whether he exposed himself to suspicion. And anyhow, people were leaving; many of the bathing-cabins stood empty, there were many vacant places in the dining-room, scarcely any foreigners were seen in the streets. The truth seemed to have leaked out; despite all efforts to the contrary, panic was in the air. But the lady of the pearls stopped on with her family; whether because the rumours had not reached her or because she was too proud and fearless to heed them. Tadzio remained; and it seemed at times to Aschenbach, in his obsessed state, that death and fear together might clear the island of all other souls and leave him there alone with him he coveted. In the long mornings on the beach his heavy gaze would rest, a fixed and reckless stare, upon the lad; towards nightfall, lost to shame, he would follow him through the city's narrow streets where horrid death stalked too, and at such time it seemed to him as though the moral law were fallen in ruins and only the monstrous and perverse held out a hope.

Like any lover, he desired to please; suffered agonies at the thought of failure, and brightened his dress with smart ties and handkerchiefs and other youthful touches. He added jewellery and perfumes and spent hours each day over his toilette, appearing at dinner elaborately arrayed and tensely excited. The presence of the youthful beauty that had bewitched him filled him with disgust of his own aging body; the sight of his own sharp features and grey hair plunged him in hopeless mortification; he made desperate efforts to recover the appearance and freshness of his youth and began paying frequent visits to the hotel barber. Enveloped in the white sheet, beneath the hands of that garrulous personage, he would lean back in the chair and look at himself in the glass with misgiving.

"Grey," he said, with a grimace.

"Slightly," answered the man. "Entirely due to neglect, to a lack of regard for appearances. Very natural, of course, in men of affairs, but, after all, not very sensible, for it is just such people who ought to be above vulgar prejudice in matters like these. Some folk have very strict ideas about the use of cosmetics; but they never extend them to the teeth, as they logically should. And very disgusted other people would be if they did. No, we are all as old as we feel, but no older, and grey hair can misrepresent a man worse than dyed. You, for instance, signore, have a right to your natural colour. Surely you will permit me to restore what belongs to you?"

"How?" asked Aschenbach.

For answer the oily one washed his client's hair in two waters, one clear and one dark, and lo, it was as black as in the days of his youth. He waved it with the tongs in wide, flat undulations, and stepped back to admire the effect.

"Now if we were just to freshen up the skin a little," he said.

And with that he went on from one thing to another, his enthusiasm waxing with each new idea. Aschenbach sat there comfortably; he was incapable of objecting to the process — rather as it went forward it roused his hopes. He watched it in the mirror and saw his eyebrows grow more even and arching, the eyes gain in size and brilliance, by dint of a little application below the lids. A delicate carmine glowed on his cheeks where the skin had been so brown and leathery. The dry, anæmic lips grew full, they turned the colour of ripe strawberries, the lines round eyes and mouth were treated with a facial cream and gave place to youthful bloom. It was a young man who looked back at him from the glass — Aschenbach's heart leaped at the sight. The artist in cosmetic at last professed himself satisfied; after the manner of such people, he thanked his client profusely for what he had done himself. "The merest trifle, the merest, signore," he said as he added the final touches. "Now the signore can fall in love as soon as he likes." Aschenbach went off as in a dream, dazed between joy and fear, in his red neck-tie and broad straw hat with its gay striped band.

A lukewarm storm-wind had come up. It rained a little now and then, the air was heavy and turbid and smelt of decay. Aschenbach, with fevered cheeks beneath the rouge, seemed to hear rushing and flapping sounds in his ears, as though storm-spirits were abroad — unhallowed ocean harpies who follow those devoted to destruction, snatch away and defile their viands. For the heat took away his appetite and thus he was haunted with the idea that his food was infected.

One afternoon he pursued his charmer deep into the stricken city's huddled heart. The labyrinthine little streets, squares, canals, and bridges, each one so like the next, at length quite made him lose his bearings. He did not even know the points of the compass; all his care was not to lose sight of the figure after which his eyes thirsted. He slunk under walls, he lurked behind buildings or people's backs; and the sustained tension of his senses and emotions exhausted him more and more, though for a long time he was unconscious of fatigue. Tadzio walked behind the others, he let them pass ahead in the narrow alleys, and as he sauntered slowly after, he would turn his head and assure himself with a glance of his strange, twilit grey eyes that his lover was still following. He saw him — and he did not betray him. The knowledge enraptured Aschenbach. Lured by those eyes, led on the leading-string of his own passion and folly, utterly lovesick, he stole upon the footsteps of his unseemly hope — and at the end found him-

self cheated. The Polish family crossed a small vaulted bridge, the
height of whose archway hid them from his sight, and when he climbed
it himself they were nowhere to be seen. He hunted in three directions
— straight ahead and on both sides the narrow, dirty quay — in vain.
Worn quite out and unnerved, he had to give over the search.

His head burned, his body was wet with clammy sweat, he was
plagued by intolerable thirst. He looked about for refreshment, of
whatever sort, and found a little fruit-shop where he bought some
strawberries. They were overripe and soft; he ate them as he went.
The street he was on opened out into a little square, one of those
charmed, forsaken spots he liked; he recognized it as the very one
where he had sat weeks ago and conceived his abortive plan of flight.
He sank down on the steps of the well and leaned his head against its
stone rim. It was quiet here. Grass grew between the stones, and
rubbish lay about. Tall, weather-beaten houses bordered the square,
one of them rather palatial, with vaulted windows, gaping now, and
little lion balconies. In the ground floor of another was an apothecary's shop. A waft of carbolic acid was borne on a warm gust of wind.

There he sat, the master: this was he who had found a way to recon-
cile art and honours; who had written *The Abject*, and in a style of
classic purity renounced bohemianism and all its works, all sympathy
with the abyss and the troubled depths of the outcast human soul.
This was he who had put knowledge underfoot to climb so high; who
had outgrown the ironic pose and adjusted himself to the burdens and
obligations of fame; whose renown had been officially recognized and
his name ennobled, whose style was set for a model in the schools.
There he sat. His eyelids were closed, there was only a swift, sidelong
glint of the eyeballs now and again, something between a question and
a leer; while the rouged and flabby mouth uttered single words of the
sentences shaped in his disordered brain by the fantastic logic that
governs our dreams.

"For mark you, Phædrus, beauty alone is both divine and visible;
and so it is the sense way, the artist's way, little Phædrus, to the spirit.
But, now tell me, my dear boy, do you believe that such a man can ever
attain wisdom and true manly worth, for whom the path to the spirit
must lead through the senses? Or do you rather think — for I leave
the point to you — that it is a path of perilous sweetness, a way of
transgression, and must surely lead him who walks in it astray? For
you know that we poets cannot walk the way of beauty without Eros
as our companion and guide. We may be heroic after our fashion,

disciplined warriors of our craft, yet are we all like women, for we exult in passion, and love is still our desire — our craving and our shame. And from this you will perceive that we poets can be neither wise nor worthy citizens. We must needs be wanton, must needs rove at large in the realm of feeling. Our magisterial style is all folly and pretence, our honourable repute a farce, the crowd's belief in us is merely laughable. And to teach youth, or the populace, by means of art is a dangerous practice and ought to be forbidden. For what good can an artist be as a teacher, when from his birth up he is headed direct for the pit? We may want to shun it and attain to honour in the world; but however we turn, it draws us still. So, then, since knowledge might destroy us, we will have none of it. For knowledge, Phædrus, does not make him who possesses it dignified or austere. Knowledge is all-knowing, understanding, forgiving; it takes up no position, sets no store by form. It has compassion with the abyss — it *is* the abyss. So we reject it, firmly, and henceforward our concern shall be with beauty only. And by beauty we mean simplicity, largeness, and renewed severity of discipline; we mean a return to detachment and to form. But detachment, Phædrus, and preoccupation with form lead to intoxication and desire, they may lead the noblest among us to frightful emotional excesses, which his own stern cult of the beautiful would make him the first to condemn. So they too, they too, lead to the bottomless pit. Yes, they lead us thither, I say, us who are poets — who by our natures are prone not to excellence but to excess. And now, Phædrus, I will go. Remain here; and only when you can no longer see me, then do you depart also."

A few days later Gustave Aschenbach left his hotel rather later than usual in the morning. He was not feeling well and had to struggle against spells of giddiness only half physical in their nature, accompanied by a swiftly mounting dread, a sense of futility and hopelessness— but whether this referred to himself or to the outer world he could not tell. In the lobby he saw a quantity of luggage lying strapped and ready; asked the porter whose it was, and received in answer the name he already knew he should hear — that of the Polish family. The expression of his ravaged features did not change; he only gave that quick lift of the head with which we sometimes receive the uninteresting answer to a casual query. But he put another: "When?" "After luncheon," the man replied. He nodded, and went down to the beach.

It was an unfriendly scene. Little crisping shivers ran all across the wide stretch of shallow water between the shore and the first sand-bank.

The whole beach, once so full of colour and life, looked now autumnal, out of season; it was nearly deserted and not even very clean. A camera on a tripod stood at the edge of the water, apparently abandoned; its black cloth snapped in the freshening wind.

Tadzio was there, in front of his cabin, with the three or four play-fellows still left him. Aschenbach set up his chair some half-way between the cabins and the water, spread a rug over his knees, and sat looking on. The game this time was unsupervised, the elders being probably busy with their packing, and it looked rather lawless and out-of-hand. Jaschiu, the sturdy lad in the belted suit, with the black, brilliantined hair, became angry at a handful of sand thrown in his eyes; he challenged Tadzio to a fight, which quickly ended in the downfall of the weaker. And perhaps the coarser nature saw here a chance to avenge himself at last, by one cruel act, for his long weeks of subserviency: the victor would not let the vanquished get up, but remained kneeling on Tadzio's back, pressing Tadzio's face into the sand — for so long a time that it seemed the exhausted lad might even suffocate. He made spasmodic efforts to shake the other off, lay still, and then began a feeble twitching. Just as Aschenbach was about to spring indignantly to the rescue, Jaschiu let his victim go. Tadzio, very pale, half sat up, and remained so, leaning on one arm, for several minutes, with darkening eyes and rumpled hair. Then he rose and walked slowly away. The others called him, at first gaily, then imploringly; he would not hear. Jaschiu was evidently overtaken by swift remorse; he followed his friend and tried to make his peace, but Tadzio motioned him back with a jerk of one shoulder and went down to the water's edge. He was barefoot and wore his striped linen suit with the red breast-knot.

There he stayed a little, with bent head, tracing figures in the wet sand with one toe; then stepped into the shallow water, which at its deepest did not wet his knees; waded idly through it and reached the sand-bar. Now he paused again, with his face turned seaward; and next began to move slowly leftwards along the narrow strip of sand the sea left bare. He paced there, divided by an expanse of water from the shore, from his mates by his moody pride; a remote and isolated figure, with floating locks, out there in sea and wind, against the misty inane. Once more he paused to look: with a sudden recollection, or by an impulse, he turned from the waist up, in an exquisite movement, one hand resting on his hip, and looked over his shoulder at the shore. The watcher sat just as he had sat that time in the lobby of the hotel when

first the twilit grey eyes had met his own.   He rested his head against
the chair-back and followed the movements of the figure out there, then
lifted it, as it were in answer to Tadzio's gaze.   It sank on his breast,
the eyes looked out beneath their lids, while his whole face took on the
relaxed and brooding expression of deep slumber.   It seemed to him
the pale and lovely Summoner out there smiled at him and beckoned;
as though, with the hand he lifted from his hip, he pointed outward as
he hovered on before into an immensity of richest expectation.

Some minutes passed before anyone hastened to the aid of the elderly
man sitting there collapsed in his chair.   They bore him to his room.
And before nightfall a shocked and respectful world received the news
of his decease.

[*Translated by* H. T. LOWE-PORTER]

James Joyce

THE DEAD

1914

❧

LILY, the caretaker's daughter, was literally run off her feet. Hardly had she brought one gentleman into the little pantry behind the office on the ground floor and helped him off with his overcoat than the wheezy hall-door bell clanged again and she had to scamper along the bare hallway to let in another guest. It was well for her she had not to attend to the ladies also. But Miss Kate and Miss Julia had thought of that and had converted the bathroom upstairs into a ladies' dressing-room. Miss Kate and Miss Julia were there, gossiping and laughing and fussing, walking after each other to the head of the stairs, peering down over the banisters and calling down to Lily to ask her who had come.

It was always a great affair, the Misses Morkan's annual dance. Everybody who knew them came to it, members of the family, old friends of the family, the members of Julia's choir, any of Kate's pupils that were grown up enough, and even some of Mary Jane's pupils too. Never once had it fallen flat. For years and years it had gone off in splendid style, as long as anyone could remember; ever since Kate and Julia, after the death of their brother Pat, had left the house in Stoney Batter and taken Mary Jane, their only niece, to live with them in the dark, gaunt house on Usher's Island, the upper part of which they had rented from Mr. Fulham, the corn-factor on the ground floor. That was a good thirty years ago if it was a day. Mary Jane, who was then a little girl in short clothes, was now the main prop of the household, for she had the organ in Haddington Road. She had been through the Academy and gave a pupils' concert every year in the upper room of the Antient Concert Rooms. Many of her pupils belonged to the better-class families on the Kingstown and Dalkey line. Old as they were, her aunts also did their share. Julia, though she was quite grey, was still the leading soprano in Adam and Eve's, and Kate, being too feeble to go about much, gave music lessons to beginners on the old square piano in the back room. Lily, the caretaker's daughter, did housemaid's work for them. Though their life was modest, they believed in eating well; the best of everything: diamond-bone sirloins, three-shilling tea and the best bottled stout. But Lily seldom made a mistake in the orders, so that she got on well with her three mistresses. They were fussy, that was all. But the only thing they would not stand was back answers.

Of course, they had good reason to be fussy on such a night. And then it was long after ten o'clock and yet there was no sign of Gabriel and his wife. Besides they were dreadfully afraid that Freddy Malins might turn up screwed. They would not wish for worlds that any of Mary Jane's pupils should see him under the influence; and when he was like that it was sometimes very hard to manage him. Freddy Malins always came late, but they wondered what could be keeping Gabriel: and that was what brought them every two minutes to the banisters to ask Lily had Gabriel or Freddy come.

"O, Mr. Conroy," said Lily to Gabriel when she opened the door for him, "Miss Kate and Miss Julia thought you were never coming. Good-night, Mrs. Conroy."

"I'll engage they did," said Gabriel, "but they forget that my wife here takes three mortal hours to dress herself."

He stood on the mat, scraping the snow from his goloshes, while Lily led his wife to the foot of the stairs and called out:

"Miss Kate, here's Mrs. Conroy."

Kate and Julia came toddling down the dark stairs at once. Both of them kissed Gabriel's wife, said she must be perished alive, and asked was Gabriel with her.

"Here I am as right as the mail, Aunt Kate! Go on up. I'll follow," called out Gabriel from the dark.

He continued scraping his feet vigorously while the three women went upstairs, laughing, to the ladies' dressing-room. A light fringe of snow lay like a cape on the shoulders of his overcoat and like toecaps on the toes of his goloshes; and, as the buttons of his overcoat slipped with a squeaking noise through the snow-stiffened frieze, a cold, fragrant air from out-of-doors escaped from crevices and folds.

"Is it snowing again, Mr. Conroy?" asked Lily.

She had preceded him into the pantry to help him off with his overcoat. Gabriel smiled at the three syllables she had given his surname and glanced at her. She was a slim, growing girl, pale in complexion and with hay-coloured hair. The gas in the pantry made her look still paler. Gabriel had known her when she was a child and used to sit on the lowest step nursing a rag doll.

"Yes, Lily," he answered, "and I think we're in for a night of it."

He looked up at the pantry ceiling, which was shaking with the stamping and shuffling of feet on the floor above, listened for a moment to the piano and then glanced at the girl, who was folding his overcoat carefully at the end of a shelf.

"Tell me, Lily," he said in a friendly tone, "do you still go to school?"

"O no, sir," she answered. "I'm done schooling this year and more."

"O, then," said Gabriel gaily, "I suppose we'll be going to your wedding one of these fine days with your young man, eh?"

The girl glanced back at him over her shoulder and said with great bitterness:

"The men that is now is only all palaver and what they can get out of you."

Gabriel coloured, as if he felt he had made a mistake and, without looking at her, kicked off his goloshes and flicked actively with his muffler at his patent-leather shoes.

He was a stout, tallish young man. The high colour of his cheeks pushed upwards even to his forehead, where it scattered itself in a few formless patches of pale red; and on his hairless face there scintillated restlessly the polished lenses and the bright gilt rims of the glasses which screened his delicate and restless eyes. His glossy black hair was parted in the middle and brushed in a long curve behind his ears where it curled slightly beneath the groove left by his hat.

When he had flicked lustre into his shoes he stood up and pulled his waistcoat down more tightly on his plump body. Then he took a coin rapidly from his pocket.

"O Lily," he said, thrusting it into her hands, "it's Christmas-time, isn't it? Just . . . here's a little. . . ."

He walked rapidly towards the door.

"O no, sir!" cried the girl, following him. "Really, sir, I wouldn't take it."

"Christmas-time! Christmas-time!" said Gabriel, almost trotting to the stairs and waving his hand to her in deprecation.

The girl, seeing that he had gained the stairs, called out after him:

"Well, thank you, sir."

He waited outside the drawing-room door until the waltz should finish, listening to the skirts that swept against it and to the shuffling of feet. He was still discomposed by the girl's bitter and sudden retort. It had cast a gloom over him which he tried to dispel by arranging his cuffs and the bows of his tie. He then took from his waistcoat pocket a little paper and glanced at the headings he had made for his speech. He was undecided about the lines from Robert Browning, for he feared they would be above the heads of his hearers. Some quotation that they would recognise from Shakespeare or from the Melodies would be better. The indelicate clacking of the men's heels and the shuffling of their soles reminded him that their grade of culture differed from his. He would only make himself ridiculous by quoting poetry to them which they could not understand. They would think that he was airing his superior education. He would fail with them just as he had failed with the girl in the pantry. He had taken up a wrong tone. His whole speech was a mistake from first to last, an utter failure.

Just then his aunts and his wife came out of the ladies' dressing-room. His aunts were two small, plainly dressed old women. Aunt Julia was an inch or so the taller. Her hair, drawn low over the tops of her ears, was grey; and grey also, with darker shadows, was her large flaccid face. Though she was stout in build and stood erect, her slow eyes and parted lips gave her the appearance of a woman who did not know where she was or where she was going. Aunt Kate was more vivacious. Her face, healthier than her sister's, was all puckers and creases, like a shrivelled red apple, and her hair, braided in the same old-fashioned way, had not lost its ripe nut colour.

They both kissed Gabriel frankly. He was their favourite nephew, the son of their dead elder sister, Ellen, who had married T. J. Conroy of the Port and Docks.

"Gretta tells me you're not going to take a cab back to Monkstown to-night, Gabriel," said Aunt Kate.

"No," said Gabriel, turning to his wife, "we had quite enough of that last year, hadn't we? Don't you remember, Aunt Kate, what a cold Gretta got out of it? Cab windows rattling all the way, and the east wind blowing in after we passed Merrion. Very jolly it was. Gretta caught a dreadful cold."

Aunt Kate frowned severely and nodded her head at every word.

"Quite right, Gabriel, quite right," she said. "You can't be too careful."

"But as for Gretta there," said Gabriel, "she'd walk home in the snow if she were let."

Mrs. Conroy laughed.

"Don't mind him, Aunt Kate," she said. "He's really an awful bother, what with green shades for Tom's eyes at night and making him do the dumb-bells, and forcing Eva to eat the stirabout. The poor child! And she simply hates the sight of it! . . . O, but you'll never guess what he makes me wear now!"

She broke out into a peal of laughter and glanced at her husband, whose admiring and happy eyes had been wandering from her dress to her face and hair. The two aunts laughed heartily, too, for Gabriel's solicitude was a standing joke with them.

"Goloshes!" said Mrs. Conroy. "That's the latest. Whenever it's wet underfoot I must put on my goloshes. To-night even, he wanted me to put them on, but I wouldn't. The next thing he'll buy me will be a diving suit."

Gabriel laughed nervously and patted his tie reassuringly, while Aunt Kate nearly doubled herself, so heartily did she enjoy the joke. The smile soon faded from Aunt Julia's face and her mirthless eyes were directed towards her nephew's face. After a pause she asked:

"And what are goloshes, Gabriel?"

"Goloshes, Julia!" exclaimed her sister. "Goodness me, don't you know what goloshes are? You wear them over your . . . over your boots, Gretta, isn't it?"

"Yes," said Mrs. Conroy. "Guttapercha things. We both have a pair now. Gabriel says everyone wears them on the continent."

"O, on the continent," murmured Aunt Julia, nodding her head slowly.

Gabriel knitted his brows and said, as if he were slightly angered:

"It's nothing very wonderful, but Gretta thinks it very funny because she says the word reminds her of Christy Minstrels."

"But tell me, Gabriel," said Aunt Kate, with brisk tact. "Of course, you've seen about the room. Gretta was saying . . ."

"O, the room is all right," replied Gabriel. "I've taken one in the Gresham."

"To be sure," said Aunt Kate, "by far the best thing to do. And the children, Gretta, you're not anxious about them?"

"O, for one night," said Mrs. Conroy. "Besides, Bessie will look after them."

"To be sure," said Aunt Kate again. "What a comfort it is to have a girl like that, one you can depend on! There's that Lily, I'm sure I don't know what has come over her lately. She's not the girl she was at all."

Gabriel was about to ask his aunt some questions on this point, but she broke off suddenly to gaze after her sister, who had wandered down the stairs and was craning her neck over the banisters.

"Now, I ask you," she said almost testily, "where is Julia going? Julia! Julia! Where are you going?"

Julia, who had gone half way down one flight, came back and announced blandly:

"Here's Freddy."

At the same moment a clapping of hands and a final flourish of the pianist told that the waltz had ended. The drawing-room door was opened from within and some couples came out. Aunt Kate drew Gabriel aside hurriedly and whispered into his ear:

"Slip down, Gabriel, like a good fellow and see if he's all right, and don't let him up if he's screwed. I'm sure he's screwed. I'm sure he is."

Gabriel went to the stairs and listened over the banisters. He could hear two persons talking in the pantry. Then he recognised Freddy Malins' laugh. He went down the stairs noisily.

"It's such a relief," said Aunt Kate to Mrs. Conroy, "that Gabriel is here. I always feel easier in my mind when he's here. . . . Julia, there's Miss Daly and Miss Power will take some refreshment. Thanks for your beautiful waltz, Miss Daly. It made lovely time."

A tall wizen-faced man, with a stiff grizzled moustache and swarthy skin, who was passing out with his partner, said:

"And may we have some refreshment, too, Miss Morkan?"

"Julia," said Aunt Kate summarily, "and here's Mr. Browne and Miss Furlong. Take them in, Julia, with Miss Daly and Miss Power."

"I'm the man for the ladies," said Mr. Browne, pursing his lips until his moustache bristled and smiling in all his wrinkles. "You know, Miss Morkan, the reason they are so fond of me is ——"

He did not finish his sentence, but, seeing that Aunt Kate was out of earshot, at once led the three young ladies into the back room. The middle of the room was occupied by two square tables placed end to end, and on these Aunt Julia and the caretaker were straightening and smoothing a large cloth. On the sideboard were arrayed dishes and plates, and glasses and bundles of knives and forks and spoons. The top of the closed square piano served also as a sideboard for viands and sweets. At a smaller sideboard in one corner two young men were standing, drinking hop-bitters.

Mr Browne led his charges thither and invited them all, in jest, to some ladies' punch, hot, strong and sweet. As they said they never took anything strong, he opened three bottles of lemonade for them. Then he asked one of the young men to move aside, and, taking hold of the decanter, filled out for himself a goodly measure of whisky. The young men eyed him respectfully while he took a trial sip.

"God help me," he said, smiling, "it's the doctor's orders."

His wizened face broke into a broader smile, and the three young ladies laughed in musical echo to his pleasantry, swaying their bodies to and fro, with nervous jerks of their shoulders. The boldest said:

"O, now, Mr. Browne, I'm sure the doctor never ordered anything of the kind."

Mr. Browne took another sip of his whisky and said, with sidling mimicry:

"Well, you see, I'm like the famous Mrs. Cassidy, who is reported to have said: 'Now, Mary Grimes, if I don't take it, make me take it, for I feel I want it.' "

His hot face had leaned forward a little too confidentially and he had assumed a very low Dublin accent so that the young ladies, with one instinct, received his speech in silence. Miss Furlong, who was one of Mary Jane's pupils, asked Miss Daly what was the name of the pretty waltz she had played; and Mr. Browne, seeing that he was ignored, turned promptly to the two young men who were more appreciative.

A red-faced young woman, dressed in pansy, came into the room, excitedly clapping her hands and crying:

"Quadrilles! Quadrilles!"

Close on her heels came Aunt Kate, crying:

"Two gentlemen and three ladies, Mary Jane!"

"O, here's Mr. Bergin and Mr. Kerrigan," said Mary Jane. "Mr. Kerrigan, will you take Miss Power? Miss Furlong, may I get you a partner, Mr. Bergin. O, that'll just do now."

"Three ladies, Mary Jane," said Aunt Kate.

The two young gentlemen asked the ladies if they might have the pleasure, and Mary Jane turned to Miss Daly.

"O, Miss Daly, you're really awfully good, after playing for the last two dances, but really we're so short of ladies to-night."

"I don't mind in the least, Miss Morkan."

"But I've a nice partner for you, Mr. Bartell D'Arcy, the tenor. I'll get him to sing later on. All Dublin is raving about him."

"Lovely voice, lovely voice!" said Aunt Kate.

As the piano had twice begun the prelude to the first figure Mary Jane led her recruits quickly from the room. They had hardly gone when Aunt Julia wandered slowly into the room, looking behind her at something.

"What is the matter, Julia?" asked Aunt Kate anxiously. "Who is it?"

Julia, who was carrying in a column of table-napkins, turned to her sister and said, simply, as if the question had surprised her:

"It's only Freddy, Kate, and Gabriel with him."

In fact right behind her Gabriel could be seen piloting Freddy Malins across the landing. The latter, a young man of about forty, was of Gabriel's size and build, with very round shoulders. His face was fleshy and pallid, touched with colour only at the thick hanging lobes of his ears and at the wide wings of his nose. He had coarse features, a blunt nose, a convex and receding brow, tumid and protruded lips. His heavy-lidded eyes and the disorder of his scanty hair made him look sleepy. He was laughing heartily in a high key at a story which he had been telling Gabriel on the stairs and at the same time rubbing the knuckles of his left fist backwards and forwards into his left eye.

"Good-evening, Freddy," said Aunt Julia.

Freddy Malins bade the Misses Morkan good-evening in what seemed an offhand fashion by reason of the habitual catch in his voice and then, seeing that Mr. Browne was grinning at him from the sideboard, crossed the room on rather shaky legs and began to repeat in an undertone the story he had just told to Gabriel.

"He's not so bad, is he?" said Aunt Kate to Gabriel.

Gabriel's brows were dark but he raised them quickly and answered:

"O, no, hardly noticeable."

"Now, isn't he a terrible fellow!" she said. "And his poor mother made him take the pledge on New Year's Eve. But come on, Gabriel, into the drawing-room."

Before leaving the room with Gabriel she signalled to Mr. Browne by frowning and shaking her forefinger in warning to and fro. Mr. Browne nodded in answer and, when she had gone, said to Freddy Malins:

"Now, then, Teddy, I'm going to fill you out a good glass of lemonade just to buck you up."

Freddy Malins, who was nearing the climax of his story, waved the offer aside impatiently but Mr. Browne, having first called Freddy Malins' attention to a disarray in his dress, filled out and handed him a full glass of lemonade. Freddy Malins' left hand accepted the glass mechanically, his right hand being engaged in the mechanical readjustment of his dress. Mr. Browne, whose face was once more wrinkling with mirth, poured out for himself a glass of whisky while Freddy Malins exploded, before he had well reached the climax of his story, in a kink of high-pitched bronchitic laughter and, setting down his untasted and overflowing glass, began to rub the knuckles of his left fist backwards and forwards into his left eye, repeating words of his last phrase as well as his fit of laughter would allow him.

．　．　．　．　．　．　．　．　．　．

Gabriel could not listen while Mary Jane was playing her Academy piece, full of runs and difficult passages, to the hushed drawing-room. He liked music but the piece she was playing had no melody for him and he doubted whether it had any melody for the other listeners, though they had begged Mary Jane to play something. Four young men, who had come from the refreshment-room to stand in the doorway at the sound of the piano, had gone away quietly in couples after a few minutes. The only persons who seemed to follow the music were Mary Jane herself, her hands racing along the key-board or lifted from it at the pauses like those of a priestess in momentary imprecation, and Aunt Kate standing at her elbow to turn the page.

Gabriel's eyes, irritated by the floor, which glittered with beeswax under the heavy chandelier, wandered to the wall above the piano. A picture of the balcony scene in *Romeo and Juliet* hung there and beside it was a picture of the two murdered princes in the Tower which Aunt Julia had worked in red, blue and brown wools when she was a girl. Probably in the school they had gone to as girls that kind of work had been taught for one year. His mother had worked for him as a birthday present a waistcoat of purple tabinet, with little foxes' heads upon it, lined with brown satin and having round mulberry buttons. It was strange that his mother had had no musical talent though Aunt Kate used to call her the brains carrier of the Morkan family. Both she and Julia had always seemed a little proud of their serious and matronly sister. Her photograph stood before the pierglass. She held an open book on her knees and was pointing out something in it to Constantine who, dressed in a man-o'-war suit, lay at her feet. It was she who had chosen the names of her sons for she was very sensible of the dignity of family life. Thanks to her, Constantine was now senior curate in Balbriggan and, thanks to her, Gabriel himself had taken his degree in the Royal University. A shadow passed over his face as he remembered her sullen opposition to his marriage. Some slighting phrases she had used still rankled in his memory; she had once spoken of Gretta as being country cute and that was not true of Gretta at all. It was Gretta who had nursed her during all her last long illness in their house at Monkstown.

He knew that Mary Jane must be near the end of her piece for she was playing again the opening melody with runs of scales after every bar and while he waited for the end the resentment died down in his heart. The piece ended with a trill of octaves in the treble and a final deep octave in the bass. Great applause greeted Mary Jane as, blushing and rolling up her music nervously, she escaped from the room. The most vigorous clapping came from the four young men in the doorway who had gone away to the refreshment-room at the beginning of the piece but had come back when the piano had stopped.

Lancers were arranged. Gabriel found himself partnered with Miss Ivors. She was a frank-mannered talkative young lady, with a freckled face and prominent brown eyes. She did not wear a low-cut bodice and the large brooch which was fixed in the front of her collar bore on it an Irish device and motto.

When they had taken their places she said abruptly:

"I have a crow to pluck with you."

"With me?" said Gabriel.

She nodded her head gravely.

"What is it?" asked Gabriel, smiling at her solemn manner.

"Who is G. C.?" answered Miss Ivors, turning her eyes upon him.

Gabriel coloured and was about to knit his brows, as if he did not understand, when she said bluntly:

"O, innocent Amy! I have found out that you write for *The Daily Express.* Now, aren't you ashamed of yourself?"

"Why should I be ashamed of myself?" asked Gabriel, blinking his eyes and trying to smile.

"Well, I'm ashamed of you," said Miss Ivors frankly. "To say you'd write for a paper like that. I didn't think you were a West Briton."

A look of perplexity appeared on Gabriel's face. It was true that he wrote a literary column every Wednesday in *The Daily Express,* for which he was paid fifteen shillings. But that did not make him a West Briton surely. The books he received for review were almost more welcome than the paltry cheque. He loved to feel the covers and turn over the pages of newly printed books. Nearly every day when his teaching in the college was ended he used to wander down the quays to the second-hand booksellers, to Hickey's on Bachelor's Walk, to Webb's or Massey's on Aston's Quay, or to O'Clohissey's in the by-street. He did not know how to meet her charge. He wanted to say that literature was above politics. But they were friends of many years' standing and their careers had been parallel, first at the University and then as teachers: he could not risk a grandiose phrase with her. He continued blinking his eyes and trying to smile and murmured lamely that he saw nothing political in writing reviews of books.

When their turn to cross had come he was still perplexed and inattentive. Miss Ivors promptly took his hand in a warm grasp and said in a soft friendly tone:

"Of course, I was only joking. Come, we cross now."

When they were together again she spoke of the University question and Gabriel felt more at ease. A friend of hers had shown her his review of Browning's poems. That was how she had found out the secret: but she liked the review immensely. Then she said suddenly:

"O, Mr. Conroy, will you come for an excursion to the Aran Isles this summer? We're going to stay there a whole month. It will be splendid out in the Atlantic. You ought to come. Mr. Clancy is coming, and Mr. Kilkelly and Kathleen Kearney. It would be splendid for Gretta too if she'd come. She's from Connacht, isn't she?"

"Her people are," said Gabriel shortly.

"But you will come, won't you?" said Miss Ivors, laying her warm hand eagerly on his arm.

"The fact is," said Gabriel, "I have just arranged to go ——"

"Go where?" asked Miss Ivors.

"Well, you know, every year I go for a cycling tour with some fellows and so ——"

"But where?" asked Miss Ivors.

"Well, we usually go to France or Belgium or perhaps Germany," said Gabriel awkwardly.

"And why do you go to France and Belgium," said Miss Ivors, "instead of visiting your own land?"

"Well," said Gabriel, "it's partly to keep in touch with the languages and partly for a change."

"And haven't you your own language to keep in touch with — Irish?" asked Miss Ivors.

"Well," said Gabriel, "if it comes to that, you know, Irish is not my language."

Their neighbours had turned to listen to the cross-examination. Gabriel glanced right and left nervously and tried to keep his good humour under the ordeal which was making a blush invade his forehead.

"And haven't you your own land to visit," continued Miss Ivors, "that you know nothing of, your own people, and your own country?"

"O, to tell you the truth," retorted Gabriel suddenly, "I'm sick of my own country, sick of it!"

"Why?" asked Miss Ivors.

Gabriel did not answer for his retort had heated him.

"Why?" repeated Miss Ivors.

They had to go visiting together and, as he had not answered her, Miss Ivors said warmly:

"Of course, you've no answer."

Gabriel tried to cover his agitation by taking part in the dance with great energy. He avoided her eyes for he had seen a sour expression on her face. But when they met in the long chain he was surprised to feel his hand firmly pressed. She looked at him from under her brows for a moment quizzically until he smiled. Then, just as the chain was about to start again, she stood on tiptoe and whispered into his ear:

"West Briton!"

When the lancers were over Gabriel went away to a remote corner of the room where Freddy Malins' mother was sitting. She was a stout feeble old woman with white hair. Her voice had a catch in it like her son's and she stuttered slightly. She had been told that Freddy had come and that he was nearly all right. Gabriel asked her whether she had had a good crossing. She lived with her married daughter in Glasgow and came to Dublin on a visit once a year. She answered placidly that she had had a beautiful crossing and that the captain had been most attentive to her. She spoke also of the beautiful house her daughter kept in Glasgow, and of all the friends they had there. While her tongue rambled on Gabriel tried to banish from his mind all memory of the unpleasant incident with Miss Ivors. Of course the girl or woman, or whatever she was, was an enthusiast but there was a time for all things. Perhaps he ought not to have answered her like that. But she had no right to call him a West Briton before people, even in joke. She had tried to make him ridiculous before people, heckling him and staring at him with her rabbit's eyes.

He saw his wife making her way towards him through the waltzing couples. When she reached him she said into his ear:

"Gabriel, Aunt Kate wants to know won't you carve the goose as usual. Miss Daly will carve the ham and I'll do the pudding."

"All right," said Gabriel.

"She's sending in the younger ones first as soon as this waltz is over so that we'll have the table to ourselves."

"Were you dancing?" asked Gabriel.

"Of course I was. Didn't you see me? What row had you with Molly Ivors?"

"No row. Why? Did she say so?"

"Something like that. I'm trying to get that Mr. D'Arcy to sing. He's full of conceit, I think."

"There was no row," said Gabriel moodily, "only she wanted me to go for a trip to the west of Ireland and I said I wouldn't."

His wife clasped her hands excitedly and gave a little jump.

"O, do go, Gabriel," she cried. "I'd love to see Galway again."

"You can go if you like," said Gabriel coldly.

She looked at him for a moment, then turned to Mrs. Malins and said:

"There's a nice husband for you, Mrs. Malins."

While she was threading her way back across the room Mrs. Malins, without adverting to the interruption, went on to tell Gabriel what beautiful places there were in Scotland and beautiful scenery. Her son-in-law brought them every year to the lakes and they used to go fishing. Her son-in-law was a splendid fisher. One day he caught a beautiful big fish and the man in the hotel cooked it for their dinner.

Gabriel hardly heard what she said. Now that supper was coming near he began to think again about his speech and about the quotation. When he saw Freddy Malins coming across the room to visit his mother Gabriel left the chair free for him and retired into the embrasure of the window. The room had already cleared and from the back room came the clatter of plates and knives. Those who still remained in the drawing-room seemed tired of dancing and were conversing quietly in little groups. Gabriel's warm trembling fingers tapped the cold pane of the window. How cool it must be outside! How pleasant it would be to walk out alone, first along by the river and then through the park! The snow would be lying on the branches of the trees and forming a bright cap on the top of the Wellington

Monument. How much more pleasant it would be there than at the supper-table!

He ran over the headings of his speech: Irish hospitality, sad memories, the Three Graces, Paris, the quotation from Browning. He repeated to himself a phrase he had written in his review: "One feels that one is listening to a thought-tormented music." Miss Ivors had praised the review. Was she sincere? Had she really any life of her own behind all her propagandism? There had never been any ill-feeling between them until that night. It unnerved him to think that she would be at the supper-table, looking up at him while he spoke with her critical quizzing eyes. Perhaps she would not be sorry to see him fail in his speech. An idea came into his mind and gave him courage. He would say, alluding to Aunt Kate and Aunt Julia: "Ladies and Gentlemen, the generation which is now on the wane among us may have had its faults but for my part I think it had certain qualities of hospitality, of humour, of humanity, which the new and very serious and hypereducated generation that is growing up around us seems to me to lack." Very good: that was one for Miss Ivors. What did he care that his aunts were only two ignorant old women?

A murmur in the room attracted his attention. Mr. Browne was advancing from the door, gallantly escorting Aunt Julia, who leaned upon his arm, smiling and hanging her head. An irregular musketry of applause escorted her also as far as the piano and then, as Mary Jane seated herself on the stool, and Aunt Julia, no longer smiling, half turned so as to pitch her voice fairly into the room, gradually ceased. Gabriel recognised the prelude. It was that of an old song of Aunt Julia's — *Arrayed for the Bridal.* Her voice, strong and clear in tone, attacked with great spirit the runs which embellish the air and though she sang very rapidly she did not miss even the smallest of the grace notes. To follow the voice, without looking at the singer's face, was to feel and share the excitement of swift and secure flight. Gabriel applauded loudly with all the others at the close of the song and loud applause was borne in from the invisible supper-table. It sounded so genuine that a little colour struggled into Aunt Julia's face as she bent to replace in the music-stand the old leather-bound song-book that had her initials on the cover. Freddy Malins, who had listened with his head perched sideways to hear her better, was still applauding when everyone else had ceased and talking animatedly to his mother who nodded her head gravely and slowly in acquiescence. At last, when he could clap no more, he stood up suddenly and hurried across the room to Aunt Julia whose hand he seized and held in both his hands, shaking it when words failed him or the catch in his voice proved too much for him.

"I was just telling my mother," he said, "I never heard you sing so well, never. No, I never heard your voice so good as it is to-night. Now! Would you believe that now? That's the truth. Upon my word and honour that's the truth. I never heard your voice sound so fresh and so . . . so clear and fresh, never."

Aunt Julia smiled broadly and murmured something about compliments as she released her hand from his grasp. Mr. Browne extended his open hand towards her and said to those who were near him in the manner of a showman introducing a prodigy to an audience:

"Miss Julia Morkan, my latest discovery!"

He was laughing very heartily at this himself when Freddy Malins turned to him and said:

"Well, Browne, if you're serious you might make a worse discovery. All I can say is I never heard her sing half so well as long as I am coming here. And that's the honest truth."

"Neither did I," said Mr. Browne. "I think her voice has greatly improved."

Aunt Julia shrugged her shoulders and said with meek pride:

"Thirty years ago I hadn't a bad voice as voices go."

"I often told Julia," said Aunt Kate emphatically, "that she was simply thrown away in that choir. But she never would be said by me."

She turned as if to appeal to the good sense of the others against a refractory child while Aunt Julia gazed in front of her, a vague smile of reminiscence playing on her face.

"No," continued Aunt Kate, "she wouldn't be said or led by anyone, slaving there in that choir night and day, night and day. Six o'clock on Christmas morning! And all for what?"

"Well, isn't it for the honour of God, Aunt Kate?" asked Mary Jane, twisting round on the piano-stool and smiling.

Aunt Kate turned fiercely on her niece and said:

"I know all about the honour of God, Mary Jane, but I think it's not at all honourable for the pope to turn out the women out of the choirs that have slaved there all their lives and put little whipper-snappers of boys over their heads. I suppose it is for the good of the Church if the pope does it. But it's not just, Mary Jane, and it's not right."

She had worked herself into a passion and would have continued in defence of her sister for it was a sore subject with her but Mary Jane, seeing that all the dancers had come back, intervened pacifically:

"Now, Aunt Kate, you're giving scandal to Mr. Browne who is of the other persuasion."

Aunt Kate turned to Mr. Browne, who was grinning at this allusion to his religion, and said hastily:

"O, I don't question the pope's being right. I'm only a stupid old woman and I wouldn't presume to do such a thing. But there's such a thing as common everyday politeness and gratitude. And if I were in Julia's place I'd tell that Father Healey straight up to his face . . ."

"And besides, Aunt Kate," said Mary Jane, "we really are all hungry and when we are hungry we are all very quarrelsome."

"And when we are thirsty we are also quarrelsome," added Mr. Browne.

"So that we had better go to supper," said Mary Jane, "and finish the discussion afterwards."

On the landing outside the drawing-room Gabriel found his wife and Mary Jane trying to persuade Miss Ivors to stay for supper. But Miss Ivors, who had put on her hat and was buttoning her cloak, would not stay. She did not feel in the least hungry and she had already overstayed her time.

"But only for ten minutes, Molly," said Mrs. Conroy. "That won't delay you."

"To take a pick itself," said Mary Jane, "after all your dancing."

"I really couldn't," said Miss Ivors.

"I am afraid you didn't enjoy yourself at all," said Mary Jane hopelessly.

"Ever so much, I assure you," said Miss Ivors, "but you really must let me run off now."

"But how can you get home?" asked Mrs. Conroy.

"O, it's only two steps up the quay."

Gabriel hesitated a moment and said:

"If you will allow me, Miss Ivors, I'll see you home if you are really obliged to go."

But Miss Ivors broke away from them.

"I won't hear of it," she cried. "For goodness' sake go in to your suppers and don't mind me. I'm quite well able to take care of myself."

"Well, you're the comical girl, Molly," said Mrs. Conroy frankly.

"*Beannacht libh,*" cried Miss Ivors, with a laugh, as she ran down the staircase.

Mary Jane gazed after her, a moody puzzled expression on her face, while Mrs. Conroy leaned over the banisters to listen for the hall-door. Gabriel asked himself was he the cause of her abrupt departure. But she did not seem to be in ill humour: she had gone away laughing He stared blankly down the staircase.

At the moment Aunt Kate came toddling out of the supper-room, almost wringing her hands in despair.

"Where is Gabriel?" she cried. "Where on earth is Gabriel? There's everyone waiting in there, stage to let, and nobody to carve the goose!"

"Here I am, Aunt Kate!" cried Gabriel, with sudden animation, "ready to carve a flock of geese, if necessary."

A fat brown goose lay at one end of the table and at the other end, on a bed of creased paper strewn with sprigs of parsley, lay a great ham, stripped of its outer skin and peppered over with crust crumbs, a neat paper frill round its shin and beside this was a round of spiced beef. Between these rival ends ran parallel lines of side-dishes: two little minsters of jelly, red and yellow; a shallow dish full of blocks of blancmange and red jam, a large green leaf-shaped dish with a stalk-shaped handle, on which lay bunches of purple raisins and peeled almonds, a companion dish on which lay a solid rectangle of Smyrna figs, a dish of custard topped with grated nutmeg, a small bowl full of chocolates and sweets wrapped in gold and silver papers and a glass vase in which stood some tall celery stalks. In the centre of the table there stood, as sentries to a fruit-stand which upheld a pyramid of oranges and American apples, two squat old-fashioned decanters of cut glass, one containing port and the other dark sherry. On the closed square piano a pudding in a huge yellow dish lay in waiting and behind it were three squads of bottles of stout and ale and minerals, drawn up according to the colours of their uniforms, the first two black, with brown and red labels, the third and smallest squad white, with transverse green sashes.

Gabriel took his seat boldly at the head of the table and, having looked to the edge of the carver, plunged his fork firmly into the goose. He felt quite at ease now for he was an expert carver and liked nothing better than to find himself at the head of a well-laden table.

"Miss Furlong, what shall I send you?" he asked. "A wing or a slice of the breast?"

"Just a small slice of the breast."

"Miss Higgins, what for you?"

"O, anything at all, Mr. Conroy."

While Gabriel and Miss Daly exchanged plates of goose and plates of ham and spiced beef Lily went from guest to guest with a dish of hot floury potatoes wrapped in a white napkin. This was Mary Jane's idea and she had also suggested apple sauce for the goose but Aunt Kate had said that plain roast goose without any apple sauce had always been good enough for her and she hoped she might never eat worse. Mary Jane waited on her pupils and saw that they got the best slices and Aunt Kate and Aunt Julia opened and carried across from the piano bottles of stout and ale for the gentlemen and bottles of minerals for the ladies. There was a great deal of confusion and laughter and noise, the noise of orders and counter-orders, of knives and forks, of corks and glass-stoppers. Gabriel began to carve second helpings as soon as he had finished the first round without serving himself. Everyone protested loudly so that he compromised by taking a long draught of stout for he had found the carving hot work. Mary Jane settled down quietly to her supper but Aunt Kate and Aunt Julia were still toddling round the table, walking on each other's heels, getting in each other's way and giving each other unheeded orders. Mr. Browne begged of them to sit down and eat their suppers and so did Gabriel but they said there was time enough, so that, at last, Freddy Malins stood up and, capturing Aunt Kate, plumped her down on her chair amid general laughter.

When everyone had been well served Gabriel said, smiling:

"Now, if anyone wants a little more of what vulgar people call stuffing let him or her speak."

A chorus of voices invited him to begin his own supper and Lily came forward with three potatoes which she had reserved for him.

"Very well," said Gabriel amiably, as he took another preparatory draught, "kindly forget my existence, ladies and gentlemen, for a few minutes."

He set to his supper and took no part in the conversation with which the table covered Lily's removal of the plates. The subject of talk was the opera company which was then at the Theatre Royal. Mr. Bartell D'Arcy, the tenor, a dark-complexioned young man with a smart moustache, praised very highly the leading contralto of the company but Miss Furlong thought she had a rather vulgar style of production. Freddy Malins said there was a negro chieftain singing in the second part of the Gaiety pantomime who had one of the finest tenor voices he had ever heard.

"Have you heard him?" he asked Mr. Bartell D'Arcy across the table.

"No," answered Mr. Bartell D'Arcy carelessly.

"Because," Freddy Malins explained, "now I'd be curious to hear your opinion of him. I think he has a grand voice."

"It takes Teddy to find out the really good things," said Mr. Browne familiarly to the table.

"And why couldn't he have a voice too?" asked Freddy Malins sharply. "Is it because he's only a black?"

Nobody answered this question and Mary Jane led the table back to the legitimate opera. One of her pupils had given her a pass for *Mignon*. Of course it was very fine, she said, but it made her think of poor Georgina Burns. Mr. Browne could go back farther still, to the old Italian companies that used to come to Dublin — Tietjens, Ilma de Murzka, Campanini, the great Trebelli Giuglini, Ravelli, Aramburo. Those were the days, he said, when there was something like singing to be heard in Dublin. He told too of how the top gallery of the old Royal used to be packed night after night, of how one night an Italian tenor had sung five encores to *Let me like a Soldier fall*, introducing a high C every time, and of how the gallery boys would sometimes in their enthusiasm unyoke the horses from the carriage of some great *prima donna* and pull her themselves through the streets to her hotel. Why did they never play the grand old operas now, he asked, *Dinorah, Lucrezia Borgia?* Because they could not get the voices to sing them: that was why."

"O, well," said Mr. Bartell D'Arcy, "I presume there are as good singers to-day as there were then."

"Where are they?" asked Mr. Browne defiantly.

"In London, Paris, Milan," said Mr. Bartell D'Arcy warmly. "I suppose Caruso, for example, is quite as good, if not better than any of the men you have mentioned."

"Maybe so," said Mr. Browne. "But I may tell you I doubt it strongly."

"O, I'd give anything to hear Caruso sing," said Mary Jane.

"For me," said Aunt Kate, who had been picking a bone, "there was only one tenor. To please me, I mean. But I suppose none of you ever heard of him."

"Who was he, Miss Morkan?" asked Mr. Bartell D'Arcy politely.

"His name," said Aunt Kate, "was Parkinson. I heard him when he was in his prime and I think he had then the purest tenor voice that was ever put into a man's throat."

"Strange," said Mr. Bartell D'Arcy. "I never even heard of him."

"Yes, yes, Miss Morkan is right," said Mr. Browne. "I remember hearing of old Parkinson but he's too far back for me."

"A beautiful, pure, sweet, mellow English tenor," said Aunt Kate with enthusiasm.

Gabriel having finished, the huge pudding was transferred to the table. The clatter of forks and spoons began again. Gabriel's wife served out spoonfuls of the pudding and passed the plates down the table. Midway down they were held up by Mary Jane, who replenished them with raspberry or orange jelly or with blancmange and jam. The pudding was of Aunt Julia's making and she received praises for it from all quarters. She herself said that it was not quite brown enough.

"Well, I hope, Miss Morkan," said Mr. Browne, "that I'm brown enough for you because, you know, I'm all brown."

All the gentlemen, except Gabriel, ate some of the pudding out of compliment to Aunt Julia. As Gabriel never ate sweets the celery had been left for him. Freddy Malins also took a stalk of celery and ate it with his pudding. He had been told that celery was a capital thing for the blood and he was just then under doctor's care. Mrs. Malins, who had been silent all through the supper, said that her son was going down to Mount Melleray in a week or so. The table then spoke of Mount Melleray, how bracing the air was down there, how hospitable the monks were and how they never asked for a penny-piece from their guests.

"And do you mean to say," asked Mr. Browne incredulously, "that a chap can go down there and put up there as if it were a hotel and live on the fat of the land and then come away without paying anything?"

"O, most people give some donation to the monastery when they leave," said Mary Jane.

"I wish we had an institution like that in our Church," said Mr. Browne candidly.

He was astonished to hear that the monks never spoke, got up at two in the morning and slept in their coffins. He asked what they did it for.

"That's the rule of the order," said Aunt Kate firmly.

"Yes, but why?" asked Mr. Browne.

Aunt Kate repeated that it was the rule, that was all. Mr. Browne still seemed not to understand. Freddy Malins explained to him, as best he could, that the monks were trying to make up for the sins committed by all the sinners in the outside world. The explanation was not very clear for Mr. Browne grinned and said:

"I like that idea very much but wouldn't a comfortable spring bed do them as well as a coffin?"

"The coffin," said Mary Jane, "is to remind them of their last end."

As the subject had grown lugubrious it was buried in a silence of the table during which Mrs. Malins could be heard saying to her neighbour in an indistinct undertone:

"They are very good men, the monks, very pious men."

The raisins and almonds and figs and apples and oranges and chocolates and sweets were now passed about the table and Aunt Julia invited all the guests to have either port or sherry. At first Mr. Bartell D'Arcy refused to take either but one of his neighbours nudged him and whispered something to him upon which he allowed his glass to be filled. Gradually as the last glasses were being filled the conversation ceased. A pause followed, broken only by the noise of the wine and by unsettlings of chairs. The Misses Morkan, all three, looked down at the tablecloth. Someone coughed once or twice and then a few gentlemen patted the table gently as a signal for silence. The silence came and Gabriel pushed back his chair and stood up.

The patting at once grew louder in encouragement and then ceased altogether. Gabriel leaned his ten trembling fingers on the tablecloth and smiled nervously at the company. Meeting a row of upturned faces he raised his eyes to the chandelier. The piano was playing a waltz tune and he could hear the skirts sweeping against the drawing-room door. People, perhaps, were standing in the snow on the quay outside, gazing up at the lighted windows and listening to the waltz music. The air was pure there. In the distance lay the park where the trees were weighted with snow. The Wellington Monument wore a gleaming cap of snow that flashed westward over the white field of Fifteen Acres.

He began:

"Ladies and Gentlemen,

"It has fallen to my lot this evening, as in years past, to perform a very pleasing task but a task for which I am afraid my poor powers as a speaker are all too inadequate."

"No, no!" said Mr. Browne.

"But, however that may be, I can only ask you to-night to take the will for the deed and to lend me your attention for a few moments while I endeavour to express to you in words what my feelings are on this occasion.

"Ladies and Gentlemen, it is not the first time that we have gathered together under this hospitable roof, around this hospitable board. It is not the first time that we have been the recipients — or perhaps, I had better say, the victims — of the hospitality of certain good ladies."

He made a circle in the air with his arm and paused. Everyone laughed or smiled at Aunt Kate and Aunt Julia and Mary Jane who all turned crimson with pleasure. Gabriel went on more boldly:

"I feel more strongly with every recurring year that our country has no tradition which does it so much honour and which it should guard so jealously as that of its hospitality. It is a tradition that is unique as far as my experience goes (and I have visited not a few places abroad) among the modern nations. Some would say, perhaps, that with us it is rather a failing than anything to be boasted of. But granted even that, it is, to my mind, a princely failing, and one that I trust will long be cultivated among us. Of one thing, at least, I am sure. As long as this one roof shelters the good ladies aforesaid — and I wish from my heart it may do so for many and many a long year to come — the tradition of genuine warm-hearted courteous Irish hospitality, which our forefathers have handed down to us and which we in turn must hand down to our descendants, is still alive among us."

A hearty murmur of assent ran round the table. It shot through Gabriel's mind that Miss Ivors was not there and that she had gone away discourteously: and he said with confidence in himself:

"Ladies and Gentlemen,

"A new generation is growing up in our midst, a generation actuated by new ideas and new principles. It is serious and enthusiastic for these new ideas and its enthusiasm, even when it is misdirected, is, I believe, in the main sincere. But we are living in a sceptical and, if I may use the phrase, a thought-tormented age: and sometimes I fear that this new generation, educated or hypereducated as it is, will lack those qualities of humanity, of hospitality, of kindly humour which belonged to an older day. Listening to-night to the names of all those great singers of the past it seemed to me, I must confess, that we were living in a less spacious age. Those days might, without exaggeration, be called spacious days: and if they are gone beyond recall let us hope, at least, that in gatherings such as this we shall still speak of them with pride and affection, still cherish in our hearts the memory of those dead and gone great ones whose fame the world will not willingly let die."

"Hear, hear!" said Mr. Browne loudly.

"But yet," continued Gabriel, his voice falling into a softer inflection, "there are always in gatherings such as this sadder thoughts that will recur to our minds: thoughts of the past, of youth, of changes, of absent faces that we miss here to-night. Our path through life is strewn with many such sad memories: and were we to brood upon them always we could not find the heart to go on bravely with our work among the living. We have all of us living duties and living affections which claim, and rightly claim, our strenuous endeavours.

"Therefore, I will not linger on the past. I will not let any gloomy moralising intrude upon us here to-night. Here we are gathered together for a brief moment from the bustle and rush of our everyday routine. We are met here as friends, in the spirit of good-fellowship, as colleagues, also to a certain extent, in the true spirit of *camaraderie*, and as the guests of — what shall I call them? — the Three Graces of the Dublin musical world."

The table burst into applause and laughter at this allusion. Aunt Julia vainly asked each of her neighbours in turn to tell her what Gabriel had said.

"He says we are the Three Graces, Aunt Julia," said Mary Jane.

Aunt Julia did not understand but she looked up, smiling, at Gabriel, who continued in the same vein:

"Ladies and Gentlemen,

"I will not attempt to play to-night the part that Paris played on another occasion. I will not attempt to choose between them. The task would be an invidious one and one beyond my poor powers. For when I view them in turn, whether it be our chief hostess herself, whose good heart, whose too good heart, has become a byword with all who know her, or her sister, who seems to be gifted with perennial youth and whose singing must have been a surprise and a revelation to us all to-night, or, least but not least, when I consider our youngest hostess, talented, cheerful, hard-working and the best of nieces, I confess, Ladies and Gentlemen, that I do not know to which of them I should award the prize."

Gabriel glanced down at his aunts and, seeing the large smile on Aunt Julia's face and the tears which had risen to Aunt Kate's eyes, hastened to his close. He raised his glass of port gallantly, while every member of the company fingered a glass expectantly, and said loudly:

"Let us toast them all three together. Let us drink to their health, wealth, long life, happiness and prosperity and may they long continue to hold the proud and self-won position which they hold in their profession and the position of honour and affection which they hold in our hearts."

All the guests stood up, glass in hand, and turning towards the three seated ladies, sang in unison, with Mr. Browne as leader:

> "For they are jolly gay fellows,
> For they are jolly gay fellows,
> For they are jolly gay fellows,
> Which nobody can deny."

Aunt Kate was making frank use of her handkerchief and even Aunt Julia seemed moved. Freddy Malins beat time with his pudding-fork and the singers turned towards one another, as if in melodious conference, while they sang with emphasis:

> "Unless he tells a lie,
> Unless he tells a lie."

Then, turning once more towards their hostesses, they sang:

> "For they are jolly gay fellows,
> For they are jolly gay fellows,
> For they are jolly gay fellows
> Which nobody can deny."

The acclamation which followed was taken up beyond the door of the supper-room by many of the other guests and renewed time after time, Freddy Malins acting as officer with his fork on high.

.   .   .   .

The piercing morning air came into the hall where they were standing so that Aunt Kate said:

"Close the door, somebody. Mrs. Malins will get her death of cold."

"Browne is out there, Aunt Kate," said Mary Jane.

"Browne is everywhere," said Aunt Kate, lowering her voice.

Mary Jane laughed at her tone.

"Really," she said archly, "he is very attentive."

"He has been laid on here like the gas," said Aunt Kate in the same tone, "all during the Christmas."

She laughed herself this time good-humouredly and then added quickly:

"But tell him to come in, Mary Jane, and close the door. I hope to goodness he didn't hear me."

At that moment the hall-door was opened and Mr. Browne came in from the doorstep, laughing as if his heart would break. He was dressed in a long green overcoat with mock astrakhan cuffs and collar and wore on his head an oval fur cap. He pointed down the snow-covered quay from where the sound of shrill prolonged whistling was borne in.

"Teddy will have all the cabs in Dublin out," he said.

Gabriel advanced from the little pantry behind the office, struggling into his overcoat and, looking round the hall, said:

"Gretta not down yet?"

"She's getting on her things, Gabriel," said Aunt Kate.

"Who's playing up there?" asked Gabriel.

"Nobody. They're all gone."

"O no, Aunt Kate," said Mary Jane. "Bartell D'Arcy and Miss O'Callaghan aren't gone yet."

"Someone is fooling at the piano anyhow," said Gabriel.

Mary Jane glanced at Gabriel and Mr. Browne and said with a shiver:

"It makes me feel cold to look at you two gentlemen muffled up like that. I wouldn't like to face your journey home at this hour."

"I'd like nothing better this minute," said Mr. Browne stoutly, "than a rattling fine walk in the country or a fast drive with a good spanking goer between the shafts."

"We used to have a very good horse and trap at home," said Aunt Julia sadly.

"The never-to-be-forgotten Johnny," said Mary Jane, laughing.

Aunt Kate and Gabriel laughed too.

"Why, what was wonderful about Johnny?" asked Mr. Browne.

"The late lamented Patrick Morkan, our grandfather, that is," explained Gabriel, "commonly known in his later years as the old gentleman, was a glue-boiler."

"O, now, Gabriel," said Aunt Kate, laughing, "he had a starch mill."

"Well, glue or starch," said Gabriel, "the old gentleman had a horse by the name of Johnny. And Johnny used to work in the old gentleman's mill, walking round and round in order to drive the mill. That was all very well; but now comes the tragic part about Johnny. One fine day the old gentleman thought he'd like to drive out with the quality to a military review in the park."

"The Lord have mercy on his soul," said Aunt Kate compassionately.

"Amen," said Gabriel. "So the old gentleman, as I said, harnessed Johnny and put on his very best tall hat and his very best stock collar and drove out in grand style from his ancestral mansion somewhere near Back Lane, I think."

Everyone laughed, even Mrs. Malins, at Gabriel's manner and Aunt Kate said:

"O, now, Gabriel, he didn't live in Back Lane, really. Only the mill was there."

"Out from the mansion of his forefathers," continued Gabriel, "he drove with Johnny. And everything went on beautifully until Johnny came in sight of King Billy's statue: and whether he fell in love with the horse King Billy sits on or whether he thought he was back again in the mill, anyhow he began to walk round the statue."

Gabriel paced in a circle round the hall in his goloshes amid the laughter of the others.

"Round and round he went," said Gabriel, "and the old gentleman, who was a very pompous old gentleman, was highly indignant. 'Go on, sir! What do you mean, sir? Johnny! Johnny! Most extraordinary conduct! Can't understand the horse!'"

The peals of laughter which followed Gabriel's imitation of the incident was interrupted by a resounding knock at the hall door. Mary Jane ran to open it and let in Freddy Malins. Freddy Malins, with his hat well back on his head and his shoulders humped with cold, was puffing and steaming after his exertions.

"I could only get one cab," he said.

"O, we'll find another along the quay," said Gabriel.

"Yes," said Aunt Kate. "Better not keep Mrs. Malins standing in the draught."

Mrs. Malins was helped down the front steps by her son and Mr. Browne and, after many manœuvres, hoisted into the cab. Freddy Malins clambered in after her and spent a long time settling her on the seat, Mr. Browne helping him with advice. At last she was settled comfortably and Freddy Malins invited Mr. Browne into the cab. There was a good deal of confused talk, and then Mr. Browne got into the cab. The cabman settled his rug over his knees, and bent down for the address. The confusion grew greater and the cabman was directed differently by Freddy Malins and Mr. Browne, each of whom had his head out through a window of the cab. The difficulty was to know where to drop Mr. Browne along the route, and Aunt Kate, Aunt Julia and Mary Jane helped the discussion from the doorstep with cross-directions and contradictions and abundance of laughter. As for Freddy Malins he was speechless with laughter. He popped his head in and out of the window every moment to the great danger of his hat, and told his mother how the discussion was progressing, till at last Mr. Browne shouted to the bewildered cabman above the din of everybody's laughter:

"Do you know Trinity College?"

"Yes, sir," said the cabman.

"Well, drive bang up against Trinity College gates," said Mr. Browne, "and then we'll tell you where to go. You understand now?"

"Yes, sir," said the cabman.

"Make like a bird for Trinity College."

"Right, sir," said the cabman.

The horse was whipped up and the cab rattled off along the quay amid a chorus of laughter and adieus.

Gabriel had not gone to the door with the others. He was in a dark part of the hall gazing up the staircase. A woman was standing near the top of the first flight, in the shadow also. He could not see her face but he could see the terracotta and salmon-pink panels of her skirt which the shadow made appear black and white. It was his wife. She was leaning on the banisters, listening to something. Gabriel was surprised at her stillness and strained his ear to listen also. But he could hear little save the noise of laughter and dispute on the front steps, a few chords struck on the piano and a few notes of a man's voice singing.

He stood still in the gloom of the hall, trying to catch the air that the voice was singing and gazing up at his wife. There was grace and mystery in her attitude as if she were a symbol of something. He asked himself what is a woman standing on the stairs in the shadow, listening to distant music, a symbol of. If he were a painter he would paint her in that attitude. Her blue felt hat would show off the bronze of her hair against the darkness and the dark panels of her skirt would show off the light ones. *Distant Music* he would call the picture if he were a painter.

The hall-door was closed; and Aunt Kate, Aunt Julia and Mary Jane came down the hall, still laughing.

"Well, isn't Freddy terrible?" said Mary Jane. "He's really terrible."

Gabriel said nothing but pointed up the stairs towards where his wife was standing. Now that the hall-door was closed the voice and the piano could be heard more clearly. Gabriel held up his hand for them to be silent. The song seemed to be in the old Irish tonality and the singer seemed uncertain both of his words and of his voice. The voice, made plaintive by distance and by the singer's hoarseness, faintly illuminated the cadence of the air with words expressing grief:

> "O, the rain falls on my heavy locks
> And the dew wets my skin,
> My babe lies cold . . ."

"O," exclaimed Mary Jane. "It's Bartell D'Arcy singing and he wouldn't sing all the night. O, I'll get him to sing a song before he goes."

"O, do, Mary Jane," said Aunt Kate.

Mary Jane brushed past the others and ran to the staircase, but before she reached it the singing stopped and the piano was closed abruptly.

"O, what a pity!" she cried. "Is he coming down, Gretta?"

Gabriel heard his wife answer yes and saw her come down towards them. A few steps behind her were Mr. Bartell D'Arcy and Miss O'Callaghan.

"O, Mr. D'Arcy," cried Mary Jane, "it's downright mean of you to break off like that when we were all in raptures listening to you."

"I have been at him all the evening," said Miss O'Callaghan, "and Mrs. Conroy, too, and he told us he had a dreadful cold and couldn't sing."

"O, Mr. D'Arcy," said Aunt Kate, "now that was a great fib to tell."

"Can't you see that I'm as hoarse as a crow?" said Mr. D'Arcy roughly.

He went into the pantry hastily and put on his overcoat. The others, taken aback by his rude speech, could find nothing to say. Aunt Kate wrinkled her brows and made signs to the others to drop the subject. Mr. D'Arcy stood swathing his neck carefully and frowning.

"It's the weather," said Aunt Julia, after a pause.

"Yes, everybody has colds," said Aunt Kate readily, "everybody."

"They say," said Mary Jane, "we haven't had snow like it for thirty years; and I read this morning in the newspapers that the snow is general all over Ireland."

"I love the look of snow," said Aunt Julia sadly.

"So do I," said Miss O'Callaghan. "I think Christmas is never really Christmas unless we have the snow on the ground."

"But poor Mr. D'Arcy doesn't like the snow," said Aunt Kate, smiling.

Mr. D'Arcy came from the pantry, fully swathed and buttoned, and in a repentant tone told them the history of his cold. Everyone gave him advice and said it was a great pity and urged him to be very careful of his throat in the night air. Gabriel watched his wife, who did not join in the conversation. She was standing right under the dusty fanlight and the flame of the gas lit up the rich bronze of her hair, which he had seen her drying at the fire a few days before. She was in the same attitude and seemed unaware of the talk about her. At last she turned towards them and Gabriel saw that there was colour on her cheeks and that her eyes were shining. A sudden tide of joy went leaping out of his heart.

"Mr. D'Arcy," she said, "what is the name of that song you were singing?"

"It's called *The Lass of Aughrim*," said Mr. D'Arcy, "but I couldn't remember it properly. Why? Do you know it?"

"*The Lass of Aughrim*," she repeated. "I couldn't think of the name."

"It's a very nice air," said Mary Jane. "I'm sorry you were not in voice to-night."

"Now, Mary Jane," said Aunt Kate, "don't annoy Mr. D'Arcy. I won't have him annoyed."

Seeing that all were ready to start she shepherded them to the door, where good-night was said:

"Well, good-night, Aunt Kate, and thanks for the pleasant evening."

"Good-night, Gabriel. Good-night, Gretta!"

"Good-night, Aunt Kate, and thanks ever so much. Good-night, Aunt Julia."

"O, good-night, Gretta, I didn't see you."

"Good-night, Mr. D'Arcy. Good-night, Miss O'Callaghan."

"Good-night, Miss Morkan."

"Good-night, again."

"Good-night, all. Safe home."

"Good-night. Good night."

The morning was still dark. A dull, yellow light brooded over the houses and the river; and the sky seemed to be descending. It was slushy underfoot; and only streaks and patches of snow lay on the roofs, on the parapets of the quay and on the area railings. The lamps were still burning redly in the murky air and, across the river, the palace of the Four Courts stood out menacingly against the heavy sky.

She was walking on before him with Mr. Bartell D'Arcy, her shoes in a brown parcel tucked under one arm and her hands holding her skirt up from the slush. She had no longer any grace of attitude, but Gabriel's eyes were still bright with happiness. The blood went bounding along his veins; and the thoughts went rioting through his brain, proud, joyful, tender, valorous.

She was walking on before him so lightly and so erect that he longed to run after her noiselessly, catch her by the shoulders and say something foolish and affectionate into her ear. She seemed to him so frail that he longed to defend her against something and then to be alone with her. Moments of their secret life together burst like stars upon his memory. A heliotrope envelope was lying beside his breakfast-cup and he was caressing it with his hand. Birds were twittering in the ivy and the sunny web of the curtain was shimmering along the floor: he could not eat for happiness. They were standing on the crowded platform and he was placing a ticket inside the warm palm of her glove. He was standing with her in the cold, looking in through a grated window at a man making bottles in a roaring furnace. It was very cold. Her face, fragrant in the cold air, was quite close to his; and suddenly he called out to the man at the furnace:

"Is the fire hot, sir?"

But the man could not hear with the noise of the furnace. It was just as well. He might have answered rudely.

A wave of yet more tender joy escaped from his heart and went coursing in warm flood along his arteries. Like the tender fire of stars moments of their life together, that no one knew of or would ever know of, broke upon and illumined his memory. He longed to recall to her those moments, to make her forget the years of their dull existence together and remember only their moments of ecstasy. For the years, he felt, had not quenched his soul or hers. Their children, his writing, her household cares had not quenched all their souls' tender fire. In one letter that he had written to her then he had said: "Why is it that words like these seem to me so dull and cold? Is it because there is no word tender enough to be your name?"

Like distant music these words that he had written years before were borne towards him from the past. He longed to be alone with her. When the others had gone away, when he and she were in the room in the hotel, then they would be alone together. He would call her softly:

"Gretta!"

Perhaps she would not hear at once: she would be undressing. Then something in his voice would strike her. She would turn and look at him. . . .

At the corner of Winetavern Street they met a cab. He was glad of its rattling noise as it saved him from conversation. She was looking out of the window and seemed tired. The others spoke only a few words, pointing out some building or street. The horse galloped along wearily under the murky morning sky, dragging his old rattling box after his heels, and Gabriel was again in a cab with her, galloping to catch the boat, galloping to their honeymoon.

As the cab drove across O'Connell Bridge Miss O'Callaghan said:

"They say you never cross O'Connell Bridge without seeing a white horse."

"I see a white man this time," said Gabriel.

"Where?" asked Mr. Bartell D'Arcy.

Gabriel pointed to the statue, on which lay patches of snow. Then he nodded familiarly to it and waved his hand.

"Good-night, Dan," he said gaily.

When the cab drew up before the hotel, Gabriel jumped out and, in spite of Mr. Bartell D'Arcy's protest, paid the driver. He gave the man a shilling over his fare. The man saluted and said:

"A prosperous New Year to you, sir."

"The same to you," said Gabriel cordially.

She leaned for a moment on his arm in getting out of the cab and while standing at the curbstone, bidding the others good-night. She leaned lightly on his arm, as lightly as when she had danced with him a few hours before. He had felt proud and happy then, happy that she was his, proud of her grace and wifely carriage. But now, after the kindling again of so many memories, the first touch of her body, musical and strange and perfumed, sent through him a keen pang of lust. Under cover of her silence he pressed her arm closely to his side, and, as they stood at the hotel door, he felt that they had escaped from their lives and duties, escaped from home and friends and run away together with wild and radiant hearts to a new adventure.

An old man was dozing in a great hooded chair in the hall. He lit a candle in the office and went before them to the stairs. They followed him in silence, their feet falling in soft thuds on the thickly carpeted stairs. She mounted the stairs behind the porter, her head bowed in the ascent, her frail shoulders curved as with a burden, her skirt girt tightly about her. He could have flung his arms about her hips and held her still, for his arms were trembling with desire to seize her and only the stress of his nails against the palms of his hands held the wild impulse of his body in check.   The porter halted on the stairs to settle his guttering candle.   They halted, too, on the steps below him.   In the silence Gabriel could hear the falling of the molten wax into the tray and the thumping of his own heart against his ribs.

The porter led them along a corridor and opened a door.   Then he set his unstable candle down on a toilet-table and asked at what hour they were to be called in the morning.

"Eight," said Gabriel.

The porter pointed to the tap of the electric-light and began a muttered apology, but Gabriel cut him short.

"We don't want any light.   We have light enough from the street. And I say," he added, pointing to the candle, "you might remove that handsome article, like a good man."

The porter took up his candle again, but slowly, for he was surprised by such a novel idea.   Then he mumbled good-night and went out. Gabriel shot the lock to.

A ghastly light from the street lamp lay in a long shaft from one window to the door.   Gabriel threw his overcoat and hat on a couch and crossed the room towards the window.   He looked down into the street in order that his emotion might calm a little.   Then he turned and leaned against a chest of drawers with his back to the light.   She had taken off her hat and cloak and was standing before a large swinging mirror, unhooking her waist.   Gabriel paused for a few moments, watching her, and then said:

"Gretta!"

She turned away from the mirror slowly and walked along the shaft of light towards him.   Her face looked so serious and weary that the words would not pass Gabriel's lips.   No, it was not the moment yet.

"You looked tired," he said.

"I am a little," she answered.

"You don't feel ill or weak?"

"No, tired: that's all."

She went on to the window and stood there, looking out.   Gabriel waited again and then, fearing that diffidence was about to conquer him, he said abruptly:

"By the way, Gretta!"

"What is it?"

"You know that poor fellow Malins?" he said quickly.

"Yes. What about him?"

"Well, poor fellow, he's a decent sort of chap, after all," continued Gabriel in a false voice. "He gave me back that sovereign I lent him, and I didn't expect it, really. It's a pity he wouldn't keep away from that Browne, because he's not a bad fellow, really."

He was trembling now with annoyance. Why did she seem so abstracted? He did not know how he could begin. Was she annoyed, too, about something? If she would only turn to him or come to him of her own accord! To take her as she was would be brutal. No, he must see some ardour in her eyes first. He longed to be master of her strange mood.

"When did you lend him the pound?" she asked, after a pause.

Gabriel strove to restrain himself from breaking out into brutal language about the sottish Malins and his pound. He longed to cry to her from his soul, to crush her body against his, to overmaster her. But he said:

"O, at Christmas, when he opened that little Christmas-card shop in Henry Street."

He was in such a fever of rage and desire that he did not hear her come from the window. She stood before him for an instant, looking at him strangely. Then, suddenly raising herself on tiptoe and resting her hands lightly on his shoulders, she kissed him.

"You are a very generous person, Gabriel," she said.

Gabriel, trembling with delight at her sudden kiss and at the quaintness of her phrase, put his hands on her hair and began smoothing it back, scarcely touching it with his fingers. The washing had made it fine and brilliant. His heart was brimming over with happiness. Just when he was wishing for it she had come to him of her own accord. Perhaps her thoughts had been running with his. Perhaps she had felt the impetuous desire that was in him, and then the yielding mood had come upon her. Now that she had fallen to him so easily, he wondered why he had been so diffident.

He stood, holding her head between his hands. Then, slipping one arm swiftly about her body and drawing her towards him, he said softly:

"Gretta, dear, what are you thinking about?"

She did not answer nor yield wholly to his arm. He said again, softly:

"Tell me what it is, Gretta. I think I know what is the matter. Do I know?"

She did not answer at once. Then she said in an outburst of tears:

"O, I am thinking about that song, *The Lass of Aughrim.*"

She broke loose from him and ran to the bed and, throwing her arms across the bed-rail, hid her face. Gabriel stood stock-still for a moment in astonishment and then followed her. As he passed in the way of the cheval-glass he caught sight of himself in full length, his broad, well-filled shirt-front, the face whose expression always puzzled him when he saw it in a mirror, and his glimmering gilt-rimmed eyeglasses. He halted a few paces from her and said:

"What about the song? Why does that make you cry?"

She raised her head from her arms and dried her eyes with the back of her hand like a child. A kinder note than he had intended went into his voice.

"Why, Gretta?" he asked.

"I am thinking about a person long ago who used to sing that song."

"And who was the person long ago?" asked Gabriel, smiling.

"It was a person I used to know in Galway when I was living with my grandmother," she said.

The smile passed away from Gabriel's face. A dull anger began to gather again at the back of his mind and the dull fires of his lust began to glow angrily in his veins.

"Someone you were in love with?" he asked ironically.

"It was a young boy I used to know," she answered, "named Michael Furey. He used to sing that song, *The Lass of Aughrim.* He was very delicate."

Gabriel was silent. He did not wish her to think that he was interested in this delicate boy.

"I can see him so plainly," she said, after a moment. "Such eyes as he had: big, dark eyes! And such an expression in them — an expression!"

"O, then, you are in love with him?" said Gabriel.

"I used to go out walking with him," she said, "when I was in Galway."

A thought flew across Gabriel's mind.

"Perhaps that was why you wanted to go to Galway with that Ivors girl?" he said coldly.

She looked at him and asked in surprise:

"What for?"

Her eyes made Gabriel feel awkward. He shrugged his shoulders and said:

"How do I know? To see him, perhaps."

She looked away from him along the shaft of light towards the window in silence.

"He is dead," she said at length. "He died when he was only seventeen. Isn't it a terrible thing to die so young as that?"

"What was he?" asked Gabriel, still ironically.

"He was in the gasworks," she said.

Gabriel felt humiliated by the failure of his irony and by the evocation of this figure from the dead, a boy in the gasworks. While he had been full of memories of their secret life together, full of tenderness and joy and desire, she had been comparing him in her mind with another. A shameful consciousness of his own person assailed him. He saw himself as a ludicrous figure, acting as a pennyboy for his aunts, a nervous, well-meaning sentimentalist, orating to vulgarians and idealising his own clownish lusts, the pitiable fatuous fellow he had caught a glimpse of in the mirror. Instinctively he turned his back more to the light lest she might see the shame that burned upon his forehead.

He tried to keep up his tone of cold interrogation, but his voice when he spoke was humble and indifferent.

"I suppose you were in love with this Michael Furey, Gretta," he said.

"I was great with him at that time," she said.

Her voice was veiled and sad. Gabriel, feeling now how vain it would be to try to lead her whither he had purposed, caressed one of her hands and said, also sadly:

"And what did he die of so young, Gretta? Consumption, was it?"

"I think he died for me," she answered.

A vague terror seized Gabriel at this answer, as if, at that hour when he had hoped to triumph, some impalpable and vindictive being was coming against him, gathering forces against him in its vague world. But he shook himself free of it with an effort of reason and continued to caress her hand. He did not question her again, for he felt that she would tell him of herself. Her hand was warm and moist: it did not respond to his touch, but he continued to caress it just as he had caressed her first letter to him that spring morning.

"It was in the winter," she said, "about the beginning of the winter when I was going to leave my grandmother's and come up here to the convent. And he was ill at the time in his lodgings in Galway and wouldn't be let out, and his people in Oughterard were written to. He was in decline, they said, or something like that. I never knew rightly."

She paused for a moment and sighed.

"Poor fellow," she said. "He was very fond of me and he was such a gentle boy. We used to go out together, walking, you know, Gabriel, like the way they do in the country. He was going to study singing only for his health. He had a very good voice, poor Michael Furey."

"Well; and then?" asked Gabriel.

"And then when it came to the time for me to leave Galway and come up to the convent he was much worse and I wouldn't be let see him so I wrote him a letter saying I was going up to Dublin and would be back in the summer, and hoping he would be better then."

She paused for a moment to get her voice under control, and then went on:

"Then the night before I left, I was in my grandmother's house in Nuns' Island, packing up, and I heard gravel thrown up against the window. The window was so wet I couldn't see, so I ran downstairs as I was and slipped out the back into the garden and there was the poor fellow at the end of the garden, shivering."

"And did you not tell him to go back?" asked Gabriel.

"I implored of him to go home at once and told him he would get his death in the rain. But he said he did not want to live. I can see his eyes as well as well! He was standing at the end of the wall where there was a tree."

"And did he go home?" asked Gabriel.

"Yes, he went home. And when I was only a week in the convent he died and he was buried in Oughterard, where his people came from. O, the day I heard that, that he was dead!"

She stopped, choking with sobs, and, overcome by emotion, flung herself face downward on the bed, sobbing in the quilt. Gabriel held her hand for a moment longer, irresolutely, and then, shy of intruding on her grief, let it fall gently and walked quietly to the window.

She was fast asleep.

Gabriel, leaning on his elbow, looked for a few moments unresentfully on her tangled hair and half-open mouth, listening to her deep-drawn breath. So she had had that romance in her life: a man had died for her sake. It hardly pained him now to think how poor a part he, her husband, had played in her life. He watched her while she slept, as though he and she had never lived together as man and wife. His curious eyes rested long upon her face and on her hair: and, as he thought of what she must have been then, in that time of her first girlish beauty, a strange, friendly pity for her entered his soul. He did not like to say even to himself that her face was no longer beautiful, but he knew that it was no longer the face for which Michael Furey had braved death.

Perhaps she had not told him all the story. His eyes moved to the chair over which she had thrown some of her clothes. A petticoat string dangled to the floor. One boot stood upright, its limp upper fallen down: the fellow of it lay upon its side. He wondered at his riot of emotions of an hour before. From what had it proceeded? From his aunt's supper, from his own foolish speech, from the wine and dancing, the merry-making when saying good-night in the hall, the pleasure of the walk along the river in the snow. Poor Aunt Julia! She, too, would soon be a shade with the shade of Patrick Morkan and his horse. He had caught that haggard look upon her face for a moment when she was singing *Arrayed for the Bridal.* Soon, perhaps, he would be sitting in that same drawing-room, dressed in black, his silk hat on his knees. The blinds would be drawn down and Aunt Kate would be sitting beside him, crying and blowing her nose and telling him how Julia had died. He would cast about in his mind for some words that might console her, and would find only lame and useless ones. Yes, yes: that would happen very soon.

The air of the room chilled his shoulders. He stretched himself cautiously along under the sheets and lay down beside his wife. One by one, they were all becoming shades. Better pass boldly into that other world, in the full glory of some passion, than fade and wither dismally with age. He thought of how she who lay beside him had locked in her heart for so many years that image of her lover's eyes when he had told her that he did not wish to live.

Generous tears filled Gabriel's eyes. He had never felt like that himself towards any woman, but he knew that such a feeling must be love. The tears gathered more thickly in his eyes and in the partial darkness he imagined he saw the form of a young man standing under a dripping tree. Other forms were near. His soul had approached that region where dwell the vast hosts of the dead. He was conscious of, but could not apprehend, their wayward and flickering existence. His own identity was fading out into a grey impalpable world: the solid world itself, which these dead had one time reared and lived in, was dissolving and dwindling.

A few light taps upon the pane made him turn to the window. It had begun to snow again. He watched sleepily the flakes, silver and dark, falling obliquely against the lamplight. The time had come for him to set out on his journey westward. Yes, the newspapers were right: snow was general all over Ireland. It was falling on every part of the dark central plain, on the treeless hills, falling softly upon the Bog of Allen and, farther westward, softly falling into the dark mutinous Shannon waves. It was falling, too, upon every part of the lonely churchyard on the hill where Michael Furey lay buried. It lay thickly drifted on the crooked crosses and headstones, on the spears of the little gate, on the barren thorns. His soul swooned slowly as he heard the snow falling faintly through the universe and faintly falling, like the descent of their last end, upon all the living and the dead.

Franz Kafka

THE METAMORPHOSIS

1916

❦

I

As GREGOR SAMSA awoke one morning from a troubled dream, he found himself changed in his bed to some monstrous kind of vermin.

He lay on his back, which was as hard as armor plate, and, raising his head a little, he could see the arch of his great, brown belly, divided by bowed corrugations. The bedcover was slipping helplessly off the summit of the curve, and Gregor's legs, pitiably thin compared with their former size, fluttered helplessly before his eyes.

"What has happened?" he thought. It was no dream. His room, a real man's room — though rather small — lay quiet within its four familiar walls. Over the table, where a collection of cloth samples was scattered — Samsa was a commercial traveler — hung the picture that he had recently cut from an illustrated paper and had put in a pretty gilded frame. This picture showed a lady sitting very upright, wearing a small fur hat and a fur boa; she offered to the gaze a heavy muff into which her arm was thrust up to the elbow.

Gregor looked toward the window; rain could be heard falling on the panes; the foggy weather made him sad. "How would it be if I go to sleep again for awhile and forget all this stupidity?" he thought; but it was absolutely impossible, for he was used to sleeping on the right side and in his present plight he could not get into that position. However hard he tried to throw himself violently on his side, he always turned over on his back with a little swinging movement. He tried a hundred times, closing his eyes so that he should not see the trembling of his legs, and he did not give up until he felt in his side a slight but deep pain, never before experienced.

"God!" he thought, "What a job I've chosen. Traveling day in, day out. A much more worrying occupation than working in the office! And apart from business itself, this plague of traveling: the anxieties of changing trains, the irregular, inferior meals, the ever changing faces, never to be seen again, people with whom one has no chance to be friendly. To hell with it all!" He felt a little itch above his stomach and wriggled nearer to the bedpost, dragging himself slowly on his back so that he might more easily raise his head; and he saw, just where he was itching, a few little white points, whose purpose he could not guess at; he tried to scratch the place with one of his feet but he had to draw it back quickly, for the contact made him shudder coldly.

He turned to his former position. He said to himself: "Nothing is more degrading than always to have to rise so early. A man must have his sleep. Other travelers can live like harem women. When I return to the hotel in the morning to enter my orders, I find these gentlemen still at breakfast. I'd like to see what my boss would say if I tried it; I should be sacked immediately. Who knows if that wouldn't be a good thing, after all! If I didn't hold back because of my parents, I would have given notice long ago; I would have gone to the boss and I wouldn't have minced matters. He would have fallen from his desk. That's a funny thing; to sit on a desk so as to speak to one's employees from such a height, especially when one is hard of hearing and people must come close! Still, all hope is not lost; once I have got together the money my parents owe him — that will be in about five or six years — I shall certainly do it. Then I'll take the big step! Meanwhile, I must get up, for my train goes at five."

He looked at the alarm clock which was ticking on the chest. "My God!" he thought; it was half-past six; quarter to seven was not far off. Hadn't the alarm gone? From the bed it could be seen that the little hand was set at four, right enough; the alarm had sounded. But had he been able to sleep calmly through that furniture-shattering din? Calmly, no; his sleep had not been calm; but he had slept only the sounder for that. What should he do now?

The next train went at seven; to catch it he must hurry madly, and his collection of samples was not packed; besides, he himself did not feel at all rested nor inclined to move. And even if he did catch the train, his employer's anger was inevitable, since the firm's errand boy would have been waiting at the five o'clock train and would have notified the firm of his lapse. He was just a toady to his boss, a stupid and servile boy. Supposing Gregor pretended to be ill? But that would be very tiresome, and suspicious, too, for during the four years he had been with the firm he had never had the slightest illness. The manager would come with the Health Insurance doctor; he would reproach his parents for their son's idleness and would cut short any objections by giving the doctor's arguments that no people are sick, only idle. And would he be so far wrong, in such a case? Gregor felt in very good fettle, apart from his unnecessary need for more sleep after such a long night; he even had an unusually keen appetite.

Just as he was quickly turning these thoughts over in his mind without being able to decide to leave the bed — while the alarm clock struck a quarter to seven — he heard a cautious knock on his door, close by his bed's head.

"Gregor," someone called — it was his mother — "It is a quarter to seven. Didn't you want to catch the train?"

What a soft voice! Gregor trembled as he heard his own voice reply. It was unmistakably his former voice, but with it could be heard, as if from below, a painful whining, which only allowed the words their real shape for a moment, immediately to confuse their sound so that one wondered if one had really heard aright. Gregor would have liked to answer fully and to give an explanation but, in these circumstances, he contented himself by saying, "Yes, yes, thank you, mother. I am just getting up." No doubt the door prevented her from judging the change in Gregor's voice, for the explanation reassured his mother, who went away, shuffling in her slippers. But because of this little dialogue the other members of the family had become aware that, contrary to custom, Gregor was still in the house, and his father started to knock on one of the side doors, softly, but with his fists.

"Gregor, Gregor," he cried, "what is the matter?" And, after a moment, in a warning tone, "Gregor! Gregor!"

At the other side door, the young man's sister softly called, "Gregor, aren't you well? Do you need anything?"

"I am getting ready," said Gregor, answering both sides and forcing himself to pronounce carefully and to separate each word with a long pause, to keep a natural voice.

His father went back to breakfast, but the sister still whispered, "Gregor, open the door, I beg you." But Gregor had no intention of answering this request; on the contrary, he complimented himself on having learned the habit of always locking his door, as if in a hotel.

He would get up quietly, without being bothered by anyone; he would dress, and, above all, he would have breakfast; then would come the time to reflect, for he felt it was not in bed that a reasonable solution could be found. He recalled how often an unusual position adopted in bed had resulted in slight pains which proved imaginary as soon as he arose, and Gregor was curious to see his present hallucination gradually dissolve. As for the change in his voice, his private opinion was that it was the prelude to some serious quinsy, the occupational malady of travelers.

He had no difficulty in turning back the coverlet; he needed only to blow himself up a little, and it fell of its own accord. But beyond that he was impeded by his tremendous girth. To get up, he needed arms and hands; but he had only numerous little legs, in perpetual vibration, over which he had no control. Before he could bend one leg, he first had to stretch it out; and when at last he had performed the desired movement, all the other legs worked uncontrollably, in intensely painful agitation. "I must not stay uselessly in bed," said Gregor to himself.

To get his body out of bed, he first tried moving the hind part. But unfortunately this hind part, which he had not yet seen, and of which he could form no very precise idea, went so slowly it proved to be very difficult to move; he summoned all his strength to throw himself forward but, ill-calculating his course, he hurled himself violently against one of the bedposts, and the searing pain he felt showed that the lower part of his body was without doubt the most sensitive.

He then tried to start with the fore part of his body and cautiously turned his head toward the side of the bed. In this he succeeded quite easily, and the rest of his body, despite its weight and size, followed the direction of his head. But when his head left the bed and was hanging in mid-air, he was afraid to continue any further; if he were to fall in this position, it would be a miracle if he did not crack his head; and this was no moment to lose his senses — better to stay in bed.

But when, panting after his efforts, he again found himself stretched out just as before, when he saw his little legs struggling more wildly than ever, despairing of finding any means of bringing peace and order into this chaotic procedure, he once again realized that he absolutely could not stay in bed and that it was perfectly reasonable to sacrifice everything to the slightest chance of getting out. At the same time he did not forget that cool and wise reflection would be far better than desperate resolutions. Ordinarily, at such moments he turned his eyes to the window to gain encouragement and hope. But this day the fog prevented him from seeing the other side of the street; the window gave him neither confidence nor strength. "Seven o'clock already," he said as he listened once more to the sound of the alarm clock. "Seven o'clock already, and the fog has got no thinner!" He lay back again for a moment, breathing weakly, as though, in the complete silence, he could calmly await the return to his normal self.

Then he said, "Before a quarter past it is absolutely essential for me to be up. In any case, someone will be sent from the office to ask for me before then, for the place opens at seven." And he began to rock on his back in order to get his whole body out of bed in one movement. In this manner he would be able to protect his head by raising it sharply as he fell. His back seemed to be hard; nothing would be risked by falling on it to the floor; his only fear was that the noise of his fall, which must surely resound through the whole house, might arouse terror, or, at the very least, uneasiness. However, that would have to be risked.

When Gregor had half his body out of bed — the new method seemed more like a game than a task, for he had only to swing himself on his back — he began to think how easily he could have got up if only he had had a little assistance. Two strong people — he thought of his father and the servant girl — would have been quite enough; they would have needed only to pass their arms under his round back, raise it from the bed, quickly lean forward with their burden, and then wait carefully till he had completed the operation of settling himself on the ground, where he hoped his feet would at last find a way of working together. But even if the doors had not been closed, would it have been wise for him to call for help? At this idea, despite his misery, he could not repress a smile.

Now he had progressed so far that, by sharply accentuating his swinging movement, he felt he was nearly losing his balance; he would have to take a serious decision, for in five minutes it would be a quarter to eight — but suddenly there was a knock at the front door. "Someone from the office," he said to himself, and he felt his blood run cold, while his little legs quickened their saraband. For a moment all was quiet.

"They're not going to the door," thought Gregor, in an access of absurd hope. But of course the maid, with a firm tread, went to the door and opened it. Gregor needed to hear only the caller's first words of greeting to know immediately who it was — the manager himself. Why was Gregor, particularly, condemned to work for a firm where the worst was suspected at the slightest inadvertence of the employees? Were the employees, without exception, all scoundrels? Was there among their number not one devoted, faithful servant, who, if it did so happen that by chance he missed a few hours work one morning, might have found himself so numbed with remorse that he just could not leave his bed? Would it not have been enough to send some apprentice to put things right — if, in any case, it was necessary to make inquiries at all — instead of the manager himself having to come, in order to let the whole innocent family know that the clearing-up of so suspicious an affair could only be entrusted to a person of his importance? These thoughts so irritated Gregor that he swung himself out of bed with all his might. This made a loud thud, but not the terrible crash that he had feared. The carpet somewhat softened the blow, and Gregor's back was more elastic than he had thought, and so his act was not accompanied by any din. Only his head had been slightly hurt. Gregor had not raised it enough, and it had been knocked in the fall. He turned over a little to rub it on the carpet, in pain and anger.

"Something fell in there just then," cried the manager, in the room on the left. Gregor tried to imagine his employer's face if such a mishap had occurred to him; for such a thing was possible, he had to admit. But, as if in brutal reply, the manager began pacing up and down in the next room, making his patent-leather boots creak.

And in the other room on the right, Gregor's sister whispered to warn her brother, "Gregor, the manager is here."

"I know," said Gregor to himself, but he dared not raise his voice enough for his sister to hear.

"Gregor," said his father in the room on the left, "the manager has come to find out why you didn't catch the early train. We don't know what to say. He wants to speak to you personally. So please open the door. I'm sure he will be kind enough to excuse the untidiness of your room."

"Good morning, good morning, Mr. Samsa," interrupted the manager, cordial and brisk.

"He is not well," said his mother to the manager, while his father went on shouting through the door. "Believe me, he is not well, sir. How else could Gregor have missed the train? The boy thinks of nothing but his work! It makes me upset to see how he never goes out after supper; do you know he's just spent a whole week here and been at home every evening! He sits down with us at the table and stays there, quietly reading the paper or studying his timetables. His greatest indulgence is to do a little fretwork. Just lately he made a small picture frame. It was finished in two or three evenings, and you'd be surprised how pretty it is; it is hanging up in his room. As soon as Gregor opens his door, you will be able to see it. I am so glad you came, sir, because without you we would never have got Gregor to open his door, he is so obstinate; and surely he must be ill, even though he denied it this morning."

"I am just coming," said Gregor slowly and carefully, but he continued to lie still, so as not to miss a word of the conversation.

"I can offer no other suggestion," declared the manager. "Let us only hope it is nothing serious. However, we businessmen must often — fortunately or not, as you will — get on with our jobs and ignore our little indispositions."

"Well, can the manager come in now?" asked his father impatiently, rapping on the door again.

"No," said Gregor. In the room on the left there was a painful silence; in that on the right the sister began to sob.

Why did she not go to the others? Possibly she had only just got out of bed and was not yet dressed. And why did she weep? Because he did not get up to let the manager in, because he risked losing his position, and because the boss would once more worry his parents about their old debts? These were misplaced troubles! Gregor was still there and had not the slightest intention of letting his family down. At this very moment he was stretched out on the carpet, and nobody seeing him in this state could seriously have demanded that he should let the manager enter his room. But it was not on account of this slight impoliteness — for which in normal times he could easily have made his excuses later — that Gregor would be dismissed. And he thought it would be more reasonable, just now, to leave him alone rather than to upset him with tears and speeches. But it was just this uncertainty which was making the others uneasy and which excused their behavior.

"Herr Samsa," now cried the manager, raising his voice, "What is the matter? You barricade yourself in your room, you don't answer yes or no, you needlessly upset your parents, and you neglect your professional duties in an unheard-of manner. I am speaking in the name of your employer and of your parents, and I beg you seriously to give us a satisfactory explanation immediately. I am astonished, astonished! I took you for a quiet, reasonable young man, and here you suddenly give yourself airs, behaving in an absolutely fantastic manner! The head of the firm, speaking to me this morning in your absence, suggested an explanation which I rejected; he mentioned the samples which were entrusted to you a while ago. I gave him my word of honor that this had nothing to do with the affair, but now that I have been witness to your obstinacy, I can assure you, Herr Samsa, that it deprives me of any wish to defend you. Your job is by no means safe! I had intended to tell you this in private but, since you oblige me to waste my time here for nothing, I see no reason for keeping quiet before your parents. I'd have you know that lately your work has been far from satisfactory; we realize, of course, that the time of the year is not propitious for big business, but you must understand, Herr Samsa, that a period with no business at all should not and can not be tolerated!''

Gregor was beside himself; in his anxiety he forgot everything else. "But, sir," he cried, "I will open the door immediately. I will open it. I felt a little ill; a slight giddiness prevented me from getting up. I am still in bed. But I feel better already. I am just getting up. Only a moment's patience. I am not quite so well as I thought. But I am all right, really. How can it be that illness should take one so quickly? Only yesterday I felt quite well, my parents can tell you; and then last evening I had a slight symptom. They must have noticed it. Why didn't I let them know at the office! But then, one always thinks one will be able to get rid of an illness without staying at home. Please, sir, spare my parents. The complaints you made just now are really without foundation. No one has even suggested them before. Perhaps you have not seen the last orders I sent in. I will leave on the eight-o'clock train; these few moments of rest have done me a great deal of good. Please don't stay, sir, I shall be at the office immediately; and please inform the director of what has happened and put in a good word for me.''

And while Gregor hastily cried these words, scarcely realizing what he said, he had, with an ease due to his previous exertions, approached the chest of drawers, against which he now tried to raise himself. He wanted to open the door; he wanted to be seen and to speak with the manager. He was curious to know what impression he would make on these people who were so imperiously demanding his presence. If he frightened them, that would be reassuring, for he would stop being cross-questioned and be left in peace. If they took everything quietly then he, too, need not be alarmed. And if he hurried he might still catch the eight o'clock train. The chest was polished, and Gregor slipped on it several times but, by a supreme effort, he managed to get upright. He paid no attention to the pains in his stomach, though they were hurting him. He let himself drop forward onto the top of a near-by chair and clung there with his little legs. Then, finding himself master of his body, he stayed very quiet in order to listen to what the manager had to say.

"Did you understand a word of what he said?" the manager asked the parents. "Is he trying to make fools of us?"

"Good heavens," cried the mother, already in tears. "Perhaps he is seriously ill, and here we are torturing him all this while! Grete! Grete!" she called.

"Mother!" cried the daughter from the other side. They were separated by Gregor's room.

"Fetch a doctor immediately. Gregor is ill. A doctor, quickly! Did you hear him speak?"

"It was an animal's voice," said the manager; after the cries of the women, his voice seemed curiously gentle.

"Anna, Anna!" shouted the father through the hall into the kitchen, clapping his hands. "Get a locksmith, quick!" And already the two young girls — how could his sister have dressed so soon? — ran along the corridor with rustling skirts and opened the front door. No one heard the door close; no doubt it had been left open, as is the custom in houses to which a great misfortune has come.

However, Gregor had become calmer. Doubtless they had not understood his words, though they had seemed clear enough to him, clearer, indeed, than the first time; perhaps his ears were becoming more accustomed to the sounds. But at least they were obliged to realize that his case was not normal, and they were ready, now, to help him. The assurance and resourcefulness with which the first steps had been taken comforted him considerably. He felt himself integrated into human society once again, and, without differentiating between them, he hoped for great and surprising things from the locksmith and the doctor. To clear his throat for the decisive conversation which he would have to hold soon, he coughed a little, but as quietly as possible, for he feared that even his cough might not sound human. Meanwhile, in the next room, it had become quiet. Perhaps his parents were sitting at table in a secret conference with the manager; perhaps everyone was leaning against the door, listening.

Gregor made his way slowly toward it with the chair; then he abandoned the chair and flung himself at the door, holding himself erect against the woodwork — for the bottoms of his feet secreted a sticky substance — and he rested a moment from his efforts. After this, he tried to turn the key in the lock with his mouth. Unfortunately, it seemed he had no proper teeth. How could he take hold of the key? In compensation, instead of teeth he possessed a pair of very strong mandibles and succeeded in seizing the key in the lock, regardless of the pain this caused him; a brownish liquid flowed out of his mouth, spread over the lock, and dropped to the floor.

"Listen!" said the manager in the next room. "He is just turning the key."

This was valuable encouragement for Gregor; he would have liked his father, his mother, everybody, to start calling to him, "Courage, Gregor, go on, push hard!" And, with the idea that everyone was following his efforts with passionate attention, he clutched the key with all the power of his jaws until he was nearly unconscious. Following the progress of the turning key, he twisted himself around the lock, hanging on by his mouth, and, clinging to the key, pressed it down again, whenever it slipped, with all the weight of his body. The clear click of the lock as it snapped back awoke Gregor from his momentary coma.

"I have dispensed with the locksmith," he thought, and sighed and leaned his head against the handle to open one panel of the double doors completely.

This method, the only possible one, prevented the others from seeing him for some time, even with the door open. Still erect, he had to grope his way round the door with great caution in order not to spoil his entry by falling flat on his back; so he was concentrating toward this end, with all his attention absorbed by the maneuver, when he heard the manager utter a sonorous, "Oh!" such as the roaring of the wind produces, and saw him — he was just by the door — press his hand over his open mouth and slowly stagger back as if some invisible and intensely powerful force were driving him from the spot. His mother — who, despite the presence of the manager, was standing by with her hair in curlers, still disordered by sleep — began to look at the father, clasping her hands; then she made two steps toward Gregor and fell backward into the family circle in the midst of a confusion of skirts which spread around her, while her face, falling on her breast, was concealed from sight. The father clenched his fists with a menacing air, as if to beat Gregor back into his room; then he looked around the dining room in perplexity, covered his eyes with his hand, and wept with great sobs which shook his powerful chest.

Gregor did not enter the room; he stood against the closed half of the double doors, allowing only a part of his body to be seen, while, above, he turned his head to one side to see what would happen. Meanwhile, it had grown much lighter; on either side of the street a part of the long, dark building opposite could clearly be seen — it was a hospital, with regular windows startlingly pitting its façade; it was still raining, but in great separate drops which fell to the ground, one by one. The breakfast crockery was spread all over the table, for breakfast was the most important meal of the day for Gregor's father; he would prolong it for hours while he read various newspapers. On the wall hung a photograph of Gregor in lieutenant's uniform, taken while he was in military service; he was smiling; his hand lay on the hilt of his sword. By his expression, he seemed happy to be alive; by his gesture, he appeared to command respect for his rank. The living-room door was ajar, and, as the front door was also open, the balcony and the first steps of the stairway could just be seen.

"Now," said Gregor, and he realized that he was the only one to have kept calm, "now I will get dressed, collect my samples, and go. Will you, will you let me go? Surely you can now see, sir, that I am not obstinate, that I do mean to work; commercial traveling is tiresome, I admit, but without it I cannot live. Where are you going, sir? To the office? Yes? Will you give them a faithful account of what has happened? After all, anyone might find for a moment that they were incapable of resuming their work, but that's just a good opportunity to review the work they have been doing, and to bear in mind that, once the obstacle is removed, they will be able to return with twice the heart. I owe so much to the director, as you know very well. I have my parents and my sister to consider. I am in an awkward position, but I shall return to work. Only, please do not make things more difficult for me; they are hard enough as it is. Take my part at the office. I know only too well they don't like travelers. They think we earn our money too easily, that we lead too grand a life. I realize that the present situation doesn't encourage the removal of this prejudice; but you, sir, the manager, can judge the circumstances better than the rest of the staff, better than the director himself — though this is between ourselves — for in his executive capacity he is often easily misled by an employee's prejudice. You know quite well that the traveler, who is hardly ever in the office the whole year round, is often the victim of scandal, of a chance, undeserved complaint against which he is powerless to defend himself, for he does not even know that he is being accused; he only learns of it as he returns, exhausted, at the end of his trip, when the sad consequences of an affair, whose circumstances he can no longer recall, painfully confront him. Please, sir, don't leave me without a word to show that you think all this at least a little reasonable."

But, at Gregor's first words, the manager had turned away and only glanced back, with snarling lips, over his trembling shoulder. During Gregor's speech, he had not stood still for a moment; instead, he had retreated furtively, step by step, toward the door — always keeping Gregor in sight — as if some secret law forbade him to leave the room. He had already reached the hall and, as he took the very last step out of the living room, one would have thought the floor was burning his shoes, so sharply did he spring. Then he stretched his hand toward the balustrade, as if some unearthly deliverance awaited him at the foot of the stairs.

Gregor realized that, if he were to keep his job, on no account must the manager be allowed to leave in this condition. Unfortunately, his parents did not realize the position very clearly; they had for so long held the idea that Gregor was settled in the firm for life and were so taken up with their present troubles that they had little thought for such a contingency. But Gregor had more foresight. The manager must be stopped, calmed, convinced, and finally won over. The future of Gregor and of his family depended on it! If only his sister were there! She had understood, she had actually begun to weep while Gregor still lay quietly on his back. And the manager, who liked women, would have listened to her; he would have let himself be guided by her; she would have closed the door and would have proved to him, in the hall, how unreasonable his terror was. But she was not there; Gregor himself must manage this affair. And without even considering whether he would ever be able to return to work, nor whether his speech had been understood, he let go of the doorpost to glide through the opening and overtake the manager (who was clutching the balustrade with both hands in a ridiculous manner), vainly sought for a foothold, and, uttering a cry, he fell, with his frail little legs crumpled beneath him.

Suddenly, for the first time that whole morning, he experienced a feeling of physical well-being; his feet were on firm ground; he noticed with joy that his legs obeyed him wonderfully and were even eager to carry him wherever he might wish. But while, under the nervous influence of his need for haste, he hesitated on the spot, not far from his mother, he saw her suddenly jump, fainting though she seemed to be, and throw her arms about with outspread fingers, crying, "Help, for God's sake, help!" She turned her head, the better to see Gregor; then, in flagrant contradiction, she began to retreat madly, having forgotten that behind her stood the table, still laden with breakfast things. She staggered against it and sat down suddenly, like one distraught, regardless of the fact that, at her elbow, the overturned coffeepot was making a pool of coffee on the carpet.

"Mother, mother," whispered Gregor, looking up at her. The manager had quite gone out of his mind. Seeing the coffee spilling, Gregor could not prevent himself from snapping his jaws several times in the air, as if he were eating. Thereupon his mother again began to shriek and quickly jumped up from the table and fell into the arms of the father, who had rushed up behind her. But Gregor had no time to bother about them. The manager was already on the stairs; with his chin on the balustrade, he was looking back for the last time.

Gregor summoned all his courage to try to bring him back; the manager must have suspected something of the sort, for he leaped several steps at a single bound and disappeared with a cry of "Huh!" which resounded in the hollow of the stair well. This flight had the unfortunate effect of causing Gregor's father — who till now had remained master of himself — to lose his head completely; instead of running after the manager, or at least not interfering with Gregor in his pursuit, he seized in his right hand the manager's walking stick, which had been left behind on a chair with his overcoat and hat, took up in his left a newspaper from the table, and began stamping his feet and brandishing the newspaper and the cane to drive Gregor back into his room. Gregor's prayers were unavailing, were not even understood; he had turned to his father a supplicating head, but, meek though he showed himself, his father merely stamped all the louder. In the dining room, despite the cold, the mother had opened the window wide and was leaning out as far as possible, pressing her face in her hands. A great rush of air swept the space between the room and the stairway; the curtains billowed, the papers rustled, and a few sheets flew over the carpet. But the father pursued Gregor pitilessly, whistling and whooping like a savage, and Gregor, who was not used to walking backward, progressed but slowly.

Had he been able to turn around, he could have reached his room quickly, but he feared to make his father impatient by the slowness of his turning and feared also that at any moment he might receive a mortal blow on his head or on his back from this menacing stick. Soon Gregor had no choice; for he realized with terror that when he was going backward he was not master of his direction and, still fearfully watching the attitude of his father out of the corner of his eye, he began his turning movement as quickly as possible, which was really only very slowly. Perhaps his father realized his good intention for, instead of hindering this move, he guided him from a little distance away, helping Gregor with the tip of the stick. If only he had left off that insupportable whistling! Gregor was completely losing his head. He had nearly completed his turn when, bewildered by the din, he mistook his direction and began to go back to his former position. When at last, to his great joy, he found himself facing the half-opened double doors, he discovered that his body was too big to pass through without hurt. Naturally, it never occurred to his father, in his present state, to open the other half of the double doors in order to allow Gregor to pass. He was dominated by the one fixed idea that Gregor should be made to return to his room as quickly as possible. He would never have entertained the long-winded performance which Gregor would have needed to rear up and pass inside. Gregor heard him storming behind him, no doubt to urge him through as though there were no obstacle in his path; the hubbub no longer sounded like the voice of one single father. Now was no time to play, and Gregor — come what may — hurled himself into the doorway. There he lay, jammed in a slanting position, his body raised up on one side and his flank crushed by the door jamb, whose white paint was now covered with horrible brown stains. He was caught fast and could not free himself unaided; on one side his little legs fluttered in the air, on the other they were painfully pressed under his body; then his father gave him a tremendous blow from behind with the stick. Despite the pain, this was almost a relief; he was lifted bodily into the middle of the room and fell, bleeding thickly. The door was slammed by a thrust of the stick, and then, at last, all was still.

II

It was dusk when Gregor awoke from his heavy, deathlike sleep. Even had he not been disturbed, he would doubtless soon have awakened, for he felt he had had his fill of rest and sleep; however, he seemed to have been awakened by the cautious, furtive noise of a key turning in the lock of the hall door. The reflection of the electric tramway lay dimly here and there about the ceiling and on the upper parts of the furniture, but below, where Gregor was, it was dark. Slowly he dragged himself toward the door to ascertain what had happened and fumbled around clumsily with his feelers, whose use he was at last learning to appreciate. His left side seemed to him to be one long, irritating scar, and he limped about on his double set of legs. One of his legs had been seriously injured during the morning's events — it was a miracle that only one should be hurt — and it dragged lifelessly behind.

When he reached the door, he realized what had attracted him: the smell of food. For there was a bowl of sweetened milk in which floated little pieces of bread. He could have laughed with delight, his appetite had grown so since morning; he thrust his head up to the eyes in the milk. But he drew it back quickly; his painful left side gave him some difficulty, for he could only eat by convulsing his whole body and snorting; also, he could not bear the smell of milk, which once had been his favorite drink and which his sister had no doubt prepared for this special reason. He turned from the bowl in disgust and dragged himself to the middle of the room.

The gas was lit in the dining room; he could see it through the cracks of the door. Now was the time when, ordinarily, his father would read aloud to his family from the evening paper, but this time Gregor heard nothing. Perhaps this traditional reading, which his sister always retailed to him in her conversation and in her letters, had not lapsed entirely from the customs of the household. But everywhere was still, and yet surely someone was in the room.

"What a quiet life my family has led," thought Gregor, staring before him in the darkness, and he felt very proud, for it was to him that his parents and his sister owed so placid a life in so nice a flat. What would happen now, if this peace, this satisfaction, this well-being should end in terror and disaster? In order to dissipate such gloomy thoughts, Gregor began to take a little exercise and crawled back and forth over the floor.

Once during the evening he saw the door on the left open slightly, and once it was the door on the right; someone had wished to enter but had found the task too risky. Gregor resolved to stop by the dining-room door and to entice the hesitant visitor as best he might or at least to see who it was; but the door never opened again, and Gregor waited in vain. That morning, when the door had been locked, everyone had tried to invade his room; but now that they had succeeded in opening it no one came to see him; they had even locked his doors on the outside.

Not till late was the light extinguished, and Gregor could guess that his parents and his sister had been waiting till then, for he heard them all go off on tiptoe. Now no one would come to him till the morning, and so he would have the necessary time to reflect on the ordering of his new life; but his great room, in which he was obliged to remain flat on his stomach on the floor, frightened him in a way that he could not understand — for he had lived in it for the past five years — and, with a half-involuntary action of which he was a little ashamed, he hastily slid under the couch; he soon found that here his back was a little crushed and he could not raise his head; he only regretted that his body was too large to go entirely under the couch.

He spent the whole night there, sometimes in a half-sleep from which the pangs of hunger would wake him with a start, sometimes ruminating on his misfortune and his vague hopes, always concluding that his duty was to remain docile and to try to make things bearable for his family, whatever unpleasantness the situation might impose upon them.

Early in the morning he had a chance to test the strength of his new resolutions; it was still almost dark; his sister, already half dressed, opened the hall door and looked in curiously. She did not see Gregor at once but when she perceived him under the sofa — "Heavens, he must be somewhere; he can't have flown away!" — she was overcome by an unmanageable terror and rushed off, slamming the door. Then, repenting her gesture, she opened it again and entered on tiptoe, as if it were the room of a stranger or one seriously ill. Gregor stretched his head out from the side of the sofa and watched her. Would she notice that he had left the milk, and not from lack of appetite? Would she bring him something which suited his taste better? If she did not do so of her own accord, he would rather have died of hunger than draw her attention to these things, despite his overwhelming desire to rush out of his hiding place, to throw himself at his sister's feet, and to beg for something to eat. But suddenly the sister saw the full bowl in astonishment. A little milk had been spilled around it; using a piece of paper, she took up the bowl without touching it and carried it off to the kitchen. Gregor waited anxiously to see what she would bring him in its place and racked his brains to guess. But he had never realized to what lengths his sister's kindness would go. In order to discover her brother's likes, she brought a whole choice of eatables spread on an old newspaper. There were half-rotted stumps of vegetables, the bones of yesterday's dinner covered with a thick white sauce, a few currants and raisins, some almonds, some cheese that Gregor, a few days before, had declared uneatable, a stale loaf, a piece of salted bread and butter, and another without salt. Besides this she brought back the bowl which had become so important to Gregor. This time it was filled with water, and, guessing that her brother would not like to eat before her, she very kindly retired, closing and locking the door to show him that he might eat in peace. Now that his meal was ready, Gregor felt all his legs trembling. His wounds seemed cured, for he felt not the slightest hindrance, and he was astonished to remember that when he had been human and had cut his finger slightly only a few months ago, it had pained him for several days after.

"Have I become less sensitive?" he wondered; but already he had begun sucking at the cheese, which had suddenly and imperiously attracted him above all the other food. Gluttonously he swallowed in turn the cheese, the vegetables, and the sauce, his eyes moist with satisfaction; as to the fresh things, he wanted none of them; their smell repelled him, and, in order to eat, he separated them from the others.

When he had finished and was idly making up his mind to return to his place, his sister slowly began to turn the key in the lock to give him the signal for retreat. He was very frightened, though he was half asleep, and hurried to reach the sofa. It needed great determination to remain beneath it during the time, however short, that his sister was in the room; his heavy meal had so swollen his body that he could scarcely breathe in his retreat. Between two fits of suffocation he saw, with his eyes filled with tears, that his sister, intending no harm, was sweeping up the remains of his meal with the very things that he had not touched, as if he needed them no more; she put the refuse into a bucket, which she covered with a wooden lid and hastily carried away. Hardly had she turned the handle before Gregor struggled out from his hiding place to expand his body to its proper size.

So he was fed each day; in the morning, before his parents and the maid were awake, and in the afternoon, when lunch was over and while his parents were taking their nap and the maid had been provided with some task or other by his sister. Certainly they did not wish Gregor to die of hunger but perhaps they preferred to know nothing about his meals except by hearsay — they could not have borne to see him — perhaps, also, in order to diminish their disgust, his sister was taking pains to spare them the slightest trouble. He must realize that they, too, had their share of misfortune.

Gregor never learned what excuses they had made to rid themselves of the doctor and the locksmith, for, as no one attempted to understand him, no one, not even his sister, imagined that he could understand them. He had to be content, when she came into his room, to listen to her invoking the saints between her sighs. It was only much later, when Grete had become somewhat accustomed to the new situation — to which she never really became reconciled — that Gregor would occasionally overhear an expression which showed some kindness or allowed him to guess at such a meaning. When he had eaten all the food off the newspaper she would say, "He liked what I brought to-day"; at other times, when he had no appetite — and lately this had become more frequent — she would say, almost sadly, "Now he has left it all."

But even if he could learn no news directly, Gregor overheard a good deal of what was said in the dining room; as soon as he heard anyone speak, he would hurry to the most propitious door and press his whole body close against it. At first, especially, there was little conversation which did not bear more or less directly on his predicament. For two whole days, the mealtimes were given over to deliberating on the new attitude which must be maintained toward Gregor; even between meals they spoke mostly on the same theme, for now at least two members of the household always remained at home, each one fearing to remain alone and, particularly, to leave Gregor unwatched.

It was not very clear how much the maid knew of what had happened, but, on the very first day, she had fallen on her knees and begged his mother to let her go; and a quarter of an hour later she had left the house in tearful gratitude, as if her release were the greatest evidence of the kindness she had met with in the house; and of her own accord she took a long and boring oath never to reveal the secret to anyone. Now his sister and his mother had to look after the cooking; this entailed little trouble, for the appetite of the Samsa family had gone. Occasionally Gregor would hear one member of the family vainly exhorting another to eat. The reply was always the same: "Thank you, I have had enough," or some such phrase. Perhaps, also, they did not drink. Often his sister would ask her father if he would like some beer; she would cheerfully offer to fetch it, or, faced with her father's silence, she would say, to remove any scruples on his part, that the landlady could go for it, but her father would always reply with a loud, "No!" and nothing more would be said.

In the course of the very first day, the father had clearly explained their precise financial situation to his wife and daughter. From time to time he would get up from the table and hunt for some paper or account book in his Wertheim safe, which he had saved from the crash when his business had failed five years before. He could be heard opening the complicated locks of the safe and closing it again after he had taken out what he sought. Ever since he became a prisoner, nothing had given Gregor such pleasure as these financial explanations. He had always imagined that his father had been unable to save a penny from the ruins of his business; in any case, his father had never said anything to undeceive him, and Gregor had never questioned him upon the matter; he had done all he could to help his family to forget as quickly as possible the disaster which had plunged them into such despair.

He had set to work with splendid ardor; in less than no time, from being a junior clerk he had been promoted to the position of traveler, with all the benefits of such a post; and his successes were suddenly transformed into hard cash which could be spread on the table before the surprised and delighted eyes of his family. Those were happy times — they had never since recovered such a sense of delight, though Gregor now earned enough to feed the whole Samsa family. Everyone had grown accustomed to it, his family as much as himself; they took the money gratefully, he gave it willingly, but the act was accompanied by no remarkable effusiveness. Only his sister had remained particularly affectionate toward Gregor, and it was his secret plan to have her enter the conservatory next year regardless of the considerable cost of such an enterprise, which he would try to meet in some way; for, unlike him, Grete was very fond of music and wished to take up the study of the violin. This matter of the conservatory recurred often in the brief conversations between Gregor and his sister, whenever Gregor had a few days to spend with his family; they hardly ever spoke of it except as a dream impossible to realize; his parents did not much like the innocent allusions to the subject, but Gregor thought very seriously of it and had promised himself that he would solemnly announce his plan next Christmas eve.

It was ideas of this kind, ideas completely unsuited to his present situation, which now passed constantly through Gregor's mind while he held himself pressed erect against the door, listening. He would get so tired that he could no longer hear anything; then he would let himself go and allow his head to fall against the door; but he would draw it back immediately, for the slightest noise was noticed in the dining room and would be followed by an interval of silence.

"What can he be doing now?" his father would say after a moment's pause, turning, no doubt, toward the door; the interrupted conversation would only gradually be resumed.

His father was often obliged to repeat his explanations in order to recall forgotten details or to make them understood by his wife, who did not always grasp them the first time. Gregor thus learned, by what the father said, that, despite all their misfortunes, his parents had been able to save a certain amount from their former property — little enough, it is true, but it had been augmented, to some extent, by interest. Also, they had not spent all the money that Gregor, keeping only a few shillings for himself, had handed over to his family each week, enabling them to gather together a little capital. Behind his door, Gregor nodded his head in approval; he was so happy at this unexpected foresight and thrift. Doubtless, with these savings his father could have more rapidly paid off the debt he had contracted to Gregor's employer, which would have brought nearer the date of Gregor's release; but under the circumstances it was much better that his father had acted as he had.

Unfortunately this money was not quite sufficient to enable the family to live on its interest; it would last a year, perhaps two, but no more. It was a sum which must not be touched, which must be kept for a case of urgent necessity. As for money on which to live, that would have to be earned. Now, despite his good health, the father was nevertheless an old man who had ceased to work five years before and who could not be expected to entertain any foolish hopes of getting employment; during these five years of retirement — his first holiday in a life entirely devoted to work and unsuccess — he had become very fat and moved with great difficulty. And the old mother would not be able to earn much, suffering as she did from asthma, for even now it was an effort for her to get about the house; she passed a good deal of her time each day lying on the sofa, panting and wheezing under the open window. And was the breadwinner to be the sister, who was still but a child, seventeen years old, so suited to the life she had led till then, nicely dressed, getting plenty of sleep, helping in the house, taking part in a few harmless little entertainments, and playing her violin? Whenever the conversation fell on this topic, Gregor left the door and lay on the leather sofa, whose coolness was so soothing to his body, burning as it was with anxiety and shame.

Often he lay all night, sleepless, and hearing no sound for hours on end save the creak of the leather as he turned. Or, uncomplainingly, he would push his armchair toward the window, crawl up on it, and, propped on the seat, he would lean against the window, not so much to enjoy the view as to recall the sense of release he once used to feel whenever he looked across the pavements; for now he was daily becoming more shortsighted, he could not even make out the hospital opposite, which he had cursed when he was human because he could see it all too clearly; and had he not known so well that he was living in Charlottenstrasse, a quiet but entirely urban street, he might have thought his window gave out on a desert, where the gray of the sky and the gray of the earth merged indistinguishably together. His attentive sister had only to see the armchair by the window twice to understand; from then on, each time she tidied the room she would push the armchair to the window, and would always leave its lower half open.

If only Gregor had been able to speak to his sister, to thank her for all she was doing for him, he could have borne her services easier; but as it was, they pained and embarrassed him. Grete naturally tried to hide any appearance of blame or trouble regarding the situation, and as time went on she played her part even better, but she could not prevent her brother from realizing his predicament more and more clearly. Each time she entered his room, it was terrible for Gregor. Hardly had she entered, when, despite the pains she always took to spare the others the sight of its interior, she would not even take time to shut the door but would run to the window, open it hastily with a single push, as if to escape imminent suffocation, and would stand there for a minute, however cold it might be, breathing deeply. Twice a day she terrified Gregor with this rush and clatter; he shrank trembling under the couch the whole time; he knew his sister would have spared him this had she been able to stand being in the room with him with the window shut.

One day — it must have been a month after Gregor's change, and his sister had no grounds for astonishment at his appearance — she came a little earlier than usual and found him looking out of the window, motionless and in such a position as to inspire terror. If she had not liked to enter, that would not have surprised Gregor, for his position prevented her from opening the window. But not only would she not enter; she sprang back, slammed the door, and locked it; a stranger might have thought that Gregor was lying in wait for his sister, to attack her. Naturally he hid himself under the couch immediately, but he had to wait till midday for Grete's return, and, when she did come, she appeared unusually troubled. He realized that his appearance was still disgusting to the poor girl, that it would always be so, and that she must fiercely resist her own impulse to flee the moment she caught sight of the tiniest part of Gregor's body protruding from under the sofa. To spare her this sight, he took a sheet on his back, dragged it to the sofa — a task which occupied some hours — and spread it in such a way that his sister could see nothing under the sofa, even if she stooped. Had she found this precaution unnecessary, she would have taken the sheet away, for she guessed that Gregor did not so completely shut himself away for pleasure; but she left the sheet where it lay, and Gregor, prudently parting the curtain with his head to see what impression this new arrangement had made upon his sister, thought he detected a look of gratitude in her face.

During the first fortnight his parents had not been able to bring themselves to enter his room, and he often heard them praising the zeal of his sister, whom they had regarded, so far, as a useless young girl and of whom they had often complained. But now, both his father and mother would wait quite frequently outside Gregor's door while is sister was tidying the room, and scarcely had she come out again before they would make her tell them in detail exactly how she had found the room, what Gregor had eaten, and, in detail, what he was doing at that moment; they would ask her, too, if there were the slightest signs of improvement. His mother seemed impatient to see Gregor, but the father and sister restrained her with argument to which she listened very attentively and with which she wholly agreed. Later, however, they had to use force, and when his mother began to cry, "Let me go to Gregor! My poor boy! Don't you understand that I must see him!" Gregor thought that perhaps it would be as well if his mother did come in, not every day, of course, but perhaps once a week; she would understand things better than his sister, who was but a child, for all her courage, and had perhaps taken on such a difficult task out of childish lightheartedness.

Gregor's wish to see his mother was soon realized. Gregor avoided showing himself at the window during the day, out of consideration to his parents; but his restricted walks around the floor did not fully compensate him for this self-denial, nor could he bear to lie still for long, even during the night; he took no more pleasure in eating, and it soon became his habit to distract himself by walking — around the room, back and forth along the walls, and across the ceiling, on which he would hang; it was quite a different matter from walking across the floor. His breathing became freer, a light, swinging motion went through his body, and he felt so elated that now and then, to his own surprise, he would let himself go and fall to the floor. But by now, knowing better how to manage his body, he succeeded in rendering these falls harmless. His sister soon noticed his new pastime, for he left sticky marks here and there in his track, and Grete took it into her head to help him in his walks by removing all the furniture likely to be a hindrance, particularly the chest and the desk. Unfortunately, she was not strong enough to manage this on her own and dared not ask the help of her father; as for the maid, she certainly would have refused, for if this sixteen-year-old child had worked bravely since the

former cook had left, it was on condition that she could stay continually barricaded in the kitchen, whose doors she would only open on
special demand. So there was nothing else for it; Grete would have
to enlist the mother's help one day when the father was away.

The mother gladly consented, but her exclamations of joy were
hushed before Gregor's door. The sister first made sure that everything
was in order in the room; then she allowed the mother to enter. In
his great haste, Gregor had pulled the sheet down further than usual,
and the many folds in which it fell gave the scene the air of a still life.
This time he refrained from peeping under the sheet to spy on his
mother but he was delighted to have her near.

"You may come in; he is not in sight," said his sister; and, taking
her mother by the hand, she led her into the room. Then Gregor
heard the two frail women struggling to remove the heavy old chest;
the sister undertook the hardest part of the task, despite the warnings
of her mother, who feared she might do herself some harm. It took a
long time. They had been struggling with the chest for four hours
when the mother declared that it might be best to leave it where it was,
that it was too heavy for them, that they would not finish moving it
before the father returned, and that, with the chest in the middle of
the room, Gregor would be considerably impeded in his movements,
and, finally, who knew whether he might not be displeased by the removal of his furniture?

The mother thought he would be; the sight of the bare walls struck
cold at her heart; might Gregor not feel the same, having long grown
so accustomed to the furniture, and would he not feel forsaken in his
empty room? "Isn't it a fact," said the mother in a low voice — she
had spoken in whispers ever since she entered the room, so that Gregor
whose hiding place she had not yet discovered, might not overhear, not
so much what she was saying — for she was persuaded that he could
not understand — but the very sound of her voice. "Isn't it a fact that
when we remove the furniture, we seem to imply that we are giving up
all hope of seeing him cured and are wickedly leaving him to his fate?
I think it would be better to keep the room just as it was before, so that
Gregor will find nothing changed when he comes back to us and will
be able the more easily to forget what has happened meanwhile."

Hearing his mother's words, Gregor realized how these two monotonous months, in the course of which nobody had addressed a word to
him, must have affected his mind; he could not otherwise explain his
desire for an empty room. Did he really wish to allow this warm, com-

fortable room with its genial furniture to be transformed into a cavern in which, in rapid and complete forgetfulness of his human past, he might exercise his right to crawl all over the walls? It seemed he was already so near to forgetting; and it had required nothing less than his mother's voice, which he had not heard for so long, to rouse him. Nothing should be removed, everything must stay as it is, he could not bear to forego the good influence of his furniture, and, if it prevented him from indulging his crazy impulses, then so much the better.

Unfortunately, his sister was not of this opinion; she had become accustomed to assume authority over her parents where Gregor was concerned — this was not without cause — and now the mother's remarks were enough to make her decide to remove not only the desk and the chest — which till now had been their only aim — but all the other furniture as well, except the indispensable sofa. This was not the result of mere childish bravado, nor the outcome of that new feeling of self-confidence which she had just acquired so unexpectedly and painfully. No, she really believed that Gregor had need of plenty of room for exercise and that, as far as she could see, he never used the furniture. Perhaps, also, the romantic character of girls of her age was partly responsible for her decision, a sentiment which strove to satisfy itself on every possible occasion and which now drove her to dramatize her brother's situation to such an extent so that she could devote herself to Gregor even more passionately than hitherto; for in a room over whose bare walls Gregor reigned alone, no one but Grete dare enter and stay.

She did not allow herself to be turned from her resolve by her mother, made irresolute by the oppressive atmosphere of the room, and who did not hesitate now to remove the chest as best she could. Gregor could bear to see the chest removed, at a pinch, but the desk must stay. And hardly had the women left the room, panting as they pushed the chest, than Gregor put out his head to examine the possibilities of making a prudent and tactful appearance. But unfortunately it was his mother who returned first, while Grete, in the side room, her arms around the chest, was rocking it from side to side without being able to settle it in position. The mother was not used to the sight of Gregor; it might give her a serious shock. Terrified, he hastened to retreat to the other end of the sofa, but he could not prevent the sheet from fluttering slightly, which immediately attracted his mother's attention. She stopped short, stood stockstill for a moment, then hurried back to Grete.

Gregor assured himself that nothing extraordinary was happening —

they were merely removing a few pieces of furniture — but the coming and going of the women, their little cries, the scraping of the furniture over the floor, seemed to combine in such an excruciating din that, however much he withdrew his head, contracted his legs, and pressed himself to the ground, he had to admit that he could not bear this torture much longer. They were emptying his room, taking away from him all that he loved; they had already removed the chest in which he kept his saw and his fretwork outfit; now they were shifting his desk, which had stood so solid and fast to the floor all the time it was in use, that desk on which he had written his lessons while he was at the commercial school, at the secondary school, even at the preparatory school. However, he could no longer keep pace with their intentions, for so absent minded had he become he had almost forgotten their existence, now that fatigue had quietened them and the clatter of their weary feet could no longer be heard.

So he came out — the women were only leaning against the desk in the next room, recovering their breath — and he found himself so bewildered that he changed his direction four times; he really could not decide what he should first salvage — when suddenly he caught sight of the picture of the woman in furs which assumed tremendous importance on the bare wall; he hastily climbed up and pressed himself against the glass, which stuck to his burning belly and refreshed him delightfully. This picture, at least, which Gregor entirely covered, should not be snatched away from him by anyone. He turned his head toward the dining-room door to observe the women as they returned.

They had had but a short rest and were already coming back; Grete's arm was round her mother's waist, supporting her.

"Well, what shall we take now?" said Grete, and she looked around. Her eyes met those of Gregor on the wall. If she succeeded in keeping her presence of mind, it was only for her mother's sake, toward whom she leaned her head to prevent her from seeing anything and said, a little too quickly and with a trembling voice, "Come, wouldn't it be better to go back to the living room for a minute?" The girl's intention was clear to Gregor: she wished to put her mother in a safe place and then to drive him from the wall. Well, let her try! He lay over his picture, and he would not let it go. He would rather leap into his sister's face.

But Grete had merely disquieted her mother; now she turned, saw the gigantic brown stain spread over the wallpaper and, before she realized that it was Gregor she was seeing, she cried, "O God! O God!"

in a screaming, raucous voice, fell on the sofa with outspread arms in a gesture of complete renunciation, and gave no further sign of life. "You, Gregor!" cried the sister, raising her fist and piercing Gregor with a look. It was the first word she had addressed to him directly ever since his metamorphosis. Then she ran to get some smelling salts from the dining room to rouse her mother from her swoon. Gregor decided to help — there was still time to save the picture — alas, he found he had stuck fast to the glass and had to make a violent effort to detach himself; then he hurried into the dining room as if able to give his sister some good advice, but he was obliged to content himself with remaining passively behind her while she rummaged among the bottles, and he frightened her so terribly when she turned around that a bottle fell and broke on the floor, a splinter wounded Gregor in the face, and a corrosive medicine flowed round his feet; then Grete hastily grabbed up all the bottles she could carry and rushed in to her mother, slamming the door behind her with her foot. Now Gregor was shut out from his mother, who perhaps was nearly dead through his fault; he dared not open the door lest he drive away his sister, who must stay by his mother; so there was nothing to do but wait, and, gnawed by remorse and distress, he began to wander over the walls, the furniture, and the ceilings so rapidly that everything began to spin around him, till in despair he fell heavily on to the middle of the huge table.

A moment passed; Gregor lay stretched there; around all was still; perhaps that was a good sign. But suddenly he heard a knock. The maid was naturally barricaded in her kitchen; Grete herself must go to the door. His father had returned.

"What has happened?" were his first words; no doubt Grete's expression had explained everything.

The girl replied in a stifled voice — probably she leaned her face against her father's breast — "Mother fainted, but she is better now. Gregor has got out."

"I was waiting for that," said the father, "I told you all along, but you women will never listen."

Gregor realized by these words that his father had misunderstood Grete's brief explanation and imagined that his son had broken loose in some reprehensible way. There was no time to explain. Gregor had to find some way of pacifying his father, so he quickly crawled to the door of his room and pressed himself against it for his father to see, as he came in, how he had every intention of returning to his own room immediately and that it was not at all necessary to drive him back with violence; one had only to open the door and he would quickly withdraw.

But his father was in no mood to notice these fine points. As he entered he cried, "Ah!" in a tone at once of joy and anger; Gregor turned his head away from the door and lifted it toward his father. He was astonished. He had never imagined his father as he stood before him now; it is true that for some time now he had neglected to keep himself acquainted with the events of the house, preferring to devote himself to his new mode of existence, and he had therefore been unaware of a certain change of character in his family. And yet — and yet, was that really his father? Was it really the same man who once had lain wearily in bed when Gregor had been leaving on his journeys, who met him, on his return, in his nightshirt, seated in an armchair out of which he could not even lift himself, throwing his arms high to show how pleased he was? Was this that same old man who, on the rare walks which the family would take together, two or three Sundays a year and on special holidays, would hobble between Gregor and his mother, while they walked slower and slower for him, as he, covered with an old coat, carefully set his stick before him and prudently worked his way forward; and yet, despite their slowness, he would be obliged to stop, whenever he wished to say anything, and call his escort back to him? How upstanding he had become since then!

Now he was wearing a blue uniform with gold buttons, without a single crease, just as you see the employees of banking houses wearing; above the big, stiff collar his double chin spread its powerful folds; under his bristly eyebrows the watchful expression of his black eyes glittered young and purposefully; his white hair, ordinarily untidy, had been carefully brushed till it shone. He threw on to the sofa his cap, ornamented with the gilded monogram of some bank, making it describe the arc of a circle across the room, and, with his hands in his trouser pockets, the long flaps of his coat turned back, he walked toward Gregor with a menacing air. He himself did not know what he was going to do; however, he raised his feet very high, and Gregor, astonished at the enormous size of the soles of his boots, took care to remain still, for he knew that, from the first day of his metamorphosis, his father had held the view that the greatest severity was the only attitude to take up toward Gregor. Then he began to beat a retreat before his father's approach, halting when the other stopped and beginning again at his father's slightest move. In this way they walked several times round the room without any decisive result; it did not even take on the appearance of a pursuit, so slow was their pace.

Gregor was provisionally keeping to the floor; he feared that if his father saw him climbing about the walls or rushing across the ceiling, he might take this maneuver for some refinement of bad behavior. However, he had to admit that he could not go on much longer in this way; in the little time his father needed to take a step, Gregor had to make a whole series of gymnastic movements and, as he had never had good lungs, he now began to pant and wheeze; he tried to recover his breath quickly in order to gather all his strength for a supreme effort, scarcely daring to open his eyes, so stupefied that he could think of no other way to safety than by pursuing his present course; he had already forgotten that the walls were at his disposal, and the carefully carved furniture, all covered with festoons of plush and lace as it was. Suddenly something flew sharply by him, fell to the ground, and rolled away. It was an apple, carelessly thrown; a second one flew by. Paralyzed with terror, Gregor stayed still. It was useless to continue his course, now that his father had decided to bombard him. He had emptied the bowls of fruit on the sideboard, filled his pockets, and now threw apple after apple, without waiting to take aim.

These little red apples rolled about the floor as if electrified, knocking against each other. One lightly-thrown apple struck Gregor's back and fell off without doing any harm, but the next one literally pierced his flesh. He tried to drag himself a little further away, as if a change of position could relieve the shattering agony he suddenly felt, but he seemed to be nailed fast to the spot and stretched his body helplessly, not knowing what to do. With his last, hopeless glance, he saw his door opened suddenly, and, in front of his sister, who was shouting at the top of her voice, his mother came running in, in her petticoat, for his sister had partly undressed her that she might breathe easier in her swoon. And his mother, who ran to the father, losing her skirts one by one, stumbled forward, thrust herself against her husband, embraced him, pressed him to her, and, with her hands clasped at the back of his neck — already Gregor could see no more — begged him to spare Gregor's life.

III

The apple which no one dared draw from Gregor's back remained embedded in his flesh as a palpable memory, and the grave wound which he now had borne for a month seemed to have reminded his father that Gregor, despite his sad and terrible change, remained none the less a member of the family and must not be treated as an enemy;

on the contrary, duty demanded that disgust should be overcome and Gregor be given all possible help.

His wound had made him lose, irremediably, no doubt, much of his agility; now, merely to cross his room required a long, long time, as if he were an aged invalid; his walks across the walls could no longer be considered. But this aggravation of his state was largely compensated for, in his opinion, by the fact that now, every evening, the dining-room door was left open; for two hours he would wait for this. Lying in the darkness of his room, invisible to the diners, he could observe the whole family gathered round the table in the lamplight, and he could, by common consent, listen to all they had to say — it was much better than before.

It must be admitted that they no longer held those lively conversations of which, in former times, he had always thought with such sadness as he crept into his damp bed in some little hotel room. Most of the time, now, they discussed nothing in particular after dinner. The father would soon settle himself to doze in his armchair; the mother and daughter would bid each other be silent; the mother, leaning forward in the light, would sew at some fine needlework for a lingerie shop, and the sister, who had obtained a job as a shop assistant, would study shorthand or French in the hope of improving her position. Now and then the father would wake up and, as if he did not know that he had been asleep, would say to his wife, "How late you are sewing tonight!" and would fall off to sleep again, while the mother and sister would exchange a tired smile.

By some capricious obstinacy, the father always refused to take off his uniform, even at home; his dressing gown hung unused in the wardrobe, and he slept in his armchair in full livery, as if to keep himself always ready to carry out some order; even in his own home he seemed to await his superior's voice. Moreover, the uniform had not been new when it was issued to him, and now each day it became more shabby, despite the care which the two women devoted to it; and Gregor often spent the evening staring dully at this coat, so spotted and stained, whose polished buttons always shone so brightly, and in which the old man slept, uncomfortably but peacefully.

As soon as the clock struck ten, the mother, in a low voice, tried to rouse her husband and to encourage him to go to bed, as it was impossible to get proper sleep in such a position, and he must sleep normally before returning to work at six the next morning. But, with the obstinacy which had characterized him ever since he had obtained his position at the bank, he would stay at the table although he regularly dropped off to sleep, and thus it would become more and more difficult to induce him to change his armchair for the bed. The mother and sister might insist with their little warnings; he stayed there just the same, slowly nodding his head, his eyes shut tight, and would not get up. The mother might shake him by the wrist, might whisper endearments in his ear; the daughter might abandon her work to assist her mother, but all in vain. The old man would merely sink deeper in his chair. At last the two women would have to take him under the arms to make him open his eyes; then he would look at each in turn and say, "What a life! Is this the hard-earned rest of my old days?" and, leaning on the two women, he would rise painfully, as if he were a tremendous weight, and would allow himself to be led to the door by his wife and daughter; then he would wave them off and continue alone, while the mother and sister, the one quickly throwing down her pen, the other her needle, would run after him to help.

Who in the overworked and overtired family had time to attend to Gregor, except for his most pressing needs? The household budget was ever more and more reduced; at last the maid was dismissed. In her place, a gigantic charwoman with bony features and white hair, which stood up all around her head, came, morning and evening, to do the harder work. The rest was done by the mother, over and above her interminable mending and darning. It even happened that they were obliged to sell various family trinkets which formerly had been worn proudly by the mother and sister at ceremonies and festivals, as Gregor discovered one evening when he heard them discussing the price they hoped to get. But their most persistent complaints were about this flat, which was so much larger than they needed and which had now become too expensive for the family purse; they could not leave, they said, for they could not imagine how Gregor could be moved. Alas, Gregor understood that it was not really he who was the chief obstacle to this removal, for he might easily have been transported in a large wooden box pierced with a few air holes. No, what particularly prevented the family from changing their residence was their own despair, the idea that they had been stricken by such a misfortune as had never before occurred in the family or within the circle of their acquaintances.

Of all the deprivations which the world imposes on poor people, not one had been spared them; the father took his day-time meals with the lesser employees of the bank, the mother was killing herself mending the linen of strangers, the sister ran here and there behind her counter at the customers' bidding; but the family had energy for nothing further. It seemed to poor Gregor that his wound reopened whenever his mother and sister, returning from putting the father to bed, would leave their work in disorder and bring their chairs nearer to each other, till they were sitting almost cheek to cheek; then the mother would say, pointing to Gregor's room, "Close the door, Grete," and he would once more be left in darkness, while, outside, the two women mingled their tears or, worse, sat at the table staring with dry eyes.

These days and nights brought Gregor no sleep. From time to time he thought of taking the family affairs in hand, as he once used, the very next time the door was opened; at the end of a long perspective of time he dimly saw in his mind his employer and the manager, the clerks and apprentices, the porter with his narrow ideas, two or three acquaintances from other offices, a provincial barmaid — a fleeting but dear memory — and a cashier in a hat shop, whom he had pursued earnestly but too slowly; they passed through his mind in confusion, mingled with unknown and forgotten faces; but none of them could bring help to him or his family; nothing was to be gained from them. He was pleased to be able to dismiss them from his mind but now he no longer cared what happened to his family; on the contrary, he only felt enraged because they neglected to tidy his room and, though nothing imaginable could excite his appetite, he began making involved plans for a raid on the larder, with a view to taking such food as he had a right to, even if he was not hungry. Nowadays his sister no longer tried to guess what might please him; she made a hasty appearance twice a day, in the morning and in the afternoon, before going to her shop, and pushed a few scraps of food into the room with her foot; in the evening, without even bothering to see whether he had touched his meal or whether he had left it entirely — and this was usually the case — she would sweep up the remains with a whisk of the broom.

As for tidying up the room, which Grete now did in the evenings, it could not have been done in a more hasty manner. Great patches of dirt streaked the wall, little heaps of dust and ordure lay here and there about the floor. At first Gregor would place himself in the filthiest places whenever his sister appeared, so that this might seem a reproach to her. But he could have stayed there for weeks, and still Grete would not have altered her conduct; she saw the dirt as well as he but she had finally decided to take no further trouble. This did not prevent her from taking even more jealous care than ever to insure that no other member of the family should presume on her right to the tidying of the room.

Once the mother undertook to give Gregor's room a great cleaning which required several buckets of water, and this deluge deeply upset poor Gregor, crouched under his sofa in bitter immobility — but the mother's punishment soon came. Hardly had the sister, coming home in the evening, noticed the difference in Gregor's room, than, feeling deeply offended, she ran crying and screaming into the dining room, despite the appeal of her mother, who raised her hands in supplication; the father, who was quietly seated at table, leaped up, astonished but powerless to pacify her. Then he, too, became agitated; shouting, he began to attack the mother, on the one hand, for not leaving the care and cleaning of Gregor's room to the girl and, on the other hand, he forbade his daughter ever again to dare to clean it; the mother tried to draw the old man, quivering with anger as he was, into the bedroom; the daughter, shaken with sobs, was banging on the table with her little fists, while Gregor loudly hissed with rage to think that no one had the decency or consideration to close the door and thus spare him the sight of all this trouble and uproar.

But even if the sister, tired out by her work in the shop, could not bother to look after Gregor as carefully as hitherto, she could still have arranged that he should not be neglected without necessarily calling on the aid of her mother, for there was always the charwoman. This old woman, whose bony frame had helped her out of worse trouble during her long life, could not really be said to feel any disgust with Gregor. Though she was not inquisitive, she had opened his door one day and had stood with her hands folded over her stomach, astonished at the sight of Gregor, who began to trot here and there in his alarm, though she had no thought of chasing him. From that day, morning and evening, the old woman never lost an opportunity of opening the door a little to peer into the room.

At first she would call Gregor to make him come out, crying in a familiar tone, "Come on, you old cockroach!" or, "Hey, look at the old cockroach!" To such invitations Gregor would not respond; instead he remained motionless beneath his sofa as if the door had not been opened. If they had only ordered the charwoman to clean his room out each day instead of allowing her to go on teasing and upsetting him! Early one morning, when heavy rain — perhaps a sign of approaching spring — beat on the roofs, Gregor was so annoyed by the old woman as she began to bait him again that he suddenly turned on her, in a somewhat cumbersome and uncertain manner, it must be admitted, but with every intention of attacking her. She was not at all frightened of him; there was a chair by the door; she took it up and brandished it, opening wide her mouth with the obvious intention of not closing it until she had brought the chair down with a crash on Gregor's back. "Ah, is that all?" she asked, seeing him return to his former position, and she quietly put the chair back in its place.

Nowadays Gregor hardly ate at all. When, by some chance, he passed by his scraps, he would amuse himself by taking a piece of food in his mouth and keeping it there for hours, usually spitting it out in the end. At first he had thought that his loss of appetite was due to the misery into which the state of his room had plunged him; no doubt this was a mistake, for he had soon become reconciled to the squalor of his surroundings. His family had got into the habit of piling into his room whatever could not be accommodated elsewhere, and this meant a great deal, now that one of the rooms had been let to three lodgers. They were very earnest and serious men; all three had thick beards — as Gregor saw one day when he was peering through a crack in the door — and they were fanatically tidy; they insisted on order, not only in their own room, but also, now that they were living here, throughout the whole household, and especially in the kitchen.

They had brought with them all that they needed, and this rendered superfluous a great many things about the house which could neither be sold nor thrown away, and which were now all stacked in Gregor's room, as were the ash bucket and the rubbish bin. Everything that seemed for the moment useless would be dumped in Gregor's room by the charwoman, who was always in a breathless hurry to get through her work; he would just have time to see a hand brandishing some unwanted utensil, and then the door would slam again. Perhaps the old woman intended to return and find the objects she so carelessly relegated here when she needed them and had time to search; or perhaps she meant to throw them all away some day, but in actual fact they stayed in the room, on the very spot where they had first fallen, so that Gregor was obliged to pick his way among the rubbish to make a place for himself — a game for which his taste began to grow, in spite of the appalling misery and fatigue which followed these peregrinations, leaving him paralyzed for hours. As the lodgers sometimes dined at home in the living room, the door of this room would be shut on certain evenings; however, Gregor no longer attached any importance to this; for some while, now, he had ceased to profit by those evenings when the family would open the door and he would remain shrinking in the darkest corner of his room, where the family could not see him.

One day the woman forgot to close the dining-room door, and it was still ajar when the lodgers came in and lit the gas. They sat down at table in the places that previously had been occupied by the father, the mother, and Gregor; each unfolded his napkin and took up his knife and fork. Soon the mother appeared in the doorway with a plate of meat; the sister followed her, carrying a dish of potatoes. When their meal had been set before them, the lodgers leaned over to examine it, and the one who was seated in the middle and who appeared to have some authority over the others, cut a piece of meat as it lay on the dish to ascertain whether it was tender or whether he should send it back to the kitchen. He seemed satisfied, however, and the two women, who had been anxiously watching, gave each other a smile of relief.

The family itself lived in the kitchen. However, the father, before going into the kitchen, always came into the dining room and bowed once with his cap in his hand, then made his way around the table. The boarders rose together and murmured something in their beards. Once they were alone, they began to eat in silence. It seemed curious to Gregor that he could hear the gnashing of their teeth above all the clatter of cutlery; it was as if they wanted to prove to him that one must have real teeth in order to eat properly, and that the best mandibles in the world were but an unsatisfactory substitute. "I am hungry," thought Gregor sadly, "but not for these things. How these lodgers can eat! And in the meantime I might die, for all they care."

He could not remember hearing his sister play since the arrival of the lodgers; but this evening the sound of the violin came from the kitchen. The lodgers had just finished their meal; the middle one had brought a newspaper and had given a page to each of the others; now they all three read, leaning back in their chairs and smoking. The sound of the violin attracted their attention, and they rose and walked on tiptoe toward the hall door, where they halted and remained very close together.

Apparently they had been heard in the kitchen, for the father cried, "Does the violin upset you gentlemen? We'll stop it immediately."

"On the contrary," said the man in the middle. "Would Fräulein Samsa not like to come in and play to us here in the dining room, where it is much nicer and more comfortable?"

"Oh, thank you," said the father, as if he were the violinist.

The gentlemen walked back across the room and waited. Soon the father came in with the music stand, the mother with the sheets of music, and the sister with the violin. The sister calmly prepared to play; her parents, who had never before let their rooms, were exaggeratedly polite to the boarders and were afraid to seem presumptuous by sitting in their own chairs; the father leaned against the door, his right hand thrust between two buttons of his livery coat; but one of the gentlemen offered the mother a chair, in which she finally sat, not daring to move from her corner throughout the performance.

The girl now began to play, while her father and mother, from either side, watched the movement of her hands. Attracted by the music, Gregor had crawled forward a little and had thrust his head into the room. He was no longer astonished that nowadays he had entirely lost that consideration for others, that anxiety to cause no trouble that once had been his pride. Yet never had he more reason to remain hidden, for now, because of the dirt that lay about his room, flying up at the slightest movement, he was always covered with dust and fluff, with ends of cotton and hairs, and with morsels of stale food, which stuck to his back or to his feet and which he trailed after him wherever he went; his apathy had grown too great for him to bother any more about cleaning himself several times a day by lying on his back and rubbing himself on the carpet, as once he used to do. And this filthy state did not prevent him from crawling over the spotless floor without a moment's shame.

So far, no one had noticed him. The family was too absorbed by the music of the violin, and the lodgers, who had first stood with their hands in their pockets, very close of the music stand — which disturbed the sister a great deal as she was obliged to see their image dancing amid the notes — had at last retired toward the window, where they stood speaking together half aloud, with lowered heads, under the anxious gaze of the father, who was watching attentively. It had become only too evident that they had been deceived in their hopes of hearing some beautiful violin piece, or at least some amusing little tune; it seemed that what the girl was playing bored them and that now they only tolerated her out of politeness. By the way in which they puffed the smoke of their cigars, by the energy with which they blew it toward the ceiling through the mouth or the nose, one could guess how fidgety they were becoming. And the sister was playing so nicely. Her face leaning to one side, her glance followed the score carefully and sadly. Gregor crawled forward a little more and put his head as near as possible to the floor to meet her gaze. Could it be that he was only an animal, when music moved him so? It seemed to him to open a way toward that unknown nourishment he so longed for. He resolved to creep up to his sister and to pull at her dress, to make her understand that she must come with him, for no one here would appreciate her music as much as he. He would never let her out of his room — at least, while he lived — for once, his horrible shape would serve him some useful purpose; he would be at all doors at once, repulsing intruders with his raucous breath; but his sister would not be forced to stay there; she must live with him of her own accord; she would sit by him on the sofa, hearing what he had to say; then he would tell her in confidence that he had firmly intended to send her to the Conservatory and had planned to let everyone know last Christmas — was Christmas really past? — without listening to any objections, had his misfortune not overtaken him too soon. His sister, moved by this explanation, would surely burst into tears, and Gregor, climbing up on her shoulder, would kiss her neck; this would be all the easier, for she had worn neither collar nor ribbon ever since she had been working in the shop.

"Herr Samsa," cried the middle lodger, and he pointed at Gregor, who slowly came into the room. The violin was suddenly silenced, the middle lodger turned to his friends, grinning and shaking his head, then once more he stared at Gregor. The father seemed to consider it more urgent to reassure the lodgers than to drive his son from the room, though the lodgers did not seem to be at all upset by the spectacle; in fact, Gregor seemed to amuse them more highly than did the violin. The father hurried forward and, with outstretched arms, tried to drive them into their room, hiding Gregor from them with his body. Now they began to be really upset, but it is not known whether this was on account of the father's action or because they had been living with such a monstrous neighbor as Gregor without being made aware of it. They demanded explanations, waving their arms in the air; and, fidgeting nervously with their beards, they retreated toward their own door. Meanwhile the sister had recovered from the distress that the sudden interruption of her music had caused her; after remaining a moment completely at a loss, with the violin and the bow hanging from her helpless hands, following the score with her eyes as if she were still play-ing, she suddenly came back to life, laid the violin in her mother's lap — the mother sat suffocating in her chair, her lungs working violently — and rushed into the next room, toward which the lodgers were rapidly retreating before Herr Samsa's onslaught. One could see how quickly, under Grete's practised hand, pillows and covers were set in order on the beds. The lodgers had not yet reached the room when their beds were already prepared, and Grete had slipped out. The father seemed so possessed by his strange fury that he had quite forgotten the respect due to lodgers.

He drove them to the door of the room, where the middle lodger suddenly came to a stop, stamping thunderously on the floor. "I wish to inform you," said this man, raising his hand and looking around for the two women, "that in view of the disgusting circumstances which govern this family and this house" — and here he spat quickly on the carpet — "I hereby immediately give up my room. Naturally, you will not get a penny for the time I have been living here; on the contrary, I am considering whether I should not claim compensation from you, damages which should easily be awarded in any court of law; it is a matter about which I shall inquire, believe me." He was silent and stared into space, as if awaiting something. Accordingly, his two friends also spoke up: "We, too, give our notice." Thereupon the gentleman in the middle seized the door handle, and they went inside. The door closed with a crash.

The father stumbled toward his chair, put his trembling hands upon the arms, and let himself drop into it; he looked exactly as if he were settling himself for his customary evening nap, but the way his head drooped heavily from side to side showed that he was thinking of something other than sleep. All this time Gregor had stayed still on the spot where he had surprised the lodgers. He felt completely paralyzed with bewilderment at the checking of his plans — perhaps, also, with weakness due to his prolonged fasting. He feared that the whole household would fall upon him immediately; he foresaw the precise moment when this catastrophe would happen, and now he waited. Even the violin did not frighten him as it fell with a clatter from the trembling fingers of his mother, who until now had held it in her lap.

"My dear parents," said his sister, who beat with her hand on the table by way of introduction. "Things cannot go on like this. Even if you do not realize it, I can see it quite clearly. I will not mention my brother's name when I speak of this monster here; I merely want to say: we must find some means of getting rid of it. We have done all that is humanly possible to care for it, to put up with it; I believe that nobody could reproach us in the least."

"She's a thousand times right," said the father. But the mother who had not yet recovered her breath, coughed helplessly behind her hand, her eyes haggard.

The sister hurried toward her mother and held her forehead. Grete's words seemed to have made up the father's mind, for now he sat up in his armchair and fidgeted with his cap among the dishes on the table, from which the lodgers' meal had not yet been cleared; from time to time he stared at Gregor.

"We must find a way of getting rid of it," repeated the sister, now speaking only to her father, for her mother, shaken by her coughing, could hear nothing. "It will bring you both to the grave. I can see it coming. When people have to work all day, as we must, we cannot bear this eternal torture each time we come home at night. I can stand it no longer." And she wept so bitterly that her tears fell on her mother's face, who wiped them off with a mechanical movement of her hand.

"But what can we do, child?" said the father in a pitiful voice. It was surprising to see how well he understood his daughter.

The sister merely shrugged her shoulders as a sign of the perplexity which, during her tears, had replaced her former assurance.

"If he could only understand us," said the father in a half-questioning tone, but the sister, through her tears, made a violent gesture with her hand as a sign that this was not to be thought of.

"If only he could understand us," repeated the father — and he shut his eyes as he spoke, as if to show that he agreed with the sister that such a thing was quite impossible. "If only he could understand us, perhaps there would be some way of coming to an agreement. But as it is . . ."

"It must go!" cried the sister. "That's the only way out. You must get the idea out of your head that this is Gregor. We have believed that for too long, and that is the cause of all our unhappiness. How could it be Gregor? If it were really he, he would long ago have realized that he could not live with human beings and would have gone off on his own accord. I haven't a brother any longer, but we can go on living and can honor his memory. In his place we have this monster that pursues us and drives away our lodgers: perhaps it wants the whole flat to itself, to drive us out into the streets. Look, father, look!" she suddenly screamed, "it's beginning again!" And in an access of terror, which Gregor could not understand, she let go her mother so suddenly that she bounced in the seat of the armchair; it seemed as if the sister would rather sacrifice her mother than stay near Gregor; she hastily took refuge behind her father, who was very upset by her behavior and now stood up, spreading his arms to protect her.

But Gregor had no thought of frightening anyone, least of all his sister. He had merely started to turn around in order to go back to his room; but it must be realized that this looked very alarming, for his weakness obliged him to assist his difficult turning movement with his head, which he raised and lowered many times, clutching at the carpet with his mandibles. At last he ceased and stared at the family. It seemed they realized his good intentions. They were watching him in mute sadness. The mother lay in her armchair, her outstretched legs pressed tightly together, her eyes nearly closed with fatigue; the father and sister were sitting side by side, and the girl's arm was round her father's neck.

"Now, perhaps, they will let me turn," thought Gregor, and he once more set about his task. He could not repress a sigh of weariness; he was obliged to rest from time to time. However, no one hurried him; they left him entirely alone. When he had completed his turn, he immediately beat a retreat, crawling straight ahead. He was astonished at the distance which separated him from his room; he did not realize that this was due merely to his weak state and that a little before he could have covered the distance without noticing it. His family did not disturb him by a single cry, a single exclamation; but this he did not even notice, so necessary was it to concentrate all his will on getting back to his room. It was only when he had at long last reached his door that he thought of turning his head, not completely, because his neck had become very stiff, but sufficiently to reassure himself that nothing had changed behind him; only his sister was now standing up. His last look was toward his mother, who, by this time, was fast asleep.

Hardly was he in his room before the door was slammed, locked, and double bolted. So sudden was the crash that Gregor's legs gave way. It was his sister who had rushed to the door. She had stood up so as to be ready immediately and at the right moment had run forward so lightly that he had not heard her come; as she turned the key in the lock, she cried to her parents, "At last!"

"What now?" asked Gregor, looking around himself in the darkness. He soon discovered that he could not move. This did not surprise him in the least; it seemed to him much more remarkable that such frail legs had hitherto been able to bear his weight. Now he experienced a feeling of relative comfort. True, his whole body ached, but it seemed that these aches became less and less until finally they disappeared. Even the rotted apple embedded in his back hardly hurt him now; no more did the inflammation of the surrounding parts, covered with fine dust, cause him any further discomfort. He thought of his family in tender solicitude. He realized that he must go, and his opinion on this point was even more firm, if possible, than that of his sister. He lay in this state of peaceful and empty meditation till the clock struck the third morning hour. He saw the landscape grow lighter through the window; then, against his will, his head fell forward and his last feeble breath streamed from his nostrils.

When the charwoman arrived early in the morning — and though she had often been forbidden to do so, she always slammed the door so loudly in her vigor and haste that once she was in the house it was impossible to get any sleep — she did not at first notice anything unusual as she paid her customary morning visit to Gregor. She imagined that he was deliberately lying motionless in order to play the role of an "injured party," as she herself would say — she deemed him capable of such refinements; as she had a long broom in her hand, she tried to tickle him from the doorway. Meeting with little success, she grew angry; she gave him one or two hard pushes, and it was only when his body moved unresistingly before her thrusts that she became curious. She quickly realized what had happened, opened her eyes wide, and whistled in astonishment, but she did not stay in the room; she ran to the bedroom, opened the door, and loudly shouted into the darkness, "Come and look! He's stone dead! He's lying there, absolutely dead as a doornail!"

Herr and Frau Samsa sat up in their bed and tried to calm each other; the old woman had frightened them so much and they did not realize the sense of her message immediately. But now they hastily scrambled out of bed, Herr Samsa on one side, his wife on the other; Herr Samsa put the coverlet over his shoulders, Frau Samsa ran out, clad only in her nightdress; and it was thus that they rushed into Gregor's room. Meanwhile, the dining-room door was opened — Grete had been sleeping there since the arrival of the lodgers — she was fully dressed, as if she had not slept all night, and the pallor of her face seemed to bear witness to her sleeplessness.

"Dead?" said Frau Samsa, staring at the charwoman with a questioning look, though she could see as much for herself without further examination.

"I should say so," said the charwoman, and she pushed Gregor to one side with her broom, to support her statement. Frau Samsa made a movement as if to hold back the broom, but she did not complete her gesture.

"Well," said Herr Samsa, "we can thank God for that!" He crossed himself and signed the three women to do likewise.

Grete, whose eyes had never left the corpse, said, "Look how thin he was! It was such a long time since he had eaten anything. His meals used to come out of the room just as they were taken in." And, indeed, Gregor's body was quite flat and dry; this could be seen more easily now that he was no longer supported on his legs and there was nothing to deceive one's sight.

"Come with us a moment, Grete!" said Frau Samsa with a sad smile, and Grete followed her parents into their bedroom, not without turning often to gaze at the corpse. The charwoman closed the door and opened the French windows. Despite the early hour, the fresh morning air had a certain warmth. It was already the end of March.

The three lodgers came out of their room and gazed around in astonishment for their breakfast; they had been forgotten. "Where is our breakfast?" the middle lodger petulantly demanded of the old woman. But she merely laid her finger to her mouth and signed them, with a mute and urgent gesture, to follow her into Gregor's room. So they entered and stood around Gregor's corpse, with their hands in the pockets of their rather shabby coats, in the middle of the room already bright with sunlight.

Then the bedroom door opened and Herr Samsa appeared in his uniform with his wife on one arm, his daughter on the other. All seemed to have been weeping, and from time to time Grete pressed her face against her father's arm.

"Leave my house immediately!" said Herr Samsa, and he pointed to the door, while the women still clung to his arms.

Somewhat disconcerted, the middle lodger said with a timid smile, "Whatever do you mean?"

The two others clasped their hands behind their backs and kept on rubbing their palms together, as if they were expecting some great dispute which could only end in triumph for them.

"I mean exactly what I say!" answered Herr Samsa and, in line with the two women, he marched straight at the lodger. The latter, however, stood quietly in his place, his eyes fixed on the floor, as if reconsidering what he should do.

"Well, then, we will go," he said at last, raising his eyes to Herr Samsa as if searching, in a sudden access of humility, for some slight approval of his resolution.

Herr Samsa merely nodded several times, opening his eyes very wide.

Thereupon the lodger walked away with big strides and soon reached the anteroom; his two friends, who for some while had ceased wringing their hands, now bounded after him, as if afraid Herr Samsa might reach the door before them and separate them from their leader.   Once they had gained the hall, they took down their hats from the pegs, grabbed their sticks from the umbrella stand, bowed silently, and left the flat.

With a suspicion which, it appears, was quite unjustified, Herr Samsa ran out onto the landing after them with the women and leaned over the balustrade to watch the three men as they slowly, but steadily, descended the interminable stairway, disappearing once as they reached a certain point on each floor, and then, after a few seconds, coming into view again.   As they went farther down the staircase, so the Samsa family's interest diminished, and when they had been met and passed by a butcher's boy who came proudly up the stairs with his basket on his head, Herr Samsa and the women quickly left the landing and went indoors again with an air of relief.

They decided to spend the whole day resting; perhaps they might take a walk in the country; they had earned a respite and needed it urgently.   And so they sat down to the table to write three letters of excuse: Herr Samsa to the manager of the Bank, Frau Samsa to her employer, and Grete to the head of her department at the shop.   The charwoman came in while they were writing and announced that her work was done and that she was going.   The three writers at first merely nodded their heads, without raising their eyes, but, as the old woman did not leave, they eventually laid down their pens and looked crossly at her.

"Well?" asked Herr Samsa.   The charwoman was standing in the doorway, smiling as if she had some very good news to tell them but which she would not impart till she had been begged to.   The little ostrich feather which stood upright on her hat and which had always annoyed Herr Samsa so much ever since the old woman had entered their service, now waved lightly in all directions.

"Well, what is it?" asked Frau Samsa, toward whom the old woman had always shown so much more respect than to the others.

"Well . . ." she replied, and she laughed so much she could hardly speak for some while.   "Well, you needn't worry about getting rid of that thing in there, I have fixed it already."

Frau Samsa and Grete leaned over the table as if to resume their letter-writing; Herr Samsa, noticing that the woman was about to launch forth into a detailed explanation, cut her short with a peremptory gesture of his outstretched hand. Then, prevented from speaking, she suddenly remembered that she was in a great hurry and, crying, "Goodbye, everyone," in a peevish tone, she half turned and was gone in a flash, savagely slamming the door behind her.

"This evening we must sack her," declared Herr Samsa; but neither his wife nor his daughter answered; the old woman had not been able to disturb their newly won tranquillity. They arose, went to the window, and stood there, with their arms around each other; Herr Samsa, turning toward them in his armchair, stared at them for a moment in silence. Then he cried, "Come, come, it's all past history now; you can start paying a little attention to me." The women immediately hurried to him, kissed him, and sat down to finish their letters.

Then they all left the apartment together, a thing they had been unable to do for many months past, and they boarded a tram which would take them some way into the country. There were no other passengers in the compartment, which was warm and bright in the sun. Casually leaning back in their seats, they began to discuss their future. On careful reflection, they decided that things were not nearly so bad as they might have been, for — and this was a point they had not hitherto realized — they had all three found really interesting occupations which looked even more promising in the future. They decided to effect what really should be the greatest improvement as soon as possible. That was to move from the flat they occupied at present. They would take a smaller, cheaper flat, but óne more practical, and especially in a better neighborhood than the present one, which Gregor had chosen. Hearing their daughter speak in more and more lively tones, Herr and Frau Samsa noticed almost together that, during this affair, Grete had blossomed into a fine strapping girl, despite the make-up which made her cheeks look pale. They became calmer; almost unconsciously they exchanged glances; it occurred to both of them that it would soon be time for her to find a husband. And it seemed to them that their daughter's gestures were a confirmation of these new dreams of theirs, an encouragement for their good intentions, when, at the end of the journey, the girl rose before them and stretched her young body.

D. H. Lawrence

THE FOX

1923

THE two girls were usually known by their surnames, Banford and March. They had taken the farm together, intending to work it all by themselves: that is, they were going to rear chickens, make a living by poultry, and add to this by keeping a cow, and raising one or two young beasts. Unfortunately things did not turn out well.

Banford was a small, thin, delicate thing with spectacles. She, however, was the principal investor, for March had little or no money. Banford's father, who was a tradesman in Islington, gave his daughter the start, for her health's sake, and because he loved her, and because it did not look as if she would marry. March was more robust. She had learned carpentry and joinery at the evening classes in Islington. She would be the man about the place. They had, moreover, Banford's old grandfather living with them at the start. He had been a farmer. But unfortunately the old man died after he had been at Bailey Farm for a year. Then the two girls were left alone.

They were neither of them young: that is, they were near thirty. But they certainly were not old. They set out quite gallantly with their enterprise. They had numbers of chickens, black Leghorns and white Leghorns, Plymouths and Wyandots; also some ducks; also two heifers in the fields. One heifer, unfortunately, refused absolutely to stay in the Bailey Farm closes. No matter how March made up the fences, the heifer was out, wild in the woods, or trespassing on the neighbouring pasture, and March and Banford were away, flying after her, with more haste than success. So this heifer they sold in despair. And just before the other beast was expecting her first calf, the old man died, and the girls, afraid of the coming event, sold her in a panic, and limited their attentions to fowls and ducks.

In spite of a little chagrin, it was a relief to have no more cattle on hand. Life was not made merely to be slaved away. Both girls agreed in this. The fowls were quite enough trouble. March had set up her carpenter's bench at the end of the open shed. Here she worked, making coops and doors and other appurtenances. The fowls were housed in the bigger building, which had served as barn and cowshed in old days. They had a beautiful home, and should have been perfectly content. Indeed, they looked well enough. But the girls were disgusted at their tendency to strange illnesses, at their exacting way of life, and at their refusal, obstinate refusal, to lay eggs.

March did most of the outdoor work. When she was out and about, in her puttees and breeches, her belted coat and her loose cap, she looked almost like some graceful, loose-balanced young man, for her shoulders were straight, and her movements easy and confident, even tinged with a little indifference, or irony. But her face was not a man's face, ever. The wisps of her crisp dark hair blew about her as she stooped, her eyes were big and wide and dark, when she looked up again, strange, startled, shy and sardonic at once. Her mouth, too, was almost pinched as if in pain and irony. There was something odd and unexplained about her. She would stand balanced on one hip, looking at the fowls pottering about in the obnoxious fine mud of the sloping yard, and calling to her favourite white hen, which came in answer to her name. But there was an almost satirical flicker in March's big, dark eyes as she looked at her three-toed flock pottering about under her gaze, and the same slight dangerous satire in her voice as she spoke to the favoured Patty, who pecked at March's boot by way of friendly demonstration.

Fowls did not flourish at Bailey Farm, in spite of all that March did for them. When she provided hot food for them, in the morning, according to rule, she noticed that it made them heavy and dozy for hours. She expected to see them lean against the pillars of the shed in their languid processes of digestion. And she knew quite well that they ought to be busily scratching and foraging about, if they were to come to any good. So she decided to give them their hot food at night, and let them sleep on it. Which she did. But it made no difference.

War conditions, again, were very unfavourable to poultry keeping. Food was scarce and bad. And when the Daylight Saving Bill was passed, the fowls obstinately refused to go to bed as usual, about nine o'clock in the summer time. That was late enough, indeed, for there was no peace till they were shut up and asleep. Now they cheerfully walked around, without so much as glancing at the barn, until ten o'clock or later. Both Banford and March disbelieved in living for work alone. They wanted to read or take a cycle-ride in the evening, or perhaps March wished to paint curvilinear swans on porcelain, with green background, or else make a marvellous fire-screen by processes of elaborate cabinet work. For she was a creature of odd whims and unsatisfied tendencies. But from all these things she was prevented by the stupid fowls.

One evil there was greater than any other. Bailey Farm was a little homestead, with ancient wooden barn and low gabled farm-house, lying just one field removed from the edge of the wood. Since the War the fox was a demon. He carried off the hens under the very noses of March and Banford. Banford would start and stare through her big spectacles with all her eyes, as another squawk and flutter took place at her heels. Too late! Another white Leghorn gone. It was disheartening.

They did what they could to remedy it. When it became permitted to shoot foxes, they stood sentinel with their guns, the two of them, at the favoured hours. But it was no good. The fox was too quick for them. So another year passed, and another, and they were living on their losses, as Banford said. They let their farm-house one summer, and retired to live in a railway-carriage that was deposited as a sort of out-house in a corner of the field. This amused them, and helped their finances. None the less, things looked dark.

Although they were usually the best of friends, because Banford, though nervous and delicate, was a warm, generous soul, and March, though so odd and absent in herself, had a strange magnanimity, yet, in the long solitude, they were apt to become a little irritable with one another, tired of one another. March had four-fifths of the work to do, and though she did not mind, there seemed no relief, and it made her eyes flash curiously sometimes. Then Banford, feeling more nerve-worn than ever, would become despondent, and March would speak sharply to her. They seemed to be losing ground, somehow, losing hope as the months went by. There alone in the fields by the wood, with the wide country stretching hollow and dim to the round hills of the White Horse, in the far distance, they seemed to have to live too much off themselves. There was nothing to keep them up — and no hope.

The fox really exasperated them both. As soon as they had let the fowls out, in the early summer mornings, they had to take their guns and keep guard: and then again, as soon as evening began to mellow, they must go once more. And he was so sly. He slid along in the deep grass, he was difficult as a serpent to see. And he seemed to circumvent the girls deliberately. Once or twice March had caught sight of the white tip of his brush, or the ruddy shadow of him in the deep grass, and she had let fire at him. But he made no account of this.

One evening March was standing with her back to the sunset, her gun under her arm, her hair pushed under her cap. She was half watching, half musing. It was her constant state. Her eyes were keen and observant, but her inner mind took no notice of what she saw. She was always lapsing into this odd, rapt state, her mouth rather screwed up. It was a question, whether she was there, actually consciously present, or not.

The trees on the wood-edge were a darkish, brownish green in the full light — for it was the end of August. Beyond, the naked, copper-like shafts and limbs of the pine-trees shone in the air. Nearer, the rough grass, with its long brownish stalks all agleam, was full of light. The fowls were round about — the ducks were still swimming on the pond under the pine-trees. March looked at it all, saw it all, and did not see it. She heard Banford speaking to the fowls, in the distance — and she did not hear. What was she thinking about? Heaven knows. Her consciousness was, as it were, held back.

She lowered her eyes, and suddenly saw the fox. He was looking up at her. His chin was pressed down, and his eyes were looking up. They met her eyes. And he knew her. She was spell-bound — she knew he knew her. So he looked into her eyes, and her soul failed her. He knew her, he was not daunted.

She struggled, confusedly she came to herself, and saw him making off, with slow leaps over some fallen boughs, slow, impudent jumps. Then he glanced over his shoulder, and ran smoothly away. She saw his brush held smooth like a feather, she saw his white buttocks twinkle. And he was gone, softly, soft as the wind.

She put her gun to her shoulder, but even then pursed her mouth, knowing it was nonsense to pretend to fire. So she began to walk slowly after him, in the direction he had gone, slowly, pertinaciously. She expected to find him. In her heart she was determined to find him. What she would do when she saw him again she did not consider. But she was determined to find him. So she walked abstractedly about on the edge of the wood, with wide, vivid dark eyes, and a faint flush in her cheeks. She did not think. In strange mindlessness she walked hither and thither.

At last she became aware that Banford was calling her. She made an effort of attention, turned, and gave some sort of screaming call in answer. Then again she was striding off towards the homestead. The red sun was setting, the fowls were retiring towards their roost. She watched them, white creatures, black creatures, gathering to the barn.

She watched them spell-bound, without seeing them. But her automatic intelligence told her when it was time to shut the door.

She went indoors to supper, which Banford had set on the table. Banford chatted easily. March seemed to listen, in her distant, manly way. She answered a brief word now and then. But all the time she was as if spell-bound. And as soon as supper was over, she rose again to go out, without saying why.

She took her gun again and went to look for the fox. For he had lifted his eyes upon her, and his knowing look seemed to have entered her brain. She did not so much think of him: she was possessed by him. She saw his dark, shrewd, unabashed eye looking into her, knowing her. She felt him invisibly master her spirit. She knew the way he lowered his chin as he looked up, she knew his muzzle, the golden brown, and the greyish white. And again, she saw him glance over his shoulder at her, half-inviting, half-contemptuous and cunning. So she went, with her great startled eyes glowing, her gun under her arm, along the wood-edge. Meanwhile the night fell, and a great moon rose above the pine-trees. And again Banford was calling.

So she went indoors. She was silent and busy. She examined her gun, and cleaned it, musing abstractedly by the lamp-light. Then she went out again, under the great moon, to see if everything was right. When she saw the dark crests of the pine-trees against the blood-red sky, again her heart beat to the fox, the fox. She wanted to follow him, with her gun.

It was some days before she mentioned the affair to Banford. Then suddenly, one evening, she said:

"The fox was right at my feet on Saturday night."

"Where?" said Banford, her eyes opening behind her spectacles.

"When I stood just above the pond."

"Did you fire?" cried Banford.

"No, I didn't."

"Why not?"

"Why, I was too much surprised, I suppose."

It was the same old, slow, laconic way of speech March always had. Banford stared at her friend for a few moments.

"You saw him?" she cried.

"Oh, yes! He was looking up at me, cool as anything."

"I tell you," cried Banford — "the cheek! — They're not afraid of us, Nellie."

"Oh, no," said March.

"Pity you didn't get a shot at him," said Banford.

"Isn't it a pity! I've been looking for him ever since. But I don't suppose he'll come so near again."

"I don't suppose he will," said Banford.

And she proceeded to forget about it, except that she was more indignant than ever at the impudence of the beggars. March also was not conscious that she thought of the fox. But whenever she fell into her half-musing, when she was half-rapt, and half-intelligently aware of what passed under her vision, then it was the fox which somehow dominated her unconsciousness, possessed the blank half of her musing. And so it was for weeks, and months. No matter whether she had been climbing the trees for the apples, or beating down the last of the damsons, or whether she had been digging out the ditch from the duck-pond, or clearing out the barn, when she had finished, or when she straightened herself, and pushed the wisps of hair away again from her forehead, and pursed up her mouth again in an odd, screwed fashion, much too old for her years, there was sure to come over her mind the old spell of the fox, as it came when he was looking at her. It was as if she could smell him at these times. And it always recurred, at unexpected moments, just as she was going to sleep at night, or just as she was pouring the water into the tea-pot, to make tea — it was the fox, it came over her like a spell.

So the months passed. She still looked for him unconsciously when she went towards the wood. He had become a settled effect in her spirit, a state permanently established, not continuous, but always recurring. She did not know what she felt or thought: only the state came over her, as when he looked at her.

The months passed, the dark evenings came, heavy, dark November, when March went about in high boots, ankle deep in mud, when the night began to fall at four o'clock, and the day never properly dawned. Both girls dreaded these times. They dreaded the almost continuous darkness that enveloped them on their desolate little farm near the wood. Banford was physically afraid. She was afraid of tramps, afraid lest someone should come prowling round. March was not so much afraid, as uncomfortable, and disturbed. She felt discomfort and gloom in all her physique.

Usually the two girls had tea in the sitting room. March lighted a fire at dusk, and put on the wood she had chopped and sawed during the day. Then the long evening was in front, dark, sodden, black outside, lonely and rather oppressive inside, a little dismal. March was content not to talk, but Banford could not keep still. Merely listening to the wind in the pines outside, or the drip of water, was too much for her.

One evening the girls had washed up the tea-things in the kitchen, and March had put on her house-shoes, and taken up a roll of crochet-work, which she worked at slowly from time to time. So she lapsed into silence. Banford stared at the red fire, which, being of wood, needed constant attention. She was afraid to begin to read too early, because her eyes would not bear any strain. So she sat staring at the fire, listening to the distant sounds, sound of cattle lowing, of a dull, heavy moist wind, of the rattle of the evening train on the little rail-way not far off. She was almost fascinated by the red glow of the fire.

Suddenly both girls started, and lifted their heads. They heard a footstep -- distinctly a footstep. Banford recoiled in fear. March stood listening. Then rapidly she approached the door that led into the kitchen. At the same time they heard the footsteps approach the back door. They waited a second. The back door opened softly. Banford gave a loud cry. A man's voice said softly:

"Hello!"

March recoiled, and took a gun from a corner.

"What do you want?" she cried, in a sharp voice.

Again the soft, softly-vibrating man's voice said:

"Hello! What's wrong?"

"I shall shoot!" cried March. "What do you want?"

"Why, what's wrong? What's wrong?" came the soft, wondering, rather scared voice: and a young soldier, with his heavy kit on his back, advanced into the dim light. "Why," he said, "who lives here then?"

"We live here," said March. "What do you want?"

"Oh!" came the long, melodious, wonder-note from the young soldier. "Doesn't William Grenfel live here then?"

"No — you know he doesn't."

"Do I? — Do I? I don't, you see. — He *did* live here, because he was my grandfather, and I lived here myself five years ago. What's become of him then?"

The young man — or youth, for he would not be more than twenty, now advanced and stood in the inner doorway. March, already under the influence of his strange, soft, modulated voice, stared at him spell-bound. He had a ruddy, roundish face, with fairish hair, rather long, flattened to his forehead with sweat. His eyes were blue, and very bright and sharp. On his cheeks, on the fresh ruddy skin were fine, fair hairs, like a down, but sharper. It gave him a slightly glistening look. Having his heavy sack on his shoulders, he stooped, thrusting his head forward. His hat was loose in one hand. He stared brightly, very keenly from girl to girl, particularly at March, who stood pale, with great dilated eyes, in her belted coat and puttees, her hair knotted in a big crisp knot behind. She still had the gun in her hand. Behind her, Banford, clinging to the sofa-arm, was shrinking away, with half-averted head.

"I thought my grandfather still lived here? — I wonder if he's dead."

"We've been here for three years," said Banford, who was beginning to recover her wits, seeing something boyish in the round head with its rather long sweaty hair.

"Three years! You don't say so! — And you don't know who was here before you?"

"I know it was an old man, who lived by himself."

"Ay! Yes, that's him! — And what became of him then?"

"He died. — I know he died —"

"Ay! He's dead then!"

The youth stared at them without changing colour or expression. If he had any expression, besides a slight baffled look of wonder, it was one of sharp curiosity concerning the two girls; sharp impersonal curiosity, the curiosity of that round young head.

But to March he was the fox. Whether it was the thrusting forward of his head, or the glisten of fine whitish hairs on the ruddy cheek-bones, or the bright, keen eyes, that can never be said: but the boy was to her the fox, and she could not see him otherwise.

"How is it you didn't know if your grandfather was alive or dead?" asked Banford, recovering her natural sharpness.

"Ay, that's it," replied the softly-breathing youth. "You see I joined up in Canada, and I hadn't heard for three or four years. — I ran away to Canada."

"And now have you just come from France?"

"Well — from Salonika really."

There was a pause, nobody knowing quite what to say.

"So you've nowhere to go now?" said Banford rather lamely.

"Oh, I know some people in the village. Anyhow, I can go to the Swan."

"You came on the train, I suppose. — Would you like to sit down a bit?"

"Well — I don't mind."

He gave an odd little groan as he swung off his kit. Banford looked at March.

"Put the gun down," she said. "We'll make a cup of tea."

"Ay," said the youth. "We've seen enough of rifles."

He sat down rather tired on the sofa, leaning forward.

March recovered her presence of mind, and went into the kitchen. There she heard the soft young voice musing:

"Well, to think I should come back and find it like this!" He did not seem sad, not at all — only rather interestedly surprised.

"And what a difference in the place, eh?" he continued, looking round the room.

"You see a difference, do you?" said Banford.

"Yes, — don't I!"

His eyes were unnaturally clear and bright, though it was the brightness of abundant health.

March was busy in the kitchen preparing another meal. It was about seven o'clock. All the time, while she was active, she was attending to the youth in the sitting-room, not so much listening to what he said, as feeling the soft run of his voice. She primmed up her mouth tighter and tighter, puckering it as if it was sewed, in her effort to keep her will uppermost. Yet her large eyes dilated and glowed in spite of her, she lost herself. Rapidly and carelessly she prepared the meal, cutting large chunks of bread and margarine — for there was no butter. She racked her brain to think of something else to put on the tray — she had only bread, margarine, and jam, and the larder was bare. Unable to conjure anything up, she went into the sitting-room with her tray.

She did not want to be noticed. Above all, she did not want him to look at her. But when she came in, and was busy setting the table just behind him, he pulled himself up from his sprawling, and turned and looked over his shoulder. She became pale and wan.

The youth watched her as she bent over the table, looked at her slim, well-shapen legs, at the belted coat dropping around her thighs, at the knot of dark hair, and his curiosity, vivid and widely alert, was again arrested by her.

The lamp was shaded with a dark-green shade, so that the light was thrown downwards, the upper half of the room was dim. His face moved bright under the light, but March loomed shadowy in the distance.

She turned round, but kept her eyes sideways, dropping and lifting her dark lashes. Her mouth unpuckered, as she said to Banford:

"Will you pour out?"

Then she went into the kitchen again.

"Have your tea where you are, will you?" said Banford to the youth — "unless you'd rather come to the table."

"Well," said he, "I'm nice and comfortable here, aren't I? I will have it here, if you don't mind."

"There's nothing but bread and jam," she said. And she put his plate on a stool by him. She was very happy now, waiting on him. For she loved company. And now she was no more afraid of him than if he were her own younger brother. He was such a boy.

"Nellie," she cried. "I've poured you a cup out."

March appeared in the doorway, took her cup, and sat down in a corner, as far from the light as possible. She was very sensitive in her knees. Having no skirts to cover them, and being forced to sit with them boldly exposed, she suffered. She shrank and shrank, trying not to be seen. And the youth, sprawling low on the couch, glanced up at her, with long, steady, penetrating looks, till she was almost ready to disappear. Yet she held her cup balanced, she drank her tea, screwed up her mouth and held her head averted. Her desire to be invisible was so strong that it quite baffled the youth. He felt he could not see her distinctly. She seemed like a shadow within the shadow. And ever his eyes came back to her, searching, unremitting, with unconscious fixed attention.

Meanwhile he was talking softly and smoothly to Banford, who loved nothing so much as gossip, and who was full of perky interest, like a bird. Also he ate largely and quickly and voraciously, so that March had to cut more chunks of bread and margarine, for the roughness of which Banford apologized.

"Oh, well," said March, suddenly speaking, "if there's no butter to put on it, it's no good trying to make dainty pieces."

Again the youth watched her, and he laughed, with a sudden, quick laugh, showing his teeth and wrinkling his nose.

"It isn't, is it?" he answered, in his soft, near voice.

It appeared he was Cornish by birth and upbringing. When he was twelve years old he had come to Bailey Farm with his grandfather, with whom he had never agreed very well. So he had run away to Canada, and worked far away in the West. Now he was here — and that was the end of it.

He was very curious about the girls, to find out exactly what they were doing. His questions were those of a farm youth; acute, practical, a little mocking. He was very much amused by their attitude to their losses: for they were amusing on the score of heifers and fowls.

"Oh, well," broke in March, "we don't believe in living for nothing but work."

"Don't you?" he answered. And again the quick young laugh came over his face. He kept his eyes steadily on the obscure woman in the corner.

"But what will you do when you've used up all your capital?" he said.

"Oh, I don't know," answered March laconically. "Hire ourselves out for landworkers, I suppose."

"Yes, but there won't be any demand for women landworkers, now the war's over," said the youth.

"Oh, we'll see. We shall hold on a bit longer yet," said March, with a plangent, half-sad, half-ironical indifference.

"There wants a man about the place," said the youth softly. Banford burst out laughing.

"Take care what you say," she interrupted. "We consider ourselves quite efficient."

"Oh," came March's slow, plangent voice, "it isn't a case of efficiency, I'm afraid. If you're going to do farming you must be at it from morning till night, and you might as well be a beast yourself."

"Yes, that's it," said the youth. "You aren't willing to put yourselves into it."

"We aren't," said March, "and we know it."

"We want some of our time for ourselves," said Banford.

The youth threw himself back on the sofa, his face tight with laughter, and laughed silently but thoroughly. The calm scorn of the girls tickled him tremendously.

"Yes," he said, "but why did you begin then?"

"Oh," said March, "we had a better opinion of the nature of fowls then, than we have now."

"Of Nature altogether, I'm afraid," said Banford. "Don't talk to me about Nature."

Again the face of the youth tightened with delighted laughter.

"You haven't a very high opinion of fowls and cattle, have you?" he said.

"Oh, no — quite a low one," said March.

He laughed out.

"Neither fowls nor heifers," said Banford, "nor goats nor the weather."

The youth broke into a sharp yap of laughter, delighted. The girls began to laugh too, March turning aside her face and wrinkling her mouth in amusement.

"Oh, well," said Banford, "we don't mind, do we, Nellie?"

"No," said March, "we don't mind."

The youth was very pleased. He had eaten and drunk his fill. Banford began to question him. His name was Henry Grenfel — no, he was not called Harry, always Henry. He continued to answer with courteous simplicity, grave and charming. March, who was not included, cast long, slow glances at him from her recess, as he sat there on the sofa, his hands clasping his knees, his face under the lamp bright and alert, turned to Banford. She became almost peaceful, at last He was identified with the fox — and he was here in full presence She need not go after him any more. There in the shadow of her corner she gave herself up to a warm, relaxed peace, almost like sleep, accepting the spell that was on her. But she wished to remain hidden. She was only fully at peace whilst he forgot her, talking with Banford. Hidden in the shadow of the corner, she need not any more be divided in herself, trying to keep up two planes of consciousness. She could at last lapse into the odour of the fox.

For the youth, sitting before the fire in his uniform, sent a faint but distinct odour into the room, indefinable, but something like a wild creature. March no longer tried to reserve herself from it. She was still and soft in her corner like a passive creature in its cave.

At last the talk dwindled. The youth relaxed his clasp of his knees, pulled himself together a little, and looked round. Again he became aware of the silent, half-invisible woman in the corner.

"Well," he said, unwillingly, "I suppose I'd better be going, or they'll be in bed at the Swan."

"I'm afraid they're in bed anyhow," said Banford. "They've all got this influenza."

"Have they!" he exclaimed. And he pondered. "Well," he continued, "I shall find a place somewhere."

"I'd say you could stay here, only —" Banford began.

He turned and watched her, holding his head forward.

"What —?" he asked.

"Oh, well," she said, "propriety, I suppose —" She was rather confused.

"It wouldn't be improper, would it?" he said, gently surprised.

"Not as far as we're concerned," said Banford.

"And not as far as *I'm* concerned," he said, with grave naïveté. "After all, it's my own home, in a way."

Banford smiled at this.

"It's what the village will have to say," she said.

There was a moment's blank pause.

"What do you say, Nellie?" asked Banford.

"I don't mind," said March, in her distinct tone. "The village doesn't matter to me, anyhow."

"No," said the youth, quick and soft. "Why should it? — I mean, what should they say?"

"Oh, well," came March's plangent, laconic voice, "they'll easily find something to say. But it makes no difference, what they say. We can look after ourselves."

"Of course you can," said the youth.

"Well then, stop if you like," said Banford. "The spare room is quite ready."

His face shone with pleasure.

"If you're quite sure it isn't troubling you too much," he said, with that soft courtesy which distinguished him.

"Oh, it's no trouble," they both said.

He looked, smiling with delight, from one to another.

"It's awfully nice not to have to turn out again, isn't it?" he said gratefully.

"I suppose it is," said Banford.

March disappeared to attend to the room. Banford was as pleased and thoughtful as if she had her own young brother home from France. It gave her just the same kind of gratification to attend on him, to get out the bath for him, and everything. Her natural warmth and kindliness had now an outlet. And the youth luxuriated in her sisterly attention. But it puzzled him slightly to know that March was silently working for him too. She was so curiously silent and obliterated. It seemed to him he had not really seen her. He felt he should not know her if he met her in the road.

That night March dreamed vividly. She dreamed she heard a singing outside, which she could not understand, a singing that roamed round the house, in the fields and in the darkness. It moved her so, that she felt she must weep. She went out, and suddenly she knew it was the fox singing. He was very yellow and bright, like corn. She went nearer to him, but he ran away and ceased singing. He seemed near, and she wanted to touch him. She stretched out her hand, but suddenly he bit her wrist, and at the same instant, as she drew back, the fox, turning round to bound away, whisked his brush across her face, and it seemed his brush was on fire, for it seared and burned her mouth with a great pain. She awoke with the pain of it, and lay trembling as if she were really seared.

In the morning, however, she only remembered it as a distant memory. She arose and was busy preparing the house and attending to the fowls. Banford flew into the village on her bicycle, to try and buy food. She was a hospitable soul. But alas in the year 1918 there was not much food to buy. The youth came downstairs in his shirt-sleeves. He was young and fresh, but he walked with his head thrust forward, so that his shoulders seemed raised and rounded, as if he had a slight curvature of the spine. It must have been only a manner of bearing himself, for he was young and vigorous. He washed himself and went outside, whilst the women were preparing breakfast.

He saw everything, and examined everything. His curiosity was quick and insatiable. He compared the state of things with that which he remembered before, and cast over in his mind the effect of the changes. He watched the fowls and the ducks, to see their condition, he noticed the flight of wood-pigeons overhead: they were very numerous; he saw the few apples high up, which March had not been able to reach; he remarked that they had borrowed a draw-pump, presumably to empty the big soft-water cistern which was on the north side of the house.

"It's a funny, dilapidated old place," he said to the girls, as he sat at breakfast.

His eyes were wise and childish, with thinking about things. He did not say much, but ate largely. March kept her face averted. She, too, in the early morning, could not be aware of him, though something about the glint of his khaki reminded her of the brilliance of her dream-fox.

During the day the girls went about their business. In the morning, he attended to the guns, shot a rabbit and a wild duck that was flying high, towards the wood. That was a great addition to the empty larder. The girls felt that already he had earned his keep. He said nothing about leaving, however. In the afternoon he went to the village. He came back at tea-time. He had the same alert, forward-reaching look on his roundish face. He hung his hat on a peg with a little swinging gesture. He was thinking about something.

"Well," he said to the girls, as he sat at table. "What am I going to do?"

"How do you mean — what are you going to do?" said Banford.

"Where am I going to find a place in the village, to stay?" he said.

"I don't know," said Banford. "Where do you think of staying?"

"Well —" he hesitated — "at the Swan they've got this flu, and at the Plough and Harrow they've got the soldiers who are collecting the hay for the army: besides in the private houses, there's ten men and a corporal altogether billeted in the village, they tell me. I'm not sure where I could get a bed."

He left the matter to them. He was rather calm about it. March sat with her elbows on the table, her two hands supporting her chin, looking at him unconsciously. Suddenly he lifted his clouded blue eyes, and unthinking looked straight into March's eyes. He was startled as well as she. He, too, recoiled a little. March felt the same sly, taunting, knowing spark leap out of his eyes as he turned his head aside, and fall into her soul, as had fallen from the dark eyes of the fox. She pursed her mouth as if in pain, as if asleep too.

"Well, I don't know —" Banford was saying. She seemed reluctant, as if she were afraid of being imposed upon. She looked at March. But, with her weak, troubled sight, she only saw the usual semi-abstraction on her friend's face. "Why don't you speak, Nellie?" she said.

But March was wide-eyed and silent, and the youth, as if fascinated, was watching her without moving his eyes.

"Go on — answer something," said Banford. And March turned her head slightly aside, as if coming to consciousness, or trying to come to consciousness.

"What do you expect me to say?" she asked automatically.

"Say what you think," said Banford.

"It's all the same to me," said March.

And again there was silence. A pointed light seemed to be on the boy's eyes, penetrating like a needle.

"So it is to me," said Banford. "You can stop on here if you like."

A smile like a cunning little flame came over his face, suddenly and involuntarily. He dropped his head quickly to hide it, and remained with his head dropped, his face hidden.

"You can stop on here if you like. You can please yourself, Henry," Banford concluded.

Still he did not reply, but remained with his head dropped. Then he lifted his face. It was bright with a curious light, as if exultant, and his eyes were strangely clear as he watched March. She turned her face aside, her mouth suffering as if wounded, and her consciousness dim.

Banford became a little puzzled. She watched the steady, pellucid gaze of the youth's eyes, as he looked at March, with the invisible smile gleaming on his face. She did not know how he was smiling, for no feature moved. It seemed only in the gleam, almost the glitter of the fine hairs on his cheeks. Then he looked with quite a changed look, at Banford.

"I'm sure," he said in his soft, courteous voice, "you're awfully good. You're too good. You don't want to be bothered with me, I'm sure."

"Cut a bit of bread, Nellie," said Banford uneasily; adding: "It's no bother, if you like to stay. It's like having my own brother here for a few days. He's a boy like you are."

"That's awfully kind of you," the lad repeated. "I should like to stay, ever so much, if you're sure I'm not a trouble to you."

"No, of course you're no trouble. I tell you, it's a pleasure to have somebody in the house besides ourselves," said warm-hearted Banford.

"But Miss March?" he said in his soft voice, looking at her.

"Oh, it's quite all right as far as I'm concerned," said March vaguely.

His face beamed, and he almost rubbed his hands with pleasure.

"Well, then," he said, "I should love it, if you'd let me pay my board and help with the work."

"You've no need to talk about board," said Banford.

One or two days went by, and the youth stayed on at the farm. Banford was quite charmed by him. He was so soft and courteous in speech, not wanting to say much himself, preferring to hear what she had to say, and to laugh in his quick, half-mocking way. He helped readily with the work — but not too much. He loved to be out alone with the gun in his hands, to watch, to see. For his sharp-eyed, impersonal curiosity was insatiable, and he was most free when he was quite alone, half-hidden, watching.

Particularly he watched March. She was a strange character to him. Her figure, like a graceful young man's, piqued him. Her dark eyes made something rise in his soul, with a curious elate excitement, when he looked into them, an excitement he was afraid to let be seen, it was so keen and secret. And then her odd, shrewd speech made him laugh outright. He felt he must go further, he was inevitably impelled. But he put away the thought of her, and went off towards the wood's edge with the gun.

The dusk was falling as he came home, and with the dusk, a fine, late November rain. He saw the fire-light leaping in the window of the sitting-room, a leaping light in the little cluster of the dark buildings. And he thought to himself, it would be a good thing to have this place for his own. And then the thought entered him shrewdly: why not marry March? He stood still in the middle of the field for some moments, the dead rabbit hanging still in his hand, arrested by this thought. His mind waited in amazement — it seemed to calculate . . . . . . then he smiled curiously to himself in acquiescence. Why not? Why not, indeed? It was a good idea. What if it was rather ridiculous? What did it matter? What if she was older than he? It didn't matter. When he thought of her dark, startled, vulnerable eyes he smiled subtly to himself. He was older than she, really. He was master of her.

He scarcely admitted his intention even to himself. He kept it as a secret even from himself. It was all too uncertain as yet. He would have to see how things went. Yes, he would have to see how things went. If he wasn't careful, she would just simply mock at the idea. He knew, sly and subtle as he was, that if he went to her plainly and said: "Miss March, I love you and want you to marry me," her inevitable answer would be: "Get out. I don't want any of that tom-foolery." This was her attitude to men and their "tomfoolery." If he was not careful, she would turn round on him with her savage, sardonic ridicule, and dismiss him from the farm and from her own mind, for ever. He would have to go gently. He would have to catch her as you catch a deer or a woodcock when you go out shooting. It's no good walking out into the forest and saying to the deer: "Please fall to my gun." No, it is a slow, subtle battle. When you really go out to get a deer, you gather yourself together, you coil yourself inside yourself, and you advance secretly, before dawn, into the mountains. It is not so much what you do, when you go out hunting, as how you feel. You have to be subtle and cunning and absolutely fatally ready. It becomes like a fate. Your own fate overtakes and determines the fate of the deer you are hunting. First of all, even before you come in sight of your quarry, there is a strange battle, like mesmerism. Your own soul, as a hunter, has gone out to fasten on the soul of the deer, even before you see any deer. And the soul of the deer fights to escape. Even before the deer has any wind of you, it is so. It is a subtle, profound battle of wills, which takes place in the invisible. And it is a battle never finished till your bullet goes home. When you are *really* worked up to the true pitch, and you come at last into range, you don't then aim as you do when you are firing at a bottle. It is your own *will* which carries the bullet into the heart of your quarry. The bullet's flight home is a sheer projection of your own fate into the fate of the deer. It happens like a supreme wish, a supreme act of volition, not as a dodge of cleverness.

He was a huntsman in spirit, not a farmer, and not a soldier stuck in a regiment. And it was as a young hunter, that he wanted to bring down March as his quarry, to make her his wife. So he gathered himself subtly together, seemed to withdraw into a kind of invisibility. He was not quite sure how he would go on. And March was suspicious as a hare. So he remained in appearance just the nice, odd stranger-youth, staying for a fortnight on the place.

He had been sawing logs for the fire, in the afternoon. Darkness came very early. It was still a cold, raw mist. It was getting almost too dark to see. A pile of short sawed logs lay beside the trestle. March came to carry them indoors, or into the shed, as he was busy sawing the last log. He was working in his shirt-sleeves, and did not notice her approach. She came unwillingly, as if shy. He saw her stooping to the bright-ended logs, and he stopped sawing. A fire like lightning flew down his legs in the nerves.

"March?" he said, in his quiet young voice.

She looked up from the logs she was piling.

"Yes!" she said.

He looked down on her in the dusk. He could see her not too distinctly.

"I wanted to ask you something," he said.

"Did you? What was it?" she said. Already the fright was in her voice. But she was too much mistress of herself.

"Why —" his voice seemed to draw out soft and subtle, it penetrated her nerves — "why, what do you think it is?"

She stood up, placed her hands on her hips, and stood looking at him transfixed, without answering. Again he burned with a sudden power.

"Well," he said and his voice was so soft it seemed rather like a subtle touch, like the merest touch of a cat's paw, a feeling rather than a sound. "Well — I wanted to ask you to marry me."

March felt rather than heard him. She was trying in vain to turn aside her face. A great relaxation seemed to have come over her. She stood silent, her head slightly on one side. He seemed to be bending towards her, invisibly smiling. It seemed to her fine sparks came out of him.

Then very suddenly, she said:

"Don't try any of your tomfoolery on me."

A quiver went over his nerves. He had missed. He waited a moment to collect himself again. Then he said, putting all the strange softness into his voice, as if he were imperceptibly stroking her:

"Why, it's not tomfoolery. It's not tomfoolery. I mean it. I mean it. What makes you disbelieve me?"

He sounded hurt. And his voice had such a curious power over her; making her feel loose and relaxed. She struggled somewhere for her own power. She felt for a moment that she was lost — lost — lost. The word seemed to rock in her as if she were dying. Suddenly again she spoke.

"You don't know what you are talking about," she said, in a brief and transient stroke of scorn. "What nonsense! I'm old enough to be your mother."

"Yes, I do know what I'm talking about. Yes, I do," he persisted softly, as if he were producing his voice in her blood. "I know quite well what I'm talking about. You're not old enough to be my mother. That isn't true. And what does it matter even if it was? You can marry me whatever age we are. What is age to me? And what is age to you! Age is nothing."

A swoon went over her as he concluded. He spoke rapidly — in the rapid Cornish fashion — and his voice seemed to sound in her somewhere where she was helpless against it. "Age is nothing!" The soft, heavy insistence of it made her sway dimly out there in the darkness. She could not answer.

A great exultance leaped like fire over his limbs. He felt he had won.

"I want to marry you, you see. Why shouldn't I?" he proceeded, soft and rapid. He waited for her to answer. In the dusk he saw her almost phosphorescent. Her eyelids were dropped, her face half-averted and unconscious. She seemed to be in his power. But he waited, watchful. He dared not yet touch her.

"Say then," he said. "Say then you'll marry me. Say — say?" He was softly insistent.

"What?" she asked, faint, from a distance, like one in pain. His voice was now unthinkably near and soft. He drew very near to her.

"Say yes."

"Oh, I can't," she wailed helplessly, half articulate, as if semi-conscious, and as if in pain, like one who dies. "How can I?"

"You can," he said softly, laying his hand gently on her shoulder as she stood with her head averted and dropped, dazed. "You can. Yes, you can. What makes you say you can't? You can. You can." And with awful softness he bent forward and just touched her neck with his mouth and his chin.

"Don't!" she cried, with a faint mad cry like hysteria, starting away and facing round on him. "What do you mean?" But she had no breath to speak with. It was as if she were killed.

"I mean what I say," he persisted softly and cruelly. "I want you to marry me. I want you to marry me. You know that, now, don't you? You know that, now? Don't you? Don't you?"

"What?" she said.

"Know," he replied.

"Yes," she said. "I know you say so."

"And you know I mean it, don't you?"

"I know you say so."

"You believe me?" he said.

She was silent for some time. Then she pursed her lips.

"I don't know what I believe," she said.

"Are you out there?" came Banford's voice, calling from the house.

"Yes, we're bringing in the logs," he answered.

"I thought you'd gone lost," said Banford disconsolately. "Hurry up, do, and come and let's have tea. The kettle's boiling."

He stooped at once, to take an armful of little logs and carry them into the kitchen, where they were piled in a corner. March also helped, filling her arms and carrying the logs on her breast as if they were some heavy child. The night had fallen cold.

When the logs were all in, the two cleaned their boots noisily on the scraper outside, then rubbed them on the mat. March shut the door and took off her old felt hat — her farm-girl hat. Her thick, crisp black hair was loose, her face was pale and strained. She pushed back her hair vaguely, and washed her hands. Banford came hurrying into the dimly-lighted kitchen, to take from the oven the scones she was keeping hot.

"Whatever have you been doing all this time?" she asked fretfully. "I thought you were never coming in. And it's ages since you stopped sawing. What were you doing out there?"

"Well," said Henry, "we had to stop that hole in the barn, to keep the rats out."

"Why, I could see you standing there in the shed. I could see your shirt-sleeves," challenged Banford.

"Yes, I was just putting the saw away."

They went in to tea. March was quite mute. Her face was pale and strained and vague. The youth, who always had the same ruddy, self-contained look on his face, as though he were keeping himself to himself, had come to tea in his shirt-sleeves as if he were at home. He bent over his plate as he ate his food.

"Aren't you cold?" said Banford spitefully. "In your shirt-sleeves."

He looked up at her, with his chin near his plate, and his eyes very clear, pellucid, and unwavering as he watched her.

"No, I'm not cold," he said with his usual soft courtesy. "It's much warmer in here than it is outside, you see."

"I hope it is," said Banford, feeling nettled by him. He had a strange suave assurance, and a wide-eyed bright look that got on her nerves this evening.

"But perhaps," he said softly and courteously, "you don't like me coming to tea without my coat. I forgot that."

"Oh, I don't mind," said Banford: although she *did.*

"I'll go and get it, shall I?" he said.

March's dark eyes turned slowly down to him.

"No, don't you bother," she said in her queer, twanging tone. "If you feel all right as you are, stop as you are." She spoke with a crude authority.

"Yes," said he, "I *feel* all right, if I'm not rude."

"It's usually considered rude," said Banford. "But we don't mind."

"Go along, 'considered rude,'" ejaculated March. "Who considers it rude?"

"Why you do, Nellie, in anybody else," said Banford, bridling a little behind her spectacles, and feeling her food stick in her throat.

But March had again gone vague and unheeding, chewing her food as if she did not know she was eating at all. And the youth looked from one to another, with bright, watchful eyes.

Banford was offended. For all his suave courtesy and soft voice, the youth seemed to her impudent. She did not like to look at him. She did not like to meet his clear, watchful eyes, she did not like to see the strange glow in his face, his cheeks with their delicate fine hair, and his ruddy skin that was quite dull and yet which seemed to burn with a curious heat of life. It made her feel a little ill to look at him: the quality of his physical presence was too penetrating, too hot.

After tea the evening was very quiet. The youth rarely went into the village. As a rule he read: he was a great reader, in his own hours. That is, when he did begin, he read absorbedly. But he was not very eager to begin. Often he walked about the fields and along the hedges alone in the dark at night, prowling with a queer instinct for the night, and listening to the wild sounds.

To-night, however, he took a Captain Mayne Reid book from Banford's shelf and sat down with knees wide apart and immersed himself in his story. His brownish fair hair was long, and lay on his head like a thick cap, combed sideways. He was still in his shirt-sleeves, and bending forward under the lamp-light, with his knees stuck wide apart and the book in his hand and his whole figure absorbed in the rather strenuous business of reading, he gave Banford's sitting-room the look of a lumber-camp. She resented this. For on her sitting-room floor she had a red Turkey rug and dark stain round, the fire-place had fashionable green tiles, the piano stood open with the latest dance-music: she played quite well: and on the walls were March's hand-painted swans and water-lilies. Moreover, with the logs nicely, tremulously burning in the grate, the thick curtains drawn, the doors all shut, and the pine-trees hissing and shuddering in the wind outside, it was cosy, it was refined and nice. She resented the big, raw, long-legged youth sticking his khaki knees out and sitting there with his soldier's shirt-cuffs buttoned on his thick red wrists. From time to time he turned a page, and from time to time he gave a sharp look at the fire, settling the logs. Then he immersed himself again in the intense and isolated business of reading.

March, on the far side of the table, was spasmodically crochetting. Her mouth was pursed in an odd way, as when she had dreamed the fox's brush burned it, her beautiful, crisp black hair strayed in wisps. But her whole figure was absorbed in its bearing, as if she herself were miles away. In a sort of semi-dream she seemed to be hearing the fox singing round the house in the wind, singing wildly and sweetly and like a madness. With red but well-shaped hands she slowly crochetted the white cotton, very slowly, awkwardly.

Banford was also trying to read, sitting in her low chair. But between those two she felt fidgety. She kept moving and looking round and listening to the wind and glancing secretly from one to the other of her companions. March, seated on a straight chair, with her knees in their close breeches crossed, and slowly, laboriously crochetting, was also a trial.

"Oh, dear!" said Banford. "My eyes are bad to-night." And she pressed her fingers on her eyes.

The youth looked up at her with his clear bright look, but did not speak.

"Are they, Jill?" said March absently.

Then the youth began to read again, and Banford perforce returned to her book. But she could not keep still. After a while she looked up at March, and a queer, almost malignant little smile was on her thin face.

"A penny for them, Nell," she said suddenly.

March looked round with big, startled black eyes, and went pale as if with terror. She had been listening to the fox singing so tenderly, so tenderly, as he wandered round the house.

"What?" she said vaguely.

"A penny for them," said Banford sarcastically. "Or twopence, if they're as deep as all that."

The youth was watching with bright clear eyes from beneath the lamp.

"Why," came March's vague voice, "what do you want to waste your money for?"

"I thought it would be well spent," said Banford.

"I wasn't thinking of anything except the way the wind was blowing," said March.

"Oh, dear," replied Banford. "I could have had as original thoughts as that myself. I'm afraid I *have* wasted my money this time."

"Well, you needn't pay," said March.

The youth suddenly laughed. Both women looked at him: March rather surprised-looking, as if she had hardly known he was there.

"Why, do you ever pay up on these occasions?" he asked.

"Oh, yes," said Banford. "We always do. I've sometimes had to pass a shilling a week to Nellie, in the winter time. It costs much less in summer."

"What, paying for each other's thoughts?" he laughed.

"Yes, when we've absolutely come to the end of everything else."

He laughed quickly, wrinkling his nose sharply like a puppy and laughing with quick pleasure, his eyes shining.

"It's the first time I ever heard of that," he said.

"I guess you'd hear of it often enough if you stayed a winter on Bailey Farm," said Banford lamentably.

"Do you get so tired, then?" he asked.

"So bored," said Banford.

"Oh!" he said gravely. "But why should you be bored?"

"Who wouldn't be bored?" said Banford.

"I'm sorry to hear that," he said gravely.

"You must be, if you were hoping to have a lively time here," said Banford.

He looked at her long and gravely.

"Well," he said, with his odd young seriousness, "it's quite lively enough for me."

"I'm glad to hear it," said Banford.

And she returned to her book. In her thin, frail hair were already many threads of grey, though she was not yet thirty. The boy did not look down, but turned his eyes to March, who was sitting with pursed mouth laboriously crochetting, her eyes wide and absent. She had a warm, pale, fine skin, and a delicate nose. Her pursed mouth looked shrewish. But the shrewish look was contradicted by the curious lifted arch of her dark brows, and the wideness of her eyes; a look of startled wonder and vagueness. She was listening again for the fox, who seemed to have wandered farther off into the night.

From under the edge of the lamp-light the boy sat with his face looking up, watching her silently, his eyes round and very clear and intent. Banford, biting her fingers irritably, was glancing at him under her hair. He sat there perfectly still, his ruddy face tilted up from the low level under the light, on the edge of the dimness, and watching with perfect abstract intentness. March suddenly lifted her great dark eyes from her crochetting, and saw him. She started, giving a little exclamation.

"There he is!" she cried, involuntarily, as if terribly startled.

Banford looked around in amazement, sitting up straight.

"Whatever has got you, Nellie?" she cried.

But March, her face flushed a delicate rose colour, was looking away to the door.

"Nothing! Nothing!" she said crossly. "Can't one speak?"

"Yes, if you speak sensibly," said Banford. "Whatever did you mean?"

"I don't know what I meant," cried March testily.

"Oh, Nellie, I hope you aren't going jumpy and nervy. I feel I can't stand another *thing!* — Whoever did you mean? Did you mean Henry?" cried poor frightened Banford.

"Yes. I suppose so," said March laconically. She would never confess to the fox.

"Oh, dear, my nerves are all gone for to-night," wailed Banford.

At nine o'clock March brought in a tray with bread and cheese and tea — Henry had confessed that he liked a cup of tea. Banford drank a glass of milk, and ate a little bread. And soon she said:

"I'm going to bed, Nellie. I'm all nerves to-night. Are you coming?"

"Yes, I'm coming the minute I've taken the tray away," said March.

"Don't be long then," said Banford fretfully. "Good-night, Henry. You'll see the fire is safe, if you come up last, won't you?"

"Yes, Miss Banford, I'll see it's safe," he replied in his reassuring way.

March was lighting the candle to go to the kitchen. Banford took her candle and went upstairs. When March came back to the fire she said to him:

"I suppose we can trust you to put out the fire and everything?" She stood there with her hand on her hip, and one knee loose, her head averted shyly, as if she could not look at him. He had his face lifted, watching her.

"Come and sit down a minute," he said softly.

"No, I'll be going. Jill will be waiting, and she'll get upset if I don't come."

"What made you jump like that this evening?" he asked.

"When did I jump?" she retorted, looking at him.

"Why, just now you did," he said. "When you cried out."

"Oh!" she said. "Then! — Why, I thought you were the fox!" And her face screwed into a queer smile, half ironic.

"The fox! Why the fox?" he asked softly.

"Why, one evening last summer when I was out with the gun I saw the fox in the grass nearly at my feet, looking straight up at me. I don't know — I suppose he made an impression on me." She turned aside her head again, and let one foot stray loose, self-consciously.

"And did you shoot him?" asked the boy.

"No, he gave me such a start, staring straight at me as he did, and then stopping to look back at me over his shoulder with a laugh on his face."

"A laugh on his face!" repeated Henry, also laughing. "He frightened you, did he?"

"No, he didn't frighten me. He made an impression on me, that's all."

"And you thought I was the fox, did you?" he laughed, with the same queer quick little laugh, like a puppy wrinkling its nose.

"Yes, I did, for the moment," she said. "Perhaps he'd been in my mind without my knowing."

"Perhaps you think I've come to steal your chickens or something," he said, with the same young laugh.

But she only looked at him with a wide, dark, vacant eye.

"It's the first time," he said, "that I've ever been taken for a fox. Won't you sit down for a minute?" His voice was very soft and cajoling.

"No," she said. "Jill will be waiting." But still she did not go, but stood with one foot loose and her face turned aside, just outside the circle of light.

"But won't you answer my question?" he said, lowering his voice still more.

"I don't know what question you mean."

"Yes, you do. Of course you do. I mean the question of you marrying me."

"No, I shan't answer that question," she said flatly.

"Won't you?" The queer young laugh came on his nose again. "Is it because I'm like the fox? Is that why?" And still he laughed.

She turned and looked at him with a long, slow look.

"I wouldn't let that put you against me," he said. "Let me turn the lamp low, and come and sit down a minute."

He put his red hand under the glow of the lamp, and suddenly made the light very dim. March stood there in the dimness quite shadowy, but unmoving. He rose silently to his feet, on his long legs. And now his voice was extraordinarily soft and suggestive, hardly audible.

"You'll stay a moment," he said. "Just a moment." And he put his hand on her shoulder. — She turned her face from him. "I'm sure you don't really think I'm like the fox," he said, with the same softness and with a suggestion of laughter in his tone, a subtle mockery. "Do you now?" — And he drew her gently towards him and kissed her neck, softly. She winced and trembled and hung away. But his strong young arm held her, and he kissed her softly again, still on the neck, for her face was averted.

"Won't you answer my question? Won't you now?" came his soft, lingering voice. He was trying to draw her near to kiss her face. And he kissed her cheek softly, near the ear.

At that moment Banford's voice was heard calling fretfully, crossly, from upstairs.

"There's Jill!" cried March, starting and drawing erect.

And as she did so, quick as lightning he kissed her on the mouth, with a quick brushing kiss. It seemed to burn through her every fibre. She gave a queer little cry.

"You will, won't you? You will?" he insisted softly.

"Nellie! *Nellie!* Whatever are you so long for?" came Banford's faint cry from the outer darkness.

But he held her fast, and was murmuring with that intolerable softness and insistency:

"You will, won't you? Say yes! Say yes!"

March, who felt as if the fire had gone through her and scathed her, and as if she could do no more, murmured:

"Yes! Yes! Anything you like! Anything you like! Only let me go! Only let me go! Jill's calling."

"You know you've promised," he said insidiously.

"Yes! Yes! I do! —" Her voice suddenly rose into a shrill cry. "All right, Jill, I'm coming."

Startled, he let her go, and she went straight upstairs.

In the morning at breakfast, after he had looked round the place and attended to the stock and thought to himself that one could live easily enough here, he said to Banford:

"Do you know what, Miss Banford?"

"Well, what?" said the good-natured, nervy Banford.

He looked at March, who was spreading jam on her bread.

"Shall I tell?" he said to her.

She looked up at him, and a deep pink colour flushed over her face.

"Yes, if you mean Jill," she said. "I hope you won't go talking all over the village, that's all." And she swallowed her dry bread with difficulty.

"Whatever's coming?" said Banford, looking up with wide, tired, slightly reddened eyes. She was a thin, frail little thing, and her hair, which was delicate and thin, was bobbed, so it hung softly by her worn face in its faded brown and grey.

"Why, what do you think?" he said, smiling like one who has a secret.

"How do I know!" said Banford.

"Can't you guess?" he said, making bright eyes, and smiling, pleased with himself.

"I'm sure I can't. What's more, I'm not going to try."

"Nellie and I are going to be married."

Banford put down her knife, out of her thin, delicate fingers, as if she would never take it up to eat any more. She stared with blank, reddened eyes.

"You what?" she exclaimed.

"We're going to get married. Aren't we, Nellie?" and he turned to March.

"You say so, anyway," said March laconically. But again she flushed with an agonized flush. She, too, could swallow no more.

Banford looked at her like a bird that has been shot: a poor little sick bird. She gazed at her with all her wounded soul in her face, at the deep-flushed March.

"Never!" she exclaimed, helpless.

"It's quite right," said the bright and gloating youth.

Banford turned aside her face, as if the sight of the food on the table made her sick. She sat like this for some moments, as if she were sick. Then, with one hand on the edge of the table, she rose to her feet.

"I'll *never* believe it, Nellie," she cried. "It's absolutely impossible!"

Her plaintive, fretful voice had a thread of hot anger and despair.

"Why? Why shouldn't you believe it?" asked the youth, with all his soft, velvety impertinence in his voice.

Banford looked at him from her wide vague eyes, as if he were some creature in a museum.

"Oh," she said languidly, "because she can never be such a fool. She can't lose her self-respect to such an extent." Her voice was cold and plaintive, drifting.

"In what way will she lose her self-respect?" asked the boy.

Banford looked at him with vague fixity from behind her spectacles.

"If she hasn't lost it already," she said.

He became very red, vermilion, under the slow vague stare from behind the spectacles.

"I don't see it at all," he said.

"Probably you don't. I shouldn't expect you would," said Banford, with that straying mild tone of remoteness which made her words even more insulting.

He sat stiff in his chair, staring with hot blue eyes from his scarlet face. An ugly look had come on his brow.

"My word, she doesn't know what she's letting herself in for," said Banford, in her plaintive, drifting, insulting voice.

"What has it got to do with you, anyway?" said the youth in a temper.

"More than it has to do with you, probably," she replied, plaintive and venomous.

"Oh, has it! It don't see that at all," he jerked out.

"No, you wouldn't," she answered, drifting.

"Anyhow," said March, pushing back her chair and rising uncouthly, "it's no good arguing about it." And she seized the bread and the tea-pot, and strode away to the kitchen.

Banford let her fingers stray across her brow and along her hair, like one bemused. Then she turned and went away upstairs.

Henry sat stiff and sulky in his chair, with his face and his eyes on fire. March came and went, clearing the table. But Henry sat on, stiff with temper. He took no notice of her. She had regained her composure and her soft, even, creamy complexion. But her mouth was pursed up. She glanced at him each time as she came to take things from the table, glanced from her large, curious eyes, more in curiosity than anything. Such a long, red-faced sulky boy! That was all he was. He seemed as remote from her as if his red face were a red chimney-pot on a cottage across the fields, and she looked at him just as objectively, as remotely.

At length he got up and stalked out into the fields with the gun. He came in only at dinner-time, with the devil still in his face, but his manners quite polite. Nobody said anything particular: they sat each one at the sharp corner of a triangle, in obstinate remoteness. In the afternoon he went out again at once with the gun. He came in at nightfall with a rabbit and a pigeon. He stayed in all evening, but hardly opened his mouth. He was in the devil of a temper, feeling he had been insulted.

Banford's eyes were red, she had evidently been crying. But her manner was more remote and supercilious than ever, the way she turned her head if he spoke at all, as if he were some tramp or inferior intruder of that sort, made his blue eyes go almost black with rage. His face looked sulkier. But he never forgot his polite intonation, if he opened his mouth to speak.

March seemed to flourish in this atmosphere. She seemed to sit between the two antagonists with a little wicked smile on her face, enjoying herself. There was even a sort of complacency in the way she laboriously crochetted, this evening.

When he was in bed, the youth could hear the two women talking and arguing in their room. He sat up in bed and strained his ears to hear what they said. But he could hear nothing, it was too far off. Yet he could hear the soft, plaintive drip of Banford's voice, and March's deeper note.

The night was quiet, frosty. Big stars were snapping outside, beyond the ridge-tops of the pine-trees. He listened and listened. In the distance he heard a fox yelping: and the dogs from the farms barking in answer. But it was not that he wanted to hear. It was what the two women were saying.

He got stealthily out of bed, and stood by his door. He could hear no more than before. Very, very carefully he began to lift the door-latch. After quite a time he had his door open. Then he stepped stealthily out into the passage. The old oak planks were cold under his feet, and they creaked preposterously. He crept very, very gently up the one step, and along by the wall, till he stood outside their door. And there he held his breath and listened. Banford's voice:

"No, I simply couldn't stand it. I should be dead in a month. Which is just what he would be aiming at, of course. That would just be his game, to see me in the churchyard. No, Nellie, if you were to do such a thing as to marry him, you could never stop here. I couldn't, I couldn't live in the same house with him. Oh-h! I feel quite sick with the smell of his clothes. And his red face simply turns me over. I can't eat my food when he's at the table. What a fool I was ever to let him stop. One ought *never* to try to do a kind action. It always flies back in your face like a boomerang."

"Well, he's only got two more days," said March.

"Yes, thank heaven. And when he's gone he'll never come in this house again. I feel so bad while he's here. And I know, I know he's only counting what he can get out of you. I know that's all it is. He's just a good-for-nothing, who doesn't want to work, and who thinks he'll live on us. But he won't live on me. If you're such a fool, then it's your own lookout. Mrs. Burgess knew him all the time he was here. And the old man could never get him to do any steady work. He was off with the gun on every occasion, just as he is now. Nothing but the gun! Oh, I do hate it. You don't know what you're doing, Nellie, you don't. If you marry him he'll just make a fool of you. He'll go off and leave you stranded. I know he will. If he can't get Bailey Farm out of us — and he's not going to, while I live. While I live he's never going to set foot here. I know what it would be. He'd soon think he was master of both of us, as he thinks he's master of you already."

"But he isn't," said Nellie.

"He thinks he is, anyway. And that's what he wants: to come and be master here. Yes, imagine it! That's what we've got the place together for, is it, to be bossed and bullied by a hateful red-faced boy, a beastly labourer? Oh, we *did* make a mistake when we let him stop. We ought never to have lowered ourselves. And I've had such a fight with all the people here, not to be pulled down to their level. No, he's not coming here. — And then you see. If he can't have the place, he'll run off to Canada or somewhere again, as if he'd never known you. And here you'll be, absolutely ruined and made a fool of. I know I shall never have any peace of mind again."

"We'll tell him he can't come here. We'll tell him that," said March.

"Oh, don't you bother, I'm going to tell him that, and other things as well, before he goes. He's not going to have all his own way, while I've got the strength left to speak. Oh, Nellie, he'll despise you, he'll despise you like the awful little beast he is, if you give way to him. I'd no more trust him than I'd trust a cat not to steal. He's deep, he's deep, and he's bossy, and he's selfish through and through, as cold as ice. All he wants is to make use of you. And when you're no more use to him, then I pity you."

"I don't think he's as bad as all that," said March.

"No, because he's been playing up to you. But you'll find out, if you see much more of him. Oh, Nellie, I can't bear to think of it."

"Well, it won't hurt you, Jill darling."

"Won't it! Won't it! I shall never know a moment's peace again while I live, nor a moment's happiness. No, Nellie —" and Banford began to weep bitterly.

The boy outside could hear the stifled sound of the woman's sobbing, and could hear March's soft, deep, tender voice comforting, with wonderful gentleness and tenderness, the weeping woman.

His eyes were so round and wide that he seemed to see the whole night, and his ears were almost jumping off his head. He was frozen stiff. He crept back to bed, but felt as if the top of his head were coming off. He could not sleep. He could not keep still. He rose, quietly dressed himself, and crept out on to the landing once more. The women were silent. He went softly downstairs and out to the kitchen.

Then he put on his boots and his overcoat, and took the gun. He did not think to go away from the farm. No, he only took the gun. As softly as possible he unfastened the door and went out into the frosty December night. The air was still, the stars bright, the pine-trees seemed to bristle audibly in the sky. He went stealthily away down a fence-side, looking for something to shoot. At the same time he remembered that he ought not to shoot and frighten the women.

So he prowled round the edge of the gorse cover, and through the grove of tall old hollies, to the woodside. There he skirted the fence, peering through the darkness with dilated eyes that seemed to be able to grow black and full of sight in the dark, like a cat's. An owl was slowly and mournfully whooing round a great oak tree. He stepped stealthily with his gun, listening, listening, watching.

As he stood under the oaks of the wood-edge he heard the dogs from the neighbouring cottage, up the hill, yelling suddenly and startlingly, and the wakened dogs from the farms around barking answer. And suddenly, it seemed to him England was little and tight, he felt the landscape was constricted even in the dark, and that there were too many dogs in the night, making a noise like a fence of sound, like the network of English hedges netting the view. He felt the fox didn't have a chance. For it must be the fox that had started all this hulla-baloo.

Why not watch for him, anyhow! He would no doubt be coming sniffing round. The lad walked downhill to where the farmstead with its few pine-trees crouched blackly. In the angle of the long shed, in the black dark, he crouched down. He knew the fox would be coming. It seemed to him it would be the last of the foxes in this loudly-barking, thick-voiced England, tight with innumerable little houses.

He sat a long time with his eyes fixed unchanging upon the open gateway, where a little light seemed to fall from the stars or from the horizon, who knows? He was sitting on a log in a dark corner with the gun across his knees. The pine-trees snapped. Once a chicken fell off its perch in the barn, with a loud crawk and cackle and commotion that startled him, and he stood up, watching with all his eyes, thinking it might be a rat. But he *felt* it was nothing. So he sat down again with the gun on his knees and his hands tucked in to keep them warm, and his eyes fixed unblinking on the pale reach of the open gateway. He felt he could smell the hot, sickly, rich smell of live chickens on the cold air.

And then — a shadow. A sliding shadow in the gate-way. He gathered all his vision into a concentrated spark, and saw the shadow of the fox, the fox creeping on his belly through the gate. There he went, on his belly like a snake. The boy smiled to himself and brought the gun to his shoulder. He knew quite well what would happen. He knew the fox would go to where the fowl-door was boarded up, and sniff there. He knew he would lie there for a minute, sniffing the fowls within. And then he would start again prowling under the edge of the old barn, waiting to get in.

The fowl-door was at the top of a slight incline. Soft, soft as a shadow the fox slid up this incline, and crouched with his nose to the boards. And at the same moment there was the awful crash of a gun reverberating between the old buildings, as if all the night had gone smash. But the boy watched keenly. He saw even the white belly of the fox as the beast beat his paws in death. So he went forward.

There was a commotion everywhere. The fowls were scuffling and crawking, the ducks were quark-quarking, the pony had stamped wildly to his feet. But the fox was on his side, struggling in his last tremors. The boy bent over him and smelt his foxy smell.

There was a sound of a window opening upstairs, then March's voice calling:

"Who is it?"

"It's me," said Henry; "I've shot the fox."

"Oh, goodness! You nearly frightened us to death."

"Did I? I'm awfully sorry."

"Whatever made you get up?"

"I heard him about."

"And have you shot him?"

"Yes, he's here," and the boy stood in the yard holding up the warm, dead brute. "You can't see, can you? Wait a minute." And he took his flash-light from his pocket, and flashed it on to the dead animal. He was holding it by the brush. March saw, in the middle of the darkness, just the reddish fleece and the white belly and the white underneath of the pointed chin, and the queer, dangling paws. She did not know what to say.

"He's a beauty," he said. "He will make you a lovely fur."

"You don't catch me wearing a fox fur," she replied.

"Oh!" he said. And he switched off the light.

"Well, I should think you'd come in and go to bed again now," she said.

"Probably I shall. What time is it?"

"What time is it, Jill?" called March's voice. It was a quarter to one.

That night March had another dream. She dreamed that Banford was dead, and that she, March, was sobbing her heart out. Then she had to put Banford into her coffin. And the coffin was the rough wood-box in which the bits of chopped wood were kept in the kitchen, by the fire. This was the coffin, and there was no other, and March was in agony and dazed bewilderment, looking for something to line the box with, something to make it soft with, something to cover up the poor dead darling. Because she couldn't lay her in there just in her white thin nightdress, in the horrible wood-box. So she hunted and hunted, and picked up thing after thing, and threw it aside in the agony of dream-frustration. And in her dream-despair all she could find that would do was a fox-skin. She knew that it wasn't right, that this was not what she could have. But it was all she could find. And so she folded the brush of the fox, and laid her darling Jill's head on this, and she brought round the skin of the fox and laid it on the top of the body, so that it seemed to make a whole ruddy, fiery coverlet, and she cried and cried and woke to find the tears streaming down her face.

The first thing that both she and Banford did in the morning was to go out to see the fox. He had hung it up by the heels in the shed, with its poor brush falling backwards. It was a lovely dog-fox in its prime, with a handsome thick winter coat: a lovely golden-red colour, with grey as it passed to the belly, and belly all white, and a great full brush with a delicate black and grey and pure white tip.

"Poor brute!" said Banford. "If it wasn't such a thieving wretch, you'd feel sorry for it."

March said nothing, but stood with her foot trailing aside, one hip out; her face was pale and her eyes big and black, watching the dead animal that was suspended upside down. White and soft as snow his belly: white and soft as snow. She passed her hand softly down it. And his wonderful black-glinted brush was full and frictional, wonderful. She passed her hand down this also, and quivered. Time after time she took the full fur of that thick tail between her hand, and passed her hand slowly downwards. Wonderful sharp thick splendour of a tail! And he was dead! She pursed her lips, and her eyes went black and vacant. Then she took the head in her hand.

Henry was sauntering up, so Banford walked rather pointedly away. March stood there bemused, with the head of the fox in her hand.

She was wondering, wondering, wondering over his long fine muzzle. For some reason it reminded her of a spoon or a spatula. She felt she could not understand it. The beast was a strange beast to her, incomprehensible, out of her range. Wonderful silver whiskers he had, like ice-threads. And pricked ears with hair inside. — But that long, long slender spoon of a nose! — and the marvellous white teeth beneath! It was to thrust forward and bite with, — deep, deep into the living prey, to bite and bite the blood.

"He's a beauty, isn't he?" said Henry, standing by.

"Oh, yes, he's a fine big fox. I wonder how many chickens he's responsible for," she replied.

"A good many. Do you think he's the same one you saw in the summer?"

"I should think very likely he is," she replied.

He watched her, but he could make nothing of her. Partly she was so shy and virgin, and partly she was so grim, matter-of-fact, shrewish. What she said seemed to him so different from the look of her big, queer dark eyes.

"Are you going to skin him?" she asked.

"Yes, when I've had breakfast, and got a board to peg him on."

"My word, what a strong smell he's got! Pooo! — It'll take some washing off one's hands. I don't know why I was so silly as to handle him." — And she looked at her right hand, that had passed down his belly and along his tail, and had even got a tiny streak of blood from one dark place in his fur.

"Have you seen the chickens when they smell him, how frightened they are?" he said.

"Yes, aren't they!"

"You must mind you don't get some of his fleas."

"Oh, fleas!" she replied, nonchalant.

Later in the day she saw the fox's skin nailed flat on a board, as if crucified. It gave her an uneasy feeling.

The boy was angry. He went about with his mouth shut, as if he had swallowed part of his chin. But in behaviour he was polite and affable. He did not say anything about his intentions. And he left March alone.

That evening they sat in the dining-room. Banford wouldn't have him in her sitting-room any more. There was a very big log on the fire. And everybody was busy. Banford had letters to write, March was sewing a dress, and he was mending some little contrivance.

Banford stopped her letter-writing from time to time to look round and rest her eyes. The boy had his head down, his face hidden over his job.

"Let's see," said Banford. "What train do you go by, Henry?"

He looked up straight at her.

"The morning train. In the morning," he said.

"What, the eight-ten or the eleven-twenty?"

"The eleven-twenty, I suppose," he said.

"That is the day after to-morrow?" said Banford.

"Yes, the day after to-morrow."

"Mmm!" murmured Banford, and she returned to her writing. But as she was licking her envelope, she asked:

"And what plans have you made for the future, if I may ask?"

"Plans?" he said, his face very bright and angry.

"I mean about you and Nellie, if you are going on with this business. When do you expect the wedding to come off?" She spoke in a jeering tone.

"Oh, the wedding!" he replied. "I don't know."

"Don't you know anything?" said Banford. "Are you going to clear out on Friday and leave things no more settled than they are?"

"Well, why shouldn't I? We can always write letters."

"Yes, of course you can. But I wanted to know because of this place. If Nellie is going to get married all of a sudden, I shall have to be looking round for a new partner."

"Couldn't she stay on here if she was married?" he said. He knew quite well what was coming.

"Oh," said Banford, "this is no place for a married couple. There's not enough work to keep a man going, for one thing. And there's no money to be made. It's quite useless your thinking of staying on here if you marry. Absolutely!"

"Yes, but I wasn't thinking of staying on here," he said.

"Well, that's what I want to know. And what about Nellie, then? How long is *she* going to be here with me, in that case?"

The two antagonists looked at one another.

"That I can't say," he answered.

"Oh, go along," she cried petulantly. "You must have some idea what you are going to do, if you ask a woman to marry you. Unless it's all a hoax."

"Why should it be a hoax? — I am going back to Canada."

"And taking her with you?"

"Yes, certainly."

"You hear that, Nellie?" said Banford.

March, who had had her head bent over her sewing, now looked up with a sharp pink blush on her face and a queer, sardonic laugh in her eyes and on her twisted mouth.

"That's the first time I've heard that I was going to Canada," she said.

"Well, you have to hear it for the first time, haven't you?" said the boy.

"Yes, I suppose I have," she said nonchalantly. And she went back to her sewing.

"You're quite ready, are you, to go to Canada? Are you, Nellie?" asked Banford.

March looked up again. She let her shoulders go slack, and let her hand that held the needle lie loose in her lap.

"It depends on *how* I'm going," she said. "I don't think I want to go jammed up in the steerage, as a soldier's wife. I'm afraid I'm not used to that way."

The boy watched her with bright eyes.

"Would you rather stay over here while I go first?" he asked.

"I would, if that's the only alternative," she replied.

"That's much the wisest. Don't make it any fixed engagement," said Banford. "Leave yourself free to go or not after he's got back and found you a place, Nellie. Anything else is madness, madness."

"Don't you think," said the youth, "we ought to get married before I go — and then go together, or separate, according to how it happens?"

"I think it's a terrible idea," cried Banford.

But the boy was watching March.

"What do you think?" he asked her.

She let her eyes stray vaguely into space.

"Well, I don't know," she said. "I shall have to think about it."

"Why?" he asked, pertinently.

"Why?" — She repeated his question in a mocking way, and looked at him laughing, though her face was pink again. "I should think there's plenty of reasons why."

He watched her in silence. She seemed to have escaped him. She had got into league with Banford against him. There was again the queer sardonic look about her, she would mock stoically at everything he said or which life offered.

"Of course," he said, "I don't want to press you to do anything you don't wish to do."

"I should think not, indeed," cried Banford indignantly.

At bedtime Banford said plaintively to March:

"You take my hot bottle up for me, Nellie, will you?"

"Yes, I'll do it," said March, with the kind of willing unwillingness she so often showed towards her beloved but uncertain Jill.

The two women went upstairs. After a time March called from the top of the stairs: "Good-night, Henry. I shan't be coming down. You'll see to the lamp and the fire, won't you?"

The next day Henry went about with the cloud on his brow and his young cub's face shut up tight. He was cogitating all the time. He had wanted March to marry him and go back to Canada with him. And he had been sure she would do it. Why he wanted her he didn't know. But he did want her. He had set his mind on her. And he was convulsed with a youth's fury at being thwarted. To be thwarted, to be thwarted! It made him so furious inside, that he did not know what to do with himself. But he kept himself in hand. Because even now things might turn out differently. She might come over to him. Of course she might. It was her business to do so.

Things drew to a tension again towards evening. He and Banford had avoided each other all day. In fact Banford went in to the little town by the 11.20 train. It was market day. She arrived back on the 4.25. Just as the night was falling Henry saw her little figure in a dark-blue coat and a dark-blue tam-o'-shanter hat crossing the first meadow from the station. He stood under one of the wild pear trees, with the old dead leaves round his feet. And he watched the little blue figure advancing persistently over the rough winter-ragged meadow. She had her arms full of parcels, and advanced slowly, frail thing she was, but with that devilish little certainty which he so detested in her. He stood invisible under the pear-tree, watching her every step. And if looks could have affected her, she would have felt a log of iron on each of her ankles as she made her way forward. "You're a nasty little thing, you are," he was saying softly, across the distance. "You're a nasty little thing. I hope you'll be paid back for all the harm you've done me for nothing. I hope you will — you nasty little thing. I hope you'll have to pay for it. You will, if wishes are anything. You nasty little creature that you are."

She was toiling slowly up the slope. But if she had been slipping back at every step towards the Bottomless Pit, he would not have gone

to help her with her parcels. Aha! there went March, striding with
her long land stride in her breeches and her short tunic! Striding
down hill at a great pace, and even running a few steps now and then,
in her great solicitude and desire to come to the rescue of the little
Banford. The boy watched her with rage in his heart. See her leap
a ditch, and run, run as if a house was on fire, just to get to that creeping
dark little object down there! So, the Banford just stood still and
waited. And March strode up and took *all* the parcels except a bunch
of yellow chrysanthemums. These the Banford still carried — yellow
chrysanthemums!

"Yes, you look well, don't you," he said softly into the dusk air.
"You look well, pottering up there with a bunch of flowers, you do.
I'd make you eat them for your tea, if you hug them so tight. And I'd
give them you for breakfast again, I would. I'd give you flowers.
Nothing but flowers."

He watched the progress of the two women. He could hear their
voices: March always outspoken and rather scolding in her tenderness,
Banford murmuring rather vaguely. They were evidently good friends.
He could not hear what they said till they came to the fence of the
home meadow, which they must climb. Then he saw March manfully
climbing over the bars with all her packages in her arms, and on the
still air he heard Banford's fretful:

"Why don't you let me help you with the parcels?" She had a queer
plaintive hitch in her voice. — Then came March's robust and reckless:

"Oh, I can manage. Don't you bother about me. You've all you can
do to get yourself over."

"Yes, that's all very well," said Banford fretfully. "You say '*Don't
you bother about me*' and then all the while you feel injured because nobody thinks of you."

"When do I feel injured?" said March.

"Always. You always feel injured. Now you're feeling injured because I won't have that boy to come and live on the farm."

"I'm not feeling injured at all," said March.

"I know you are. When he's gone you'll sulk over it. I know you
will."

"Shall I?" said March. "We'll see."

"Yes, we *shall* see, unfortunately. — I can't think how you can make
yourself so cheap. I can't *imagine* how you can lower yourself like it."

"I haven't lowered myself," said March.

"I don't know what you call it, then. Letting a boy like that come so cheeky and impudent and make a mug of you. I don't know what you think of yourself. How much respect do you think he's going to have for you afterwards? — My word, I wouldn't be in your shoes, if you married him."

"Of course you wouldn't. My boots are a good bit too big for you, and not half dainty enough," said March, with rather a miss-fire sarcasm.

"I thought you had too much pride, really I did. A woman's got to hold herself high, especially with a youth like that. Why, he's impudent. Even the way he forced himself on us at the start."

"We asked him to stay," said March.

"Not till he'd almost forced us to. — And then he's so cocky and self-assured. My word, he puts my back up. I simply can't imagine how you can let him treat you so cheaply."

"I don't let him treat me cheaply," said March. "Don't you worry yourself, nobody's going to treat me cheaply. And even you aren't, either." She had a tender defiance, and a certain fire in her voice.

"Yes, it's sure to come back to me," said Banford bitterly. "That's always the end of it. I believe you only do it to spite me."

They went now in silence up the steep grassy slope and over the brow through the gorse bushes. On the other side the hedge the boy followed in the dusk, at some little distance. Now and then, through the huge ancient hedge of hawthorn, risen into trees, he saw the two dark figures creeping up the hill. As he came to the top of the slope he saw the homestead dark in the twilight, with a huge old pear-tree leaning from the near gable, and a little yellow light twinkling in the small side windows of the kitchen. He heard the clink of the latch and saw the kitchen door open into light as the two women went indoors. So, they were at home.

And so! — this was what they thought of him. It was rather in his nature to be a listener, so he was not at all surprised whatever he heard. The things people said about him always missed him personally. He was only rather surprised at the women's way with one another. And he disliked the Banford with an acid dislike. And he felt drawn to the March again. He felt again irresistibly drawn to her. He felt there was a secret bond, a secret thread between him and her, something very exclusive, which shut out everybody else and made him and her possess each other in secret.

He hoped again that she would have him. He hoped with his blood suddenly firing up that she would agree to marry him quite quickly: at Christmas, very likely. Christmas was not far off. He wanted, whatever else happened, to snatch her into a hasty marriage and a consummation with him. Then for the future, they could arrange later. But he hoped it would happen as he wanted it. He hoped that to-night she would stay a little while with him, after Banford had gone upstairs. He hoped he could touch her soft, creamy cheek, her strange, frightened face. He hoped he could look into her dilated, frightened dark eyes, quite near. He hoped he might even put his hand on her bosom and feel her soft breasts under her tunic. His heart beat deep and powerful as he thought of that. He wanted very much to do so. He wanted to make sure of her soft woman's breasts under her tunic. She always kept the brown linen coat buttoned so close up to her throat. It seemed to him like some perilous secret, that her soft woman's breasts must be buttoned up in that uniform. It seemed to him moreover that they were so much softer, tenderer, more lovely and lovable, shut up in that tunic, than were the Banford's breasts, under her soft blouses and chiffon dresses. The Banford would have little iron breasts, he said to himself. For all her frailty and fretfulness and delicacy, she would have tiny iron breasts. But March under her crude, fast, workman's tunic, would have soft white breasts, white and unseen. So he told himself, and his blood burned.

When he went in to tea, he had a surprise. He appeared at the inner door, his face very ruddy and vivid and his blue eyes shining, dropping his head forward as he came in, in his usual way, and hesitating in the door-way to watch the inside of the room, keenly and cautiously, before he entered. He was wearing a long-sleeved waistcoat. His face seemed extraordinarily a piece of the out-of-doors come indoors: as holly-berries do. In his second of pause in the doorway he took in the two women sitting at table, at opposite ends, saw them sharply. And to his amazement March was dressed in a dress of dull, green silk crêpe. His mouth came open in surprise. If she had suddenly grown a moustache he could not have been more surprised.

"Why," he said, "do you wear a dress, then?"

She looked up, flushing a deep rose colour, and twisting her mouth with a smile, said:

"Of course I do. What else do you expect me to wear, but a dress?"

"A land girl's uniform, of course," said he.

"Oh," she cried nonchalant, "that's only for this dirty mucky work about here."

"Isn't it your proper dress, then?" he said.

"No, not indoors it isn't," she said. But she was blushing all the time as she poured out his tea. He sat down in his chair at table, unable to take his eyes off her. Her dress was a perfectly simple slip of bluey-green crêpe, with a line of gold stitching round the top and round the sleeves, which came to the elbow. It was cut just plain, and round at the top, and showed her white soft throat. Her arms he knew, strong and firm muscled, for he had often seen her with her sleeves rolled up. But he looked her up and down, up and down.

Banford, at the other end of the table, said not a word, but piggled with the sardine on her plate. He had forgotten her existence. He just simply stared at March, while he ate his bread and margarine in huge mouthfuls, forgetting even his tea.

"Well, I never knew anything make such a difference!" he murmured, across his mouthfuls.

"Oh, goodness!" cried March, blushing still more. "I might be a pink monkey!"

And she rose quickly to her feet and took the tea-pot to the fire, to the kettle. And as she crouched on the hearth with her green slip about her, the boy stared more wide-eyed than ever. Through the crêpe her woman's form seemed soft and womanly. And when she stood up and walked he saw her legs move soft within her modernly short skirt. She had on black silk stockings and small, patent-leather shoes with little gold buckles.

No, she was another being. She was something quite different. Seeing her always in the hard-cloth breeches, wide on the hips, buttoned on the knee, strong as armour, and in the brown puttees and thick boots, it had never occurred to him that she had a woman's legs and feet. Now it came upon him. She had a woman's soft, skirted legs, and she was accessible. He blushed to the roots of his hair, shoved his nose in his teacup and drank his tea with a little noise that made Banford simply squirm: and strangely, suddenly he felt a man, no longer a youth. He felt a man, with all a man's grave weight of responsibility. A curious quietness and gravity came over his soul. He felt a man, quiet, with a little of the heaviness of male destiny upon him.

She was soft and accessible in her dress. The thought went home in him like an everlasting responsibility.

"Oh, for goodness sake, say something, somebody," cried Banford fretfully. "It might be a funeral." The boy looked at her, and she could not bear his face.

"A funeral!" said March, with a twisted smile. "Why, that breaks my dream."

Suddenly she had thought of Banford in the wood-box for a coffin.

"What, have you been dreaming of a wedding?" said Banford sarcastically.

"Must have been," said March.

"Whose wedding?" asked the boy.

"I can't remember," said March.

She was shy and rather awkward that evening, in spite of the fact that, wearing a dress, her bearing was much more subdued than in her uniform. She felt unpeeled and rather exposed. She felt almost improper.

They talked desultorily about Henry's departure next morning, and made the trivial arrangement. But of the matter on their minds, none of them spoke. They were rather quiet and friendly this evening; Banford had practically nothing to say. But inside herself she seemed still, perhaps kindly.

A nine o'clock March brought in the tray with the everlasting tea and a little cold meat which Banford had managed to procure. It was the last supper, so Banford did not want to be disagreeable. She felt a bit sorry for the boy, and felt she must be as nice as she could.

He wanted her to go to bed. She was usually the first. But she sat on in her chair under the lamp, glancing at her book now and then, and staring into the fire. A deep silence had come into the room. It was broken by March asking, in a rather small tone:

"What time is it, Jill?"

"Five past ten," said Banford, looking at her wrist.

And then not a sound. The boy had looked up from the book he was holding between his knees. His rather wide, cat-shaped face had its obstinate look, his eyes were watchful.

"What about bed?" said March at last.

"I'm ready when you are," said Banford.

"Oh, very well," said March. "I'll fill your bottle."

She was as good as her word. When the hot-water bottle was ready, she lit a candle and went upstairs with it. Banford remained in her chair, listening acutely. March came downstairs again.

"There you are then," she said. "Are you going up?"

"Yes, in a minute," said Banford. But the minute passed, and she sat on in her chair under the lamp.

Henry, whose eyes were shining like a cat's as he watched from under his brows, and whose face seemed wider, more chubbed and cat-like with unalterable obstinacy, now rose to his feet to try his throw.

"I think I'll go and look if I can see the she-fox," he said. "She may be creeping round. Won't you come as well for a minute, Nellie, and see if we see anything?"

"Me!" cried March, looking up with her startled, wondering face.

"Yes. Come on," he said. It was wonderful how soft and warm and coaxing his voice could be, how near. The very sound of it made Banford's blood boil.

"Come on for a minute," he said, looking down into her uplifted, unsure face.

And she rose to her feet as if drawn up by his young, ruddy face that was looking down on her.

"I should think you're never going out at this time of night, Nellie!" cried Banford.

"Yes, just for a minute," said the boy, looking round on her, and speaking with an odd sharp yelp in his voice.

March looked from one to the other, as if confused, vague. Banford rose to her feet for a battle.

"Why, it's ridiculous. It's bitter cold. You'll catch your death in that thin frock. And in those slippers. You're not going to do any such thing."

There was a moment's pause. Banford turtled up like a little fighting cock, facing March and the boy.

"Oh, I don't think you need worry yourself," he replied. "A moment under the stars won't do anybody any damage. I'll get the rug off the sofa in the dining-room. You're coming, Nellie."

His voice had so much anger and contempt and fury in it as he spoke to Banford: and so much tenderness and proud authority as he spoke to March, that the latter answered:

"Yes, I'm coming."

And she turned with him to the door.

Banford, standing there in the middle of the room, suddenly burst into a long wail and a spasm of sobs. She covered her face with her poor thin hands, and her thin shoulders shook in an agony of weeping. March looked back from the door.

"Jill!" she cried in a frantic tone, like someone just coming awake. And she seemed to start towards her darling.

But the boy had March's arm in his grip, and she could not move.

She did not know why she could not move. It was as in a dream when the heart strains and the body cannot stir.

"Never mind," said the boy, softly. "Let her cry. Let her cry. She will have to cry sooner or later. And the tears will relieve her feelings. They will do her good."

So he drew March slowly through the door-way. But her last look was back to the poor little figure which stood in the middle of the room with covered face and thin shoulders shaken with bitter weeping.

In the dining-room he picked up the rug and said:

"Wrap yourself up in this."

She obeyed — and they reached the kitchen door, he holding her soft and firm by the arm, though she did not know it. When she saw the night outside she started back.

"I must go back to Jill," she said. "I *must!* Oh, yes, I must!"

Her tone sounded final. The boy let go of her and she turned indoors. But he seized her again and arrested her.

"Wait a minute," he said. "Wait a minute. Even if you go you're not going yet."

"Leave go! Leave go!" she cried. "My place is at Jill's side. Poor little thing, she's sobbing her heart out."

"Yes," said the boy bitterly. "And your heart, too, and mine as well."

"Your heart?" said March. He still gripped her and detained her.

"Isn't it as good as her heart?" he said. "Or do you think it's not?"

"Your heart?" she said again, incredulous.

"Yes, mine! Mine! Do you think I haven't *got* a heart?" — And with his hot grasp he took her hand and pressed it under his left breast. "There's my heart," he said, "if you don't believe in it."

It was wonder which made her attend. And then she felt the deep, heavy, powerful stroke of his heart, terrible, like something from beyond. It was like something from beyond, something awful from outside, signalling to her. And the signal paralysed her. It beat upon her very soul, and made her helpless. She forgot Jill. She could not think of Jill any more. She could not think of her. That terrible signalling from outside!

The boy put his arm round her waist.

"Come with me," he said gently. "Come and let us say what we've got to say."

And he drew her outside, closed the door. And she went with him darkly down the garden path. That he should have a beating heart!

And that he should have his arm round her, outside the blanket! She was too confused to think who he was or what he was.

He took her to a dark corner of the shed, where there was a tool-box with a lid, long and low.

"We'll sit here a minute," he said.

And obediently she sat down by his side.

"Give me your hand," he said.

She gave him both her hands, and he held them between his own. He was young, and it made him tremble.

"You'll marry me. You'll marry me before I go back, won't you?" he pleaded.

"Why, aren't we both a pair of fools!" she said.

He had put her in the corner, so that she should not look out and see the lighted window of the house, across the dark yard and garden. He tried to keep her all there inside the shed with him.

"In what way a pair of fools?" he said. "If you go back to Canada with me, I've got a job and a good wage waiting for me, and it's a nice place, near the mountains. Why shouldn't you marry me? Why shouldn't we marry? I should like to have you there with me. I should like to feel I'd got somebody there, at the back of me, all my life."

"You'd easily find somebody else, who'd suit you better," she said.

"Yes, I might easily find another girl. I know I could. But not one I really wanted. I've never met one I really wanted, for good. You see, I'm thinking of all my life. If I marry, I want to feel it's for all my life. Other girls: well, they're just girls, nice enough to go a walk with now and then. Nice enough for a bit of play. But when I think of my life, then I should be very sorry to have to marry one of them, I should indeed."

"You mean they wouldn't make you a good wife."

"Yes, I mean that. But I don't mean they wouldn't do their duty by me. I mean — I don't know what I mean. Only when I think of my life, and of you, then the two things go together."

"And what if they didn't?" she said, with her odd sardonic touch.

"Well, I think they would."

They sat for some time silent. He held her hands in his, but he did not make love to her. Since he had realized that she was a woman, and vulnerable, accessible, a certain heaviness had possessed his soul. He did not want to make love to her. He shrank from any such performance, almost with fear. She was a woman, and vulnerable, accessible to him finally, and he held back from that which was ahead, almost with dread. It was a kind of darkness he knew he would enter finally, but of which he did not want as yet even to think. She was the woman, and he was responsible for the strange vulnerability he had suddenly realized in her.

"No," she said at last, "I'm a fool. I know I'm a fool."

"What for?" he asked.

"To go on with this business."

"Do you mean me?" he asked.

"No, I mean myself. I'm making a fool of myself, and a big one."

"Why, because you don't want to marry me, really?"

"Oh, I don't know whether I'm against it, as a matter of fact. That's just it. I don't know."

He looked at her in the darkness, puzzled. He did not in the least know what she meant.

"And don't you know whether you like to sit here with me this minute, or not?" he asked.

"No, I don't, really. I don't know whether I wish I was somewhere else, or whether I like being here. I don't know, really."

"Do you wish you were with Miss Banford? Do you wish you'd gone to bed with her?" he asked, as a challenge.

She waited a long time before she answered:

"No," she said at last. "I don't wish that."

"And do you think you would spend all your life with her — when your hair goes white, and you are old?" he said.

"No," she said, without much hesitation. "I don't see Jill and me two old women together."

"And don't you think, when I'm an old man, and you're an old woman, we might be together still, as we are now?" he said.

"Well, not as we are now," she replied. "But I could imagine — no, I can't. I can't imagine you an old man. Besides, it's dreadful!"

"What, to be an old man?"

"Yes, of course."

"Not when the time comes," he said. "But it hasn't come. Only it will. And when it does, I should like to think you'd be there as well."

"Sort of old age pensions," she said drily.

Her kind of witless humour always startled him. He never knew what she meant. Probably she didn't quite know herself.

"No," he said, hurt.

"I don't know why you harp on old age," she said. "I'm not ninety."

"Did anybody ever say you were?" he asked, offended.

They were silent for some time, pulling different ways in the silence.

"I don't want you to make fun of me," he said.

"Don't you?" she replied, enigmatic.

"No, because just this minute I'm serious. And when I'm serious, I believe in not making fun of it."

"You mean nobody else must make fun of you," she replied.

"Yes, I mean that. And I mean I don't believe in making fun of it myself. When it comes over me so that I'm serious, then — there it is, I don't want it to be laughed at."

She was silent for some time. Then she said, in a vague, almost pained voice:

"No, I'm not laughing at you."

A hot wave rose in his heart.

"You believe me, do you?" he asked.

"Yes, I believe you," she replied, with a twang of her old tired nonchalance, as if she gave in because she was tired. — But he didn't care, His heart was hot and clamorous.

"So you agree to marry me before I go? — perhaps at Christmas?"

"Yes, I agree."

"There!" he exclaimed. "That's settled it."

And he sat silent, unconscious, with all the blood burning in all his veins, like fire in all the branches and twigs of him. He only pressed her two hands to his chest, without knowing. When the curious passion began to die down, he seemed to come awake to the world.

"We'll go in, shall we?" he said: as if he realized it was cold.

She rose without answering.

"Kiss me before we go, now you've said it," he said.

And he kissed her gently on the mouth, with a young, frightened kiss. It made her feel so young, too, and frightened, and wondering: and tired, tired, as if she were going to sleep.

They went indoors. And in the sitting-room, there, crouched by the fire like a queer little witch, was Banford. She looked round with reddened eyes as they entered, but did not rise. He thought she looked frightening, unnatural, crouching there and looking round at them. Evil he thought her look was, and he crossed his fingers.

Banford saw the ruddy, elate face of the youth: he seemed strangely tall and bright and looming. And March had a delicate look on her face, she wanted to hide her face, to screen it, to let it not be seen.

"You've come at last," said Banford uglily.

"Yes, we've come," said he.

"You've been long enough for anything," she said.

"Yes, we have. We've settled it. We shall marry as soon as possible," he replied.

"Oh, you've settled it, have you! Well, I hope you won't live to repent it," said Banford.

"I hope so too," he replied.

"Are you going to bed *now*, Nellie?" said Banford.

"Yes, I'm going now."

"Then for goodness sake come along."

March looked at the boy. He was glancing with his very bright eyes at her and at Banford. March looked at him wistfully. She wished she could stay with him. She wished she had married him already, and it was all over. For oh, she felt suddenly so safe with him. She felt so strangely safe and peaceful in his presence. If only she could sleep in his shelter, and not with Jill. She felt afraid of Jill. In her dim, tender state, it was agony to have to go with Jill and sleep with her. She wanted the boy to save her. She looked again at him.

And he, watching with bright eyes, divined something of what she felt. It puzzled and distressed him that she must go with Jill.

"I shan't forget what you've promised," he said, looking clear into her eyes, right into her eyes, so that he seemed to occupy all her self with his queer, bright look.

She smiled to him, faintly, gently. She felt safe again — safe with him.

But in spite of all the boy's precautions, he had a set-back. The morning he was leaving the farm he got March to accompany him to the market-town, about six miles away, where they went to the registrar and had their names stuck up as two people who were going to marry. He was to come at Christmas, and the wedding was to take place then. He hoped in the spring to be able to take March back to Canada with him, now the war was really over. Though he was so young, he had saved some money.

"You never have to be without *some* money at the back of you, if you can help it," he said.

So she saw him off in the train that was going West: his camp was on Salisbury plains. And with big dark eyes she watched him go, and it seemed as if everything real in life was retreating as the train retreated with his queer, chubby, ruddy face, that seemed so broad across the cheeks, and which never seemed to change its expression, save when a cloud of sulky anger hung on the brow, or the bright eyes fixed themselves in their stare. This was what happened now. He leaned there out of the carriage window as the train drew off, saying good-bye and staring back at her, but his face quite unchanged. There was no emotion on his face. Only his eyes tightened and became fixed and intent in their watching, as a cat when suddenly she sees something and stares. So the boy's eyes stared fixedly as the train drew away, and she was left feeling intensely forlorn. Failing his physical presence, she seemed to have nothing of him. And she had nothing of anything. Only his face was fixed in her mind: the full, ruddy, unchanging cheeks, and the straight snout of a nose, and the two eyes staring above. All she could remember was how he suddenly wrinkled his nose when he laughed, as a puppy does when he is playfully growling. But him, himself, and what he was — she knew nothing, she had nothing of him when he left her.

On the ninth day after he had left her he received this letter:
"DEAR HENRY,

"I have been over it all again in my mind, this business of me and you, and it seems to me impossible. When you aren't there I see what a fool I am. When you are there you seem to blind me to things as they actually are. You make me see things all unreal and I don't know what. Then when I am alone again with Jill I seem to come to my own senses and realize what a fool I am making of myself and how I am treating you unfairly. Because it must be unfair to you for me to go on with this affair when I can't feel in my heart that I really love you. I know people talk a lot of stuff and nonsense about love, and I don't want to do that. I want to keep to plain facts and act in a sensible way. And that seems to me what I'm not doing. I don't see on what grounds I am going to marry you. I know I am not head over heels in love with you, as I have fancied myself to be with fellows when I was a young fool of a girl. You are an absolute stranger to me, and it seems to me you will always be one. So on what grounds am I going to marry you? When I think of Jill she is ten times more real to me. I know her and I'm awfully fond of her and I hate myself for a beast if I ever hurt her little finger. We have a life together. And even if it can't last for ever, it is a life while it does last. And it might last as long as either of us lives. Who knows how long we've got to live? She is a delicate little thing, perhaps nobody but me knows how delicate. And as for me, I feel I might fall down the well any day. What I don't seem to see at all is you. When I think of what I've been and what I've done with you I'm afraid I am a few screws loose. I should be sorry to think that softening of the brain is setting in so soon, but that is what it seems like. You are such an absolute stranger and so different from what I'm used to and we don't seem to have a thing in common. As for love the very word seems impossible. I know what love means even in Jill's case, and I know that in this affair with you it's an absolute impossibility. And then going to Canada. I'm sure I must have been clean off my chump when I promised such a thing. It makes me feel fairly frightened of myself. I feel I might do something really silly, that I wasn't responsible for. And end my days in a lunatic asylum. You may think that's all I'm fit for after the way I've gone on, but it isn't a very nice thought for me. Thank goodness Jill is here and her being here makes me feel sane again, else I don't know what I might do, I might have an accident with the gun one evening. I love Jill and she makes me feel safe and sane, with her loving anger against me for being such a fool. Well, what I want to say is won't you let us cry the whole thing off? I can't marry you, and really, I won't do such a thing if it seems to me wrong. It is all a great mistake. I've made a complete fool of myself, and all I can do is to apologize to you and ask you please to forget it and please to take no further notice of me. Your fox skin is nearly ready and seems all right. I will post it to you if you will let me know if this address is still right, and if you will accept my apology for the awful and lunatic way I have behaved with you, and then let the matter rest.

"Jill sends her kindest regards. Her mother and father are staying with us over Christmas.

"Yours very sincerely,

"ELLEN MARCH."

The boy read this letter in camp as he was cleaning his kit. He set his teeth and for a moment went almost pale, yellow round the eyes with fury. He said nothing and saw nothing and felt nothing but a livid rage that was quite unreasoning. Balked! Balked again! Balked! He wanted the woman, he had fixed like doom upon having her. He felt that was his doom, his destiny, and his reward, to have this woman. She was his heaven and hell on earth, and he would have none else-where. Sightless with rage and thwarted madness he got through the morning. Save that in his mind he was lurking and scheming towards an issue, he would have committed some insane act. Deep in himself he felt like roaring and howling and gnashing his teeth and breaking things. But he was too intelligent. He knew society was on top of him, and he must scheme. So with his teeth bitten together and his nose curiously slightly lifted, like some creature that is vicious, and his eyes fixed and staring, he went through the morning's affairs drunk with anger and suppression. In his mind was one thing — Banford. He took no heed of all March's outpouring: none. One thorn rankled, stuck in his mind. Banford. In his mind, in his soul, in his whole be-ing, one thorn rankling to insanity. And he would have to get it out. He would have to get the thorn of Banford out of his life, if he died for it.

With this one fixed idea in his mind, he went to ask for twenty-four hours leave of absence. He knew it was not due to him. His conscious-ness was supernaturally keen. He knew where he must go — he must go to the Captain. But how could he get at the Captain? In that great camp of wooden huts and tents, he had no idea where his Captain was.

But he went to the officers' canteen. There was his Captain standing talking with three other officers. Henry stood in the door-way at attention.

"May I speak to Captain Berryman?" — The Captain was Cornish like himself.

"What do you want?" called the Captain.

"May I speak to you, Captain?"

"What do you want?" replied the Captain, not stirring from among his group of fellow officers.

Henry watched his superior for a minute without speaking.

"You won't refuse me, sir, will you?" he asked gravely.

"It depends what it is."

"Can I have twenty-four hours leave?"

"No, you've no business to ask."

"I know I haven't. But I must ask you."

"You've had your answer."

"Don't send me away, Captain."

There was something strange about the boy as he stood there so everlasting in the door-way. The Cornish Captain felt the strangeness at once, and eyed him shrewdly.

"Why, what's afoot?" he said, curious.

"I'm in trouble about something. I must go to Blewbury," said the boy.

"Blewbury, eh? After the girls?"

"Yes, it is a woman, Captain." And the boy, as he stood there with his head reaching forward a little, went suddenly terribly pale, or yellow, and his lips seemed to give off pain. The Captain saw and paled a little also. He turned aside.

"Go on then," he said. "But for God's sake don't cause any trouble of any sort."

"I won't, Captain, thank you."

He was gone. The Captain, upset, took a gin and bitters. Henry managed to hire a bicycle. It was twelve o'clock when he left the camp. He had sixty miles of wet and muddy cross-roads to ride. But he was in the saddle and down the road without a thought of food.

At the farm, March was busy with a work she had had some time in hand. A bunch of Scotch fir-trees stood at the end of the open shed, on a little bank where ran the fence between two of the gorse-shaggy meadows. The furthest of these trees was dead — it had died in the summer and stood with all its needles brown and sere in the air. It was not a very big tree. And it was absolutely dead. So March determined to have it, although they were not allowed to cut any of the timber. But it would make such splendid firing, in these days of scarce fuel.

She had been giving a few stealthy chops at the trunk for a week or more, every now and then hacking away for five minutes, low down, near the ground, so no one should notice. She had not tried the saw, it was such hard work, alone. Now the tree stood with a great yawning gap in his base, perched as it were on one sinew, and ready to fall. But he did not fall.

It was late in the damp December afternoon, with cold mists creeping out of the woods and up the hollows, and darkness waiting to sink in from above. There was a bit of yellowness where the sun was fading away beyond the low woods of the distance. March took her axe and went to the tree. The small thud-thud of her blows resounded rather ineffectual about the wintry homestead. Banford came out wearing her thick coat, but with no hat on her head, so that her thin, bobbed hair blew on the uneasy wind that sounded in the pines and in the wood.

"What I'm afraid of," said Banford, "is that it will fall on the shed and we'll have another job repairing that."

"Oh, I don't think so," said March, straightening herself and wiping her arm over her hot brow. She was flushed red, her eyes were very wide-open and queer, her upper lip lifted away from her two white front teeth with a curious, almost rabbit-look.

A little stout man in a black overcoat and a bowler hat came pottering across the yard. He had a pink face and a white beard and smallish, pale-blue eyes. He was not very old, but nervy, and he walked with little short steps.

"What do you think, father?" said Banford. "Don't you think it might hit the shed in falling?"

"Shed, no!" said the old man. "Can't hit the shed. Might as well say the fence."

"The fence doesn't matter," said March, in her high voice.

"Wrong as usual, am I?" said Banford, wiping her straying hair from her eyes.

The tree stood as it were on one spelch of itself, leaning, and creaking in the wind. It grew on the bank of a little dry ditch between the two meadows. On the top of the bank straggled one fence, running to the bushes uphill. Several trees clustered there in the corner of the field near the shed and near the gate which led into the yard. Towards this gate, horizontal across the weary meadows came the grassy, rutted approach from the highroad. There trailed another rickety fence, long split poles joining the short, thick, wide-apart uprights. The three people stood at the back of the tree, in the corner of the shed meadow, just above the yard gate. The house with its two gables and its porch stood tidy in a little grassed garden across the yard. A little stout rosy-faced woman in a little red woollen shoulder shawl had come and taken her stand in the porch.

"Isn't it down yet?" she cried, in a high little voice.

"Just thinking about it," called her husband. His tone towards the two girls was always rather mocking and satirical. March did not want to go on with her hitting while he was there. As for him, he wouldn't lift a stick from the ground if he could help it, complaining, like his daughter, of rheumatics in his shoulder. So the three stood there a moment silent in the cold afternoon, in the bottom corner near the yard.

They heard the far-off taps of a gate, and craned to look. Away across, on the green horizontal approach, a figure was just swinging on to a bicycle again, and lurching up and down over the grass, approaching.

"Why it's one of our boys — it's Jack," said the old man.

"Can't be," said Banford.

March craned her head to look. She alone recognized the khaki figure. She flushed, but said nothing.

"No, it isn't Jack, I don't think," said the old man, staring with little round blue eyes under his white lashes.

In another moment the bicycle lurched into sight, and the rider dropped off at the gate. It was Henry, his face wet and red and spotted with mud. He was altogether a muddy sight.

"Oh!" cried Banford, as if afraid. "Why, it's Henry!"

"What!" muttered the old man. He had a thick, rapid, muttering way of speaking, and was slightly deaf. "What? What? Who is it? Who is it do you say? That young fellow? That young fellow of Nellie's? Oh! Oh!" And the satiric smile came on his pink face and white eyelashes.

Henry, pushing the wet hair off his steaming brow, had caught sight of them and heard what the old man said. His hot young face seemed to flame in the cold light.

"Oh, are you all there!" he said, giving his sudden, puppy's little laugh. He was so hot and dazed with cycling he hardly knew where he was. He leaned the bicycle against the fence and climbed over into the corner on to the bank, without going in to the yard.

"Well, I must say, we weren't expecting *you*," said Banford laconically.

"No, I suppose not," said he, looking at March.

She stood aside, slack, with one knee drooped and the axe resting its head loosely on the ground. Her eyes were wide and vacant, and her upper lip lifted from her teeth in that helpless, fascinated rabbit-look. The moment she saw his glowing red face it was all over with her. She was as helpless as if she had been bound. The moment she saw the way his head seemed to reach forward.

"Well, who is it? Who is it, anyway?" asked the smiling, satiric old man in his muttering voice.

"Why, Mr. Grenfel, whom you've heard us tell about, father," said Banford coldly.

"Heard you tell about, I should think so. Heard of nothing else practically," muttered the elderly man with his queer little jeering smile on his face. "How do you do," he added, suddenly reaching out his hand to Henry.

The boy shook hands just as startled. Then the two men fell apart.

"Cycled over from Salisbury Plain have you?" asked the old man.

"Yes."

"Ha! Longish ride. How long d'it take you, eh? Some time, eh? Several hours, I suppose."

"About four."

"Eh? Four! Yes, I should have thought so. When are you going back again?"

"I've got till to-morrow evening."

"Till to-morrow evening, eh? Yes. Ha! Girls weren't expecting you, were they?"

And the old man turned his pale-blue, round little eyes under their white lashes mockingly towards the girls. Henry also looked round. He had become a little awkward. He looked at March, who was still staring away into the distance as if to see where the cattle were. Her hand was on the pommel of the axe, whose head rested loosely on the ground.

"What were you doing there?" he asked in his soft, courteous voice. "Cutting a tree down?"

March seemed not to hear, as if in a trance.

"Yes," said Banford. "We've been at it for over a week."

"Oh! And have you done it all by yourselves, then?"

"Nellie's done it all, I've done nothing," said Banford.

"Really! — You must have worked quite hard," he said, addressing himself in a curious gentle tone direct to March. She did not answer, but remained half averted, staring away towards the woods above as if in a trance.

"*Nellie!*" cried Banford sharply. "Can't you answer?"

"What — me?" cried March starting round, and looking from one to the other. "Did anyone speak to me?"

"Dreaming!" muttered the old man, turning aside to smile. "Must be in love, eh, dreaming in the day-time!"

"Did you say anything to me?" said March, looking at the boy as from a strange distance, her eyes wide and doubtful, her face delicately flushed.

"I said you must have worked hard at the tree," he replied courteously.

"Oh, that! Bit by bit. I thought it would have come down by now."

"I'm thankful it hasn't come down in the night, to frighten us to death," said Banford.

"Let me just finish it for you, shall I?" said the boy.

March slanted the axe-shaft in his direction.

"Would you like to?" she said.

"Yes, if you wish it," he said.

"Oh, I'm thankful when the thing's down, that's all," she replied, nonchalant.

"Which way is it going to fall?" said Banford. "Will it hit the shed?"

"No, it won't hit the shed," he said. "I should think it will fall there — quite clear. Though it might give a twist and catch the fence."

"Catch the fence!" cried the old man. "What, catch the fence! When it's leaning at that angle? — Why it's further off than the shed. It won't catch the fence."

"No," said Henry, "I don't suppose it will. It has plenty of room to fall quite clear, and I suppose it will fall clear."

"Won't tumble backwards on top of *us*, will it!" asked the old man sarcastic.

"No, it won't do that," said Henry, taking off his short overcoat and his tunic. "Ducks! Ducks! Go back!"

A line of four brown-speckled ducks led by a brown-and-green drake were stemming away downhill from the upper meadow, coming like boats running on a ruffled sea, cackling their way top speed downwards towards the fence and towards the little group of people, and cackling as excitedly as if they brought news of the Spanish Armada.

"Silly things! Silly things!" cried Banford going forward to turn them off. But they came eagerly towards her, opening their yellow-green beaks and quacking as if they were so excited to say something.

"There's no food. There's nothing here. You must wait a bit," said Banford to them. "Go away. Go away. Go round to the yard."

They didn't go, so she climbed the fence to swerve them round under the gate and into the yard. So off they waggled in an excited string once more, wagging their rumps like the sterns of little gondolas ducking under the bar of the gate. Banford stood on the top of the bank, just over the fence, looking down on the other three.

Henry looked up at her, and met her queer, round-pupilled, weak eyes staring behind her spectacles. He was perfectly still. He looked away, up at the weak, leaning tree. And as he looked into the sky, like a huntsman who is watching a flying bird, he thought to himself: "If the tree falls in just such a way, and spins just so much as it falls, then the branch there will strike her exactly as she stands on top of that bank."

He looked at her again. She was wiping the hair from her brow again, with that perpetual gesture. In his heart he had decided her death. A terrible still force seemed in him, and a power that was just his. If he turned even a hair's breadth in the wrong direction, he would lose the power.

"Mind yourself, Miss Banford," he said. And his heart held perfectly still, in the terrible pure will that she should not move.

"Who me, mind myself?" she cried, her father's jeering tone in her voice. "Why, do you think you might hit me with the axe?"

"No, it's just possible the tree might, though," he answered soberly. But the tone of his voice seemed to her to imply that he was only being falsely solicitous and trying to make her move because it was his will to move her.

"Absolutely impossible," she said.

He heard her. But he held himself icy still, lest he should lose his power.

"No, it's just possible. You'd better come down this way."

"Oh, all right. Let us see some crack Canadian tree felling," she retorted.

"Ready then," he said, taking the axe, looking round to see he was clear.

There was a moment of pure, motionless suspense, when the world seemed to stand still. Then suddenly his form seemed to flash up enormously tall and fearful, he gave two swift, flashing blows, in immediate succession, the tree was severed, turning slowly, spinning strangely in the air and coming down like a sudden darkness on the earth. No one saw what was happening except himself. No one heard the strange little cry which the Banford gave as the dark end of the bough swooped down, down on her. No one saw her crouch a little and receive the blow on the back of the neck. No one saw her flung outwards and laid, a little twitching heap, at the foot of the fence. No one except the boy. And he watched with intense bright eyes, as he would watch a wild goose he had shot. Was it winged, or dead? Dead!

Immediately he gave a loud cry. Immediately March gave a wild shriek that went far, far down the afternoon. And the father started a strange bellowing sound.

The boy leapt the fence and ran to the figure. The back of the neck and head was a mass of blood, of horror. He turned it over. The body was quivering with little convulsions. But she was dead really. He knew it, that it was so. He knew it in his soul and his blood. The inner necessity of his life was fulfilling itself, it was he who was to live. The thorn was drawn out of his bowels. So, he put her down gently, she was dead.

He stood up. March was standing there petrified and absolutely motionless. Her face was dead white, her eyes big black pools. The old man was scrambling horribly over the fence.

"I'm afraid it's killed her," said the boy.

The old man was making curious, blubbering noises as he huddled over the fence.

"What!" cried March, starting electric.

"Yes, I'm afraid," repeated the boy.

March was coming forward. The boy was over the fence before she reached it.

"What do you say, killed her?" she asked in a sharp voice.

"I'm afraid so," he answered softly.

She went still whiter, fearful. The two stood facing each other. Her black eyes gazed on him with the last look of resistance. And then in a last agonized failure she began to grizzle, to cry in a shivery little fashion of a child that doesn't want to cry, but which is beaten from within, and gives that little first shudder of sobbing which is not yet weeping, dry and fearful.

He had won. She stood there absolutely helpless, shuddering her dry sobs and her mouth trembling rapidly. And then, as in a child, with a little crash came the tears and the blind agony of sightless weeping. She sank down on the grass and sat there with her hands on her breast and her face lifted in sightless, convulsed weeping. He stood above her, looking down on her, mute, pale, and everlasting seeming. He never moved, but looked down on her. And among all the torture of the scene, the torture of his own heart and bowels, he was glad, he had won.

After a long time he stooped to her and took her hands.

"Don't cry," he said softly. "Don't cry."

She looked up at him with tears running from her eyes, a senseless look of helplessness and submission. So she gazed on him as if sightless, yet looking up to him. She would never leave him again. He had won her. And he knew it and was glad, because he wanted her for his life. His life must have her. And now he had won her. It was what his life must have.

But if he had won her, he had not yet got her. They were married at Christmas as he had planned, and he got again ten days leave. They went to Cornwall, to his own village, on the sea. He realized that it was awful for her to be at the farm any more.

But though she belonged to him, though she lived in his shadow, as if she could not be away from him, she was not happy. She did not want to leave him: and yet she did not feel free with him. Everything around her seemed to watch her, seemed to press on her. He had won her, he had her with him, she was his wife. And she — she belonged to him, she knew it. But she was not glad. And he was still foiled. He realized that though he was married to her and possessed her in every possible way, apparently, and though she *wanted* him to possess her, she wanted it, she wanted nothing else, now, still he did not quite succeed.

Something was missing. Instead of her soul swaying with new life, it seemed to droop, to bleed, as if it were wounded. She would sit for a long time with her hand in his, looking away at the sea. And in her dark, vacant eyes was a sort of wound, and her face looked a little peaked. If he spoke to her, she would turn to him with a faint new smile, the strange, quivering little smile of a woman who has died in the old way of love, and can't quite rise to the new way. She still felt she ought to *do* something, to strain herself in some direction. And there was nothing to do, and no direction in which to strain herself. And she could not quite accept the submergence which his new love put upon her. If she was in love, she ought to *exert* herself, in some way, loving. She felt the weary need of our day to *exert* herself in love. But she knew that in fact she must no more exert herself in love. He would not have the love which exerted itself towards him. It made his brow go black. No, he wouldn't let her exert her love towards him. No, she had to be passive, to acquiesce, and to be submerged under the surface of love. She had to be like the seaweed she saw as she peered down from the boat, swaying for ever delicately under water, with all their delicate fibrils put tenderly out upon the flood, sensitive, utterly sensitive and receptive within the shadowy sea, and never, never rising and looking forth above water while they lived. Never. Never looking forth from the water until they died, only then washing corpses, upon the surface. But while they lived, always submerged, always beneath the wave. Beneath the wave they might have powerful roots, stronger than iron, they might be tenacious and dangerous in their soft waving within the flood. Beneath the water they might be stronger, more indestructible than resistant oak trees are on land. But it was always under-water, always under-water. And she, being a woman, must be like that.

And she had been so used to the very opposite. She had had to take all the thought for love and for life, and all the responsibility. Day after day she had been responsible for the coming day, for the coming year: for her dear Jill's health and happiness and well-being. Verily, in her own small way, she had felt herself responsible for the well-being of the world. And this had been her great stimulant, this grand feeling that, in her own small sphere, she was responsible for the well-being of the world.

And she had failed. She knew that, even in her small way, she had failed. She had failed to satisfy her own feeling of responsibility. It was so difficult. It seemed so grand and easy at first. And the more you tried, the more difficult it became. It had seemed so easy to make one beloved creature happy. And the more you tried, the worse the failure. It was terrible. She had been all her life reaching, reaching, and what she reached for seemed so near, until she had stretched to her utmost limit. And then it was always beyond her.

Always beyond her, vaguely, unrealizably beyond her, and she was left with nothingness at last. The life she reached for, the happiness she reached for, the well-being she reached for, all slipped back, became unreal, the further she stretched her hand. She wanted some goal, some finality — and there was none. Always this ghastly reaching, reaching, striving for something that might be just beyond. Even to make Jill happy. She was glad Jill was dead. For she had realized that she could never make her happy. Jill would always be fretting herself thinner and thinner, weaker and weaker. Her pains grew worse instead of less. It would be so for ever. She was glad she was dead.

And if she had married a man it would have been just the same. The woman striving, striving to make the man happy, striving within her own limits for the well-being of her world. And always achieving failure. Little, foolish successes in money or in ambition. But at the very point where she most wanted success, in the anguished effort to make some one beloved human being happy and perfect, there the failure was almost catastrophic. You wanted to make your beloved happy, and his happiness seemed always achievable. If only you did just this, that and the other. And you did this, that, and the other, in all good faith, and every time the failure became a little more ghastly. You could love yourself to ribbons, and strive and strain yourself to the bone, and things would go from bad to worse, bad to worse, as far as happiness went. The awful mistake of happiness.

Poor March, in her goodwill and her responsibility, she had strained herself till it seemed to her that the whole of life and everything was only a horrible abyss of nothingness. The more you reached after the fatal flower of happiness, which trembles so blue and lovely in a crevice just beyond your grasp, the more fearfully you become aware of the ghastly and awful gulf of the precipice below you, into which you will inevitably plunge, as into the bottomless pit, if you reach any further. You pluck flower after flower — it is never *the* flower. The flower itself — its calyx is a horrible gulf, it is the bottomless pit.

That is the whole history of the search for happiness, whether it be your own or somebody else's that you want to win. It ends, and it always ends, in the ghastly sense of the bottomless nothingness into which you will inevitably fall if you strain any further.

And women? — what goal can any woman conceive, except happiness? Just happiness, for herself and the whole world. That, and nothing else. And so, she assumes the responsibility, and sets off towards her goal. She can see it there, at the foot of the rainbow. Or she can see it a little way beyond, in the blue distance. Not far, not far.

But the end of the rainbow is a bottomless gulf down which you can fall for ever without arriving, and the blue distance is a void pit which can swallow you and all your efforts into its emptiness, and still be no emptier. You and all your efforts. So, the illusion of attainable happiness!

Poor March, she had set off so wonderfully, towards the blue goal. And the further and further she had gone, the more fearful had become the realization of emptiness. An agony, an insanity at last.

She was glad it was over. She was glad to sit on the shore and look westwards over the sea, and know the great strain had ended. She would never strain for love and happiness any more. And Jill was safely dead. Poor Jill, poor Jill. It must be sweet to be dead.

For her own part, death was not her destiny. She would have to leave her destiny to the boy. But then, the boy. He wanted more than that. He wanted her to give herself without defences, to sink and become submerged in him. And she — she wanted to sit still, like a woman on the last milestone, and watch. She wanted to see, to know, to understand. She wanted to be alone: with him at her side.

And he! He did not want her to watch any more, to see any more, to understand any more. He wanted to veil her woman's spirit, as Orientals veil the woman's face. He wanted her to commit herself to him, and to put her independent spirit to sleep. He wanted to take away from her all her effort, all that seemed her very *raison d'être.* He wanted to make her submit, yield, blindly pass away out of all her strenuous consciousness. He wanted to take away her consciousness, and make her just his woman. Just his woman.

And she was so tired, so tired, like a child that wants to go to sleep, but which fights against sleep as if sleep were death. She seemed to stretch her eyes wider in the obstinate effort and tension of keeping awake. She *would* keep awake. She *would* know. She *would* consider and judge and decide. She *would* have the reins of her own life between her own hands. She *would* be an independent woman, to the last. But she was so tired, so tired of everything. And sleep seemed near. And there was such rest in the boy.

Yet there, sitting in a niche of the high wild cliffs of West Cornwall, looking over the westward sea, she stretched her eyes wider and wider. Away to the West, Canada, America. She *would* know and she *would* see what was ahead. And the boy, sitting beside her staring down at the gulls, had a cloud between his brows and the strain of discontent in his eyes. He wanted her asleep, at peace in him. He wanted her at peace, asleep in him. And *there* she was, dying with the strain of her own wakefulness. Yet she would not sleep: no, never. Sometimes he thought bitterly that he ought to have left her. He ought never to have killed Banford. He should have left Banford and March to kill one another.

But that was only impatience: and he knew it. He was waiting, waiting to go west. He was aching almost in torment to leave England, to go west, to take March away. To leave this shore! He believed that as they crossed the seas, as they left this England which he so hated, because in some way it seemed to have stung him with poison, she would go to sleep. She would close her eyes at last, and give in to him.

And then he would have her and he would have his own life at last. He chafed, feeling he hadn't got his own life. He would never have it till she yielded and slept in him. Then he would have all his own life as a young man and a male, and she would have all her own life as a woman and a female. There would be no more of this awful straining. She would not be a man any more, an independent woman with a man's responsibility. Nay, even the responsibility for her own soul she would have to commit to him. He knew it was so, and obstinately held out against her, waiting for the surrender.

"You'll feel better when once we get over the seas, to Canada, over there," he said to her as they sat among the rocks on the cliff.

She looked away to the sea's horizon, as if it were not real. Then she looked round at him, with the strained, strange look of a child that is struggling against sleep.

"Shall I?" she said.

"Yes," he answered quietly.

And her eyelids dropped with the slow motion, sleep weighing them unconscious. But she pulled them open again to say:

"Yes, I may. I can't tell. I can't tell what it will be like over there."

"If only we could go soon!" he said, with pain in his voice.

THE LIFE AND DEATH OF YUKIO MISHIMA
Henry Scott Stokes
318 pages, 39 b/w photos
0-8154-1074-3
$18.95

EDGAR ALLAN POE
A Biography
Jeffrey Meyers
376 pp., 12 b/w photos
0-8154-1038-7
$18.95

THE FAIRY TALE OF MY LIFE
Hans Christian Andersen
New introduction by Naomi Lewis
610 pp., 20 b/w illustrations
0-8154-1105-7
$22.95

HEMINGWAY
Life into Art
Jeffrey Meyers
192 pp.
0-8154-1078-6
$27.95 cloth

SCOTT FITZGERALD
A Biography
Jeffrey Meyers
432 pp., 25 b/w photos
0-8154-1063-8
$18.95

GRANITE AND RAINBOW
The Hidden Life of Virginia Woolf
Mitchell Leaska
536 pp., 23 b/w photos
0-8154-1047-6
$18.95

 Cooper Square Press

150 Fifth Avenue
Suite 814
New York, NY 10011

Available at bookstores;
or call 1-800-462-6420

13192580R00373

Made in the USA
Lexington, KY
18 January 2012